C000226208

SACR

Christopher Mitchell is the author of the epic fantasy series The Magelands. He studied in Edinburgh before living for several years in the Middle East and Greece, where he taught English. He returned to study classics and Greek tragedy and lives in Fife, Scotland with his wife and their four children.

Brigdomin Books Ltd
First Edition, June 2019
ISBN 978-1-912879-12-0

For my family

ACKNOWLEDGEMENTS

I would like to thank the following for all their support during the writing of the Magelands - my wife, Lisa Mitchell, who read every chapter as soon as it was drafted and kept me going in the right direction; Graeme Innes for reading the manuscripts and sharing many discussions over whisky; my parents for their unstinting support; Amy Tavendale, Sandra and Donna Wheat and Vicky Williams for reading the books in their early stages; James Aitken for his encouragement; and the Film Club and Stef Karpa for their support.

Thanks also to my Magelanders ARC team, for all your help during the last few weeks before publication.

DRAMATIS PERSONAE

Holdings

    Daphne HoldFast, Vision Mage
    Karalyn Holdfast, Daphne's daughter
    Godfrey Holder Fast, Daphne's father
    Lady Rosalind Holdfast, Daphne's mother
    Jonah Holdfast, Daphne's brother
    Celine Holdfast, Daphne's sister-in-law
    Ariel Holdwick, Daphne's sister
    Faden Holdwick, Ariel's husband
    Teddy Holdwick, Ariel's son
    Lydia Holdwick, Ariel's daughter
    Emperor Guilliam, Holder of the World
    Mirren Blackhold, Queen of the Realm
    Prior, Imperial Chamberlain
    Arnault, Lord Vicar to the Prophet
    Yosin, Deacon and leader of the One True Path
    Chane Hold Clement, former advisor to Agang
    Weir, former cavalry trooper
    Flora Hold Cane, friend of the Fire Mage
    Ghorley, Governor of Rahain

Sanang

    Agang Garo, ex-King of Sanang
    Echtang Gabo, Agang's nephew
    Hodang Tipoe, Agang's Chief Minister

Rahain

    Laodoc, ex-Chancellor of Rahain
    Baoryn, Renegade

Kellach Brigdomin

    Keira ae Caela, Mage of Pyre

    Killop ae Kellan, ex-Chief of the Severed Clan

    Kylon, Fugitive

    Conal, Freed slave

    Kallie, Returning refugee

    Kelpie ae Kylanna, Former leader of Kell

    Kendrie, Former warrior

    Bay, Keira-fan

    Bridget, Chief of the Severed Clan

    Bedig, Bridget's Boyfriend

    Bonnie, Hunter

    Brodie, Head Brewer, Severed Clan

    Brynt, Severed Clan leader

    Lola, Hunter

    Draewyn, Severed Clan leader

    Dyam, Severed Clan leader

    Dean, Young Fire Mage

    Dora, Keira-fan

    Duncan, Chief of the Plateau Clan

Rakanese

    Shella, Flow Mage and Princess

    Sami, Brother of Mage Shella

    Thymo, Noli's son

THE PEOPLES OF THE STAR CONTINENT

There are five distinct peoples inhabiting the Star Continent. Three are descended from apes, one from reptiles, and one from amphibians. Their evolutionary trajectories have converged, and all five are clearly 'humanoid', though physical differences remain.

1. **The Holdings** – the closest to our own world's *Homo sapiens*. Excepting the one in ten of the population with mage powers, they are completely human. The Holdings sub-continent drifted south from the equator, and the people that inhabit the Realm are dark-skinned as a consequence. They are shorter than the Kellach Brigdomin, but taller than the Rakanese.

2. **The Rakanese** – descended from amphibians, but appear human, except for the fact that they have slightly larger eyes, and are generally shorter than Holdings people. They are descendants of a far larger population that once covered a vast area, and consequently their skin-colour ranges from pale to dark. Mothers gestate their young for only four months, before giving birth in warm spawn-pools, where the infants swim and feed for a further five months. A dozen are born in an average spawning.

3. **The Rahain** – descended from reptiles. Appear human, except for two differences. Firstly, their eyes have vertical pupils, and are often coloured yellow or green, and, secondly, their tongues have a vestigial fork or cleft at their tip. Their heights are comparable to the Holdings and the Sanang. Skin-colour tends to be pale, as the majority are cavern-dwellers. Their skin retains a slight appearance of scales, and they have no fingerprints. They are the furthest from our world's humans.

4. **The Kellach Brigdomin** – descended from apes, and very similar to the Holdings, they are the second closest to our world's humans. Their distinguishing traits are height (they are the tallest of the five peoples), pale skin (their sub-continent drifted north from a much colder region), and immunity to most diseases, toxins and illnesses. They are also marked by the fact that mothers give birth to twins in the majority of cases.

5. **The Sanang** – descended from apes, but evolved in the forest, rather than on the open plains that produced the Holdings. As a consequence, their upper arms and shoulders are wider and stronger than those of people from the Holdings or Rahain. They are pale-skinned, their sub-continent having arrived from colder climates in the south, and they occupy the same range of heights as the Holdings and Rahain. The males bear some traits of earlier *Homo sapiens*, such as a sloping forehead and a strong jaw-line, but the brains of the Sanang are as advanced as those of the other four peoples of the continent.

NOTE ON THE HOLDINGS
CALENDAR

In this world there is no moon, so there are no months.

Instead, the four seasons are divided into '**thirds**', each lasting thirty days. To make the year up to 365 days, five extra days are added, two between Winter and Spring, and one between the other seasons, roughly corresponding to each solstice and equinox.

New Year starts on the vernal equinox (our 21st March).

--- New Year's Day – 21st March

- First Third

- Second Third

- Last Third

--- Summers Day – 20th June

- First Third

- Second Third

- Last Third

--- Autumns Day – 19th September

- First Third

- Second Third

- Last Third

--- Winters Day – 19th December

- First Third

- Second Third

- Last Third

--- Year's End – 20th March

Examples:

Daphne's fort was built in the last third of spring (i.e. our 21st May to 19th June)

The goat gave birth on the fourth day of the second third of autumn (i.e. our 23rd October)

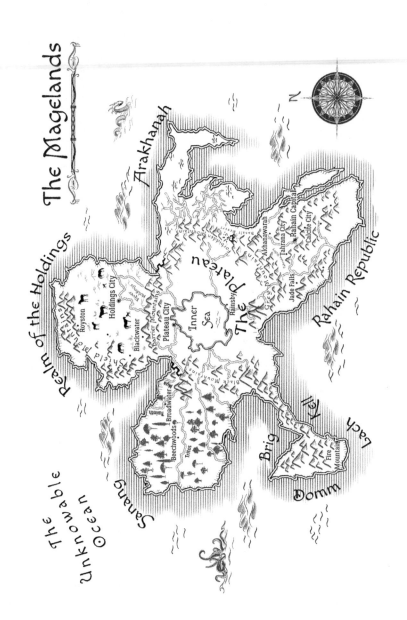

The Magelands

Arakhanah

Realm of the Holdings

The Unknowable Ocean

Sanang

Shield Mountains
Royston
Holdings City
Blackwater
Plateau City
Barrier Mountains
Holdings River

Inner Sea

The Plateau

Forbidden Mountains
Basalt Desert
Akhanawarah
Tahrana City
Rahain Capital
Calcite City
Jade Falls
Rahain Mountains

Rahain Republic

Rainsby

Beechwoods
Broadwater
Twinn
Trinn
Black Mountains

Brig

Kell

Lach

Domm
Fire Mountains

CHAPTER 1
SIDELINED

Hold Fast, Realm of the Holdings – 11th Day, Last Third Spring 507

Killop brought his left index finger and thumb close together, and concentrated.

A crackling spark of white fire arced across the gap.

'Daddy burn!' Karalyn cried. 'Again!'

He laughed, watching the delight in his daughter's eyes.

'Maybe later, wee bear,' he said. 'I'm hot enough as it is. Let's see if we can find your mummy.'

They gazed out from the shade of the wagon at the endless plains of Daphne's homeland. Killop felt almost dizzy at the sight. No mountains were visible, and not even a hillock ruined the perfect flat line of the horizon. The world was divided by that line. Greens and browns below, a vast sky of blue above. Another cloudless day, in the land where the sun ruled from its burning throne as it scorched the earth below. Dust billowed up from the wheels of the wagon trundling down the road, drying their throats and covering their skin and clothes.

He gripped the reins in his right hand and reached under the driver's bench for the water bottle, sweat streaking the dirt on his arms.

'Mummy there,' Karalyn pointed.

Killop stared into the distance, following her finger, but could see nothing.

'Are you seeing her in your mind, wee bear?'

'Aye, daddy. Mummy on the horse.'

He took a large swig of lukewarm water. The closer they had got to Hold Fast, the more Daphne had gone out on her stallion. Though she did her best to hide it, her growing anxiety was clear to him.

Karalyn pointed again, and he looked up. Ahead was a small cloud of dust, moving towards them. Half a minute later, the rider beneath became visible, racing across the green pasturelands. He half-filled a mug with water and passed it to Karalyn.

'Drink,' he said.

She took the mug and slurped the water, much of it going down her chin.

The horse and its rider grew closer. Killop smiled. Daphne never looked more beautiful than when she was in the saddle, as if she had been born to be on the back of a horse. He gazed at the expression on her face as she guided the stallion towards the wagon, trying to fix it in his memory.

Daphne slowed the racing beast to a trot as she came alongside.

Killop threw her the water bottle, and she splashed a handful over her face, wiping the dust from her dark skin.

'We close to Hold Fast?' he asked.

'Close?' she said. She smiled. 'We're in it.'

'I didn't notice any signs.'

'You passed a marker stone about a mile back.'

'We did?'

She nodded, and took a drink.

'Welcome home,' he said. 'Does it feel good?'

She threw back the bottle, and jumped across to the wagon, the reins looped round her crippled left hand. She tied them to the side post by the driver's bench, and sat down next to Karalyn and Killop under the shade of the canopy.

'I'm a bit nervous,' she said.

'There's still time to use your powers to let them know we're coming.'

She shook her head. 'I've checked to make sure they're all at home,' she said, 'but I still want our arrival to be a secret.'

'Word will get out,' he said. 'Once you're home, the church will know you're back.'

'I know, but it's important that they find out after I get there, so they can't try to stop me.'

'The roads you've led us,' he said; 'hugging the coastline – we've barely seen another person in days. If I didn't know any better, I'd think the Holdings was empty.'

'I didn't want to risk the crowds in the River Holdings,' she said, 'not when the imperials are out recruiting.'

'Do you think they'll come up here?'

Daphne glanced over the empty lands on either side of the road.

'It looks as though they've already been.'

Killop frowned.

'These plains should be teeming with horses,' she went on, 'but I haven't seen one since we crossed into Hold Fast. That usually only means one thing: that the army have come. Traditionally, the cavalry gets its troopers from the River Holdings, its officers from the noble estates, and its horses from Hold Fast. I would imagine that the imperial army is doing the same.'

'What does the Emperor want with another army?'

Daphne raised an eyebrow. 'After your sister killed so many soldiers, there are barely enough left to form a regiment.'

He looked away, biting his tongue.

'Sorry,' Daphne said, 'although, this is something we need to talk about. If we tell everyone who you are, then they're going to know you're Keira's brother.'

'I'm not responsible for her actions.'

'I know that,' she said, 'but people are still going to make comments. You have to decide how you're going to act when they do.'

'I suppose punching them's out of the question?'

She shrugged. 'Depends who says it, and what they say. And you have to remember that you're a Kellach Brigdomin. A punch from you could kill someone from the Holdings.'

He glanced down at Karalyn. 'Maybe I could just think bad thoughts about them, and let wee bear fry their minds.'

Daphne frowned.

Killop suppressed a smile, and gazed ahead, as the sweltering horses pulled their wagon along the dusty road. Overhead, the sun bore down upon the land, and Killop felt the heat soak through him. It was hotter than he had ever experienced, and even under the shade of the canopy, he could sense his skin burn. By the time the sun set each day, his limbs and face had usually reddened; but when dawn came, his skin had turned a shade more tanned, and he guessed his natural Kellach healing abilities were keeping him from suffering too much sunburn.

Ahead, a whitewashed stone wall appeared, lining the road on the left, before turning and stretching across the plain. On the other side of the road, a large building emerged from the heat haze, its high walls dazzling white, and its roof laid with deep-red tiles.

Beyond the line of the wall, the road became paved, and the wagon wheels clattered over the smooth flagstones as they left the dirt track behind.

'We're close,' said Daphne.

Killop glanced at the building on their right as they passed it. Its windows and doors were boarded up, and no one was in sight. Along a flat, whitewashed section of wall was a sign painted in flaking red paint, *Southern Troops 21-40*. Behind the building stretched lines of stone stables, all deserted.

'Usually this place is busy,' Daphne said. 'I've only ever seen it like this when the first invasion of Sanang was being planned. Just about every horse troop in Hold Fast was involved in that. My father ended up paying for half of the invasion force. Still, he forgot about that once the money started to pour in.'

She glanced at him. 'Are you ready to practise your Holdings?'

4

'I'll give it a try.'

'We'll see how well I've taught you.'

'I don't know if taught is the right word for whatever it was you did to my head.'

She shrugged. 'It worked on me when Kalayne put your language into my mind. I just tried the same on you, but in reverse.'

Killop nodded. Daphne's native language tingled in his brain as if it had been burned into place. He hadn't admitted to her how much the process had hurt as, night after night, she had linked her mind to his and imprinted words and grammatical structures into him.

More buildings appeared through the haze, lines of cottages set back from the road, and a cluster of farm structures surrounding a well. A couple of men were standing, drawing water. They turned to gaze up at the wagon, their hands shielding their eyes from the sun.

Daphne nodded to them as they passed, saying nothing.

The road grew wider, and the buildings larger, though all wore the same appearance, with whitewashed stone walls and red roofs. They passed a mason's yard on their left, with an ironsmith's beyond, while a pair of long, low buildings stretched away to their right. Outside were several Holdings men and women in light-green uniforms.

'Members of the Hold Fast Company,' Daphne said. 'I used to ride with them before I went up to Holdings City to join the cavalry.'

A few curious glances were aimed in their direction, and Killop wondered if any had ever seen a Kellach Brigdomin before.

Karalyn pointed ahead. 'Big house, mummy.'

Killop looked up. Two hundred yards in the distance loomed a great mansion, dazzling white in the sunlight, with balconies and terraces stacked up across its exterior, and fountains glistening and sparkling by the roadside.

'Your home?'

Daphne nodded.

The road grew busier as they reached a long row of watering troughs on their right, as estate workers filled buckets and horses drank. A few glanced up at the wagon, but most paid no attention.

Daphne kept her head down as Killop steered the horses past the troughs. A large street opened up to the right, leading to a high tower and an enormous pavilion, with canopies like the sails on the ships he had seen when they had been travelling along the shores of the Inner Sea.

Killop squinted as he caught sight of something on the other side of the wide street.

'Trees,' he said. 'I didn't think there were any here.'

'That's the family nursery,' Daphne said. 'I remember my father planting the first saplings, taken from Sanang about ten years ago. It's too hot and dry for some of the species, but a few seem to have flourished.'

Killop gazed at the thin trunks and dust-covered leaves, not recognising any of the varieties within the fenced enclosure. Beyond, the road opened up, surrounding the great mansion. Unlike the solid, simple block that had comprised the Slateford estate house, the Hold Fast home spread out on multiple levels, with colonnades down the sides, and squat towers on each corner. As they approached, he saw a large elevated porch at the centre.

'Maybe we should have come by the main entrance,' Daphne said. 'The front of the house looks much more impressive.'

Killop said nothing, his eyes taking in the wealth and power symbolised by the great mansion.

He noticed Daphne's smile fade. He glanced back at the porch, and saw a small group sitting out on the long chairs and benches. A tall woman stood as the wagon approached. She narrowed her eyes and took a step forwards.

Killop swung the wagon to the side of the porch, where polished marble steps led up to where the woman stood. He flicked the reins and brought the wagon to a halt.

He glanced at Daphne, waiting for her to say something, but she was sitting in silence, her right fist clenched.

'Are you all right?' he whispered.

She nodded. Killop jumped down from the wagon, a wall of heat hitting him as soon as he had emerged from under the shade of the canopy. He held up his arms and Daphne passed Karalyn to him. She climbed down, her riding boots crunching on the gravel in front of the marble steps. She gazed up at the porch.

'Daphne,' the tall woman said.

'Mother.'

'Welcome home.'

'Thank you.'

An older woman, dressed in a plain grey tunic, came forwards, leading two small children by the hand. She glanced at Daphne's mother as if awaiting instruction, but the tall woman said nothing, her face expressionless.

Daphne took Karalyn from Killop.

'This is my daughter,' she said. 'Our daughter.'

'I recall hearing the news,' her mother said. 'Congratulations.'

'And this is Killop.'

'How do you do?' said Killop, in accented Holdings.

The tall woman's eyes flickered over him for a second, then her gaze returned to Daphne.

'Your father will be happy to see you, I'm sure,' she said. 'Come out of the sun, and I'll have someone fetch him.'

Killop followed Daphne and Karalyn up the wide steps, the sweat starting to pour from him in the scorching light. The porch was covered with a large white awning, and they slipped back under the shade.

'Excuse me for a moment,' Daphne's mother said, then she glided through the open doors into the interior of the house, her long gown flowing.

The older woman smiled at Daphne.

'Welcome back, miss,' she said. 'You'll be needing refreshments?'

'Thanks, Jean,' Daphne said.

Jean walked to a nearby table, and Daphne crouched down next to the two children.

'Teddy, Lydia,' she said. 'I'm Aunty Daphne. I've come from far away to see everyone.'

She stood Karalyn on the ground next to them.

'This is your cousin, Karalyn.'

'Hello, Karalyn,' said Lydia. 'I'm nearly three.'

Karalyn buried her face in Daphne's cloak.

Jean handed Killop a glass of a cold, golden liquid. Expecting a beer, he took a long gulp, and grimaced. Daphne took a glass, and drank it down in one long draught. She sighed.

'That's the best iced tea I've had in years.'

Jean gazed down at Karalyn. 'And how old is your little girl, miss?'

'One year and four thirds.'

Jean's mouth opened. 'But she's bigger than Lydia, miss.' The woman knelt down next to the children. 'Come on, Karalyn,' she said. 'Let me have a look at you.'

'I don't like you,' the girl replied in Kellach, one eye peering out from behind Daphne's cloak.

'What did she say?' said Jean.

'She's just being shy,' Daphne said. 'Kara-bear, say hello to Mistress Jean.'

Karalyn scowled at the Holdings woman, then noticed the doll that Lydia was clutching in her hands.

'Mine,' she cried, ripping it from Lydia's grasp. The Holdings girl burst into tears.

'You give that back to my sister,' Teddy yelled.

Karalyn shot him a dark look, and the boy's eyes widened, and he started to tremble.

'Kara-bear,' Daphne said, as Lydia continued to cry, 'that's not nice.'

Teddy let out a whimper and cowered backwards. Jean raised an eyebrow, glancing from one child to the next.

Killop heard a low cough, and looked up.

'I've sent out a call for your father,' Daphne's mother said from the doorway. She looked down at the doll in Karalyn's hands and frowned. 'What's going on here? Are you unable to control your daughter?'

Daphne's eyes smouldered, but she said nothing.

'We'll make sure she gives it back,' said Killop.

Daphne's mother ignored him, and he fell silent as the two Holdfast women glared at each other.

'Maybe I should take Ariel's children inside, my lady,' Jean said.

'Why on earth would you do that?' Daphne's mother said. 'This is their home. They are not the strangers here.'

She reached down to take the doll from Karalyn, but froze when her hand was an inch away. She swayed, then put her hand to her forehead.

'My lady, are you all right?' said Jean.

'A slight headache, that's all,' she said, straightening. 'Lydia, would you please stop that wailing.'

The little girl quietened, though tears continued to run down her cheeks.

'Daphne!' a voice cried.

A man strode through the open doors and straight towards them.

'Father,' Daphne said, a tight smile on her lips.

'Daffie, my girl,' the man said, embracing his daughter. 'It's wonderful to see you. Why didn't you send me a message that you were coming?'

'I wanted it to be a surprise.'

Her father turned to Killop, and extended his hand.

'And you must be Killop of the Kellach Brigdomin. Chief of the Severed Clan, if I'm not mistaken.'

'An honour to meet you, sir,' Killop said, shaking the man's hand.

'The honour is mine, of course,' Daphne's father said, a smile on his lips. His glance lowered to Karalyn, and his features opened. A tear rolled down his cheek as he crouched down by her. 'Little Karalyn, so pretty.' He glanced up at Daphne. 'What a beautiful girl,' he said, his voice almost breaking. He reached out with his arms, and Karalyn smiled and approached. Daphne's father wrapped his arms around her and gave her a hug.

'Really, Godfrey?' Daphne's mother said. 'Tears? It's a little early to have started drinking, is it not? Well, perhaps not for you.'

'I haven't touched a drop,' he said, beaming. He stood, picking Karalyn up. She smiled and cuddled into his shoulder. 'You're a big girl,' he said. 'I had wondered if the mixture of Kellach blood would influence your development, and I was right. You can call me Papa, like Lydia and Teddy do.'

He glanced down at the other children, both of whom looked terrified.

'What's the matter with you two?'

'Perhaps you should ask your daughter,' Daphne's mother said.

'Sister,' said a female voice. Killop turned back to the door to see two more women approach. One looked quite similar to Daphne, though less athletic and a little taller, while the other was clad in black from head to toe.

Daphne smiled 'Ariel and Celine, it's good to see you.'

Ariel and Daphne embraced, while Celine stood back. Her eyes seemed empty and tired.

Daphne noticed a bulge at Ariel's waist. 'You're not…?'

Ariel laughed. 'I am. Number three is on its way.'

'Congratulations. Is Faden here with you?'

'He's working in Holdings City,' Ariel said. She glanced down at Lydia and Teddy. 'I see you've already met my little monsters. Oh.'

She knelt, and her two children ran weeping into her arms. 'Oh dear.'

'How are you, Celine?' Daphne said.

'How do you think?' said her mother. 'Are you blind? She's in mourning, as are we all.'

Daphne swallowed. 'Not Vince?'

For the briefest moment, Daphne's mother looked like she might break, but her features hardened.

'Yes, Daphne,' she said, her voice devoid of emotion. 'Your brother Vince is dead.'

Daphne sobbed, then turned to her father, who nodded.

'He fell at the Sanang frontier wall last Winter's Day.'

Killop's heart filled with sorrow for Daphne as she began weeping, her face crumpling up in tears. Her father, still holding on to Karalyn, reached out for her and held her close.

Killop stayed silent, glancing at the Holdings folk on the porch.

'At least she's crying,' Daphne's mother said. 'I've yet to see my boy's widow shed a single tear.'

Celine said nothing, her eyes cast downwards.

'Mother,' Ariel snapped. 'Don't be like that. Celine is allowed to mourn in her own way.'

'You're so naïve at times, Ariel,' her mother said. 'When you're older, you'll learn how to spot people who try to take advantage of your generosity and family name.'

'Rosalind, enough,' Godfrey said, his eyes dark as he glared at his wife. 'Celine is family now. She's a Holdfast.'

There was an icy silence. Killop wondered if he should say something.

'Holder Fast?' said Jean.

'Yes?'

'Shall I organise getting Miss Daphne's things unloaded? Where shall we be putting our guests? The south wing has an empty suite on the first floor.'

'Yes, of course,' Godfrey said, disentangling himself from Daphne, and passing Karalyn to her. Killop stepped forward and put his arm around her.

'The south wing will be fine,' Godfrey said.

'But first,' said Rosalind, 'we will pay our respects.'

The Hold Fast family shrine was a short walk across the baking-hot gravel to a low marble building shaded by the trees of the nursery. Killop hung at the back while they trooped along the path, leading Karalyn by the hand. She was crying, the doll having been forcibly removed by Daphne before they had left the porch.

Servants lowered their parasols as the Holdfasts entered the nursery. No servant had been tall enough to hold one over Killop's head, and so he had borne the beating sun, and was sweating by the time the thin shade of the trees covered him.

Godfrey and Rosalind led the way towards the white stone building, with Daphne, Ariel and Celine following. Lydia and Teddy had been left with Jean back at the house. Mistress Jean had tried to persuade Karalyn to stay behind as well, but she had clung to her father's leg, and had refused to be parted from him. He ducked his head to get through the front entrance of the building, and exhaled in relief at the cool air circulating within. A hallway opened out into a large chamber, where the walls were lined with dozens of alcoves. Most contained stone or metal urns, while old skulls sat in some of the higher spaces. The family gathered around an alcove by the right end of the wall, where fresh flowers had been arranged in vases on either side of a small silver urn.

Godfrey rested his hand on the urn for a second, closing his eyes.

Rosalind frowned, and turned to Daphne. 'You should say a few words.'

Daphne nodded, and approached the alcove. Her eyes were red from weeping, and she kept her gaze downwards.

Godfrey moved back to give her room, and the family stood and waited for her to speak.

'Should we wait for Jonah?' she said.

'He's out for the day,' her father said, 'working with the northern herds, what's left of them. I doubt he'll be back before nightfall.'

Daphne nodded. 'Vince was my hero when I was little,' she said, her words slow. 'In my earliest memory of him, he was riding a horse; he seemed like a giant up there, so brave...' She paused, her head bowed. 'And he was kind, and would have made a great father. I know he wanted children...' She glanced over to Celine, but the other woman had her eyes closed. 'I loved him,' Daphne went on, 'and I'll miss him.' She turned to face the urn. 'Goodbye, Vince.'

'Thank you, Daphne,' her mother said. 'Good girl. Now I would like to say something.'

Daphne nodded and stood to the side, where Killop put his arm around her. He kissed her on the top of her head, as her mother reached the alcove.

'Sweet words are all very nice,' Rosalind said, 'but the grief I bear burns with a mother's rage for all the years wasted. Vince was the heir to Hold Fast, and no woman could have been prouder to name him as their son. That honour was mine, and now he has been lost to us forever, snuffed out while trying to protect his homeland from the vile savages that invaded on Winter's Day; and anger now fills my heart.' She gazed into Godfrey's eyes. 'And so,' she went on, 'I give thanks to the blessed Emperor for striking down the evil witch Keira, the monster that took Vince from us.'

Killop tensed, his heart burning, but remained silent. Godfrey glared back at his wife, but also said nothing.

'I am comforted by my faith,' Rosalind said. 'I know that Vince is now in paradise, whereas the soul of the witch will be tortured for all eternity. The Creator will see that justice is done.'

She glanced at Daphne. 'Don't you agree?'

Daphne's face hardened. 'I don't want to argue with you, mother. Not here.'

'I thought you were a believer now,' Rosalind said. 'Did you not claim to have spoken to the Creator?'

'It's complicated,' Daphne said. 'I'll tell you all about it, every last detail if you want, but not now. Now, I just want to sleep. I'm so tired.'

'Of course,' her father said. 'You've had a long journey; you must be exhausted. Ariel and Celine can show you to your rooms.' He glanced at his elder daughter, and Ariel nodded. He turned back to Rosalind. 'I would like a word with your mother.'

Rosalind snorted. 'There is nothing you can say that I want to hear.'

She turned her back to him and strode from the chamber.

Ariel shrugged at Daphne and Killop. 'Some things never change. Come on.'

Killop picked up Karalyn, and she was asleep in his arms in seconds. Ariel took Daphne's hand, and they followed Rosalind out of the chamber, Celine shuffling behind.

'Sorry you had to hear all that,' Ariel said to Killop, as they walked along the path through the nursery.

'Your mother has a right to be angry,' he said.

'I think your arrival was a shock to her. Well, it was a shock to us all. I'll admit that I never thought you'd come all this way. I wish you'd sent word.'

Servants with parasols were waiting on the gravel by the edge of the nursery, and Killop felt the wall of raw heat hit him as they emerged back out into the sunlight. He took a parasol from a servant, and held it over Karalyn as they walked back to the mansion.

———

Godfrey held up a bottle in the candlelight.

'This is the finest rum on the estate,' he said, gazing at Daphne sitting across from him by the fire. 'I've been saving it for a special occasion and, well, your homecoming would seem appropriate.'

Killop glanced at Daphne. They were both dressed in clean clothes, after having bathed, and then slept for several hours in an enormous bed in their new rooms. A servant had awoken them a few hours after sunset, and invited them downstairs to her father's study. They had left Karalyn sleeping, and were now sitting on comfortable chairs while Godfrey poured them drinks.

Daphne lit a cigarette.

'Is anyone else coming?' she said, as her father passed her a glass.

Godfrey shook his head. 'Ariel's in bed, Celine has smoked enough dreamweed to fell a carthorse, and Jonah's not returned home. I suspect he's decided to stay up north for the night. I didn't ask your mother.'

They raised their glasses.

'To your health,' Godfrey said, and they drank.

Killop savoured the rich sweetness of the rum.

'Now,' Godfrey said, gazing at Daphne, 'I'm going to make some guesses. Please oblige me by pointing out where I err.'

'All right.'

'You have fled the civil war in Rahain?'

She nodded.

'Governor Ghorley is firmly in charge?'

She nodded again.

'The Severed Clan has evacuated?'

Daphne glanced at Killop.

'Aye,' he said. 'The clan didn't feel safe in Rahain any more. Both sides wanted us out. They've gone back to Kellach Brigdomin.'

'A pity,' he said. 'Strategically speaking, your presence was a useful wedge. Without it, there's nothing to stop the church's takeover of the entire country.'

Killop frowned.

'So,' Godfrey went on, 'you are no longer their chief? Am I to understand that you chose my daughter over your position?'

'Aye, I did.'

'Another pity.'

Daphne glared at him. 'What?'

'Strategically speaking, Daffie,' he said. 'As a father, I'm grateful that Killop escorted you home. However, the withdrawal of the Severed Clan from Rahain is a victory for the empire.'

'Who cares about the empire?' Daphne said.

'All those who love the Holdings should care about the empire,' Godfrey said, lighting a cigarette, and refilling their glasses. 'You must have seen the poverty on your way here. The Emperor has bled the River Holdings dry of recruits and supplies.'

'We avoided the towns,' Daphne said. 'We came up the old coast road.'

'But you saw the empty fields when you entered the estate?'

Daphne nodded.

'The imperial army took every fighting-age horse we had. Every one, Daphne.' He paused, and sipped his rum. 'And didn't pay a penny.'

'The army didn't pay us?'

'Not a single coin. Nothing but promises of payment from future campaigns. But against whom? The recruitment has gone well beyond the simple replacement of the old alliance field army that was destroyed at the Sanang frontier. The Emperor is assembling a truly stupendous force, about as large as the Sanang horde that invaded on Winter's Day.'

Daphne said nothing.

'So,' Godfrey went on, 'what does the Emperor intend to do with his new army? Rahain is finally settling down, and Governor Ghorley already has his own army; he doesn't need any help. To send an army of that size to Sanang would seem pointless, considering that as much as a third of its men-folk were slaughtered last year.'

'That many?' said Killop.

'Indeed,' said Godfrey. 'Your sister left half of Sanang ablaze before she invaded the Plateau, and her entire army, some hundred thousand strong, was annihilated outside the walls of the imperial capital by the Emperor himself, if the tales are true.'

'So what does he want?' Daphne said.

'Come now, Daffie; you must have heard.'

She shook her head.

'Mages. He wants mages.'

'Why?'

'I've heard whispers, from sources deep within the capital, that the Emperor had the Lord Vicar murder five mages during some kind of sordid sacrifice, in order to steal their powers.'

'A news-teller in the Plateau said that the Creator had given him those powers.'

'Maybe, but it also required the deaths of five mages, one from each land.'

'But if he's got all those powers,' Daphne said, 'why is he looking for more mages?'

'I don't know. Maybe he wants even more power. But there's no doubt; every one of his proclamations since defeating the firewitch has been repeating the same message: all high mages must report to the imperial capital. As far as the Holdings are concerned, that means anyone with inner-vision and above.'

He held Daphne's gaze for a moment.

'With your return,' he said, 'I am in breach of the law, by knowingly harbouring a high mage. And I would imagine the imperial authorities might also wish to question the brother of the lately-deceased firewitch, to ask if you know the whereabouts of her corpse.'

'What?' Killop said, his eyes narrowing.

'It's gone missing, you see,' Godfrey said. 'Thousands up on the city walls watched her die, but apparently it was dark when scouts went out to look for the body, and by the time they got there it had disappeared.'

'Thousands saw her die?' said Daphne.

'Half the city claim to have watched it happen. The Emperor is furious; he wants the body back. The chief suspects are Keira-worshippers among the Kellach living in the capital. The latest imperial edict has demanded that they hand over the body, or soldiers will go in to retrieve it.'

'Worshippers?'

'The Sanang treated her as a god,' Godfrey said. 'Keira kill-kill.'

Killop bowed his head. 'They won't find the body,' he said. 'She's still alive.'

Godfrey's eyes widened. 'You know this for certain?'

'No.'

'Hmm,' Godfrey said. 'Regardless, the Emperor looks as though he is planning to assault the Kellach quarter in Plateau City soon. He might be using the body as a pretext, but his true aim is, I believe, to scour the area for any hidden mages.'

Killop turned to see Godfrey staring at him, and he felt an odd sensation behind his temples.

'Father!' Daphne said.

He flinched away, a look of confusion on his face.

Daphne glared at him. 'Trying to read Killop's mind without asking? That's very rude.'

Godfrey's mouth hung open. 'How did you know? And how did you stop me?'

Daphne smiled, but her eyes remained cold. 'Killop's an honest man,' she said. 'If you want to know something, all you need do is ask.'

Godfrey took a gulp of rum. 'I have never felt power like it. Never in my life. Daphne, my beloved daughter, I feel proud and slightly terrified at the same time.'

'I learned a lot while I was away.'

Godfrey chuckled, and refilled their glasses.

'Tell me everything. I want to know what my little girl's been up to.'

CHAPTER 2
WORLD'S END

W estgate, Domm Pass – 14th Day, First Third Summer 507
'Keira, ya lazy cow,' the voice cried. 'Get yer arse out here; the place is filling up.'

'Aye,' she muttered, as she lay sprawled over the bed, a multitude of blankets wrapped round her.

She closed her eyes, and began snoring.

'Don't you think you should get up?' another voice said. 'They've been banging on your door for an hour.'

Keira cracked open an eye and squinted at the young man sitting on the bed next to her.

'Who the fuck are you?'

His face fell. 'Do ye not remember last night?'

'No,' she said, closing her eyes again. 'Did we...?'

'You were too out of it. I had to carry you onto the bed.'

'And ye never took advantage of me?'

'Of course not.'

Keira peered under the blankets, and saw she was still in her clothes from the night before.

'Just as well,' she grunted.

'Can I see you again?'

'Are ye not looking at me right now?'

'Well, aye; but what I mean is, would you at all be interested...?'

'No.'

'But...'

'Are ye fucking deaf? Now fuck off and give me some peace. I'm trying to sleep off a bastard of a hangover.'

She heard the young man get up and walk to the door. He unbarred the lock and swung it open.

'Wait,' Keira yelled. 'Don't open the... Shit.'

Another man, dark haired and angry-looking, strode into the room as the other left.

'What are you doing still in bed?' he cried. 'Get yer arse out front. There's a whole crowd waiting. Kelpie's going mental.'

'Aye, aye,' Keira mumbled, swinging her legs off the bed. 'I need to wash first.'

'No time for that,' the man said. 'Folk are starting to leave; they're saying that you're not coming today.'

'I could do with a day off, right enough.'

'Ye get one every ten days. You've got seven to go.'

'Yer a fucking slave driver, Kendrie,' she said. 'Not like the sweet young man I used to know.'

She stood, swayed, then staggered to a bucket of water atop a small table. She splashed her face, and bowed her head, her mind swimming. The days were blurring into one. She opened a small pouch by the bucket and took a look inside. At the bottom were three small weed-sticks, all she had left. She had managed to stock up when they had run into a band of Sanang bandits as they had been crossing the Plateau, but the supply was almost done.

She picked up one of the remaining weedsticks and took a match from the box on the table. She lit it and sat back onto the bed.

Kendrie sighed. 'Five minutes?'

She nodded, and the man left the room.

Keira's headache started to fade as she inhaled, and she felt life course through her.

20

'I thought this would be your dream job.'

She looked up, and saw a young woman standing by the doorway.

'It is, Flora,' she said, 'but it takes me a wee bit to get going each day.'

The Holdings woman smiled. 'It's beautiful outside. The warmest I've felt it since we got here. I might even take my coat off for a bit later, if the wind quietens down.'

'You never know,' said Keira, 'it might be one of the three days a year it doesn't rain in Domm.'

Flora nodded, then frowned. 'Who was that I saw coming out of your room?'

'That guy?' Keira said. 'Fuck knows.'

The Holdings woman turned away.

'What's the matter?' Keira said. 'Did ye fancy him for yourself?'

'No.'

Keira frowned. 'Yer a strange woman at times, Flora.'

She nicked the weedstick halfway down, and put the unburnt end behind her ear for later. She got to her feet and stretched.

'Right,' she said, 'let's get back to work.'

'So there I was, staring up at thousands of flying lizard carriages, just like the ones those wee bastards used to invade Kell and Brig. The entire fucking Sanang army was hungover to fuck, seeing how we'd just stolen a shitload of wine, and...'

'What's wine?' said a voice from the listening crowd.

'Booze that tastes like sour juice,' Keira went on. She held up her glass of whisky. 'Not as good as this, mind; but drink enough and it'll mangle ye all the same.'

The patrons of the packed tavern laughed.

Keira glanced at the woman who had spoken. 'If ye interrupt me again, hen, I'll fucking brain ye. Stick yer hand up if ye've got questions.'

The woman nodded, her eyes wide.

Keira took a drink. 'Where was I? Oh aye. The Sanang army were sleeping off this massive session we'd had the day before, and so it was all up to me to save their arses. The first wave of carriages were smashing into the army. One of them smacked right into my fucking tent, whack! If I hadnae been up drinking, it would have smeared me right across the hillside. Every numpty was running about, panicking and screaming like bairns, and I was like, "cool it, ya fuds; I've got it under control." Then I raised my arms, and made this great big cloud of fire, and shot down every one of those flying bastards from the sky...'

'Bullshit,' muttered someone.

Keira narrowed her eyes and scanned the crowd. At a table to her left, past where Flora sat next to her, was a group of young travellers, a mixture of young men and women. A few were laughing, and most wore sceptical expressions.

'Are you calling me a liar?'

'Just enjoying your stories,' one said. 'Carry on.'

Keira scowled. 'They're not just stories.' She gazed over the rest of the full tavern. To her right sat a large group of regulars, who came every day to hear her speak, and even though she had recycled her tales several times over, the stupid bastards never seemed to get enough. The rest of the tavern was filled with travellers, mostly those arriving as refugees from Rahain or the Plateau, on their way down to the new settlements in the Domm lowlands; or merchants, carrying their wares to the numerous towns and communities spreading across the long Domm Pass. Everyone was watching her, waiting for her words.

'What happened next?' said one.

Keira finished her whisky, and held out her glass to Flora, who re-filled it.

'I killed them all.'

The crowd hushed, waiting, but Keira said nothing more.

'She lit up the night sky,' Flora said. 'I was there; I saw it. Hundreds of burning carriages fell, and crashed into the fields in front of the army; it was like nothing...'

'Who are you?' shouted someone.

'She's my wee white-faced witch,' Keira said.

'But she's dark-skinned.'

Keira shrugged. 'You had to be there.'

The crowd began to glance at each other as Keira drank her whisky in silence.

'And then?' said someone. 'Did you go to the capital of the Plateau?'

'I'm bored,' Keira said. 'That's enough for today.'

The crowd groaned and complained.

'Tell us more,' cried someone from her group of regulars.

'Aye,' said a man from the table on the left. 'Tell us about the Rakanese camp.'

Keira glared at him. 'What the fuck did you say?'

The tavern quietened.

'Who are the Rakanese?' said Bay, one of her regular listeners.

'Never you mind,' Keira snapped. She gestured to Kendrie. 'Get those wankers out of here.'

Kendrie nodded, and he and a couple of other tavern workers approached the group on the left.

Keira stood, and began shooing the crowds away. 'We're done for today.'

Amid mutterings, the people started to disperse, leaving the tavern by its wide front doors.

'Wait!' called out an older woman. 'We have an offer on lunch; a free ale for every meal ordered.'

The woman frowned at the backs of the leaving patrons, and within a minute the tavern was quiet, with just a few regulars propping up the bar.

She glared at Keira.

'It's not my fault,' Keira said. 'I'm just not in the fucking mood for it today.'

'Sorry, Miss Kelpie,' said Flora.

'It's not your fault, hen,' Kelpie said. 'I saw you trying to help.'

'Those guys were arseholes,' said Bay, approaching Keira's table with Dora, another of Keira's regular followers.

Kelpie frowned at the two young women as they sat next to Keira.

'I told ye girls,' Keira said. 'We're done for today.'

'We just want to sit here,' said Dora. 'We'll pay for yer drinks.'

Keira smirked.

'Don't worry yourself, lass,' Kelpie said. 'Keira gets her food, drink and rooms for her and her two friends all paid for, and all she has to do is speak to folk for a few hours each day.' She sat at the table next to Flora and poured herself a whisky. 'And let's see; ye managed a whole twenty minutes today. Still, better than yesterday.'

'Don't give me yer shite,' Keira said. 'The money Agang's bringing in more than pays for me and Flora.'

Kelpie frowned. 'Not in front of company, please.'

'Where is he, anyway?' Flora said.

'Working,' Kelpie said. 'He'll be finished soon.'

Keira pulled the half-smoked weedstick from behind her ear and lit it.

'A large group will be passing by on their way to the lowlands this evening,' Kelpie said.

'So?'

'Well,' Kelpie said, 'to make up for this lunchtime, I'll need you to speak to them.'

'Forget it,' Keira said. 'I'm getting rat-arsed.'

'It's too late; I've already put out word on the road that you'll be here this evening. They'll burn the place down if you don't show up, and then where would you sleep, or get your booze?'

Keira glared at the older woman as she finished her whisky and got to her feet.

'See you this evening,' Kelpie said, and walked away.

'We should get some sleep,' said Flora. 'It's going to be a long night.'

When Keira stumbled back into the tavern it was quiet, with a handful of patrons sitting drinking. The shutters had been opened along the entire western wall, and the sky was lit with shades of peach and red as the sun fell over the lowlands beyond the high pass where the tavern perched.

Agang was sitting alone at a table by the windows, watching the vast sunset.

Keira and Flora joined him, and a bar-boy brought over ales.

'Such beauty,' Agang said, his face shining in the reflected glow.

'Aye, it's braw,' Keira said, taking a drink.

'You been busy?' said Flora.

Agang nodded.

'You look exhausted.'

'I am. I must have mended a dozen broken bones today.'

'Get paid well?' Keira said.

He frowned. 'Using my powers for money is wrong. And besides, the Kellach barely require a healer. Your people don't get diseases, and recover quickly from accidents. It's been mostly alcohol-related injuries that I've been fixing. An ignoble use of my gifts.'

'Quit whining,' Keira said. 'It's only while we settle in and decide what to do.'

Flora pulled her eyes from the sunset to gaze at Keira. 'You mean you don't intend to stay here at Kelpie's?'

'Are we going back to the Plateau?' Agang said.

'Probably not, and definitely not,' Keira said. 'In that order.'

'I thought the plan was to keep our heads down,' Flora said. 'With every day that passes, more people learn who you are. Soon, the whole of Domm will be aware that Keira the fire mage has returned.'

'Aye,' Keira said. 'Kelpie's got it into her head that that's a good thing.'

'But the Emperor will come looking if he finds out you're down here.'

'Come on,' Keira said. 'We're at the arse end of fucking nowhere. More folk are still coming here, but nobody's leaving. And even if someone did, and walked all the way back to Rainsby, and started telling folk there was a drunken woman in Domm claiming to be me, no one would believe it anyway.'

Flora and Agang shared a glance.

'So,' Agang said, 'are you considering the offer the Domm Council made you?'

'Nah,' Keira said. 'I must have told ye a hundred fucking times, I'll not be using my powers again, not ever. That's the one thing guaranteed to get the Emperor's attention.'

'So what are we going to do?' said Flora.

Keira shrugged.

Kendrie walked over. 'Evening,' he said. 'You wanting fed?'

'Aye,' Keira said.

Kendrie nodded and turned to go.

'And bring us a bottle of whisky,' Keira said.

Kendrie frowned.

'Do as she says,' Kelpie called over from the bar. 'Agang's more than earned their pay today.'

'Fine,' Kendrie said.

Keira grinned. 'Cheers, Kelpie.'

Flora glanced at her. 'Maybe you should hold back a bit, at least until you've spoken to this new group that's coming.'

Keira snorted. 'Fuck that.'

She turned and gazed at the sunset. The sky was blood red, and darkening. A brisk wind gusted by the open windows, and she breathed in a good lungful.

'Nothing beats the air in Kellach Brigdomin,' she said. 'Every other place stinks. Especially Sanang.'

'You've never been to the Holdings,' Flora said.

'True, but I bet it reeks of horseshit.'

'At least it's warm.'

'It's warm now,' Keira said.

'What?' Flora said. 'This is the middle of summer, right? As good as it gets? And I'm still wearing three layers to keep the wind out.

Even our winter is better than this. And don't get me started on the rain.'

'I don't mind a wee bit of rain.'

They paused as Kendrie put a bottle of whisky onto their table, along with three glasses.

'Could I have some water, please?' Agang said.

Keira frowned. 'A pair of pansies, the both of ye. One's moaning about the fucking weather, and the other needs water to put in his whisky. Might I remind ye that I'm not forcing anyone to stay here with me. Yer more than welcome to fuck off if ye don't like it.'

Agang glowered, while Flora looked away.

Keira poured herself a large whisky, as Kendrie returned with a jug of water and a bowl of bread.

'Your fans have arrived,' he muttered.

Keira turned, and saw Bay and Dora waving at her from the tavern's front doors. She sighed as they began to walk over.

'Don't be mean to them,' Flora said. 'They look up to you.'

The two young Kellach women approached the table.

'Can we sit with you, please?' said Dora.

'Will you be quiet?' Keira said.

'Aye.'

Keira nodded at a couple of spare chairs, and they sat down, beaming.

'Have you been in a fight?' Flora said, peering at them.

'Aye,' Bay said. 'A few of us caught up with those pricks from lunch; you know, the ones who were giving Keira grief.'

Dora gazed at Keira. 'They won't be disrespecting you again, mage.'

Keira smirked, and sipped her whisky.

'Can I ask you something, please?' Bay said. 'What did they mean? What happened at the Rakanese camp?'

Keira continued to stare out of the window. The light was fading, and lamps were being lit inside the tavern. She finished her glass of whisky, and poured another.

'Is it true you destroyed a whole city?' Dora said.

Keira said nothing.

'That's what those folk told us,' said Bay.

'I thought ye were going to be quiet,' Keira said. 'If ye don't shut up, ye can fuck off.'

The young women lowered their eyes, and sat in silence.

After an awkward minute, Flora spoke up. 'So, girls, you always seem to know what's going on – have you heard anything about the group coming in this evening?'

'Just more refugees from Rahain,' Bay said.

'Eight thousand,' said Dora. 'All heading down to the lowlands.'

'Call themselves a clan.'

'It's their leaders coming here tonight. Apparently, some of them say they know Mage Keira.'

Keira glanced at them. 'Who are they?'

Dora and Bay shrugged.

'Don't know any names,' Bay said.

'It could be anybody,' Keira said, putting her feet up onto a nearby stool. 'I know loads of folk.'

'Do you know when they'll get here?' Flora said.

'We can find out for you,' said Bay.

'Aye,' Keira said. 'You go do that, girls.'

The two young women stood and hurried from the tavern.

Agang poured himself a small whisky, and topped it up with some water.

'At some point,' he said, 'you should probably tell me and Flora what happened at the camp. I think we have a right to know.'

'Do ye now?' Keira said. 'Anyway, I thought ye already knew.'

'In the Plateau, King Guilliam, as he was then, told me that the Rahain had slaughtered an entire city of Rakanese refugees. He didn't mention you. But last year, a Holdings priest told me that it was you who had done it. That's all I know.'

Keira nodded to Flora. 'She knows. You can ask her. Just wait until I'm not around.'

'I know about as much as Agang,' Flora said. 'Just that you burned up a whole city. Half a million refugees, or something like that.'

'What did I just say, ya silly cow?' Keira cried. 'I ask ye not to speak about it, and off you go, spouting fucking numbers at me.' She glared at them. 'I'm not going to talk about it, do you understand? Fuckwits.'

Flora pushed back her chair and stood. 'I'm going back to bed.'

Keira shook her head as the Holdings woman strode from the still-empty tavern.

'You should be nicer to her,' Agang said.

'What's it to you, eight-thirds?' She downed her glass of whisky. 'You fancy her, don't ye? Ye just want to get into her pants.'

'Sometimes,' Agang said, 'you are completely clueless.' He stood. 'Good night.'

'What the fuck's that supposed to mean?' Keira yelled, as he walked away. She turned back to the windows, filled her glass, and watched the last lingering light of the sunset, its final glow diminishing into the horizon.

'You should treat your friends better,' Kelpie said, sitting at the table and pouring herself a whisky. 'As far as I can tell, they've stuck with you this long; they deserve a bit more respect.'

Keira snorted. 'You're one to talk. The way yer milking Agang, like he was a prize cow. Doesnae sound like respect to me.'

'Keira, my dear,' Kelpie said, shaking her head, 'I'm just trying to help you. Agang, it is true, is earning your keep here, but the important thing is that everyone knows you're home. You give the people hope, Keira.' She smiled. 'From the moment I saw you at Marchside, when you destroyed the attacking ranks of Rahain, I knew that you were special. Our folk have been scattered to the far corners of the world, those of us who have survived invasion, slavery and war, but now they are returning home.'

'And what the fuck's that got to do with me? I just want a quiet life.'

Kelpie laughed. 'You must know there's no chance of that. Whatever happened in the past, you're still Keira the fire mage, the one who rallied the clansfolk after the Rahain invasion, and cleared the lands of Kell and Lach of the lizards, until you were captured.'

Keira smirked.

'That's what most folk here remember about you,' Kelpie went on. 'You're still a hero to them. Most of the refugees coming in are from slave camps in Rahain, yet each night you talk of wars in Sanang, and fighting outside the walls of the empire's capital city. These lands are so far away for most folk that they may as well be listening to fables or legends.'

'Ye saying that I'm lying?'

Kelpie sighed. 'Of course not.'

The front doors of the tavern opened, and Bay and Dora ran in.

'They're coming,' Dora yelled. 'And there's loads of them.'

Keira stood, picking up the bottle of whisky and her glass.

'Close the shutters, Kendrie,' Kelpie said. 'Let's get ready.'

'And then the bastard appeared, high up on the city walls,' Keira said, a glass of whisky in one hand, the other gesticulating at the listening crowd. She scanned their faces, but recognised no one. 'He raised his arm and, just like that, the heads of every fucking Sanang warrior exploded, covering everything in brains and blood. A hundred thousand heads, bursting like ripe fruit. Pyre's arsehole, the fucking noise it made, it shook the ground like a low, long rumble. Mental.'

'How did ye get away?' cried someone amid the crowd.

'I ran for it,' Keira said. 'It was dark, and there were so many bodies around, no one noticed me go.'

'How many wars have ye been in?'

Keira frowned. 'Umm, let me think. The Rahain invasion, then when the Alliance attacked Rahain, and finally when the Sanang invaded the Plateau. Three.'

'You were with the alliance forces?' someone said. 'They liberated us from slavery.'

'Aye,' Keira said; 'that was our plan. Free all the slaves.'

'Tell us a story from that war.'

'Aye, all right.' She paused as the main doors opened, and another group of travellers entered. The crowd seemed to know who they were, and parted for them. Keira squinted through the dim lamplight as the group approached.

'Conal, ya wee bastard,' she yelled, standing and grinning. 'Yer alive!'

The young man gazed across the tavern at her, his mouth falling open.

'Clear a path,' Keira said, stepping out from behind her table. Alongside Conal were the others from the new group, and she spotted a solitary old Rahain man lurking near the back.

'Keira!' Conal cried, as she reached where he was standing.

She embraced him, squeezing hard and lifting him off the floor.

'I cannae tell ye how good it is to see a friendly face,' she said, releasing him. 'Are ye with the lot that's just come in from Rahain?'

'Aye,' Conal said, 'from Slateford.'

Keira nodded, the name meaning nothing to her.

A woman with short, dark hair stepped in front of her. 'Hello, Keira.'

'Who the fuck are you?'

The woman blinked. 'I'm Bridget. I was in your squad at Fallsie Castle, and under the Fire Temple.'

'Bridget?' Keira squinted. 'Oh aye, I mind ye now. A right wee sarcastic cow.'

Conal coughed. 'She's our chief.'

'I was,' Bridget said. 'We're in Domm now.'

A pale, blonde woman came to Bridget's side. 'Yer still our chief, no matter what the Domm Council says.'

'This is Dyam,' Bridget said, 'my herald.'

'Whatever,' Keira said. She glanced over to Kelpie. 'Talk's over. I'm getting drunk with my old squad.'

Kelpie frowned, but nodded.

'Come on,' Keira said. 'Sit with me. We'll crack open another bottle of whisky and ye can tell me what ye've been up to.'

As they began to move past her, she noticed a tall red-haired man.

'Bedig, you as well?' Keira said, slapping the big man across his back. 'How the fuck did you end up with these guys?'

'It's a long story,' he said, grinning, 'involving Kylon. By the way, do you know where he is?'

Keira shook her head. 'Last time I saw the prick, we were on the Plateau. We had a fight, I might have called him a useless dipshit, and he fucked off.'

Kendrie came over. 'Old friends?'

'Aye,' she said. 'They'll be needing food and plenty of booze.' She glanced at the small party sitting around her table. As well as Dyam and the three familiar faces, there were another half dozen that she didn't recognise, including the old Rahain man. 'Where are ye all staying?'

'A few of us have booked rooms here,' Bridget said, 'once we found out the World's End tavern was hosting Keira the fire mage.'

'See?' Keira smirked at Kendrie. 'Told ye I was good for business.'

She sat, and waited while bar-boys and girls filled the table with plates, ale and whisky.

'Here's to us,' Keira said, raising her glass and taking a drink. 'So,' she said, 'ye decided to get out of Rahain?'

'It's a mess,' Conal said. 'Slateford wasn't safe any more.'

'Slateford? Where the fuck's that?'

'It's the estate we were living on in Rahain,' Bridget said. 'Laodoc here gifted it to us.' She nodded at the grey-haired Rahain man sitting slouched over at the end of the table. He was the only one without a drink in his hand.

Keira eyed the folk at the table as an awkward silence fell. She narrowed her eyes.

'Is there something yer not telling me?'

Bridget downed her whisky. 'It's about your brother.'

'Killop?' Keira cried. 'Ye've seen him?'

'I've spent the last three years by his side,' Bridget said. 'In captivity, as a rebel, and then in Slateford.'

Keira's temper burned. 'Then where the fuck is he now?'

'He went off after Daphne,' Bridget said, 'his Holdings woman. He didn't come back.'

'Did you look for him?'

'We sent out a squad, but they lost track of him near the tunnel to the Plateau.'

Keira stood, clenching her fists. 'You lost him? Ye fucking lost him?'

'Wait...' said Bridget.

Keira lashed out with her right fist, striking Bridget in the eye and sending her flying back off her seat.

'Ye lost ma wee brother?' Keira screamed.

She raised her fist to strike again, but Bedig reached up and gripped her arm, and Dyam shoved herself in front of Bridget.

'Don't you touch her,' the blonde woman said, her eyes dark.

Keira yanked her arm free of Bedig and glared around the table.

'Ye bunch of cowardly shitstains. If ma brother's dead because of you, I'll fucking kill the lot of ye.'

She picked up the bottle of whisky, and barged past Bedig.

'Out of my way, ya prick.'

The crowd in the tavern parted in silence, and Keira strode out into the dark night sky before anyone could see the tears in her eyes.

CHAPTER 3
SHAMED

Westgate, Domm Pass – 15th Day, First Third Summer 507

Laodoc eased past the sleeping bodies to the door of the small room he was sharing with five Kellach Brigdomin. He crept out onto the landing, descended the deserted stairs, and went outside into the bright light of morning. It was too early for the tavern staff to be up, and there was no sign of any guests, so he wandered round the perimeter of the building until he came to the terrace overlooking the lowlands of Domm.

A sharp wind was blowing up from the west, and Laodoc pulled his cloak and scarf around him as he took in the panoramic view. The World's End tavern sat next to the road, at the far western end of the Domm Pass, just next to where the road led down a steep, switch-backed path to the lowlands below. White clouds scudded across the sky, rolling in from the great ocean, which was out of sight over the horizon. Domm spread out beneath the terrace, a vast carpet of green, dotted with farmsteads and villages.

Laodoc gazed over the little fence at the edge of the terrace at the straight drop down to the lowlands. A hundred feet, or more.

Why had he come here? He was useless to Bridget and the others, just a sad old man who contributed nothing. Although they tried not to show it, he knew they blamed him for Killop leaving, after he had cajoled Daphne into hunting down Douanna. If only he could discover if she had been successful. If he knew Douanna was dead, then perhaps he might feel some peace. Instead, the worst had occurred. Daphne and Killop had gone, and he didn't know if Douanna still lived.

She could be laughing at him at that moment.

Hatred billowed through him, the only genuine emotion he continued to experience.

He had fled Rahain, but he couldn't flee from himself. Maybe he should jump. His life was as good as over, anyway. No one would miss him.

He heard voices coming from his left. Round the corner of the terrace, by the back door of the tavern, Bedig and Dyam were standing.

'I don't know what to do,' Bedig said. 'She's inconsolable. Anything I say just makes it worse.'

'I'm raging at that cow Keira,' Dyam said. 'She humiliated Bridget. If I see her today...'

'Just stay clear of her,' Bedig said. 'She's mental.'

'And pretending she didn't recognise her,' Dyam said, scowling. 'Bitch.'

'She probably didn't. That's just Keira. I was a bit surprised she remembered who I was, to be honest.'

'She thinks she's something special.'

'She was upset about her brother, but.'

'But it wasn't Bridget's fault,' Dyam spat. 'She wanted to take half the clan to go looking for Killop, but Draewyn and the rest outvoted her. There was nothing she could do.'

'I know.'

Dyam shook her head, then frowned. 'Laodoc,' she said, 'you can stop eavesdropping and come over.'

Laodoc's face reddened, and he turned towards them.

'Morning,' Bedig said.

'Good morning,' Laodoc said. He walked over to where they stood.

'Sleep well?' Dyam said.

'Fine.'

'Are you sure?' Dyam said. 'You don't look so good.'

'I can assure you, Miss Herald, I am perfectly well.'

'I worry about you,' she said, 'and so does Bridget. You're not eating enough.'

'I fail to see the point.'

'In eating?'

'In anything.'

'Come on,' Bedig said; 'we've just survived a civil war, and we're almost at the end of our journey.' He pointed out over the Domm lowlands. 'In a few days we'll be down there, ready to begin new lives.'

'And what is it that you think I'll be doing down there?' Laodoc said. 'Farming? Milking cows? I know nothing about this kind of life, and am too old to learn.'

'We'll find you something to do,' said Dyam. 'How does teaching sound? I plan on setting up a few schools for the clan when we get settled. You could help with lessons in Rahain.'

Laodoc frowned, and gazed out at the view. 'I don't like children.'

Dyam shrugged. 'You don't have to do anything. You're retired; you can put your feet up and relax. The clan will always look after you.'

He bowed his head and said nothing.

'You could write a book or something,' Bedig said. 'Your biography.'

'Autobiography,' Dyam said.

'Who on earth would want to read that?'

'Me, for one,' Dyam said.

'I'm too bitter to write. It would come out all twisted.'

'I'll see about getting you paper and pencils,' Dyam said, 'in case you change your mind.'

Laodoc said nothing.

Bedig stretched his arms. 'We should go in for breakfast.'

'Do you think Keira will be there?' Laodoc said.

'I spoke to the owner last night,' said Dyam. 'After apologising, she told me that Keira doesn't usually get up before noon. She spends her nights drinking, either in the tavern, or in her room.'

Laodoc shook his head. 'So this is how the world's most powerful mage spends her time? The great Keira, a violent drunk.'

Bedig shrugged. 'So what's new? She's always been like that, when she's not fighting some war.'

He opened the door, and they went back into the tavern. A large fire was blazing in a hearth to their left, and they sat at a table close to its warmth.

Kendrie walked over. 'Porridge?'

'Aye, please,' Dyam said. 'Plenty of salt on mine.'

'Can I get an extra portion for Bridget?' Bedig said.

Kendrie nodded and walked off to the kitchens, while a bar-girl put a jug of ale and some mugs on the table. Bedig muttered a thank you and poured himself an ale.

'Nice,' he said. 'Good ale, good whisky, good food. I can see why Keira stayed.'

'It's just ordinary Domm stuff,' Dyam said.

'Maybe, but after years of Rahain and Holdings food, it tastes like the best thing ever.'

A bar-boy came over with a tray, and unloaded four large bowls of steaming porridge, a salt cellar and a pot of honey.

'Thanks,' Dyam said.

Laodoc spooned a large helping of honey into his bowl, while Bedig downed his ale and stood. He picked up two bowls.

'I'll see if Bridget's hungry,' he said.

'See you later,' Dyam said, as the tall Brig walked away. She turned to Laodoc, and eyed him as she put salt on her porridge.

'You're depressed,' she said.

He said nothing.

'It'll pass,' she went on. 'It might take a while, but it will pass. And until it does, we're here for you. If ever you want to talk about anything, I'll be happy to listen.'

Laodoc stirred his porridge, his appetite fading. He felt so worthless; he didn't deserve their help.

'I know you mean well,' he said, 'but I'm fine.'

Dyam nodded as she ate her porridge, her eyes unconvinced.

Laodoc pushed his bowl away and gazed out of the window at the clouds racing across the sky. He heard the main doors of the tavern open, and watched as a small group of uniformed Kellach entered. He glanced at Dyam, and nodded at the doors.

She turned.

The group approached the bar and spoke to Kendrie, who pointed over at their table.

Dyam put down her spoon. 'Can I help you?'

The group walked over and stopped in front of Dyam. A woman stepped forward.

'We're looking for the leadership of the Severed Clan.'

'I'm the herald. What do you want?'

'Apologies for disturbing your breakfast, ma'am, but we have been sent by the Domm Council at Threeways Junction,' the woman said. 'They have delivered their verdict regarding the legal status of the clan.'

Dyam nodded. 'Then we'll need to get Chief Bridget.' She gazed over at the bar. 'Kendrie, could we please have somewhere private?'

'The back room should be free,' Kendrie said. 'Give me a few minutes to get it ready.'

Dyam turned back to the uniformed group. 'Take a seat,' she said. 'I'll go and find the chief.' She started to walk for the door, then stopped.

'This is Laodoc,' she said. 'I know he's Rahain, but he's a benefactor and friend of the Severed Clan. Please treat him with courtesy.'

The group took seats next to him at the table.

'Nice to meet you, Laodoc,' said one.

The old man said nothing, and turned to gaze out of the window.

Ten minutes later, Kendrie emerged from a side door, and beckoned towards the group of uniformed Kellach. They stood, and walked in his direction. Laodoc got to his feet and followed them. They passed through the door and into a large, windowless chamber, with a long table and rows of seats.

'I'll have drinks brought through for you in a moment,' Kendrie said, as he left.

Laodoc took a seat at the end of the table, while the other Kellach stood, waiting. After a few minutes, the door opened, and several bar-boys and girls came in with trays of ale and food. As they were laying them out on the table, the door opened again, and Bridget walked in.

Her left eye was swollen and a greenish-purple bruise covered her temple. She looked tired, but wore a determined expression on her face. Behind her entered Dyam, Draewyn, Brodie, Liam and Brynt, the members of her clan leadership council.

'This is Chief Bridget of the Severed Clan,' Dyam said.

'Greetings,' said the uniformed woman who had spoken before. 'We are representatives of the Domm Council.'

Bridget nodded. 'I understand that you bring news?'

'We do.'

'Please, have a drink; make yourselves comfortable.'

They sat round the table, the clan on one side, and the council representatives on the other, with Laodoc at one end. No one paid him any attention, so he remained where he was, listening.

'The council have thought long and hard about the Severed Clan,' the woman said, 'and their position within Domm society. On the one hand, we wish to be fair to you, and understand that you have suffered together, in slavery, and under the oppression of foreign regimes. However, it is intolerable that any one group is ruled by a different set of laws, with different leaders. Here in Domm, we are all equal under the same law.'

'Excuse me for interrupting,' Dyam said, 'but what about the Domm Highlands? Isn't it the case that they rule themselves?'

The woman frowned. 'It is true,' she said, 'that in certain highland glens, renegade Domm live outwith the control of the council. The folk up there refuse to accept any incomers from Brig, Lach or Kell, and do not recognise the council's authority. It is for precisely that reason that we cannot tolerate another separate enclave. Believe me, one is bad enough.'

'So,' Dyam said, 'in practical terms, what does this ruling mean for us?'

'We want it to mean as little as possible,' the woman said. 'We encourage you to hold on to your cultural cohesion. Set up your own villages, your own schools and temples, and carry on with your traditions. You can continue to call yourselves the Severed Clan,' she said, pausing as she gazed around the table, 'but understand that none of it has any legal standing. The law, the courts, the militia, taxation, all of it, is under the authority of the Domm Council.'

Laodoc coughed. 'May I ask a question?'

The woman looked at him. 'Sure.'

'The Domm Council,' he said, 'does it have people on it from the other clans?'

'You mean Brig and so on?'

'Yes.'

'Aye,' the woman said, 'a man and a woman from each, making up eight altogether on the council.'

'And how are these members chosen?'

'They were selected three years ago, after we came down from the Domm Highlands.' She took a drink. 'The lizards had evacuated Brig, and for the first time we felt safe enough to venture down to Threeways, where the Domm Pass meets the road to the old Fire Temple. All the village elders got together and picked the eight members of the council.'

'Are they members for life, then?' said Laodoc, ignoring the 'lizards' comment.

The woman frowned.

'Laodoc is something of a constitutional scholar,' Bridget said, a weak smile on her lips.

He glanced at her. 'I am just trying to establish what kind of governmental structure has been implemented. I'm guessing that their arrangements were probably drawn up under considerable stress, and I think it quite remarkable that they have created such stability. The Domm Pass seems much more civilised than I'd been led to expect.'

'Thank you,' the woman said. 'It's not quite the same down in the lowlands. Our militia can only do so much, and the settlements down there are spread far and wide. You may have to look to your own security at times.'

'We can handle ourselves,' said Dyam.

'I've no doubt you can.' The woman finished her drink. 'I think we're finished here. I'd love to stay, and catch the fire mage speak, but we're wanted back at Threeways by nightfall.' She stood. 'Any questions? Is everything understood?'

Bridget looked at the tabletop. 'It is.'

'Then we'll be leaving.' She opened a purse, and passed over a handful of coins to Kendrie, who had been lurking by the doorway. She nodded to Bridget, and they trooped out of the chamber. Kendrie followed them out, closing the door behind him.

Bridget broke down in tears.

The others glanced at each other. Dyam put her arm over Bridget's shoulder, but she shrugged it off.

Brodie poured himself an ale. He took a sip, and nodded. 'That's it, then. The clan's done.'

'No, it's not,' said Dyam. 'You heard what she said. We can form our own settlements and farm our own land. We can keep on being the Severed Clan.'

'What's the point?' Brodie said. 'If given the choice, I'd rather go back to Brig. I heard that more villages are being repopulated there, just beyond the eastern end of the Domm Pass.'

'Don't be ridiculous,' Draewyn said. 'We should stick together. I'm looking forward to setting up a village with a few of the lassies that I knew at Slateford.'

'But you're Domm,' Brodie said. 'This is your home.' He pointed to the east. 'My home's that way, over the pass to Brig.'

'We're all Kellach Brigdomin now,' said Dyam.

Brodie shook his head. 'What a surprise; you're Domm as well. Of course you're saying that, because it's like we're all guests in your home. We all know that the majority of folk that survived are Domm; you just want the rest of us to become Domm as well.'

'That's not true,' said Dyam.

'We wouldnae have ye, anyway,' Draewyn chuckled.

'I know what he means,' said Liam, the old sparker, 'but at least settlers are starting to return to Brig. Lach is a wasteland.'

'Aye,' said Dyam. 'It'll be a while before anyone lives there again, but one day they will, Liam. One day.'

The pale blonde woman paused, and glanced at Bridget, who was sitting with her head in her hands.

'You'll always be chief to me, Bridget,' she said, 'no matter what anyone says.'

'Ye did a grand job,' Draewyn said. 'Ye should be proud.'

Bridget looked up, and dried her tears. 'How soon can we get out of here?'

'The clan's already moving down the road into the lowlands,' Dyam said, pulling a map from her cloak and unfolding it onto the table. 'We can be on our way first thing tomorrow morning. I'm for taking what the council said literally, and forming our own settlement area.' She pointed at the map. 'Now, Draewyn's old village is here, aye?'

Draewyn nodded.

'And we agreed to re-settle this area,' Dyam said, tracing out a region of the map. 'So we stick to our plan, and send the clansfolk to assemble here.' She glanced at Bridget. 'That's what I think, anyway.'

'And that's what we'll do,' Bridget said. 'You and Draewyn know the geography, and you know what we're looking for.'

'You can see the ocean from here,' Draewyn said, pointing at the map.

'So it'll be windy, then,' Brodie said. 'Does the wind ever stop in this fucking place?'

Bridget frowned at him. 'You don't have to come. Go back to Brig if you want. Personally, I'd rather you stayed with us. I've got plans for a great big clan brewery and distillers, to see if we can make gin, ale and whisky like we did at Slateford, then maybe we can sell it to the other settlers.'

Brodie narrowed his eyes. 'And how would we afford to build such a facility?'

'Don't worry,' Bridget said; 'I have the gold for it, and for all the houses and schools we'll need.'

'You have gold?' said Draewyn.

'I do,' Bridget said, 'and I apologise for telling no one except Dyam about it until now; but I wanted to ensure it remained intact to fund our settlement.'

The others glanced at each other.

'Where did you get it?' said Draewyn.

Bridget smiled, for the first time in many days. 'Let's just say that Daphne Holdfast wasn't a poor woman.'

Laodoc leaned against the fence, watching the vast sunset unfold before him. He was standing in the same spot as he had that morning. It was a good spot, he reflected, away from the prying eyes of most.

He looked down the sheer slope, and considered jumping. Today had been a good day. He had felt a flicker of interest in the workings of the Domm Council, and it was a rare day when he was interested in anything. And Bridget had smiled, also a rarity. Leading the clan while it had journeyed from Rahain to Domm had borne down upon her shoulders with the weight of a mountain. He wondered if she would feel relieved once it dawned on her that she was now without any legal responsibility for anyone else, but he doubted it. She cared too much, like he once had.

No, he wasn't going to jump that day.

He frowned as he remembered that they were leaving in the morning. He would quite like the chance to see if he felt like jumping every day.

'Hello,' a voice said.

Laodoc's frown remained. 'I came out here for some quiet, thank you very much.'

'Do you not remember me?' the voice said.

Laodoc turned to glance at the stranger, and his tongue flickered in surprise. 'Agang?'

'May we talk?'

Laodoc sighed. 'Very well.'

'Dyam told me I'd find you out here.'

'And so you have. Well done.'

'I thought you'd want to talk.'

Laodoc snorted. 'Really? Just because we are two failed rulers of our respective countries, you think we share a bond?'

'Why are you being so rude?'

'Let's just call it my revenge for the way you treated me during the alliance invasion of Rahain,' Laodoc spat. 'Do you think I have forgotten your behaviour? You were insufferable.'

Agang bowed his head. 'You are right. I apologise. I've changed.'

Laodoc laughed. 'Strange how humiliation does that to people. I see that you are now a friend of the woman who overthrew you. You must have wallowed deep in the pit of shame and self-loathing; how else would you be able to look at Keira without breaking?'

'You know nothing,' cried Agang, his face turning red. 'You haven't the faintest idea of what happened to the Emperor, of what he's now capable of doing. I saw him use the powers of many different mage lines: fire, water, stone, vision.'

Laodoc frowned. 'What?'

'The Emperor is now like a god.'

Laodoc shook his head. 'We did hear some fanciful rumours when we were entering the Kellach Littoral a couple of thirds back. Are you saying you were there?'

Agang nodded. 'You need to hear Keira speak.'

Laodoc's tongue flickered again. 'No, thank you.'

'Look,' Agang said; 'I'm sorry for getting angry. I know you've been through a lot, but I need to explain to you what's been happening.

You're one of the few people here who will grasp the full significance of the events in Plateau City that we witnessed.'

Laodoc shrugged. 'I don't care. Now, if you would kindly leave me alone.'

He stared back out at the sunset, its red hues spanning the vast sky.

'Then I have to apologise again,' said Agang.

'For what?'

'For this.'

Agang reached out with his hand and took Laodoc's arm in a tight grasp. Laodoc opened his mouth to protest, but he began to feel a powerful surge of energy grow within his body. He arched his back, as every strain and sprain disappeared in a golden glow of well-being. All the old aches that he had lived with for years vanished in an instant. He felt the surge pass into his head, and he nearly passed out, and would have fallen, had Agang let go of his arm. He felt euphoric as the power passed through his mind, and a feeling of pity and love flooded him.

He broke down and began to sob, and Agang put his arm round his shoulder.

'Sorry,' he said. 'I must have used too much power; you're not supposed to be weeping.'

'It's all my fault,' Laodoc cried. 'Killop would never have left if I hadn't bullied Daphne into looking for Douanna. It's my fault he's not here with his sister, all because of my blindness, my selfish stupidity. I cared more about Douanna's death than the lives of my friends.'

'It's all right,' Agang said. 'It is what it is.'

Laodoc glanced at the Sanang man. 'You're a mage?'

Agang nodded. 'I've been hiding it for years.'

'You healed me.'

'How do you feel?'

'Amazing,' Laodoc said. 'Thank you.'

'Dyam told me you were feeling...'

'And I'm healed?'

'No,' Agang said. 'The mind doesn't work like that. I've corrected the balance within your brain, but if there's something else that's making you depressed, then it might come back. Your memories, for example. My power doesn't reach them.'

'I still feel wonderful,' he said. 'The pain and grief haven't gone, but I feel as though I am capable of hope again.' He smiled. 'I also feel like hearing your tale of what happened to the Emperor, but unfortunately, the Severed Clan is due to leave in the morning.'

'That's the other reason I'm out here,' Agang said, 'to try to persuade you to stay.'

'Here with the fire mage?' said Laodoc, narrowing his eyes.

'And me and Flora, a Holdings woman,' Agang said. 'If you don't like it, you could always re-join the clan.'

'So tell me,' Laodoc said; 'is living with Keira tolerable?'

Agang shrugged. 'I like her. She takes a bit of getting used to. She drinks too much, a bit like the Sanang do, and I've had to heal her more than once after a bar fight; but you need to hear her story.'

Laodoc turned from the sunset, his heart full. 'And where is Keira just now? I think I would like to talk to her.'

Keira was holding court in a small alcove within the busy tavern. The shutters along the western wall were spread open, allowing the last rays of the day to flood into the room. At Keira's table sat four others. Two were young and pretty Kellach women, one was the older owner of the place, and the fourth was a dark-skinned Holdings woman, clutching a glass of whisky as Keira talked.

'If we'd been born in Sanang, none of us would have seen the light of day until we were led out to be married. And even then we'd be covered up in big sheets, so nae bastard could look at us.'

'Why?' said one of the young women.

'The men there treat women like possessions,' Keira said, 'and get jealous if any other man speaks to them, or even looks at them. It's mental.'

The Holdings woman looked up and saw Laodoc and Agang approach.

'We could ask the man himself,' Flora said. 'Here he is, the ex-king of Sanang.'

They reached the table.

'Keira,' Agang said, 'this is Laodoc.'

The fire mage glanced over. 'Aye? I met him last night. A right miserable bastard; didn't say one fucking word to me.'

'You barely gave me a chance, madam,' Laodoc said. 'You punched Bridget in the face not two minutes after you sat down. And then, I believe, the evening was over.'

Keira squinted at him. 'Think yer funny?'

'Not at all, madam. I am merely interested in listening to the tales you tell here each day. Agang has assured me that I would find them fascinating.'

He sat, and poured himself a glass of whisky. He held it up.

'The fabled whisky of Kellach Brigdomin?' he said. 'In all the chats I used to have with Killop, when he lived in my house in Rahain with Bridget and Kallie, they never failed to mention how much they missed whisky.'

He took a sip, as Keira sat in silence watching him.

'Lovely,' he said. 'Now, madam mage, I would like to stay here in World's End and listen to your tales, and in return I will tell you everything I know of Killop. Where he lived, what he did, right up until the day he risked his life to save the woman he loved.'

Keira frowned, then raised her glass. 'Alright.' She glanced at the older Kellach woman.

'That's fine by me,' she said. 'I'm Kelpie, by the way, proprietor of this establishment. I can put you on the same ticket as the others, Laodoc, which means you get a room, shared with Agang, and your food and drink. All you have to do is sit by Keira each day as she speaks.'

'It's a deal, madam,' said Laodoc.

Kelpie chuckled. 'Just think, my tavern will be hosting folk from three foreign countries – the ape-folk, the dark-skinned folk, and now the lizard-folk.' She looked around the table. 'No offence.'

'There's one more,' Keira said.

'Eh?'

'Where is he?' Keira muttered, scanning the people in the tavern. 'There he is. Hoi! Over here.'

Laodoc's tongue flickered as Dean emerged from the crowd and walked over.

'This is Dean, Kelpie,' Keira said.

'Aye, so?'

'We need to add him to the ticket.'

'And why would I do that?'

'Because he wants to stay here, with me.'

'So what?' Kelpie said.

Keira leaned over, grinning. 'He's a fucking fire mage.'

CHAPTER 4
HOLD FAST

Hold Fast, Realm of the Holdings – 20th Day, First Third Summer 507

Daphne muffled a cry and fell back onto the warm straw, listening to the sound of Killop breathing, and feeling the touch of his skin next to hers.

There was a rustling noise, and she opened her eyes. A horse in the neighbouring stall was looking over the partition wall at Daphne and Killop as they lay together.

'We might have an audience,' Daphne whispered, reaching down and pulling her underwear and leggings back up.

Killop laughed.

'We'd better go back out before anyone notices that we've been gone a while,' she said.

He refastened his clothes and sat up. 'That was great.'

'I lost my virginity in a stable.'

Killop raised an eyebrow.

'Not in these stables, I should add,' she said. 'At the academy in Holdings City. I didn't have any proper boyfriends until I'd left home.'

They got to their feet, and smoothed their clothes and hair.

'I lost mine in the toilets behind a tavern,' Killop said. 'Not exactly romantic.'

'How old were you?'

'Sixteen.'

Daphne opened the stall door and peered out. 'It's clear; come on.'

They came out into a long passageway with lines of stalls down either side. Sunlight was pouring in from great openings in the roof, and the heat, mixed with the heady smell of the stables, felt more like home to Daphne than anything else in the world. She gazed up at Killop and smiled. He took her hand.

As they walked towards the exit, they passed the stall with the white stallion they had brought from Rahain.

Daphne stopped. 'How are you this morning, boy?' she said, rubbing the horse's flank. 'Shall we go out for a ride later?' She glanced at Killop. 'I must choose a name soon. I can't keep calling him "boy".'

'What about using the name Karalyn has for him?'

'What, Bedig?'

Killop shrugged. 'She must miss the big oaf. Either that, or she sees a resemblance.'

Daphne laughed. 'If he had a tuft of red hair on his head, maybe. I don't know; I named my last horse after a friend who had died.'

She paused, her thoughts going back to Vince. Over a third had passed since she had learned the news, and she felt her sorrow return, though it was never far from the surface. The stallion nuzzled into the side of her face.

'You all right?' said Killop.

She nodded, then glanced up at the horse. 'See you soon, boy.'

Killop took her hand again, and they walked to the open sliding doors of the huge stable block. Outside, the sun was shining, and the roads around the Holdfast mansion were starting to get busy. Garlands and flags were festooned from every rooftop and balcony, and the tall tower ahead of them was decorated in swathes of coloured banners.

To their left, the enormous covered pavilion was filled with traders and merchants setting up stalls, and sellers hawking food and drink wandered through the growing crowds.

'I love festival time,' Daphne said.

Killop narrowed his eyes at the crowds. 'Does every Hold have its own?'

'Yes,' Daphne said, 'though ours is held last. The festivals mark the anniversary of a Hold joining the Realm in the Founding Year of the Kingdom, so most are clustered around the start of spring. Hold Fast was the last to join, so we have ours in summer.'

'Did the first king conquer all the other Holds?'

'Most of them surrendered,' Daphne said. 'The first king had the first prophet by his side, and was pretty much invincible in battle. Hold Fast held out the longest, but by then all the other Holds were allied against us, and so we joined the Realm. It might have been five hundred years ago, but the Holdfasts have always been proud that we were the last to surrender our independence.'

She glanced at him. 'Are you ready for the heat?'

'Aye,' he said, and they stepped out into the road, where the sun beat down upon them with a searing light.

'It's hot today,' she said, as they walked down the road to their right.

'It's like being in a furnace.'

'It'll be shaded over by the market,' she said, 'and we can get something to drink.'

They followed the road to where it opened out into a large square, with low stone buildings on three sides, and the Holdfast mansion set back on the left. In the centre of the square was a great marble fountain, twelve yards in diameter, sending cascades of water into the air. Children splashed and ran in the shallows by the outer circumference, shouting and laughing in the sunshine.

Around the fountain was a market, with lines of stalls selling cold drinks and warm food. Slabs of beef hung from hooks, and boxes of vegetables and fruit were on display. Daphne and Killop ducked under the canvas canopies of the stalls, and wandered down the line. They bought two cold ales from an old woman, and Daphne lit a cigarette.

'Morning, miss,' an old man said as they passed, bowing his head.

'Morning,' Daphne replied.

They passed out of the market and approached the mansion. They walked round to the rear porch, and ascended the steps. Daphne gazed up at the clock face on the side of the old tower in the distance.

'Let's sit here and finish our drinks,' she said. 'We've got a few minutes.'

They sat down on a long, cushioned bench and watched the people in the market.

'This place seems so untouched by all the wars,' said Killop.

'You may not see it, but I do,' she said. 'The festival this year is about half as busy as I last remember it, and there's hardly anything for sale. And there are not many people of my age around. They've all been enlisted. Or killed.'

Killop said nothing.

'And it's getting worse,' she went on. 'The Emperor's raids on the Kellach quarter in Plateau City and his invasion of Rainsby have killed hundreds more, on both sides.'

'Holdings fighting Kellach,' he said, shaking his head.

'And for three days now they've been sacking Rainsby, searching for hidden mages.'

'And my sister's body.'

'The Emperor's a fool.'

Killop nodded at the road. 'Your brother is coming.'

Daphne frowned and looked up. Jonah was approaching the mansion with two other men. A few paces behind, a small retinue of servants were carrying trays.

Jonah climbed the steps, then paused when he saw Daphne.

'Good morning,' he said.

'Good morning,' said Daphne.

The two other men joined Jonah at the top of the steps and there was an awkward silence.

'Are you wanting the porch?' Daphne said.

'No, no,' Jonah said. 'It's fine. We can go somewhere else.'

'Don't be silly,' Daphne said; 'we were just leaving.'

She stood, and Killop got to his feet after her. He nodded to Jonah as he followed Daphne into the house, but her brother and his friends ignored him. They entered the cool air of the rear hall, where a water fountain bubbled in a corner.

Daphne frowned, as the voices of Jonah and his friends came through from the porch.

'I should go back there and speak to him,' she said. 'I saw him ignoring you.'

'Don't,' he said. 'He's not the only one that does it.'

'I know,' she said, 'and I don't like it. I can see them starting to get to you.'

'It's fine.'

She looked away from Killop's frown, and gazed out of the door where her brother sat. Servants were serving them drinks, and they were smoking and chatting. She had stopped caring what Jonah thought years before, but she felt insulted that he was treating Killop as if he were invisible. Her mother was doing much the same. She felt her temper rise.

'Come on,' he said. 'You'll be late for lunch.'

Daphne turned her back on the porch, and they walked through the hall. Servants bowed as they passed, and they made their way to a small chamber on the southern side of the mansion. In its centre was a low pool, fed by four small fountainheads, and the roof above was open. Around the walls were long couches, covered by a vaulted ceiling held up by slim pillars.

'There you are,' her father said.

Daphne smiled, and she and Killop walked through the pillars to where her father sat reclining on a couch. A low table was set out before him, covered in dishes and jugs. Finely woven sheets were hanging from the ceiling, providing more shade.

'Mummy,' Karalyn cried, running out from behind the couch.

'Hiya, Kara-bear,' Daphne said, picking her up. 'Have you been a good girl for Papa?'

'She has been perfectly behaved,' her father said. 'What have you two been up to?'

Daphne put Karalyn down, and sat on the couch opposite her father. 'I showed Killop round the pavilion stables, and visited our stallion.'

'A fine beast,' her father said. 'He's one of the best on the estate right now, the Emperor having taken most of the others.'

Killop hoisted Karalyn up onto his shoulders.

'Have a nice lunch,' he said. 'I'll see you later.'

'Good day, Killop,' her father said.

Daphne waved. 'See you this evening. And remember to duck when you go through doorways.'

Killop smiled, and set off.

'A good man,' her father said.

'Yes.'

Her father poured drinks. 'It's been a while since we talked, Daffie; how are you holding up?'

'Fine,' she said. 'I mean, I hadn't seen Vince in a while, but I always thought in the back of my mind that I'd be able to speak to him again. And now I never will.'

She bowed her head.

'It was the worst moment of my life when I learned the news from the Sanang frontier,' her father said, 'but I can't allow myself to wallow in grief, not when I have three other children to worry about.'

'You needn't worry about me.'

'Daffie, my dear, how could I not? Up until now, we have managed to keep your presence here fairly quiet, but dozens will see you during the festival. The Emperor may be busy in Rainsby right now, but he's bound to learn that you have returned.'

'I'm not running away again,' she said. 'All I've done for the last few years is go from one end of the world to the other, and now that I'm back home, the Emperor will have to come here in person to shift me.'

Her father frowned. 'That's what worries me.'

She lit a cigarette. 'Are there many One True Path in the Holdings?'

He shook his head. 'There are probably a few agents about, but they keep to themselves. When Guilliam moved his throne to Plateau City, he took the entire government with him, and the church followed. The Lord Regent officially rules from Holdings City as the Emperor's representative, but he has no army, and no money. The Holds have been left to fend for themselves, in the main.'

'Then I should be safe here, for the moment, anyway.'

Her father nodded. 'I have a guest arriving soon, but before that, I wanted to ask you something.'

'All right.'

'Yesterday, I saw you practising battle-vision.'

'I try to do a few hours every week.'

'But you're a high mage.'

'I suppose so. I mean, I have every power on the vision scale, and a few extra.'

'But no mage can master more than one or two powers,' he said. 'If you're practising battle, what have you sacrificed?'

'Nothing, I can do them all.'

Her father spluttered. 'What? But no, Daffie dear; that is simply impossible.'

Daphne frowned. She recalled hearing her lecturers at the academy say similar things.

'It's clearly not impossible,' she said; 'because I can do them all. Actually, not all. I can't speak to the Creator whenever I feel like it, but that's not a power I'd want to have.'

'So you're saying that you can do battle, line, range, inner and outer-vision?'

'Not only that,' she said; 'I can do them one after the other, without a break between.'

Her father frowned. 'Now I know you're exaggerating.'

'Well,' she said, 'I sometimes need five minutes. And a bottle of something strong helps.'

'If what you're saying is true,' her father said, shaking his head, 'then you are one of the most powerful mages alive today.'

'I'm good at what I do,' she said, 'but one of the best? I don't know about that.'

'You're probably not aware of this,' he said, 'but the toll on mages over the last few years has been devastating. And I'm not just talking about the Holdings, though we have suffered grievously. Kellach, Rahain and Rakanese high mages have been killed off in their dozens. Ten mages are now believed to have died in the ritual that gave the Emperor his powers.'

'Ten? I thought you said five.'

'I have learned from my sources that a further five Holdings mages died, acting as some kind of conduit. Furthermore, I believe Father Rijon was one of them.'

'Rijon?' Daphne said, masking a smile.

'He was ranked at the very highest level, as were several others who have perished in the wars. What I'm getting at, my dear Daffie, is that you are most likely one of the few high mages remaining.'

She shrugged. 'There's still Arnault, and Ghorley, and Princess Shella.'

'Your friend Shella is missing, I'm afraid.'

Daphne glared at him. 'How long have you known this?'

'For a while,' he said, 'but I didn't want to burden you with even more worry.'

'What happened to her?'

'The known facts are that she was arrested by the One True Path for refusing to answer the summons for all mages to hand themselves over to the imperial authorities, and taken into custody. After that, no one knows what happened to her. There was a rumour that she might have been killed in the ritual that empowered the Emperor, but no remains have ever been found.'

'Another missing body.'

'Yes, but unlike Fire Mage Keira, nobody saw Shella die. My sources believe that she was helped to escape, and the Emperor is too embarrassed to admit it.'

'Killop believes Keira is still alive.'

Her father nodded. 'After what he said the night you arrived, I decided to carry out my own investigations.' He paused. 'Unfortunately for Killop, I have spoken to three people I trust, who saw her fall with their own eyes. The Emperor flicked his hand from the walls of the city and, surrounded by the headless remains of her army, she collapsed, dead.'

Daphne picked up a glass of iced tea and drank, saying nothing. She wasn't sure if she should relay this news to Killop, or whether it would be better to allow him to hold onto his hopes.

A servant entered from an archway.

'My Lord Holder,' she said, bowing, 'your guests have arrived.'

A man and a woman appeared, and approached the low table.

'Greetings, Faden,' her father said. 'Did you have a good journey from the capital?'

'Long and uncomfortable, Godfrey,' the man said. He noticed Daphne. 'Miss Holdfast,' he bowed, 'a pleasure to meet you, as always.'

Daphne stood, and curtsied. 'And you, Lord Holdwick. May I offer my congratulations?'

Faden raised an eyebrow.

'On Ariel's pregnancy,' Daphne said. 'Your third child.'

'Of course,' Faden said. 'Thank you.'

'I know how much my sister and the children have missed you.'

'I have just spent a most delightful morning in their company,' he said. 'I wish I could be with them more, but my work keeps me in Holdings City.'

'Please sit,' her father said.

Faden reclined on one of the couches as a servant poured him a drink.

The woman approached.

'This, Daphne,' her father said, 'is Annifrid, commander of the Hold Fast Company.'

'Hello,' said Daphne.

The woman bowed, and sat. She was a few years older than Daphne, and had the look of a cavalry veteran.

They all lit cigarettes, and drank iced tea.

'When I arrived this morning,' Faden said, 'I couldn't help but notice that the festival seems quiet this year.'

Her father sighed. 'It's the lowest attendance in decades. The country's largest horse fair, and no damn horses to buy or sell. We even had to cancel most of the competitions.'

'It's the same everywhere, old chap,' Faden said. 'The imperial army has stripped the Holdings bare. The economy's on the verge of collapse, trade is almost non-existent, and with the Emperor's insane invasion of Rainsby, the only major trade link to Rahain has been cut. The River Holdings are seething with rage; it'll only take one spark and they'll explode.'

'No, no,' her father said, shaking his head. 'It's bad, I'll grant you, but I don't believe a collapse is imminent. There is opportunity here, my friend, for the Holds to unite. If we band together, the Lord Regent will be unable stop us.'

Faden frowned.

Her father chuckled. 'Daphne is completely trustworthy, Faden; you needn't worry about what you say in front of her.'

'With all due respect, Godfrey, did she not used to work for the church?'

'Just the one time,' Daphne said; 'when I rescued Princess Shella from the Rakanese camp, which I certainly don't regret. The church themselves call me a renegade.'

'And what are your thoughts on the empire?'

'I'm not against it in principle, I suppose,' she said, 'if it was fairly done. You may not agree with this, but from the outside world, it looks as though the Holdings are in charge. Rakana is firmly under the thumb, and Rahain is ruled by Governor Ghorley. And the Emperor himself, of course, is Holdings. To every other race of people, we are the imperial overlords, and our church is feared even more than our soldiers.'

'If only they knew how much resistance there is here to the Emperor and the church,' her father said. 'Guilliam lost a lot of love when he moved to the Plateau. Did you know he hasn't been back once since his coronation? In the early days of the alliance, the people remained hopeful and proud, but with the endless losses in war, and the savage recruitment for the new army, the poor in the River Holdings have suffered much. And we, the Holds of the great plains, have been taxed and stripped of our resources.'

'We wouldn't mind so much,' Faden said, 'if there were some terrible necessity or grand strategy underpinning the Emperor's actions. But all he seems to care about is the gathering up of every mage in the world, and for what? No one seems to have an answer.'

'To become even more powerful?' Daphne said.

Her father shook his head. 'Annifrid here has not long returned from the imperial city, where she saw the Emperor in person. Tell her about it, Anni.'

The commander flushed a little as she caught Godfrey's eyes, and Daphne frowned.

'I was staying with an old cavalry officer that I used to know,' Annifrid said, turning to Daphne, 'and she was called up as part of the force that assaulted the Kellach quarter. Emperor Guilliam himself came down to the barracks on the morning of the attack, and I heard him speak to the soldiers.' She shook her head. 'Then he personally led the assault. I went along, and saw what he did. He was... unstoppable. He must have killed hundreds.

'The soldiers followed behind, searching for the body of the fire mage. From a basement under a tavern, I saw them haul out a Sanang hedgewitch, or at least that's what I was told. I left the Kellach quarter after that; I couldn't stand any more.'

'The irony,' said Daphne's father. 'They went in looking for a dead fire mage, and came out with a living hedgewitch.'

Daphne caught Annifrid smile at her father. She narrowed her eyes.

'I wonder who they'll find in Rainsby,' Faden said. 'There are bound to be one or two mages hiding down there. And then we face the most important question: where will the Emperor strike next?'

Her father nodded. 'It's imperative that we hold our nerve until the

Emperor's aims are clear. If we act in haste, then Guilliam may very well decide to bring his army here. After all, one of the most powerful mages in the land is sitting before you.'

Faden raised an eyebrow, and sipped his iced tea.

Daphne lit another cigarette. 'What do you plan to do?'

'For now, nothing,' her father said. 'Keep the Holdings running while we wait and see what the Emperor does next. But our dream? Do you wish to know our ultimate aim?'

Daphne nodded.

'We wish for nothing less than to overthrow the Lord Regent that sits in Holdings City, and proclaim a republic. We wish to rule ourselves again, reform the Royal Council into a Senate of the Holds, and throw off the shackles of monarchy.'

'Like Rahain?'

'Without the slavery, of course.'

'What about the church?'

'The people will be free to follow their faith; we would never interfere with that, but the church will have no role in any constitution or government.'

'And the empire?'

'It was a foolish idea from the beginning,' Faden said. 'I'm all for peace and trade, but each nation should look after its own interests.'

'I'm not sure Guilliam would agree.'

'Which is why we do nothing,' her father said. 'Quite clearly, the Emperor is a threat to the stability of the world, and wherever he chooses to go is in grave danger. He seems to care nothing for the well-being of his subjects.'

'The power's gone to his head,' Faden said. 'He thinks he's almighty.'

'Perhaps you're right,' Daphne said, 'though there must be some reason behind his madness, some plan he's following. Presumably, he's carrying out the Creator's wishes, or thinks he is.'

Faden shook his head. 'I do not accept the existence of the Creator. It is nothing more than a legend.'

'You still don't believe?' Daphne said. 'Even after what happened? How then did the Emperor get his powers?'

Faden shrugged. 'Through some arcane mage-craft of which I have no knowledge. Some foul ritual that involved the slaughter of ten mages.'

Daphne shook her head.

'We may never agree on the Creator, Daffie,' her father said, 'but we can still work together to further our aims. Are you with us?'

'I'll do whatever it takes to protect my family.'

Her father smiled. 'Good enough for me.'

After lunch, Daphne went up to her quarters. She had expected to find Killop and Karalyn there waiting for her, but the rooms were empty. A note was on a table, written by Killop. It asked her to meet him outside by the pavilion.

She washed off the heat and dust, changed her clothes and smoked half a weedstick from her dwindling supply. The afternoon was wearing on when she headed back out into the sunshine, and the temperature had dipped from earlier. The market square was quiet as she passed through it, and few were on the road to the old tower and the pavilion. She spotted Killop, standing in the shade of the stables.

'Hi,' she said. 'Where's Karalyn?'

'I left her with Celine.'

Daphne raised an eyebrow.

'Jean was there too,' he said. 'I have something I need to show you.'

'What?'

'Come on,' he said, turning towards the line of temporary bars that had been constructed by the side of the great pavilion.

'Are we going for a drink?' she said.

'You might need one after you see this.'

The bars were quiet, and Killop entered one that was almost empty, with just a few tables occupied. They walked over to a couple sitting in the corner.

Daphne's mouth fell open as she saw who was there.

The woman stood.

'Daphne,' she said. 'It's good to see you.'

'Chane,' said Daphne. 'What are you doing here?'

'It's a long story.'

Daphne looked at the other occupant of the table. She narrowed her eyes. 'Kylon.'

'Hello, Daphne,' he said, continuing to sit and drink his ale.

She turned to Killop, who shrugged. 'We knew he was coming,' he said.

Kylon frowned. 'How?'

'Another long story,' Daphne said. 'You should know that I haven't forgiven you for telling Killop I was dead.'

'An unfortunate but necessary lie,' Kylon said. 'But you're together now, which just proves you were meant to be.'

Daphne frowned.

'Sit with us,' Kylon said.

Killop and Daphne took seats round the table, and a waiter brought over a large jug of ale.

Daphne glanced at Chane. 'So you and Kylon know each other?'

'We met in spring,' she said. 'Weir brought us together.'

'Sergeant Weir?'

'Yes. He found me first, in some drinking dive in the River Holdings. One of the regulars was also ex-cavalry, and he told Weir I was back. And then, in spring, he found Kylon.'

'I'd been asking around the towns for anyone who knew how to find Daphne Holdfast,' Kylon said, 'but the imperial recruiters were out in force, and I had to lie low. Eventually, someone told me about a sergeant who had served with you in Sanang, and I was introduced to Weir. He took me to a safe house, where I met Chane. A little while back, he told us that you had returned to Hold Fast, and we waited for the festival, so we wouldn't stand out too much.'

'Did you come by yourselves?'

'Aye,' Kylon said. 'Weir stayed in the River Holdings. He's in charge of putting up roadblocks if and when the recruiters return. The folk down there are angry; angry enough to put up a fight if the army tries to enlist any more of them.'

'A lot of people are talking about resisting,' Chane said. 'And they're furious with the church.'

'Is that why you're here?' Daphne said. 'To tell me this?'

Chane chewed her lip. 'I don't know, to be honest. It was Kylon who kept insisting that he needed to see you, and when Weir told us you were back, he asked if I'd go along with him, since I knew the way, and I said yes.' She lit a cigarette. 'I'm sorry about how we parted, and for some of the things I said. I was in a dark place at the time. It took me until we'd got back to Sanang to realise that Agang was never going to change, and I got out. Just in time, as it happens. Keira arrived not long after.' She nodded at Kylon. 'With him by her side.'

'You were with my sister?' Killop said.

Kylon nodded. 'Right up until the final battle before the walls of Plateau City.'

'Are the imperials looking for you?' said Daphne.

'Aye,' he said. 'I'm a wanted man.'

Killop leaned forward. 'Did you see what happened to my sister?'

'No, but I've heard nothing else since I left the Plateau and entered the Holdings.' He picked up his ale and took a long draught. 'The rumours are untrue, Killop,' he said, his dark eyes glinting in the dim light. 'Keira is alive.'

'But if you left before the battle,' Daphne said, 'how do you know that? Have you seen her?'

'The morning after the battle,' Kylon said, 'Kalayne came to me in my dreams, and gave me a message. He told me to go to the Holdings, and said that he was taking Shella to meet up with Keira in Kellach Brigdomin.'

'Kalayne was with Shella?' Daphne said.

'Aye. He'd rescued her from where she was being held, and was going to smuggle her out of the city.'

Killop narrowed his eyes and stared at Kylon. 'So Kalayne told you my sister was alive?'

Kylon nodded. 'And when was he ever wrong?'

Killop bowed his head, and clenched his eyes shut.

'And he's taking Shella to Kellach Brigdomin?' Daphne said.

'I don't know any more,' Kylon said. 'That was the last time I've been in contact with Kalayne. He said he'd visit me in my dreams again, but hasn't. Also, some time ago he told me there was a point beyond which he'd never seen himself in a vision. We have now passed that point, and I fear the worst.'

'You believe he's dead?'

'I can't think of any other reason that would prevent him from contacting me. He had a plan, and my coming to the Holdings was part of it.'

Daphne took a sip of ale. Keira was alive, but Kalayne dead? She wasn't sure if she should trust anything Kylon said, not after the way he had lied to them before. She glanced at him. He looked almost spectral, thin and gaunt, pale-skinned with his straight black hair falling over his shoulders. He was wearing his long leather overcoat, but looked untroubled by the heat.

'I am here,' he said, 'to fulfil what may be the final task Kalayne has set me.'

'And what's that?' said Daphne.

Kylon gazed at her with his dark eyes. 'Your daughter, Miss Hold-fast. Kalayne told me to stay close by, and protect her with my life.'

'What makes you think I'll let you anywhere near my daughter?'

'Because my intentions are true,' he said. 'From this moment forwards, I pledge my life to protect Karalyn Holdfast, unto death. And I'll do that, whether you give me permission or not.'

CHAPTER 5
DRUNK IN DOMM

Westgate, Domm Pass – 29th Day, First Third Summer 507

'And then,' Laodoc said, raising his arm, 'as the first rays of dawn broke over the eastern horizon, the Lord Commander of the great Alliance army gave the order to attack, and the glistening ranks of Holdings heavy cavalry began rumbling towards the walls of the Rahain Capital. To their right marched the forces of Lord Agang, and to their left charged the gallant battalions of Kellach Brigdomin. In the centre of the walls directly ahead of them lay the blocked gatehouse...'

'That's where I was,' said Keira, as the packed crowd listened.

'Yes, indeed,' Laodoc said, 'and Miss Flora as well, I believe?'

Flora nodded as she sipped her whisky.

'Now,' Laodoc said, 'between the gatehouse and the charging Alliance soldiers was the army of the lawless and cruel regime that ruled Rahain, the regime that had previously committed such heinous atrocities as the invasion of your lands, and the destruction of the Rakanese refugee camp...'

Keira coughed, and shook her head.

'This army,' Laodoc carried on, 'began loosing their thousands of crossbows at the advancing Alliance forces, while above the gatehouse, on a platform carved out of the rock, a dozen stone-throwing machines were unleashed, bombarding the lines of horses and soldiers below, inflicting calamitous ruin wherever they struck. Just as it seemed that disaster was about to strike down the noble Alliance forces, suddenly there appeared a great blazing fire on the hillside.'

The crowd inside the tavern cheered, drowning out the sound of the rain hitting the closed shutters.

Keira smirked. The folk in the tavern knew this story well, and Laodoc had been asked to tell it for three nights running.

'It was Killop,' Laodoc cried over the noise of the crowd. 'The great chief of the mighty Severed Clan, who, having brought his army of brave Kellach Brigdomin over the snow-covered mountains in the middle of winter, had arrived to save the day!'

The crowd cheered again, and raised their mugs.

'His young fire mage, Lilyann, destroyed the stone-throwers, smashing them into flaming pieces, and then she dropped her fire onto the ranks of enemy soldiers below. At once, the Alliance army took heart, and charged on with renewed vigour, capturing the gatehouse and entering the city. And so, my friends, the day was won, and the slaves of Rahain were freed.'

Applause mixed with the cheers as the crowd acknowledged the old man.

'Thank you, my friends; thank you,' he said, blushing.

Keira glowered. 'Look at him milking it.'

'Jealous?' said Flora.

'Fuck off,' Keira said. 'I'm glad he's getting the attention. It means I can just relax and get pished while he does all the talking.'

'Yeah, right.'

Keira glared at her. 'Yer a right wee lippy cow these days.'

Kelpie came over to their table as the crowds began to disperse. She grinned as she sat down, and put her arm over the Rahain man's shoulder. Keira sniggered.

Kelpie ignored her. 'Once again, Laodoc, my fine Rahain gentleman, you've done the job for me. Takings are up, and the place has been mobbed for days. You're quite the draw.'

'It's my pleasure, Madam Kelpie,' he said. 'I am flattered and surprised that anyone would want to listen to the tales of a boring old man like me.'

Kelpie laughed.

'You two can borrow my room if you want,' Keira said.

Kelpie tutted. 'What's the matter with you?'

'It's disgusting watching the pair of ye. I don't want to have to see old folk getting it on.'

'Ignore her,' Flora said. 'She's just jealous that Laodoc's stolen all her attention.'

'Am I fuck,' Keira snorted.

'It does seem that way,' said Agang from her right.

Keira turned to him. 'And when are you going to speak up? Why don't you tell the crowds a tale? What about the one where I kicked yer arse?'

'Maybe I should,' he said. 'I'm sure all of your admirers would love to hear how you rained down fire on a town of innocent men, women and children; and I had to surrender to stop you slaughtering them.'

'You were in our way,' she said. 'We did what we had to do to stop the Emperor.'

'But you didn't, did you?'

She growled at him. 'Fuck you, eight-thirds; at least I managed a better go of it than you did.'

'Behave, Keira,' Kelpie said. 'Anyway, that's you lot done. You've got the rest of the night off.'

She stood, and walked off to the bar. Bay and Dora, who had been hanging around like flies, came over to their table.

'Can we sit?'

'No,' said Keira, as Laodoc said 'Yes' at the same time.

Keira frowned. 'Fuck it, all right.'

The two young women sat, and Dora looked around.

'Where's Dean?' she said.

'How should I know?' said Keira.

'I think he's coming along later,' Flora said. 'I don't think he likes the crowds.'

'Fancy him, do ye?' Keira said.

Dora went red.

'She does, aye,' said Bay.

'He's about your age, Dora,' Flora said, 'and he's a good looking boy. Why not?'

'You knew him in Rahain, Mister Laodoc,' Bay said. 'Did he have any girlfriends?'

'Not that I know of, dear,' Laodoc said, 'but Killop was quite strict, and he kept Dean in the estate house most of the time.'

'Why?' said Dora. 'Was he a troublemaker?'

'No, it was to keep secret the fact that he was a fire mage.'

Keira snorted. 'He's not a fire mage yet, if he'll ever be one.'

'Aye, he is,' said Dora. 'Not in the same league as you, of course.'

Flora started to refill everyone's glasses with whisky.

Laodoc put his hand over his glass. 'No more for me, Miss Flora, thank you.' He turned to Keira. 'Would now be a good time to hold a discussion?'

Keira scowled. 'About what?'

'About our plans for the future.'

Keira sighed, downed her whisky, and poured herself another.

'I have been listening to everything Agang has told me,' Laodoc went on, 'and I've heard the tales you have to tell. In my opinion, if everything you say is correct, then the world is in a most perilous situation.'

'Ach, well,' Keira said. 'It's a shite world anyway.'

'The Emperor has gained powers beyond all measure,' Laodoc said. 'And sooner or later, he will discover that you are alive and well, and living out your days in a tavern in Domm.'

'We're endangering everyone with our presence here,' Agang said. 'Maybe it'll take some time for the Emperor to cast his eye southwards, but it's inevitable that he'll come, if he knows you're here.'

'Let's hear it, then,' Keira said.

'What?' said Laodoc.

'Yer plan, lizardface. I assume you've fucking got one?'

Laodoc's tongue flickered. 'Indeed. We should organise a small force, of perhaps two dozen, and search for Mage Shella.'

Keira started to laugh. 'Yer kidding me, right? Search for Shella? Yer out of yer fucking minds.'

Laodoc frowned.

'She's drunk,' said Flora. 'Maybe now's not the best time to engage her in constructive dialogue.'

'I think you're right, Miss Flora,' Laodoc said. He glanced at Agang. 'Shall we?'

Agang nodded, and the two men got to their feet.

'Night all,' Agang said, and they left the tavern.

'Pair of eejits,' Keira muttered, slugging back more whisky.

'Mage Keira,' said Bay, 'are we in danger?'

'Nah. We're safe down here.'

'But the Emperor...?'

'Can kiss my arse,' Keira said. 'Wanker.'

'The Emperor's got a lot more to worry about than us,' Flora said. 'Rahain's in a civil war, Sanang's in anarchy and who knows what's going on in the rest of the world? It'll be a long time before he even hears about Domm.'

'But when he does?'

'Don't worry about it, hen,' Keira said. 'Any bastard comes to Domm, I'll fry his arse off.'

Bay nodded, but her eyes were troubled.

'Here he comes,' Dora whispered.

Keira glanced up, and saw Dean walk past the bar towards them, looking younger than his seventeen years.

He flushed when he noticed Dora sitting at the table.

'Hi, Dean,' Flora said. 'Do you want an ale?'

'Aye, thanks,' Dean said, taking a seat while Flora poured him a mug.

Bay shook her head at Dora, whose eyes were fixed on the table, her cheeks flushed.

'What you been up to?' Flora asked him.

'Not much,' Dean said. 'Just reading in my room.'

'Fucksake,' Keira said. 'Call yerself a fire mage? Reading? At your age, ye should be out raising havoc and causing mischief, and fighting off the lassies with a shitty stick. Is this how my brother raised ye?'

Dean lowered his head. 'Me and a hundred other kids were locked up in a Rahain camp for years, and Chief Killop rescued us. But I never got to go out. I wasn't allowed to leave the big house because I was a fire mage, so I didn't have any friends. Except for Lilyann, but she ran away.'

Dora gazed at the boy, her eyes full of pity.

'Boo hoo,' said Keira. 'Sounds like Killop kept ye safe enough, but now that yer here ye can relax.' She filled a glass with whisky and passed it across the table to him. 'Drink this; ye've got some catching up to do.'

Two hours later, Keira opened another bottle of whisky.

'I think Dean's had enough to drink,' Flora said.

'Fuck off,' Keira muttered. 'The boy's got to learn sometime.'

Dean picked up his refilled glass, grinning. Dora was sitting next to him, the whisky having emboldened both of them. Bay sat looking bored to the side, as Dora whispered in the boy's ear.

'I wish I had some weed,' Keira said.

'So do I,' said Flora.

'You miss it, eh?'

'Not really, but you're less of an arsehole when you smoke, compared to when you just drink.'

'Are you here just to fucking nip ma head?'

'I enjoy winding you up; it's one of the few pleasures I have left.'

'Ye should get yourself laid,' Keira said. 'A bit of Kellach love action is what you're needing.'

'One can hope.'

'I'll set ye up, hen,' Keira said. 'Just leave it to me. I've noticed Kendrie eyeing ye up. He smells a bit funny, but I could make him have a bath first.'

Flora frowned and shook her head.

'All right, maybe not him,' Keira said, her eyes scanning the few remaining regulars at the bar, 'but I'll find ye a sturdy lad.'

'Please don't.'

'What? I thought ye wanted to get laid?'

'Never mind,' Flora said. 'Can we talk about something else?'

Keira smirked. 'Come on; when's the last time ye had a cock between yer legs?'

'Shut up, Keira.'

Keira laughed and downed her whisky. She glanced over to Dean and Dora, who were both giggling.

'So, my wee fire mage,' she said, 'yer feeling a bit braver after a few whiskies, it looks like.'

Dean grinned at her.

'I think it's time ye showed us what ye can do,' Keira said. 'I mean, ye say yer a fire mage, but I've not seen any proof of yer claim.'

'What, now?' Dean said, looking bewildered.

'Aye, ya numpty, now,' Keira said. She reached over and unlatched a lamp from the wall and set it on the table between her and Dean. The young man stared at it. Keira smiled.

'I see it in yer eyes,' she said, lifting the glass covering off the lamp, and exposing the naked flame. 'Now, show us.'

'I'm.. I'm too drunk,' he said. 'I'm not ready.'

'If yer not ready now, wee man, ye'll never be fucking ready.'

Dean glanced to his side, but Dora said nothing, her eyes wide. Bay shuffled forwards in her seat.

'Leave the boy be if he doesn't want to do it,' Flora said.

'No,' Keira said. 'Either he proves to us he is what he says he is, or he can fuck off out of this tavern.'

Fear swept across Dean's face.

'Are ye nothing but a shitebag, Dean?' Keira said.

'Try,' said Dora. 'Please.'

'Come on,' said Bay.

Dean closed his eyes. 'All right; I'll try.'

'Hey!' shouted Kelpie, as she strode towards them. 'What in Pyre's name do ye think yer doing? Are you trying to burn the place down?' She pointed at the door. 'Outside, if yer going to be up to that sort of thing.'

Keira laughed. 'Calm yerself, hen. I doubt very much that Dean's capable of burning anything down.'

'I don't give a shit,' Kelpie cried. 'No fire-magery indoors. House rules.'

Keira picked up the lamp and the bottle of whisky and got to her feet. 'Fair enough. Come on then, wee man.'

She walked to the back door, the others following. Outside, the rain was pelting down, and Keira stood under the wide eaves of the sloping tiled roof. A few yards ahead of her was the low fence next to the cliff-side.

'It's too wet for this shite,' cried Bay, ducking out of the rain, and huddling next to Keira.

'Bollocks it is,' Keira said. 'Just watch; the lad'll do fine.'

Flora, Dora and Dean joined her outside. Keira placed the lamp on the top of an upright barrel, her hands shielding the flame from the breeze. Dean stepped forward, and stood next to the lamp.

'Right, my wee pyromaniac,' Keira said. 'I'm not expecting anything fancy, mind; just lift up the flame and fire it over the cliff as far as ye can.'

Dean nodded, closed his eyes and breathed.

'You can do it, Dean,' Dora said.

'Aye,' Keira laughed, 'but she'll dump yer arse if ye cannae.'

Dora's face flushed as Bay sniggered.

Dean said nothing, his cheeks puffing in and out. Keira took a long swig of whisky.

A thin tendril of flames began to rise into the air, climbing inch by inch upwards, then Dean cried out, and it fell back down again.

Keira frowned at the lad. 'What was that supposed to be?'

'Have another try, Dean,' Flora said.

He nodded, though to Keira he seemed on the verge of tears. He closed his eyes again, and raised his hand close to the lamp. The flame rose again, stronger than before. When a ball the size of a skull had formed, the link to the lamp fell away, and the mass of fire hovered in the air, just above their heads.

Dean grunted, and hurled his arm towards the cliff.

The fireball flew out from under the eaves, but just as Dora began to let out a cheer, it fizzled, broke up, and fell to the sodden ground, where the rain extinguished it in seconds.

The young man stood in silence, his mouth open, staring at the smoking patch of grass.

'That was fucking embarrassing,' Keira said, taking another swig of whisky. 'You're crap.'

Bay laughed, while Dora remained stony-faced. She gazed at Dean.

'Now I know why Killop kept ye locked up,' Keira went on. 'It was cause he didnae want anyone to see just how shite ye were. Cause if they knew, nobody would be scared of ye. What a fucking disappointment. Stick to books from now on, cause yer no fire mage.'

'Leave him alone, Keira,' said Flora.

'Or what, ya whiny wee bitch?'

Flora's face twisted in rage. 'Don't call me that.'

Keira swaggered, her head swimming. 'I'll call ye what I like. I'm a fucking goddess.'

'You're a fucking arsehole,' said Flora, and stormed off back into the tavern, slamming the door behind her.

Keira tutted, took a swig of whisky, and leered at Dean, who had tears in his eyes.

'Stop greetin'; yer like a wee bairn.'

She began to laugh, but stopped when she saw Dora glaring at her.

The young woman took Dean's hand. Without a word, she led Dean away through the rain and out of sight behind the tavern.

'I was only having a fucking laugh,' said Keira. 'Can they not take a joke?'

Bay said nothing.

'Come on,' Keira said. 'Let's get another drink.'

'I think I'll just go home,' Bay said, and walked off.

Keira shrugged. She shook the bottle of whisky. It still had enough in it for a decent slug, so she held it to her lips and drained it, then fell headfirst into the mud.

She awoke fully clothed, lying on top of her bed. A trail of vomit led from the side of the mouth, down the blankets, and on to the wooden floor.

'Ya bastard,' she groaned, her head pounding.

She attempted to get up, but toppled off the bed, her hand smearing through the pool of sick as she landed. She crawled to the table that held her washbasin, and pulled herself up. The water inside the basin hadn't been changed since the previous morning, but she washed her hands, and splashed her face. She peered into her weed pouch, even though she knew she would find it empty.

She needed food, she decided, and a drink. She staggered to the door of her room and stumbled down the flight of stairs. The passageway leading to the tavern was deserted, so she carried on, and went into the tavern's main room. It was nearly empty, with just a handful of patrons. The shutters were open, and the day was sunny outside. Kendrie spotted her from the bar and shook his head.

'Check the state of you.'

She straightened herself, and strode to the bar. 'Give me an ale.'

Kendrie smiled. He reached under the counter for a mug, and poured her a pint of water.

'This first,' he said.

She stared at him, but took the mug, and downed its contents.

He refilled it with water. 'Again.'

'Yer being a right prick this morning,' she muttered, taking the mug. She held it to her lips and drank it down, her stomach feeling heavy and unsettled.

'All right,' he said; 'now ye can have an ale.'

He took her mug to one of the kegs stacked against the back wall of the bar and filled it.

'About fucking time,' she said. She took a sip, then felt an urgent need for the toilet.

'See what ye've done,' she cried. 'I need a piss now.'

'Yer hangover will lift soon,' he said, as she stomped off, 'then ye can thank me.'

A freezing wind was blowing through the backyard where the wooden outhouse was located. She opened the door of a stall, and gagged from the stench. She closed the door, pulled down her leathers and squatted over the pit, shivering in the bitter breeze.

She had a vague feeling that she had been out of her face the night before, but couldn't remember much. She grinned as she remembered she it was her day off. She might have a whisky with her breakfast.

She stood, re-fitted her clothing, and went back into the warmth of the tavern. She walked to the bar and picked up her mug.

'That feels a whole lot better.'

'See?' said Kendrie. 'Now, are ye wanting something to eat?'

'Aye,' she said. 'Fry whatever ye've got in the kitchen and pile it all up on a plate for me; I'm fucking starving.'

'Will I bring it over to the table where yer mates are?'

Keira frowned, and turned to scan the tavern. In the corner, Flora, Agang and Laodoc were sitting.

'Aye,' she said. 'Cheers.'

She took her mug, and ambled over to the table. The three sat there stopped talking and turned to look at her.

'Morning,' she said, sitting down.

Laodoc frowned. 'Madam mage, you appear to have mud in your hair.'

'Aye?' She scratched her head. 'So I do. Weird.'

She noticed Flora glaring at her.

'You were completely out of order last night,' the Holdings woman said.

Keira shrugged.

'You should find Dean, and apologise to him.'

'Eh?' Keira said. 'Dean? Oh aye, I remember, he was here last night. Him and Dora were getting all frisky with each other.'

'You don't remember humiliating him?'

'Nope,' she said; 'though if I did, he probably deserved it.'

She took a drink of ale.

'And Dora,' Flora said. 'I'm not sure if she'll be back.'

'So what?' Keira said. 'It's not like I need more hangers-on. I've already got you.'

Flora stood. Keira expected to see rage on her face, but she seemed calm.

'I know what you're doing,' she said. 'You're trying to push us all away. It won't work with me.'

She walked over to the front doors and left the tavern.

Keira narrowed her eyes. 'What the fuck was that about?'

'She means,' Laodoc said, 'that, consciously or not, you are attempting to show us how undeserving you are of our loyalty and friendship; perhaps due to a deep-seated realisation that you are not a nice person.'

Keira burst out laughing. 'I think ye might have me confused with someone else.'

Agang's face reddened.

'You got something to add, eight-thirds?' Keira snarled.

'I think the way you treat Flora is abysmal.'

'There ye go again,' Keira said; 'sticking up for poor wee Flora. Is there something going on between you pair?'

Agang shook his head, sighing. 'How can you say that?'

'Say what?'

'You know what Niall told us.'

'What?'

'Niall,' Agang said. 'That night we were up talking, right before we were attacked by the flying gaien carriages. Do you not remember what Niall said? About Flora?'

Keira frowned. 'Was I drunk at the time?'

'Yes,' Agang said, 'you were. But still, I thought you'd remember.'

'Well? What did he say?'

Agang looked down. 'I'm not sure if I should tell you now.'

'If it's important, then I should fucking know.'

'All right.' He lowered his voice. 'Flora prefers girls.'

'Is that it?' Keira scowled. 'Big deal. Wait a minute; she doesnae fancy me, does she?'

Agang shrugged.

Keira sipped her ale. 'Shit.'

Kendrie arrived with a large tray. He deposited three bowls of porridge and a large plate of fried meat and eggs, nodded, and went back to the bar.

Keira picked up a fork. 'Ya fucking beauty.'

'Madam Keira,' Laodoc said, 'as we eat breakfast, I was wondering if we could resume our conversation from last night?'

'What was that, then?'

'About searching for Mage Shella.'

Keira groaned and put down her fork.

'Kalayne said she was essential to achieving victory over the Emperor,' Agang said. 'His vision showed you and her together.'

'Shella's the last person on earth that I want to see,' Keira said. 'I hear she can kill folk with a wave of her hand.'

'I've seen her do it,' Laodoc said.

'Then she'll try to kill me for sure if she ever catches sight of me. The only thing I can do is blast her with a fucking firebolt before she can raise her arm.'

'Don't be ridiculous,' Agang said; 'you and her are on the same side.'

'So she's just going to forgive me for wiping out her city of frog-folk? Hardly.'

'But you'll have to meet her some time,' Agang said. 'Kalayne saw it.'

'Fucksake, eight-thirds; I remember when you used to laugh whenever we mentioned that mad old bastard's visions. Now yer more of a devoted believer than Kylon was. And anyway, if me meeting her is destined to be, then I may as well stay here and get drunk. I mean, she'll come here eventually, won't she?'

Laodoc frowned. 'It pains me, I admit it, to sit here in Domm, while the rest of the world endures the rule of this new, powerful Emperor. I yearn to know what is happening elsewhere.'

'Then go,' Keira said. 'No one's keeping ye here.'

'I would,' Laodoc said, 'but according to Agang, you are the key to everything. Only you can save the world. As much as my sceptical mind finds it hard to understand, let alone believe that an old Kell man can somehow see into the future, I have come to trust Agang, and am ready to accept what he has told me. Therefore, madam, if we do leave, then you must come with us.'

'Forget it.'

'The world needs you, Keira,' Agang said.

Keira picked up her ale, and smiled. 'The world can go fuck a donkey.'

CHAPTER 6
MIRREN BLACKHOLD

H old Fast, Realm of the Holdings – 17th Day, Second Third Summer 507

'Keira's more fragile than you think,' Kylon said.

Killop gazed out at the sunset from the guesthouse terrace and raised an eyebrow. 'She is?'

'Aye,' Kylon said. 'I could see it getting to her after a while. The burden.'

'The poor dear,' Chane said, flicking ash from her cigarette. 'After killing hundreds of thousands of people, you mean she actually started to feel bad?'

Killop shook his head. 'Hundreds of thousands? No way.'

Chane shrugged. 'Add 'em all up.'

'Three, at the most,' Kylon said.

'Oh sorry,' Chane said; 'a mere three hundred thousand people. I apologise. She's barely a mass murderer at all.'

Killop frowned at the Holdings woman. 'Mass murderer or not, she's still my sister.'

'And we'll need her to defeat the Emperor,' Kylon said, 'no matter what she's done.'

'Didn't you already try that?' Chane said.

'Then we'll try again. Would you rather the Emperor remained in power?'

'I honestly don't know. He does appear to be insane, I'll grant you that, but if the alternative means the return of the fire witch, then frankly, both options seem undesirable.'

'The Emperor will destroy the world, Chane. He's already devastated the Kellach quarter in Plateau City, and laid waste to the town of Rainsby. And now his army is poised to enter Rakana, which, I'll remind you, has no armed forces to speak of, just a few militia with pointy sticks. And when he's finished there? Where next?'

'But he's Holdings,' Chane said. 'Why would he injure his own country? The soldiers would rebel, for one thing. The majority of recruits in the imperial army are from the River Holdings, do you think they'd be happy to rampage through their own towns?'

'I used to think the same about Rahain,' Killop said, 'but once the bloodshed started, they couldn't stop hating and killing each other. Brother against brother. Parents against their own children.'

He paused, and gazed at Chane. 'What is that you're smoking?'

'This?' she said, holding up her lit smokestick. 'River Holdings dreamweed. Not bad.'

'They're growing that shit in the Holdings now?'

'Yes. Some enterprising troopers returned with cuttings a few years ago. It's not as good as the Sanang stuff, obviously, but it's getting there. Their keenweed's pretty decent as well.'

'So Daphne's been getting it from you? I did wonder.'

Chane smirked. 'Has Daphne been a bad girl? Has she been keeping her weed habit from you?'

'It's her business.'

'But I get the sense that you don't approve?'

He picked up his glass of rum. 'She's a grown-up.'

Chane smiled. 'I was there when she started smoking. She was in excruciating agony from the injury to her arm, so a friend of Agang's got her some dullweed. Then it was dreamweed and keenweed, to relieve the boredom of captivity.'

'I'll take some,' said Kylon.

Chane passed him the weedstick. 'I thought you were on duty tonight.'

Kylon took a draw and shook his head. 'Celine's doing it.'

'How did you talk her into that?'

'She offered.'

Killop shook his head. 'I can understand why you want to guard Karalyn, since Kalayne asked you to, but Celine? I don't get it; why?'

'I told you,' he said. 'She came to me and asked. Daphne had mentioned to her that I was being taken on as an estate worker, but that really I'd be watching Karalyn's back, and Celine told me she wanted to help.'

'And you trust her?' Chane said.

'Karalyn trusts her,' he said, 'and Daphne told me she'd read Celine's mind, and she's happy with the arrangement. I mean, have you seen her with Karalyn?'

'Celine's a changed woman,' Killop said. 'When we first got here she hardly said a word, mourning for her husband.'

'Do you know what I believe?' Kylon said. 'I think Karalyn has been altering Celine's mind. Changing her. Kalayne told me something like this could happen.'

Killop nodded, recalling when Karalyn had repaired his own mind.

'That would make sense,' Chane said, 'but we should keep this to ourselves. You must have seen the way Daphne's mother looks at the girl. I don't think she likes her at all.'

'Of course,' said Killop. 'The fewer folk know about what Karalyn can do, the better.' He bit his tongue to prevent himself from saying more, still rankling that Kylon had seen fit to inform Chane of everything Kalayne had told him about Karalyn.

'Daphne's mother could be a problem,' Kylon said.

'I don't think she's a threat to Karalyn,' Chane said. 'She actually seems to be afraid of her.'

'I wasn't meaning that,' Kylon said. 'I was referring to her professed love for the Emperor and his holy church.'

'Daphne thinks she's just putting it on,' Killop said. 'If her father says white, she'll say black. They oppose each other in everything, apparently.'

'Why?' Kylon asked.

Killop tried to remember anything Daphne might have said.

'I think there was a rumour going around that Daphne's father was having an affair with the old queen, Guilliam's sister. Daphne said it wasn't true, but maybe her mother believes it.'

'I can believe it,' Chane said. 'Her father's eyes do have a tendency to wander, and if I had to put money on it, I'd be prepared to bet that he's having an affair with Annifrid, the commander of the local guard.'

'Nah, you think?' Killop said. 'He seems like a good guy. He always treats me with respect.'

'Well, no offence, but he doesn't want to sleep with you.'

Kylon's eyes darkened. 'Has he behaved in any way dishonourably towards you?'

'And what would you do if I said yes?' Chane said. 'Would you rush to protect my fragile honour, and challenge him to a duel, or would you just punch him in the face?'

Kylon took a draw of the weedstick. 'I would punch him in the face.'

Chane laughed. 'My hero. But the answer is no. Dear old Godfrey has been nothing but a gentleman, aside from the half-dozen times I've caught him looking at me.'

'You are an exceptionally beautiful woman,' Kylon said.

'You know,' Chane said, 'I used to fancy a guy like you. He always said that I was beautiful, but whenever I tried to get him into bed, he would push me away. Turned out in the end that he preferred guys.'

'My heart belongs to someone else,' Kylon said. 'The woman you referred to moments ago as a mass murderer.'

'You told me she dumped you.'

'She did. It didn't affect how I feel about her.'

'In that case, you shouldn't be calling another woman exceptionally beautiful.'

'But you are.'

Sacrifice

Chane sipped her rum, and turned her gaze out over the plains before them, the last light of the day fading. The temperature was starting to drop, and Killop relaxed in the cooler air.

'Kylon of Kell,' Chane said, 'you're not right in the head.'

Killop stood. 'I'd best be off; I'm meeting Daphne.'

'Yes?' Chane said. 'What's she been up to?'

'More meetings with the Holders. More plotting.'

'Good,' said Kylon. 'We should all be preparing.'

'Unless you're Rakanese,' Chane said, 'then you should be running.'

Killop nodded, and left the terrace by the sliding doors into the guest house. Apart from Kylon and Chane, the large building was empty, another sign adding to the sense of anxiety evident in Hold Fast. When the imperial army had left Plateau City, the Holdings had held its breath, and when they had turned east towards Arakhanah City, the relief had been palpable. And then the nervous rounds of chatter had started all over again; the worry that sent Godfrey, Daphne, and whichever other aristocratic Holder was visiting into endless secret meetings. Everyone came to Hold Fast, Killop had noted. Godfrey never left to visit anyone; his seat was the centre the others attended.

Lamps were being lit along the main street as Killop stepped outside. To his left, the fountains glistened in front of the mansion, and he began to make his way there. An old woman curtsied to him as he passed, his position as Miss Daphne Holdfast's consort long established among the estate workers.

To the right of the mansion, Killop noticed a cluster of carriages parked along the route to the market square. Handlers were out, leading the horses to the nearby guest stables. Killop smiled. Another Holder must have arrived, filled with their tales of woe and outrage at the Emperor's latest unreasonable demand.

At the back porch, Celine was playing with Karalyn. The woman was holding onto the girl's arms and spinning, so that Karalyn was flying through the air, screaming with delight.

'Evening,' Killop said, as he ascended the steps.

'Hi, Killop,' Celine said, coming to a stop, and swaying.

'Should you be getting her all excited before bedtime?'

'She'll be fine,' Celine said. 'Do you want to do her story?'

'Celine do story!' Karalyn yelled.

'I don't mind,' Celine said.

'I should do it.'

Karalyn started to cry. 'Daddy not do story. I want Celine do story.'

Killop sighed.

Celine went down on one knee. 'You know, your daddy has been looking forward to telling you a story all afternoon. I would be very happy if you were a good girl and listened to daddy tell you a story.'

Karalyn sniffled.

'I'll be in the next room,' Celine said, 'and I'll come and see you before you fall asleep.'

Karalyn smiled, and took Killop's hand.

'Come on, wee bear,' he said; 'let's get you to bed.'

———

Daphne flicked the ash from her cigarette over the edge of the balcony into the dark night air.

'I need to spend more time with Karalyn,' she said. 'I seem to sit all day in stupid meetings, or doing the paperwork my father can't be bothered to look at. How did she go down?'

'Fine.'

'And did you see Kylon?'

'It was Celine,' he said. 'They'd swapped shifts.'

Daphne shook her head. 'They're both insane.'

'Kylon thinks that Karalyn has done something to Celine's mind.'

Daphne took a large sip of rum. 'He's right. Our daughter has bonded with her. Celine's mind was a mess; she was overwhelmed with guilt when Vince was killed, and tried to blot it all out with dreamweed and alcohol. Karalyn's been in her head. She saw that Celine was in pain, and I guess she's trying to heal her.'

'Like she healed me?'

'Emotions are different from memories,' Daphne said. 'With you, she was helping you remember, but with Celine?'

'She does seem devoted to Karalyn.'

'And knowing Celine's vulnerability, how much of that is due to her own free will?'

Killop said nothing, not wanting to imagine his daughter capable of what Daphne was suggesting.

He frowned. 'Guilt?'

'What?'

'You said Celine was overwhelmed with guilt. What did she have to feel guilty about?'

Daphne frowned. 'She'd been having an affair with Bedig, back when we lived in Plateau City. At the time, I'd hoped that she and Vince would get back together when he returned home after his service, and it would all be forgotten about.'

'I assume your parents don't know?'

'No one else does, I think, apart from a few servants at the old Hold-fast townhouse in Plateau City. Celine was as down as anyone I've ever seen when we got here, but now she's like a blinding ray of sunshine whenever she's in the company of our daughter. I wish I knew what to do, but Karalyn's powers are beyond my control. She can break through any protection I put over Celine; they don't even slow her down any more.'

Daphne bowed her head.

'I worry about my own thoughts, too. Whenever I feel annoyed at Jonah, or my mother, I picture what Karalyn could do to them if I allowed my anger to develop. It frightens me.'

'What's the alternative?' he said. 'We go and live in the mountains until she's old enough to control her powers?'

'She's never going to fit in, is she?' Daphne said. 'She's never going to have a normal life.'

Killop gazed at her, his heart aching as he thought about their daughter's future.

There was a knock on the glass door, and Godfrey stepped out onto the balcony.

'Apologies for interrupting,' he said.

'That's all right, Father,' Daphne said. 'Is the meeting ready to restart?'

Godfrey closed the door behind him. 'No,' he said. 'Something rather curious has occurred. A new guest has arrived at Hold Fast.'

'Not just another Holder, I presume?'

Godfrey smiled. 'We're arranging a spot of late supper for them in the old library. I think you should attend. In fact, you should both come.'

'All right,' Daphne said. 'Who is it?'

'Why,' Godfrey said, 'only the Queen.'

Queen Mirren Blackhold was seated in the high-backed chair usually reserved for Holder Godfrey. She was clad in long black robes, and a hood half-covered her face. To either side stood stern-faced guards, while Faden Holdwick sat a few seats down.

A servant held the door open for Godfrey, Daphne and Killop to enter, then left the room, closing it behind her.

'Your Majesty,' Godfrey said, bowing low, 'welcome to Hold Fast. You do me and mine great honour with your visit...'

'This is not a social call, Godfrey,' Mirren said. 'Please sit.'

Godfrey took a seat across from Faden. 'This is my daughter Daphne,' he said, 'and her companion Killop, former chieftain of the Severed Clan.'

'I recall Daphne from her visits to court,' Mirren said. 'I believe you were pregnant when you last attended?'

'Yes, your Majesty. I now have a young daughter. Killop is the father.

'Sit,' Mirren said, 'before my neck muscles cramp from leaning up to look at you.'

Daphne and Killop sat.

Mirren stared at Killop. 'So, you are the Kellach Brigdomin who intervened at the Battle for the Rahain Gates? An act which decisively swung the outcome, I believe?'

'I commanded the clan forces that day,' Killop said.

Mirren nodded, her fingers drumming the tabletop. 'I had assumed I'd be speaking only to yourself and Faden, Godfrey. However, Daphne and Killop may remain. I will assume they are in your confidence.'

'Please do so, your Majesty,' Godfrey said. 'Both have my complete trust.'

'First of all,' Mirren said, 'my thanks to Faden for bringing me here, a duty performed without the slightest clue as to why.' She smiled as she glanced at Faden. 'I could see you bursting with curiosity for the entire journey. Well, fear not, for now I will tell you all why I am here.'

She paused to light a cigarette and, on her cue, the other Holdings in the room also began to smoke. Godfrey opened a bottle of rum, and filled five glasses.

'Thank you,' Mirren said.

The others gazed at her, waiting.

'As I'm sure you are all aware,' she said, 'the great imperial army has recently crossed the frontier wall into Arakhanah, with my beloved husband the Emperor at its head. Over one hundred thousand soldiers, did you know?'

'We have indeed heard the news, your Majesty,' Godfrey said.

'The Emperor will remain in Arakhanah for several thirds, I would imagine,' Mirren said, 'which is why we must act now.'

'Act, your Majesty?'

'There is something I must tell you,' she said; 'something that you may find hard to believe. When Keira the fire mage attacked the city, we had been evacuated to the Great Fortress in the Old Town, and from its rooftop battlements I watched fireballs destroy the palace.' She turned to Killop. 'Your sister was exceptionally thorough; I doubt one brick of the building now stands upon the other. My condolences for your loss, of course. When she had finished, she moved round to opposite the merchants' quarter, and opened up a great breach in the walls. As the Sanang hordes began to pour into the streets of the city, I genuinely felt for a moment that the capital was lost, and that that day would be my last.'

She took a sip of rum.

'Then,' she went on, 'quite to my surprise, I noticed my husband standing alone on the city walls, just yards from the breach.' She sighed. 'Do I need tell of what he did then? I am sure you have all heard. And no, the tales have not been exaggerated.'

The room fell into silence for a moment.

'Afterwards,' Mirren said, 'I awaited my husband in our rooms in the Great Fortress. I was a little nervous, having not the faintest idea of how Guilliam had obtained such power. I waited, listening to the roars and cheers from the crowds in the streets outside the fortress, gathered in their thousands to give thanks to the Emperor. Eventually, the door to our bedchamber opened, and he walked in.'

She stubbed out her cigarette, and lit another.

'It's not him.'

'What?' said Faden.

'Whoever that man is,' she said, 'it's not Guilliam. It's not my husband.'

Godfrey frowned. 'An impersonator, your Majesty?'

Mirren shook her head. 'That's what the logical half of my brain is telling me, but if it is, then he's the best impersonator in history. Every physical detail is accurate, except improved upon, somehow. His hair is softer, his eyes deeper, his skin smoother; I can't explain it. But it's not him on the inside.'

Godfrey and Faden glanced at each other.

'You think I'm crazy,' she said. 'Of course you do. I would, were I in your position.'

'But, your Majesty,' Faden said, 'if his skin and hair are different, then surely this man must be an impostor?'

'I have an idea which may explain it, your Majesty,' Daphne said.

All eyes turned to her.

'If we imagine that the Emperor was granted all mage powers, as seems evident from what he did to the Sanang army, then presumably he also has the skills of a hedgewitch. If so, then he would have been able to heal every part of his body, make himself stronger, and appear younger.'

'Yes,' Mirren said. 'I think that may be it. He looks like a younger, fitter version of himself. That would explain the physical differences.'

'So he's not an impostor, then?' Faden said.

Mirren frowned at him. 'At the risk of repeating myself, it may indeed be Guilliam's body, but the man inside is not my husband.'

'Then who is he?'

'Someone... not very nice.'

'Did he hurt you, your Majesty?' Faden said, his eyes narrowing.

'No, but I felt fear in his presence, which is something that I could never say about Guilliam.' She glanced at the two men. 'I am perfectly aware of your opinion of my husband, but you are wrong. Guilliam is a good man, who truly has the best interests of the world close to his heart. However, the being who resides within my husband's body is a different matter. He is a monster.'

'Two alternatives suggest themselves, your Majesty,' Godfrey said. 'One, that the process which granted the powers to the Emperor somehow changed him, made him into a different person. If that is the case, then the old Guilliam may be lost forever.'

Mirren shook her head.

'Two,' Godfrey went on, 'a powerful mage has taken over the body of the Emperor.'

Faden snorted. 'There's no mage in the world who could do that.'

'Then I am at a loss, my friend,' Godfrey said.

Mirren picked up her glass of rum. 'Have you guessed why I've come here, to the Hold of the throne's most outspoken opponent?'

Godfrey said nothing.

'The Holdfasts have been a thorn in Guilliam's side for years, plotting and conspiring behind his back at every opportunity. You were allowed to become too powerful under the old queen, and thought you were entitled to have a say in the running of the realm because you used to be her favourite. My husband has never liked you, for reasons I am sure you are aware of. Nevertheless, it is to you that I have come. It is you I seek to ally myself with, as the only Holder capable of organising a rebellion large enough to succeed.'

Godfrey's mouth fell open.

'And it must be now,' Mirren said, 'while the creature inhabiting my husband's body is occupied with the slaughter of recalcitrant Rakanese. We must unite the Holds and arm ourselves, ready to resist the Emperor upon his return.'

'But if we do this,' Godfrey said, 'he will invade the Holdings.'

Mirren smiled. 'My dear Godfrey, after the Emperor has finished scouring the Rakanese marshes for mages, the invasion of the Holdings is next on his list. Somehow, he has the notion that high mages are being hidden in the old realm.' She glanced at Daphne. 'This is why I have come here, to warn you.'

Godfrey nodded. 'You have given us much to think about, your Majesty.'

'Don't spend too long thinking,' she said. 'I must now depart for Holdings City.'

'Tonight, your Majesty?'

'Indeed. I am expected at the Lord Regent's residence. Officially, I am visiting the old realm; my trip here was merely a long detour. But I will be in touch soon, Godfrey, and I shall expect you to have a plan prepared. Now, if you would all please excuse me, I would like to eat in silence before I take my leave.'

'Of course, your Majesty,' Godfrey said, rising. The others did the same.

The Holdings men bowed, while Daphne performed a low curtsy. Killop nodded his head, unable to keep a frown from his lips.

Celine was sitting up, reading a book by lamplight outside Karalyn's door, when Killop and Daphne returned to their chambers.

She smiled as she saw them enter.

'Good evening, Celine,' Daphne said. 'I hope you remembered to eat something.'

'You'll never guess what Karalyn did today, Daphne,' said Celine, a wide grin on her face. 'She managed to get her dress on this morning, all by herself. She's so clever.'

'That's good,' Daphne said. 'Now that we're back, you can go and relax; get some sleep.'

'No. I'm fine, thanks.'

For a moment, Daphne looked like she was going to say something else, but instead she opened the door to her daughter's room, and snuck in.

Killop poured himself an ale from a silver decanter.

'What you reading?' he said.

'A story.'

'Aye? Any good?'

'Yeah. It's about a young Holdings girl who rises to become the leader of a band of ruthless mercenaries.'

'Sounds a bit like my sister.'

Celine looked away.

'Sorry,' he said.

'It's all right. I've never blamed you for what happened to Vince. You weren't in charge of what your sister did.'

Killop nodded, and took a drink of ale.

Daphne re-emerged from Karalyn's room.

'We'll leave you to it, Celine,' she said. 'Help yourself to food, drinks, whatever you want.'

Celine went back to her book. 'Night, then.'

Killop and Daphne went through to their own large bedchamber, as big as the one they had shared in Slateford. Daphne went straight to her bedside table and extracted a pouch. She reached inside and withdrew a weedstick.

'Join me on the balcony?' she said.

Killop picked up a bottle of rum and followed her outside. He sat at the small table as Daphne leaned against the railings. He poured rum into two glasses and watched her, the smoke from the lit weedstick trailing up into the cold air. Overhead, the seven stars were visible in the dark, cloudless sky.

'We came all this way to escape a war,' he said. 'Now it looks like we're heading back into one.'

Daphne nodded, her gaze directed out into the darkness.

'Do you wish we'd gone to Kellach Brigdomin?' she said.

'No.'

'Good, because I'll be needed here, to prepare for when the Emperor comes. My father can't do this on his own. He's going to need my help.'

'I know,' he said. 'We must try to do what Keira and an army of Sanang failed at, and defeat the Emperor, or whoever he is. Did you read the queen's mind?'

Daphne nodded. 'She wasn't lying, about any of it. She's genuinely scared of Guilliam, and beneath her calm exterior I could sense her desperation.'

'She seems like a powerful ally.'

'We'll find it a lot easier to unite the Holds with Mirren alongside us, but we shouldn't be in any doubt about what we're doing.'

She bowed her head. 'Many will remain loyal to the Emperor,' she said, 'and we will have to fight them.'

Killop nodded. 'Civil war.'

CHAPTER 7
THE RAT

Domm Lowlands, Domm – 25th Day, Second Third Summer 507

Laodoc's eyes opened as the wagon went over a bump in the road. Overhead, the sky was grey, pricked in several places by glowing shafts of sunlight, illuminating the land below in a hundred shades of green, from verdant summer to dark emerald. Low hills and gentle valleys were criss-crossed with drystane dykes, and crofter's cottages dotted the landscape.

The twin pair of oxen lumbered along the road, oblivious to the flies buzzing around their heads.

'You're awake,' Agang said, holding the reins next to him on the wagon's bench. 'The rain's stopped.'

Laodoc peered up at the sky. 'For now.'

'You all right?'

'Fine,' he said, though he felt like he wanted to go into the back of the wagon and curl up into a ball rather than talk to anyone.

'We're nearly there,' Agang said. 'Just a couple more miles, according to Conal's directions.'

The wind from the west picked up, bringing the scent of ocean salt.

'This is truly the far end of the world,' Agang said. 'The furthest place from anywhere.'

'Rahain soldiers made it here, once,' Laodoc said, 'back when we fancied ourselves an imperial power. Little did we suspect that the Holdings would so thoroughly outdo us on that score.'

'We knew about them from the beginning,' Agang said. 'They did to us what you did to this place, only for a lot longer.'

'Rahain forces still occupy Northern Kell, though,' Laodoc said. 'They've managed to cling on by their fingertips, guarding their walled-off mines, so they can send home the coal to keep the city caverns warm in winter. You must have seen them on your way here?'

'We didn't see much of Kell,' Agang said. 'We stuck to the mountain paths and avoided the lowlands. We were worried that the Rahain might recognise Keira.'

'You did the right thing,' Laodoc said. 'If she had witnessed the full scale of what the Rahain have done to her land, she might have done something rash. The empire would surely take notice if the coal supply to Rahain was disrupted. I can sense it rankle in quite a few of the people however; the feeling that the war isn't really over, and cannot be, while a part of their land remains under foreign occupation.'

'I've heard it from a few Kell and Lach,' Agang said, 'but the Domm don't seem to care much. I did overhear Kelpie suggest to Keira that she should head north and clear their old clan's homeland. You can imagine her response.'

'She has certainly widened my vocabulary.'

Agang chuckled. 'I wonder how she's getting along in the tavern without you there to do most of the speaking? For five nights, she's had to do it on her own, and it'll be a lot more by the time we get back.'

The sun broke out from behind the thick, grey clouds, bathing the land around the wagon in golden light. To either side of the road were low walls and stone cottages, some lying derelict, while others had smoke billowing up from chimneys. Cattle and sheep filled the fields ahead, where lines of trees provided some shelter from the never-ceasing wind. Laodoc smiled, savouring the wild beauty.

'I hope she's expecting us,' Agang said. 'I know Conal said he would let her know we were coming, but I'm sure he had a hundred things to do when he got back.'

'Does it matter?' Laodoc said. 'We're about to disrupt her existence; try to persuade her to put her life in danger again. I doubt she's going to welcome us with flowers and party favours when she learns why we're coming to see her.'

'Do you think we're doing the wrong thing?' Agang said. 'My friend, we've been over this countless times. It's our only option.'

Laodoc stared out of the wagon, as the clouds moved to cover the sun again, and the land was cast into shadow. He considered asking Agang for a brief healing, but knew the look the Sanang man would give him. He rationed out his powers like a miser, saving it for when Laodoc was at his lowest, and even then sometimes he would be loath to help him, always worrying that he might become dependent on it, and urging him to try to work through it on his own.

Nothing felt better than when he had just been healed, but it only lasted for a few days before it began to wear off. After ten, and he was back where he started, and that was when he usually began to cast sideways glances at Agang, wondering how and when to ask him for more.

'I think I can guess what's going through your mind,' Agang said.

Laodoc's tongue flickered. 'Do you now?'

'I can see it in your eyes. Every day since we left the World's End, the black cloud above your head has grown.'

Laodoc eyed him. 'Is that it? No lecture this time?'

'No,' Agang said. He turned to face Laodoc. 'I realise I might have been a bit over-bearing recently, nagging you about healing and depression and so on, but I've never done this sort of thing before. So, what I am saying is that I'll try to be less judgemental.'

Laodoc turned away. He knew that Agang was trying to help, but still wanted to yell at him. He felt a rush of anxiety surge upwards through his body, and a sense of panic about nearing their journey's end. He closed his eyes, taking control of his breathing as Dyam had taught him, letting the wave pass through him and dissipate.

As he opened his eyes again, he saw Agang turn the oxen up a small lane to their right. The way was flanked with tall trees, heavy with thick, green leaves, and the sun split the clouds, lighting up the path.

'It's a very charming place in the sunshine,' Laodoc said, glancing around. 'So green.'

'It's a beautiful country, no doubt about it.'

The wagon followed the path for a few miles, up the side of a low ridge facing the west. As they mounted the top of the hill, Laodoc saw the vastness of the great ocean, just a few hundred yards ahead, where it crashed against the cliffs.

Agang stopped the wagon, put down the reins and stared out over the endless water.

'Quite a sight,' Laodoc said, taking in the great sweep of ocean before them. 'It puts our troubles into perspective, I think. No matter what foolishness we do on the land, the endless sea will continue, oblivious to our petty lives.'

'Is it really endless?'

Laodoc smiled. 'My dear Agang, is that what you were taught in the schools of Sanang? The world is round, like a ball. That ocean in front of us stretches for thousands of miles, until it finally reaches the eastern coast of Arakhanah.'

'The world is round?' Agang said.

'The scientists of Rahain discovered this many years ago.'

'And, apart from our piece of land, is the rest just sea?'

'That is not known for certain,' Laodoc said, 'though we have no evidence of anyone else sharing this world with us. It has been many centuries since Rahain tried to explore the ocean. The storms out there are devastating, and too many ships did not return. It may have been different before the Collision.'

Agang nodded. He flicked the reins, and the oxen began pulling the wagon down the path on the far side of the ridge, towards a lonely cottage.

'Something about the Collision bothers me,' Agang said. 'You say it happened ten thousand years ago?'

'Indeed,' Laodoc said, 'our records detail it.'

'But the five land masses must have been moving before that?'

'Indubitably.'

'Then don't you think it an unlikely coincidence that they all smashed into each other, as if they were attracted to a central point?'

'A mystery, my friend,' Laodoc said; 'one that has exercised the best minds of Rahain for millennia.'

Agang frowned. 'Does it not point to the Holdings' Creator being real?'

'I think chance just as likely. And if not chance, then perhaps some geological phenomenon currently beyond our understanding.'

'Kalayne thought the Creator was real. He said that he could see into his mind.'

'I would very much like to meet this Kalayne fellow,' Laodoc said, 'and put a few questions to him.'

'Who knows, you might get the chance one day,' Agang said. He pulled on the reins, and the oxen halted on the path before the lone cottage. 'Here we are.'

Laodoc gazed at the low stone structure. Signs of repair were evident on its roof, with fresh thatch covering one side. A thin trail of smoke rose from a chimney. Agang jumped down off the wagon and stretched his legs. He walked round to the other side and raised his arm for Laodoc.

'Thank you,' the old man said, taking Agang's hand and climbing down to the ground. He wrapped his cloak around him as a blustery breeze came in from the ocean. They walked to the front of the cottage and knocked on the door.

It opened, and Bedig appeared in the doorway.

'Laodoc!' he cried, lifting the old man into the air and embracing him.

'It's nice to see you too, Bedig,' Laodoc said.

'What are you doing here?' Bedig said, lowering Laodoc to the ground.

'Didn't Conal tell you?'

Bedig rubbed his chin. 'Maybe. He was round a few nights ago.'

'This is Agang,' Laodoc said, gesturing to the Sanang man.

Bedig eyed him up and down.

'I remember you.'

'Have we met?' Agang said.

'No. But I was in Plateau City with Daphne when you and your army put it under siege.'

'That was before I joined the alliance,' Agang said.

'May we go inside?' Laodoc said. 'My old bones are weary from travelling.'

Bedig laughed. 'Of course, sorry.' He swung the door open, and they went into the cottage. There was a fire burning in a hearth on their left, and a single other door led off to the right. The interior was furnished with a few odds and ends, a couple of wooden chairs, a bench and a scarred old table.

'Bridget,' Bedig yelled, 'we've got visitors.'

'If it's Dyam,' a voice cried from behind the door, 'just send her through.'

'It's not.'

'I'll just be a minute.'

Bedig turned to Laodoc and Agang. 'Whisky? Ale?'

'Water, please,' Laodoc said.

'I'll have to go out to the burn for that,' Bedig said, picking up a large jug. 'Be back in a minute.'

He went out by the front door just as Bridget emerged from the other room.

'Laodoc,' she said.

'Miss Bridget, a pleasure to see you again,' Laodoc said, bowing. 'This is Agang Garo.'

'Aye,' she said, nodding, 'Keira's friend.'

'The way she behaved was reprehensible,' Agang said. 'I'm not here to defend her.'

'Then why are you here?'

'We'll come to that soon enough,' Laodoc said. 'For now, I just want to hear how you've been.'

Bridget shrugged. The lines under her eyes were deeper than before, though the bruising on her face had healed.

The front door opened, and Bedig came back in, splashing water onto the rug by the fire.

'Oops,' he said. He put the jug down, and scooped a mugful. 'Here you are,' he said, handing it to Laodoc.

'Thank you,' Laodoc said.

'What were you after, Agang?' said Bedig.

'Could I have a whisky and some water, please?'

'Sure,' Bedig said.

Bridget took a seat while Bedig prepared the drinks.

'Sit down,' she said.

Laodoc perched on the end of the bench, Agang sitting a foot to his left.

'I'm not as busy as I used to be,' Bridget said. 'Draewyn and Dyam are pretty much handling the settlement by the clan, distributing houses and farms, and using Daphne's gold to purchase whatever we need.'

'So you've been taking a well-deserved break,' Laodoc said. 'You've been working hard for years; you should enjoy your time off.'

Bedig passed out drinks to Agang and Bridget, and sat, holding a giant mug of ale.

'We're going to be farming this land,' he said, 'Bridget and I. We'll have to learn how first, of course.'

'It sounds fascinating,' Laodoc said. 'Were you thinking of cattle or crops? Perhaps a vegetable garden? I tried my hand at growing, when I was staying in Slateford in my youth.'

'The last people to live here had sheep,' Bedig said, 'but we haven't decided yet.'

Laodoc glanced at Bridget. Her face was relaxed, but she was gripping onto her cup of whisky.

'How you been getting on with Keira?' said Bedig.

Bridget muttered something under her breath.

'I have been learning,' Laodoc said. 'Keeping my ears open, to the fire mage, and to what Flora and Agang have told me.'

'Have you seen much of Dean?'

'Yes,' Laodoc said. 'He has a girlfriend. Dora, a young woman his age.'

Bedig laughed. 'Good for him. Is she cute?'

'She's a delightful young lady.'

Bridget sighed.

'What's up with you?' Bedig said.

'They're not here to chat about Dean's girlfriend,' she said. 'They're here because they want something.' She faced Laodoc. 'Is that not correct?'

'We should have a few more drinks first,' Bedig said, 'and some food. Then get all their stuff brought in. I take it they're staying here? Get that out of the way before we start on some heavy discussion, where we'll probably shout at each other and fall out.'

'I certainly hope that isn't the outcome,' Laodoc said, 'but what we have to talk about is serious, so perhaps you're right.'

'I just want to get it over with,' Bridget said.

Bedig stood. 'I'll make a start on dinner.'

Laodoc glanced at Agang.

'Miss Bridget,' the Sanang man said, 'have you ever heard of a Rakanese high mage called Shella?'

She narrowed her eyes. 'Aye. Daphne rescued her from the refugee camp in Rahain, the one that Keira destroyed.'

Agang nodded.

'What about her?'

'Do you believe in the prophecies of Kalayne?'

Bridget frowned. 'I remember the name from somewhere.'

'I know him,' Bedig said from the stove, where he was stirring a pot. 'He helped us when we were fighting in Kell. I believe in his visions. He always knew exactly where the enemy was, and what they were going to do.'

'Was he the one who saw Killop and Daphne getting together?' Bridget said.

'Aye,' Bedig said.

Bridget nodded, and glanced back at Agang. 'All right, so I know of Kalayne.'

There was a knock at the door, and Dyam peered in.

'Smells good, Bedig,' she said, then noticed the others. 'Visitors.'

'Hi, Dyam,' Bedig said. 'You eaten? It'll be ready in twenty minutes if you can wait.'

'If that's alright,' she said, coming in and closing the door.

Laodoc stood. 'Greetings, Dyam. Have you met Agang?'

'I have,' she said, glancing from them to Bridget. 'Am I interrupting something?'

'They were just about to tell me why they're here,' Bridget said.

Dyam raised an eyebrow. 'I thought getting away from Keira would be reason enough.'

Laodoc sat again. 'It's certainly nice to have a break,' he said, 'but there is something we need to discuss with Bridget.'

A suspicious look crossed the Domm woman's face. 'Mind if I listen?'

Bridget shook her head. 'Get yourself a drink and sit down.'

Dyam took a mug of ale and sat. 'Have I missed anything?'

'Not really,' Bridget said.

'I think it best if Agang tells his story,' Laodoc said. 'Then we can talk.'

Bridget nodded. 'Go for it.'

Agang cleared his throat. 'The first time I heard the name Kalayne, I was a captive. It was Winter's Day. Keira had conquered Sanang, and she was assaulting the Holdings frontier wall, and I asked Kylon why they were trying to destroy the world...'

Agang spoke for an hour, continuing while they ate the dinner served up by Bedig at the small table. Bridget and Dyam remained silent throughout, as he described the visions of Kalayne, and the attack on the imperial capital by Keira. Their expressions grew more intense as he told of what the Emperor had done from the battlements.

When he finished, the others sat without speaking for a long while.

'Thank you for dinner,' Laodoc said.

'No problem,' said Bedig. 'If you're planning on staying for a while, I can nip over to the market for some blood pudding and bread in the morning.'

The Brig man got up, and started to clear the table of plates.

'Let me get this straight in my head,' Dyam said. 'You're saying that this emperor, Guilliam, now has the powers of every mage in the world?'

'We think so,' said Agang. 'We saw him use fire, flow, vision and stone. We are assuming he has life powers as well.'

'So Keira failed to stop him,' Bridget said. 'Kalayne was wrong.'

'No,' Agang said. 'Kalayne was right. He said that the church was planning something, and they were. We arrived too late, though.'

'And the Emperor slaughtered the entire Sanang army?' Dyam said. 'Leaving who, just you and Keira?'

'And Flora,' Agang said.

'I don't understand. How did you three manage to survive?'

'We ran away.'

'Bullshit.'

'Excuse me?'

Dyam shook her head and turned to Bridget. 'They must think we're as gullible as bairns.'

Agang said nothing, biting his lip.

'Come, my friend,' Laodoc said. 'Everything you have said is the truth, is it not?'

Dyam laughed. 'Only if you believe that the Emperor was clever enough to use different powers to destroy a whole army, but then somehow he missed the fire mage. Are you saying he just let her go?'

Agang bowed his head. 'No.'

'Tell us what really happened,' Bridget said, 'or you're not welcome here. I won't have liars staying in this house.'

Laodoc's tongue flickered, and his heart pounded. He gazed at Agang, willing him to speak.

'When he was finished with the army,' Agang said, his voice a low whisper, 'the Emperor then struck down Keira. He stopped her heart. I guess he didn't want to mutilate her body like he had with the Sanang, so he could show it off to the people of the city; I don't know.'

'He killed her?' Bridget said.

'And Flora. And me.'

Laodoc frowned. 'You left out that part of the story when you told me, my friend.'

'I'm sorry,' Agang said.

'Wait,' Bridget said. 'The Emperor killed you and Keira and Flora?'

'He stopped our hearts.'

The others looked at each other in bewilderment.

Agang stood, and walked over to where the bottle of whisky sat. He poured himself a large measure and drank.

With the eyes of the others on him, he raised his head.

'I am a life mage,' he said. 'As Laodoc knows, I can heal.'

Laodoc nodded. 'He can; I've seen it.'

'But I'm not just a hedgewitch. My powers go... further.'

'My friend,' Laodoc said, 'what does that mean? I have researched all the skills of the various mages that inhabit this world, and have read nothing of any higher Sanang power.'

'When the Emperor stopped my heart,' Agang said, 'my healing power restarted it. And then I restarted the hearts of Keira and Flora, and put life back into their bodies.'

Bridget gasped. 'You brought them back from the dead?'

'I did.'

The room fell into silence.

'I heard Leah died outside the walls,' Bedig said. 'Could you not bring her back too?'

'The Emperor had burnt her body,' Agang said. 'I couldn't do anything for her; I'm sorry.'

Bedig bowed his head.

'My friend,' Laodoc said. 'I'm confused, but at the same time exhilarated to think that you possess such power. Bringing life back to the dead?'

Dyam frowned. 'I might need to see some proof.'

'How?' Bridget laughed. 'Yer not suggesting he kills one of us first, are ye? Or are ye expecting him to bring our dinner back to life?'

Bedig rubbed his stomach. 'Please don't.'

'You may make light of it,' Agang said, 'but every mage of my kind is hunted down and killed in Sanang. That's why I've kept it a secret for so many years, and why I found it so hard to tell you.'

'We're not making light of it,' Bridget said; 'it's just a lot to take in. So, how does it work? Can ye go to a graveyard and summon the bodies to rise?'

'No,' Agang cried. 'The person has to have been dead for a few minutes at the most. Their brain, heart and other organs must still be capable of working, otherwise, otherwise...'

'What?'

Agang bowed his head. 'If life is given to a corpse that is cold and beginning to rot, then the thing that rises is no longer the person they once were. Mindless abominations, grotesque puppets, under the control of the mage that raised them. Keira and Flora had been dead for only a few moments For them it would have been like being in a deep, dreamless sleep.'

'Could you do it to something small, like a rat?' said Dyam.

Bridget smirked. 'I didn't know you had a pet.'

Dyam scowled at her. 'I'm the kind of person who needs evidence to believe the unbelievable.'

'I've never tried,' said Agang.

'But you'd be willing to?'

'I suppose so, if it'll make you believe me.'

Dyam stood. 'Stay right here.'

She darted to the front door, and left the cottage.

Bedig laughed. 'Is she really away to get a rat?'

'Who knows?' said Bridget. She took a sip of whisky. 'So, boys, that was all very interesting, but I have to ask, what the fuck's it got to do with me?'

'Just before Keira began the assault on the city,' Agang said, 'Kalayne spoke to her. He said that only she could save the world; but also that he'd had a vision of her with Shella, the Rakanese mage.'

'So?'

'Well, Miss Bridget,' Laodoc said, 'it would seem that in order to set events in motion, Keira and Shella must meet. Agang and I have already failed to persuade Keira to seek out Shella, so therefore only one alternative is open to us.'

'Which is?'

'We find Shella, and bring her to Keira.'

'Do you know where she is?'

'No, we do not,' Laodoc said. 'The last time I saw her she was in Plateau City, before the alliance forces set out for Rahain. As chancellor, however, I did hear that she had become the Rakanese ambassador to the Emperor's court; but I don't know if she still holds that position. In fact, with the current situation in the imperial capital, I would doubt very much that she still resides there.'

'So you want to find Shella,' Bridget said, 'but you have no idea where she is, or even if she's still alive. She might have died in the siege.'

'No,' said Agang. 'Kalayne saw a vision of her in the future. She's alive.'

Bridget rolled her eyes. 'Let's just say for now that that's true. I'm guessing you want me to help you?'

'We want you to lead the expedition,' Laodoc said.

Bridget laughed, long and hard. Laodoc glanced at Agang, and shrugged.

'Ye think I'm just going to pack up and leave, so soon after we got here?' she cried. 'Yer out of yer minds. We could be hunting this Shella for thirds, years, and never find her. She's probably gone back to Arakhanah.'

'I doubt it,' said Bedig, looking up from washing the dishes. 'She'd never go there to hide; too many folk know her there, and hate her.'

The others turned to the tall Brig man.

'Of course,' said Laodoc, 'you were with Shella in Akhanawarah, and Plateau City. Do you have any idea where she might have gone? Where would she consider safe?'

Bedig rubbed his chin and stared into the fire.

'Leave him a moment,' Bridget said. 'The gears of his brain grind slower than most.'

The door opened, and Dyam burst in, holding a leather bag at arm's length.

'Got one,' she cried, walking over to the table. She held the writhing bag aloft. 'Everyone see it moving, aye?'

Before anyone could reply, Dyam swung the bag down, battering it off the surface of the table, making the whisky glasses jump. She did it again, and a third time, then emptied the bag out onto the floor at Agang's feet. Laodoc peered down at the dead rat, hiding a grimace. Bridget got up, and walked round so she could see.

'Go on then,' said Dyam.

Agang leaned forwards, stretching out his arm until his fingers touched the body of the rodent. He closed his eyes, and felt for the creature's heart through a tangle of broken bones and bruised tissue. He sent a powerful wave of healing to repair its flesh, then jolted its heart.

The rat wheezed, opened its eyes, swayed, then scurried off through a gap in the floorboards.

'Great,' Bridget yelled, 'now we've got a fucking rat in the house. Good thinking, Dyam.'

'That was amazing,' Dyam said, glancing at Agang. 'I believe you now.'

'I remember,' said Bedig.

They all turned.

'There was a little town that Shella used to talk about,' he said. 'I've never been there myself, but it was a secret; in other words, even her sister the queen knew nothing about it. Shella said that she had gone against orders and let a small group of refugees settle, and set up a town.'

'And where is this town?' Laodoc said.

'I'm not sure of its exact location,' Bedig said, 'but Shella told us it was at the first river they came to after crossing the Basalt Desert into Rahain.'

'And do you know its name?'

'Aye,' he said. 'Silverstream.'

CHAPTER 8

BLOODLESS

Holdings City, Realm of the Holdings – 3rd Day, Last Third Summer 507

'Men are arseholes,' Chane said. 'Most are too shy to talk to me, and the good-looking, confident ones are already taken. Or it turns out they like guys.'

'You've just been unlucky,' said Daphne, passing her a weedstick as they leaned back against a wall. 'You'll find someone. Which one of them likes guys, by the way?'

Chane took a draw. 'Don't laugh,' she said. 'Agang.'

Daphne raised her eyebrows. 'Really? Why would I laugh?'

'Because I spent so much time chasing him, even after I found out. It's embarrassing.'

'It happens, Chane. Don't worry about it; at least you got away in time.'

Chane said nothing.

'Did you sleep with him?'

'We shared a bed,' Chane said. 'Most nights, in fact. But he just lay there like he was my brother.'

Daphne grimaced. 'Awkward.'

'That doesn't even begin to describe it.'

A young man in a pale green uniform approached.

'Ma'am,' he said to Daphne. 'The company is in position.'

Daphne nodded. 'Tell them to wait for my signal, then move in.'

The man ran back up the alleyway.

Daphne scanned the rooftops. The day's light was darkening into dusk over the city, and a long shadow was being cast by the outcrop of rock where the Upper City sat. She glanced at Chane, pulled on her battle-vision, and set off.

The streets were deserted, and there was no noise except for the low roar of fighting elsewhere in the city, fuelled by the numerous diversionary units sent in to attack the old capital's key points. Daphne sprinted down a lane, with Chane close behind, until they reached a high wall. They halted, and Daphne pushed a line of vision up to the roof of the building opposite.

'Clear,' she said, and Chane braced herself against the wall, the fingers of her hands interlocking. Daphne stepped back a few paces, surged her battle-vision, and ran at Chane. She leapt into the air, her foot landing in Chane's grip, and hurled herself up onto the top of the wall, and over to the other side. She glanced around, but the barracks of the cavalry garrison were quiet and empty.

She stayed under the shadow of the wall and ran to where a postern gate was positioned. There were no guards on duty at the gate, the widespread disturbances having ensured that the entire garrison had been called out.

Daphne swung the bar from the gate and pushed it open. She signalled to the militia of the Hold Fast Company, who were waiting in the shadows of a side street, and they began to file towards the gate.

Chane entered first.

She grinned at Daphne, her eyes dancing, as the troopers followed through after her.

'This way,' Daphne said, and ran by the wall towards the compound's corner tower, a square block that rose above the height of the exterior walls. She paused to allow the troopers to catch up, and they lined up against the wall behind her. She steadied herself and scanned the top of the tower with line-vision. Up on the battlements, a squad of troopers were gazing out over the city, watching the lights from several fires that were burning. None were looking back within the compound.

She ran on, and reached the doors of the tower.

'Crossbows,' she said to the troopers nearest her, and they passed the word down the line.

She nodded to Chane, and kicked the door in. They burst into the tower, the Hold Fast troopers spreading through the building as fast as they could enter. Daphne led a detachment up the stone stairs, and emerged onto the open rooftop.

'Put down your weapons,' she cried to the squad of imperial soldiers, who turned to stare at Daphne and the crossbow-wielding troopers on either side of her. 'This is the Hold Fast Company, and you are now our prisoners. Who's in charge?'

A woman stepped forwards, her arms raised. 'I'm the sergeant here.'

'Order your squad to disarm.'

The woman scanned the group of green-uniformed troopers, many of whom were fresh-faced.

'You heard her,' she said. 'Drop your bows.'

Daphne turned to one of her officers as the imperial soldiers threw down their arms. 'Collect their weapons and take the prisoners downstairs. Put a guard on them, and leave a squad up here to watch the compound.'

'Yes, ma'am.'

Daphne returned to the ground floor, where the rest of the company was waiting. Chane was standing by an enormous winch, around which was coiled a thick chain.

'Open up the bridge,' Daphne ordered, and a squad of troopers took hold of the winch's long handles, and began to turn. The chain tensed, then started winding round the iron mechanism, foot by foot as the troopers grunted with the effort.

Daphne nodded to Chane. 'Send the signal.'

'Yes, ma'am.'

Chane ran up the stairs and out of sight.

'This is treachery,' shouted one of the imperial soldiers as they were being led off to a side room.

Daphne smiled.

'The signal's up,' said Chane, as she bounded back down the steps.

'Open the gate,' Daphne cried, and troopers removed the long bar from the wide doors that led out onto the street. They pushed them open, and Daphne strode outside. The sound of the river mixed with the cries of hundreds of approaching troopers, the force her father had gathered.

The tower gates led to the widest bridge over the great river of the Holdings, one of three crossings from the sprawling Lower City to the sheer cliffs of the Upper City. The other bridges were narrow, and led to steep flights of steps hewn from the cliff-face, but the crossing that led from the city garrison could accommodate a pair of carriages side by side. The portcullis that blocked the way was hanging high, raised above the road as it led on to the bridge.

Chane stood at her side as the Holdings rebels grew nearer.

'Excellent job, Miss Holdfast,' cried an older man, who stopped as he drew near to the tower, out of breath.

'Thank you, Lord Holdsmith,' Daphne said.

The man spat and coughed, and lit a cigarette. 'Feels like I've run through half the damn city.'

Chane nudged her, and she turned to see a trooper leading a pair of horses towards them.

'Ma'am,' the trooper saluted, 'as you requested.'

'Thank you,' Daphne said. She glanced at Lord Holdsmith. 'If you'll excuse me.'

She leapt up onto the saddle, and took the reins, while Chane mounted the other horse. They kicked their heels, and their mounts took off, galloping through the gates and onto the bridge, while the troopers cleared a path for them.

On the other side of the bridge was the wide royal ramp, which went up a gradual slope to the buildings clustered on the summit of the

Upper City. They overtook the leading troopers of the rebel force, and the clatter of their horses' hooves against the bridge changed as they started up the ramp. The cobbles beneath them sparked as they cantered up the slope, leaving the force behind.

Daphne slowed as they approached the top, her vision-assisted eyesight taking in every detail of the buildings crowded together upon the summit. To the left, rising above low stables, was the Old Tower, its roof gone, and its walls crumbling and blackened with fire damage. Ahead was the road leading to Holders Square, where the palace lay. Daphne gazed up at the great edifice, squeezed into the tight space of the Upper City. Added to and modified over centuries, it wore many differing styles and architectural fashions. As a young woman, she had always pictured it as the grandest building she had ever seen, but now knew it was tiny in comparison to the great buildings of state she had seen in Rahain, and much smaller even than the palace in Plateau City that Keira had destroyed.

'What now?' said Chane. 'Should we wait for the others?'

Daphne gazed at the empty road leading to the palace.

'No,' she said, kicking her horse into movement, 'let's take a look.'

They spurred their mounts to a trot, and made their way down the wide street. The buildings to either side looked deserted, and many had been neglected, their windows broken and their roofs leaking.

'The entire government left years ago,' Chane said, as she gazed at the dilapidated structures. 'I'm surprised the Lord Regent stays up here. It's like a ghost town.'

'The Prophet's up here too,' she said.

'That miserable old fart? Is he still alive?'

'I think so, skulking somewhere deep within the citadel.'

'He probably smokes dreamweed all day,' Chane said, 'and wallows in nostalgia about how he used to be important, but now everybody's forgotten he even exists.'

'Let's focus on the Lord Regent first,' Daphne said. She slowed as they entered Holders Square. Lamps had been lit, illuminating the façade of the palace. Pillars and arched windows ran in rows along the front of the building, with a stately entrance in the centre. There was a low platform abutting the grand stone steps that led down from the palace, and Daphne gazed at the spot where she had nearly been executed three and a half years before.

They trotted over to the steps, and climbed down next to a low railing. After securing their horses, they ascended the stairs towards the open doors of the palace.

Four soldiers were on duty, guarding the entrance. They lowered their crossbows at Daphne and Chane as they approached.

'I am Daphne Holdfast,' she said. 'I'm here to see the Lord Regent.'

The soldiers stared at her.

'What do you know about the fighting in the city?' said one. 'What's going on?'

'There's an uprising in progress,' Daphne said. 'That's why I need to speak to the Lord Regent urgently.'

'You'll have to leave your weapons at the door.'

'Of course.'

The lead soldier nodded, and Daphne and Chane passed into the great entrance hall of the palace. It was poorly lit, with a handful of lamps burning against the walls. Daphne unbuckled her sword belt and handed it to a soldier. Chane frowned, and did the same.

The two women turned, and strode across the marble floor of the hall towards an arched opening opposite.

'I hope you know what we're doing,' Chane said. 'Cause I haven't a clue.'

'Maybe this can end without bloodshed,' Daphne said. 'Let's see if the Lord Regent is a reasonable man.'

At the entrance to the adjoining hall, a courtier was standing. She bowed as they approached, but her eyes were lit with suspicion.

'We're here to see the Lord Regent,' Daphne said.

'And do you have an appointment?'

'No. But there's a force of several thousand rebel Holdings troopers currently running up the royal ramp towards the palace. I imagine the Lord Regent would want to know.'

The courtier's mouth opened. She glanced at their beltless waists.

'Follow me,' she said, and turned for a grand set of stairs.

They climbed to the first floor, and the courtier led them to a massive reception room, equal in beauty and grandeur to any Daphne had seen on her travels. At the far end was a podium, upon which sat a great throne, flanked by lesser thrones. All three were empty, and the room was quiet and still. The courtier led them on to a door in the far wall, and they went through to a small chamber. Guards lined the walls around a large table, at which four people sat.

'Lord Regent,' the courtier said as they entered.

A man looked up. Next to him was a uniformed woman, and across the table sat Faden Holdwick and Queen Mirren Blackhold.

'What is it?' the man muttered.

'Visitors, Lord Regent,' the courtier said, gesturing to Daphne and Chane.

The man squinted at them. 'I wasn't expecting anyone.'

Daphne stepped forwards. 'Your regime is at an end, Lord Regent. I'm here to see if you wish that end to be bloody or peaceful.'

The man's face twisted in contempt. 'How dare you...?'

'A force of three thousand troopers, from eleven different noble Holds, is on its way up the royal ramp. They will be in Holders Square any moment, and then they are coming here for you, Lord Regent. If you surrender now, we can prevent the loss of any lives.'

The guards lining the walls of the room tensed, their hands going to the hilts of their swords.

'You walk in here, unarmed, and make demands of me?' the Lord Regent cried. 'I was appointed by the Emperor to rule the old realm, and only the Emperor can remove me.'

He stood.

'Do you surrender?' Daphne said.

'Of course I don't, you silly little girl,' he sneered.

She visioned into his mind and took control of it, forcing his body to freeze.

I am in your head, Lord Regent. Listen very carefully to what I have to say. Do you feel my power on your memories, your thoughts? Do you see how fragile they are, how easily I could tear and shred them? Do you know I could scour your mind clean, or wreck it so that you weep and scream every day for the rest of your life? I could make you forget who you are, or fill your mind with endless torment. Nod if you understand me.

The Lord Regent nodded, while the guards stood frozen, waiting for his command.

Good. Now, you will do exactly as I say.

Daphne relinquished control of the Lord Regent's body, but kept a part of herself hidden in his mind.

'I will ask you again,' she said. 'Do you surrender?'

Fear swept across his face. On the other side of the table, Mirren and Faden were watching.

The woman in uniform got to her feet, and drew her sword. 'Lord Regent,' she said, 'should I place them under arrest?'

Tell her to put the sword down.

'Stand down, Major,' the Lord Regent cried. He bowed his head. 'I surrender.'

The woman's mouth opened in shock, and she glanced from the Regent to Daphne.

'Get on your knees,' Daphne said.

The Regent stood still for a moment, then did as she ordered.

'What is happening?' the major said. 'Lord Regent?'

'Put your sword away,' he said, his eyes welling with tears.

Daphne nodded at him. 'Good. Now swear allegiance to the new Chancellor of the Holdings, Lord Faden Holdwick.'

The man stared up at Faden. 'You? You betrayed me?'

'It is you who have betrayed the Holdings,' Faden said. 'Now we can take back control of our own land.'

'But the empire...?'

'The empire has stripped the Holdings bare, you fool,' Faden said. 'The Emperor's insane quest for mages is the cause of children starving in the River Holdings, and the endless toll of war dead. Thousands have already fallen in the marshes of Arakhanah City, prey to disease and pestilence. No more. No more.'

The Lord Regent bowed his head.

'I swear allegiance.'

Daphne glanced at the uniformed woman. 'Major, please take the former Lord Regent into custody.'

The woman frowned. 'Under whose authority?'

'Mine,' said Faden. 'As chancellor, I command it.'

The major remained expressionless. She glanced from person to person.

Mirren stood and bowed her head to Faden. 'I acknowledge you as chancellor, Lord Holdwick. May you rule the Realm of the Holdings wisely.'

The major frowned, then nodded at the guards. 'Take him to the cells.'

Four soldiers approached, and escorted the Lord Regent from the room. The major got down onto one knee.

'I swear allegiance to you, Lord Holdwick.'

'Excellent,' said Daphne. She gestured to the queen and the new chancellor. 'Shall we?'

They left the small chamber, and went back into the enormous reception hall. Faden mounted the platform, and sat in the great throne, and the queen took the smaller throne to his right. Daphne and Chane took up position one step down from the podium, and the remaining guards were ordered by the major to secure the hall.

'What was that, Daphne?' Chane whispered. 'What did you do to him back there?'

'I showed him the true meaning of fear.'

'You are one scary bitch, Daphne Holdfast, even without a sword.'

The front doors of the hall burst open, and squads of militia began running in. Their uniforms ranged from pale green to brown and dark blue, detachments from all eleven rebel Hold forces present as they filled the hall. She saw Lord Holdsmith walk to the front, panting.

Daphne raised her right arm.

'The Lord Regent has surrendered, and is in custody,' she cried out, loud enough for the hall to hear. The militia let out a cheer. 'Lord Holdwick is now Chancellor of the Realm, and Queen Mirren Blackhold is his First Minister. Do you pledge your loyalty to them?'

The crowd of militia roared and cheered.

Lord Holdsmith approached the thrones, and knelt, while other noblemen and women gathered to offer their congratulations and pledges of allegiance.

'Look at them,' Chane whispered. 'All wanting to be the first to kiss the arse of the new leader, hoping to get the pick of the plum jobs.'

'Let's leave them to it,' Daphne said. 'I want to make sure the rest of the Upper City is secure.'

She bowed to Faden, who nodded and smiled at her, then she and Chane descended the steps.

'Stay here, Major,' she said to the officer, 'in case any imperial soldiers arrive who are yet to hear the news.'

'Who are you?' she asked.

'Daphne Holdfast.'

The major shook her head. 'So the Holdfasts have finally got what they wanted, to rule the Holdings?'

'I think you'll find that Lord Holdwick is chancellor, Major, not my father.'

'And where is your father, ma'am?'

'At home on the estate,' she said, 'with the rest of my family.'

'He sent you in his stead,' the major said, 'so his hands would appear clean.'

Daphne stopped. 'Do we have a problem, Major?'

'I am an officer of the imperial army, ma'am. This coup of yours will bring nothing but despair and destruction to the Holdings. The Emperor will have no choice but to intervene in force.'

'The Emperor was planning to invade regardless,' Daphne said. 'We are merely taking action to defend ourselves.'

The major said nothing, her eyes conflicted.

'I have no desire to see Holdings kill Holdings,' Daphne said, 'but I will take any action necessary to protect this land. If you wish, I can have you arrested, and then your conscience will be clear.'

The major bit her lip.

'Is your loyalty to the empire or the Holdings?' Daphne said.

'The Holdings, ma'am.'

'Good.'

Daphne turned, and caught Chane's eye. As she was about to speak, she felt a voice in her mind.

Miss Daphne Holdfast, I have been expecting a visit from you for a long time.

Daphne paused, recognising the voice from years before.

And now you are here, the voice went on, *there is much for us to discuss. Come to the citadel; I will be waiting for you.*

Daphne nodded.

'Let's go to the citadel,' she said. 'I want to look in on the Prophet.'

Chane frowned. 'I thought we were going to check the steps down to the middle bridge?'

'The Holdwain militia are assigned there; I'm sure they can handle it.'

Chane shrugged.

They set off through the maze of corridors within the palace, turning at a junction that led to a small gate on the western side. They emerged out onto a dark street, marking the boundary between the secular and ecclesiastical halves of the Upper City. Behind them stood the bulk of the palace complex, while ahead lay the piled-high buildings of the headquarters of the church, with the spires of the cathedral dominating the skyline.

A pair of armed church wardens were guarding the main gates to the headquarters, and they raised their spears as Daphne and Chane approached.

'This is church ground,' cried one. 'You are forbidden to enter.'

'I have an invitation from the Prophet,' Daphne smiled.

One of the guards staggered, his eyes glazing over. His head snapped up, his sight clear again.

'Let them through,' he said.

The other guard nodded, and swung open the great iron-rimmed door.

Daphne entered, followed by Chane. Inside, the passageways were dim, lit with low burning lamps. There was a musty smell of abandonment, and dust covered most surfaces.

Chane peered into the gloom. 'Where do we go?'

Daphne reached out with her vision, feeling for the presence of the Prophet. His power shone like a beacon in her mind's eye.

'This way,' she said.

They walked through long, dark corridors, past empty offices and deserted halls, deep into the warren of buildings, until they reached a large set of double doors lying open.

'The cathedral,' Chane muttered. 'This is the first time I've been here in years.'

'The first time anyone has, by the look of it,' Daphne said.

They entered the great space within the cathedral. The ceiling was lost above them in the gloom and shadows, held up by lines of enormous pillars. At the far end was a raised throne, upon which sat a small figure, hunched over and wrapped in a thick cloak.

At the foot of the steps below the throne stood half a dozen men and women, dressed in the black robes of the One True Path.

'How did you get in here?' shouted one of the deacons. 'Stop at once!'

Daphne smiled. 'Or what?'

One of the deacons drew a sword, and advanced.

'Shit,' muttered Chane, feeling the empty space on her waist where her belt had been.

Daphne pulled on her battle-vision and ran at the deacon. She ducked under a sword lunge, drew a knife from her boot and planted it into the side of the man's neck. She took the sword from the dying man's grasp and threw it to Chane.

'Happy now?'

Chane grinned, and charged. Daphne retrieved her knife, and the pair cut their way through the remaining deacons, slaying them on the steps before the throne, blood spraying onto the marble floor.

Daphne sheathed her knife and ascended the steps. The gnarled old figure on the throne was motionless. His eyes were closed, and he seemed to be sleeping, or dead. He looked at least a hundred years old.

I am a mere ninety-three, Miss Daphne, said the voice. Not yet dead, but the day is not too far off, I think. My body is old and dying, and only my mind is keeping it alive. I thank you for disposing of those vile deacons; they have made my life a misery for years, trapped up here alone in the citadel, shunned by the church and forgotten by the people. The Lord Vicar will quickly realise what you have done to his spies, however, when he next attempts to make contact with them.

'I'm not worried about the Lord Vicar.'

No? What about the Emperor?

Daphne smiled. 'I have a few concerns.'

He will be coming, Miss Daphne, make no mistake about that. Your coup may slow him down a little, but once he learns what you have done, his fury will be without limit or restraint.

'He was coming anyway.'

I know. His thirst for mages is insatiable. You are near the top of his list, I believe.

'I'm flattered.'

You should be afraid. I can sense great power in you, but even that is modest next to what the Emperor is now capable of. But I can help you.

'The Prophet would aid us against the Emperor? Why?'

My girl, as yet you have no inkling of what the Emperor wants, or of what he plans. The empire is rotten and Guilliam is drunk with power. I have been shunned for years, ever since I refused to accompany him to his new city in the Plateau. Even then, I knew the plans of the Creator, and knew they would destroy the world.

Daphne felt Chane nudge her arm.

'Is he alive?'

She nodded. 'He wants to help us.'

'Is he in your head?'

'Or I'm in his, it's hard to tell.'

You feel it too? the Prophet said. *You and I, Daphne, we share much in common. We both possess traces of an older magecraft, lost and forgotten to even the wisest. How else would you have been able to give birth to such a child? Did you think it was through chance alone that your daughter has such power?*

Daphne gasped. 'You know about Karalyn?'

Indeed. As I said, Daphne, we have much to discuss.

CHAPTER 9
LEAVING PARTY

Westgate, Domm Pass – 4th Day, Last Third Summer 507

Keira staggered down the muddy street, the drizzle on the high pass clinging in the air like mist, covering her in moisture. Passers-by avoided her as she splashed through puddles and swayed round corners. Her hair was lank and unwashed, and her clothes stank of smoke.

She gazed around, the thick cloud cover making it impossible to tell what time it was. She laughed. She didn't know which day it was, never mind the time. Her stomach turned and she retched. She needed a drink, and she needed to pee. She spotted the tavern up the slope to her left, and stumbled towards it. The large faded sign reading 'World's End' was swinging in the breeze as she reached the front entrance. She hesitated, then walked round to the back of the building, and went in through a side door. She climbed up the steps to her room, her legs aching from the effort, and she nearly fell through the door when she got to it.

Flora was lying on her bed.

Keira grinned. 'That was the best weed I've had in fucking ages,' she said, staggering into the room. She crashed down into the only chair as Flora opened her eyes and sat up.

'You been greetin'?' Keira said.

'Where have you been, Keira?' Flora yelled. 'I thought you'd died or something.'

'Already done that, hen, and I'm still here.'

'You've been gone for four days!'

'That long, eh?' Keira chuckled. 'It was some session, right enough.'

'You don't give a shit about anyone but yourself.'

'Now hang on, hen,' Keira snarled. 'Yer not my ma; ye dinnae control me. All I did was go out for a bit.'

Flora shook her head.

'Ye should have seen the stash of weed these folk had, but,' Keira said. 'It was mental. Dream, dull, keen... you fucking name it, they had it. They were just in from the Sanang borderlands, part of some team working up there.'

'Bandits, you mean.'

Keira shrugged. 'Maybe. It wasn't my business to ask them where they got it from; all I wanted to do was smoke it. Met them over at Dermot's Bar, had a few drinks with them, and they invited me up to their room when they discovered who I was.'

'And you've been there for four days?'

'If you say so. I cannae remember much, to be honest.'

'Me and Kendrie searched the whole town for you. We even looked over the cliff to see if you'd fallen down, drunk.'

'That's funny as fuck,' Keira sniggered. 'And all the time I was out of my nut.'

Flora wrinkled her nose. 'You stink.'

'Aye, well, so would you, if ye'd spent four days lying about in some dingy wee room with a bunch of hairy-arsed bandits.'

Flora stood. 'I should go.'

'What were ye doing in my room anyway?' Keira said, narrowing her eyes.

'Nothing.'

Keira watched Flora walk to the door.

'Wait a wee minute,' she called out. 'If I was gone for four days, what's Kelpie been doing with me not around?'

'Cursing your name, mostly. Trying to persuade customers not to leave because you haven't shown up. It was lucky that Laodoc came back from the lowlands. He's been covering for you.'

'They're back, are they? About time.'

'Get cleaned up, and come to the tavern,' Flora said. 'There's something you might want to see.'

'What?'

'Come, and you'll see,' she said, leaving and closing the door.

'Awkward wee cow,' Keira muttered, getting up and jumping onto the bed. She lay down with her head on the pillow. Just a quick nap. She felt something under her cheek, and moved up to look. There was a damp patch on the pillow, from where Flora's face had been when Keira had entered the room. The wee cow had been crying on her bed.

Keira sat up and shook her head. A twinge of guilt crept up her, but she brushed it aside. It wasn't her fault if wee Flora fancied her. She had never done anything to lead her on, and she had always been completely open about preferring guys. She hoped Flora wasn't going to be a pain in the arse about it; that was the last thing she needed.

She got up, and staggered over to her wash bowl.

An hour later, clean and in fresh clothes, Keira strode through to the tavern.

'Alright, Kendrie?' she cried at the barman.

He looked up and did a double take.

'Yer back?'

'Yer getting brighter every day, I swear it,' Keira cackled. 'Now, how about an ale?'

'And how are ye going to pay for it?'

'Pay?' Keira curled her lip. 'What the fuck are ye talking about?'

'I think Kelpie might be having second thoughts about yer arrangement,' Kendrie said, folding his arms. 'After all, ye've stood us up for four shifts in a row, without a word about where ye were, or if ye were coming back...'

'Yawn, yawn, Kendrie,' Keira muttered. 'I'm back now, am I not? And correct me if I'm wrong, but I never used my room, ate any of yer food, or drank any of yer booze while I was away, right? So give me a fucking drink for today's shift, and stop being a cantankerous wee prick.'

Kendrie frowned.

'See?' Keira laughed. 'I knew my logic would bamboozle ye. So, an ale?'

Kendrie looked over her shoulder. 'I think yer friends are wanting ye.'

'Oh aye?' she said, turning.

In the centre of the tavern floor stood a large pile of boxes, trunks and baggage had been piled up. Agang stood close to it, frowning and rubbing his chin, while Laodoc and Flora sat at a nearby table. Flora waved her over.

'What's going on?' Keira said to Laodoc as she sauntered over to the table. 'Flora told me that you'd got back a few days ago. Too lazy to unpack, eh?'

Laodoc smiled. 'My dear Mage Keira, please sit. I'd like to talk with you.'

Keira noticed a large jug of ale on the table, and sat. She poured herself a mug, and took a drink.

'Ahh,' she sighed, putting her feet up onto a stool.

'Mage Keira,' Laodoc said, 'if I may, please. I would like to inform you that Agang and I have decided to leave.'

Keira shrugged, and looked out of the window at the rain.

'It was a difficult decision,' Laodoc went on. 'On the one hand, here we can enjoy peace and the freedom to live our lives in the manner we wish; while on the other hand, the world is in peril, and if we sit here and do nothing then, sooner or later, that peril will come to Domm and consume us.'

Laodoc glanced over at Agang.

'We feel there is no other option,' the Sanang man said, walking over. 'The hardest choice I ever made was to believe that Kalayne was speaking the truth. So when he said that only you could save the world, I believe it. I, we, also believe that Shella must be found...'

Keira turned her head to glare at them. 'I thought ye said ye were leaving? Ye seem to be doing a lot of talking instead.' She pointed. 'There's the door.'

Laodoc smiled. 'Our desire to leave matches your wish to see us gone, but we have to wait for our companions to arrive. But do not fear, we will be gone as soon as that happens.'

'I hope not,' said Kelpie, walking over. 'I have a leaving party planned for you. Just a wee chance to say our goodbyes, ye know?'

'Madam Kelpie,' Laodoc said, 'my most earnest thanks, but please don't put yourself out on our account.'

'It's no bother,' she said. She turned to Keira, her face calm.

'Yer working tonight, don't forget.'

Kelpie marched away, without waiting for Keira to respond.

Keira smirked.

Agang sat, and poured himself a water.

'Come with us, Keira,' he said. 'Please.'

'Not a fucking chance, eight-thirds.'

'You're wasting your time, my friend,' Laodoc said. 'Mage Keira would rather remain here and wallow in her sense of self-pity and failure.'

'Failure?' Keira snarled. 'Fuck you, ya scaly wee bastard. I've packed more winning into a few short years than you arseholes have managed in yer entire lives. Do ye have any fucking idea of how many bastards I've killed?'

'I have a vague notion,' Laodoc said; 'but whatever the exact number, it's proved enough of a burden to send you to the very end of the world.'

'And ye want me to go out and kill more?' Keira cried, her rage building. She could feel her cheeks burning as the others gazed at her.

'Have I not given enough? Have I not killed enough for ye? Ye want more?'

Flora swallowed, and looked away.

Keira bared her teeth, her knuckles clenched.

'I apologise, Mage Keira,' Laodoc said into the nervous silence. 'We have no desire to force you to use your powers again if you do not wish to do so. However, the Emperor is coming, and you are one of the only mages strong enough to give the inhabitants of this world any hope.'

'I'm sick of being everyone's hope,' she cried. 'Life is short, cruel and doesn't give a fuck, and most people are either stupid or selfish or both. Fuck them all. Fuck this world; I hope the bastard Emperor fucking wins.'

She got to her feet, kicking the chair over, and stormed from the tavern. She slammed the door shut behind her, and paused as the rain poured down, drenching her. She raised her face, letting the drops fall onto her cheeks, mixing with the tears so that nobody would know.

'You should really come and say goodbye, you know,' Flora said, sitting on the chair in her room as Keira lounged on the bed, a bottle of whisky in her hand.

'I knew ye were going to say that,' she said, not bothering to look up, 'and if that's all ye came for, ye can fuck off.'

'They're your friends. Well, Agang is.'

'Is he fuck. Do friends walk out on each other? Now that he's best friends with that scaly bastard, he couldnae give a shit about me or you. He'd rather pretend to be a hero, when he's just trying to impress Grandpa Laodoc.'

'But everyone's in the tavern; they're all wondering where you are.'

Keira swigged the whisky.

Flora sat back, frowning. 'They'll think you're scared.'

Keira snorted. 'Of what?'

'I don't know, of facing them, I suppose. Scared of breaking down and admitting that you'll miss them.'

'Agang and Laodoc? Miss them? Ha, yer just being ridiculous now.'

'Do you know that Dean's going as well?'

'Is he? So what. He's a useless wee twat; we're better off without him.'

'He's too inexperienced to be going on some crazy mission,' Flora said. 'I've tried to talk him out of it, but he seems set. If you could speak to him, Keira, he'll listen to you.'

'Why the fuck would I want to do that?'

'Because he's just a kid.'

'If he's old enough to be shagging Dora, he's old enough to get himself killed in some pointless fight.'

'That doesn't make any sense.'

'Stop nagging me, Flora. Go back to the party and leave me be.'

The Holdings woman stood.

'Do you want me to open those shutters for you?' she said. 'The sun's come out.'

'I like it dark.'

Flora nodded, then left her room, closing the door on the way out.

Keira took a swig of whisky, then leaned over to the floor and picked up the cloak she had worn for four days over at Dermot's place. She rifled through the pockets, then smiled as she found what she was looking for. She withdrew her hand, a tight bundle of stolen weedsticks grasped in her fingers.

She pulled one free of the bundle, lit it off the bedside lamp, and inhaled.

An hour later, fuelled by whisky and a potent blend of Sanang narcotics, Keira decided it was time to go to the party. She tucked a weedstick into her belt pouch, and tossed the empty bottle of whisky into the corner of the room to join the others.

She heard the noise coming from the tavern as she went down the back stairs, a low roar of conversations, laughter and music. Bar boys and girls squeezed past her in the corridor, taking plates filled with lunch from the kitchens out to the customers, and her stomach growled. She entered the tavern, and swaggered through the crowds, passing a small group of guitar-strumming musicians playing by the hearth. The shutters were wide open, letting in the afternoon sunshine, and the blustery wind smelled of the ocean.

The pile of luggage had gone from the floor, and Keira glanced around. She spotted Flora and the others sitting in the corner. Their tables were filled with plates, jugs and bottles, and everyone was eating and drinking. Keira frowned as she saw Bridget and Bedig sitting with them, along with the pale, blonde-haired lassie whose name she had forgotten.

Those that noticed her approach fell silent. She reached the table, and poured herself an ale from the jug.

'Alright, ya stupid goat-shaggers,' she said. 'I thought I'd come and laugh at you, off on yer fucked up wee mission to find the frog-woman. Ye'll be lucky if ye make it past Kell.'

'And a good afternoon to you, Mage Keira,' Laodoc said, before anyone else could react. 'Many thanks for your words of encouragement; I will treasure them in my heart.'

Keira frowned at him, and sat. She glared at Bridget.

'I see all the losers are leaving,' Keira said. 'The old, the bairns, the useless.'

'Go fuck yourself,' said the pale, blonde woman.

'Leave it, Dyam,' said Bridget. 'She's just trying to get a rise out of us.'

'Indeed,' said Laodoc, 'and using bravado to cover the fact that she's too afraid to leave the security of Domm and venture back out into the world.'

Keira's rage boiled over. 'Just because yer an old bastard, don't think I won't punch yer fucking teeth in.' She gazed around the table at the angry faces. 'I'll kick all yer arses.'

The table sat in silence, and Keira drank down her ale and poured another.

'It's not too late, Flora,' Agang said.

'You're more than welcome to join us,' said Bridget.

The Holdings woman shook her head. 'I've made my decision.'

'Good luck to you, young lady,' Laodoc said. 'It has been a privilege to get to know you during my stay here.'

'Thanks,' Flora said. 'I'll miss you all, especially you, Agang; we've been through so much together, and I don't think I ever actually thanked you for saving my life. So, thank you.'

Agang smiled.

Flora turned to Dean, who was sitting next to Dora. 'One last time,' she said, 'please stay, Dean.'

The young man stared at the table. 'Sorry, but I'm going.'

Dora sobbed.

Keira sniggered. 'You should go with them, Dora, at least then I wouldn't have to put up with all yer snivelling.'

'I want to,' she said, 'but my ma and da say I can't.'

Keira laughed. 'At your age I did what the fuck I wanted, not what I was told to do.'

Two women approached the table, longbows slung over their shoulders.

'Boss,' said one to Bridget, 'both wagons are loaded up and ready to go.'

'Thanks,' Bridget said. 'Everyone, this is Bonnie and Lola; they're coming along with us. I figured we were a bit light on muscle for this trip, and these two have seen plenty of action. Brynt recommended them to me; they were part of his hunting squad back in the Severed City.'

The two women nodded at the group.

'Nice to meet you,' Laodoc said. 'That brings the number of our party up to eight.'

'Hopefully small enough to travel unnoticed,' Bridget said.

'Ye'll never make it past Kell,' Keira muttered. 'The lizard soldiers are too scared to go near large mobs of refugees heading south, but they'll mince a wee group like you.'

'What would you know?' Dyam said.

'A shitload more than you, ya cow. I've been all round this fucking world.'

'And all it seems to have taught ye is how to be a twisted bitch.'

Keira clenched her fists.

'Dyam, enough,' Bridget said.

Kelpie walked over.

'I hope you all enjoyed your lunch?'

'Very much, Madam Kelpie,' Laodoc said. 'Thank you for your generosity.'

'Aye, thanks,' Bridget said, standing.

'No problem,' Kelpie said. 'It's been a pleasure to host ye, Laodoc, and I'll be sad to see ye go.'

'Aye,' Keira said, 'sad that yer takings will be down.'

Kelpie nodded. 'That too.'

'Goodbye, Flora, Kelpie,' said Bridget. 'And to you, Keira.'

'Whatever.'

The others got to their feet. Bonnie, Lola and Dyam left the tavern, while Flora gave Agang a hug.

'Take care,' she said.

'And you.'

Laodoc paused in front of Keira. 'We will see you again, mage, of that I have no doubt.'

She ignored him.

Dean pushed away Dora's embrace and ran from the tavern, his cheeks wet. Bridget frowned, and caught Laodoc's eye.

'Time to go,' she said.

The old man nodded, and they left the tavern.

'Farewell, Keira,' Agang said, and followed them.

Bedig approached, and got down on one knee. He leaned over to whisper in her ear.

'Sort yourself out, Keira; you're a mess.'

She said nothing, continuing to stare out of the window, and she heard him walk away.

'There, there,' Kelpie said, as Dora collapsed in tears.

Keira turned. Flora was sitting shaking her head, while Dora and Kelpie sat opposite, the older woman comforting the younger.

'You should have stayed in your room,' said Flora.

'Misbehaving, was she?' Kelpie said.

'Just the usual.'

'That bad, eh?'

'Shut it, the pair of ye,' Keira snapped.

'Don't you speak to me like that,' Kelpie said, 'not after ye don't show up for four days. Ye've lost me a lot of money.'

'Well, I'm back now.'

'Aye,' Kelpie said, standing, 'and ye'd better start paying yer way, now that Laodoc and Agang aren't here.'

She strode off towards the bar.

Keira removed the weedstick from her pouch, and lit it. She put her feet back up onto the stool and inhaled.

'Stop wailing,' she said to Dora. 'Yer ruining ma smoke.'

She gazed at the red-faced lassie, tears rolling down her cheeks.

'Ye'll forget him soon enough,' she said. 'Here, have some of this.' She passed Dora the weedstick. 'That'll shut ye up for a while.'

The afternoon wind picked up as they sat in the corner of the tavern, drinking; Flora matching her whisky for whisky. Dora was snoring, her head on the table, as the crowds began to gather to hear Keira speak.

'What story have you got lined up for them?' Flora slurred.

'Fuck knows, hen,' Keira said. 'I've done the flying carriages to death, and the exploding heads.'

'Maybe it's time for something they've not heard before.'

'Aye, or I could just make something up,' she laughed, filling her whisky glass. 'The stupid arseholes would never notice.'

Bay approached the table.

'Hi, Mage,' she said. 'Is Dora all right? Is she drunk?'

'She's upset about Dean going,' Flora said.

'Aye?' Bay said, sitting. 'Was that today?'

'Yeah,' said Flora, 'a few hours ago.'

Bay nudged Dora with her elbow, and the snoring ceased.

'Never knew what she saw in him, to be honest,' Bay said. 'He always had his head in a book.'

Keira saw Kelpie over by the bar. The older woman nodded, signalling it was time for Keira to begin.

She banged her glass on the table. 'Settle down, folks,' she cried. 'It's time for a wee story.'

The crowd quietened, filling every table in the place.

Keira swallowed. Here we go again.

'I want to tell ye about the time I was leading the Sanang army, and we were attacked by thousands of flying carriages, and...'

'We've heard it a hundred times,' shouted someone, amid a murmur of agreement.

'Where's the old Rahain guy?' cried another voice.

'Aye, we want to hear him speak!'

Keira scowled. 'Well, ye've got me today. The scaly old bastard's gone, probably for good.'

The faces of the crowd looked disappointed.

'All right,' she said, 'there was the time, back when I was in the alliance army, that we assaulted a gatehouse of the Rahain Capital...'

'Heard it before,' cried someone.

Kelpie was giving her worried glances as the crowd grew restless. Keira downed her whisky.

'Ya bunch of ungrateful bastards,' she said, refilling her glass. 'Here's one ye'll have not heard before, I promise you that.'

She paused, for a second unsure, then drank her whisky and ploughed on.

'It was after I had been captured by the Rahain. They kept me chained up, with a bag over my head. My brother was also a prisoner, and they showed him to me, then told me that they were going to kill him if I didn't do what they said. Then they flew me off, wrapped in chains at the bottom of a flying carriage, with fifty crossbows pointed at my back.'

She took another drink, her head swimming. The crowd remained silent, waiting for her next words.

'The carriage landed, and I was dragged outside. We were on top of a ridge, overlooking this city. It was weird; they'd told me I was going to see a refugee camp, but this place was built up, bigger than any town in Kell or Domm. Then they told me that everyone in the city was dead, poisoned by chemicals in the water, and all I had to do was burn it all up, purify the land with fire.

'So I stood there, looking down at the city. It stank. The streets were covered in a thick layer of poisoned mud, but the folk there weren't all dead. I saw hundreds of them, thousands, diseased and dying, staggering like walking corpses. There were piles of them heaped up on every corner, skeletal and rotten, children...'

She paused again. The tavern sat in absolute stillness, with every eye on her. Flora's mouth was open.

'The lizards ordered me to burn the city, and I told them to go fuck themselves; but they said they would kill Killop, and then me, and I looked down into the camp, and the folk there, they were already dying, already as good as dead, and all I was doing was ending their pain; and so I hardened my heart and did it.

'I burned them,' she said. 'I burned an entire city of refugees.'

Some in the crowd stared at her, while many looked away. A few were weeping.

An old woman approached. She shook her head at Keira, spat on the ground in front of her, and walked out of the tavern. Others followed, and before long, the place was empty and quiet.

'Was that true?' said Bay, her eyes wide.

Keira nodded.

Bay stood up and walked away.

'What were ye thinking, Keira?' said Kelpie, marching over.

'Just giving them what they wanted.'

'Well, if I hear that story again, yer out; understand?'

Keira watched her stride back to the bar, then turned to Flora.

'It's just you and me now, hen.'

CHAPTER 10
BABYSITTING

Holdings City, Holdings Republic – 13th Day, Last Third Summer 507

'Come and fly, daddy,' Karalyn whispered as he slept, and Killop felt his dreaming mind lift into the air and hover over the sleeping citizens of Holdings City. Around him whirled the consciousness of his daughter, laughing and spinning.

He looked down over the Lower City, the streetlamps marking out the main routes and landmarks. The university, the courts and market halls, and the great cavalry fortress, that used to house the garrison of imperial soldiers, and was now home to the army of the new regime. Across the river, the Upper City was bathed in shadow and darkness, with a few lamps marking the royal ramp and Holders Square, close to where he was sharing a room with Karalyn and Daphne. The twin clusters of palace and cathedral sat side by side atop the rocky summit, rivalling each other in bulk and height.

'Let's fly,' urged Karalyn.

'Shall we wait for mummy?'

'Mummy not sleeping.'

Killop frowned.

'All right, wee bear. Let's fly.'

Karalyn squealed, and took off over the plains at lightning speed, dragging Killop with her. They sped west, crossing fields and plantations, and great herds of cattle.

The air pressure changed, and they slowed as a force began to pull them back the way they had come.

'Daddy,' Karalyn cried, as fear shot through him. 'It's alright, daddy.'

Their speed increased tenfold, and the land beneath became a blur. They crossed two rivers, then a patch of ocean, then travelled above the spine of a great mountain range running south-east for mile after mile. They slowed as they came out of the mountains, and Killop saw a mighty city lie before him, larger than anything he had believed possible. It stretched out for dozens of miles in each direction, and was criss-crossed by a vast network of canals. Large sections of the city lay unlit and abandoned, with a glow of lights coming only from the centre, where they were headed.

'Do you know where we're going, wee bear?'

Karalyn nodded. 'The bad man.'

Killop frowned. It could only mean the Creator, and they were going in without Daphne.

They hurtled over the canals, and entered a tall brick-built structure. In a large hall, a man was seated upon a throne, raised high above the gathered army officers and government officials, and Killop flinched as they passed through his eyes and into his mind.

Killop froze, trying not to breathe or make a sound.

He opened his eyes, and saw that he was looking out from the point of view of the man on the throne.

Guilliam? Killop frowned. How was this happening?

'Your Majesty,' said the officer on his knees before the throne, 'yesterday's casualties from ill health and disease came to five hundred and sixty-two.'

'An average day, then,' the Emperor said. 'Why are you even bringing this to my attention?'

'But your Majesty, thousands more are sick, and the lack of sanitary conditions endured by the soldiers is sure to mean that more will die unnecessarily.'

'I factored that in, you idiot,' the Emperor snapped. 'Why do you think I assembled such a large army? I knew that the feeble constitution of most Holdings soldiers wouldn't stand up well in the fly-ridden swamps of Arakhanah. I took a guess that maybe half would perish from the conditions alone, and the numbers would seem to bear me out.'

'Half, your Majesty?' the officer said. 'Such a toll.'

'Soldiers die. Next.'

The officer got up from his knees, bowed, and backed away. An official took his place, kneeling before the Emperor.

'I bring a message from Lord Chancellor Prior in the imperial capital, your Majesty,' she said. 'He advises that troops are required to enforce the blockade of the Old Realm. It appears that the rebel Holds have been successful in smuggling in more arms and supplies to bolster their illegitimate regime.'

'Tell him no,' the Emperor said. 'I can't spare any troops for him. Once Ghorley has finished recruiting my new army in Rahain, then he will be welcome to some, but until then, no.'

'Yes, your Majesty. However, Lord Chancellor Prior requested that I inform you that he feels that the rebel Holds will be a formidable force militarily, if the smuggling is allowed to continue.'

The Emperor snorted.

'Tell Prior that he worries too much,' he said. 'Whatever rabble those rebel bastards are able to assemble will be swept aside once I have finished in Arakhanah. Next.'

The woman got to her feet.

As she was backing away, a soldier ran into the hall, making straight for the throne.

'Your Majesty!' he cried, shoving past the official who was next in line.

'Speak,' the Emperor said.

The soldier fell to his knees, his eyes cast downwards.

'The captive Rakanese mages, your Majesty, they are dead.'

Killop felt a surge of rage ripple through the Emperor's body. He pointed at the soldier, and his head evaporated in a cloud of red mist that covered everything within a five-yard radius. The body slumped to the floor.

The Emperor stood, and stormed down the steps. Guards ran to flank him as he marched from the hall and down a set of stairs to the lower levels of the building. Along the way, soldiers and Rakanese staff cowered out of his path, recoiling in terror.

He reached a large chamber, with barred cells down one side. Within each lay several dead Rakanese.

'You!' he shouted at an officer who was present. 'What happened?'

The officer got down on her knees.

'Your Majesty,' she said, trembling, 'they committed suicide, all at once. We couldn't stop them.'

'They were supposed to be chained and bagged,' the Emperor raged. 'Did I not give explicit orders?'

'You did, your Majesty.'

'And?'

'The process of securing the captives was still under way when it began, your Majesty. Those unchained first killed the others, and then themselves.'

'How long have they been dead?'

'Ten minutes, maybe, your Majesty.'

The Emperor stared at her, then turned. 'Open up the cells.'

He glanced back at the officer.

'I shall require a considerable amount of energy for what I am about to do,' he said, 'and as this was your mistake, Captain, it seems only fair that you should be the one to pay the price.'

He stepped forwards, and lowered his hand onto the kneeling woman's head, clasping her skull. Killop sensed a shift of power within the Emperor, and then a sudden and brief surge as he drained the officer. She fell to the floor, dried up and lifeless.

Killop's mind began to grow dizzy under the weight of energy that the Emperor was carrying within him, and as the Emperor began walking towards the first open cell, he felt himself whipped out of his head, and within seconds, he was back in his own bed.

He shot up, sweat pouring from him.

Daphne looked over from the desk where she was working, a solitary candle lighting the room.

Killop rolled off the bed onto his knees and retched, but nothing came. He panted, feeling as if he had run the distance from Rakana. He gazed at the cot. Karalyn was sitting up, smiling and looking at him.

'You alright?' Daphne said, walking round to where Killop crouched on the floor.

He glanced up at her, drool running down his chin.

'Bad dream?' she said, then turned to Karalyn. 'Hold on, were you two in the Creator's head?'

'Daddy see bad man,' Karalyn said.

'Damn it,' Daphne said. 'And I was up working. Sorry. So what happened? Did you learn anything?'

Killop fell back into a sitting position.

Daphne filled a mug with ale and passed it to him, then lit a cigarette.

He took a long drink.

'It wasn't the Creator,' he said. 'We weren't in the Creator's mind.'

Daphne frowned.

'A force took us, just like it did the last time, except we didn't go upwards. Instead, we flew across the mountains to Rakana.'

'What? Are you sure?'

'Well, I've never been, but I know it was Rakana, because the Emperor and his army were there.'

'You saw the Emperor?'

'Saw him? It was his head we were in, Daphne.'

Daphne frowned, and smoked her cigarette.

'Tell me everything.'

Daphne listened as Killop told his story. Afterwards, she got up and walked to the cot.

'She's sleeping again,' she said. 'Just like before, she doesn't seem to take any ill effects from being in his mind.'

'His mind? Whose, the Emperor's?'

She turned.

'The Creator's. What if the Creator was in the mind of the Emperor when you were there? What if he was watching through Guilliam's eyes, and you were watching through his?'

Killop frowned.

'If the Emperor has the skills of every mage, then he must have vision power, all the way up to the ability to talk to the Creator. Their minds must have been bound together when you went in, it's the only explanation.'

'I don't know,' he said. 'It felt like the mind we were in was doing all the talking and thinking. I couldn't sense any other presence there.'

'If Kalayne were here, he might be able to work it out,' she said. 'Still, interesting intelligence about the thinking of Lord Chancellor Prior; seems we have him worried. We should step up smuggling operations; send him into even more of a tizzy. And I wonder what happened with the Rakanese mages? How many were there, do you think?'

Killop shrugged. 'Two dozen, maybe.'

'What on earth was the Emperor planning to do with two dozen corpses?'

'Whatever it was, it needed a lot of power. All he could get from that officer he drained.'

'And she died from it?'

'Aye. She was all wrinkled up, as if all the liquid had been sucked out of her.'

Daphne grimaced.

There was a knock at the door.

'Everything all right in there?' Kylon's voice called through the door panels.

'Fine,' Daphne said, shaking her head. 'Those two. Insane.'

Killop smiled. 'At least we'll always have babysitters.'

———

Daphne had left for work when Killop next arose. He dressed himself and Karalyn, and went out into the grand reception chamber that formed the heart of the suite of apartments where they were staying. The room had a view of the palace across Holders Square, where companies of Hold militia drilled.

Kylon and Celine were the only others in the chamber, lounging across large couches.

'You're a remarkable woman, Celine,' he heard Kylon say, 'and you've been through so much. I have watched in wonder as you have changed into a confident, smart and hopeful person. It has been a most beautiful transformation to behold.'

Celine smirked, then caught sight of Killop and Karalyn.

'Kara-bear,' she said, grinning and getting up. 'How's my little lady this morning? You hungry for breakfast?'

'Celine make pancakes,' Karalyn said.

Celine put her hands on her hips and smiled. 'Me? My little bear, we're living like royalty. All we have to do is ask a kind servant, and they'll make us whatever we like. Shall I show you?'

'Aye,' Karalyn cried, jumping up and down.

Celine led her off by the hand to a side door of the chamber.

'Morning, Killop,' said Kylon.

'Morning,' he said, sitting. 'Is there anything to drink?'

Kylon smiled. 'Depends what you mean. We're in the Holdings, where getting drunk before midday is frowned upon, at least in the company we've been keeping. But if you want a hot drink, there's plenty of tea and coffee.'

Killop sighed.

'Any plans for today?' Kylon said.

'Don't think so.'

Kylon raised an eyebrow.

'I know what you're thinking,' Killop said. 'We have to remember that this conflict is internal to the Holdings; it's not ours to fight.'

'So it doesn't strike you as odd?'

'What?'

'That Godfrey Holdfast has not called upon you to serve? I mean, you've led armies to victory in battle, Killop, and have as much experience of fighting as anyone else here. You were a chief.'

'It's just politics, Kylon. Some of the Holds in the rebel coalition would feel uncomfortable about taking orders from a foreigner, and they can't exactly put me in the ranks.'

'They're a bunch of elitist snobs,' Kylon said.

'Daphne also said that it was partly because I couldn't ride a horse. That's why I'm taking lessons. If and when the Emperor invades, I'm going to be fighting one way or another; we all will.'

Kylon smiled. 'Ye see yourself as a cavalryman?'

'No. I can barely stay on, never mind swing a sword at the same time. You should think about learning.'

'I already know,' Kylon said. 'How do you think I got to the Holdings?'

'You rode?'

'Stole a horse. Got thrown a couple of times, but I got the hang of it in the end.'

Killop shook his head. 'I might have known.'

He glanced through the great bay windows at the palace. 'There's something I've been meaning to ask you.'

'Aye?' said Kylon.

'Why did you tell Chane everything about Karalyn?'

'Do you not like her?'

'She's all right,' Killop said, 'and Daphne seems to be friends with her again, which is good. But that's not the point. You should have asked us before you said anything.'

Kylon nodded. 'At the time, I was alone in the River Holdings, surrounded by thousands of strangers, searching for you. I was also struggling with having left your sister, wondering if it was the right thing to do, and then I was stuck in a small house with Chane for a long time, unable to go outdoors in case the imperial recruiters got hold of us. I saw something in her that I trusted.'

His dark eyes caught Killop's.

'I apologise if I did the wrong thing.'

'Are you sleeping with her?'

'Who, Chane? No.'

'Celine?'

'Killop,' Kylon said, 'I am faithful to your sister.'

'Even though she broke up with you?'

'We were both going through a lot of shit at the time,' he said. 'I was pushing her hard, making sure we followed Kalayne's plan, and I think she started to resent me for it.'

Killop frowned. 'You pushed my sister into murdering all those folk?'

'Murder? It was war, Killop. We were trying to stop the Emperor.' He gazed at him. 'We have all done things in war we regret.'

'And it sounds like you've added a lot to your list.'

Kylon bowed his head, his long black hair falling in sheets. 'I do have regrets about the Sanang campaign. We were ruthless, and utterly focussed on getting to the imperial capital in time. But we failed. The Emperor got his powers, and destroyed our army. In the end, it was all for nothing.' He looked up. 'But there's still hope. Karalyn is the key, somehow. Kalayne told me much about her, but even he didn't know exactly what role she will play.'

'She's one year old,' Killop said. 'She won't be playing any role in what's coming.'

Kylon shrugged. 'The other part of the plan involves Shella and Keira. Your sister remains the one who will save the world, but Kalayne said she has to meet Shella first.'

'If my sister really has gone to Domm,' Killop said, 'then she'll be on the other side of the world when the Emperor invades the Holdings.'

'If the Emperor invades.'

'He will,' Killop said. 'Last night, when you banged on our door, you were right, something had happened.'

Kylon narrowed his eyes. 'What?'

'Did Kalayne ever tell you that Karalyn could see inside the Creator's mind?'

'He did,' said Kylon. 'Did she travel there last night?'

'Aye,' Killop said, 'and she wasn't alone.'

———

'That's enough for today,' the woman called out to the students.

Killop grunted in relief, his legs and rear in agony, and swung himself off the horse and down to the ground. He towered over the other students, a mix of teenage Holdings youths, while the horse he was practising on was a good head higher than the others.

'You did well,' the trainer nodded to him. 'You're getting better.'

Killop shook his head, as a stablegirl led his beast away.

'Bravo,' cried Daphne, from the fence enclosing the small compound. Behind her stood the burnt-out and abandoned remains of the Old Tower.

Chane smirked as he approached the fence half-limping. 'Where did they find you that old nag?'

'It was the only one big enough to take me,' he said.

'You alright?' said Daphne.

'My arse is killing me.'

'I remember those days,' Chane laughed. 'Don't worry, your arse cheeks will toughen up in a third or two.'

'He's Kellach,' Daphne said, 'so it'll probably just take a few days.'

She opened the gate, and Killop left the enclosure.

'I could do with an ale.'

Daphne pursed her lips. 'You drink too much.'

Killop shrugged. 'You smoke too much.'

'I have a solution,' Chane said. 'Let's go back to yours, and we can drink and smoke.'

'Is that you done for the rest of the day?' Killop asked.

'Yeah,' Daphne said. 'We're off until the morning.'

They set off through the winding maze of backstreets towards Holders Square.

'I told Kylon about last night,' Killop said. 'Wanted to see if he had any ideas.'

'And did he?'

'He suggested the same thing as you,' Killop said, 'that the Creator was in Guilliam's head at the same time as me and Karalyn.'

'It does sound the most reasonable explanation,' said Chane.

Killop glanced at Daphne.

'You told Kylon,' she said. 'I told Chane.'

'But that's it, though?' Killop said. 'Just the four of us know about Karalyn?'

'Five,' said Chane. 'You're forgetting about Celine.'

'Five,' he repeated, shaking his head.

'I'm never going to breathe a word of it to anyone,' Chane said. 'Who would I tell? You're the only people I know here, and you're certainly the only ones I trust. Kylon and Celine are both mad, but they'd do anything to protect your daughter.'

Killop nodded. 'I know. Listen, there's something I remembered when I was telling Kylon what had happened, that I forgot to mention to you.'

'Yeah?' said Daphne.

'It was about the lord chancellor's request for reinforcements. The Emperor said that he could have more when Ghorley had finished recruiting a new army.'

Daphne narrowed her eyes.

'A new army?' said Chane. 'What for?'

'The Emperor will use it to invade the Holdings,' Daphne said. 'He thinks he'll lose half of his present army in Rakana, and he won't want to invade us with Holdings soldiers anyway. It makes much more sense for him to do it with fresh Rahain troops.'

They came out onto Holders Square as the sun was setting over the vast expanse of plains to the west, visible from the top of the Upper City.

'It's getting chilly already,' Daphne said. 'Summer's nearly done.'

'At last,' Killop said. 'It's still hotter during the day than it ever gets in Kell. But I admit, I love the nights, nice and cool.'

'Freezing, you mean,' Daphne smiled.

'I thought all that time in Rahain had toughened you up?'

'It didn't mean I liked it. That time I walked to Slateford in a blizzard was nearly the end of me. I never want to be that cold again.'

They paused in front of a large guest house, filled with apartments for visiting aristocracy, where Killop and Daphne were staying.

'You coming up?' Daphne asked Chane.

'If you're asking,' she grinned, and they entered the building.

They climbed to the third floor, and went through into their suite. Celine and Karalyn were playing on a rug in front of the enormous bay windows, while Kylon was sitting in an armchair, reading a book. He peered over the top of it as they approached.

Killop and Daphne went over to see their daughter. She looked up from playing to smile at them.

'She's been a very good girl today,' Celine said. 'I showed her how to order food from the servants.'

Daphne laughed. 'I hope they're prepared for endless requests for pancakes and biscuits.'

'Karalyn eat pancakes for dinner and tea,' said the girl.

Daphne frowned. 'Really, Celine, she can't have that for every meal. You shouldn't always be saying yes to her. You give in too easily.'

'I just like to see her smile,' Celine said. 'But I know. It won't happen again, ma'am.'

'Please don't call me that,' Daphne said. She turned to Killop. 'Time for that ale, I think.'

Chane spoke to a servant, who returned in a few minutes with ale, coffee and rum, glasses, and bowls of nuts and strawberries. Killop and Daphne sat by Kylon, who put down his book.

'So, Miss Holdfast,' he said, 'how goes your civil war?'

'Much the same as yesterday, Kylon,' she said, pouring drinks. 'The same group of Holds are refusing to join us, and the imperial garrisons in the forts along the border with the Plateau are still holding out.'

'You have accomplished much without bloodshed.'

'So far,' she nodded. 'Aside from the riots in the River Holdings that killed a hundred imperials, we've managed to avoid any large confrontations.'

Kylon nodded, and took a glass of rum from the low table.

'The Prophet has been a great help,' Daphne went on. 'His range-vision is amazing, and he's been telling us the positions of every group of imperial soldiers, and what the militia of the unaligned Holds are doing. He's enabled us to avoid traps, and stay a step ahead of Lord Chancellor Prior's forces.'

'Much like Kalayne did for us in Kell,' Kylon said.

'I should tell the Prophet about last night,' she said. She glanced at Killop. 'Make that six people who know. But he's on our side. He hates Lord Arnault and the Creator as much as we do.'

'We'll need him when the Emperor invades,' Kylon said. 'His control of communications will allow you to be the tip of the spear, Daphne, where you belong. You will face the Emperor when he comes to this city. You're the strongest among us, it has to be you. But we'll be at your side, with your daughter's power to shield us, and scour the enemy...'

'What?' Daphne cried. 'No, Kylon. Karalyn will be as far away from the fighting as possible, with you and Celine to guard her, as you promised. If I'm to be the tip of the spear, as you put it, then I need to know that Karalyn is safe.'

Kylon frowned, his dark eyes piercing her.

'I will give my life to protect your daughter, Daphne Holdfast, do not insult me by doubting my resolve on this. But Karalyn is not just an innocent bystander or a hapless victim in the coming storm. She has powers, mighty powers, and she will be needed if we are to defeat the Emperor.'

'No,' said Killop, 'that's not going to happen. Karalyn will be nowhere near the battlefield, and you must decide now if you're going to obey our orders on this. If Daphne and I command you and Celine to take Karalyn away from a battle, will you obey us?'

'He'd better,' Celine said, walking towards the table, holding Karalyn's hand as she toddled along. She stared at the Kell man. 'Well, Kylon?'

'Of course,' Kylon said, 'Kalayne told me to protect Karalyn. I will follow your orders, Killop; and yours, Daphne, as long as those orders don't put Karalyn in danger.'

'They never would,' said Daphne.

'Then we are agreed,' said Kylon.

'Good,' said Celine. She glanced at Daphne. 'I'm just taking little bear to bed, do you want to read her a story?'

Daphne smiled. 'Yes,' she said, standing.

Killop gave Karalyn a kiss, and watched as she was led to their bedroom by Celine and Daphne. Kylon filled his glass with rum, and sat back in his chair. Chane extracted a weedstick from a pocket of her uniform and lit it.

'Well?' she shrugged at Killop. 'Karalyn's away to bed.'

'Just open a window,' Killop said. He glanced at Kylon as the Holdings woman tutted and got up.

Kylon glanced back at him.

'My daughter is not a weapon.' Killop said, 'I don't care what Kalayne told you.'

Kylon's dark eyes held him as he nodded. 'You're the boss.'

CHAPTER 11
AVOIDANCE TACTICS

Northern Kell – 26th Day, Last Third Summer 507

'This is shit,' said Dean. 'We've been waiting here for hours.'

'Be patient,' Dyam said. 'Bonnie and Lola will return soon, and hopefully they'll give us the all clear.'

The young fire mage's eyes darted round the rocky crevasse where the two wagons lay hidden, the frustration plain upon his face.

'I'm cold,' he said. 'Can we light a fire?'

Dyam shook her head. 'If the lizards see the smoke, they'll be all over us.'

Laodoc reached under the driver's bench of the wagon and pulled out a blanket.

'Wrap this round yourself, Dean,' he said. 'It'll keep you warm while we wait.'

The young man frowned. 'I'm not an invalid.'

Laodoc sighed. They had been stuck in the crevasse since breakfast, and the day was wearing on. Their pace had ground almost to a halt since they had passed into the occupied zone of Northern Kell three days previously. They had made good time through Brig, and had crossed into Kell without any problem or delay, after checking in with the Kellach Brigdomin forces that patrolled the Brig Pass. Their progress through Southern Kell had also been rapid. Despite the devastation and pollution covering the landscape, it was empty of people, and the roads had been clear. The first sign of the Rahain had come when they had entered the pass to Northern Kell, where they had been forced to cross several blockades and lines of wooden palisades. The soldiers there had been happy to let the two wagons through to the occupied zone, after relieving them of most of their gold.

Since entering, however, they had been harassed on a daily basis by patrols of Rahain soldiers, as they had tried to make their way through the broken land. Enormous slagheaps of mining waste littered the grey and dead countryside. Every town and village had been destroyed, buried under landslides or burned to the ground. The Rahain military sat within walled-off mining compounds, some of which covered hundreds of acres, with accommodation for the legions of slave labour that were required to keep the coal flowing to the cities of Rahain.

On their way south, when they had been travelling with the entire Severed Clan, the Rahain soldiers had given them a wide berth, and had allowed them to pass unmolested, but now, with their small party of eight, it seemed that every group of soldiers they met tried to rob and abuse them.

Agang jumped down from the lead wagon and walked back to where Laodoc sat next to Dean and Dyam.

Laodoc nodded to him as he approached.

'Looks like we might be stuck here for the night,' Agang said. 'Bridget says that if Bonnie and Lola are not back within an hour, then we should get the camp set up.'

Dean groaned.

'It is what it is, Dean,' Agang said.

'But we're never going to get out of Kell if we keep hiding.'

'That was a whole company of lizards we almost ran into this morning,' she said. 'Over a hundred soldiers, Dean. They looked like they hadn't eaten in a third. One look at our oxen, and we'd be walking.'

'If Keira was here, she could fight them off.'

'But she's not here, Dean,' Dyam said, 'so stop moaning.'

'Bonnie and Lola are trying to find us a quieter route,' Agang said, 'then we can get back on the road.'

Dean said nothing, staring out of the wagon as it started to rain. Dyam stood, and untied the cords to release the canvas hood. Agang got up and helped her fix it into position, covering the passengers and their luggage from the heavy drops.

There was a low whistle, and Laodoc glanced up. Through the dim shadows cast by the dark clouds above, he saw two figures scrambling down the loose scree of the crevasse.

'There they are,' he said, watching them head towards the lead wagon. 'They're back.'

'I'd better go,' Agang said, 'in case we get moving quickly.'

He turned, and jogged up to where the two scouts were talking to Bridget. After a minute, Lola strode back towards Laodoc as the lead wagon began to pull away, its wheels turning through the thick mud at the bottom of the crevasse.

'Success?' Dyam said, as Lola climbed up onto the driver's bench and took hold of the reins.

'Aye.'

'You find a route?'

'Aye.'

She flicked the reins, and the oxen took off, plodding along a few yards behind the lead wagon.

'It'll be slow going,' the Lach woman said, 'and treacherous at times, but it should keep us off the main roads.'

'You see many lizards?'

'Aye, a few.' She glanced at Laodoc. 'Do you not mind her calling you that?'

'It's not my favourite word,' he said, 'but my people did this to Kell, and I can understand the anger directed at us.'

Dyam looked away. 'Shit, I don't mean anything by it.'

They sat in silence as the wagon was pulled through the narrow valley.

'I won't say it again,' Dyam muttered after a while.

Lola smiled.

———

They travelled for several hours, on through the afternoon and into the evening. It grew dark, and Laodoc was unable to see the path ahead, but still the Kellach kept on, their natural night vision allowing them to see what he couldn't. The rain continued, dripping down the inside of the sodden canvas as they negotiated the winding and narrow track. They stopped often, to clear away branches, rocks and other debris from the path, or to dig wheels out of the thick mud. Laodoc was spared such duties, and watched shivering from the driver's bench each time, until they were under way again.

He was frozen stiff when they stopped for the night, close to a deep cave with a narrow entrance. They tied up the oxen, and gathered within the dry cave with their blankets and supplies. Dyam lit a lamp, and Bedig prepared a small fire near the entrance, as the rain pelted down outside.

'Good work today, you two,' Bridget said to Bonnie and Lola, who were positioning their blankets side by side.

'Sorry it took so long,' Bonnie said. 'The hills are crawling with Rahain.'

'They're searching for someone,' Lola said.

'Us?' said Dean.

'Unlikely,' said Bridget. 'Why would they bother with us? I mean, they'll rob us if they get the chance, they're hungry and pissed off, but they're not going to send out half the army to look for us.'

'So we just have to avoid them,' Laodoc said, 'until we're out of Kell.'

'I hate this place,' Dean said. 'It's an ugly wasteland.'

'It used to be beautiful,' said Bridget. 'I'm glad Killop's not here to see it.'

'What has happened here is a terrible crime,' Laodoc said, 'carried out by stupid people who thought they were better than everyone else.'

'I don't want to argue with you, Laodoc,' Bridget said, 'but as chancellor of Rahain, you didn't exactly do much to fix the situation.'

'I inherited it, as you know,' he said. 'The old regime had been spending a huge amount for the upkeep of the garrisons here, but the treasury was empty when I came into power. Most had gone on the siege of Akhanawarah, and the rest was stolen by a certain Sanang gentleman sitting not too far away.'

He smiled at Agang, who shrugged.

'So there was no money to pay for the operations in Kell,' Laodoc went on, 'and the garrisons and mining communities effectively became self-sufficient, and looked to their own needs. And without any government cash, they began selling the coal directly to the cities, moving further beyond my authority, until they became in fact, if not in law, an independent little state.'

'You're saying it was out of your control?' Bridget said.

'Indeed. What could I have done? To re-assert authority, I would have needed to send in more troops, and I was rather occupied with fighting the New Free rebellion at the time. And if I had ordered the garrisons to withdraw from Kell, they would have ignored me, just as they ignored the general order to emancipate their labour force. Certain elements among the Rahain leadership in Kell have become exceedingly wealthy from the coal, and have no desire to give it up.'

'So you abandoned Kell because it was too complicated to deal with?'

'I was working night and day to prevent Rahain from splitting apart. I failed, I know I did, but I did my best. I apologise if my performance fell short of your expectations, Miss Bridget.'

'We were never equal partners in the alliance,' she said. 'From day one, the Kellach Brigdomin were sidelined, their conquered territories administered by the same army that did the conquering, while that arsehole Duncan sat up in Plateau City pretending he represented us all. The sad fact is that we were sold out for coal. Keeping the cities of Rahain warm and lit was more important than seeing justice done.'

'I accept that I played my part in that,' Laodoc said, his voice low as everyone in the cave watched him. 'I'm sorry. I believed at the time that a mere handful of Kellach Brigdomin still lived in your lands. I didn't imagine that so many would return home.'

Agang glanced at him. 'I'm surprised that the Kellach forces haven't tried to kick the Rahain out of Kell.'

'The Domm Council isn't stupid,' Dyam said. 'They know that any disturbances in Kell might bring them to the attention of the Emperor.'

'Their priority is the safety of everyone in Domm,' Bridget said. 'I think they're happy to keep the border at the Brig Pass, with Southern Kell as a buffer between them and the Rahain.'

'Something will have to change soon, though,' Dyam said. 'The speed the Rahain are stripping the coal out of the ground, they're going to run dry at some point.'

Laodoc shook his head. 'Unfortunately, that is not so. I have read the detailed geology reports from Kell, made by the expedition undertaken by my son Likiat. At current rates of consumption, there's enough coal in Northern Kell to supply Rahain for hundreds of years.'

The others stared at him.

'Not only that,' Laodoc went on, 'but there are untapped reserves of iron, copper, silver, lead and other minerals, and plentiful supplies of timber. I fear that without intervention, the occupation will remain in place for a considerable time yet. The biggest risk to their existence is the gradual depletion of their reserves of slave labour. Unless a fresh source of workers can be found, then they will run into difficulties in a decade or so.'

Bridget shook her head. 'Once we've sorted everything out with Shella and the Emperor, then we can fix Kell. Until then, we get the fuck out as fast as we can.'

'Makes me feel sick, boss,' Bonnie said. 'Skulking our way across our own lands, and hiding from those we should be fighting.'

'I don't like it either,' she said, 'but we have to keep our eyes on the job, and remember what we're out here to do. Now, eat your food, and get some sleep; we have another full day of skulking tomorrow to look forward to.'

They passed the night in the cave, cold but dry. In the morning, Bedig cleared away the remains of the fire, and they packed up the wagons. The sun shone down from an almost cloudless sky.

'The last days of summer,' Bedig said, as he helped Laodoc climb up onto the rear wagon.

'Not sick of travelling by now?'

'It all depends on the company,' he said, 'though I'll be glad to get out of Kell. The place makes me sad.'

When the two wagons were ready, they set off along the path, flanked on either side by tall rocky escarpments. Lola held the reins of the rear wagon, with Laodoc, Dyam and Dean next to her on the driver's bench.

'Let's see how many miles we can do today,' Dyam said.

The lumbering oxen made hard work of the slippery path, labouring up long steep slopes, and through narrow defiles, following the course of a small stream northwards towards the mountains. They saw no one for the whole morning – just the land, broken as if from countless earthquakes.

After a short stop for lunch, they continued, and the path led down into a wider valley, where a road ran. Bridget called a halt.

'Should we risk crossing in daylight?' she said, as they conferred together. 'If anyone comes along that road before we reach the other side of the valley, we'll be spotted for sure.'

'How far is it?' Laodoc said.

'Three miles or so,' said Bonnie. 'Should only take us twenty minutes.'

Bridget scanned the road, chewing her lip.

'Let's do it,' she said.

They got back into their wagons and set off. The ground was boggy, and more than twenty minutes had elapsed before they reached the road, which ran halfway across the valley. The road was carried on a broad causeway of packed earth and stones, and rose two feet above the level of the marshy path they had been following. The oxen pulled the wagons up the bank, and Laodoc gasped. On the other side of the road, down a similar bank to the one they had ascended, lay dozens of bodies. Bridget, Dyam and the others leapt down to look.

They covered their noses from the stench.

'Rahain,' Bridget muttered.

Laodoc was the last to reach the side of the road and peer over. Flies buzzed in swarms over the muddy corpses of the Rahain soldiers. Sword wounds and arrow holes pierced their bodies, and some had been mutilated, their heads severed and lying in a small mound.

'Looks like an entire company,' Dyam said, 'and their weapons have been taken.'

'Rebel Kellach,' Agang said. 'It must be.'

'The folk the army are out looking for,' Bridget said. 'Pyre's tits. I always thought there might be a few rebels up here, living in the mountains, but if they're strong enough to do this...'

'Boss,' said Bonnie, 'I'm getting nervous. We're sticking out like a prize cow, we should get going.'

'Aye,' Bridget said, ushering the others back to the wagons, 'let's go.'

The oxen hauled the wagons down the embankment, and began plodding across the sodden ground towards a gap in the valley side.

Time dragged. Laodoc's neck was hurting from turning to glance at either end of the road behind them. Dyam was staring ahead, silently urging them on.

'We're nearly there,' Lola said.

'Shit,' said Dean. 'They're coming!'

The others turned. At the head of the valley, a group of figures were moving down the road.

'They haven't seen us yet,' Dyam said. 'Keep going, Lola.'

'What do ye think I'm doing?'

'Well, keep doing it.'

The figures on the road were marching east, toward the coastal region. Any moment, Laodoc realised, they would reach the bodies of their fallen comrades. He glanced ahead, his tongue flickering. The shelter of the narrow gap in the valley was still over a hundred yards away, and the oxen were toiling through the deep mud.

'Come on, ya bastards,' Lola grunted, lashing the oxen.

The figures on the road halted, and shouts echoed across the valley to the wagons from the spot where the bodies lay.

'They're looking over at us,' Dean cried.

'Quiet, Dean,' Dyam said, staring back at the road as figures began clambering down the bank. 'The mud'll slow them down.'

'They can still run faster than we're going,' Dean yelled. 'They're going to catch us up.'

Dyam frowned. 'Lola,' she said, 'give me the reins and get yer longbow ready. Dean, light up the storm lamp, be prepared to do whatever ye can to help. Laodoc, stay down.'

Lola threw the reins to Dyam, and pulled the covering from her longbow. She sat still, taking care to string the bow and check it over.

'They're getting closer!' Dean cried from the back of the wagon, where he was attempting to light the storm lamp.

Laodoc raised his head. Dozens of Rahain soldiers were splashing and running through the marsh they had just traversed. Some at the front were swinging their crossbows down, and loading them as they ran.

One fell, an arrow through his left eye socket.

Laodoc glanced over. Lola was on one knee, her longbow at an angle as she crouched. She notched a second arrow, aimed, and loosed.

'Dean,' Dyam yelled, 'how's it going with that lamp?'

'It's lit,' he cried.

'Good lad. We're almost there.'

A crossbow bolt ricocheted off the iron rim of a rear wheel, causing them all to flinch.

'More of them will be in range soon,' Dyam yelled. 'Keep yer heads down.'

There was a whoosh, and a cloud passed overhead. Laodoc looked up, and saw a dozen Rahain fall, arrows through their bodies. There was another whoosh, and more fell. The ranks of Rahain turned and began running back towards the road, leaving a score dead on the marsh.

The wagons pulled into the narrow valley, the oxen hauling them up onto drier ground. On either side, tall cliffs shut out most of the light.

'You all right back there?' Bedig cried out from the lead wagon.

'We're fine,' Dyam yelled. 'Did ye see who...?'

Her voice tailed off as the wagons were surrounded by a group emerging from the shadows of the cliffs. All were Kellach Brigdomin, and all were aiming their longbows at the wagon's occupants.

'What the fuck are ye doing?' a man cried at them. 'Are ye trying to lead those lizard bastards right to us?'

'Thanks for saving our arses,' Bridget said. 'We didn't know you were here. We were trying to avoid the Rahain ourselves.'

'Fucking amateurs,' the man said. 'Crossing Northern Kell with two wagons? We're taking them, by the way. And yer oxen.'

'Boss,' cried another warrior. 'Look over here, one of them's a fucking lizard.'

The man strode round to the rear wagon, his face reddening.

'Ya treacherous bastards,' he shouted. 'Ye've got a lizard with ye.'

He drew his sword.

Agang jumped down from the lead wagon, and several longbows were trained on him. He raised his hands.

'This Rahain is a friend.'

'And who, or what, are you?' the man said.

'He's Sanang,' Bridget said. 'They're both friends. We're on the same side.'

'I'll never be on the same side as those lizard bastards; just look what they did to our folk, our land.' He shook his head. 'Ye don't get it, ye're not Kell.'

Bridget gazed at the warriors. 'Are you all Kell?'

'Damn right we are,' the man said. 'While everyone else has fucked off, we're still here, fighting. Fuck those arseholes down in Domm; they've forgotten all about us.'

'No one has forgotten,' Bridget said.

'But they haven't lifting a finger to help us, have they? Not unless you lot are our fucking reinforcements.'

The warriors laughed.

'No,' the man went on, 'this is your unlucky day. We're taking the wagons and oxen, and killing the lizard. The rest of you can go free, as long as you don't make any trouble.'

'You're not touching my friend,' Agang said.

The man shrugged. 'You can stand and watch, or you can die. Your choice.'

He reached up and grabbed Laodoc's cloak. Dyam punched him in the face, and he stepped back, blood pouring from his nose.

'That hurt, ya cow,' he said, then he hauled Laodoc off the wagon. The old man fell, hitting the hard ground, and the man pointed his sword at him.

Laodoc raised his eyes at Agang and shook his head.

'Wait,' cried a woman's voice, and a hooded figure stepped through the ring of warriors.

The man lowered his sword, watching as the woman approached.

'What is it?' he said.

The woman knelt before Laodoc's shaking body.

'Laodoc?' she said, and pulled back her hood.

He gasped. 'Kallie?'

After being blindfolded and made to sit in the back of the wagons, they were led by the warriors through the mountains for an hour. They were then taken deep within a network of caves, to a warm hall where a large fire was burning.

They pulled their blindfolds off.

Bridget's eyes darted across the crowd of warriors in the room looking at them, until she saw Kallie, then rushed forwards and embraced her.

The leader of the warriors shook his head as the two women wept and hugged each other. 'Ye know her too, eh?'

'This is Bridget,' Kallie said. 'We were slaves together for a long time. And that man,' she said, pointing at Laodoc, 'was our master.'

'More reason to kill him, then,' the man said.

Kallie shook her head. 'No. He was kind to us.' She turned to the warriors. 'Two of this group are old friends. I ask you all to accept them as guests, and do them no harm while they are here.'

'You vouch for them all, eh?' the man said. 'Even that one?' He pointed at Agang.

'Bridget?' Kallie said.

'This is Agang Garo,' she said, 'from the forest nation of Sanang. I will vouch for him.'

Kallie turned to the man and nodded.

'Alright,' he said. 'On your head be it if they get up to no good. Put them in the northern caves.'

'Thank you,' Kallie said. She turned to the group. 'Follow me.'

She led them through a series of tunnels, past a sparkling waterfall, and down a steep flight of stairs into a small cavern, with alcoves in the walls. She lit a lamp.

'You can sleep here,' she said. 'There's a hearth in the corner. You hungry?'

'All our food's in the wagons,' Bridget said.

'I'll bring you some. Get yourselves settled.'

Kallie disappeared up the steps.

When she was out of sight, Dyam nudged Bridget.

'Can we trust her?'

Bridget nodded. 'We parted badly, but we went through a lot together before that.'

'She saved my life,' Laodoc said. 'That man was going to kill me.' He glanced at Dyam. 'My thanks for punching him, miss.'

Dyam shrugged. 'Any time.'

Bedig built a fire from a stack of wood by the hearth, and they warmed themselves. Kallie returned down the steps, followed by three other women, all carrying baskets. They laid them down onto a table in the cavern, then the other women departed back up the steps.

Kallie smiled at them, and Laodoc remembered how beautiful she was.

'Let's eat,' she said.

They sat round the table, filling their stomachs with meat, cheese and bread. Ale and whisky had also been provided, and the group relaxed as the drinks began to flow.

Bridget introduced everyone to Kallie.

'And this is Bedig,' she said, 'my um, boyfriend.'

'Nice to meet you, Kallie,' he said. 'Heard a lot about you.'

Kallie smiled and glanced at Bridget. 'I suppose I should ask you what happened to Killop. We met a couple of Kell a few thirds ago, they said that he was the chief of a clan in Rahain.'

Bridget shook her head. 'He was, but he chose to leave with Daphne.'

Kallie looked away.

'So,' Bridget said, 'where's wee Lacey?'

'No idea,' Kallie said. 'Lost touch with her ages ago.'

'What did you do?'

'We walked as far as the Rahain border with the Plateau, then fell in with a group of bandits living in the hills.'

'You were a bandit?' Bedig laughed.

'We didn't intend to stay, but after a while it was hard to leave. The group didn't want us to go, we had to slip away in the night and run for days. When we eventually crossed into Kell, we met a group of refugees heading for Domm. Lacey joined them.'

'But you didn't?' Laodoc said.

'I couldn't,' she said. 'When I saw Kell, my heart broke all over again, and I knew I had to fight. I joined this group about a year ago, and have been fighting alongside them ever since.'

'I understand,' Laodoc said, 'but you must see that if the coal supply from Kell ceases, then you risk bringing the wrath of the empire down on you, and those living safely in Domm. The Emperor is a dangerous man.'

'Who?' Kallie said.

Laodoc glanced at Agang.

'An emperor rules the world,' Agang said, 'and he wields power beyond mortal imagining. He will destroy everything unless he's stopped.'

Kallie raised an eyebrow. 'I don't care about what goes on in the outside world. I'm only interested in clearing Kell of Rahain soldiers.'

'But there are thousands of them in Kell,' Laodoc said. 'How many are in your armed company?'

'Fifty,' she said, 'but it doesn't matter. We're only keeping the flame alive until Keira returns to lead us.'

'What?' Bridget said.

'The fire goddess,' Kallie said. 'She will return. You remember the other part of Kalayne's prophecy, don't you? That I would be reborn when the fire goddess returns? And when she does get back, how do you think she'll react when she sees the state Kell's in? She'll go mental.'

The room fell silent.

Kallie gazed at them. 'What is it?'

'Miss,' Laodoc said, 'Keira is already in Domm. She passed through Kell on her way there some time ago.'

Kallie's mouth fell open. 'You've seen her?'

'I travelled with her,' Agang said, 'all the way from the Plateau. We tried to persuade her to come with us, to carry on the fight, but she refused.'

Kallie shook her head. 'But what's she doing in Domm?'

Bridget frowned. 'Getting drunk, mostly.'

CHAPTER 12
HITTING HOME

Holdings City, Holdings Republic – 13th Day, First Third Autumn 507

Daphne rose before dawn. She made no sound as she put on her uniform, kissed Karalyn and Killop and left their room. Chane was sitting waiting for her in the reception chamber, drinking coffee and smoking a cigarette.

'Morning,' she said.

'Hi, Chane. I didn't think you were getting back from the River Holdings until tomorrow.'

Chane downed her coffee and stood. 'I rode through the night.' She gestured to the heap of boxes and luggage sitting on the floor. 'You going somewhere?'

'Killop's taking Karalyn back to Hold Fast today,' Daphne said, lighting a cigarette. 'We're making sure she's somewhere safe before the Emperor gets here.'

Chane nodded. 'I thought you'd be taking the morning off, then.'

'I just need to get a couple of hours of work done before they wake up.'

They walked to the front door of the apartment, and descended the stairs to Holders Square. The sun was rising over the eastern horizon, and the clear sky promised another warm day. Across the square, companies of Holdings cavalry were out training, and the air was filled with the clatter of hooves on cobblestones.

'How'd it go?' Daphne said as they walked towards the palace.

'All right,' Chane said. 'The preparations are as advanced as we could hope for. All the roads to the Plateau have been blocked, and the majority of the bridges over the Lesser River have been dismantled. I met Weir, by the way.'

'Yeah? How's he doing?'

'Fine,' Chane said. 'He's a good leader. His teams have been working all hours, collecting weapons, drilling recruits, holding practice evacuations. Most of them are too old, or too young, but they're keen, I'll give them that.'

'Do they understand the role they have to play when the Emperor invades?'

Chane nodded. 'They do, but they don't like it. Asking them to destroy their homes and farms as they pull back will hurt, but they'll do it.'

'Forcing the Emperor to lead his army onto the plains is our only chance,' Daphne said.

'Are we going to have enough cavalry, though?'

'We've bought every horse left in the realm.'

Chane smiled. 'The republic, you mean?'

'Yes, the republic,' Daphne laughed. 'I'm still not used to calling it that. Especially as we have a queen back in the palace.'

'Yeah, but she's not the same as the old queen.'

'No,' Daphne sighed. 'She's not.'

'We didn't realise how lucky we were, back then.'

'That reminds me,' Daphne said, stopping. 'Don't repeat a word of this to anyone, not that it would make any difference now, but while you were away, the Prophet told me everything he knew about the plot against the old queen.'

'So she was poisoned?' Chane said. 'I knew it. Did that old bastard order it?'

'He completely denies it,' Daphne said. 'He admitted that he approved the plan to frame me for the collapse of the front in Sanang, but says he knew nothing of the attempt to assassinate the queen until after it had occurred.'

'And you believe him?'

'Yes. I could feel his anger about it, even after so long has passed. He said Arnault was behind it.'

'The Lord Vicar? Doesn't surprise me in the slightest. It's a pity the Prophet's waited so long to tell the truth.'

Daphne thought back to her time in prison. 'Yeah.'

They began walking again, strolling between the lines of drilling cavalry as they neared the front of the palace.

'So it was Rijon, then?' Chane said. 'He put that vision of our fort into Agang's head? The Prophet confirmed it?'

'Yeah.'

'Did you know he did it a second time?'

'When?'

'Outside Plateau City,' Chane said. 'Agang told me that the Sanang war god had appeared to him, and told him to join Guilliam's alliance, rather than attack.'

Daphne laughed. 'What?' She shook her head. 'I did wonder what had changed his mind, everyone assumed it was the king's diplomacy that had converted him.'

'Deep down, I think Agang was relieved,' Chane said. 'He never really wanted to attack the Plateau. He wanted to build schools and roads, and bring civilisation to his country. He only invaded because the other chiefs pressured him into it. And even then, he wanted a limited campaign, just terrorise some farmers, steal a few herds of cattle, and get back to Sanang as quickly as possible.'

'Do you miss him?'

'Sometimes. He could be a right arsehole, but I'm sorry he's dead.'

'His body was never found, you know.'

'I heard they were burning piles of headless Sanang bodies for days on end outside the walls of the imperial capital. If he was there, he's nothing but a pile of ash.'

Soldiers saluted them as they ascended the steps to the main entrance of the palace.

They went into a large chamber near the entrance, where a dozen tired-looking staff were standing around a long table, which was covered in maps and papers. More maps were hung up on the walls, detailing the countryside and towns of the River Holdings.

'Ma'am,' they saluted as Daphne approached.

'Good morning,' she said. 'I'll only be here for a short while, so Captain Chane will be looking after you today. Are your daily reports ready?'

The staff shuffled their papers and nodded.

Daphne smiled. 'Let's get started.'

'I'm going to miss you, Kara-bear,' Daphne said, holding her daughter close.

'Mummy come too,' the girl said.

'I want to, but I can't right now. Daddy's going to be taking you back to the big house in Hold Fast, where you'll get to see Papa, and play with Lydia and Teddy.'

'I don't want them, I want mummy.'

Daphne crouched down and wiped the tears from her daughter's face.

'You can come and find me every night in your dreams,' she said.

Karalyn folded her arms and glowered. 'No.'

Killop picked her up. 'She'll be fine once we're on the road.'

Daphne stood, and embraced him. 'I'm going to miss you as well.'

'Me too,' he said.

Kylon coughed from the door leading to the stairs. 'Wagon's ready.'

'All right,' Killop nodded. 'We'll be down in a minute.'

'Sure, boss,' Kylon said, leaving them alone in the apartment.

'Are we doing the right thing?' Killop said. 'I know we agreed this, but I'm starting to have doubts. What if the imperial army moves between Hold Fast and Holdings City, and cuts us off from each other?'

Daphne shook her head. 'The Emperor will head straight for the city, right through the River Holdings, and attack from the south. Hold Fast is too far to the north to be in the line of attack. If our plan works, we'll draw his army out to the west of the city, and destroy it on the plains.'

'You sound very sure about how the Emperor will act.'

'The Prophet has seen his thoughts,' Daphne said. 'The Emperor may be powerful, but he is rash and careless. He lost over half his army in Rakana in exchange for a handful of flow mages. His over-confidence is our greatest weapon against him.'

'I wish I was fighting by your side.'

'So do I, but if we can force a battle on the plains, it'll be decided by cavalry. The Rahain army that the Emperor has assembled are all foot-soldiers. If we can get them to the plains, we can sweep them away.'

He frowned.

'I know you want to fight,' she said, 'but I need you to look after Karalyn.'

'We have Kylon and Celine to help look after her now,' he said, 'just like we had Bedig in Slateford.'

Daphne said nothing.

'If Bedig was here,' he said, 'things would be different. You don't completely trust them, do you?'

'I trust Celine.'

'But not Kylon?'

'There's something dark and empty about him,' she said. 'Something I can't put my finger on.'

'I trust him. He's always been true to any purpose he's set his heart on, and he's devoted himself to protecting our daughter, so he can obey the last command that Kalayne gave him. I think we're lucky to have him around.'

'Well, you know him better than I do,' she said, 'but when the

Emperor invades, I want Karalyn to be with her father. I know you'll keep her safe.'

'Alright,' he said. He turned to their daughter. 'Shall we go, wee bear?'

'I want mummy.'

Daphne took her from Killop's arms and hugged her.

'We'll see each other soon,' she said as they walked to the stairs. Outside, a large covered wagon was parked. Kylon was up on the driver's bench, while Celine was chatting to Chane at the rear of the wagon, where the luggage had been placed.

Celine saw them approach, and held her arms out for Karalyn.

Daphne kissed her daughter, reluctant to let her go.

'It'll be all right, little bear,' Celine said. 'We've got some snacks ready for you when we set off.'

Karalyn sniffled, and Daphne passed her over, a tear escaping from her eye. She embraced Killop, then stood back as he boarded the wagon. He leaned over and helped Celine and Karalyn climb up.

Kylon cracked the whip, and the wagon began to move, pulled by a twin pair of horses. Karalyn let out a wail, tears and snot running down her cheeks as she waved from the back of the wagon. Killop crouched by her, raising his hand in farewell.

Daphne watched until the wagon passed from sight as it left Holders Square. She bowed her head, more tears falling. The thought of going back up to her empty apartment sent a wash of regret through her.

'It's for the best,' Chane said. 'You said it yourself, you don't want them here when the Emperor arrives.'

'I know.'

'Do you want to get a drink?'

'I can't. I need to get back to work.'

Daphne went to her office in the palace and worked through the afternoon and into the evening, organising troop movements and completing requisition and purchase orders for everything from grain to boots. Her signature sent convoys of wagons filled with food supplies out of the River Holdings heading towards depots in the safety of the western plains. She signed orders for squads of volunteer militia to stay hidden when the invasion came, so that they could harass the enemy from the rear, even though few would doubtless survive. Her right hand grew sore from holding the pen, as it flicked over documents, amending figures and correcting estimates, or scrawling revised orders across the margins in red ink.

She picked up her cigarette case. Empty.

Her mind was buzzing from the countless cups of tea and coffee, and her head was starting to hurt. She rubbed her neck. Lamps were burning in the room, and the shutters had been closed to keep out the chill night air. A junior staff officer leaned by the door, always ready to carry off her signed documents to wherever they needed to go, and always bringing her more when he returned. He straightened himself as he noticed her gaze.

'That's enough for today,' she said. 'Dismissed.'

'Good night ma'am,' he saluted, and departed down the corridor.

She wondered if Chane was still up for a drink.

There was a knock at the door, and a young officer peered in.

'Major Holdfast,' she said, 'the chancellor requests your presence in the war room.'

Daphne nodded and stood.

The officer escorted her through the well-lit hallways and corridors of the palace, to the chamber close to the front entrance where Daphne had been that morning. Standing by the long table was Faden Hold-wick, flanked by senior officers. The queen was a few paces away, gazing up at a large map of the Holdings on the wall.

Daphne nodded to her staff officers as she entered. Chane caught her eye from across the room.

'Major Holdfast,' Faden said as she approached. 'Thank you for joining us. I understand that Killop and Karalyn departed the city today?'

'They did, Chancellor.'

'A wise move,' he said. 'I'm glad Lydia and Teddy are safe up there with Godfrey. And with dear Ariel so far on in her pregnancy, I would rather she was as far away from danger as possible.'

Daphne gazed down at the map Faden had been studying. It showed the border area between the Holdings and the Plateau.

'Your staff have done a remarkable job of organising the defence of the republic,' Faden said. 'I'm told that the Emperor has moved his army close to the border. Some sixty thousand Rahain infantry are preparing to invade, with the Emperor himself at their head, but the work you have done here fills me with confidence that we shall prevail.'

'Thank you, Chancellor.'

'Do you have a tally of current troop numbers?'

'Of course, Chancellor,' she said, gesturing to one of her staff officers, who rose from her seat with a sheaf of papers.

'Six thousand heavy cavalry,' Daphne went on, reading from the documents the staff officer was holding out for her. 'Two thousand light cavalry, and twenty thousand heavy infantry.'

Faden stared at the map on the table. 'So we still only have half the enemy's numbers?'

'Yes, Chancellor. However, they have no cavalry, and our regular infantry are far better equipped and trained. And as well as these official numbers, we estimate somewhere in the region of ten to fifteen thousand irregulars are armed and ready in the River Holdings, under the command of local militia.'

Faden raised an eyebrow. 'The bait?'

'I wouldn't quite use that expression, Chancellor,' Daphne said, 'but their job is to lure the imperial army on towards Holdings City, where the regular army will be waiting for them.'

'And that will be our cue to evacuate?'

Daphne nodded. 'Yes, Chancellor.'

He frowned. 'This is the part of the plan that irks me. Having to give up the River Holdings and our capital city without even putting up a proper fight.'

'I understand, Chancellor, but the cavalry would be useless in the towns of the River Holdings. We need to meet the imperial army on the open plains.'

'Yes, yes, but it looks bad. It will appear to outsiders that we are running away.'

'Forgive me, Chancellor,' Daphne said, 'but that is precisely the impression we wish to create. If the Emperor thinks we are in disarray, he will be more likely to do something rash.'

'I don't know,' Faden said. He pointed at the map. 'Perhaps we should move our light cavalry here.'

'Right down to the border, Chancellor?'

'As you said, they have no cavalry of their own. If we strike when they first invade, we can give them a bloody nose, and show the Emperor we're not afraid.'

'But, Chancellor, we cannot afford to throw away one quarter of our cavalry strength simply to make a gesture.'

Faden narrowed his eyes.

'Now, now, Faden,' the queen said, walking over. 'We talked about this. Major Holdfast has the best officers in the republic at her disposal, and we must trust their judgement.' She smiled at him. 'Let's leave the tactics and strategy to the experts, shall we?'

'Very well,' Faden frowned.

'I would like a moment with Major Holdfast if that's all right, Faden,' the queen said, glancing at Daphne. 'Walk with me.'

Daphne nodded. 'Yes, your Majesty.'

The queen tutted, but smiled at the same time as they walked off together towards the door. 'First Minister, please.'

'Apologies, First Minister, I keep forgetting we're a republic now.'

The queen laughed as they left the chamber. 'It's all nonsense really. Now that we're out of earshot, you can call me Mirren, and I will call you Daphne.'

'All right.'

'Follow me,' she said. 'I want to show you something.'

The queen led Daphne up a long spiral staircase, into one of the palace's many towers. At the top, they came into a beautiful chamber, filled with elegant furnishings and art.

'This was going to be my favourite place,' Mirren said. 'I had it decorated after Guilliam's coronation, but no sooner was it completed than we were on our way to our new city in the Plateau. Do you like it?'

Daphne nodded, strolling to the narrow windows. 'Nice view.'

'Yes,' Mirren said, coming to stand alongside. 'In the daytime, you can see almost the entire city from up here.'

Daphne said nothing.

'I wanted you to know, Daphne,' Mirren went on after a moment, 'that despite the long years of bad blood between Guilliam and I and your family, I feel it is time to heal the wounds of the past. I for one have said many cruel and hurtful things about the Holdfasts. When you next see your father, I would very much like you to tell him that I hope he forgives me, as I forgive him.'

'I'm sorry, Mirren, but why would you need to forgive my father?'

Mirren raised an eyebrow, as a look of incredulity swept across her face.

'Oh my,' she said. 'You mean to tell me that you don't know?'

'Know what?'

'You must be aware of the rumours,' Mirren said. 'Even the miners in the northern iron fields have heard the rumours.'

Daphne felt her temper rise.

'It was the most talked-about affair in the realm,' Mirren went on, 'Godfrey Holdfast and the Queen of the Holdings. For over a decade they brazened it out. She loved him, but refused to allow him to divorce your mother, and also refused to take a husband to get herself an heir. Guilliam hated your father for it, with a passion he rarely exhibited elsewhere.'

'No,' Daphne said.

'No?' Mirren repeated. 'Come now, why on earth would I lie to you? I swear to you that if I had known you were ignorant of this, I would have held my tongue and said nothing. I merely assumed you knew what every other person in the realm knows. I'm sorry that you had to find out this way.'

Daphne felt sick. For years, she had believed her father's vehement denials but, as she looked back over her parents' relationship, and the way they had always seemed to hate each other, she knew that what Mirren had told her was the truth. She lowered her head, ashamed of feeling so stupid. How had she not realised? She needed to speak to her mother.

Mirren touched her arm. 'Truly, Daphne, I'm sorry. This will sound trite to your ears, but please don't dwell on it. After all, it's over and done with now.'

Daphne felt a surge of hatred for her father. Liar and coward.

She glanced at Mirren. 'He would have left his family if the queen had let him?'

Mirren sighed. 'I'm afraid so. Please sit, take a moment. Would you like a glass of brandy? There's a bottle around here somewhere.'

Daphne sat on a plush armchair, while Mirren fetched the brandy and poured two glasses. She handed one to Daphne and sat across from her.

'Cigarette?' she said, opening her silver case.

Daphne nodded and took one.

'Oh dear,' Mirren said, lighting the cigarettes. 'I appear to have upset you. It was not my intention.'

Daphne took a sip of brandy. 'When did the affair begin?'

'Not long after her coronation,' Mirren said, 'in four-eight-eight. When you were about six?'

'Seven.'

'They kept it fairly quiet for the first few years, but here in the city at least, it became open knowledge. When Guilliam found out, he wasn't too opposed at first, he assumed his sister was just having a casual relationship, but as the years passed, and she showed no sign of taking a husband, his anger began to stir.'

'Guilliam made them break it off?'

Mirren smiled. 'No one could force the queen to do anything she didn't want to do. No, what finally ended it was the fact that Godfrey's children were all growing up, and presumably he was concerned about you finding out. Nevertheless, he remained very close to the queen, and used all his influence to persuade her to invade Sanang in five-oh-one. After that, I don't believe Guilliam ever talked to his sister again.'

Daphne shook her head. She thought about the years the affair had covered. Her father must have broken it off as Daphne herself was about to arrive in the capital to start university. She remembered being teased by some students about her father and the queen, but had always believed his denials. She wondered if this meant that her siblings knew the truth, and that as the youngest, the rest of the family had colluded to keep Daphne in blessed ignorance.

She finished her drink, and stood.

'Thank you for the brandy, Mirren,' she said, 'and for being honest. If you'll excuse me, I'm going to get drunk with Captain Chane.'

'Ah,' said Mirren. 'Before you go, just one more thing. I visited the Prophet this morning, for the first time since I got back. I admit that I have been wary of going to see him, as I was one of those who had been scathing about him, back when he refused to move to the Plateau with Guilliam. I should not have worried. The Prophet was perfectly gracious, and we discussed many things. When I was leaving, he asked me to pass on his request that you attend him this evening.'

Daphne sighed. 'To the citadel, then.'

The night air was still and dark as Daphne crossed from the palace to the headquarters of the church. The guards and small number of servants knew her face well, and saluted or bowed as she passed. She entered the Prophet's private apartment, where the old man was sitting hunched in a wicker chair next to a blazing fire, while a young man fed him soup with a spoon.

'Good evening,' Daphne said.

The Prophet turned to her and smiled.

'That's enough for now,' he said to the young man, his voice hoarse and quiet.

The young man bowed low, and left the room.

The Prophet gestured to a chair, and Daphne sat.

'Thank you for coming,' he said. 'You know by now to help yourself.'

Daphne nodded, and poured herself a glass of white rum.

'Troubled?' he said. 'Ah, I see. You learned tonight of the great scandalous affair between your father and the old queen.'

'Why did you not tell me?'

'At first I assumed you knew, but when I realised you didn't, I felt it wasn't my place. Mirren Blackhold, on the other hand, has no such compunctions.'

'It was a mistake,' Daphne said. 'Mirren didn't mean to tell me.'

'I don't think Mirren does many things by mistake. But the reason I have called you to the citadel tonight is not to rake over old wounds. Mirren was round here today, I assume she told you that?'

'Yes.'

'It was beholden upon me to read her thoughts,' the Prophet said, 'as I knew she has seen the Emperor in person, after he had received his mage abilities. I wanted to discover if she had gleaned any insight into his strength or behaviour, but instead, I found out something considerably more disturbing.'

Daphne leaned closer.

'What?'

'The Emperor is dead.'

Daphne frowned in confusion. 'He's dead? When...?'

'He died the moment the Creator possessed his body. The god of the Holdings has come to earth in mortal form. I saw it, as clear as day, when I looked into Mirren's mind, and witnessed everything she had seen. His voice, his eyes, the little personal details. Mirren is right, that man is not her husband. He is the Creator.'

'But you've been in his mind,' Daphne said. 'You've read his thoughts, his plan for the invasion. Why could you not see who he really was?'

'This is what disturbs me the most, Daphne. When he was alone with Mirren, his mind was open, and his true identity was clear to me, but now he is shielding it, and if he is shielding it, it is because he suspects that others might be trying to see inside his thoughts. And if he suspects that...'

'He may have been giving you the wrong information.'

'Exactly. He knows that I am here, and has an inkling of how powerful you have become. I don't believe he is yet aware that Karalyn can enter his mind, but he will assume that you or I would try.'

'Who else knows?'

'That he is the Creator? Just the two of us sat here, for the moment. I feel it might be unwise if we reveal the truth to others, however. Half would refuse to believe, and those who did would be too terrified to resist.'

Daphne lit a cigarette. 'Should we be terrified?'

'That the Creator has descended from the heavens and walks the earth in the company of his creation?' the Prophet said, smiling. 'He views us as mere insects, mere things that he made. He cares nothing for the lives of anyone in this world, as he proved when he threw away fifty thousand soldiers in the Rakanese campaign, not to mention the tens of thousands of civilian deaths that the invasion was responsible for. And now it is the turn of the Holdings. His chosen people have rebelled against him, Daphne, and he is coming in wrath and might to destroy us.'

He gazed at her, the smile gone from his face.

'Yes, Daphne, we should be terrified.'

CHAPTER 13
IN THE GUTTER

Westgate, Domm Pass – 28th Day, First Third Autumn 507
'This is ridiculous,' said Flora, as Keira peered down the passageway at the rear of the tavern.

'Shut it, ya numpty,' Keira said. 'She'll hear us.'

They slipped through the corridor, and opened the side door to the outside.

'Bollocks,' Keira said, looking over her shoulder as the main door to the tavern opened. 'Run.'

Keira and Flora raced through the door and out into the rain.

'I know yer there, Keira!' Kelpie cried. She appeared at the side door as Flora and Keira reached the alleyway leading to the main street of Westgate village. 'Yer meant to be working tonight!'

Keira laughed, and kept running, Flora just behind.

'Come back now,' Kelpie yelled, 'or don't come back at all!'

Keira and Flora ran out onto the muddy street and down the hill, away from the World's End. They slowed as they grew out of sight of the tavern.

'That was hilarious,' Keira said. 'Did ye see her face?'

'I hope she's not being serious this time,' Flora said.

'About what, not letting us back in?' Keira smirked. 'Of course she will, she needs us more than we need her.'

'But you're missing another night of work.'

'So what? I need a break.'

Flora shook her head. 'One of these times, we're going to push Kelpie too far. What'll we do if she throws us out?'

'It wouldnae be too bad. I mean, I'm getting sick of telling the same old stories every night. Nobody listens any more, they've heard them so many fucking times.'

'But we've no money. Where would we stay?'

'You worry too much. There's always my ma and da's if we get desperate.'

Flora frowned. 'What?'

'Are ye deaf? I said we could always stay at...'

'No, I heard you alright, Keira,' Flora said. 'My mind just refused to comprehend it. Are you telling me that we've been in Domm for nearly five thirds, and your parents live here? And you've never once mentioned them, or gone to visit them? Do they even know you're back? Where do they live?'

'Enough with the questions.'

Flora stopped in the middle of the street, the rain running down her face. She stared at Keira.

'What is it now?' the mage groaned.

'Do your parents live here?'

'Aye. Well, I think so. They used to anyway, last time I was in Domm.'

'So you haven't bothered to find out?'

'I'm a grown fucking woman, not a wee bairn.'

'Do you not get along with them?'

Keira shrugged. 'Come on. I need a drink, and I'm getting wet standing here like a donkey.'

She set off again, and Flora followed a few steps behind. After another minute, they reached a low stone building, with a chimney belching smoke. Two large Kellach stood to either side of the door, above which hung a sign reading 'Dermot's Bar'.

'Hold it,' the tall Kellach woman on the left said. 'I'm not sure we should be letting ye in, not after what happened last time.'

'Come on, Bella,' Keira said, 'that wasnae my fault. Those two Domm arseholes were winding me up all night.'

'Will ye behave if we let ye in?' asked the large man on the other side of the door.

'Of course I will,' Keira said. 'Promise.'

The two door wardens glanced at each other, frowned, and nodded.

'Cheers!' Keira cried, and entered with Flora.

The interior of the bar was quiet, with few patrons. A handful sat at a couple of stained tables next to the great fire that roared at one end of the room. Keira strode over to the bar, on the wall opposite the fire.

'Evening,' she said. 'Two ales and a bottle of whisky.'

The woman behind the bar eyed her for a few moments, then looked over at an older man who was sitting alone. He nodded.

'All right,' the woman said, and began to prepare the drinks.

Keira waved to the man. 'Cheers, Dermot.'

'This is yer last chance, Keira,' he said. 'Fuck up again, and yer barred.'

She opened her palms wide, grinning. 'I'll be good.'

The man frowned.

Keira turned to Flora and winked.

The bar woman placed the ales, whisky and glasses onto the bar. 'That'll be twelve bits.'

'Stick it on my tab.'

The woman turned to Dermot, who shook his head.

'Sorry, dear,' the bar woman smiled. 'No more credit.'

'Fucksake,' Keira muttered, counting out the coins from a pouch on her belt. 'Here ya go, ya greedy bastards.'

She dropped the coins onto the bar top, took the drinks, and found a table near the fire. She sat, and Flora joined her. Keira poured two large whiskies, and took a slug of ale.

'That's better.'

She glanced at Flora. 'What's up with the sour face, hen?'

Flora muttered something.

'Speak up,' Keira said. 'Stop mumbling.'

'I said you're an idiot.'

Keira laughed. 'Let's hear it then, oh wise Flora. How exactly am I an idiot?'

'Domm is full of refugees, people whose lives have been thrown up in the air. They've been torn apart from their loved ones. Sisters, brothers, children. You must have seen the countless posters, nailed to every house and shop-front on the main road, where people are searching for their relatives. Yet you've sat on your arse for thirds, while your mum and dad might just be a few miles away?'

Keira wagged her finger. 'See, that's where yer wrong. Fuck knows where my ma and da are. I only said they were probably in Domm. Think about it, why should I spend ages searching for them? I might be looking for a year, who knows? Is it not a better idea to stay in the same place, and let them find me?'

She sat back, smug in her certainty.

Flora shook her head. 'So you're saying that this has been your plan all along? That you've been expecting them to turn up?'

'Exactly.'

'You're full of shit.'

'Steady on,' Keira frowned. 'Ma parents are no fucking business of yours. Do ye hear me asking about your ma and da?' She smirked. 'Like I'd give a shit.'

Flora lowered her eyes, and she took a sip of whisky.

'Keira,' she said, 'are we friends?'

The mage raised an eyebrow. 'Why are ye getting all heavy on me? We only came here for a drink.'

'Would you please answer the question?'

'No,' Keira said, 'I won't. It's bullshit, that's what it is. Ye shouldnae be questioning me on shit like this. Maybe folk in the Holdings go on about their feelings and crap like that, but yer in Domm now, hen.'

'I count you as a friend.'

Keira groaned.

'My only friend, in fact.'

'I cannae handle this,' Keira said, downing her whisky and pouring another. 'I'm sitting somewhere else if ye keep this shit up.'

Flora fell silent.

'That's better,' Keira said. 'Now, keep yer eyes open for they bastards from before that I was telling ye about. I want to see if they've got anything to smoke. I'm gagging for a bit of weed.'

'They haven't been in for ages,' Flora said. 'They moved on thirds ago.'

Keira shrugged as she scanned the bar. 'They might be back, ye never know. In the meantime, let's get manky.'

'Shut that fucking door!' cried someone, as the wind and rain gusted into the bar.

Flora shivered in the chill draught.

The departing customer closed the door, and the warmth returned.

'It's nasty out there the night,' Keira slurred. She squinted at the bottle of whisky. 'Shit, we're nearly out of the good stuff.'

She glanced up at the bar.

'Last orders have been and gone,' said Dermot.

'Fuck you,' Keira sneered. 'Surely ye can give us a couple more ales at least.'

Dermot shrugged. 'Ye can get more at Kelpie's. I'm closing up in ten minutes.'

Keira glanced over the remaining patrons. 'Maybe one of these jokers has got some booze.'

She got to her feet, swayed, then staggered towards a nearby table, where two women and three men were sitting.

'Hoi,' she said, approaching. 'What ye doing after this? Ye got anything to drink?'

One of the men shook his head. 'No, Keira. We're off to bed. Got work in the morning.'

Keira scowled. 'Pansies.'

She looked over the rest of the bar. In a dark corner, three men were sitting, huddled round a lamp. She strode across to them and sat down at their table.

'Evening, fuckheads,' she said.

They gazed at her, their eyes narrow.

'I don't think I've seen you lot round here,' Keira went on. 'You new?'

One of the men put down his glass. 'Who's asking?'

'Ye must be new if ye don't know who I am,' she said. 'Anyway, have ye come from the Plateau, or lizard land?'

'What it to you?'

'Is it not fucking obvious?' Keira smirked. 'I'm wanting a smoke, and if ye've come from the Plateau, then there's a much better chance ye're carrying weed.'

The men glanced at each other and laughed.

'We've come from Rainsby,' said one.

'Excellent,' she said. 'I mean, it's a shithole, but every bastard was smoking weed when I was there.'

'Not any more, they're not.'

Keira frowned. 'How come?'

'Rainsby got well and truly fucked over by the Emperor,' the man said. 'You not heard? Him and his army sacked the place, then burnt it to the ground.'

'He killed thousands of Kellach,' said another. 'The whole town's just a smear now.'

'What a shame,' she said. 'So, have ye got any weed?'

'Maybe.'

'Any ye'd like to donate?'

'No.'

'Any to sell?'

'Maybe. What you got?'

'About twenty bits.'

'We've got plenty of money. What else you got?'

'What ye after?'

The man looked over to where Flora was sitting.

'Is she yours?'

Keira shrugged. 'Aye.'

'Lend us her for the night, and ye can have all the weed ye can smoke.'

She narrowed her eyes at them. 'How much exactly are we talking about?'

The man rubbed his chin for a moment. 'An ounce.'

Keira glanced over at Flora. Enough weed for a third. She got to her feet.

'Be back in a minute, boys.'

She staggered over to the table where Flora sat, stumbling as she reached her chair. She scrambled, and crashed down into the seat.

'Did ye see that?' she laughed. 'Nearly fell on my arse there.'

'So,' Flora sighed, 'did you find any?'

'Aye, maybe,' she said. 'I've been thinking about what ye were saying earlier, about us being friends.'

'Yeah?'

'Yer a good friend, Flora,' she said, pouring the dregs from the whisky bottle into her glass.

Flora snorted. 'I know you're pissed, but you're not that pissed. What do you want?'

Keira put on her hurt expression. 'Here I am, opening up to ye, and ye throw it back in my fucking face.'

She turned away, lowering her eyes.

'Sorry,' Flora said. 'I'm just not used to you being like this. It's good. I'm glad I'm your friend.'

Keira looked up. 'I need a favour.'

'What?'

'See those guys over there?'

'Yes.'

'They've got weed, right? A shitload. But here's the thing. They're ready to hand it over, but they've got their heart set on spending the night with you first…'

'What?' Flora cried, getting to her feet. 'You want to hand me over to some random guys so you can get a smoke? What is wrong with you?'

She slapped Keira across the face, and as the mage blinked from the shock, she heard laughter coming from the table in the corner where the men sat. Before she could say anything, Flora stormed out of the bar, slamming the door behind her.

Keira rubbed her cheek. 'Fucksake.'

She staggered to the bar, ignoring the three men in the corner.

Dermot looked up from drying a row of glasses. 'Aye?'

'I'll give ye twenty bits for a bottle of whisky.'

Dermot laughed and shook his head.

'Kelpie cut ye off, eh?' he said.

'Not yet,' she grinned, 'but the cow had a right fucking mood on before, and I'd rather not have to ask her, if ye know what I mean.'

Dermot sighed and put down the glass. He reached under the bar and lifted a bottle. He placed it in front of her and held out his hand. She smirked, and emptied the contents of her money pouch onto the top of the bar. She picked up the bottle and headed for the door.

'Hey you,' cried one of the men in the corner.

She turned.

The three men got up and approached her.

'Where's yer wee friend gone?'

'She thought you were the ugliest wee pricks she'd ever laid eyes on. She's away to throw up in the fucking street.'

'You reneging on the deal?' he said. 'If yer friend's done a runner, then you owe us a favour. But we're reasonable. We'll take you instead.' He smirked at his friends. 'For half an ounce.'

Keira punched him in the face.

'Half an ounce, ya cheeky bastard?' she cried, as the other two men rushed her, lashing out. She felt a blow to her chin, and flinched back-wards. Another punch struck her in the stomach. She gasped, and staggered. She brought her arm up and over one of the men's heads, and began to choke him.

'Take that out of here!' cried Dermot, and at the sound of his voice, the two door wardens ran into the bar. Without a word, they began piling into the three men and Keira. The mage rolled to the floor as the fists flew all around her. She clutched onto her bottle of whisky, and dodged the legs between her and the door. A last punch struck her back as she flew out of the building and hurtled down the muddy street into the darkness. After a few hundred yards she paused, gasping for air. She glanced back up the street, but could see no one.

She opened the bottle of whisky, and laughed.

The dawn was grey, with a chill breeze blowing from the west. The rain had stopped at some point during the night, but the street was still wet and muddy. The cold had worked its way into Keira's bones as she lay sprawled out in the gutter next to a row of cottages. Her clothes were sodden and covered in mud, and her head ached liked an evil sprite was hitting it with a hammer.

She opened her eyes, then shut them again, the dim grey light too much for her to take. She heard footsteps walk by on the road, as folk avoided where she lay. A few tutted in her direction, or muttered disapproving comments. Arseholes.

Where was wee Flora? Was she not supposed to prevent this sort of shit from happening?

She cracked open her eyes a slit and glanced at the street. She was at least a mile from the World's End, and half that from Dermot's Bar. She tried to get up, but her limbs were stiff and frozen, and she collapsed back into the mud. Ignoring the laughs from a couple of passers-by, she put one hand in front of the other, and began to crawl up the street. The gutter had an inch of water at its bottom, and she grew colder as she struggled up the hill towards the tavern.

After a hundred yards, she fell down into the mud, exhausted. She rolled onto her back and stared up at the low clouds covering the sky. A drop of rain hit her face.

Shit.

She opened her mouth as the rain started, catching some on her dried and parched tongue, and closed her eyes.

After a moment, she felt the rain stop, although she could still hear it falling around her.

'Pyre's tits,' said a voice. 'What a state to get into.'

'Ye found her?' another voice said, one that she recognised as Kendrie's.

Keira opened her eyes. A woman with long red hair was standing over her, looking down with a frown on her face.

'Aye,' the woman said. 'Ye were right. Drunk in a ditch.'

'You get her arms,' Kendrie said, 'I'll take her legs.'

Keira tried to speak, but it came out as a mangled groan. Kendrie chuckled, walking to where her feet lay in the mud. The red-haired woman reached down and grasped Keira's wrists, and she felt herself lifted into the air, her backside swaying.

Kendrie groaned. 'She's heavier than she looks.'

'Fuck you,' Keira tried to say, then she passed out.

When she next awoke, she was in her bed in the tavern. Her head was splitting, and her bones ached, but at least she was warm and dry. She peered under the blanket and saw she was wearing a clean night-shirt, and her temper rose.

She gazed around the empty room. Someone had tidied away the piles of dirty clothes and rubbish that had littered the floor, and removed the collection of empty whisky bottles that had been accumulating in the corner. The window had been opened an inch, and even the smell in the room was better than she remembered.

'Fucking Flora,' Keira muttered, 'messing with my stuff again.'

'No, it was me.'

Keira nearly fell off the bed in surprise. She turned, and saw the red-haired woman, sitting on a chair in the corner by the door. Keira's mouth fell open.

'Good afternoon, Keira.'

'Kallie?'

The woman filled a mug with water and passed it to the mage.

Keira took it, and drank deep.

'When Bridget told me what was going on down here,' Kallie said, 'I didn't believe it.'

'You met Bridget?' Keira said, her voice hoarse and raspy.

'Aye, in Kell.'

'Wee cow.'

'Shut yer mouth, Keira. Bridget's a hero. After all the shit she's been through, and she's still fighting, she's still trying, while you're sat on yer arse in Domm, getting wasted day and night. Yer a disgrace, that's what ye are.'

'Hey,' Keira croaked. 'That's not fair.'

Kallie shook her head. 'Fair? I was being generous. If I told ye what I actually thought of ye... But I won't. All this time, I've been fighting up north, watching my comrades get killed, and having to live in the night-mare that Kell has become. All that time, we were waiting for you. "When Keira returns, that's when we'll kick the lizards out of Kell at last", that's what we used to say.' She laughed, but her eyes remained dark. 'But ye were down here all along, getting hammered while we were dying. I never thought ye'd give up, Keira.'

'Fuck you.'

Kallie's left arm reached out in a flash, grabbing Keira by the throat. She formed her other hand into a fist, and raised it.

'I'm not scared of you, Keira, not any more. Ye speak to me like that again and I'll kick the shit out of you. Understand?'

Keira struggled, but Kallie's grasp on her throat was strong and firm, and her own limbs were still weak and aching from being out all night in the cold. She bared her teeth at Kallie, and glared at her, but said nothing.

Kallie released her, and sat back down in her seat. Keira rolled away and clambered off the bed, stumbling and clattering into her bedside table, one hand on her bruised throat.

'Ye've no clue what I've been through,' she said. 'No fucking idea.'

'I spoke to Laodoc and Agang as well as Bridget,' Kallie said. 'I know enough.'

'Then ye know yer being unreasonable. Ye know that I've had to kill thousands, over and over again. Rahain, Rakanese, Sanang, Holdings, you fucking name them, I've slaughtered them. And yer seriously asking me to go out and do it again?'

'Aye.'

'Well, I'm not.'

Kallie stood. 'Aye ye are. Get dressed and get yer arse through to the tavern. I'll be waiting.'

She opened the door, and left Keira's room.

The mage sat on her bed. Did nobody understand that she couldn't face killing again? They just demanded shit from her, without caring about how she felt about any of it. The Rahain, the Alliance, Kylon, she had just been a tool in their sweaty hands, a killing machine, pointed in the direction of their enemies, and let loose.

She gazed at the small lamp burning by her bedside. The joy she used to feel when she was connected to a living flame had gone, replaced by bitter resistance. She hadn't used her powers since outside the walls of the imperial capital, when she had felt those powers vanish. For an hour, she had been unable to summon even the slightest reserve of her skills, but instead of feeling downhearted about it, she had felt nothing but relief, the lifting of a great burden from her shoulders. She had been crushed when she had felt her powers return.

What kind of fire mage was she, that wished she could scourge her powers from her body? She longed to be free of the curse of being a mage.

Not just any mage, but the best. A fucking goddess.

A goddess.

She stood and got dressed, finding her cleanest clothes from where someone had folded them into a drawer. She brushed her tangled hair, and drank another full mug of water.

Then she remembered Flora.

Shit.

What had she done?

She tried to summon up her cocky sneer, but lacked the energy, so walked into the tavern looking like death warmed up. Kendrie was at the bar, serving a couple of patrons. He glanced up at her, smirking, but she ignored him. She gazed around the quiet room, and saw Kallie sitting by the window, Kelpie and Flora next to her.

She went over and sat down in silence.

Kelpie raised an eyebrow, and glanced at Kallie. Flora was also looking at Kallie, the expression on her face like she was gazing at a vision.

'I believe you owe this lassie an apology,' Kallie said.

Keira narrowed her eyes. 'For what? I was only joking last night. I wouldnae really have let those guys do anything to her.'

'Stop lying,' Kallie said. 'For once just be honest, and admit ye made a mistake.'

Keira looked from one woman to the other, her head pounding. She gagged, and tasted bile in her mouth.

'I fucked up.'

'And?' Kallie said.

Keira gazed at Flora. 'Sorry,' she muttered.

Kelpie snorted. 'By the arse cheeks of Pyre himself, there's something I never thought I'd hear.'

Flora looked into Keira's eyes. 'Thank you.'

'She's coming with us, Keira,' Kallie said, 'when we head north tomorrow.'

Keira shook her head.

'She can carry the lamp for ye,' Kallie went on, 'just like Lacey used to. Once we get to Northern Kell, we spread the word that yer back, and then hit the lizards where it hurts. There will be justice at last.'

'I'm in,' said Flora. 'Laodoc and Agang were right. The longer we sit here, the more likely the Emperor will come, and when he does, he'll destroy everything. All the families here trying to rebuild their lives will be devastated. We can't wait until that happens, we owe it to them to fight.'

'Owe them?' Keira said. 'What do I owe them?'

'By coming here, ye've endangered everybody,' Kallie said. 'Yer wee holiday's over. Ye've got today to sort yer shit out.'

Keira glanced at Kelpie.

The older woman shook her head. 'I've looked after ye the best I can, but I've always wanted ye to head back into the world when ye were ready. Keira, despite yer best attempts to piss me off, I'll always be fond of ye. I'll always remember what ye did for Kell when the lizards first invaded. But our deal's over. It's time to go.'

'Yer kicking me out?'

'Aye, if it comes to that.'

'So yer all ganging up on me?'

Flora shrugged. 'It's because we love you.'

Keira tried to fire back with something, but the words stuck in her throat. Pyre's tits, her head was splitting.

'I've got something to show you,' Kallie said. 'The Severed Clan left a load of stuff here when they cleared out, luggage and boxes. I was looking through one of Laodoc's crates this morning when ye were sleeping. I wanted to see if he'd left anything behind that he might want kept safe, ye know, before Kelpie chucks it all out. At the bottom, I found a load of women's clothing in a bag.' She reached into her pocket. 'I also found this.'

She placed something onto the table.

Keira stared at it.

It was a small wooden bear, rearing up on its hind legs, its claws and teeth carved to sharp points.

'Killop's wee bear.'

Kallie nodded. 'I took it from yer home in Kell years ago, then left it in the Rahain Capital when I was arrested with Killop and Bridget. I've no idea how it got mixed up with that luggage, but I thought ye might want it.'

Keira picked it up. It felt so light.

'Yer da made it, aye?' said Kallie.

Keira smirked. 'That's what Killop thinks.'

Kallie frowned.

'Our da did make one for him,' Keira said, gazing at the carved beast, 'but I broke it one night by accident, and then buried the bits in the garden to hide the evidence. The next morning, Killop went mental looking for it, so I went away and made him another one. Took me days. I had to dig up the broken one, so I could copy it, then I hid the new one under his bed so he could find it.'

'You made it?' Kallie said.

'Aye. My copy was so good he never noticed it was different.'

'And now it's back with you.'

'But it belongs to my wee brother.'

'Then you should take it to him,' Kallie said, 'after we've cleared Kell of lizards.'

Keira laughed, then caught the expressions on the faces of the others.

'Fucksake, alright,' she said. 'We'll go to Kell, but I'm not making any promises about what I'll do when we get there.'

Kallie nodded, then glanced at Kelpie.

'We'll be leaving quietly in the morning,' she said. 'No announcements, no big farewells.'

'Folk'll realise that the mage has left,' Kelpie said. 'I won't be able to keep it a secret for long.'

'Tell them she's away to visit folk in the lowlands,' Kallie said. 'I'd rather we were well on our way before everybody realises where we've really gone.'

'Alright,' Kelpie said.

'Now,' Keira said. 'We've got the rest of the day free, let's get the whisky in.'

Kallie shook her head. 'No chance. I want ye sober until we leave.'

'What?' Keira groaned.

'Ye heard me,' the red-haired Kell woman said. 'And don't bother trying to get some. Every place in Westgate's been told not to sell ye any, and Kendrie's going to be keeping an eye on the bar here.'

Keira frowned. 'I'm beginning to regret this already.'

CHAPTER 14

THE PRESENCE OF ROYALTY

Hold Fast, Holdings Republic – 8th Day, Second Third Autumn 507

'Sorry I'm late,' Killop said as he entered the grand dining room. He nodded at Godfrey, sitting at the head of the long table, then at the other adult members of the Holdfast family, who were lining the sides. He got a curt frown from Rosalind as he took his seat next to Celine, and opposite Ariel and Jonah.

'That's fine, Killop,' Godfrey said. 'We were just getting started.'

'Was Karalyn not wanting to leave her daddy?' Ariel smiled, her swollen abdomen visible.

'Aye,' Killop said. 'She was a wee bit reluctant, but Jean's got it under control.'

'She's quite a handful, is young Karalyn,' Rosalind said. 'It's what comes from her mother always being away, playing soldiers when she should be looking after her daughter.'

'The Kellach style of parenting is more relaxed,' Killop said. 'We tend to give our wee ones free rein when they're that small.'

'So you think we're too strict?'

'No,' Killop said, 'just different.'

'I believe that discipline is at the heart of every successful example of child-rearing,' Rosalind said. 'It might very well be what has propelled the Holdings race to the forefront of the world, rather than languishing in some backwater.'

Killop pondered the wisdom of entering into another argument with Lady Holdfast.

'You can't be serious, mother,' said Ariel. 'Are you trying to say that the misfortunes that have struck the Kellach Brigdomin are because they don't cane their children enough?'

'I'm merely suggesting that it may be part of what makes ours the superior culture,' Rosalind said. 'There will be other factors, of course. Literacy, for example. I believe that the Kellach see no use in learning how to read or write.'

'I agree with you there,' Killop said. 'That's why we set up schools in Slateford. It's true that we never saw any need for literacy before we were invaded, though there was at least one scribe in most villages. But now?'

'I fear it may be a little too late,' Rosalind said. 'With the Emperor having cleared all of the Kellach Brigdomin from the Imperial Capital and Rainsby, and with the Rahain in control of what remains of your homeland, I wonder if your race has any future in this world, except as ever-dwindling numbers of beggars, recruits for the army, or bandits.'

Killop took a sip of water from a tall crystal goblet on the table, as servants began to serve their opening course.

'And which of those three would you say I am?' he said.

Rosalind smiled. 'Oh, you're a special case.' She paused as a plate was set before her.

'Really, dear,' Godfrey said. 'I'm sure Killop doesn't need to hear any more about the ill luck afflicting his people.'

Rosalind stared at her husband. 'And might I enquire why you have been so quiet? You usually aren't so reserved at the dinner table.'

'If you must know,' Godfrey said, his expression dark, 'I've just been at a briefing with my intelligence officers. The first detailed reports of the casualties resulting from the Emperor's Rakanese campaign have arrived. They make grim reading.'

He picked up a spoon and stirred his soup, his eyes cast down.

'Well?' said Jonah.

'Please,' Rosalind said, 'not while we're eating.'

'I have friends who were conscripted into the imperial army,' Jonah said. 'Father?'

Godfrey looked up. 'Over fifty thousand dead. Another twenty thousand in their beds, too sick to return to the Plateau. The rest were abandoned when the Emperor departed Rakana, and ordered to make their way to Rainsby, to re-populate the town there.'

The table sat in silence.

'And every horse that accompanied the army,' Godfrey went on. 'Dead.'

Jonah closed his eyes.

'We shall have to rebuild our stocks from scratch,' Godfrey said. 'It'll take years before we have anything like our previous numbers, maybe a generation.' He glared at Rosalind. 'See what your precious Emperor has done to us. You may be able to blind yourself to the fact that a Rahain army is currently occupying the River Holdings, but you can't ignore the empty fields and paddocks right here on the estate.'

'The army is here because of you, Godfrey,' Rosalind spat. 'You're the one who has put our lives in danger. Your foolish and selfish rebellion against the Creator-appointed ruler of the world will do nothing but damage to our country, and you try to blame me for it? Of course the Emperor has moved his army into the River Holdings. He had to. All order had broken down, with the ignorant peasants following your puppet, Faden Holdwick. But I'm not overly concerned. The Emperor will overthrow the pathetic new government and restore order.'

'And what about Daphne?' Killop said.

'She was naïve to get herself caught up in it,' Rosalind said, 'but once again, she believed whatever her father told her. He barked, and she jumped up and down like an eager little puppy.'

'Shut up, mother,' Jonah said.

Rosalind glared at her son. Killop shared a glance with Celine.

'What did you just say to me, young man?' Rosalind said.

'Tell me, mother,' Jonah said, 'what exactly would the Emperor have to do before you condemn him? Slaughter half the River Holdings? Kill Ariel's husband, and your youngest daughter? Even then, I believe you'd find some way to justify his actions. We all know you hate Father, but now I wonder how far you'd go.'

'How dare you!' she said. 'I expect as much from the others, but you, Jonah? After everything I've done for you, you turn on me now?'

Ariel and Jonah shouted at the same time, and Killop sat back as the table descended into a row. He frowned at Celine.

'Another happy family dinner,' she whispered to him.

'Quiet!' Godfrey roared, and Jonah and Ariel fell silent.

Rosalind smiled, her arms folded.

'You two,' Godfrey said, 'apologise for raising your voices at your mother.'

'Sorry,' muttered Jonah.

Ariel tutted.

Godfrey glared at her.

'Fine, I'm sorry,' she said.

'Remember,' Godfrey said, 'Celine and Killop are new to the family. What must they think when they see you behave like that?'

'Killop's not part of the family,' Jonah said.

'That's not his fault,' Godfrey said. 'Marriage is prohibited between Holdings and Kellach Brigdomin under imperial law, otherwise I'm sure he and Daphne would have wedded.' He glanced at Killop. 'Isn't that right?'

'Aye.'

'Did you not live together for a considerable period under your own laws in Rahain?' Rosalind said. 'I would have thought you'd have had ample time for a wedding ceremony there, if you were serious about committing to my daughter.'

Killop clenched his fists under the table. 'The way you said that, it sounded for a moment as if you actually care about Daphne.'

The others fell quiet. A tiny smile appeared on Celine's lips.

'I care about the reputation of the family,' Rosalind said.

'Then you should be very proud of your daughter, Lady Holdfast,' Killop said. 'Daphne is a credit to your family.'

'She appeals to a certain class among the ill-educated, I'll grant you,' she said, 'but I assure you, the better bred amongst us do not share that view.'

'And when we get married, what will the so-called better bred think then?'

'I hesitate to say, in case I ruin everyone's appetites.'

Killop pushed his untouched bowl of soup away. 'Too late for that.'

'Come now, Killop,' Godfrey said. 'Don't play her game. She wants you to get up and walk away, so she can present it to everyone as further proof that you don't fit in.' He glanced at his wife. 'Isn't that right, dear?'

Rosalind performed a false smile.

'If one cannot speak freely at the dinner table,' she said, 'then I fear for the future under Faden's regime. Well, I would fear, were it not for the fact that the Emperor will soon be in Holdings City to put things in order, and hold those responsible to account.'

Ariel started crying.

'Oh, do be quiet,' Rosalind said. 'Don't waste your tears on that foolish man. He doesn't deserve them, Ariel, not after he betrayed you the same way your father betrayed me.'

Godfrey's face twisted in rage. 'What have I told you about bringing that up?'

Rosalind ignored him. 'Some men just can't help themselves,' she said to Ariel, 'especially, it seems, when they are in the presence of royalty.'

'It's not true,' Ariel wept.

Rosalind sighed. 'You're such a dreamer, Ariel. I remember feeling the way you do now, faced with the realisation that the father of your children had chosen a woman so far above your station that she may as well be a goddess.' She shook her head. 'Unfortunately, daughter, I learned one cannot compete with a queen.'

'Enough!' Godfrey roared, getting to his feet.

Killop tensed, as the air in the room grew chill.

As Rosalind began to say something, a side door burst open, and Karalyn rushed into the dining room, wearing a princess outfit. Behind her, Jean was puffing, her arms stretching out for the girl.

'Daddy!' she cried.

'Come now, Jean,' Rosalind said. 'I know that girl can be badly behaved, but surely it's not beyond your abilities to keep her confined to a secure room?'

'Sorry, ma'am,' Jean said, as Karalyn ran to Killop and grabbed hold of his legs.

'What is it, wee bear?'

'Daddy, daddy,' she said, hiding her face and clinging on.

Jean began to pull her away, but the girl wriggled and held on tight.

Killop leaned down. 'What's wrong, wee bear?'

The bad man, daddy, he's coming.

He gasped.

Celine got off her seat and knelt by Karalyn, as Killop froze, his mouth hanging open.

'Come on, little bear,' Celine said, trying to prise Karalyn from Killop's leg, 'we'll take you back to play with Teddy and Lydia.'

Killop stood, and turned to where Godfrey and Rosalind sat. They frowned up at him.

'We need to leave,' he said. 'We have to get out of here.'

Rosalind laughed. 'You're rather excitable today.'

'I'm serious,' he said. 'We need to go.'

'Whatever are you talking about?' Godfrey said. 'We don't finish meals because of an upset child.'

Killop picked up Karalyn, and held her close. Celine raised an eyebrow.

'What's going on?' she said.

He leaned next to Karalyn's ear. 'Wee bear,' he whispered, 'show me the bad man.'

In a second, his eyesight distorted, as colours whirled and whipped across his vision. It cleared. He was looking out of a small, round port-hole at the plains rushing by a hundred feet below.

Someone next to him coughed.

'Five minutes, your Majesty,' said the officer.

He glanced over the interior of the flying carriage at the dense ranks of Rahain soldiers strapped to their seats, and smiled.

Killop's vision snapped back to his body, and he staggered.

'Are you well?' Godfrey said. 'Jean, fetch the doctor.'

'No!' cried Killop. 'The Emperor, he's coming.'

Godfrey stood. 'I'm sorry?'

Killop stared at him. 'Use your vision powers.'

'There's no need, old chap,' Godfrey said. 'Our intelligence has the entire imperial army well within the bounds of the River Holdings.'

'Look to the skies.'

Godfrey strode to a large bay window, and opened the sliding door to the balcony. Jonah and Ariel followed, while Rosalind sat back and sipped her water.

Killop whispered to Karalyn. 'Find Kylon, wee bear, tell him to get ready.'

'Aye, daddy,' she said.

Godfrey stumbled back into the dining room, his face distraught. He put a hand onto the back of a chair to steady himself. Jonah and Ariel gathered next to him.

'What did you see?' said Ariel.

'Killop's right,' her father said. 'A dozen flying carriages from Rahain are approaching from the south. They'll be here in minutes.'

Rosalind rose. 'What? Here? They're coming here?'

Godfrey looked like he was about to explode at her, but his features softened, and he took her hand.

'I'm afraid so, dear.'

'Oh, Godfrey.'

Jonah ran back out onto the balcony, and Killop followed, holding onto Karalyn. Jonah leaned over the railings.

'Alarm!' he cried. 'Sound the alarm! The Emperor's coming!'

Down below, the workers close to the mansion looked up.

'Sound the alarm!' Jonah cried again, and some of those below reacted, running in the direction of the Old Tower. Killop gazed into the south, and scanned the horizon.

'I see them,' he said. 'Coming in low.'

Jonah stood next to him, and squinted into the distance.

'How did you know?' he cried.

'The wee girl can sense things,' he said. 'Like her mother.'

'I have to go,' Jonah said. 'With the Hold's militia down in the capital, someone has to rally the workers.'

'Tell them to run.'

'No,' Jonah said. 'I'm not giving up Hold Fast without a fight.'

He ran back into the dining room, and disappeared through a door. Killop walked back in. Celine was comforting Ariel, who was weeping. Godfrey and Rosalind were still standing in the same place, saying nothing.

'We must evacuate,' Killop said. 'There's still a few minutes.'

Godfrey put his hand on Killop's shoulder.

'Take Ariel, Celine and the children,' he said. 'Go to the stables by the square, and flee.'

'And you?'

'My place is here.' He turned to Rosalind. 'Our place is here.'

Killop nodded, and began pushing Celine and Ariel towards the door. He turned to Jean. 'You heard Holder Fast, get the children and meet me by the back porch in two minutes.'

Jean swithered for a second, then ran out of the room.

He leaned close to Karalyn. 'Where's Kylon, wee bear?'

His sight blurred and flickered, as his vision was transported to a dark bedroom, where a man was scrambling to get dressed.

Kylon, he said. *It's Killop.*

What happening? Kylon cried. *I got a garbled message from the wee one. Trouble?*

Half a dozen flying carriages filled with imperial soldiers are about to land, Killop said. *I've got Karalyn, Celine and Ariel, and Jean's away to fetch the other children.*

Kylon frowned. *Are we taking them along, boss?*

Aye.

They'll slow us down.

Don't start, Killop said. *We're heading to the rear porch, get your arse there as fast as you can.*

Kylon nodded, and Killop's vision zipped back to his own head.

He turned to Ariel. 'Listen to me,' he said, looking into her red eyes. She was shaking, despite Celine's arm over her shoulders. 'We're going to get out of here. You have to move. Your children need you.'

There was a loud noise from outside, the sound of something heavy striking the ground. The floor shook. A second later, Rahain voices shouted, and someone screamed.

Killop grabbed hold of Ariel's right arm and, with Celine on the other side, they pulled Ariel out of the room and ran towards the stairs. He didn't look back. They hauled Ariel down the steps, Killop gripping onto Karalyn at the same time, and raced towards the rear porch. As they reached the anteroom next to it, they skidded to a stop. Rahain soldiers were climbing the steps, armed with crossbows. The bodies of several estate workers lay sprawled across the gravel.

'Back,' Killop cried. 'Through the kitchen. There's a side exit.'

He kicked down a door, and they bolted through a servants' passageway, the sound of screaming coming from other parts of the mansion. They reached a large laundry room, which had a window facing the front of the great house. They ran to it, and peered out.

Two flying carriages were lying within yards of the steps leading up to the main doors, and dozens of Rahain soldiers were running towards the great house. Among them walked a solitary Holdings man, in black armour.

'Guilliam,' Celine whispered.

Ariel turned to Killop. 'My children.'

'Stay here,' he said to them. He passed Karalyn to Celine.

'Where are you going?' she said.

'To get Jean.' He kissed Karalyn on the forehead. 'Love you, wee bear. Back soon.'

He gazed around the laundry room, picked up a long wooden

paddle used for stirring the giant vats of washing, and ran to the door. He calculated the route from the children's room to the rear porch, and sprinted down the corridors of the mansion, the noise of struggle and terror all around.

He ran out into a wide passageway, and stumbled to a halt as a squad of Rahain wheeled round to face him. He dived back as crossbow bolts flew past him and over his head. One glanced off his right shoulder, taking half an inch of flesh with it. He cursed his lack of armour or weapons, and retreated, slamming a door behind him and barring it with the paddle. He doubled back and sprinted down another passageway. He reached a door, and opened it a crack, keeping silent.

The hall on the other side was clear. He went through, then ducked as he saw a large group of Rahain through an arched opening on the hall's right. He crouched behind the base of a marble fountain and stole a glance at them.

They had rounded up some of the staff, and were guarding them with crossbows. Killop swore as he saw Jean and the two children among them.

Teddy and Lydia were both shaking, their eyes fearful, as the soldiers lined them up against the wall. At the end of the passageway, the man in black armour appeared. Killop looked at him. He seemed like a normal Holdings man, though maybe taller than most. Apart from the blackened steel plate, he was unarmed. He approached the group of prisoners.

The Emperor stopped when he reached Jean.

'Where is Holder Fast?'

His voice was strong, and almost caused pain to Killop's ears. The prisoners cowered.

Jean shook her head.

'He's upstairs, in the dining room,' cried one of the staff, his eyes wild.

The Emperor pointed at him, and the man's head disintegrated in a flash of red. The body toppled to the floor, amid screams and wailing from the staff. The two children wept, near hysterics.

'I hate telltales,' the Emperor said, 'but I hate having to listen to this racket even more.' He glanced at the Rahain soldiers. 'Kill them all.'

He strode from the passageway, and walked past where Killop was hiding. Killop kept himself low until he had gone, then sprang to his feet. He ran heedless towards the passageway, as the soldiers aimed their crossbows at the prisoners.

Killop roared as they loosed. He reached the first soldier and throttled him, cracking his neck. He gazed down at the fallen bodies of the prisoners, then punched the next soldier, breaking his nose into his face. The other soldiers were reloading, and the thought of Karalyn swept over his mind. His red rage receded, and he ran back the way he had come. Crossbow bolts hit the wall next to his head, and he felt a sting in his left thigh. He crashed through a doorway, and ran for his life, barrelling through storage rooms and empty corridors. The smell of smoke reached his nose.

As soon as he knew the pursuit had ceased, he fell to his knees, and vomited over the floor. The imprint of what he had seen shone in his mind, and guilt surged through him. He had been too slow. He had frozen when the Emperor had walked past his hiding place. He should have acted sooner.

Teddy and Lydia.

He imagined how he would feel if it had been Karalyn, and he almost broke. Instead, he hauled himself to his feet, and began running back towards the laundry room. As he approached, there was a great roar from above, and the ceiling over his head burst into flames. He ducked down, and kept running, the heat intensifying. In every room and corridor he passed through, the wooden beams holding up the floor above were burning, as if a great inferno had consumed the upper storeys of the mansion.

At last, he reached the corridor leading to the laundry room. As he was about to sprint across the gap, the door to his left flew open, and the Emperor strode through. He walked into the laundry room, and paused.

Killop could see Celine, Karalyn and Ariel huddling in the corner as the Emperor approached them. He clenched his fists, rage taking hold of him. He ran into the room, whispering a silent apology to Daphne. He had failed, but at least he would die defending his family.

The Emperor's glance passed over the group crouching in the corner, and he strode from the room.

Killop stopped, his mouth open in disbelief.

'Daddy,' Karalyn cried, and ran to him, hugging his leg.

Celine rose to her feet. 'Did you see that?' she sobbed. 'He walked right past, like he didn't even see us.'

'Karalyn hide from the bad man,' the little girl said, as Killop picked her up and hugged her.

Ariel glanced over. 'My children? Did you see them?'

Killop swallowed. 'They're waiting for us at the stables.'

Ariel nodded, and got to her feet.

Celine took Karalyn, and they left the laundry room, keeping silent as they headed towards the kitchens. They passed the bodies of two young servants lying dead, bleeding from their vacant eye sockets.

'Bastard,' Celine muttered. 'Why's he doing this? If he's after mages, he must know Daphne's in the old capital.'

Ariel shook her head, her eyes tired and red. 'Revenge against the Holdfasts. The Emperor's always hated us. Daddy's rebellion has given him the excuse he needed.'

They crept through the kitchens, past abandoned pots bubbling on the stoves, and a dead servant lying sprawled among a pile of broken dishes.

'There's the door,' Celine whispered, pointing ahead.

They ran into the deserted hallway. The side door was lying open, letting in a shaft of sunlight. Killop peered through the gap. Across the gravel was the market square, its canvas covering aflame in a sea of fire. To the left, the stables were also burning. Dozens of Rahain soldiers were outside, corralling a large group of workers. Killop squinted through the smoke. There was no sign of Kylon.

'We can't leave this way,' he said. 'Too many soldiers.'

'Let me look,' said Ariel as she leaned towards the door.

CHRISTOPHER MITCHELL

'What'll we do, boss?' Celine said, clutching on to Karalyn.

There was a great roar from outside, and Killop edged to the door beside Ariel. A large group of armed Holdings was charging the Rahain. Several fell as the soldiers aimed their crossbows at them, but the Holdings soon reached the Rahain, and engaged at close quarters.

'Leave them to me,' a voice echoed, and Killop flinched from its raw power.

The Emperor strode towards the fray. With a wave of his hand, the Rahain soldiers were flung backwards, leaving the Holdings exposed. In their centre stood Jonah.

'A Holdfast,' the Emperor said. He waved his other hand, and every Holdings fighter fell, their eyes bulging and bleeding, except for Ariel's brother.

Jonah stood alone and defiant as the Emperor smirked, and strode towards him.

'Do you want to hear how your mother and father begged for their lives?' he said, his voice like a razor through the mind. 'How they pleaded on their knees before me? Your family has long been a hindrance to my plans.' He stopped a yard from Jonah. He flicked his finger, and the Holdings man fell to his knees. 'But the main reason I'm here,' he said, 'is to hurt your sister. She betrayed me, and I want her to know her family is dead before I kill her.'

He raised his hand, and Jonah's eyes burst from his head. His body collapsed to the ground.

'No!' screamed Ariel, and before Killop could grab her, she bolted from the door, flying towards her brother.

The Emperor turned, and stretched out his arm. Ariel exploded into a thousand pieces of flesh, her remains covering the gravel outside the mansion in a circle of deep red.

Killop fell back behind the door, as the Emperor stared in their direction. Karalyn burrowed her head into his chest.

'Wee bear hide,' she said, as Celine huddled in from the other side.

'Come on,' Killop said, getting up. He picked up a large knife from the kitchen counter. 'Follow me.'

They retraced their steps through the burning mansion, passing the corpses of dead servants, and skirting groups of soldiers. They reached the south wing, where the flames had yet to reach, and stole their way through deserted chambers until they came to Godfrey's private study. Killop bolted the door, and Celine crashed down into an armchair, out of breath, Karalyn clinging to her.

There was an old sword attached to the wall above Godfrey's desk, and Killop reached up and took it down. He strapped it to his belt, and walked to the balcony doors. The view from the study overlooked a steep slope, at the bottom of which were workers' cottages, all aflame. Rahain soldiers stood before them, watching them burn. A pile of bodies lay in the middle of the road.

He turned to Celine and Karalyn.

'We're getting out of here,' he said.

Celine nodded.

'Help me,' he said, and they began ransacking the room. Celine found a bag, and they packed it with the snacks they knew Godfrey kept in a drawer, along with a full water skin, and a bottle of rum. They shoved a map into the bag, and Celine slid an old hunting knife they found into her boot.

Killop knelt by Karalyn.

'Where's the bad man?' he said. 'Is he close?'

Karalyn shook her head. 'The bad man is killing the horses in the stables.'

Killop nodded. He got up, and gazed out of the window. There were at least eight soldiers at the bottom of the steep slope.

'Wait here,' he said, as Celine joined him at the balcony door. 'Bring Karalyn when I signal.'

Before she could respond, Killop slipped out of the door, and jumped over the balcony railing, landing on the gravel. He crouched in the deep shadow of the mansion, and began to edge his way down the slope. The soldiers were all watching the fires consume the workers' cottages, and as Killop reached the bottom of the slope, he drew his sword.

He took a breath, and crept across the gravel without making a sound. He slashed down, striking a soldier from behind, then jumped into their midst, swinging his arm at anything within reach. He felled another, then another, charging and rushing, before a crossbow bolt hit his right thigh. He sprang forwards, grabbing a soldier by the throat in his left hand, while he lashed out with the sword, killing another. He spun round, and saw the remaining four soldiers aiming their crossbows at him.

'Shit.'

The soldiers fell, their hands grasping their faces as their eyes rolled up into their heads. Killop blinked. His daughter?

He looked up.

'That was stupid,' said Celine, reaching the bottom of the slope with Karalyn in her arms. 'Are you trying to get yourself killed? You're lucky little bear was here to save you.'

Killop sheathed his sword, reached down, and pulled the crossbow bolt from his thigh, grunting with pain. Celine handed him a rag from her pack, and he tied it round his leg.

'Can you walk?' she said.

Killop nodded, then drew his sword again as an armed figure appeared by the cottages, running towards them.

'Kylon,' he said.

'Back porch is swarming with Rahain,' Kylon said, catching his breath. He gazed at Celine and Karalyn. 'Ariel and her bairns not make it?'

Killop shook his head.

He pushed on, despite the pain, and the others followed, half-running, along the bottom of the steep slope towards the wide driveway that led from the front of the mansion. Two flying carriages were sitting before the grand steps leading to the main entrance, and soldiers were standing guard. Killop peered in the opposite direction. The road leading away from the estate house was empty, and they set off again, keeping the main road to their right.

The slope levelled off, and they stopped. Killop looked back. The mansion, and every other building of the estate, was burning. Great pillars of smoke were rising, and among them were flying carriages, taking off and departing, one after the other.

'I messed up, boss,' said Kylon behind him. He turned.

'How?'

'I'm supposed to be looking after Karalyn,' he said, 'and when I was needed, I was sleeping off a hangover.'

'It was Celine's shift,' Killop said, 'and she did fine.'

'It doesn't matter,' Kylon said, his eyes burning. 'From now on, I'm always on shift. I won't let you down again.'

They gazed at the cauldron of fire engulfing the estate. Celine joined them, holding Karalyn, who turned her head to watch the fires.

Killop kissed his daughter on the top of her head.

'You're a brave wee girl,' he said. 'You saved us today.'

He glanced at Celine and Kylon, and covered his daughter's ears.

'Let's get the fuck out of here.'

CHAPTER 15
THE SCENE OF THE CRIME

T ahrana Valley, Imperial Rahain – 15th Day, Second Third
Autumn 507

A chill autumnal wind blew off the Rahain mountains, blustering down the long and deep valley. The small group of travellers sat together, sheltering behind the remains of a brick wall. To their right flowed a river, its clear waters glistening through the abandoned and devastated remains of Akhanawarah City. Acres of burnt-out streets and buildings lined the banks of the river, while mud and pools of viscous, oily liquid covered the ground. By the edge of the water, some life was returning. Reeds and grasses bent in the wind, and a few thorny bushes clung to the deteriorating brickwork of the old quays, their roots reaching down into the clean water.

'This place stinks,' said Dean.

'Yes,' said Laodoc. 'Maybe we were wrong to come here.' He glanced at his companions. 'I'm sorry my sense of morbid curiosity has led us to this place of death, but I felt I couldn't pass it without stopping by to take a look.'

'Should we head back to the wagons?' said Dyam.

'We're close to the centre,' Bedig said. 'I think I'd like to see it again.'

'Thank you for guiding us, my friend,' Laodoc said. 'I know it must be painful for you, but maybe something here will spark your memory about the location of Silverstream.'

'I don't see how,' Bridget said, gazing around at the charred brick walls and toppled masonry. 'Keira did a pretty thorough job.'

Dyam nodded. 'I had no idea how big this place was.'

Agang pulled the stopper from a water skin, drank, then passed it to Laodoc.

'Remember to keep some of that for later,' Bridget said. 'That's the only clean water we've got. The rest of us will be fine, but you two should drink only that until we're clear of the city.'

Laodoc nodded as he took a sip.

'I should be able to heal myself if I ingest any toxins,' Agang said.

'I'm the only frail one here,' Laodoc smiled. 'What with your healing powers, and the Kellach's natural immunity, it appears that, here in Rahain, I am the one in danger. Ironic.'

'Why did they do it?' asked Dean. 'The city, I mean. Why did the Rahain destroy it?'

'Fear,' said Laodoc. 'The government was afraid that the Rakanese would spread, that this city was only a first step to overwhelming the Rahain population. Lies, exaggerations and ignorance did the rest. It was like the ruling party was in the grip of mass hysteria. The siege nearly bankrupted the republic, leaving it open to invasion. The alliance was supposed to be in response to this great crime, to bring justice to those who had carried it out, but now I believe it was just an excuse, and that the Holdings wanted to dominate the world from the beginning.'

'Not all the Holdings,' said Bedig. 'I met plenty of fine folk up in Plateau City, when I was living with Daphne and her family.'

'Aye,' said Dyam, 'and how many young ladies did you get to know?'

'One or two.'

Bridget whacked him on the arm.

'Ow,' he yelled. 'I couldnae help it.'

'He has a point,' Laodoc smiled. 'Being a tall, handsome, exotic foreigner in the imperial capital turned a few heads towards Bedig. I remember it well.'

'Aye?' Bridget said. 'But I'd rather not fucking have to hear it, thank you very much.'

They laughed, and Laodoc thought what a strange noise it made in such bleak surroundings. Though most of the bodies had long gone, rendered to ash by Keira, or disintegrated over time, a few blackened bones still littered the side of the river, or protruded from stagnant pools like pale reeds. A sense of shame thickened his blood, and he bowed his head.

'Are you alright?' Agang asked.

He shook his head. 'This is where everything turned bad. My sons, my country. We committed the most heinous of crimes, and our punishment has been commensurate. We have lost everything.'

'I like you, Laodoc,' Dyam said, 'but don't expect me to have much sympathy for Rahain. I lost my family too, when your soldiers invaded our lands.'

'We have all been wronged,' said Agang. 'My land was stripped bare by the Holdings for years before we were organised enough to fight back. But then we went and did the same to them.' He shook his head. 'It pains me to say it,' he went on, 'but the empire is a good idea. Imagine all five peoples living in peace, deciding their differences by talking, instead of killing each other. I'd love to see the other lands of this world. The wide plains of the Holdings that Daphne used to talk about, or the city of Arakhanah, where Shella comes from. It's all out there, waiting for us to stop slaughtering our neighbours and come to our senses.'

'It sounds like a dream,' said Bridget.

'It is,' said Laodoc. 'It is we who have turned it into a nightmare. Our petty prejudices, our greed, and our pride. They have brought us to our knees.'

'So we find Shella,' Bridget said, 'and bring her and Keira together. Then hope Kalayne was right.'

'What if Shella doesn't want to see Keira?' Lola said.

'Aye,' said Bonnie. 'I mean, look around and imagine this used to be your home. Would you want to meet the person that destroyed it?'

'We'll worry about that if it happens,' Bridget said.

'Shella knows it was the Rahain that did it,' Bedig said.

Dean glanced at the big Brig man. 'Can she really kill folk just by waving her hand at them?'

Bedig nodded. 'Aye.'

'Like the Emperor,' said Agang, 'and Keira.'

Bedig frowned. 'So, is the plan that Keira and Shella will fight the Emperor?'

'Who knows?' said Bridget. 'Agang?'

The Sanang man shrugged. 'Kalayne didn't say how it would happen, just that they have to meet.'

Bonnie shook her head.

'Don't bite yer tongue,' Bridget said. 'If ye've got something to say, say it.'

'I'm committed to the job, boss,' Bonnie said, 'but it seems like a fool's errand to me.'

'Maybe it is,' Bridget said. 'It's better than sitting on our arses doing nothing, but. Talking of which, let's get moving. I want to be out of the city by nightfall.'

They got to their feet, some pulling packs over their shoulders. They had left the majority of their luggage with the wagons, hidden in some trees where the edge of the hills met the city, and were travelling light. Laodoc was carrying nothing but a walking stick, and he used it to help him stand.

Bedig took the lead, and they left the shelter of the wall, and walked to the edge of the river, avoiding the oily, stinking pools of mud along the way. By the water ran a long brick-paved walkway. Parts of it had fallen away into the river, but it was easier to navigate than the debris-strewn streets. Laodoc had a light headache from the tainted air, but he managed to keep up with the others as they made their way towards the centre of the ruined city. The remains of the buildings to their left grew taller, with some over one storey high, though the inner floors had been destroyed. Blackened and charred bricks were everywhere, heaps of them littering the streets. They came to a canal branching to their left.

'This way,' said Bedig, and they turned to follow it. The waterway was full, its gate long broken, and it stretched for a hundred yards until they reached a great open square, covered in oily patches and bones.

Bedig halted.

'That was the palace,' he said, pointing to the ruins on the right hand side of the square. He swung his arm round to the left. 'And that was Shella's headquarters, where I lived.'

'With Leah?' said Agang.

'Aye, and Kylon.'

'Shit,' said Bonnie. 'Everyone, get down.'

She crouched by the remains of a wall at the edge of the square, the others joining her.

'What is it?' asked Bridget.

'Someone's been here,' she said, 'recently. Look.'

She pointed over in the direction of the palace. The ruins were surrounded by a large, walled garden, its orchards shrivelled and dead.

Dyam frowned. 'What am I supposed to be looking at?'

'There,' Bonnie said. 'That's a fresh midden, among the stumps of the trees.'

Laodoc squinted, and peered into the gardens. At last he saw what Bonnie was pointing at. There was a knee-high pile of rubbish over in the furthest corner from the ruins of the palace.

'How do ye know it's fresh?' asked Bridget, her voice low.

Bonnie shook her head. 'Ye can tell that none of ye are hunters. There's fish bones on the top, I can see them from here.'

'Let's take a closer look,' Bridget said. 'Follow me and stay low.'

She set off at a run, crouching as she raced across the square towards the wall enclosing the palace gardens. Agang helped Laodoc to his feet, and they followed Bridget, keeping to the dry sections of the brickwork underfoot. The wall was three feet high, and they huddled behind it, peering over.

Laodoc gazed into the gardens. The rubbish heap was clear to him now, but more alarming were the tents and wagons positioned under the eaves of the palace wall to their left.

'Pyre's tits,' muttered Bridget. 'Who are they?'

'Judging by the number of tents,' said Bonnie, 'I'd say there's a dozen or so of them. No one seems to be home at the moment, though.'

'If they're Rakanese,' Laodoc said, 'they might be able to help us find Silverstream.'

'Want me to go and check, boss?' Bonnie said.

'Aye,' nodded Bridget.

'Be careful,' said Lola. 'They could be in the palace right now, watching us.'

Bonnie caught her eye and smiled. She pulled off her pack, laid it on the ground, and ran by the side of the wall towards the palace gates. She gazed around, then sprinted into the gardens, keeping low through the lines of ruined tree trunks. At the corner of the palace, she disappeared out of sight, and the others stared at the tents, waiting for her to re-appear.

There was a strangled cry.

'Shit,' said Lola, rising.

'Wait,' said Bridget.

'No way.'

'If Bonnie just walked into a trap,' Bridget said, 'then I don't want you following her in. We need to think.'

'No,' said Lola, 'we need to fight.'

Bridget frowned, scanning the gardens for movement. 'Right, here's what we're going to do...'

'Come out from behind the wall,' shouted a voice in Rahain. 'We have your friend.'

'Who are you?' Bridget called out.

'Come out or we'll kill her.'

'Lola,' Bridget said, 'stay down. Take Dean with you, and find another way in.'

The Lach hunter nodded.

Bridget and the others stood, their arms raised. She gave a quick nod to Lola and Dean, who were still crouching, and began to walk towards the palace gates.

'We're not here to fight,' she shouted as they reached the edge of the gardens. 'Show us our friend.'

'Come over and you'll see her,' cried the voice.

Bridget glanced at the others. Dyam frowned.

'I'll go,' said Laodoc. 'They won't shoot an old man.'

'No,' said Agang.

Laodoc smiled, and strode through the gates before anyone could stop him.

'Greetings,' he said, coming closer to the tents. He glanced around, but could see no one. 'We are merely passing through this place, and desire nothing more than to be on our way.'

He passed the corner of the ruined palace and halted, his tongue flickering. Bonnie was lying in a pool of blood, three crossbow bolts protruding from her chest. Her lifeless eyes stared up at the sky.

As he was about to cry out, he saw a Rahain woman staring at him from a scorched window frame, her crossbow aiming at his head. The woman smiled.

'Keep your hands in the air,' cried the voice, and Laodoc glanced up. More Rahain were on the upper storey, pointing their weapons down at him from the ruins. One man was out on a half-collapsed balcony. 'Call for the others,' he said.

'How dare you,' Laodoc said. 'We are peaceful travellers.'

'Of course you are,' the man said, 'and you just happened to sneak into our camp as we were about to pack up and leave? Do you think I'm stupid? We haven't spent the last third working our arses off just to be robbed at the last minute.'

Laodoc gazed up at the Rahain, and frowned. Their bodies were covered in sores and rashes, and several looked underweight.

'You've been looting the palace?' he said.

'None of your fucking business,' the man said. 'Now, call the others.'

'No.'

'I'll have you shot.'

'I don't care.'

'Tiana!' the man yelled. 'Grab that son of a whore. Put your crossbow to his fucking head.'

The woman on the lower floor jumped through the window, and approached Laodoc. She too, he noticed, had blisters and rashes on her face and arms.

'You crazy old bastard,' she cried, raising her crossbow and pointing it in his face. She wheeled round, until she was facing Bridget and the others.

'Get over here,' Tiana cried, 'or I'll shoot him in the eye.'

Laodoc watched in silence as Bridget, Bedig, Dyam and Agang approached. Tiana kept her crossbow an inch away from his nose.

The group stopped when they saw Bonnie.

'You bastards,' Bridget cried. 'What the fuck did ye do that for?'

'She was sneaking through our property,' the man yelled from the balcony. 'Now, throw down your weapons.'

'We can take them,' muttered Bedig, his face twisted in anger. 'Rush the entrance, get up there and kill them.'

'But how many would die?' whispered Bridget. 'You and Agang are the only hand to hand fighters here.'

'But we cannae just surrender.'

'Lola and Dean,' she said, unbuckling her sword belt, 'they'll find a way.'

Agang followed her lead, and threw down his sword, then Dyam did the same.

'You too,' shouted the man, 'you giant red-headed freak. Drop your sword.'

Bedig cursed, and did so.

The Rahain woman named Tiana backed away from Laodoc, and turned her weapon to Bridget.

'Are you in charge?' she said.

'Aye.'

The woman pulled the trigger, and shot Bridget in the stomach. She grunted, and staggered backwards. Bedig raised his fists, but Agang grabbed his arm, pulling him back.

'I'll heal her,' he said. 'Don't get yourself shot too.'

Dyam and Agang rushed to Bridget, who was writhing on the ground in agony.

'All of you,' shouted the man on the balcony. 'Get inside.'

The Rahain woman waved her crossbow, and shepherded them into the ruins of the palace, with Agang and Dyam carrying Bridget. Laodoc noticed the Brig woman's cries fade, and glanced over. Agang was sweating in concentration as he helped carry her. He noticed Laodoc's gaze, and nodded.

'I can't do too much just now,' he whispered, 'or they'll get suspicious. But I've eased her pain.'

They were led into a large, empty chamber, where they were met by the Rahain from the upper storey. Dyam and Agang put Bridget down by a wall, and Bedig knelt by her, taking her hand.

Their leader paced up and down, staring at them.

'Three Kellach, an old Rahain and a Sanang,' he said. 'Are you their guide?' he asked Laodoc.

'Let us go.'

The man smirked. 'I'm guessing that you hired yourself some muscle,' he said, 'and came to see what you could find. Well, tough shit, old man, we were here first. Everything in those wagons is ours.'

'We don't want whatever you've robbed from this tomb,' Laodoc said. 'You make me sick.'

The man nodded to Tiana, and the woman sprang forward and clubbed Laodoc with the butt of her crossbow. He fell to the floor. Agang crouched by his side, raising a protective arm. Laodoc gazed up from where he lay. Agang placed his hand on his arm, and within seconds, he felt himself heal.

'Think yer a bunch of heroes, do ye?' Dyam shouted. 'Punching old men, and shooting unarmed women.'

The man leered at her. 'We might keep you, blondie. There's Old Free still willing to pay for young Kellach flesh.'

'We should kill them all, boss,' Tiana said.

'Yeah, probably,' he said, 'though the red-haired guy might get us some cash, as well as the blonde one.'

'Too much hassle, boss.'

The man rubbed his chin. 'I'll think on it.' He turned to the rest of his crew. 'Get the last of the stuff into the wagons, then dismantle the camp. We're leaving in an hour.' He glanced at Tiana. 'Take three and guard the prisoners.'

The Rahain woman nodded.

The man left the chamber, accompanied by the majority of the others, leaving Tiana and three Rahain, all armed with crossbows. Laodoc moved into a sitting position, and the others crouched down as well. Bedig remained by Bridget, ignoring everything else in the room. Agang edged along to them.

'Pull out the bolt,' he muttered.

'No speaking!' Tiana yelled.

The Brig man blinked.

'Sorry, babe,' he whispered, and yanked the bolt from Bridget's stomach. She convulsed in agony, blood pouring from her wound. Agang raised his hand towards her.

'Get away from her!' screamed Tiana. 'Stop moving, and stop talking, or I'll kill you all.'

Laodoc caught Agang's eye, and stood.

'Please, miss,' he said, his arms outstretched.

Tiana strode forwards and struck him again, as Agang's fingers reached out and made contact with Bridget's side. Laodoc smiled as he fell. Dyam knelt by him, shaking her head.

'Thank you,' she mouthed.

This time, Laodoc had to ride the pain out on his own, as Agang was next to Bedig and Bridget, out of arm's reach. He felt his cheek, and his fingers came away bloody.

The prisoners sat in silence and the guards settled down, squatting or sitting against the opposite wall. Through the open doorway behind them, Laodoc watched as other members of the crew passed by with filled crates, on their way outside to where the wagons were parked.

The next few minutes seemed like an eternity to Laodoc, his head sore and his body aching from his fall. The crew stopped work and filed outside. Their leader came back into the room, leading a young Rakanese woman by a chain linked to a collar round her neck. The woman's face was bruised and covered in the same rashes as the Rahain, and her hands were tied behind her back.

'We're ready to go,' he said.

Tiana leapt to her feet. 'Let me kill them, boss.'

The man frowned, gazing down at the row of prisoners.

'I don't know,' he said. 'I'm still inclined to take the blonde one, and him.' He pointed at Bedig. 'I know it'll be a right pain in the ass, but we'll get a good price for those two.'

'So I can kill the rest?'

As the man was about to speak, there was a loud noise from outside of something catching fire, followed by shouts and cries from the Rahain crew.

'Shit,' the man said, turning. 'Stay here.'

He ran from the room.

'But...' Tiana said, then frowned. She stared at the prisoners. 'You know,' she said, 'I'm gonna pretend I heard him say yes.'

She glanced at the other three guards. 'Get over here and cover me.'

They got to their feet and approached, their crossbows levelled.

'Please,' Laodoc said. 'You can't...'

'Watch me,' Tiana said. She walked to the end of the line, where Bedig sat next to Bridget. The Brig woman was lying unconscious, but her bleeding had stopped.

'Let's start with her,' the Rahain woman said, and shot Bridget in the throat.

She began to reload, but Bedig sprang up and slammed into her. As they fell to the ground, her crossbow went off, and a bolt struck Agang's chest, sending him falling to the ground. The three other guards jumped back in fright. One of them aimed at Bedig, and shot him in the back. Dyam pulled a knife from her boot and jumped at the nearest guard.

Laodoc shrank back against the wall, pulling Agang towards him. The Sanang man's eyes were closed. Laodoc reached out with both hands and freed the bolt from Agang's chest. He threw it down and held onto his friend.

He ducked as the Rahain woman was flung over his head, crashing into the wall, and falling lifeless to the ground. Laodoc glanced up. Bedig was strangling a Rahain man, as Dyam faced off against another guard, her knife bloodied. As Bedig crushed the guard's skull, the leader burst back into the room, a sword in his hand. He lunged forwards and slashed Bedig down the back, then thrust the blade between his shoulder blades, the point protruding from his ribs.

Bedig collapsed to the ground, and the man pulled his sword from his back. He smiled at Dyam, who retreated, her knife grasped in her right hand, the other guard dead by her feet.

'Your friends set fire to my wagons, you bitch,' he cried, advancing with his sword. Dyam moved back until she was against the wall. 'I'm going to enjoy killing you.'

He raised his sword.

Agang grunted, and reached out with his hand, grabbing hold of the Rahain man's ankle. He dropped the sword, his face contorted in pain, and fell to his knees. His eyes sank back into their sockets, and he collapsed to the floor, dead.

Laodoc clung onto Agang. 'My friend, you are alive!'

Agang nodded. He tried to speak, but coughed, his breath raspy.

Lola ran into the chamber, her sword dripping blood, and her eyes in a fighting frenzy. She glared about the room, her teeth bared.

'Lola!' cried Dyam. 'It's us.'

Lola gazed at the bodies of Bridget and Bedig, and broke down, sobs wracking her body. Dean appeared in the doorway, his empty hands shaking.

Dyam staggered forward. 'Dean. What's going on outside? Dean?'

The young mage looked up. 'Lola went mental when she saw Bonnie. She killed them all.'

Dyam dropped the knife and fell to her knees, staring at the bodies of Bridget and Bedig.

Laodoc felt Agang pull himself from his grasp, and crawl across the floor to where the bodies of the two Brig lay. The Sanang man drew himself up and sat on the ground between them, gazing from one to the other. His head hung low, and exhaustion was etched into his face.

'Who?'

Dyam looked at him, her eyes wide. 'Who what?'

'Who do I try to save?'

Dyam's mouth hung open, but no words came out. Laodoc moved to Agang's side.

'Please do what you can, my friend,' he said.

Agang turned to Bridget.

'Pull the bolt out for me.'

The others gathered round and Laodoc ripped the crossbow bolt from Bridget's neck. Blood seeped from the wound. Agang placed his hands on the sides of Bridget's head, and closed his eyes, while the others stared in silence.

For a long moment nothing happened, then Laodoc saw the hole in Bridget's neck heal, and some colour return to her pale skin. Sweat was pouring down Agang's face. He cried out, and collapsed onto the ground. Dyam put her face to his chest.

'He's breathing,' she said.

'What about Bridget?' Dean said, his voice wavering.

Dyam reached out and held onto the Brig woman's hand.

Bridget coughed up blood, her eyes opening. Dyam leaned her head to the side, and she vomited blood down her tunic and onto the ground. Dyam started crying, the tears rolling down her cheeks.

Bridget tried to speak, but her voice was husky and hoarse.

'Rest,' said Laodoc, stroking the hair from her eyes. 'Rest.'

Lola leaned over with a skin of water, and held it to Bridget's lips.

She drank. Her eyes were cloudy and red, and her breath sounded painful and harsh.

Laodoc stood, as tears threatened to come. He watched the others crowd round Bridget, staring at her with a mixture of relief and disbelief. A few yards away, Bedig's body lay alone, the blood pooling under him. Laodoc walked to the door, went through the corridor, and emerged back into the grey light of the afternoon. The wagons were burnt-out shells. Smoke still rose from the smouldering remains of the valuables that had been packed into the crates and boxes. The corpses of the Rahain looters littered the ground. Four had arrows piercing them, while the others had been hacked to pieces. Bonnie's body remained where she had fallen, blood soaking the earth around her.

Laodoc wept.

He heard a noise, and noticed Dean standing beside him.

Laodoc turned to the young man. 'We might all have died, were it not for you and Lola.'

Dean nodded, but kept his eyes downcast.

They both turned as a strange voice called to them. Laodoc scanned the side of the palace wall and saw the Rakanese woman, chained to a twisted railing by a gate.

'Hello,' he said to her.

The young woman gazed at him. She looked to be in her teens, but the bruises and rash on her face made it difficult to tell. Laodoc approached. He opened his hands.

'You're free now,' he said. 'You're safe.'

She said something in a language he didn't understand.

'Help me, Dean,' he said. 'Go back inside and search their leader's body for keys.'

The young man ran off. Laodoc smiled at the woman, then pointed at himself.

'Laodoc,' he said.

The woman frowned, then did the same. 'Tara.'

Dean re-emerged from the palace with a set of keys, passed them to

Laodoc, and the old man unlocked the heavy padlock connecting the woman to the chains. She threw them to the ground, and spat on them.

'Does anyone speak Rakanese?' Dean said.

Laodoc paused. 'Only Bedig did, I think.' He gazed at Tara. 'Silverstream?'

The woman blinked. She stared at Laodoc and Dean, then nodded.

'Let's get her some water,' he said to Dean, 'she's probably...'

His voice was cut off by the sound of a scream, ripped from Bridget's lungs. Laodoc bowed his head.

He walked back into the palace, Dean and Tara following. They came into the chamber. Bridget was leaning over Bedig's body, crying and keening; while around her, the others wept. Agang was sitting in silence next to them, his face drained of energy and emotion.

Laodoc put his hand onto the Brig woman's shoulder, then knelt and embraced her. Dyam joined them, and together they mourned over the body of Bedig.

CHAPTER 16
HOLDER FAST

Holdings City, Holdings Republic – 16th Day, Second Third Autumn 507

'You're not thinking straight,' said Chane. She passed the lit weed-stick to Daphne, as they sat crouched by the wall of the stables. 'Not that I blame you. After what happened, you're entitled to freak out, but don't throw your life away. Killop and Karalyn are safe in the Red Hills, remember the plan.'

Daphne said nothing. She gazed down at her uniform, the steel chestplate, the leathers, the armour covering her left arm, and the sword buckled to her belt. Her right hand was shaking, not from fear at the approaching army of Rahain, but with the desire to kill.

From all around came the noise of the emptying city. Most of the civilians and loyal republican forces had already left the Holdings capital, the militia of Hold Fast having elected to be the last to leave. She glanced over at the Upper City, searching for the signal flag that would let them know the evacuation was complete, and they could withdraw, but saw nothing.

'We'll be out of here soon,' Chane said, following her gaze. She smiled. 'We've just got to keep it together for a few more days. You're as tough as a nag's hide, Daphne. I can only imagine what you're feeling right now, but the soldiers are looking for you to lead them out of here, not to their deaths.'

'I kill him, I end the war.'

'Yeah,' Chane said. 'Just the small problem of sixty thousand Rahain soldiers protecting him. Look, I understand. If it were me, I'd want to go out there and kick his arse. But you can't. You have a daughter, not to mention being a proper lady now. You've got responsibilities.'

Daphne took a drag of the weedstick. Vast acres of her thoughts gave her nothing but pain, and smoking helped numb her a little. Part of her wished she could lie down in a darkened room and take some dullweed to block everything out, but she knew Chane was right. She had two thousand soldiers depending on her orders. If she did what she wanted to do, and charged out to fight the Creator, what would happen to them? What would Annifrid, their commander, do? And Chane? Would she run away, or would she die by Daphne's side? She thought back to her vision meeting with Karalyn that morning. Her daughter was still withdrawn and quiet after the massacre on the estate, and had pleaded with her mother, begging her to come north to where she and Killop were sheltering in safety.

Her mind turned to Ariel, and the children. She closed her eyes.

'Holder Fast?'

Daphne gazed up to see a tall officer standing close by.

'Yes, Lieutenant?'

'The commander would like to inform you that the imperial army has been spotted on the road south, marching towards the city.'

Daphne nodded.

'Shall I pass on a message, my lady?'

'No,' Daphne said, getting to her feet and stubbing the weedstick beneath her heel. 'I'll speak to her myself. Is she still in the south tower?'

'Yes, my lady.'

She waited until Chane was standing next to her, then turned for the main street, keeping her head high as she walked, a mask of calm impenetrability fixed to her face. Soldiers bowed as she passed, some muttering greetings. She nodded to them, her eyes hard and determined. Ahead was the great enclosing wall of the Holdings capital, the stone-built defensive line surrounding the narrow streets of the Lower City. The main road south went through a massive set of gates, and to their left was the south tower, a four-storey fortification that had stood for hundreds of years, guarding the way to the River Holdings.

Guards saluted her as she passed into the ground floor of the tower. She ascended the steps to the roof level, where a group of junior officers had assembled. Annifrid stood at their centre, her hands grasping the stone battlements as they gazed south.

'Commander,' Daphne said, walking into their midst, and taking her place by the wall. She looked down at the great road heading south by the river. On either side were fields and cottages, and in the distance, the towns of the River Holdings could be seen. A great cloud of dust covered half the horizon. At its base marched the imperial army, sixty thousand Rahain infantry, their front lines carrying enormous door-sized shields.

'Holder Fast,' Annifrid bowed, 'the company are ready to evacuate on your orders.'

Daphne glanced over at the Upper City. No flag. She gazed back at the advancing Rahain. Somewhere, amid the mass of armour and flesh, was the Creator. She clenched her right fist. Chane elbowed her way to the front to stand next to her, and looked out at the approaching army.

'Our cavalry will trash those bastards once we get them onto the plains,' she said, casting her voice loud enough for the rest of the officers to hear.

Daphne ignored her. She sent her vision out towards the army, flying over the road, then passing the line of door-shields. She saw him. The Creator made flesh. Flanked by thousands of Rahain soldiers, he was riding a grey horse. His body was covered in black armour, but he bore no weapon.

Lady Holdfast? his voice echoed, cutting through her thoughts. *Spying on me? Come to see the man who killed your family?*

Daphne pulled on every defence Kalayne had taught her, and snapped back to her body. She swayed, her face almost cracking. Chane put a hand on hers.

'Take a breath,' she whispered.

Daphne wanted to scream, but instead she turned to face her officers.

'The evacuation of the city is almost complete,' she said, gazing at them. 'Our job now is to make sure the Hold Fast Company get out in one piece, while slowing down the enemy army's advance if possible. To that end, I want every even-numbered squadron to pull back immediately to the defensive line at the junction of Nethertown and Market Lane.' She nodded to her lieutenants. 'Now, if you please.'

Half of the officers bowed, then rushed down the stairs to their units.

'Holder Fast,' Annifrid frowned, 'may I point out that the evacuation signal flag has not yet been raised over the Upper City?'

'It hadn't escaped my notice, Commander,' Daphne said. 'It will take thirty minutes to get half the company through to the defensive line. If we wait until the flag is raised, then we won't have enough time to get everyone out before the enemy attacks.'

'But my lady, there won't be sufficient soldiers to defend the wall.'

Daphne shook her head. 'This wall isn't going to stop the Emperor. If Keira the fire mage could blow a hole through the defences of the imperial city, which are thicker and taller than these, then the Emperor isn't going to have much of a problem getting through.'

Annifrid opened her mouth to speak.

'Don't worry, Commander,' Daphne said, 'I'll be here until the flag is raised, you can count on that.'

'Very well, my lady.'

Daphne glanced at the advancing army, about two miles away.

'All right,' she said, 'get every soldier down from the wall. I want first, third and fifth squadrons operating the catapults, and all the others positioned at least two streets back. Have them assemble into their squads, and wait for the Emperor to break through. He'll probably go for the gates, so concentrate in that area, but he may hit anywhere on the southern perimeter, so be ready to move wherever you're needed. And remember to keep an eye on the Upper City. As soon as you see that flag, get your soldiers to the assembly point by the royal ramp. Understood?'

They bowed, and left the roof, departing by the stairs to the lower floors. Annifrid joined Chane and Daphne by the battlements, and they watched the slow advance of the Rahain. Chane passed round cigarettes, and they smoked in the morning sunshine.

Annifrid fidgeted. 'May I say something, my lady?'

'Please do.'

'I've said this to you already, my lady, but I implore you to leave the front line and join those evacuating the city. This is not the place for a Holder of the Realm to be standing.'

'If the Realm is threatened,' Daphne said, 'then it's exactly the right place to be.'

'Excuse me, my lady, but I must disagree. If you were to die, then the line of Hold Fasts would be extinguished. By being here, you are risking the future of the Hold.'

Daphne shook her head. 'If I die, then Celine Holdfast can look after Karalyn Holdfast until she is old enough to be named Lady Holder.'

'Forgive me, my lady, but the people do not see Celine as a true scion of the Hold, as she was adopted. And your daughter...'

'What about her?' Daphne frowned.

Annifrid looked away. 'She was born out of wedlock, my lady, and has a foreign father. I don't know if she'd be acceptable to the people as a Holder.'

Daphne glared at her commander.

'It's a Republic now,' said Chane, leaning over the battlements. 'You both said Realm.'

'Quite right,' Daphne said, smiling. 'My apologies, Captain.'

Chane winked at her.

Annifrid sighed, and left the rooftop.

'She's still hurting,' Chane said, 'but you should sack her anyway, once we're clear of the city. She can't say things like that about Karalyn.'

'She's probably just echoing what others are thinking,' Daphne said, watching the front ranks of the Rahain army spread out to the left and right of the south road. They formed their door-sized shields into a long line, covering the entire southern side of the city. In their midst, a great bonfire was being piled up, with carts and beams thrown on. Beside it sat the figure of the Emperor on his horse, his face looking up at the walls. She felt a presence searching for her, and tried to block her mind.

I know you're up there somewhere, Daphne Holdfast, the Creator said, *using your little tricks to hide from me.*

He scanned the battlements, stopping when he reached the south tower.

Ah, there you are.

He raised his hand, and Daphne dived to the wooden floor, dragging Chane with her, as a pulse of power swept over their heads.

'Come on,' Daphne yelled, crawling for the stairs. 'He's seen us.'

They leapt down the steps. A scout saluted them at the bottom.

Daphne dusted down her uniform.

'Tell the catapult squadrons that they may commence their bombardment,' she said to the wide-eyed scout.

'Yes, my lady,' he said, and ran off.

'Did the Emperor know it was you?' Chane said.

'Yeah,' Daphne said. 'I tried to block him out, but he still saw me.'

She lit a cigarette. The Prophet had been right. If everyone knew that it was the Creator who was before the walls, rather than merely the Emperor, they would run away in panic. She controlled her breathing.

They left the south tower, coming out onto the main street leading from the great gates. Barricades had been heaped up behind the enormous iron-rimmed doors, and many of the side streets had been blocked. Fifty yards up the road was a blockade, behind which crouched a full squadron of soldiers, each armed with a crossbow. Daphne and Chane strode up the street. They came to an alleyway that had been left open, where another squadron had lined up. Daphne joined them, and turned to watch the gate.

'My lady,' said the lieutenant in command.

Daphne nodded in reply.

The air over their heads whooshed, and Daphne glanced up to see half a dozen giant boulders fly above the streets. They passed the walls, and Daphne heard the crashes as they impacted. She stole a glance at the Upper City. No flag.

They waited.

Chane smoked another cigarette, as more boulders were flung over the wall at the imperial army.

Daphne resisted the temptation to use her line-vision to see what the enemy was doing. The Creator, she sensed, would be able to see her if she revealed her powers. She readied her battle-vision, her eyes scanning the empty battlements.

There was a deafening roar and a blinding flash, and Daphne was flung off her feet, along with the others in the alleyway as a powerful shockwave surged past. With her ears ringing, she opened her eyes. A cloud of dust filled the air. She coughed, covered in small fragments of rubble. Next to her, Chane groaned, and struggled to her feet. She stared towards the gates, her mouth hanging open.

Daphne stood, putting her right hand onto the wall of the alley for support. She stared.

The gates were gone.

In their place was a great gap, a breach in the city's walls as wide as a dozen carts. Broken masonry lay scattered down the street, and the houses closest to the gates were smoking ruins, their roofs caved in. The air felt hot, and the back of Daphne's throat was as dry as sand.

She turned to the squadron in the alleyway.

'Get up. Check your kit. Any second, the Rahain are going to burst through. Lieutenant, send a squad into the shop in front of us. I want crossbows on the upper floor. Now.'

The lieutenant staggered to his feet, his uniform and dark skin covered in a film of grey dust.

'Yes, my lady,' he gasped. He pointed at a sergeant. 'You heard the Holder. Get your squad inside and upstairs.'

The sergeant kicked in the side door of the shop and a dozen soldiers followed her in. Daphne drew her sword. She checked the Upper City. No flag.

There was a roar of voices, and the first Rahain appeared in the breach, their large shields held up. They bunched together as they avoided the piles of debris, leaving their sides exposed.

'Crossbow squads, form up,' Daphne yelled. 'Shoot at will.'

As the Holdings troopers ran forwards with their weapons, a hail of bolts came from the blockade up the main street, twenty yards to their right. Most struck shields, but a few hit Rahain flesh, and the first cries of dying echoed through the air. More bolts were shot down from the shop, and from the squads kneeling by the alleyway. Hundreds of Rahain were pouring through the gap, and the number falling grew, until the ground was carpeted in the dead and injured.

There were screams from within the shop. Daphne found the nearest sergeant.

'Get in there and help them,' she yelled.

The sergeant grunted, and pulled his soldiers through the side door. Ahead, the Rahain were advancing along the main street, their numbers increasing as more crammed through the gap in the wall.

'Where is that flag?' cried Chane, huddling behind the corner of the alleyway, her hand on the hilt of her sword.

The front ranks of the advancing Rahain were now level with the alleyway. Daphne glanced at the remaining soldiers behind her. Two squads of swords.

'Get ready,' she muttered to Chane, then she turned to the others, her sword in the air. 'Follow me!'

She surged her battle-vision and sprang from the alleyway. She kept to the left of where the row of kneeling crossbow squads were shooting, and charged into the enemy's flank. Her sword flashed, slicing through light leather armour and Rahain flesh, severing limbs and cleaving torsos. On either side, the sword squads formed a wedge, with her at its head and Chane a yard behind her.

Daphne forgot everything else as she satisfied an urge to kill. She moved faster than anyone around her could keep up with, her blade a crimson blur. Not one death made the slightest difference to her pain, but she felt freer than she had since learning the fate of her family. Every Rahain she struck down she imagined was the Creator, and no matter how many versions of him she killed, she never tired of it, her battle-vision thrumming its rhythm through her.

She felt hands grip her shoulders and pull her back. She spun, ready to kill again.

'Steady!' Chane yelled. She pointed up. 'The flag!'

Daphne glanced at the Upper City. Flying from the ruins of the Old Tower was a great green standard.

Chane grabbed her arm and started running, dodging the dozens of dead Rahain that lay bloody on the ground. Daphne followed, sheathing her sword and keeping her head down, while around her the other Holdings soldiers were also fleeing, scattering down the maze of side streets and alleyways away from the southern gate. The Rahain pursued, but the narrowness of the roads, and the prepared roadblocks, slowed them down.

Daphne turned a corner and stopped. They had reached a large, marble fountain marking the edge of Nethertown, where a great barricade had been erected. It lay in silence. She turned, and gazed back the way they had come, as dozens of Holdings soldiers ran into the square.

'Looks clear,' Chane said. 'We've lost them, for a few moments at least.'

She pulled a hipflask from her armour, and took a swig.

Daphne called over the officers present: two lieutenants and a handful of sergeants.

'Get everyone through the barricade,' she said. 'Split up into squads and run for the garrison bridge. Horses will be there for you. Good luck.'

'Are you not leaving with us, my lady?' said a young lieutenant.

'I'll wait until we're all through, but I'll be right on your heels.'

The officers and sergeants nodded. They began to lead their squads into a house flanking the main barricade, where a path had been kept open through to the other side.

Chane offered Daphne a cigarette.

She took it and leaned against a wall, watching as the remaining Holdings soldiers lined up by the fountain, queuing to enter the house.

'All going to plan, then,' said Chane.

Daphne laughed.

'How you feeling?' Chane said.

'I'm going to kill him, just not today.'

'And I'll be by your side when you do it.'

'Thanks, Chane. You know, I'm sorry about everything that happened between us. We shouldn't have left you in Sanang. It was a mistake.'

'Yeah, well, it was a long time ago,' she said. 'I hated you for it. I mean, you took that arsehole Mink along with you.'

'Did you know he testified against me at my appeal?'

'No, but it doesn't surprise me. He probably got a cushy job, some-where safely behind the lines. It's always the same. The competent get punished, and the idiots get rewarded.'

The last of the soldiers entered the house, and Daphne stubbed out her cigarette. Down the street towards the southern gate, she could hear the noise of the approaching Rahain.

'Come on,' she said. They sprinted across the square and entered the house. At the end of a dining-room, a large hole had been knocked through the wall, and a half-squad stood on the other side.

'My lady,' said the sergeant, 'are you the last?'

She nodded, and they passed through the hole and into the back room of a shop.

The sergeant raised his arm, and the other members of the squad kicked away a series of wooden supports that were braced against the wall. There was a loud crash as the ceiling fell, blocking the way. They emerged from the house into an empty street, the enormous barricade behind them. Empty houses and shops flanked either side of the road, and a light breeze was blowing rubbish across the deserted cobbles. The city felt cold, despite the warm autumn sunshine.

'To the cavalry garrison, everyone,' Daphne yelled, and they set off.

After twenty minutes of hard running, Daphne, Chane and the squad neared the long walls encircling the garrison. The gate to the river was lying open, and they sped through.

'Holder Fast!' an officer cried out. She approached. 'You're safe, thank the Creator. Come this way, your horse is ready. The rest of the company has already departed, except for us, who were awaiting your return.'

There were a few dozen soldiers and horses clustered by the gate, preparing to depart.

'Did Chancellor Holdwick and Queen Mirren get away in good time?' Daphne said.

'Yes, my lady. They requested that I pass on their thanks for standing fast at the southern gate while the rest of the city could finish evacuating. They also said that they hope to see you soon at the Red Hills assembly point.'

Daphne nodded. 'And the Prophet?'

The officer stopped. 'He refused to leave the citadel, my lady.'

'Damn,' Daphne muttered. She gazed at the Upper City. 'He's up there on his own?'

'Yes, my lady.'

A soldier led out Daphne's white stallion, saddled and ready to go. Daphne rubbed his flank with her right hand, then mounted. Around her, the last members of the Hold Fast Company still in the city climbed into their saddles. They formed up, with Daphne in the centre. Chane manoeuvred her mare to Daphne's right. The officer whistled, and they began to troop out of the gate. They turned right, and trotted onto the bridge leading to the royal ramp. At the other end, a new gate had been punched through the city wall, and a road had been laid to connect it to the ramp. On the far side of the gap stretched the endless Holdings savannah, and in the distance, Daphne could see thin trails of dust made by those who had evacuated before them.

As the officer spurred her mount towards the new roadway, Daphne paused.

'Wait,' she said.

She turned back in the saddle, and gazed up the ramp to the Upper City.

Damn Prophet.

'My lady?' said the officer.

Daphne frowned.

I know what you're thinking, said a voice in her head. *Please don't.*

But I can't leave you up there to die.

I'm staying in the Upper City so that you can all get away, the Prophet said. *Don't ruin my plan by trying to rush to my rescue.*

Daphne bowed her head, a tear coming from her eye.

Don't weep for me, Daphne dear. I don't deserve it. I am responsible for much of the pain in your life, but please let me do this so I can pay back some of what I owe you.

But the Creator will kill you.

I know, but by staying here he will have to deal with me, instead of pursuing you. He will have to fight me. He will win, but I intend to make the price of his victory high. Now, go. Be on your way. And when you see your daughter, give her a kiss for me. And maybe, when she's older and you mention me, I hope you will tell her about this day, and not about the times I let you down. Farewell, Daphne.

She wiped her cheek. The other soldiers were gazing at her, their horses stationary.

'Are you alright?' asked Chane.

Daphne nodded. She wheeled the stallion around, taking a good look back over the city, the capital of her nation, now under occupation.

'I can't believe we're really leaving,' Chane said.

'We'll be back.'

Daphne kicked her heels, and the stallion cantered forward. They raced down the new road, through the gap in the city wall, and out into the plains. Low grass covered the land ahead all the way to the horizon. The hooves of their horses thundered over the hard ground, sending a cloud of brown dust into the air behind them. After a few miles, Daphne slowed. She brought the stallion to a halt, and turned, Chane and the others joining her.

Chane pointed. 'Look!'

Tiny black specks were circling the Upper City in the distance, like flies buzzing round a dungheap. Some swooped in, trying to land, but every time they got close, their winged gaien would wheel away, as if in terror.

'The old bastard's holding them off,' Chane said.

The cycle repeated, but no matter how many carriages were brought near to the citadel, their flying mounts would turn back at the last moment, as if they were encountering an invisible barrier. After a few minutes, all of the winged gaien flew away; except for one, which took up position hovering above the palace.

'The Emperor,' muttered Chane.

The Holdings stared at the Upper City from their horses, but for a long moment nothing happened, then the buildings crowding the surface of the tall promontory began to melt as if they were made of butter left out in the midday sun; their stone walls collapsing and toppling. Great chunks of masonry fell into the river below, as the palace and the cathedral disintegrated into rubble. A grey cloud of dust rose from the ruins, and the grinding noise of tortured stonework reached their ears across the plains.

Chane pulled her hipflask from her armour.

'To the Prophet,' she said, taking a swig and passing it to Daphne.

Holder Fast gazed up at the ruined palace and citadel, and lifted the alcohol to her lips. She passed it back to Chane, then turned her stallion.

She raised her right arm, the reins wound through the crippled fingers of her left hand.

'To the Red Hills,' she cried. 'Follow me.'

CHAPTER 17

A DOZEN DAYS IN KELL

Northern Kell, Kellach Brigdomin – 23rd Day, Second Third Autumn 507

'Damn this weather,' moaned Flora, as a gale threatened to send her off the narrow path and down a ravine.

Keira cackled, the sound of her laughter lost in the howling wind. The rain was driving hard, and the path slippery. Flora looked up at her and pointed at an old abandoned goat shed, halfway down the hillside.

'We've got miles to go yet,' Kallie said.

'I need to get out of this rain,' cried Flora, 'just for a couple of minutes.'

Keira shrugged, and Flora ran down the slope and into the goat shed.

'I like her,' said Kallie, as they followed the Holdings woman, 'but she's slowing us down.'

'Tough shit, Kallie-Wallie, she's coming.'

They stepped into the rough stone building, and out of the wind and rain. Flora had already taken her pack off, and was drying her face with a towel. She was shivering.

'Light the storm lamp,' Keira said to her, then gazed around the interior of the shed. Old, rotting heaps of straw covered most of the floor, and a wooden workbench sat in a corner. She pulled her pack off and released the handaxe from its straps. She hacked the workbench to pieces, then turned to see Flora lighting the lamp she carried everywhere. Keira threw the wood into a pile and shot a flame out from the lamp, igniting it.

Flora put her hands right next to the roaring fire, smiling. 'Thanks.'

Keira gazed at her hand.

'There, that wasn't so hard now, was it?' Kallie said, unwrapping food from her pack, and laying out cheese, dried beef strips and hard bread onto a cloth on the ground.

'Using fire to get warm is one thing,' Keira frowned. 'Using it to massacre folk is another.'

'Baby steps,' Kallie said. 'When we left Domm, you insisted that you wouldn't use your powers for anything.'

'It's because I'm lazy, but,' Keira said. 'I mean, I could've spent ten minutes carefully building the fire up by hand, but I couldnae be arsed.'

'All I'm saying is…'

'I know what yer saying, and all I'm saying is that it's not the fucking same.'

'It's not exactly the same, but it's a start.'

'Stop saying that,' Keira yelled.

'You know,' said Flora, looking up, 'you two argue like sisters.'

Keira snorted.

'It once felt like we were,' said Kallie.

'Before my wee brother dumped yer arse,' Keira said.

'Before he betrayed me by sleeping with that Holdings woman.'

'Her name's Daphne; have ye forgotten?' Keira said. 'Daphne fucking Holdfast.'

'You ever met her?' Flora said.

'Who, me?' said Keira. 'Nope.'

'I have,' said Kallie. 'She rescued us from a Rahain prison. I didn't know it at the time, but she and Killop had just been together before they turned up.'

'Been together?' Flora said. 'You mean?'

'Aye,' laughed Keira. 'They stopped off for a quick shag on the way before rescuing Kallie, can ye fucking believe it?'

'She was lucky I didn't know,' said Kallie. 'I would've ripped her head off.'

'No chance,' Flora said. 'She's a high mage, from what I've heard about her. A battle-vision specialist. She'd have cut you up into small pieces if you'd tried.'

Kallie frowned. 'She was pretty handy with a blade, right enough.'

'Beaten in every department,' Keira chuckled.

'In every department?' said Flora. 'She must be gorgeous.'

Kallie shrugged. 'I'm not one to judge folk from the Holdings, but she seemed pretty ordinary to me. Lacey kept saying that she'd put some sort of spell on Killop, used her vision powers to make him love her.'

'And do you believe that, Kallie?'

'No. Killop wasn't bewitched, he was besotted. Anyway, can we stop talking about it now? It took me ages to get over it.'

'Ye know they've got a bairn, though eh?' Keira said.

Kallie frowned. 'No.'

'A wee lassie.'

'That's nice.'

'I'm an auntie.'

'So ye are.'

'Auntie Keira.'

Kallie gave Keira a cold stare, then got up and left the goat shed.

'You shouldn't do that,' said Flora.

Keira shrugged. 'She dragged my arse all the way up here, and anyway, I'm only telling her the truth, it's not my fault it hurts.'

'That's bullshit, Keira. You found a weakness, and you just enjoy poking at it.'

'And you're some sort of expert, are ye?' Keira said. 'If yer so packed full of wisdom, how come I've never seen ye with anyone? Your problem is that ye think yer smarter than everyone else. Puts folk off.'

Flora scowled, but said nothing. She picked up a stick and prodded the fire.

The door opened, and Kallie came back in. She crouched by the flame.

'We should get going,' she said. 'Got another eight miles to go before we hit the road to the coast. From there, our camp's a twenty-minute hike up the glen.'

'If yer friends are still there,' Keira said.

'You're right,' Kallie said, 'they might have been discovered while I was gone. We'll need to be careful. We'll be passing close to a mining compound on the way, so we'll have to keep our heads down.'

'Why?' said Keira. 'I thought we were here to fight.'

Kallie raised an eyebrow. 'The compound covers hundreds of acres, Keira, and is guarded by an entire battalion of soldiers. Their camps are ten times the size of the old ones you fought after the invasion. You must have seen them on the way in, they're too big to attack on our own.'

Keira frowned.

'We stuck to the mountain trails on our way south,' said Flora. 'We didn't see any Rahain.'

Kallie nodded. 'Makes sense.'

'What does?' said Keira.

'I've often wondered how you were able to pass through Northern Kell without stopping to fight. You still haven't seen what the Rahain have done to it.'

'But we're in Northern Kell now,' said Flora.

Kallie laughed and shook her head. 'We're still in the mountains, away from the nightmare the lowlands have become. We even avoided the garrisons on the main pass to Southern Kell. We haven't seen anything yet.'

'So we'll need help?'

'Aye, Flora,' Kallie said, 'we'll need to sit down and make a plan. Rally every rebel in the hills, and then choose where to strike.'

'Sounds too fucking complicated,' Keira said. 'Just point me at the lizards. The sooner we've burnt them out of Kell, the sooner I can go back to Domm.'

Kallie got to her feet, shaking her head. Flora stood, and slung her pack back over her shoulder.

'Back into the sideways rain,' she said. 'Oh joy.'

Keira extinguished the fire, and they left the goat shed. The wind and rain had eased, and thick grey clouds covered the sky. They followed the path down the narrow glen, then through the shelter of a long stretch of trees, their brown and faded leaves piled deep on the wet ground. Moss covered every rock next to the tiny burn. Keira smiled. Home.

Kallie led the way as they emerged from the trees. They came out onto a high platform, the lowlands of Northern Kell spread out before them. Keira stood by Kallie's side and gazed out.

She squinted through the murk. The land was unrecognisable. Mountains of ash and slagheaps littered the landscape. There were still some green patches here and there, but the ground was mostly broken rock, with landslips and giant, jagged crevices crossing the hillside. Every tree had gone, and smoke rose from a dozen locations. In the distance, Keira could see lines of high walls, enclosing an enormous camp, where row after row of squat buildings were laid out, amid guard towers and hills of mined coal.

Kallie spat. 'Now do you see?'

Keira said nothing. She wanted to look away, to pretend she had never seen it, but remained frozen where she stood. Her anger began to grow.

'The Rahain did all this?' asked Flora.

'Aye,' said Kallie. 'Their stone mages levelled every village and opened up the hillsides to reach the coal easier. The whole land's been ripped apart by earthquakes and mining. And they chopped down all the forests and woods, and dumped their mining waste into every river.'

Keira felt her fists clench.

'This,' Kallie said, stretching out her arm, 'is what we're up against. That compound there is one of the largest in this area. There are a couple of bigger ones further north, but that's the main one here. It sits where an old village used to be, about thirty miles from the pass to Southern Kell.'

'Aye,' muttered Keira, 'I remember it.'

'Where's your camp from here?' Flora said.

Kallie pointed to a range of hills to their left. 'That way.'

She turned, and began walking down the path. Flora glanced at Keira.

'The Rahain really kicked your arses.'

'Aye?' Keira said. 'Now it's my turn.'

It was dark when Kallie led them up another narrow glen. Flora struggled with the lack of light, and they had to take their time, as she stumbled over every rock and tree root on the path. When they reached a waterfall, Kallie told them to wait, and she continued up the track on her own. She returned a few minutes later, and gestured for them to follow her.

They clambered up a steep incline to the mouth of a cave, where a Kellach was guarding the entrance. He nodded at Kallie and moved aside to let them pass.

The cave stretched into a wide, twisting tunnel, and they emerged into a well-lit chamber, where a few rebels were sitting by a roaring fire. More were coming in from other entrances, and all were staring at Keira.

'Is it really her?' said one.

A tall man frowned as he approached, walking as if he thought he was important.

'Is this the fire mage?'

'Aye,' said Kallie. She gazed around at the faces in the chamber. 'This is Keira. She has returned.'

About forty or so rebels had now gathered, forming a circle around Keira and Flora, who stood close to her.

'Ya beauty!' cried someone, and the chamber rang out in cheers.

'We'll give it to those fucking lizards now!'

The tall man continued to frown. 'The fire mage, eh?'

Keira frowned back at him. 'Aye. And who the fuck are you?'

'I'm the leader of the rebels in these hills,' he said. 'If you're here to fight, then you'll be under my command.'

'The fuck I will,' Keira said. 'I commanded an army of a hundred thousand Sanang. I'm not going to be taking any orders from you.'

He turned to Kallie.

'Did you not explain the situation to her before you came here?'

Kallie shrugged. 'She's the fire mage, and I'm following her from now on.'

'But...'

'Me too, boss,' said a female warrior with an enormous battle-axe strapped to her back. 'Sorry.'

The folk in the chamber began to chant her name, Keira, Keira.

She smiled and raised her arms in the air. 'Let's plan our first attack over some whisky. Ye have got whisky, haven't ye?'

'Oh aye,' said an old woman. 'Loads.'

'Ye know, Kallie,' Keira said. 'I might get used to being here after all.'

Keira gazed through the lens of the long lizardeye at the enormous mining compound. It was several times bigger than any town in Kellach Brigdomin had ever been, and included the minehead, where a great wooden tower stood, surrounded by mountainous bins of extracted coal. Beyond that, a quarter of the compound was given over to dozens of long, low buildings where the slave-miners lived. It was surrounded by its own palisade fence. An army garrison occupied the third quarter of the compound, laid out like its own little town, while the final quarter was sealed off with a high wall, the area where the rich merchants and senior officers lived their pampered existence.

The entire compound was enclosed by a series of ditches and

palisade walls, and was protected on its landward flank by a fortress. On the other side, long palisade fences stretched a mile down to the cliff-edge. In this protected area, herds of cattle grazed, and fields were being farmed.

She felt a nudge in her side, and passed the lizardeye to Flora, who was lying on the raw stones of the hillside next to her, a look of deep fatigue in her eyes.

'This the last one?' she said.

'Aye. The last big one, anyway. Kallie said there's a few smaller places we've missed, but they can be mopped up after we've finished.'

'They're panicking,' Flora said, peering through the Rahain-made instrument. 'Loading up wagons, and soldiers are running around all over the place.'

Keira chuckled. 'Guess word reached them of our wee tour across Northern Kell.'

'It's only two days since we attacked the last place,' Flora said. 'Are you sure the imperials don't have a vision mage?'

'That's what Kallie says. Think about it though. The bastards seemed surprised when we hit them, they never saw us coming. These guys down there must have seen the smoke rising from the last place, or maybe a survivor managed to escape.'

'I don't know, you were pretty thorough.'

'As always.'

'How you coping with it? I must admit, I wasn't sure you'd do it all again, not after the Plateau.'

Keira shrugged.

'You sleeping alright?'

'Whisky helps.'

'You seem calm on the surface, but...'

'Enough. Let's just blow the shit out of this place, and get back to Domm.'

She turned her head and glanced at the dozens of Kellach rebels standing among the giant boulders of the broken hillside. The wood they had salvaged from the previous compound was being unloaded from six wagons, creating a great mound of fuel.

Keira jumped down the slope towards them, and Kallie saw her approach.

'How's the range?' she said.

'I can hit the front half of the compound from here,' Keira said, 'and the fortress. I'll start with that, then work my way to the minehead.'

Kallie nodded. 'Where do you want the strike squads?'

'Straight through the front gate,' Keira said, 'as soon as the fortress is ablaze. Make sure they stay clear of the coal bins; I'm going to light those fuckers up, they'll burn for days, the amount of coal that's been stockpiled.'

Kallie nodded again, and started issuing orders to the others.

Keira rubbed her hands, waiting for everyone to get into their positions. The warriors trooped off, leaving Kallie and a half-squad as the mage's personal protection. Flora opened the storm lamp.

'Not yet,' Keira said. 'Anyone got a drink?'

A grizzled older man reached into his belt and pulled out a bottle. He bit off the cork and spat it out, then passed it to Keira.

'Good man,' she said, and took a long drink of whisky. She gazed at her right hand. Steady.

'Alright,' she said to Flora, 'now.'

The dark-skinned woman opened the storm lamp, exposing the flame within. Keira closed her eyes, feeling for the living fire, sensing its desire to spread and consume. She drew back her fingers as if taking a pinch of salt, and a thin tendril of fire leapt out of the lamp, igniting the heap of wood in a great whoosh of flame. Flora stepped back, the heat intense. Keira smiled.

'Someone spot for me,' she said, and Kallie gestured to a warrior, who ran up the slope and lay down at the top.

Keira flicked her wrist, and a ball of fire the size of a pumpkin soared through the air. Seconds later she heard it crash, and she glanced at the spotter.

'You hit the inner wall to the right of the fort,' the warrior yelled. 'Pull back twenty yards, and angle thirty to the left.'

Keira nodded, and sent over another fireball.

'You hit a building inside the fortress,' cried the warrior.

'Good enough,' she said. She increased the size of the next fireball to that of a wagon, and sent it on the same trajectory. She then fired off a dozen more in quick succession, sprinkling them around the same area.

'The fortress is burning!' the warrior called down to her.

'The coal bins next,' she shouted back. 'Same routine.'

She gazed at the pillars of smoke rising over the edge of the ridge, trying to remember exactly where the giant stores of coal lay. She flicked her wrist, and a smaller fireball whooshed towards the compound.

'Too far to the left,' cried the warrior. 'Angle fifty yards to the right.'

She tried again, and again, narrowing in on the bins, until the warrior whooped. Above his head, the flames could be seen rising.

'You got it!' he yelled. 'Pyre's arsehole, it's burning like an inferno.'

Keira glanced at her diminishing supply of fuel. She weaved her hand through the air, pulling up everything that remained, and sent it over to the compound, over to where she knew the minehead lay. She waited for the whump as it hit, and smirked.

They clambered back up the ridge, leaving a smouldering black circle on the ground behind them, and gazed down at the compound. The fortress at the front was burning, flames ripping through its towers and interior buildings. The minehead had collapsed, and was on fire, but the light it made was insignificant next to the raging conflagration by the coal bins. Black smoke was pouring up into the sky from where the mountains of coal lay, and the heat from it was igniting the structures around it.

Keira stared at the white-hot flames. From her attacks on the other compounds, she knew that the fire would rage on and on, until all the coal had been consumed, melting the rocks underneath the inferno, and scarring the land for years. She also knew that the cavern cities of the Rahain would be cold and dark that winter, and felt a savage revenge satisfied. Let those bastards suffer. Let their lizard arses freeze in the dark.

'There's the attack squads,' yelled one of the warriors, pointing.

'We'd better get down there,' said Kallie. 'There are still over a thousand soldiers in that garrison.'

Keira nodded, smiling to herself.

They sprinted down the loose rubble of the hillside, and ran towards the ruins of the fortress. They grew close enough to hear the screams from within, then turned and made for the main gates of the compound. Keira held her arm up as they ran, lifting a mass of fire from the burning fortress, and throwing it at the gates in front of where the attack squads had gathered. The gates exploded, their doors shattering from the burst of fire, and the attack squads funnelled through. Kallie swung her longbow off her shoulder, notched an arrow and shot down a Rahain guard up on the wall. Keira took another fireball from the fortress, and cleared the rest of the wall's battlements, incinerating the other Rahain guards that were up there.

They followed the squads through the broken gates, and into the compound. To their right was another wall, enclosing the wealthy quarter, while to their left was the great inferno consuming the coal bins. Ahead, the Rahain garrison was forming up, row upon row of soldiers with shields and crossbows, all marching up the road at a trot.

'Dear oh, dear,' said Keira, raising her arm. 'Yer going the wrong way, ya numpties.'

She swung her arm down, and a sheet of white flame rose from the coal bins and cut through the air, like a whirling circular blade. It soared over the heads of the attack squads then, as Keira moved her fingers, it grew closer to the ground until it was at waist-height. It sliced through the ranks of Rahain soldiers, cutting them in two as it filled the width of the road.

Keira pushed with her hand, and the blade of fire went spinning down the road, annihilating everything that stood there. At the end of the street, Keira flicked her wrist, and the fiery wheel slammed into the gatehouse of the garrison barracks. She spread her fingers, and the flames moved through the buildings, leaping from roof to roof.

The squads stood and stared at the carnage carpeting the road all the way to the burning garrison.

Keira winked at Kallie. 'A thousand, did ye say?'

She turned to the walled-off inner compound, where the wealthy merchants that controlled the coal trade lived. She strode to the gates marking the entrance, Kallie, Flora and the half-squad following. Warriors held up shields before the fire mage, but she could see no one up on the wall. She raised a ball of hot flame from the centre of the fire at the coal bins, and blew the gates apart.

'Get out here,' she yelled, 'or I'm burning the place down.'

A group of Rahain soldiers appeared, their hands in the air. They scrambled through the smouldering wreckage of the gates, where Kallie lined them up against the wall, their weapons piled up by the road.

'Where are your masters?' Keira said to them in Rahain.

The prisoners glanced at each other.

'Most have already fled,' said one. 'Last night, or at dawn this morning.'

'North, I hope?'

The Rahain soldier nodded. 'Back to the Plateau.'

'Taking all their wealth with them.'

'Whatever they could carry, ma'am.'

Kallie strode forward. 'You said most. Are there still some inside?'

'Yes, ma'am. Barricaded into the Merchants' Hall.'

'And you were supposed to stop us getting there?'

The prisoner nodded.

Keira nodded at Kallie, and stepped into the enclosed quarter. Once past the gates, she ignored the sounds of Kallie's half-squad killing the prisoners, and gazed around. It was like being in a different town. The streets were filled with grand-looking houses, with shops, taverns and tree-lined avenues.

'Looks quiet,' said Flora.

'That lamp lit?'

The Holdings woman nodded.

'Keep it ready.'

They set off as soon as the half-squad had gathered round her. They strode down the wide street, passing a broken fountain, its stonework green with slime. On the far side of the square stood the Merchant Hall. Its front entrance had been blocked, and its windows were boarded up.

'Good afternoon,' Keira yelled, 'my wee colony of rich lizards. Have ye got anything to say before I burn yer hall to the ground?'

A white flag poked out from a balcony window.

She looked up. 'Aye?'

'This is imperial property,' cried a voice. 'The Emperor will hear of this. Word has already been sent to the governor of Rahain. An army will come, and you...'

'Aye, whatever,' Keira muttered. 'Flora, the lamp.'

The Holdings woman opened the door of the lamp, and Keira fired a small sliver of flame across the square to the Merchant Hall. It affixed itself to the eaves under a sloping side roof, and the fire began to lick up the wall. Keira moved her hand in a gentle swirl, and the flames spread, and grew, leaping across gaps to other parts of the hall, until the flames took a firm hold of the building. Keira lowered her hand.

She waited for the screams.

They didn't take long to reach her ears. Men, women, and children. Their cries rose up into the sky as the flames whipped through the building. Kallie glanced over at the mage, her eyes full of pain as the last sounds of the dying echoed through the square, but Keira kept her features impassive.

Desperate cries of terror and agony sounded much the same, no matter which race of folk she incinerated. The sound of bairns screaming, in particular. Didn't matter if it was Rahain, or Sanang, or Rakanese, or Holdings. They all sounded the same.

Keira turned and walked from the square, the half-squad trooping in silence behind her.

The rest of the attack squads had formed up outside the wealthy quarter, their forms silhouetted by the coal bins burning behind them.

'Garrison accounted for?' Kallie asked a group of officers.

'Aye, boss,' said one. 'There weren't many left after the mage's attack. It's just the slaves to deal with.'

'How many?'

'I'm guessing in the region of four thousand, boss, based on the size of the sheds where they're housed.'

Keira glanced over to the palisade wall surrounding the slave quarter, in the opposite corner to the wealthy area. She began walking towards it. Flora ran to catch up, while the Kellach watched her go in silence.

'What are you going to do?' Flora said.

'What the fuck do ye think?'

'You can't, not again.'

Keira snorted. 'Ye care about the lizards now, do ye?'

'Not really, if I'm honest,' she said, 'but I care about you. About what slaughtering these slaves will do to you.'

Keira ignored her, and upped her pace.

'Wait,' Flora cried, sprinting after her. 'I know you, Keira, I know you. I saw everything you did with the Alliance, and in that shithole Sanang, and on the Plateau. Don't do this. Please, Keira, you're so far gone, I don't want to lose you...'

Keira stopped a few yards from the slaves' enclosure. The stout palisade walls reared up in front of her, and through the gaps in the planks she could see the faces of those locked within, the faces of the slave labour force that went down into the earth every day, digging for the black rocks. Their eyes were filled with terror as they watched her gazing at them.

Stupid lizard bastards.

Flora tugged her arm.

'Please, Keira.'

'Get off me.'

'Don't do it.'

Keira pushed Flora, sending her sprawling to the ground. 'What the fuck's it to you, anyway?'

'I love you.'

Keira stared at the Holdings woman, unsure whether to laugh or fly into a rage.

'Pyre's cock,' she muttered, shaking her head. She held out her hand. 'Get up.'

Flora took it, and the mage pulled her to her feet. Keira glanced at the slaves for a moment, then turned and began walking back towards Kallie and the attack squads, Flora running to keep up.

'What's happening?' said Kallie as she approached.

'Ask her,' Keira said, nodding at Flora. She walked past Kallie and sat on a white-washed boulder marking the edge of the road. 'Somebody get me a fucking whisky.'

A warrior ran over with a bottle and Keira drank deep.

'So, yer not going to kill the miners?' Kallie said.

Keira shook her head. 'I'm done.'

'What will we do with them all?'

'Fuck knows, whatever ye want. I'm out of here.'

Kallie sat next to her on the boulder. 'Back to Domm?'

'Aye.'

Kallie sat in silence for a minute. Flora came over, and took a swig of whisky.

'And you, Flora?' Kallie said. 'What do you want to do?'

The young Holdings woman gazed at the burning compound.

'I want to go home.'

'You mean the Holdings?' said Kallie.

'Yeah.'

'What?' said Keira. 'I thought ye were coming back with me to Domm?'

Flora gazed at her. 'If I thought there was any chance that you'd ever feel the same way that I do about you, then I'd be by your side forever. But I have to be realistic. You never will.'

Keira stared at her in silence. Something within her began to hurt.

'Well,' Kallie said, 'if you're going to the Holdings, then we may have found something that might interest you.'

'What?' Flora said.

Kallie stood. 'Come and see.'

'What is it?' said Keira.

'It's of no concern to you if yer going back to Domm.'

Keira stood. 'I want to see it.'

Kallie sighed. 'Come on then.'

She led Flora and Keira back into the wealthy quarter and down an alleyway to a large paddock, where four winged gaien were tethered. Next to them lay a long carriage.

'Wow,' Flora said, her eyes lighting up.

Kallie smiled. 'We have no idea how it works, but...'

'I can fly it,' Flora said, walking towards the carriage. 'Learned when we fled from the Rahain Capital. Leah showed me.'

Flora neared the carriage, and put her hand up to run her fingers over the wooden frame, and the thick steel bands that held it together. She turned back to Kallie.

'Do you mean I can take it?'

'Aye,' Kallie said, 'if it'll help ye get home.'

'Thanks,' Flora said, 'though I wouldn't be able to fly it alone. It needs a crew of three, at the very least.'

Kallie rubbed her chin. 'That could be a problem. I suppose we could see if there are any volunteers, who are up for an adventure to the Holdings.' She turned to Keira. 'You could take the bear you carved to Killop.'

'I can see what yer trying to do,' said Keira. 'I'm not stupid.'

'The world needs you, Keira,' Kallie said. 'I realise that now, after everything you've accomplished here. In a dozen days ye've cleared Northern Kell, and killed close to, I don't know, twenty thousand Rahain.' She shook her head. 'You are a goddess. You have to go. Fight the Emperor, do whatever you have to do to make sure no more armies ever come marching towards Kellach Brigdomin.'

Keira frowned. She turned away from Kallie and Flora's beseeching eyes.

Why did it always fall to her? Could the rest of the world not look after itself for once?

She spat on the ground.

'Three?' she said to Flora. 'That thing needs three to crew it?'

'Yes.'

'Alright then. I'll fucking do it, but on one condition.'

She smirked at Kallie.

'You're coming with us.'

CHAPTER 18
THE RED HILLS

The Red Hills, Imperial Holdings – 5th Day, Last Third Autumn 507

Killop held Daphne close, his bare arms pressed against the cold steel of her armour, his face in her hair. He kissed her.

'Up, up,' cried Karalyn from the floor of the tent, her arms raised. Daphne leaned down and picked her up.

'Mummy stay,' the child said.

'I can't, Kara-bear,' Daphne said. 'Mummy has to fight the bad man, but I'll be back soon.'

Karalyn started to cry.

'It's alright,' Daphne said. 'Everything's going to be fine. Daddy'll look after you.'

She glanced up at Killop, and he gazed into her green eyes.

'I'd better go.'

Killop reached out and took Karalyn, and the crying girl buried her face into his shoulder.

Daphne scanned the tent, and picked up her cavalry helmet from the low bed. She adjusted the buckle on her sword belt, and took a breath.

They walked the few paces to the entrance, and Daphne pushed the canvas aside, revealing a blue sky over the great plains. Chane and the Hold's senior officers were outside, their armour shining, and they saluted as she left the tent. Killop remained in the entranceway, watching as Daphne nodded her greetings.

'Holder Fast,' said a man bowing low, his uniform and armour decorated with medals. 'Chancellor Holdwick and First Minister Blackhold request your presence to discuss the strategy of today's battle.'

Daphne nodded. The army camp was situated on a gentle slope of the Red Hills, which stretched behind them, growing into the great Shield Mountains. She gazed across the plains in front of her. The Holdings infantry had already assembled – twenty thousand soldiers formed up into their Holds were arranged half a mile from the foot of the hill. Beyond them in the far distance was a dust cloud, marking the approaching imperial forces, commanded by the Emperor.

'It'll need to be quick,' Daphne said. She turned a final time to Killop and Karalyn, smiled, then with Chane at her side, she walked along the path to the chancellor's command post, a terraced platform dug into the side of the hill a hundred yards away.

Karalyn waved, and they watched Daphne disappear, flanked by her officers.

'She'll be back soon, wee bear,' Killop said. He walked to a smaller tent, alongside Daphne's. 'Ye can come out now, she's gone.'

Kylon emerged from within, a sour look on his face. Celine followed, but kept her distance from her colleague. Kylon walked off alone, and stared out over the plains.

'He's still in the huff,' Celine said.

Killop shrugged. 'He was out of order last night. I thought at one point that Daphne was actually going to hit him.'

'He has a problem with getting told no,' Celine said. 'I think he's used to giving orders, not taking them.'

Killop glanced at the black-clad Kell standing alone at the edge of the ridge.

'What did you think of what he was suggesting?'

Celine shook her head. 'Madness. You can't take a child into battle.'

Killop nodded.

'This must be weird for you,' she went on. 'You were a soldier, and an officer. You've fought in battles, right?'

'Aye.'

'And here you are, standing unarmed with the children and civilians, about to watch a battle that could decide the fate of the world.'

Killop said nothing.

'Do you not wish you were down there?' she asked, nodding at the soldiers lined up on the plains before them.

'Not really,' he said. 'I wish I was with them.' He pointed to the right, where at the bottom of the slope, the Holdings heavy cavalry was beginning to assemble. 'But you've seen me ride, aye? I mean, I can stay on the damned beast, but I'm years away from being good enough to make the cavalry.'

Celine nodded.

'I was told I could join the infantry if I fancied it,' Killop went on, 'but I knew Daphne wanted me up here, making sure Karalyn is alright.'

'She doesn't trust us?'

Killop lowered his voice. 'She trusts you.'

Celine frowned. 'Kylon would die for Karalyn.'

'I know he would.'

From Killop's arms, Karalyn gazed over at the lone Kell man. 'Kylo sad.'

'Is he?' said Celine. 'He looks more angry to me.'

'No,' Karalyn said. 'Kylo sad. Kylo miss his family.'

Celine raised an eyebrow, and leaned close to Killop. 'Do you know anything about Kylon's family?'

Killop shook his head. 'He's always refused to talk about his past. I only know about his life from the day he joined my squad, back during the Rahain invasion of Kell. Before that, I have no idea.'

'Karalyn show you,' the girl said.

'No, wee bear,' her father said. 'If Kylon wants to keep it a secret, then we must respect that.'

Celine's eyes were conflicted, and she looked away.

A group of uniformed officers strolled up the hillside towards the Hold Fast tents.

'Chief Killop,' said one, 'the Chancellor would like to invite you and your party to the command platform to watch the battle, now that the cavalry have received their orders.'

'Aye, thanks.'

The officer nodded. 'Should we wait a few minutes until you are suitably attired, Chief?'

Celine chuckled as Killop looked down at his scruffy tunic and stained leathers.

'Aye, alright,' he muttered. He passed Karalyn to Celine, and strode back to the big tent. Inside, he washed and put on his cleanest clothes, then picked out his best armour, and the steel chestplate emblazoned with the Hold Fast insignia that had been a gift from Godfrey. He strapped on the armour, then laced up his infantry boots, and pulled a comb through his wild hair. He stood in front of Daphne's tall mirror, though he had to crouch to see his head.

How much simpler life was when you couldn't see how you appeared to others.

He began to walk towards the exit, then remembered his weapon. He reached over by the bedside, slid a scabbard out from under the mattress and buckled it to his belt. Inside was a fine Holdings longsword, light but strong, and made from steel that kept its edge better than any blade forged in Kell.

Celine laughed when he re-emerged into the open.

'You look like a different person,' she said. 'One I could actually believe used to be a chief, rather than a vagrant.'

He shook his head.

The officer smiled, and gestured in the direction of the platform. 'This way, please.'

The terraced area was dominated by a pair of raised chairs. Both were empty, as Faden Holdwick and Queen Mirren mingled with the officers and aristocrats who had gathered to observe the battle. Killop walked into their midst, Celine on his left, carrying Karalyn, and Kylon on his right, wordless and brooding.

Killop gazed around. He and Kylon were a good head taller than anyone else on the platform, and he could see a few gazes in their direction. As Holder Fast's barbarian consort, he engendered a mixture of responses. Some appeared to admire his past, and respect what he had achieved, while others made no attempt to hide their contempt at the savage upstart who had the audacity to presume he was a suitable match for a Holder of the Realm.

Everyone gave Kylon a wide berth, his deep frown acting as a repellent to anyone wishing to engage in small talk. The queen caught Killop's eye, and she approached.

'Chief,' she said, smiling, 'and Miss Celine Holdfast.' She gazed at Karalyn. 'And the little one. What a beautiful girl, you must be proud.'

'Aye,' said Killop.

'I hear you did a fine job in rescuing your daughter from that awful tragedy on the Hold Fast estate,' Mirren said. 'I hope today that the new Holder Fast is presented with ample opportunity for revenge.'

'There's only one person she needs to kill,' he said. 'Your husband.'

A flash of sadness swept over the queen's face. 'Indeed. I wish it were not so. However, as you already know, I believe that the man out there leading the invasion of the Holdings is not my beloved Guilliam. I will not shed a tear when the Emperor falls today.'

Faden walked up to Mirren's side.

'Ah, Killop, my good man,' he said, swaying a little, as if he had taken a drink.

'Chancellor,' Killop nodded.

'May I say how sorry I am, Chancellor,' Celine said, 'about your loss.'

'Thank you, my girl,' he said, his features falling. 'That terrible day of infamy was meant to scare the people of the Holdings, but rather than being cowed, the Emperor will instead find us steadfast and united against him.' He turned to Killop. 'So, what's your prediction for today's little set-to? Am I to assume that you've never seen the magnificent Holdings heavy cavalry in action before?'

'I watched them charge the gates of the Rahain Capital during the alliance invasion,' Killop said. 'It was quite a sight. They were vulnerable to the catapults and ballista, but I'm told the imperial army have no machines with them today.'

'Quite right,' Faden said, his eyes bright. 'Can you believe their arrogance? The Rahain armed forces have always been famed for their artillery, and yet here they are, marching towards us with nothing but shields and crossbows.'

'Did you fight against the Rahain when you were younger, Chancellor?' Celine asked.

'No,' he frowned. 'The wars came at a bad time for me. I was nineteen and still in officer training when the great Rahain Wars ended, and then when the last queen ordered the assault against Sanang, I was too old to go. I spent my military prime during years of peace. My career in the cavalry consisted of nothing but exercises and getting rather drunk.'

'My dearest Faden,' Mirren laughed, 'that's why we keep reminding you to leave the tactics to our experts. I would imagine that Killop here far out-reaches your knowledge of warfare.' She turned to him. 'I believe you have led armies against the Rahain on multiple occasions, yes?'

'Aye,' Killop said. 'I've fought and commanded in many battles.'

'Well then,' Faden said, stretching his arm out toward the plain below. 'I'd be intrigued to hear your opinion of today's engagement. Your critique, as it were.'

Killop gazed down at the Holdings infantry in their positions, where they had been all morning. To their right, the heavy cavalry had assembled, formed into four detachments. He couldn't see where the light cavalry had been placed, so he guessed it was off to the left, to fend off any Rahain attempt to outflank the Holdings infantry on that side.

Ahead, the sky was filled with dust. Now only two miles away, the imperial army was approaching them in a line twice as wide as that of the Holdings, and their ranks were deeper. At the front, their soldiers held out the great door-sized shields he had seen so many times before.

He glanced at Faden. 'It depends what you're going to do with your heavy cavalry. I'd guess you want your infantry to hold theirs for as long as possible, while the cavalry does something else to win the battle.'

Faden grinned. 'And what would that be, do you think?'

'If it were up to me,' Killop said, turning back to face the armies below, 'I'd ram them straight down the Emperor's throat. Have them circle the flanks, find a gap, and strike for the centre.'

'A rather succinct summation of our battle plan, don't you think, Faden?' said Mirren. 'Perhaps we should find a job for this young man on the staff?'

'It's pointless,' said a low voice to Killop's right.

'I'm sorry?' said Faden. 'I didn't quite catch that.'

Kylon glared at him. 'I said it was pointless. This whole battle, you're just wasting time and soldiers. You should be hiding your mages away up the mountains, and sheltering your folk, not throwing their lives away. Look at you all up here, swanning about like you think you're important. Don't you realise that the Emperor is about to annihilate your entire army before your eyes? He killed a hundred thousand Sanang in front of the walls of the imperial capital. They had the greatest fire mage the world has ever seen on their side, and he still smashed them. Do you think he's going to balk at a few horses?'

Faden stared in silence, his mouth open, as several officers on the platform bristled and tensed.

Mirren suppressed a smile. 'It's so refreshing to hear a contrary opinion. As queen, I always felt that people were too scared or syco-phantic to truthfully express their inner thoughts, and I continually had a niggling feeling that I was being humoured.' She stared at Kylon. 'And what is your name?'

Killop opened his mouth to speak. 'He's...'

'My name is Kylon. I led the Sanang army that invaded the Plateau last winter, along with Keira the fire mage, Killop's sister.'

There was a collective gasp from the officers on the platform, and Killop heard Celine groan.

Mirren nodded, her eyes bursting with amusement.

'A wanted man.'

'Only under imperial law,' Kylon said. 'I have already faced the enemy your army is about to meet. I urge you to pull back, scatter, and flee for the mountains. The Emperor wants your mages, that's why he's here. He's doesn't care about your little rebellion; it's the mages, that's all he's after.'

'We are aware of that,' Mirren said. 'Our high mages have already been withdrawn. In fact, I believe the only one on the field today is Holder Fast, who unfortunately could not be dissuaded from donning armour and mounting her horse.' She glanced at Killop. 'I tried my best, believe me.'

'All the more reason to call off the battle,' said Kylon. 'If there are no mages here to defend, then the Emperor will destroy your army for nothing.'

Faden stepped forward. 'Do not humour this man any longer, Mirren,' he said. 'Chief Killop, please escort your companion from the platform. His defeatism is souring the mood.'

Killop nodded.

He glanced at Kylon, and the two Kellach men walked away to the edge of the platform.

'I'm only speaking the truth,' Kylon said.

Killop looked out over the plain. The heavy cavalry, Daphne among them, were preparing their lines, wheeling into formation, their hooves kicking up a cloud of dirt. Their armour glistened in the sunlight, and their long green pennants fluttered in the breeze. They looked as if nothing could stop them.

'Are you sure?' he said.

'Aye, Killop. The Emperor will destroy them all.'

'How do you know? I thought you'd left the battlefield before the Emperor made his appearance at Plateau City.'

'You're right, I wasn't actually there,' Kylon said, 'but I saw what a hundred thousand Sanang looked like before the battle, and where are they all now? Every eyewitness account says the same thing, and Kalayne also vouched for the truth of it. The Emperor killed them, single-handed. That's why he hasn't brought any catapults or ballista. He doesn't need them.'

Killop nodded, his gaze on the plain. The imperial army was in the process of coming to a halt, a quarter of a mile in front of the Holdings infantry. Horns were blowing, and the front line of shields closed up into a firm wall.

'Get horses prepared,' Killop said. 'Get ready to go. I'll send Celine and Karalyn to you as soon as the battle's under way.'

'And you?'

'Just concern yourself with getting Karalyn to safety,' Killop said. 'Don't worry about me.'

Kylon nodded, then turned and walked back down the path towards the tents.

Killop re-joined Celine. Mirren and Faden had moved on, and were speaking to a small group of elderly officers by a table laid out with refreshments.

'Daddy,' Karalyn squealed, and he took her into his arms. She rapped her knuckles on his steel breastplate. 'Shiny.'

Celine raised an eyebrow at him. 'Well?'

'He's gone back to his tent.'

'And? Why did he tell them his real name, after we've spent thirds trying to hide it from everyone?'

Killop shrugged.

'He's lucky he wasn't arrested.'

'Let's watch the battle,' Killop said.

Celine frowned, and gave him a narrow-eyed stare. 'What are you not telling me?'

'Just stay ready, that's all.'

'Ready for what?'

'Ready to get the fuck out of here, if what Kylon says turns out to be true.'

Her expression changed, and she nodded.

There was a great blast of horns, and the imperial army began advancing, their great shield wall rumbling towards the lines of Holdings.

Killop gazed over the field below them. The Holdings infantry remained where it was, their shields to the front, waiting for the Rahain to get closer, while the heavy cavalry was beginning to pull away to the right, the huge formations of horse-flesh and steel thundering across the plain, as if they were departing the battlefield.

When the Rahain army had closed to a hundred yards, the Holdings artillery opened up, sending a shower of boulders raining down on the imperial lines, each one ploughing into the Rahain ranks.

There was a series of horn-blasts, and the Rahain lines picked up speed. They ran forward ten yards, stopped and, as one, aimed their crossbows through the slits in their shields and loosed. A hailstorm of bolts flew towards the Holdings infantry, peppering their shields and felling several soldiers. The Rahain sprinted forward another ten yards, grounded their shields and shot again. Each time, more Holdings fell. Their soldiers began to shoot their own crossbows into the Rahain lines, but the door-sized shields absorbed the bolts with ease. The outer wings of the Rahain army began to swing round to envelop the flanks of the smaller Holdings force. Killop saw the light cavalry appear from the far left, charging at the right wing of the imperial army from the side and rear, darting back and forth with their lances. They were unopposed, and ripped through the rear of the Rahain units, but there were so many imperial soldiers that overall, they were having little impact.

There were a few concerned mutterings from the officers on the platform.

'This is all part of the plan,' said Faden, holding a glass. 'A little patience, everyone.'

They tensed as the front ranks of Rahain reached the Holdings infantry. Both sides were relying on their shield walls, and along the entire front, the lines met in a crash of wood and steel. Killop tried to locate the position of the Emperor among the masses of soldiers, but the dust and dirt hung too thick in the air to be sure.

The ground rumbled, and all eyes darted to their right, where the Holdings heavy cavalry appeared, split into its four divisions, each charging a separate area of the Rahain back lines. They had formed into thick wedges of lances and armour, and the leading edges pierced through the imperial ranks like an oar through water.

There was a great cheer on the platform, and several glasses were raised.

There were now two battles going on, and Killop's eyes darted between them. Near the base of the hill, the struggle between the two sets of infantry was continuing, with the Rahain gaining ground step by step, while a hundred yards behind them, the heavy cavalry were ripping great holes through the enemy ranks, getting closer and closer to the centre of the imperial army.

'Too noisy,' said Karalyn, holding her ears.

Killop leaned in close to her. 'Is the bad man there?'

'Aye, daddy.' She pointed to the midst of the battle, where two of the heavy cavalry divisions were nearing.

The nervous chatter among the officers on the platform grew.

'Come on,' cried a voice.

'They're going to do it!' said Faden.

At that moment, there was a deafening cry, a sickening sound as thousands of horses reared up in agony, throwing their riders, or collapsing and crushing them. All over the battlefield, the cavalry stumbled and crashed to a halt. Horses cried out as they fell, creating heaps of armoured flesh. In the midst of the carnage, a lone figure stood, clad in plates of black steel, with his arms raised.

The voices on the platform fell silent. Someone sobbed.

Killop passed Karalyn to Celine. 'Now,' he said. 'Go.'

Celine took the child, her eyes wide and staring, and ran down the path towards the tents. Killop turned. Faden was walking towards the edge of the platform, his mouth open, tears rolling down his cheeks. He stared at the devastation. The officers around him said nothing, weeping at the sight of thousands of slain horses clustered on the battlefield. Around them, Holdings troopers were staggering to their feet. Many had been killed or injured when their mounts had fallen, and Rahain infantry were moving in to surround the survivors.

At the base of the hill, the Holdings infantry remained shield to shield with the Rahain, unaware of the disaster that had overtaken the cavalry. The two wings of the imperial army had now closed in on the flanks of the Holdings, and were beginning to push them back.

'It's over,' cried someone. 'We must order the retreat.'

Faden said nothing. Mirren took his hand.

Killop slipped off the platform, and ran straight down the side of the hill. He glanced over at the tents, but couldn't see Celine or Karalyn. He hoped Kylon was getting them far away. He reached the foot of the hill and kept running, veering to the right to avoid the Holdings catapults and artillery, now lying abandoned, their crews gone. Ahead of him were the rear ranks of the Holdings infantry, pushing and shoving the backs of their comrades ahead of them as the Rahain forced them back. Killop ran past them, swooping to pick up a shield that had been cast to the ground. A small paddock was laid out to the side of the catapults, where the heavy cavalry had been based that morning, and Killop vaulted the fence.

'Stop!' cried a Holdings soldier. 'You can't come in here.'

Killop pushed him aside, sending him flying to the ground. He picked up a saddle from a fence post, and prepared the largest horse in the paddock. He leapt up into the saddle. The beast reared, and stamped its hooves.

'Come on, you stupid bastard,' Killop muttered, kicking his heels and pulling on the reins. The horse took off, galloping across the paddock, and jumping over the fence. Killop pulled hard, and they skidded to the right, the horse kicking up great sods of earth as he clung on. He raced the horse across the length of the rear ranks of Holdings, and broke out past the advancing left wing of the Rahain, who dived out of the way of the charging beast.

He burst through the remaining lines of infantry and wheeled to the left. Rahain soldiers turned to stare as he sped past, and a few bolts were aimed in his direction. Killop pointed the nose of the horse at where he had seen the figure in black, and urged it on. They approached the area where the heavy cavalry had attacked, and the ground became littered with dead horses, Rahain infantry, and Holdings troopers. A multitude of small confrontations were taking place, with pockets of troopers holding off attacks from larger Rahain units.

Killop saw the Emperor. He was striding across the battlefield, surrounded by a tight bodyguard of Rahain soldiers, pointing his arm at any group of Holdings he approached. Killop dismounted by a piled mound of horse flesh, and drew his sword, crouching. The Emperor reached a group of Holdings, who were fighting back-to-back against a circle of advancing Rahain. He flicked his wrist, and the troopers fell to the ground, their eyes bursting from their heads.

Killop crouched lower amid the carpet of dead, and took a breath.

Where was she?

The battlefield covered a hundred acres; he was an idiot for thinking he would be able to find Daphne among such slaughter.

'Killop!'

He turned, and Daphne crashed into him from the other direction. She was shaking, blood coming from a wound to her left temple. Her sword was drawn, and was bloody and notched. She kissed him, and he tasted the blood on her lips.

He stared at her.

'Karalyn told me you were out here,' she yelled, as they crouched with their backs to the mound of dead horses. 'She wasn't pleased you ran off like that.'

'I'll make it up to her,' he grunted, 'as soon as I get you out of here.'

Daphne peered over the mound in the direction of the Emperor. 'If only I could get close enough to him,' she said, 'then we could salvage something from today.'

Killop leaned up next to her. The black-clad figure of the Emperor was now a hundred yards away. He was standing as a pile of wood was being built, made from discarded shields and broken-up wagons.

Daphne withdrew a whistle from her belt, and let out a long, low blast. Within a minute, several other troopers had crawled out of their hiding places, and were assembling behind where Daphne and Killop sheltered. Groups of Rahain forces still scoured the area, but the great majority of the enemy was continuing to engage the Holdings infantry over to their left.

'We're going to give it one last try,' Daphne said to the troopers, 'while he's distracted getting that fire ready. Split up into pairs, and make your way over there. Attack if you get close enough. Come on.'

Daphne ran off, keeping her head low, and sprinted to another heap of corpses. Killop frowned, but followed, and the other troopers began to set off on their own routes towards the Emperor. Daphne and Killop dodged from cover to cover, running and crouching, until they reached a deep ditch. They clambered down to its bottom and looked over the edge. The Emperor had his back to them, a mere twenty yards away.

'You should stay here,' Daphne said to Killop, 'in case this goes wrong.'

'Forget it,' he said. 'Where you go, I go.'

She nodded. 'Cover me, then.'

As she was about to launch herself up over the side of the ditch, a pair of Holdings troopers rushed out from the left, straight at the Emperor. From ten yards away they knelt, and each loosed a crossbow bolt, striking the Emperor in his side and chest, and knocking him off his feet.

'Yes!' Daphne cried, scrambling up the bank.

Killop leapt up after her, as the Rahain in charge of building the fire turned to face the attacking troopers. Killop and Daphne slammed into the group of Rahain side by side, cutting them down. The other troopers joined them, and they began to push the Rahain back.

The Emperor staggered to his feet, and ripped the bolts from his body. He glared at the Holdings troopers, his teeth bared, and raised his hand. He moved his fingers from right to left, and the heads of the troopers exploded. Daphne dived to the ground, Killop next to her. He reached an arm over her as the Emperor turned to face them. Killop stared back in silence, ready to die.

The Emperor's gaze passed over them. He spat on the ground, then turned and ordered the Rahain to continue building up the fire. Killop stayed frozen. Every Holdings trooper lay dead, only he and Daphne were unharmed. In silence, they crawled back to the ditch, and fell in.

'How?' Daphne whispered. 'How are we still alive?'

Killop lay back, panting, his hands shaking.

A hand touched his arm.

'Daddy!'

He jumped back in shock as he saw Kylon next to him in the ditch, Karalyn strapped to his back.

'What the fuck?' he cried.

Daphne sprang over him, her right fist connecting with Kylon's nose.

'You bring my daughter to a battle?' she yelled. 'I'll kill you.'

Kylon struggled, but Daphne clung on, punching him again.

'I saved you,' Kylon gasped.

Killop pulled Daphne off Kylon. 'Not now,' he whispered. 'We get Karalyn to safety first, then you can kick his arse.'

Daphne had murder in her eyes, but backed off.

'Mummy angry,' said Karalyn.

'Come on,' Killop said, 'let's move.'

'Wait,' said Daphne. 'Kara-bear, is Aunty Chane still alive? Can you see her?'

Killop peered over the lip of the ditch as Karalyn gazed around. The Emperor was urging the Rahain on, driving them to make the pile of fuel larger. Killop slid back down the ditch as Karalyn nodded.

The girl pointed back towards where the initial cavalry charge had floundered, out among the sea of horse-flesh.

They set off, running at a crouch along the bottom of the ditch until they came to a mound of corpses, with both horses and Holdings mingled in a heap.

'Chane there,' Karalyn said.

'Good girl,' Daphne muttered, and started to pull the bodies from the pile. Killop and Kylon helped, dragging the corpses from the heap, until their hands and arms were thick with blood and gore. At the bottom of the heap, they found her. Chane was unconscious, and had multiple wounds.

'Her armour saved her from getting crushed,' Kylon said. 'We'll carry her back.'

'Getting through the Rahain lines might be tricky,' said Daphne.

'Ye still don't get it, do you?' Kylon said. 'It's not just the Emperor who's blind to her. When she hides, no one can see her, or us, if we stick close to her. All we have to do is walk back through their lines. Celine is waiting with horses for us on the other side of the ridge.'

'Celine agreed to this?'

'I might have lied to her about what I was going to do.'

The sound of an explosion reached them, and the ground trembled. Killop looked up at the hillside. The command platform, where he had been standing with Faden and Mirren, was bathed in flames. Figures on fire ran from the terrace screaming, or toppled off the edge and fell down the slope. At the bottom of the hill, the Holdings infantry were in full retreat, streaming back over the hills, throwing their shields and weapons behind them as they ran.

'Shit,' said Killop. 'This battle's over.'

'We'll fight on,' said Kylon. 'We must.'

Daphne stared at him. She unstrapped Karalyn from his back, and held her close. Killop and Kylon picked up the body of Chane, and they began the long walk back across the battlefield.

Rahain soldiers marched or ran past without noticing them, and they were ignored all the way to the ridge. Kylon led them on for another mile to the left, down into a thick dell, where Celine was standing. Next to her, four horses were saddled and ready to go.

Daphne fell to her knees, exhausted. Killop took Karalyn, and helped Daphne onto a horse.

Celine gazed at them. 'How did you get away?'

Killop frowned as he leapt up into the saddle of his horse, Karalyn in one arm. He settled her down in front of him, and took the reins.

Celine also mounted. 'Killop?'

He glared at Kylon, who was getting into his own saddle.

'Ask me later.'

Celine gazed from Killop to Kylon, then to Daphne, frowning.

'What did you do?' she said to the Kell man in black.

Kylon shrugged. 'What I had to.'

Celine leaned over in her saddle and slapped him across the face.

'You endanger that child again, and I'll kill you myself.'

Daphne looked up, her eyes half closed. 'Not if I get to him first.'

Killop turned, and gazed up at the great peaks of the Shield Mountains, which ran across the northern edge of the Holdings, continuing on into the far west. They kicked their heels, and their horses took off at a trot along the path at the base of the dell, growing further from the noise on the battlefield with every stride, until there was nothing but the still silence of the plains.

CHAPTER 19
CRY FOR HELP

Northern Rahain City, Imperial Rahain – 10th Day, Last Third Autumn 507

Bridget sat alone, her cloak wrapped round her to keep out the chill breeze. She stared out at the hills and valleys of Northern Rahain, the wild lands above the Tahrana Valley, where no one dwelt. Laodoc watched her from where he sat with the others round a warm camp fire. Dyam and Dean were preparing a meal from two large birds that Lola had shot earlier that morning. It would be their first warm food in several days, and Laodoc's stomach was grumbling.

Agang sat to his left, deep in thought, while Lola and Tara, the young Rakanese woman, were on his right.

'Thank you for catching our breakfast,' said Laodoc amid the silence.

Lola grunted.

Tara rattled off a string of angry-sounding words in her own language, staring at Laodoc as she said them. He smiled at her, but she seemed to become annoyed, and looked away, shaking her head.

'She's probably just hungry,' Agang muttered.

Laodoc sighed. 'No, she's angry with me, and she has a right to be, I suppose. She would have been home days ago if it weren't for me slowing you all down.'

'It's not your fault.'

'It is. I'm a foolish old man who should have realised that a journey such as this would be too much for me. You're all young and fit, my friend. The reason we're only managing a few miles each day is entirely down to my old bones.'

'You should have built some roads up here when you were chancellor,' Dyam said, winking at him. 'Then we could have taken the wagons with us, and we could all be relaxing, instead of lugging our gear over these hills.'

She finished skewering the two plucked birds, and placed them over the fire.

'Turn them every minute or so,' she said to Dean, who nodded, his eyes staring at the ground. She opened her pack and pulled out a water skin. 'At least there are plenty of streams,' she said. 'Could be a lot worse.'

'It's just a few more miles to Silverstream,' said Agang, 'if we understand Tara correctly.' He turned to Laodoc. 'You've done fine,' he smiled, 'for an old man.'

Laodoc nodded, but felt shame creep through him. He was slowing everything down, his weak and stupid limbs growing tired after only a mile or two into each march. Agang and Dyam had tried to make light of it, but he could sense the frustration from the others, and had earned many a dirty look from Tara whenever they had stopped for another break to accommodate him.

At least she was looking healthier, he reflected. The rashes and bruises on her skin had faded since they had left the poisoned city of Akhanawarah. While the rest of them had lost weight, she had put on a little, as even their meagre rations were better than what she had survived on in captivity. Despite her impatience with him, Laodoc had spent many hours trying to communicate with Tara. They had established that she had been on a scouting expedition from Silverstream, when she and a number of companions had been captured by the

Rahain looters. She had signalled her ignorance of the name of Shella, but Laodoc wasn't convinced, believing that she might be lying to protect her.

'Pay attention, Dean,' scolded Dyam. 'Yer letting them burn.'

She pushed him out of the way, and re-arranged the two birds on the fire. Dean sat down, misery darkening his young features.

'Do you want to get some practice in?' asked Laodoc. 'There's no one about to see.'

Dean shook his head.

'I wanted to say,' Laodoc went on, 'what a good job you did with burning those looters' wagons.'

Lola snorted, as Dean's face went red.

Laodoc raised an eyebrow.

'I set them alight,' Lola said. 'He froze.'

Dean's face twisted into a snarl. He leapt to his feet, and ran off through the trees next to where they had camped.

Dyam gave Lola a look.

'Ye need to stop mothering him,' the Lach hunter said. 'The laddie needs to toughen up. Ye all do. Apart from Agang, yer all falling to pieces.'

The others said nothing. Laodoc knew that Lola had lost more than just a fellow hunter in Bonnie, but she seemed to be able to put her grief aside and stay focussed on doing her job. Dyam poked at the fire, her pale blonde hair untidy and unwashed. To his left, Agang looked his usual composed self, somehow managing to appear smart and clean despite the hardships they had experienced walking for long days through barren valleys and up rocky slopes.

'We'll have time to recover once we get to Silverstream,' the Sanang man said. 'We can rest and heal our wounds there.'

Dyam looked up. 'Food's ready.'

She took the birds off the fire, and used a knife to slice the meat into a row of bowls. Laodoc picked one up.

'I'll see if Bridget wants any.'

Dyam nodded.

He got to his feet, his walking stick in his left hand, and climbed the dusty slope to where Bridget sat on a large boulder. She was looking up at the great mass of mountains to the west. He sat down next to her, the bowl of warm food resting on his lap.

'Snow,' she said.

Laodoc gazed up, and noticed the white peaks through the clouds in the distance.

'Yes,' he said. 'The highest summits of the Grey Mountains can get snow, even before winter has begun.' He smiled. 'Not far to go, Bridget. Today, maybe.' He held out the bowl. 'I've brought you some food.'

She glanced at it.

'How long's it been?'

Laodoc frowned. 'What?'

'Since Bedig died.'

'Twenty-five days.'

She nodded, her eyes returning to gaze at the mountains.

'Are you hungry?' he said.

She shook her head.

'You should eat. I'll share it with you.'

'I don't want it.'

'Is there anything I can do to help?'

'I just want to get to Silverstream,' she said. 'And then sleep. For a long time. Maybe if I'm lucky, I won't wake up again.'

Laodoc remembered how he had felt after Simiona's death, and said nothing.

'I wish Killop was here,' she said after a while. 'I miss him. For so many years, we were closer than I've ever been to anyone, it was like we shared the same thoughts. He knew everything about me, and I knew everything about him. He was my brother. When he left, it felt worse than it did when I lost my real sisters in the war. I want to talk to him, tell him about Bedig. He'd get it.'

'You can talk to us,' Laodoc said. 'We've all lost somebody we loved.'

'See?' she said. 'I knew you wouldn't understand.'

Laodoc paused. He wanted to say that he did understand, and that the pain of Simiona's death had left his emotions shredded, but he swallowed, and nodded.

'Help me understand.'

She glared at him. 'If Bedig had died on the battlefield,' she said, 'then it would have been hard to take, but easier than this.'

'Why?' Laodoc said. 'He fought bravely to the end.'

'Aye, while I was lying on the ground with an arrow in my throat. He was killed thinking I was dead. I was dead. And then someone made the decision that my life was worth more than his, and here I am, alive again.' She shook her head. 'I should be dead. I don't deserve life more than Bedig did. Why was I chosen?' She started to cry. 'It's bullshit, all of it.'

'It wasn't like that,' Laodoc said, his heart breaking. 'No one knew what to do. Amid all the blood and confusion, nobody was thinking rationally. Agang had a split-second choice to make, please don't blame him for doing what he thought best.'

'So it was him? He left Bedig to die?'

'And if he hadn't?' Laodoc said. 'Imagine he had raised Bedig instead of you. Imagine how Bedig would be feeling right now. Would he want to go on, knowing that he had been chosen over you? Oh, Bridget, I'm so sorry, for everything. It is I who dragged you all on this journey, a "fool's errand", as Bonnie called it. If anyone's to blame, it's me.'

'Don't be stupid.'

Laodoc glanced at the bowl of food on his lap, his appetite gone.

He heard a whistle from the campsite below, and glanced up to see Dyam waving at them to come down. The tents were being packed up, and the fire extinguished.

'Time to go,' he said.

Bridget nodded, and they got to their feet.

'You should eat that,' Lola said when they got to the bottom of the slope.

'I don't want it,' he said. 'You have it.'

Lola shrugged, and took the bowl. She took half of the food in her hands and swallowed it down, then passed the rest to Tara.

'We all ready?' Agang said, gazing round the clearing. Everyone nodded, including Dean, who Laodoc noticed had re-appeared.

The Sanang man approached Tara, whose mouth was full of her second helping of breakfast.

'Which way?' he said, pointing.

Tara smiled, and strode off through the trees. The others followed, Laodoc leaning on his stick.

'Just a few more miles,' Agang said to him, picking up a heavy pack and slinging it over his broad shoulders.

Laodoc smiled, though his heart was heavy.

'I'll keep you company,' Agang said.

'Thank you, my friend.'

They followed the line of narrow forest, hemmed in between high rocky cliffs on either side. The trees towered above them, sheltering them from the cold wind that gusted down the valley. The ground was uneven, and slippery, and Laodoc felt his calves ache as they started to lag behind.

Agang glanced at him. 'How was Bridget this morning?'

'The same,' he said. 'It breaks my heart to see her in such pain. Are you sure you can't help her, heal her mind?'

'I can't,' he said. 'I've told you, grieving is a natural process, I can't interfere.'

'You interfered with me quickly enough.'

'All I did was temporarily fix the imbalance in your brain, to ease your depression. Bridget's in mourning, it's different.'

'But there must be something you can do,' Laodoc said. 'The guilt she's carrying is too much for anyone to bear.'

'Guilt?' Agang said, his eyes tightening. 'I'm not sure you under-stand how my powers work. I can encourage a body to physically heal itself, or I can give a piece of my own life-force to bring someone back. I can't cure guilt, my friend.'

'So we're just going to leave her to suffer?'

'Keep talking to her,' Agang said. 'She'll get over it eventually. We all do.'

Laodoc glanced ahead at the group. Tara and Lola were out in front, almost out of sight through the trees. The two Domm came next. Dyam was chatting to Dean, who was glowering in silence. Bridget followed them alone, her gaze fixed, but her eyes vacant. She was as thin as she had been when he had first seen her, in the cess-pit of a holding cage in the Rahain Capital, bound in chains next to Killop and Kallie.

'What about you?' Agang said.

'I'm fine.'

'You don't have to pretend with me.'

Laodoc frowned at him. 'I said I was fine. You may not believe it, but you'll have to accept it. It was most certainly not an invitation for you to pry.'

Agang scowled and looked away, and they continued on in silence.

———

They walked for a few hours, as Laodoc's limbs grew wearier, the joints in his legs and back aching. He said nothing, refusing to be the one who called for a rest, not when Tara's excitement was visibly growing with every step. They were close, they just had to keep going.

Agang passed him a water skin.

Laodoc reached out to take it, but staggered forward. Agang grabbed his arm, stopping him from falling.

'You're pushing yourself too much,' he said, then turned to the front. 'Everyone! Time for a break.'

Bridget sat down on a rock, and Dyam and Dean trudged back to where Agang was supporting the old Rahain man. He lowered him onto a smooth boulder, and held the water skin to his lips.

'I'm not a child,' he snapped, taking the skin from Agang's grasp.

Agang backed off.

'It's time for lunch anyway,' said Dyam, pulling off her pack. 'Dean, help me unpack whatever we've got left.' Tara barged past her, heading for Laodoc. She stood in front of him, and unleashed a torrent of Rakanese in his face.

'Enough,' said Lola, and the young woman fell silent, but continued to glare at Laodoc.

'Sorry, everybody,' he said. 'Damn these old legs.'

'Let's just recover our strength,' Agang said. 'We can get a few more miles done this afternoon.'

Lola snorted. 'Maybe; if you carry him.'

'Look,' said Agang, 'I understand that you're all frustrated, but we have to deal with the situation we're in. We need to stick together, now more than ever. Soon we'll be in Silverstream, a town where we won't understand anything that people are saying, a town that's stayed hidden for years. They're probably going to be suspicious, and worried that the world has finally caught up with them.'

He gazed at them all.

'We're hoping to meet Shella there,' he went on, 'so remember this. The only person among us that she's ever met before is Laodoc. This old man is the only link we have to her. To help us, he's walked over a hundred miles through these hills. Is a little patience too much to ask?'

Lola frowned. 'Ten minutes,' she said, and walked off, Tara close behind.

Dyam glanced over at Agang, and smiled.

'Thank you,' said Laodoc.

Agang shrugged. 'I meant what I said.'

He knelt, his hands out-stretched. 'Now, where does it hurt?'

Their route that afternoon took them through a tight ravine, its bottom muddy and littered with fallen boulders. They scaled a long rocky slope, scrambling over the rough ground, and down into a deep valley, thick with spruce trees. Laodoc pushed himself on, Agang's healing keeping him on his feet for hours.

As they descended the slope, Tara cried out, pointing. Laodoc glanced up, and lost his footing on the loose rocks. The ground shifted beneath his feet and he slid down the hillside, his arms flailing. His leg hit a tree trunk, and he swivelled, coming to a halt next to a great boulder. He groaned, and clenched his eyes shut, the pain in his leg excruciating. He heard footsteps close by.

'Shit,' said Dyam. 'Agang, get over here.'

Laodoc opened his eyes, biting his lip to keep himself from screaming. Agang was running towards him, while Dyam knelt by his side. Agang put a hand on his leg.

'Broken.'

Lola came into view. Behind her, Tara was standing. 'Fix him,' said the Lach hunter.

'I can't,' Agang said. 'He's too weak. I don't think he's eaten anything today. If I try to heal his leg, he'll go into a coma, maybe worse.'

'But you're a fucking mage.'

'I can only work with what I've got,' Agang yelled, his eyes narrowing at Lola. 'The body needs some reserves for my powers to work. Older people have less reserves anyway, and Laodoc's are utterly exhausted.' His voice lowered. 'I've already healed him so many times, he has nothing left to give.'

Agang faced him. 'But I can ease his pain.'

Laodoc felt a soothing sensation through the Sanang man's touch, and he gasped in relief.

'Thank you,' he said.

'I'll make him a splint,' said Dyam. 'Dean, help me.'

'Why do I always have to help you?' the young mage said.

'Don't test me,' Dyam snarled. Dean backed away.

Tara started talking, her voice rising in an angry tirade. She kept pointing further into the forest.

'Look,' said Lola, 'the lassie's obviously desperate to get home. I reckon from the way she's carrying on, it must be close. Maybe I should go with her. If it's nearby, she can show me the way, and then I can come back for the rest of ye.'

'That's a good idea,' said Agang. 'We're not going to be able to move Laodoc for a while. He needs rest and food before I can heal his leg.'

Lola swung her pack to the ground. 'I'll leave this here with ye.' She turned to Tara. 'Come on, then. Silverstream.'

Tara grinned, and the two walked off through the trees.

Laodoc lay still as Dyam prepared a splint, using an axe to pare down and trim a sturdy branch, while Dean sat watching. Agang straightened his leg, dulling his pain with every slow movement, until it lay flat.

'How bad is it?'

'Two breaks,' Agang said, not looking up.

'Could I have some water, please?'

'Of course,' Agang said. He folded a cloak, and slid it under Laodoc's head to prop him up, then passed him the water skin. The old man took a drink. Dyam held the splint out against his broken leg, then removed it and began to make adjustments.

Laodoc frowned. 'Where's Bridget?'

Dyam glanced around. 'Shit. Where's she got to?'

'I didn't see her come down the slope,' Agang said.

'Bridget!' Dyam yelled. 'Shit. I'd better look for her.'

She passed the splint to Agang, and stood. 'Dean, come with me, help me look.'

The young mage grunted and got to his feet.

'You go that way,' she pointed, and they split up, each taking a separate route back up the rocky hillside.

'I hope she's all right,' Laodoc said, as Agang started to strap the splint to his leg.

'Just focus on staying still,' Agang said, leaning over to tighten the straps. 'Right, the splint's on. How's the pain?'

'Bearable.'

Agang slumped back against a tree. He opened Lola's pack, and pulled out a cloth package. He unwrapped it, and offered Laodoc a greasy strip of dried pork. He took one for himself, and started chewing.

Laodoc stared at the piece of gristle, and laid it down.

'No,' Agang said. 'You have to eat. If you don't, I won't be able to heal you.'

The Rahain man picked it up, closed his eyes, and took a bite. A wave of nausea washed over him, but he swallowed, and managed to keep it down. He raised it to his mouth again, then stopped, as a piercing cry rang out over the hillside, echoing off the other side of the valley.

Agang sprang to his feet, his hand on the hilt of his sword, and gazed around.

'It came from where Dean was headed,' he said, turning to Laodoc.

'You'd better go.'

Agang frowned, his eyes darting between Laodoc and the hillside.

'I'll be back as soon as I can,' he said, and sprinted up the hill.

Laodoc watched him leave, and took another bite.

A voice hissed at him in a foreign language.

He turned, and saw two Rakanese approach, each aiming a Rahain-made crossbow at him. They glared at him with venom in their eyes. One of them shouted at him, and he picked out 'Rahain' among the stream of words.

Laodoc dropped the strip of pork and raised his hands.

One of the Rakanese lifted his crossbow and took aim.

There was a blur of movement and Bridget appeared, running out from the cover of the trees. She grasped the crossbow and ripped it out of the hands of the Rakanese, then shoved him to the ground. She then punched the other Rakanese in the face before she could raise her weapon, and sent her flying into the undergrowth.

'Behind you,' Laodoc said, as the male Rakanese got back to his feet, a knife in his hand.

Bridget turned, a look of rage on her face. The two began to pace round in a circle, each staring at the other. Bridget was unarmed, but stood a good foot and a half taller than the Rakanese with the knife.

'We're looking for Shella,' Laodoc cried. 'Shellakanawara.'

The man's eyes glanced towards him, and Bridget leapt forwards. She gripped the man's wrist and squeezed. He yelled out in pain and dropped the knife. There was a crashing noise of sliding rocks, and Dyam stumbled down the hill.

She gazed at the two Rakanese. Bridget was still grasping onto the man's arm, and was forcing him down to his knees. Dyam picked up his crossbow.

'Let him go,' said Laodoc to Bridget.

'He was going to kill you.'

'I know, but you stopped him. Let him go, Bridget.'

She released the man. He raced off ten yards, then turned, and hurried back to where his companion lay in the undergrowth. He reached her side and crouched down.

'We need to go,' said Bridget.

'How?' Dyam said. 'Laodoc can't walk.'

'I'll carry him.'

The Rakanese man let out a loud cry. They turned to face him. He was staring at Bridget, hatred twisting his features.

'What did you do, Bridget?' Dyam said.

The Brig woman said nothing.

'She punched her,' said Laodoc.

Tears were rolling down the face of the Rakanese man.

Laodoc saw figures run from the forest. They surrounded the small group, crossbows pointed at them. All were Rakanese.

Dyam dropped the crossbow, and put an arm out to touch Bridget.

'Don't move,' she whispered.

The Rakanese man cried out to the new group, and Laodoc could see rage grow in their wide eyes. They gestured with their crossbows, and Bridget and Dyam raised their arms. Several approached, and threw hoods over their heads. Crossbows were shoved into their backs, and they were marched off into the forest. Others came to where Laodoc lay. They took an arm or leg each, and lifted him.

Laodoc cried out in agony as the splint on his leg buckled under the strain. He closed his eyes.

When he came to, his leg was on fire. Pain seared up from his foot to his hip. He opened his eyes. He was lying inside a cold wooden hut. Dyam and Bridget were sitting on one side of him, Agang and Dean on the other.

As soon as the Sanang man heard his cry, he placed his hands onto Laodoc's leg, and the pain faded to a dull ache. Laodoc shivered, shaking on the packed earth floor of the hut. Dyam pulled off her cloak and laid it over him, while Agang took his hand.

'Once again,' Laodoc said, 'I owe you all my thanks. Why on earth you ever agreed to travel with such a feeble old man is beyond me.'

'You're a tough old bastard,' Bridget said.

Laodoc gazed at her. 'Did you kill that woman?'

Bridget nodded. 'Aye. I didn't mean to, but I was just so angry. I had no idea I could kill someone with one punch. I tried to say sorry, but they didn't understand me.'

'The Rakanese are frail creatures next to the Kellach Brigdomin,' Agang said. 'To them, you must appear like ferocious giants.'

'And the cry we heard?'

Agang nudged Dean.

'That wasn't my fault,' said the young mage. 'I thought they were going to shoot me.'

Dyam raised an eyebrow. 'It was you that let out that howl?'

Dean glowered.

'I found him surrounded by Rakanese,' Agang said. 'I tried to communicate with them, tell them who we were looking for, but they weren't in the mood for a discussion.'

'Where are Lola and Tara?' asked Laodoc.

'We were hooded all the way here,' said Dyam. 'Didn't see anyone.'

'Same with Dean and I,' said Agang. 'Hopefully they'll come along soon, and get us out of here.'

'Where is here, do ye think?' said Dyam. 'Are we in Silverstream?'

Agang leaned over to the wall, and put his eye up to a narrow gap in the slats.

'Maybe,' he said. 'I can see other huts.'

There was a sound from outside of people approaching. The wooden door opened, and a Rakanese man entered, followed by more with crossbows. The small group of captives edged back.

'Is Shella here?' said Agang. 'Shella?'

A hooded figure came through the door.

'Who are you and what do you want?' said a woman's voice from under the hood. 'Holy shit. Laodoc?'

She pulled back her hood.

'A pleasure to meet you again, princess,' Laodoc said, trying to raise his head.

She stared at him, then at Agang and the others.

'How did you find me?'

Agang stood. The Rakanese guards in the room tensed.

Shella turned to them and yelled something. The guards nodded, then filed out of the hut, leaving Shella alone with the captives.

'You were going to say something, Agang?' she said.

'How do you know my name?'

'We've met,' she smirked. 'Do you not remember? Outside the walls of Plateau City, while your army was besieging it.'

'You were there?' Agang said. 'With the Emperor?'

'He was only a king at the time. Anyway, don't get distracted. How did you find me?'

'We met a young woman, called Tara. We saved her from some Rahain bandits, and she led us here.'

'Tara? Thought she was dead. The border guards told me you killed one of them. If you hadn't been mentioning my name, they would have executed you all by now.'

'That was me,' said Bridget. 'I did it.'

'It was an accident,' said Laodoc. 'I saw it happen. Bridget didn't intend to kill her.'

Shella frowned.

'Laodoc needs help,' Agang said. 'He's hurt.'

Shella approached the old man.

'Don't bullshit me, you fork-tongued old bastard,' she said. 'Why are you here?'

'To tell you something,' Laodoc said. 'We're here because of a prophecy made by the Kellach mage Kalayne, in which he saw you and Fire Mage Keira together. We beseech you to help us fulfil this prophecy, so that the Emperor's hold over this world can end.'

Shella starting laughing.

'Kalayne's dead.'

'What?' said Agang, his face greying.

'Yip. He didn't see that coming. I know all about his prophecies.'

'Then you'll help us?' said Laodoc.

'Nope,' she said. 'I want you to leave Silverstream and forget that you were ever here. Here's the deal. I'll stop the militia from executing you for murder, and you can say thank you and go.'

'I'm afraid my leg is broken,' Laodoc said. He caught Agang's eye. 'I'm not able to walk at the moment.'

'He can't be moved,' said the Sanang man. 'Not until his leg's properly healed. At his age, that might take some time.'

Shella frowned. 'How bad is it?'

'Fractured in two places.'

'Fucksake,' Shella muttered. 'Okay, you can stay until it heals, but not a day longer.'

The door opened, and Tara walked in, followed by Lola. Shella glanced at the tall Lach woman.

'Another one?' She shook her head. 'I suppose you'll want housed and fed. What a ball-ache.'

'It'll give us time to catch up,' said Laodoc.

Shella smirked. 'Oh yeah, professor snake-eyes? I bet my story blows the shit out of yours.'

CHAPTER 20
WEIGHING THE ODDS

Outside Royston, Imperial Holdings – 12th Day, Last Third Autumn 507

'This is insanity,' Kylon muttered, as Daphne lit another cigarette. 'Four days we've been camped here. At any moment of the Emperor's choosing, his forces could wipe out every trooper that survived the battle. What are your leaders thinking?'

Daphne said nothing, her gaze scanning the long lines of tents by the main road outside the town of Royston. She knew Kylon was right. Troopers had been arriving in small groups every day since the defeat at the Red Hills. Most were unarmed, and many were injured. They had been refused access to Royston, and had been left to look after themselves, while the remainder of the rebel leadership were safe behind the high walls of the town. Daphne had been the highest ranking rebel to stay outside with the soldiers, where she could keep an eye on the remnant of the Hold Fast company that had made it off the battlefield.

'It'll end today,' she said, 'one way or another.'

Kylon frowned as they sat on the low bank overlooking the fields of tents.

'That's if they listen to you.'

'I hope they do,' she said, 'but I'm not completely out of ideas about what to do if they don't.'

'The Emperor's laughing at us,' he said. 'He's picking off the rebel Holds one at a time, while the only force in the country large enough to stand up to him sits here and festers. Correct me if I'm wrong, but doesn't Royston supply the steel that makes your weapons? Why haven't these troopers been re-armed? Why is no one training and drilling them? Why are none of their officers out here? Why...?'

'Enough, Kylon,' she said. 'You know the answer.'

'Aye, but I can hardly believe it. All it took was your father and Faden to be killed, and the entire rebellion crumbles into ash and dust.'

'The other Holders are still in shock after seeing our cavalry annihilated,' she said, 'but that's not why I wanted to talk to you.'

'It's because you don't trust me.'

She took a draw of the cigarette. 'A judgement I've arrived at based on the evidence of your own actions. I explicitly forbade you from bringing Karalyn onto the battlefield, and you disobeyed me.'

'If I'd obeyed you, dear Lady Holdfast, then we wouldn't be having this conversation. Your corpse would be rotting with the others in the shadow of the Red Hills. As would Killop's. I took a calculated risk.'

Daphne frowned.

'Your daughter put a vision of the future into my mind,' Kylon went on, 'seen from your eyes. In it, the Emperor was about to kill you, so I knew what would happen if I did nothing. She also demanded that I take her out there, to save you.'

'So you listen to the word of a one-year-old, but not me?'

'I do, when that one-year-old happens to be the most important person in the world. Remember that my oath is to her, not to you, or Killop. Karalyn is my mistress, and I am her servant.'

'Then your primary duty is to protect her, even if she asks you to put her in danger. If a similar situation occurs again, Kylon, I want you to remember that duty, and say no. It's alright to say no to her, she's one. If I gave in to her every request, she'd eat nothing but cake and biscuits. Do you want her to eat nothing but cake and biscuits?'

Kylon frowned, and looked away. Daphne sighed. Compared to Kylon, Killop was an open book, and she struggled to understand what he was thinking most of the time.

'You Kell,' she muttered. 'I miss Bedig and Bridget, they're so straightforward in comparison. Tell me, are the Kell known for their brooding bloody-mindedness?'

'Maybe if the Brig had been invaded first,' Kylon said, 'they'd have a greater understanding of the price we paid. Tell me, Lady Holdfast, apart from Killop, how many Kell did you see when you lived in Slateford? I'll bet it wasn't many.'

Daphne paused. She remembered Kalden, but he had died. There were others, weren't there?

'Conal,' she said. 'He was there. He knew Killop from before.'

Kylon smirked. 'So, one? Among how many Brig and Domm?'

'Damn,' she said. 'I hadn't really thought of it that way. The Rahain attacked Kell first.'

'And our folk took the brunt of it. So, forgive us if we are melancholy, for few of us remain. The haven at Domm, if it survives, will end up an amalgam of the other three clans. The Kell songs and stories, they'll be the ones forgotten first.'

Daphne nodded. 'Then you know how it feels to see your country trampled underfoot, by an invader who cares nothing for the lives of your people, who burns, destroys and kills his way across the land you love. For that is now the fate of the Holdings.'

'I sympathise,' he said, 'which is why I'm still arguing with you about strategy. This war is not lost yet. The rebels still have four high mages sheltering in Royston. If they scattered into the mountains, with supplies and soldiers to protect them, then the Emperor's army will have to hunt them. If you take up guerrilla tactics, and harass the Rahain forces constantly, they'll run out of supplies, and have to head back to the Plateau before winter comes along to starve them.'

Daphne shook her head. 'And then what? He comes back next year?'

'Ultimately, we need to strike, we need to kill him. But for now, I just want the survival of those who are prepared to resist him.'

'Then our aims are aligned. You know, if the situation were different, I might offer you a place on my command.'

'I have your ear,' he said. 'I just hope you listen to my words.'

She glanced at him, his dark eyes hiding whatever schemes were going through his mind.

'If only I could trust you,' she said.

He said nothing, turning his glance back to the lines of tents.

'Here you are,' said Killop, walking along the low ridge towards them. 'A messenger's arrived from Queen Mirren for you.'

'Yeah?' Daphne said. 'Have I been summoned?'

Killop sat next to them.

'Aye,' he said, 'looks like it.'

His gaze wandered over the tents. He shook his head.

'Are you going along?' said Kylon.

Killop shrugged. 'Doubt I'm invited.'

'I want you to stay here,' Daphne said, 'but not because I care about what the other Holders think. I want you here so you're ready.'

He nodded.

'We'll be ready,' said Kylon.

Daphne glanced at the two men. 'Don't you want to know what for?'

'We're Kell,' said Kylon. 'We're ready for anything.'

Daphne took Commander Annifrid with her, and they accompanied the messenger into the town of Royston. The town's wealth was based on the rich iron seams in the hills to the north, and the walled settlement lay piled up the side of a mountain. The entrance gates were on the level of the plains, while the aristocratic quarters were reached by steep paths up the hillside. Mirren Blackhold's temporary accommodation was located in the heart of the noble district, in an old stone mansion across a square from the town hall, where the rebel command was based.

The streets of the town were quiet, with most shops closed, and many houses boarded up. Much of the population had already fled into the hills. Those with mining connections had journeyed up to the large communities nestled by the iron seams, while others had simply run.

Daphne, Annifrid and their small honour guard ascended the paths to the upper quarter. The square where the town hall lay was guarded, with militia wearing the insignia of Hold Smith, the most powerful noble house of Royston. They were waved through, the soldiers saluting her as they passed.

The square was deserted, and they crossed to Mirren's mansion. More guards let them enter, and a courtier escorted them to a private reception chamber, where the queen sat, drinking tea.

'My dear Daphne Holdfast,' she said, 'thank you for coming. Tea?'

'Please.' She nodded to her guard, and they took up positions outside the chamber. She walked forward, Annifrid by her side, and they sat by the low table across from Mirren. The queen poured three hot cups of golden liquid.

'Are you hungry?'

'No, ma'am,' Daphne said, opening her cigarette case and offering it to the others.

'Thank you,' said Mirren. They lit their cigarettes and drank tea.

'The meeting due to be held this evening,' Mirren said, 'will be attended by every Hold in the rebellion. I thought it might be in our interests if we were to go over a few salient points before we attend.'

Daphne shook her head. 'I harbour some doubt as to whether anything we say will have any influence with what remains of the leadership.'

'You and I have been frozen out by the others since the battle,' Mirren said. 'I trust you know why that is? We two were the only ones mentioned by name in the Emperor's letter.'

Annifrid looked up. 'The Emperor sent a letter?' she said. 'Why? He could destroy us all if he wanted to.'

'He wants our mages,' Daphne said. 'He knows we're hiding them, and doesn't want to risk killing them if he attacks.'

'Indeed,' said Mirren. 'However, with Faden's death, you and I have been relegated from leadership to bargaining chips.'

'Do you think the others wish to trade us? For what?'

'For a promise that the Emperor will spare their lands. He has already scoured Holds Cane and Clement, and he is currently employed in burning Hold Vale to the ground. Holders Terras, Wain and Smith naturally feel that their turn is next. If you're asking if I think they would sell us out if the Emperor promised to spare them, then I would have to say yes, of course they would.'

'The Emperor's promises are worth nothing.'

'I know that, you know that, but a whisper of water to a man dying of thirst can do wonders for changing his mind. Tell me, how many troopers of Hold Fast do you have battle-ready?'

'Three hundred.'

Mirren nodded.

Daphne sat back in her chair. 'Not tempted to go running back to Guilliam?'

Mirren put down her teacup, and swept a stray hair from her face. Daphne smoked, watching her.

'I know you don't like me,' Mirren said. 'I can see why. I was having an affair with your sister's husband, after all.' She shook her head. 'Faden was weak. It should have been your father who led the rebellion...'

'Did you want to screw him as well?' Daphne said. 'Two queens might have been too much, even for him.'

Annifrid made a choking sound, and put a hand to her face.

Mirren glanced at Daphne, raising an eyebrow.

Daphne shrugged. 'Probably.'

'Godfrey was a good man,' sobbed Annifrid.

'I'm sure he was,' Mirren said, offering her a hankie. 'Now, Lady Daphne, what I meant earlier by referencing your father, was that the Hold Fast name remains the only one capable of uniting any resistance to the Emperor. I am a patriot. Above all else, I love this country, and will fight to my last breath to protect it.'

Daphne nodded, sipping her tea.

'To this end,' Mirren went on, 'I pledge my support to you, Holder Fast. I am willing to kneel to you, as leader of whatever rabble we have to cobble together to defend this land. Do you understand? So long as you don't submit to any notion of surrender, then I'm your woman. Lead us.'

'I accept your pledge, ma'am,' Daphne said, stubbing out her cigarette. 'My trust is never given out lightly, but I believe you love the Holdings, and will fight for it. I have orders for you, that I want you to carry out tonight, but before I tell you them, I wanted to say that you were right all along.'

Mirren smiled. 'What about?'

'The Emperor is not your husband.'

Her face fell. She lit a cigarette. 'Tell me. What do you know?'

'Guilliam's dead,' Daphne said. 'The man you knew has gone. He was killed by the spirit that took over his body. I'm sorry.'

'A spirit?'

'The Creator.'

Mirren narrowed her eyes, and Annifrid looked up.

Daphne put down her tea. 'The Creator has taken on flesh, and inhabits the body of your husband. He has every power that the world's mages possess, and he wants to ensnare every other mage that's still alive.'

Mirren stared at her in disbelief.

Daphne smiled at her. 'And he wants his queen back.'

The town hall of Royston was a grand building on the top level of the town. It was partly dug out of the hillside, and was fronted by a solemn row of pillars. Above the main entrance were the insignia of the noble Holds that dominated the iron industry. Among them, only Hold Smith was on the side of the rebels. The others had awaited the result of the Red Hills battle before declaring, and had abandoned the town at the news of the Emperor's victory.

Daphne ascended the steps to the great doors, a single armed cavalryman from her company as escort. She wished Chane was by her side, but her injuries from the battle had her confined to bed.

The guards at the entrance saluted, and Daphne entered. She went through the lobby, her escort a pace behind, and proceeded into the great hall. A dozen large chairs were arranged in a semi-circle in the middle of the floor, with rows of tiered benches to either side. Several guards had been posted at each of the doorways, and Daphne noted their numbers and positions. The doors were closed behind her, and a courtier showed Daphne to her seat among the rebel leaders. Her chair had the insignia of Hold Clearwater, a minor aristocratic house that had fled as soon as the rebels had arrived after the battle. As she sat, she caught a glance from Mirren, who was seated opposite her.

Lord Holdsmith nodded to Daphne and smiled. 'Now that Holder Fast is present,' he said, 'we may commence our deliberations.'

'Commence?' Daphne said. 'And here I thought you scamps had been plotting for hours already.'

'See?' Lord Holdwain said. 'This is the very attitude I was talking about.'

'Would you care to withdraw that statement, Lady Holdfast?' Lord Holdsmith said.

'Why? Was it factually incorrect?'

'It was impertinent,' said Mirren.

'Fair enough,' said Daphne. 'I withdraw the part where I called you all scamps. Would conspirators be more apt? Traitors? Tell me, which word adequately describes one party that is about to betray another?'

'We must act for the greater good,' said Lord Holdwain, his eyes tight. 'Flinging insults and accusations around helps no one.'

'Of course, Holder Wain,' Daphne said, 'and I apologise if anyone feels insulted.'

She smiled at him, her mask of calm confidence hiding her rage.

She took a measure of the man's mind, reading his emotions, and saw contempt for her, and fear.

'We shall continue,' said Lord Holdsmith. He took a parchment from the small table next to his chair. 'This is the draft of a possible reply to the Emperor's letter that arrived some days ago, acceding to his demands. In order for it to become valid, it must be voted on by we who are gathered here this evening.'

'May I read it?' Daphne said.

'Certainly.'

Lord Holdsmith passed the letter to a courtier, who bowed and carried it across the hall to Daphne. She took it, and scanned down the single sheet. It announced the unconditional surrender of the Holders' rebellion, and denounced the late Lord Holdwick as a traitor to the imperial throne. Almost as an afterthought, at the bottom it mentioned that all mages held by the rebels would be delivered to the Emperor, along with his queen.

'Interesting,' she said, sliding a thread of vision into Lord Holdsmith's mind. 'By the way, where are the mages?'

The Holder's thoughts flashed to a heavily guarded building in the lower town, near the main gates. Daphne saw four hooded figures, chained and surrounded by soldiers. She recognised the street, and pulled her vision out, and sent it flying down the hill to the tents outside the town. As quickly as she was able, she pushed the image into Annifrid's head, then found Killop, and gave him the signal to go.

'That, Lady Holdfast,' Lord Holdsmith said, 'is not what we are here to discuss. Have you read the letter?'

'What, this letter?' she said, ripping the parchment in two, and letting the pieces fall to the floor. 'How about I draft you a new one? "Dear Emperor, kiss my arse." That should do it.'

Lady Terras laughed.

Daphne glanced at her. 'You think it's funny? It's a pity your brother Quentin isn't Lord of Hold Terras. I knew him when he was the ambassador in Rahain. He would never betray me, or Mirren, or the four mages.'

The elderly woman shrugged. 'What you call betrayal, I call survival. It's simple, really. If we fight on, then the Emperor will obliterate us one by one, wiping out our lands, and our family names. This way, we only lose six people, instead of thousands.'

Daphne sighed, and gazed around the room. 'Are you really all so stupid? You actually believe the Emperor's promises? After everything he did to the River Holdings? And Holder Vale, didn't she surrender? Yet the Emperor still had her executed, and still destroyed her lands. What makes you think he won't do the same to you, after you've handed us over?'

'It's not an easy decision,' said Holder Elance, a young man whose father had been killed at Red Hills. He shook his head. 'But I can see no alternative to accepting the Emperor's demands. Sorry.'

'Your father should never have instigated this rebellion,' said Holder Wain. 'It was a strategic error that we are all paying for. It is right and proper that Holder Fast carries some of that cost.'

'My head on a stick, you mean?' Daphne said. 'Next to the queen's, if she's lucky and the Emperor hasn't devised some other torment for her.' She dropped her mask for a second, making plain her disgust for them. 'Go on, then. Have your vote.'

Lord Holdsmith signalled to a courtier, who produced a rolled up scroll from within his tunic.

'I took the liberty of making a copy,' the Holder said, glancing at Daphne. He turned to address the hall. 'Would those in favour of the draft letter, which signals our surrender, and our acquiescence to his Imperial Majesty's demands, please raise their hands.'

Except for Daphne and Mirren, every Holder lifted their right hand in the air.

'A clear majority,' said Lord Holdsmith. He nodded to a nearby officer. 'Captain, please take Holder Fast and Queen Mirren Blackhold into custody.'

There was a scuffle by the main doors, as Daphne's cavalryman escort was disarmed and put under guard. Daphne glanced at Mirren, nodded, then turned to face the approaching troopers. She raised her right hand, and a wave of energy surged out from her, sending the troopers collapsing to the ground, their eyes vacant, their swords and crossbows clattering across the marble floor.

'I'm assuming control of the rebellion,' Daphne said to the lords and ladies sitting open-mouthed around her. 'The soldiers camped outside the town walls are now under my authority, as are the four mages.'

Lord Holdwain sprang to his feet, drawing a knife from under his cloak.

'Die, Holdfast,' he cried.

Daphne raised a finger and scoured his mind clean. He staggered, made a choking, gargling sound, then toppled over.

'Would anyone else like to comment?' Daphne said.

Lady Terras raised her hand.

'Yes, Holder?'

The elderly woman glanced at the troopers lying on the floor. 'Will they be all right?'

'They'll awaken in an hour or so,' she said. 'They'll be fine.'

'And him?' she pointed at Lord Holdwain.

Daphne shook her head.

'Do you intend to kill us, Holder Fast?'

'Yes.'

'In that case,' the old lady said, 'I ask to be spared. I have two hundred loyal troopers, who will join with yours, and I have information.'

'Yeah? What?'

Lady Terras gazed round at the other Holders. 'The deal with the Emperor,' she said, 'was struck before you walked into the room. Lord Holdsmith has already sent the letter announcing our surrender, and our intention to hand over those requested.'

Daphne shrugged. 'You'll have to do better, my lady, I'd already guessed that.'

Lady Terras smiled. 'Yes, but did you guess that the Emperor is on his way to Royston at this very moment, carried through the air by winged gaien?'

'No,' Daphne said, 'that I didn't know. Get up, if you want to live.'

Lady Terras got to her feet, smoothing down her robes, as the other Holders stared at her, their hatred obvious.

Daphne turned to Mirren. 'Your Majesty?'

The queen stood.

Lord Holdsmith shook his head. 'Betrayed by those we wished to betray?'

'What did you expect, Holder Smith?' Mirren said. 'Did you think we would meekly fall into the Emperor's hands?'

There was a loud crash, and the main doors of the chamber were flung open. Hold Fast militia streamed in, and surrounded the Holders. Annifrid approached.

'Commander,' Daphne said, 'please report.'

Annifrid bowed. 'The mages are safely in our custody, my lady, and the town gates and armoury are under our control.'

'Thank you, Commander,' Daphne said. 'Lady Terras has come over to our side. Please ensure her troopers are armed as a priority. Also, we'll need to evacuate sooner than planned. Issue orders to flee immediately to the designated assembly points in the mountains.'

'Immediately, my lady?'

Daphne nodded. 'The Emperor's on his way.'

She glanced at Mirren and Lady Terras. 'Let's go.'

They began to walk to the doors.

'And the others?' Annifrid said.

'As we planned, Commander. No mercy.'

Daphne strode through the entrance to the hall, followed by the noise of crossbows thrumming and screams. More Hold Fast troopers were in the town square, along with others dressed in Blackhold colours from Mirren's personal guard. A line of Holdsmith militia were on their knees by a wall, under guard.

The troopers hailed Daphne as she stood at the top of the steps,

Mirren to her right, and Lady Terras to her left. They raised their weapons and roared out a cheer.

She lifted her right arm until there was silence.

'Troopers of the Holdings,' she cried, 'this is a victory, but it's a painful one. We have removed those who wished to betray us to the empire, but the damage caused by their treachery means that the Emperor himself will soon be here.'

Many soldiers peered up into the dark sky.

'We have no time to waste,' Daphne went on. She pointed at the group of Holdsmith militia. 'Free them,' she said. 'Our fight is not with the troopers who were let down by their treacherous leaders, our fight is with the Emperor and his army of Rahain. Every trooper loyal to the Holdings must be allowed to arm themselves and evacuate, for when the Emperor arrives, and discovers that we have ruined his plans, I imagine his rage will be dark indeed.'

She paused, watching the troopers' expressions grow grimmer.

'This war is not over,' she said, 'but to carry on, we must hide our mages away, and scatter. We must learn a new way to fight, as rebels, and we will teach the Emperor and his invading army a bloody lesson they'll never forget.'

She pointed to the great mass of rock behind her. 'To the mountains.'

Six hours later, Daphne sat by the edge of a high pass, looking down on the smoking ruins of Royston. The Emperor had gone, his flying gaien taking him away as quickly as they had brought him to the town a few hours earlier. In the intervening time, he had taken out his fury on the buildings of Royston, devastating it with an earthquake, and then incinerating the remains, along with hundreds of his loyal subjects, who had refused to flee with the rebels.

Killop passed her a hip flask, and she took a drink.

'This is your area of expertise,' she said, 'mountain warfare, hit and run, guerrilla tactics.'

She glanced at him.

'I want you as my commander,' she went on. 'Annifrid knows everything there is to know about heavy cavalry, but she doesn't know how to fight the next stage of this war.'

He nodded. 'I'll do it, though you'll have to get used to me calling you "my lady" in public.'

'I look forward to it, Commander,' she smiled. 'Chane will be your second, once she's recovered.'

'This means we'll have to leave Karalyn with Celine and Kylon more.'

'I know,' she said, 'but she's in danger wherever we go now. We can't hide her away.'

'They'd both die for her.'

'Yes. They would.' She stood. 'Come on, the rest are waiting for us. You ready to go?'

'Aye,' he said, standing. 'I am, my lady.'

CHAPTER 21
SHOPPING TRIP

Imperial Rainsby – 20th Day, Last Third Autumn 507

'Check the face on her,' Keira smirked. 'Like a fox licking piss off a nettle.'

Flora smiled, but said nothing, her long cloak trailing along the wet ground. Apart from their tramping feet, the woods were quiet.

'Go on, Kallie,' Keira went on, 'give us a smile.'

Kallie glowered, but refused to take the bait.

'Ye'll be grateful once we're back at the flying carriage,' Keira said.

'No, I won't,' Kallie snapped. 'I'll be playing nursemaid while you two get out of yer faces.'

Keira grinned.

'You should join us,' she said. 'I cannae wait to take some dreamweed when we're flying through the clouds.'

Kallie tutted. 'Somebody has to be the grown up.'

'Look, I don't see the fucking problem,' Keira said. 'We had to stop anyway, and Rainsby's only a few miles away. It'd be stupid to go right past it and not take a wee look.'

'I don't want to take a look,' Kallie said, 'and that's not why we're going. It's so you can buy drugs and booze, and don't pretend otherwise.'

302

'Alright, I won't,' Keira snarled. 'Pyre's fanny, you're no fun at all.'

Kallie shook her head. 'I should have stayed in Kell.'

'Yer fucking right ye should have,' Keira said. She nudged Flora. 'We should have got somebody else to come along. Somebody who wouldnae whine as much.'

They walked along the trail in silence, the trees close on either side, as dark, heavy clouds edged across the sky.

'The way I see it,' Keira said, 'is that we're heading to the Holdings, right? And what are the Holdings famous for? Being prudish wee wanks that try to ban everything that folk enjoy. There'll be no weed or whisky up there, that's why we have to stock up now. We've plenty of gold from the lizard mining compound, we should be able to put together a pretty good deal.'

'That money's supposed to be for emergencies,' Kallie said.

'Aye, well, being sober all the time is an emergency,' she laughed, 'of the highest fucking order.'

Flora frowned at her. 'Quiet. Anyone within a mile's radius will hear us if you keep making that racket.'

'Alright, twinkletoes,' Keira whispered, 'is that better?'

To their left, the trees began to thin, and Keira saw the town of Rainsby in the distance, down the flank of a gradual slope. She stopped.

'There it is,' she said. 'Shithole central.'

'And behind it,' Kallie said, 'is that the sea?'

'Aye,' Keira said, 'the Inner fucking Sea.'

Kallie raised an eyebrow. 'You sailed across that?'

'Twice. Was spewing ma load the entire time. Thank Pyre we're flying; I couldnae handle a boat again.'

'I can't see any ships,' Flora said, squinting into the distance.

'So?'

'The last time we were here, the bay was filled with boats,' the Holdings woman said, 'and that large mound over there didn't exist.' She pointed towards a grassy hillock by the town gates.

'There used to be a shanty town there,' Keira said. 'Or was that on my first visit, I cannae mind.'

'So who lives here now?' Kallie asked.

'Not sure,' Keira said. 'Was full of Rahain, but Agang's Sanang mob slaughtered them, and Kellach refugees moved in. But from what those arseholes I met in Domm said, they got kicked out by the Emperor.'

'Or they were killed,' said Flora. 'Something's under that mound.'

Keira shrugged. 'Aye, maybe. Folk are living here now, but. There's smoke coming from those chimneys.'

They walked on further down the trail, edging closer to the town. The old refugee camp had been cleared away along with the shanty town, and the walls looked as if they had been recently repaired. A new gatehouse sat astride the main entrance, and Keira saw figures on the wooden battlements.

'Holdings,' she muttered. 'Shit.'

'The prudes?' Kallie laughed. 'Let's get back to the carriage; there'll be no weed for you here.'

'Hold on,' Keira frowned. 'Just cause they're guarding the walls, doesnae mean that their church is in charge. Plenty of Holdings folk smoke and drink.' She nudged Flora. 'Don't they?'

Flora shrugged. 'I guess. Just depends if the One True Path are in control.'

'Only one way to find out.'

'Yer still thinking about going?' Kallie said. 'We've no idea what to expect inside, and that's if they let us through the gates and don't shoot us on sight.'

'Let me do the talking,' Keira said, and began to stride towards the main road that led to the open gates. She heard a groan behind her and smiled. Time to teach Kallie a bit about the world.

They reached the road, and were a hundred feet from the gates when the rain started. Keira pushed her hair to the side as they got soaked by the downpour, the road turning to mud under their boots.

'Halt!' cried a voice in the Holdings language as they neared the open entrance. A squad of soldiers stared at them. A sergeant stood smoking. 'What do you want?'

Keira raised an eyebrow. 'In.'

'No Kellach are allowed through the main gates,' the sergeant said. He glanced at Flora. 'She can come in, but you pair will have to go round to the west gate.'

'And can she come in the west gate with us?'

'Of course she can, she's Holdings,' the sergeant grinned. 'This is our town now, Kellach, we go where we please.'

Without a word, Keira turned, and started walking in the direction of the other gate, Kallie and Flora following.

'See?' she said. 'I can be calm. I could've punched that guy's face in, but I restrained myself.'

Flora smirked. 'Yeah, I can see how getting arrested might interfere with your plan to find weed.'

'Exactly. I can be as professional, if there's something worth doing.'

'So, the Holdings are in charge,' Flora said, 'but Kellach are still living here, presumably.'

'Aye,' Keira said, 'and probably in the shittest part of town, as per fucking usual.'

'I was hoping they spoke Rahain here,' Kallie said. 'I don't know any Holdings.'

'Shit, really?' Flora said. 'Well, we're going to a separate gate for the Kellach.'

Keira spat on the ground. 'Ye don't speak Holdings? Ye do know where it is we're going, aye?'

'Ye never asked me if I could when ye dragged me along,' Kallie said. 'I've picked up a wee bit from Flora, but. I know how to swear pretty well.'

'I'll teach you,' Flora said. 'More than just how to swear, I mean.'

'Thanks.'

Keira decided she didn't like the way that Flora was looking at Kallie. Even unwashed, and dressed in worn and dirty travelling clothes, Kallie was stunning. She frowned. Why did she care?

They reached the western road, and the smaller set of gates that gave entry to the town. A squad of Holdings soldiers were standing by the open entrance, sheltering from the light rain. They moved aside as the three women approached.

'That was easy,' Keira said, as they walked into the narrow streets. Tall wooden tenements lined the road, and rubbish was piled high in the gutters. 'Stinks, but.'

She waited until Flora and Kallie stood by her, and they gazed around.

A Kellach man staggered across the street. He turned to leer at them.

'Hello, ladies,' he slurred. 'Looking for a good time?'

'Fuck off, ya bandy-legged old prick,' Keira said, clenching her fists.

The man stopped, his breath reeking of cheap whisky. 'I was only being friendly, ya stuck-up cow. And anyway, I wasnae talking to you, I was speaking to the good-looking one.'

Keira kneed him in the groin. He folded, gasping, his hands clutching his nethers as he fell to the ground.

'Learn some fucking manners,' Keira said, and they walked round him and continued up the street.

She smiled as they saw a row of taverns down a side alley.

'This is working out better than I'd hoped,' she said. 'The Kellach are bound to have stuff to sell, and this way, we won't even have to speak to any more Holdings.'

'What's the plan, then?' said Flora.

Keira pointed to the line of bars. 'We start there.'

By the fourth tavern, Keira was beginning to enjoy being back in Rainsby.

'This is the worst ale I've ever tasted,' said Flora, 'and yes, that includes what we had to endure in Sanang.'

'I reckon the barman's just emptying the pissing trough back into the barrels,' Keira said. 'Still, it'll do.'

She scanned the bar. It was half-full, with elderly and crippled

Kellach comprising the majority of the patrons. The table of three young women was attracting a lot of glances, she noticed, though most of them were aimed at Kallie.

'Not having some?' she asked her.

'No thanks,' Kallie said.

'They've got food, if you're hungry.'

'If ye think I'm eating anything in this dump, yer crazier than I thought.'

'Suit yerself, hen.'

An old man on a crutch hobbled over to them.

'You girls new in Rainsby?'

Keira thumbed at Flora. 'Me and her have been here before.'

The man sat.

'Friends with a Holdings, eh?'

'Aye, so?'

The man shrugged. 'It's nothing to me, but there might be a few about who'd take exception. Ye have to remember that it's not so long ago that the Emperor brought in boatloads of the dark-skinned bastards to kick our arses.'

Flora looked up. 'We heard about that. Were you here when it happened?'

'Aye, lass, that I was. The Emperor's mad. He killed hundreds of clansfolk, hunting for mages.'

'Did he find any?' said Keira.

'Aye, just the one though. An old sparker. Once he'd been hauled off in chains, the Emperor left, and took all the soldiers with him. That's when we moved back in. Had the whole town to ourselves for a while, not that there was that many of us left, mind. And then, about a third ago, this new lot arrived. They pushed us all into this wee corner of the town, and walled us in. Now they're living like kings and queens in the rest of the town, each of them with their own pet Rakanese.'

Keira frowned. 'Eh?'

'Aye,' the man said. 'So much for the Holdings being against slavery.

The new soldiers brought a load of they frog-folk with them, ones they'd captured in the summer campaign.'

'The Holdings invaded Rakana?' Flora said.

The man looked at them like they were stupid. 'Where the fuck have you girls been?'

'Grey Mountains,' said Keira, before the others could open their mouths.

The man nodded. 'Well, everything's changed since the Emperor went mental and killed the Sanang army. He cleared the Kellach out of the imperial capital, and then he attacked Rainsby. After that, he took a great big army and stomped all over the swamps of Rakana, and now he's up in the Holdings, doing the same thing to them.'

Flora's face fell. 'The Emperor's in the Holdings?'

'Aye, fighting rebels. Or he was. I heard he won a big battle up there, wiped out their cavalry.'

'A rebellion,' Flora said, shaking her head. 'Shit. How could they be so stupid?'

The man squinted at her. 'You an Emperor-lover? If ye are, then I advise ye keep that opinion to yerself around here.'

'I hate the bastard.'

The old man slapped his thigh. 'Then yer alright by me, hen.'

'But what about all the Holdings here in the town?' Flora said. 'What do they think about what's been happening?'

The man shrugged. 'Some of them treat us like shit, but the rest are alright. I know a few folk with work permits who labour for them out in the fields. They said that most are conscripts, who didn't want to join the army, or go to Rakana, or come here for that matter. They just want to go home, or they did, before they found out that the Emperor's been kicking the shit out of it.'

'Any One True Path?'

'Aye, a few. They never come into our wee district though, too scared we'll rip their heads off.'

Keira drummed the tabletop with her fingers. 'This has all been so very fucking interesting, but I want to get on to business.'

The man raised an eyebrow. 'What kind of business?'

'I want to buy a shitload of weed.'

'And I took ye for sensible lassies,' the man said, shaking his head. 'Ye don't want to be getting mixed up in that nonsense.'

'Can ye point us in the right direction, but?'

He frowned. 'I don't want ye to get into trouble.'

'We're big girls,' Keira said. 'We can look after ourselves.'

'Sorry,' he said. 'I'm not helping ye. The folk that deal in weed are a bad lot.'

'Ach, well,' Keira said, finishing her ale. 'Next tavern?'

She stood. Flora said goodbye to the old man, and they walked outside. Keira stretched.

'Excuse me,' a voice said.

A younger man stepped out of an alleyway.

'Aye?' Keira said.

'I couldnae help but hear what ye were saying to that auld guy in there.'

Keira frowned.

'I can help you,' he said, 'if yer serious. Ye said a shitload.'

'Aye, I did,' she said. 'And who the fuck are you?'

'Me, I'm nobody, but for a small cut, I can introduce ye to somebody.'

'I'll give ye two gold if the deal pans out.'

'Five.'

'Three.'

'Done.' He grinned. 'Follow me, ladies.'

He set off down an alleyway, away from the main road, into a twisting warren of narrow lanes. High tenements hemmed them in, while rubbish and human waste ran down a trough in the centre of the street. Flora earned a few rough glances, while Kallie caused more than one man to turn his head. Keira frowned.

'I should have brought the storm lantern,' muttered Flora.

'And my longbow,' said Kallie.

'Quit whining,' Keira said, 'the pair of ye. I've done weed deals in the forests of Sanang; this'll be a piece of piss in comparison.'

They reached a huge wall that cut the street ahead in two. It extended on both sides as far as Keira could see. The man halted, and glanced at her.

'This the first time ye've seen it, aye?' he said. 'Holdings bastards, walling us in like we were wild animals.'

'Watch yer tongue,' Keira said. 'My friend here's a fucking Holdings. If ye call them that again, the deal's off, and I'll kick yer nuts in.'

The man glowered. 'Wait here,' he said, then turned and disappeared down an alleyway that ran by the wall.

'This is no good,' Kallie said. 'We should get out of here.'

'Yeah,' said Flora. 'I agree.'

Keira glared at them.

'You two head back, then,' she said. 'Go on, I don't need ye here, I can take care of this on my own, ya pair of useless fuds.'

'Alright,' Kallie said. 'We'll meet ye back at the tavern where we met that auld guy. Might buy him a drink, and see what else he knows. Come on, Flora.'

The Holdings woman swayed, glancing at the two Kell women.

'Go on,' Keira said. 'Fuck off.'

Flora shook her head, and walked off with Kallie. Keira stared at them until they were out of sight.

She sighed. She just needed to get this deal over with.

'Where have the others gone?' the man said.

Keira turned. 'They were starting to piss me off, so I sent them away.'

He eyed her for a moment. 'This way.'

He darted off towards the alleyway, and Keira followed. They entered the shadow of the dark lane, with the great wall cutting through the town on one side, and a tall row of run-down tenements on the other. The man knocked on a door, leaned close and whispered something.

The door opened, and a burly Kellach stared out.

'Thought ye said there were three?'

'The other two bailed,' Keira said, 'but I'm still in.'

'Ye got the cash on ye?'

'Depends how much ye've got to sell.'

'Weapons?'

'Knife.'

The man at the door nodded, and stood aside to let her enter. As she passed, he held out his hand, and she plucked the knife from her boot and handed it to him. The other man tried to enter, but the door-keeper slammed the door in his face.

'Wee runt,' he frowned.

She shrugged.

He gestured towards a set of stairs leading down. She stepped in front of him, and he followed her into the basement. Another large Kellach was sitting by a door, a crossbow across her knees. She got up as Keira approached, and opened the thick door. She stepped through, and the door was closed behind her.

Faces looked up from a table, where six sat, drinking, smoking and poring over a large map of Rainsby. Keira scanned the room. Three lamps. She smiled. Against the walls behind the table were crates, stacked up to the ceiling. The six were mostly Kellach, but a Holdings officer in uniform and a Rakanese man sat among them.

A Kellach woman in leather armour glanced up at her.

'So,' she said, 'define shitload.'

Keira flexed her fingers. 'I want dream, keen and dull. What's yer price for a pound of each?'

The woman smiled. 'One-fifty for the dream and keen, two hundred for dull.'

'Give me a second,' Keira said, counting in her head. 'Alright, I'll take three dream, three keen and one dull.'

The folk at the table laughed.

'Ye want seven pounds of weed?' the woman said.

'Aye. I think that qualifies as a shitload.'

'Yer full of crap,' said a long-haired Kellach man. 'There's no way ye've got over a thousand gold on ye.'

She shrugged. 'Show me the weed, and I'll show ye the cash.'

The woman shook her head. 'Cash first.'

Keira unbuttoned her tunic, revealing belts wrapped round her midriff, thick with gold.

'Your turn,' she said, buttoning it back up.

'You silly bitch,' said the Holdings officer. 'You walk in here with all that money? No friends, and unarmed. You know what's going to happen now. You're going to give us that money, and if you don't make a fuss, then we'll probably let you walk out alive.'

'I'm not unarmed.'

The woman laughed. 'What? Have ye got a wee knife tucked away somewhere?' She drew her sword and laid it on the table. The others next to her also pulled out their weapons.

Keira gazed at the swords and bows, and smirked. 'Toys for bairns.'

She flicked her fingers, and a whoosh of fire spun up from one of the lamps, extinguishing it. She coiled the flame into a long whip, and ran it over the table, slicing it in two. It collapsed, the weapons clattering to the ground. The Holdings officer went for a knife on his belt, and she spat a dart of flame from the fiery whip. It struck his hand and he yelled in pain, grasping his injured and scorched palm.

The others backed off, their eyes wide, and Keira pointed her finger upward, and the fiery whip rose, and began circling the room, a foot over their heads.

'Now,' she said, 'where's my weed?'

'Get it, get it!' the Kellach woman yelled. The Rakanese man and a Kellach ran to the back of the room. They ripped open the crates, and began throwing large packets to the ground.

'Put them in a sack,' said Keira. She glanced at the Holdings man, who was crouching on the floor, a yard from the broken table, his hand burnt and bleeding.

'Who are you?' he said. 'A rogue fire mage; what are you doing here?

If the town knew you were here, they'd send every soldier they've got after you. The Emperor would come himself if he knew.'

'And are you going to fucking tell him?' Keira snarled.

'We're fighting against the Emperor, you stupid bitch.'

'Aye? Yer not doing a very good job.'

She unbuttoned her tunic, and slung the coin-filled belts to the ground.

'Deal's a deal,' she said. She picked up the sack, glanced inside, then backed to the door. 'It's been a pleasure.'

The others stared at her. She opened the door and slammed it behind her, knowing that the fiery whip would only last a few more seconds. She smiled at the woman guarding the door, nodded, then sprinted up the steps, the bulky sack over her shoulder.

She ran to the front door. As she was yanking the bolts clear, the doorman came out of a side room. He frowned at her.

'Nice doing business with ye,' she yelled, and leapt out of the door and into the alleyway. The young man who had guided her was sitting on a low wall opposite.

'Hey!' he shouted. 'What about my three gold?'

She threw him a small purse from her belt.

'Ye can keep whatever's in that, if ye show me the fastest way out of here.'

He opened the bag, his face lighting up.

'Stop her!' came a voice from the building, and the doorman bounded towards her.

Keira grabbed her guide and hauled him off down the street, sprinting. The young man glanced over his shoulder at their pursuers, his eyes wide.

'Shit,' he cried. 'What did ye do?'

'Never mind that, just keep running.'

Her guide sped off through the warren of streets like a hare, and Keira put her head down and followed, running until her breath was coming in thick gasps, her chest aching. They skidded through refuse-strewn alleys and under low arches, where it was pitch dark in the shadows. Her knees gave first, and she stumbled to a halt, leaning over and vomiting against a tenement wall.

'Pyre's arsehole,' the young man cried, glancing back the way they had come. 'I'll never be able to go back there again.'

'Did we lose them?'

'Aye.'

She wiped her mouth and straightened.

'That was fucking funny,' she laughed. 'Ye should've seen yer face.'

He weighed up the purse in his hand. 'I hope it was worth it, ya mental cow.'

'Fucking right it was.'

She grinned, and he started to laugh. A crossbow bolt struck him in the side of his head, and he tumbled to the cobbles.

Keira turned, and a bolt hit her left side, above her hip. She grunted, and fell to one knee.

'Bitch,' said the Holdings officer, reloading, his right hand swathed in bandages. 'This is your own fault, you know,' he said, pointing the bow at her head. 'If you'd listened to me, we would have let you live.'

'Eat shit, ya donkey-shagging prick.'

There was a blur of movement to her right, and a staff swung out, clattering the Holdings man on the back of the head. His eyes went blank as he sank to the ground. Kallie stepped forward, Flora just behind. They gazed at the bodies lying in the alleyway.

Flora raised an eyebrow. 'Were those really going to be your last words?'

'Sorry I wasnae more poetic,' Keira muttered. 'I was a bit distracted with this fucking bolt in my side.'

Kallie leaned forward and yanked it from the wound.

'Ah, ya bastard,' Keira cried, holding her side. She ripped a length of cloth from her cloak and wrapped it round her waist, grunting in pain.

'This guy was the only one that chased you,' Flora said, kicking the Holdings officer. 'The rest gave up pretty quickly.'

'That's cause I paid the bastards,' Keira said, straightening. 'He was just pissed off that I burnt his hand.' She glanced down at her dead guide. 'And he was just unlucky.'

She took the purse from his grip and put it back in her belt, then she hoisted the sack.

'Let's go.'

'Wait,' said Flora. She knelt by the Holdings officer, and drew a knife. She slapped him. 'Wake up.'

'What the fuck are ye doing?' Keira said.

'Hold him down,' Flora said.

Keira shrugged and bent over, gripping the officer's arms. Kallie opened her water bottle and sprinkled some over his face. He sputtered, his eyes opening.

Flora placed the knife against his throat. He stared at them.

'Listen,' said Flora, 'I'm going to ask you a few questions. Do you understand?'

The officer gave a slight nod.

'Good,' said Flora. 'Now, we heard the Emperor invaded the Holdings. Is it true?'

He nodded.

'And he's destroying it?'

'He's been burning the lands of the rebel Holds,' the officer gasped.

'The rebels. Give me some names.'

'Holdfast, Holdwick, Blackhold, they were the main ones,' he said. 'Others too. Terras, Cane, Elance...'

'Cane?' Flora's hand started to shake.

'You from Hold Cane, are you?' the man said.

Flora said nothing, a tear rolling down her cheek.

'We done?' Keira said.

'Yes.'

Keira grabbed the officer's hair and smacked his head off the cobbles, knocking him out.

They stood, and Keira watched as Flora put her knife away.

'Come on,' said Kallie, and they headed off into the alleyways.

Flora was silent the whole way back to the forest covering the hills next to Rainsby. They had departed the town without trouble, even managing to buy a few bottles of whisky from a store by the gates, from the money in the purse that Keira had retrieved.

When they were a mile away from where they had hidden the carriage, Flora broke down, fell to her knees and began weeping. As Keira frowned, Kallie went to the side of the Holdings woman, putting an arm over her shoulder.

'Those stupid bastards,' Flora sobbed. 'Idiots. Following the Hold-fasts like they always have. I knew it.'

'Holdfast?' said Kallie. 'Isn't that...?'

'Aye,' said Keira. 'That's Daphne's clan or Hold, or whatever.'

'It'll have been Daphne's father,' Flora said. 'The famous Godfrey, who used to sleep with the old queen.'

Kallie frowned. 'I wonder if Killop's up there.'

'So you're Hold Cane?' said Keira.

'Yeah.'

'Does that mean yer nobility, like Daphne?'

'Don't be ridiculous,' Flora said, wiping her eyes. 'I'm Flora of Hold Cane, she's Daphne Holdfast. My family are tenants on the Hold Cane estate. Workers, not lords or ladies.'

'What do ye want to do?' said Kallie. 'We still planning on going up there?'

Flora stood, and hardened her features. 'Yes. I get it if you don't want to come, but I need to go back, to see if my family are still alive.'

Kallie smiled. 'We'll be with ye all the way. Keira?'

'Aye. Sure.'

They resumed their journey through the forest.

Kallie let out a cry, and began running. Keira frowned, then saw the smoke rising through the branches of the forest. They ran, racing between the trees towards the clearing where their carriage was hidden. They burst out into the open.

'Shit!' Kallie yelled, clenching her fists.

The carriage was a burnt-out wreck. Parts were still smouldering, and wafts of smoke trailed up into the darkening sky. Their clothes and possessions lay scattered on the muddy ground, along with their ransacked luggage. A lone winged gaien circled overhead.

Keira stumbled through the wreckage, picking up items of her clothing. She saw the wooden bear, and tucked it into her pocket.

'They've taken the food and weapons,' said Flora. 'Shit, looks like we're walking.'

Kallie shook her head. 'This is your fault, Keira. We should never have left the carriage unguarded.'

'What?' Keira cried. 'Do ye think if we'd left Flora here, she'd have been able to stop a bandit attack on her own? From the tracks, it looks like a whole fucking pack of them were here.'

Kallie sat on a crate, her head in her hands.

'So,' she said, 'we've no money, no food, and no transport.'

'Aye,' Keira smirked, 'but we've got a shitload of weed.'

CHAPTER 22
SHIELD

Shield Mountains, Imperial Holdings – 23rd Day, Last Third Autumn 507

Killop raised his hand for quiet, his eyes scanning the narrow gorge beneath them. The squad of Holdings troopers stilled, watching him for the signal. Through the tangled thorn bushes and branches of spruce trees, a group of Rahain soldiers were entering the valley from their left. They scrambled over the loose rocks, their heads down. The lead pair had their crossbows out, while the twenty or so behind them had their bows slung over their shoulders.

Killop extended a finger, and the squad took up their positions on the ridge above. Two troopers took hold of a tree trunk that had been felled and wedged under a great boulder, and the others aimed down the shafts of their crossbows.

They waited, Killop staring into the gorge. As soon as the last pair of Rahain had come into view, he drew his sword. All along the ridge, his squad loosed their bows, a dozen bolts flying down to where the Rahain clustered in the narrow ravine. At the same time, the two troopers heaved on their wooden lever, and the boulder creaked and toppled over the edge, rolling down the slope and crashing to the bottom of the ravine, cutting off the enemy's retreat.

Killop bounded down the steep side of the gorge, leaping from rock to rock, as the squad continued to pepper the Rahain. He landed at the bottom, and leaned back against a giant boulder, keeping out of sight. The first Rahain came into view, as they ran from the hail of bolts. Killop stepped out in front of them, swinging his sword. His lunge caught the lead Rahain in the side, cleaving him in two. He reached out with his left hand and grabbed the throat of the second Rahain. He shook him like a rag doll, and threw him at the others sprinting towards him.

Battle frenzy gripped him, and he charged into their midst, his sword lashing out from side to side, clearing a path. The ravine was too narrow for the Rahain to get out of his way, and some tried to run back down the gorge, but were hit by the Holdings squad above, who were still shooting. Killop pressed on, slashing and lunging, until the last Rahain fell to the ground, her head split open.

He stood, panting, his right arm aching, and stared at the corpses littering the gorge. The Holdings climbed down from their positions. They gazed from the bodies to Killop and back again, their eyes wide.

'Check for survivors,' he said to a pair of young troopers.

'Are we taking prisoners, sir?'

'No. Kill them all,' he said. 'The rest of you, get these bodies cleared. Throw them off the cliff, then pick up all the bolts and anything else lying about. We've got twenty minutes to get everything looking normal again.'

He walked down the gorge, as the squad got to work. He kept half an eye on the two troopers looking for survivors, and examined the dead Rahain, shaking his head.

'You've fought the Rahain many times before, haven't you, sir?' asked a trooper.

'Aye,' he said, 'though none as poorly equipped or trained as this lot. They're more like peasants with crossbows, rather than real soldiers.'

He noticed the two young troopers standing over the body of a Rahain. He walked over, and looked down. One of the troopers frowned.

'She's still breathing, sir.'

'I can see that. You know what to do.'

The troopers aimed their crossbows at the injured Rahain, but neither loosed.

'Something wrong?' Killop asked.

'Sorry, sir,' said one. 'It's just that we've always been taught that executing prisoners, especially wounded ones was... wrong.'

Killop swung his sword down, and drove it through the throat of the Rahain.

'I understand,' he said, as the two troopers stared at him, 'but this is not a pitched battle between two sides who are playing by the rules. This is an all-out war for survival. There are no rules.'

The troopers bowed their heads.

'Throw her off the cliff,' he said, 'then get back to your posts.'

One looked up at him. 'Are we in trouble, sir?'

He shook his head. 'Forget it.'

Killop watched as the pair picked up the body of the slain soldier, and carried her up the gorge to where a steep cliff fell down the side of the mountain. A sadness swept over him, and he felt the loss of something within his heart. If someone had to be the monster, he would rather it were him, than a pair of young troopers.

Once the ravine was clear, he assembled his squad.

'Good job,' he said. 'We're going to move the ambush a hundred yards down the gorge. Let's go.'

The troopers secured their weapons and scrambled up the side of the slope. At the top, they followed a trail along the ridge, past where they had toppled the boulder. As they were getting settled into their new positions, Killop crouched by a rocky summit and peered down the valley. Low clouds scudded by in the breeze, and all around were the bare peaks and jagged cliffs of the Shield Mountains, threaded with deep ravines and treacherous passes. Thousands of Rahain were in the mountains, pushing up the valleys in search of the rebels, and destroying every village they came across.

Killop gestured to a pair of troopers and they approached, kneeling alongside him.

'Get yourselves up there,' he said, pointing to a cliff opposite their position. 'There's enough scree for a small rockslide, and you'll have a better view down the gorge than us. Signal when you see them coming, and I'll signal back when it's time to set off the rockslide. Got it?'

They nodded.

'Off ye go.'

They sprinted back along the ridge, and out of sight.

'Get some rest,' he said to the remainder of his young squad. 'I'll keep watch.'

He turned and leaned his back against a boulder, his eyes scanning the gorge.

'Sir?' said a voice.

'Aye, trooper?'

'Will you teach me how to kill like you do?'

'Just follow my orders,' he said, looking away. 'You'll pick up the rest on your own.'

'I'm not sure I will, sir. I don't think I'm cut out to be a soldier.'

'Did you shoot your crossbow?'

'Yes, sir,' the trooper said, his voice low, 'but I closed my eyes, and nearly peed myself.'

'Then you've already done better than many,' he said. 'You've nothing to be ashamed of.'

The trooper gazed out at the mountains.

'This your first fight?' Killop said.

'I was in the battle at Red Hills, sir,' he said, 'but I was stationed near the rear of the infantry, and didn't come close to any Rahain.'

'And did you obey orders when you were there?'

'Yes, sir.'

'So you've been in two fights, and haven't run away or disobeyed your officers?' Killop said. 'It's too late, you're a soldier whether you like it or not. Now, I'm ordering you to get some rest, so you're ready for your third fight.'

The trooper nodded and rejoined the others. Killop glanced at them. Sooner or later, some of them would die, and he needed to harden his heart, and not get attached. He turned back to face the gorge, and settled down to wait.

The signal from the cliffs came two hours later. Killop nudged the trooper next to him.

'Everybody up. Get ready.'

The squad began to move, scratching their backs and stretching.

Killop scanned the gorge, but saw no one. He glanced back up to the cliff. The pair of troopers were crouching by a heap of loose scree, staffs in their hands.

'Into position, crossbows checked and ready,' Killop whispered down the line as he glimpsed the first Rahain make their way up the gorge. As before, he waited until the group of two dozen Rahain were directly beneath them, then raised his hand. There was a rumble of stone as the rockslide began to clatter down the slope, drowning out the sound of crossbows thrumming. The soldiers in the gorge began to fall. Some ran, but they were hemmed in between the rockslide and the enormous boulder they had dislodged in the first ambush.

Killop waited, his squad cutting down the trapped Rahain without any assistance from him. The survivors began to plead for mercy, throwing down their crossbows and getting to their knees, and some of the squad hesitated.

'Stop shooting,' Killop cried. He glanced at the squad. 'Cover me.'

He got to his feet and jumped down the slope. The five remaining Rahain cowered on the ground before him as he approached.

'Kellach,' one cried.

Killop faced him.

'Don't kill me, I'm a friend,' the soldier shouted in Killop's language. The other Rahain stared at him, their eyes wide.

'A friend?' Killop said. 'Somehow, I doubt that.'

'I know the fire mage, and I know Kylon, I was in their squad in Kell,' the Rahain man said, his words coming out in a rush as he knelt, his arms raised.

Killop stared at him. 'Or you fought against us in Kell, and learned our language.'

'It's true, I did,' the man wept, 'but I was captured, and Kylon spared me, and I worked for Keira, helping her. And then I went with Kylon to the city of the Rakanese, and after it was destroyed, we went looking for the fire mage's brother in Rahain, to tell him his lover was dead...'

'Stop,' Killop cried, leaning closer. 'I recognise you.'

The Rahain man blinked, his tongue flickering.

Killop almost laughed. 'I'm the fire mage's brother. We've met.'

'You're Killop?' the man said, squinting. 'Sorry, all you Kellach look the same to me. I'm Baoryn.'

'I remember,' Killop said. 'When you visited, did you know Daphne was alive?'

'Yes, I did,' Baoryn said. 'I apologised to Daphne for it in person, after I was released from jail in Plateau City.'

'You've met Daphne?'

'I have.'

Killop frowned. The four other Rahain soldiers were staring at them.

'These your friends now?' Killop said.

'No. I've been looking for Kylon for nearly two years. I lost him when he went into Sanang, and only picked up his trail a while ago. I let myself be conscripted, hoping I would find the rebels. Do you know where Kylon is?'

'I might do,' Killop said.

He glanced up to the squad on the ridge, and beckoned them down.

'This is Baoryn,' he said. 'Bind his hands and hood him, we're taking him back to the camp.'

Baoryn stood, and held his arms out to the approaching troopers.

'Thank you, Killop,' he said. 'As the fire mage's brother, I want you to know that you have my trust.'

Killop said nothing as the troopers put a bag over Baoryn's head, and bound his wrists with rope.

'What'll we do with the others, sir?'

Killop gazed at the four terrified Rahain kneeling before him.

'Start making your way to the camp,' he said. 'Keep the prisoner guarded at all times. I'll finish off here.'

'Yes, sir.'

He waited until their steps had faded into the distance, and drew his sword.

It was a six-hour hike up to the camp, their third base since fleeing Royston. Keep moving, that had been Killop's first piece of advice to Daphne. Move and strike, move and strike. Never give the enemy a moment's peace, and put up with whatever discomforts come along without complaint. He had been taking different squads out on raids, sometimes for the day, sometimes staying out overnight for a dawn ambush. He had noted the best from each squad, and was compiling a list of names of those he thought capable of more daring and arduous raids.

The four remaining Holdings mages had been split up and sent to locations further up the chain of mountains, close to where the great ocean battered the cliffs. Daphne had positioned herself with two hundred soldiers as the force closest to the Rahain advancing through the rocky valleys.

They retreated every time they shifted base, but they were making the Rahain pay for every step they took, with hundreds of casualties inflicted by the rebels' tactics. If only he had a squad of veteran Kellach in the mountains, he thought, as he gazed at the jagged, barren peaks, instead of inexperienced Holdings militia, some of whom were barely out of childhood.

The camp was nestled in a flat-bottomed ravine, where a patch of trees stood by a narrow mountain stream, which tumbled down from the grey slopes. A sentry greeted them as they approached, and Killop nodded.

They clambered down the steep slope of the ravine, and walked through the untidy rows of tents. Daphne's tent was higher than the others, and stood in the centre, a cluster of soldiers on guard outside. They saluted as they saw Killop draw near.

'Squad,' he said, turning to face his raiders, 'good work today, you're learning. I'm going back out tomorrow, so be ready in case any of you are selected. Dismissed.'

He put his arm on Baoryn's shoulder, and approached Daphne's tent.

'You're back early,' said Celine, who was standing outside having a cigarette.

'Found this guy,' he said, nodding to the bound and hooded Rahain. 'Are the rest of them inside?'

'Yeah.'

Killop called over a couple of guards.

'Watch this prisoner for me,' he said. 'Keep him here until I call for him.'

'Yes, sir.'

Killop glanced down at the hooded figure. 'I'll be back soon,' he said in Rahain, then stepped into the tent. He went through a small hallway, and entered Daphne's quarters.

Karalyn squealed, and ran to him, hugging his leg. He ruffled her hair.

'Hiya, wee bear.'

Kylon grunted at him from where he sat in the corner of the tent. Daphne was sitting on a chair next to Chane, who was lying on a camp bed, bandages still covering her ribs. They were smoking a weedstick.

'I see you two are having fun,' Killop said, smiling, 'while I'm out doing all the work.'

Chane shook her head and started to laugh. 'You're in trouble now,' she said. 'Poor Daphne here's been slaving her guts out all day.'

CHRISTOPHER MITCHELL

Killop slung his sword belt over a bench, and unbuckled his armoured chestplate.

Daphne glanced up at him, her eyes exhausted. 'I thought you were going to be out longer, I wasn't expecting you back until tomorrow morning. How did it go?'

He sat on a chair, and unlaced his boots. 'Fine. Hit two patrols. Forty-seven Rahain killed. No casualties our end.'

She nodded.

'What you been doing?' he asked.

Daphne sighed. 'Ranging,' she said, 'and checking in with the other detachments. Our positions to the south-west have become compromised and we're going to have to move location soon, probably tomorrow.'

'And the Emperor?'

'A hundred miles to the east, burning the last of the mining towns.'

'He see you?'

'No, Karalyn shielded me. He had no idea I was watching him.'

'Good.' He paused. 'There's a reason I'm back early. I found someone.'

Daphne frowned. 'Who?'

'A man who claims to know us. Says we've met, and I think I recognise him, but I'm not sure. It was a long time ago.' He glanced over at Kylon. 'You're going to want to see this.'

He got up and walked to the tent entrance.

'Bring him,' he called to the guards.

They all watched as the two Holdings troopers escorted the hooded figure in.

'Thanks,' Killop said. 'You can go.'

The troopers saluted and left the tent.

Daphne leaned forward in her chair as Killop removed the captive's hood.

'Baoryn!' cried Kylon, rising. He ran to the Rahain man and embraced him, holding him close to his chest. The two men began to weep.

Killop nodded. 'Guess he was telling the truth.'

He stepped forward, and cut the cords that bound the wrists of the Rahain. Baoryn put his arms round Kylon's back, sobbing as he hugged the Kell man.

Chane frowned. 'Are they going to need their own room?'

Killop glanced at Daphne. 'Do you recognise him?'

'Yeah,' she said. 'He came round to see me once, when I was pregnant in Plateau City. He knew about Kalayne.'

Baoryn broke off, and stared at Daphne. He rubbed his eyes.

Kylon gazed down at him. 'Kalayne's dead, old friend.'

'I know,' the Rahain man said, 'or, I guessed, when he didn't send a vision when he said he would.'

'He was putting visions into your head?' Daphne asked.

Baoryn nodded. 'Just once. He told me that Kylon was going to the Holdings, to look for you. He said he would let me know how to find him, but he never did.'

'Was this last winter?' said Kylon.

'Yes,' said Baoryn, 'just after the fire mage's army was wiped out by the Emperor.'

'Come and sit down,' Daphne said. 'We'll get some food and drink, and talk.'

The Rahain man nodded. 'From the moment I left your home, Miss Holdfast, I have been searching for Kylon. Thank you for welcoming me here.'

Daphne nodded.

'By the way,' said Chane, 'it's Lady Holdfast now.'

Baoryn bowed. 'My lady.'

The sun was setting over the mountains to the west as dinner was prepared. Celine came in, and they gathered chairs and a table next to Chane's camp bed. A hot wood stove was brought in to heat the tent, its chimney poking up through a slit in the canvas ceiling. Their rations were small and bland, but the ale was plentiful.

Baoryn stayed quiet most of the time, listening to Kylon tell the long tale of Keira's invasion of the Plateau. Whenever Killop glanced at the Rahain, he would be gazing up at the black-cloaked Kell man, his wide eyes looking like they wanted to consume him.

Daphne and Killop gave a shorter account of their lives, which entertained Chane and Celine more than Baoryn, whose attention remained fixed on Kylon. Chane passed round a few weedsticks. Killop abstained, preferring to keep his mind unclouded. He picked up Karalyn and sat her on his lap.

Baoryn glanced at her.

Karalyn smiled, and the Rahain man glanced away, his tongue flickering.

'She's beautiful,' he said, 'just like her mother.'

'Thank you,' said Daphne. 'In your vision, what else did Kalayne say to you?'

'He reminded me that many years ago I pledged my life and service to Kylon, and told me to help him in any way I could.'

Daphne turned to Kylon. 'Did you know about this?'

'No,' he said. 'To be honest, I had no idea that Kalayne was in contact with him.'

'It was only one vision,' Baoryn said. 'I was in Rainsby at the time, on my way back from Rahain.'

'What were you doing in Rahain?' Daphne said.

'After I left Plateau City, my lady, I discovered that Kylon had been enlisted in the alliance army, and was fighting down there. But by the time I got to Rahain, he was no longer with the army, and I lost track of him completely. I wandered through the Grey Mountains, thinking that maybe he and the fire mage had been living in the wild up there, but found nothing. When I got to Rainsby, all everyone was talking about was the invasion of the fire witch from Sanang, and I realised what had happened.'

He glanced at Kylon. 'I'm sorry it took so long to find you.'

'I knew you would in the end,' Kylon said.

'And how did you find him?' said Daphne.

'I travelled up to Plateau City, though didn't get too close to it. The Emperor was in Rakana, hunting for mages. I heard that a Rahain army had been summoned, so I walked up to the border with the Holdings, and waited. It was easy to fall in with the soldiers that arrived from Rahain, though I stuck out at the start. The rest of them were raw recruits, and most hadn't been given any training, and I was about the only veteran who knew what he was doing. So I played dumb, and mingled in.'

'Did you fight at Red Hills?' Killop said.

'I was there, sir, but I stuck to the back. I just wanted to survive. After it was over, we were led to the mountains, and I made sure I was sent out with the lead units, hoping that if I got to speak to the rebels, then I could talk my way here. I was lucky it was you that found me.'

Daphne narrowed her eyes and took a draw of her weedstick.

'I'm going to look inside your mind,' she said. 'Nothing personal.'

'That's unfair,' said Kylon. 'I believe him, and I trust him.'

Daphne shrugged, and her eyes hazed over for a few moments, as Baoryn sat still. She shook her head and grimaced. She picked up a mug of ale and took a long swig.

'Well?' said Chane.

'He's telling the truth,' she said.

Kylon glowered. Baoryn glanced at him. 'It's all right, I understand why they need to be sure. I've been away a long time.'

'So he's a good guy?' said Celine.

'Of course he is,' said Kylon.

'Don't get your knickers in a twist,' said Chane. 'You'd have done the same.'

'It's settled,' Daphne said. 'Baoryn can stay. Kylon, you look after him for now. I'll have a think about where to assign him later.'

'Thank you, my lady,' the Rahain said, bowing.

Kylon stood. 'I'll get you kitted out, come on.'

Baoryn got to his feet, bowed at Daphne again, and they left the tent.

'I don't like him,' said Chane.

'Did you see the way he was looking at Kylon?' said Celine.

Daphne frowned. 'I said he could stay, but I'm not sure I want him too close; not yet, at any rate.'

'I thought he was telling the truth?' said Killop.

'He was,' said Daphne. 'All the same, let's keep him at arm's length for now.'

Celine turned to Karalyn. 'What did you think of the Rahain man, little bear?'

'Karalyn sleepy.'

Celine put down her drink and took the girl from Killop's lap. 'Bed-time for you.' She stood. 'I'll get to my own bed as well, I want to be fresh in the morning.'

'Night, then,' Daphne said, kissing Karalyn.

Celine carried the child to a curtained-off section at the rear of the tent.

Daphne glanced at Killop and Chane. 'Commanders,' she smiled, 'we need to discuss tomorrow.'

Killop refilled their mugs with ale.

'Get the map,' Daphne said, and Chane reached into a chest by her camp bed. She unrolled a large scroll, displaying the region in fine detail.

'Is that new?' Killop said.

'I made it,' Chane said. 'I was so bored just lying about all day. I put it together from all the routes the scouts have been marking out, along with some older charts I found.'

Killop examined it, bringing a lamp closer to read the neat script.

'It's beautiful.'

Chane laughed. 'It's a map.'

'Still, I've never seen one like it.' He pointed. 'We're here, aye?'

'Yeah.'

He glanced at Daphne. 'And the Emperor?'

'Over there,' she said, tapping the other end of the map. She picked up a pouch, and began to place small pebbles on the map to mark the different locations. 'I think our next base should be at the mouth of where these two valleys split. It should take us two days to get there, so we'll stop off halfway for the night.'

Killop nodded. 'Shall we leave in the morning?'

'Yes, although I want you to stay here with a couple of squads. Make sure no one finds the path we take.'

'Send me a signal when you arrive,' he said, 'and we'll pull out. We'll cover the distance to the new camp in a day.'

'I've ordered the other detachments to move as well,' Daphne said, laying out more pebbles. 'These are their current positions, and these are where they're going. Annifrid's unit will cover the gorge over here, to watch our flank.'

Chane shook her head. 'Every time we relocate, the Emperor gets a little bit closer to the mages.'

'I agree,' said Killop. 'Next time we move, we should push everyone westward, including the mages.'

Daphne nodded. 'I'll send out scouts to find some suitable locations.'

Chane sighed. 'It's a game, isn't it? A damn game. Can the Emperor's army catch us before they run out of food and supplies? No offence, Killop, but your raiding squads haven't made much of a dent in their numbers.'

'That's not their purpose,' he said. 'They're to sow fear and confusion. The more the enemy doubt themselves, the sooner they'll want to go home.'

'But the Emperor will just force them to stay.'

'I don't think he can,' Killop said. 'We know he's powerful, and stronger than any normal mage, but he can only be in one place at a time. I want to speak to Baoryn about this, but from everything I've seen, the Emperor is running the army on his own, which is fine when he's on the battlefield, but in these mountains? We keep hitting the Rahain, and some units are going to desert, and run home.'

'You sound confident,' Daphne said.

'Back in Kell,' he said, 'the Rahain were a different army. They had discipline, and a rigid command, with officers everywhere. This lot are a rabble. Half have no boots or winter coats, and most seem never to have loosed a crossbow before. In the patrols we've hit, there never seems to be anyone in charge, no sergeants, or anyone who looks like they've seen a day's training. I don't know how the Emperor raised them, but he scraped the bottom of the barrel with this lot.'

'How's your elite squad coming along?' Daphne asked.

'I've taken over a hundred out on raids now,' he said, 'and I've made a list.' He pulled out a scrap of paper from his pocket. 'Fourteen names, so far.'

'Good. Select them as part of the force that stays here in the morning. As usual, we'll keep this to ourselves until then, and issue the orders at dawn.'

Chane and Killop nodded, and the map was put away, Daphne sliding the pebbles back into the pouch.

'I think I'll have one last smoke, then get to sleep,' Chane said.

Daphne glanced at Killop. 'Want some fresh air?'

'Aye.'

Killop pulled on his boots and they left the tent, nodding to the guards at the entrance. They walked through the bottom of the valley, among the trees and lines of tents. Many soldiers were still up, sitting round small fires smoking, or drinking rum from mugs. Daphne and Killop came to the edge of the cliff, and she took a narrow path upwards, their way illuminated by the glow of the campfires. They reached a quiet spot, and halted, gazing into the darkness of the mountains. Above, the seven stars shone bright and clear. Killop put his arms round her, and she leaned back into him.

He kissed her on the neck.

'I love you.'

'I love you too, Killop.'

They stood a moment in silence.

'Daphne,' he said, 'this war...' He paused, unsure how to form his thoughts into words.

She remained quiet.

'I think I'm...' he went on.

'What?'

'Changing. When I led the slave revolt in Rahain, I used to kill unarmed soldiers who'd surrendered, I didn't even think about it, I just did it. But when I saw the Sanang slaughter hundreds of prisoners outside the gates of the Rahain Capital, my heart broke, and I swore I'd never do it again. Today, I killed five unarmed prisoners, one of whom was injured, while the others were on their knees, begging for mercy. I wanted to shield the squad from having to do it. They're so young, Daphne. I looked at them, and I remembered what I'd been like, before the wars started. So I killed the prisoners myself.'

He paused, closing his eyes. 'I remember my sister used to say that I was self-righteous, that I thought I was better than everyone else. Maybe I did back then, but now I know it's bullshit. I'm not a good man.'

She turned in his arms to face him, her body close.

'Killop, what are you fighting for?'

'You,' he said, 'and Karalyn. And for the hope that one day we might be able to live in peace.'

She leaned up and kissed him. The fingers of her right hand traced a scar down his cheek, and her green eyes gazed up at him.

'We will, Killop,' she said.

CHAPTER 23
TRADING SECRETS

Silverstream, Imperial Rahain – 29th Day, Last Third Autumn 507

'How much longer do I have to fake it, do you think?' Laodoc said.

'A while yet, I'm afraid,' said Agang, sitting by the old man's bedside. 'It's only been nineteen days since you broke your leg.'

'And eighteen since you healed it.'

'Would you rather I hadn't?'

Laodoc shook his head. 'No, I'm grateful not to be in pain. It's just that I'm not a good liar.'

'I thought you used to be a politician?'

The old man frowned. 'That's completely different. When I was a city councillor, I may have exaggerated, reinterpreted, or even twisted the truth on occasion, but it was still the truth. I never used to tell flat-out lies.'

Agang raised an eyebrow. 'I lied all the time as king, and as chief before that. Sometimes, the Sanang people weren't prepared for the truth. For example, I was never honest about my plans to free the slaves. If I had been, I probably would have been lynched.'

'But, my friend,' Laodoc smiled, 'you were lynched by Keira.'

'Eight-thirds, she used to call me,' he glowered. 'That's how long my reign lasted.'

'Maybe being more honest would have helped?'

'Against the fire witch? No. Only one thing would have worked against her. Running.'

There was a loud cheer from outside, and they paused to listen.

'I wish we could see what was going on,' said Laodoc. 'This damnable house, so cramped and lightless. How I long for some fresh air.'

'We all do,' Agang said. 'You might be stuck in this bed, but we're all stuck in this house. It could be a lot worse, I suppose. It's clean, we have our own rooms, and the food's plentiful, if not particularly appetising.'

He picked up a mug of water and took a drink.

'The Rakanese do like their spices,' Laodoc said, 'and admit it, the burning sensation at least hides the fact that we're eating river slugs and grasshoppers.'

Agang grimaced.

'So,' the Sanang man said, 'how do you think she's doing?'

'I'm optimistic,' Laodoc said, 'judging by that cheer we heard.'

'Unless it was to announce her execution.'

'No, surely not. Shella told us that the town had dropped the charges against her.'

'But speaking with them may have re-opened the wounds.'

'I hope not,' Laodoc said. 'I think it was a very brave thing for her to do. And the work she put into preparing for it was admirable. Studying the Rakanese language day after day, and practising her speech. At least it's taken her mind off Bedig for a while.'

'I hadn't realised how intelligent she is,' Agang said.

Laodoc smiled. 'Bridget's sometimes robust demeanour has fooled more than one person. I suspect that showing off is frowned upon by the Kellach Brigdomin, unless one has the bravado of a Keira to carry it off.'

'You taught her the Rahain language, didn't you? In your academy?'

'Not exactly,' Laodoc said. 'I hired a professor to do it. At the time, I was still a little stand-offish with them. Bridget, Killop and Kallie were my captives after all, and I was worried what the other councillors would make of it. Nevertheless, I read the reports that were made for me, and kept up with their progress. While the other two showed reasonable intelligence, Bridget was outstanding, and her appetite for learning seemed insatiable. She devoured difficult books on history, and science, and poetry. It would have been wonderful to have seen where it could have led, had fate not intervened.'

'You sound proud of her, my friend.'

'I was, and I remain so. Bridget is a born leader, Agang, and one whose heart is as steadfast as they come.'

Agang bowed his head. 'Then I was right to choose her.' He shook his head. 'That choice still preys on my mind, my friend. I can only imagine how she feels.'

Laodoc nodded.

'How are the rest of our travelling companions?' he said. 'With the exception of yourself and Bridget, not many have visited me for a few days.'

'They're fine. Bored, mostly. Dyam and Dean niggle each other constantly. She nags, and he glowers. I don't know how she keeps it up; that boy's obstinacy and bad manners make me want to give him a good slapping. You know, he's the only one I regret bringing. He should have stayed in Kell, then Dyam wouldn't have to waste all her time nannying him.'

'We brought him because he's a mage.'

Agang snorted. 'He's yet to show any evidence of that. It's a pity we can't leave him here when we go.'

'You're being a little hard on the boy. What about Lola?'

'Keeps to herself. Stays in her room, getting drunk.'

'Has Tara come to visit her?'

Agang shook his head. 'Only Shella and Bridget's language tutor have entered this house since we got here.'

Laodoc frowned. 'Poor Lola.'

Sacrifice

'She's mourning her lover, just like Bridget,' Agang said. 'She needs time.'

'At least they're getting some here, away from the fighting and troubles elsewhere.'

There was a tap on the door, and Bridget came in.

'Hello, boys,' she said.

'Well?' said Laodoc, looking up. 'Sit down and tell us how it went.'

Bridget walked over, plucking a jug of Rakanese spirits from the table as she fell into a seat. She poured herself a tall measure, and exhaled.

'They didn't kill me,' she said, and took a large swig of the clear spirit. She pursed her lips, and Laodoc caught a spark in her eye.

'And your speech?' he said. 'It was received well?'

'It wasn't a speech,' she said, 'it was an apology.'

'Of course,' he said. 'Was it accepted?'

She grinned. 'Aye. Pyre's cracked nipples, I'm glad that's over, but. I've never been so nervous in my life. Standing up there in front of hundreds of Rakanese, each of them staring at me with their great big eyes. Shella helped. She stood right next to me the whole time, and made sure I got the words right. I fucked up a few transitive verbs, which was annoying. They're back to front in Rakanese, and I can't get my head around them. Anyway, when I was done, they had a vote, and they agreed to absolve me of the guard's death. They accepted it was an accident, and that I was remorseful.'

Agang nodded. 'That took courage.'

She shrugged. 'It had to be done. I regret killing that lassie. Did ye know her family were in the front row when I was up speaking?' She paused. 'That was hard.'

Laodoc leaned forward, putting a hand on her arm. 'You did well, Bridget.'

She took a swig. 'And how have you been? Not gone mental from having to stay in bed for yet another day?'

'It's frustrating, I'll grant you,' he said. 'It'd be nice to walk around the house, but one never knows who might come in.'

Bridget shook her head and laughed. 'Yer being paranoid. No one's going to know if ye take a quick five minute walk about the room once a day.'

'I can't take the risk,' said Laodoc. 'The only reason we're still here is because I'm supposed to be healing my broken leg. If I were found out, then...'

Bridget took another swig. 'Come on,' she said. 'Get up. It's time to stretch yer legs.'

She stood, and held out her hand.

'I'm not sure this is wise,' said Agang.

'Never mind wise,' she said, taking hold of Laodoc's fingers.

He smiled.

'All right,' he said. He pulled back his cover, revealing a long white tunic that reached to his bony knees. A splint was attached to a lower leg, secured at ankle and shin. He swung his feet off the bed.

Laodoc's heart rose as Bridget smiled. He placed his bare feet onto the wooden floor, and put some weight onto them. He stood, his joints throbbing. Bridget kept a firm hold of his arm, and helped him edge forwards.

'How does that feel?' she said.

'Sore, but good.'

'Sounds like a summary of life,' Bridget said.

Agang laughed. 'It should be our motto.'

Laodoc gazed at his two friends, his love for both sharpened by their joy. He walked round the bed, stretching his limbs, Bridget at his elbow.

'You lying bastards.'

Laodoc turned, his tongue flickering. Shella was standing in the doorway, glaring at him.

'Wait, I can explain,' Laodoc said.

'I come here to give you some good news, and find this? You faked your injury to stay?'

Laodoc glanced at Agang.

'I want you all out of here,' Shella said.

'It's time to be honest,' Agang said.

'It's too late for that,' Shella cried. She turned to go.

'Please,' said Laodoc. 'Don't leave. Come in and shut the door.'

'It's worth hearing,' Bridget said, 'believe me.'

Shella paused for a moment, her face dark with anger. She slammed the door and folded her arms.

'Okay,' she said. 'This had better be good.'

Laodoc sat on the bed. 'I did break my leg, we didn't lie about that.'

'The fuck you did,' Shella said. 'There's no way it could have healed by now.'

'Unless...' Agang said.

'Unless what?'

Laodoc tried to smile. 'Do you know what Sanang mages can do?'

Shella frowned, then stared at Agang. 'You?'

He nodded.

'Prove it.'

Agang glanced at the others. 'How? Does anyone have any wounds?'

Shella pulled a knife from her cloak, and slammed it down on the table.

Laodoc raised an eyebrow.

'Fucksake,' said Bridget, leaning forwards and picking up the blade.

'Try not to get any blood on the bed,' Laodoc said.

She glared at him, shook her head, then crouched before Agang. She lifted the knife, and ran it down her forearm, a line of red seeping from the cut. Shella furrowed her brows and stared. Agang put his hand onto Bridget's arm, and within seconds, the cut healed. The Brig woman flexed her fingers, and wiped the blood away, showing smooth skin where the wound had been.

Shella sat.

'You still lied,' she said.

'We did,' said Laodoc. 'We're sorry. We were desperate. You were going to send us away, after we'd journeyed so far, and lost so much. It was my idea to lie to you, but I was in considerable agony at the time, and I'm not proud of what I did.'

'My answer's the same,' she said. 'I'm not leaving Silverstream. You've bought yourselves a few more days here, though.'

'Thank you,' he said. 'May I ask why?'

'Now that I know he's a mage, I want him to attend the clinic and help out. He can cure the sick and injured, and pay the town back for the kindness they've shown you.'

Agang nodded. 'I am at your service.'

'Good.'

'However, I have one condition,' he said. 'No one must discover I'm a mage. Tell the clinic that I'm a doctor, and I'll work my powers subtly.'

Shella frowned. 'Why all the subterfuge? I mean, why would you keep being a healer secret anyway?'

'I'm not just a healer.'

'What?'

'I can do more than just heal wounds.'

'Yeah?'

'I can bring people back from death.'

'No way.'

'Have you heard of soulwitches?' Laodoc said.

'Nope, and I've never heard of any mage skill that can beat death.'

'It's kept secret by the Sanang,' Agang said. 'We don't speak of it to outsiders.'

'Bullshit.'

'I'm telling the truth,' Agang said, his face reddening.

'Oh yeah?' Shella smirked. 'And has anyone ever seen you do it?'

Bridget coughed. Shella turned to face her, and the Brig woman nodded.

'You? You've seen him bring someone back from the dead?'

'No,' said Bridget. 'I was the one he brought back.'

'I witnessed it happen,' said Laodoc, 'as did Dyam, Dean and Lola.'

Shella's mouth opened.

'It doesn't make sense,' she said. 'What about Bedig? You told me he was killed. Why didn't you bring him back?'

The others sat in silence.

'I knew the red-headed oaf when he lived with Daphne in Plateau City,' Shella went on, her voice rising. 'He was at the birth of her child. He was our friend, and you just let him die?'

'It's a little more complicated than that,' Laodoc half-whispered, 'and the wounds are still raw.'

Shella glowered at them. 'Explain it to me.'

'Agang had been seriously wounded,' Laodoc said, 'and he needed to heal himself first.'

Agang nodded. 'I didn't have enough strength to bring back both Bridget and Bedig. I wish I had, but I didn't. I hope you understand.'

'Oh, I get it alright. You chose her over Bedig. Over my friend.'

Bridget got to her feet, her face grey, and stumbled towards the door.

'Wait,' said Laodoc, 'Bridget, please.'

'I can't do this,' she cried, and rushed from the room.

Laodoc felt his temper rise. He turned to Shella.

'I think you should go,' he said, 'before I say something I'll regret.'

Shella tutted. 'Get over yourself, you lying old bastard. I'm not the one at fault here. Perhaps if you'd told me the truth in the first place...'

Laodoc exploded. 'Have you any idea of the pain that young woman's gone through? She didn't choose to be raised from the dead, she loved Bedig, do you understand? The guilt she's been carrying would crack granite. Today I saw her smile for the first time since Bedig died, and then you go and open your foolish mouth, and say the cruellest, most stupid thing you can think of, just to hurt us. Well, it's Bridget you hurt, and I'm not sure I can forgive you.'

Shella sat back in her seat. 'You finished?'

'I am,' said Laodoc, his heart racing.

She nodded. 'You're right. I'll apologise to Bridget. She's not to blame, you two assholes are. She's just another victim of your bullshit. You dragged her halfway across the world, getting Bedig killed in the process, and for what?'

'To persuade you to come with us,' said Agang, 'to leave Silver-stream, and help us rid the world of the Emperor.'

'No chance,' she said. 'I've seen the Emperor.'

'So have I,' said Agang. 'I stood before the walls of the imperial capital while he annihilated a hundred thousand warriors.'

'And you still want to fight him?'

'I must.'

She shook her head. 'All that proves is that you're more stupid than I am.'

'The Emperor may be powerful,' Agang said, 'but we can still beat him, if we can unite the strongest mages against him. You and Keira would be formidable together.'

'I'm sure we would, if I didn't just kill her on sight,' Shella said. 'But you're wrong. We can't beat the Emperor.' She sighed. 'Look, if it's time for trading secrets, then there's something you should know, if you're truly crazy enough to believe you can beat him.'

The others leaned in, listening.

'I was there when Guilliam, when the Emperor... received his powers. I saw it all.'

Laodoc gasped. 'What happened?'

'It was a fucked-up ritual, a bloodbath, but that doesn't matter. What's important is that it's not Guilliam in there any more.'

'In where?'

'In his body. The spirit of the Creator came down and took possession of it. It's him in there now.'

'The Holdings god?' said Agang.

'Exactly, and I ain't fighting a god.'

'You're sure?' said Laodoc.

'Yeah, and Kalayne confirmed it was true. That mad old bastard had a plan to beat him, but he died and well, that's that.'

'He had a plan?'

'Yeah. Don't know the details, but it hinged on Kalayne. He had a weird power, where he could make himself almost invisible, so people wouldn't see him.'

'I saw him do it once,' said Agang.

'He said it worked on the Creator too, that he could get close without being seen, and hide others next to him, so they were invisible as well. That was the only way the old bastard could see us beating him, and like I said, he's dead.'

Agang frowned. 'Shit.'

'You said it, death-raiser.' She smirked. 'So tell me, how many people have you brought back?'

'Not many,' he said. 'I kept my powers hidden.'

'He raised Keira,' Laodoc said, 'after the Emperor killed her.'

'No shit?' Shella said. 'Well, good for her. She slaughters half the world, and when she finally pays the price, she's rewarded with a new life.'

'Kalayne said she was essential,' said Agang, 'that she would save the world.'

'What?' Shella laughed. 'There'll be peace because she's killed everyone? She's a homicidal bitch! Why you guys think I'll ever want to meet her, let alone work with her, is beyond me. You said you went to Akhanawarah City, you saw what she did?'

'We saw,' said Laodoc.

'She was doing the same to Plateau City when the Emperor stopped her,' she said. 'Of course, that time I happened to agree with her, but it doesn't mean I want to help her, or be in any way involved with her. And anyway, if she wants to meet me so badly, why didn't she come in person?'

Laodoc glanced at Agang.

'Let me guess,' she said. 'You asked her, and she told you to fuck off. Not having much luck getting us together, are you?'

'It would appear not,' Laodoc said, 'but I still have hope we can persuade you.'

'Go on then,' Shella smiled, 'give it another try. I'm all ears.'

Laodoc opened his mouth, then frowned. What else could he say that would make any difference? He and Agang had attempted several times to convince her, but nothing had come close to working.

'No,' he said. 'I need to think about what we've learned. The Emperor being possessed by the Creator changes less for me than you might imagine. Whoever it is, he remains absurdly powerful, and will be difficult to defeat. What troubles me more is the failure of Kalayne's plan. I think I am only now beginning to understand what his loss means.'

'It means we're fucked,' Shella said, 'but only if we go looking for trouble. We stay here, we're safe.'

'My dear Shella,' Laodoc said. 'Are you inviting us to stay?'

'No, I was being rhetorical. Nice try, but I still want you all on your way, once Agang's put in some work at the clinic.'

'Then you can go back to hiding?' Agang said.

'Pretty much.'

She stood. 'It's been a lovely chat, boys, but I should go and say sorry to Bridget.'

'One moment,' Laodoc said. 'When you came in, you said you had some good news for us.'

'Oh yeah. After Bridget's speech, the town voted to host a welcoming party for you all tonight.'

'Is that what the cheer was for?'

'Yeah,' she smirked, 'any excuse for a party. You're all expected to attend, so be in the town square for sunset.'

'We're being allowed out?' said Agang.

'Yeah. They also voted to give you the freedom to walk the streets of Silverstream.'

'What about me?' Laodoc said. 'Should I go? I mean, my leg...?'

Shella smiled. 'You're coming, but I want you on crutches all night, hobbling around as if you're in pain. And I want a good performance.'

'I suppose so,' Laodoc said. 'I wouldn't want the town knowing we'd lied to them.'

'Indeed,' she said, 'and it'll be funny.'

The six strangers washed and put on their cleanest clothes as the sun fell beyond the mountains to the west. Laodoc had wondered if anyone would refuse to go, but they were so sick of being stuck inside the house that even Dean didn't complain.

He noticed Bridget come out of her room and enter their small communal hall, where they were waiting.

'Did you speak to Shella?' he asked, as the others got ready to go.

'Aye,' she said, her breath strong with Rakanese spirits. 'Said she was sorry, in her own sort of way.'

'She's always been one to speak without thinking,' Laodoc said, putting on his coat. He picked up the two crutches, and placed them under his shoulders.

Bridget shook her head. 'Just walk, for Pyre's sake. Shella's having ye on. No one in the town even knows ye were injured, or maybe at most they heard ye had a sore leg. Just tell them ye sprained yer ankle, and let's see Shella's face when she realises.'

Laodoc smiled. He glanced at Agang.

'Do it,' he said. He turned to the others. 'Listen. If anyone asks, Laodoc had a sprained ankle, and he's all better now. Nobody mention broken bones, and nobody mention anything about me being a mage.'

Dyam sighed. 'We know; ye've told us often enough.'

'Just making sure,' he said. 'Shella knows, but that's it.'

They nodded.

Agang stepped forward and put his hand on the entrance door. He glanced at the others, then turned the handle. It opened. He smiled, and stepped outside, the others following. Laodoc watched them, then gazed back at the crutches.

'Getting cold feet?' Bridget said.

He placed the crutches back against the wall, and took his walking stick instead. They went outside, and Laodoc got his first proper look at his surroundings. Wooden and brick-built houses were raised on stilts, with low walkways connecting them, creating streets through the town. Lamps were being lit as the sun set, and trees lined the avenues. Beneath the houses and walkways, the waters of the river reflected the lamplight. The Rakanese had breached its banks, and inundated the area to create a large freshwater marsh. Insects buzzed about the lamps, and birds nested on the wide rooftops.

Laodoc shook his head. 'All this time, I had no idea we were above water. We'll have to get all the shutters in the house opened up; I feel like we've been living underground.'

'Ye should have felt at home, then,' Bridget said. She took a swig from a hip flask, and gazed around. A small crowd had gathered, gawking at the strangers. A couple stepped forward.

'Good evening,' said one in Rahain. 'We're here to escort you to the town hall for the celebrations.'

Agang bowed to them, much to the amusement of the crowd. 'My thanks,' he said, ignoring the laughter.

'Come on,' Bridget said, and they set off, a path clearing before them. The escorts led them along several wide avenues, the trees leafless and bare. A chill wind was blowing down from the mountains, and most of the locals were wrapped up warm. They came to a square, fronted on all sides by the tallest buildings in the town. Ahead was the largest, a wooden-framed brick edifice, with its great doors wide open.

'The town hall,' Bridget muttered, before their escorts could speak.

'I heard your speech there today,' said one. 'It was very moving.'

Bridget nodded and glanced away.

The escort turned. 'This way, please.'

They crossed the square and entered the hall. They passed through an entrance lobby, and went into a large, high-ceilinged chamber, where great fires burned at either end. Tables had been laid out, and hundreds of Rakanese were already sitting. They hushed when they saw the strangers. Shella stood, and stepped forward.

She opened her mouth to speak, then noticed Laodoc and frowned. She turned to face the Rakanese.

'These are our guests,' she said, 'and we're holding this dinner to welcome them to Silverstream, and to acknowledge Miss Bridget's gracious apology, made before the town council earlier today.'

There was a smattering of applause, and a few banged their cups on the tables.

'So, without further ado,' she went on, 'let's get them seated, and dinner can begin.'

She led them to a table at the end of the room, where several Rakanese were sitting. Laodoc sat next to Shella, with Dyam on his right, and Agang and Bridget opposite. In front of them were jugs of water, and the clear spirit alcohol that the locals drank. The Brig woman filled her mug.

Laodoc smiled out of politeness as servers placed a great variety of small dishes onto their table.

'Help yourselves,' Shella said, picking up a spoon and scooping a portion of something with tentacles from a bowl.

Laodoc spotted a dish of rice and vegetables, and heaped some onto his plate. It came in a thick sauce that scorched the back of his mouth, and he poured himself a large water.

'Your people's range of foods,' said Agang, glancing at Shella, 'is unique.'

Bridget snorted. 'That's one way to put it. Insects and slugs, and things with too many eyes.'

'You seem to be enjoying it,' Shella said, nodding at Bridget's heaped plate.

'The rice is good,' she said. 'It's the rest of it I'm not touching. I've put up with worse than a spicy grasshopper, but never through choice.'

'Your loss,' Shella said, biting the head off a long fried stick insect.

The plates were replenished as soon as they ran low, and dozens of new dishes appeared. Laodoc found a bowl of plain rice, and pulled it towards him. Bridget laughed, and emptied her mug. He watched as she refilled it.

'Thirsty tonight?' he said across the table, his voice lowered.

'Aye, so?'

'We can drink back at the house later,' he said. 'Maybe we should rein it in a little while we're here?'

She shrugged. Laodoc looked across to Agang for support, but the Sanang was chatting to a Rakanese man on his left.

Dyam nudged him. 'This reminds me of the parties we used to have in Slateford. Do you remember Killop's birthday party, when Bridget went mental and trashed half the dance-floor?'

'I think I missed that one,' Laodoc said.

'Maybe it was before you got there,' she said.

Shella nudged him from the other side.

He turned.

'What was that?' Shella said. 'Something about a birthday?'

'Aye,' said Dyam. 'Last year.'

'Whose did you say it was?'

'Our chief's. Killop.'

'Chief Killop?' Shella said, frowning. 'Wait. All this time you've been here, no one mentioned that you were in Chief Killop's clan, or tribe? Whatever it's called.'

'Clan,' said Bridget. 'The Severed Clan.'

'Right,' Shella said. 'Laodoc, you didn't think this was important?'

'Is it?' he said. 'I admit, it never came up, so I didn't think it worth mentioning.'

'But what about Daphne, you dozy old lizard?' Shella said. 'This is Daphne's Killop we're talking about, right? You didn't think I'd want to hear about my best friend?'

'Sorry.'

'She did make it there, didn't she? She must have done, if Bedig made it.' She groaned. 'I can't believe I didn't put it together myself.'

'She made it to Slateford,' Dyam said, 'with Bedig and her daughter.'

Bridget snorted.

Shella frowned at her, then turned to Laodoc and Dyam.

'So, how was old Daffers? When did you last see her?'

Laodoc's tongue flickered.

'Not always a good sign,' Shella said, 'but go on.'

'Daphne Holdfast was happy in Slateford, with Killop and the baby. They lived a good life there, from what I saw. Daphne was at her usual best. She rescued me from the Rahain Capital when the rebels took over the government.' He paused.

'Ha,' laughed Shella. 'Good old Daffers.'

'When we parted,' he went on, 'she was on her way to settle an old debt.'

'Aye,' grunted Bridget, 'and tell her what happened next.'

Shella glanced across the table, frowning.

Laodoc swallowed. 'Killop left the clan and went after her.'

Bridget shook her head and mumbled something.

'What was that?' snapped Shella.

The Brig woman looked up. 'I said I hate that cow.'

'Who?'

'Daphne fucking Holdfast,' Bridget muttered. 'All that time I thought she was my friend, I was fooling myself. She was never my friend. She didn't give a shit about anybody but Killop and Karalyn.' She swayed, and put a hand on the table to steady herself, as the others stared.

'I wish she'd stayed away,' Bridget went on, 'then Killop would never have left. That girl fucked with his mind.'

'Love does that,' Shella said.

Bridget stared at her. 'Not Daphne, ya idiot; Karalyn. She fucked with Killop's mind.' She gazed around the table, her heavy eyes narrowing. 'None of you know, eh? Not one of ye knows.'

'Knows what?' said Shella.

'About Daphne's daughter. About what she can do.'

Laodoc frowned. 'And what can she do?'

'She's a mage,' Bridget said, 'a one-year-old mage, more powerful than either of you two sitting here.' She nodded to Agang and Shella. 'She can read minds, mess with yer thoughts, and Pyre knows what else.'

She put down her mug. 'Just like Kalayne. That's what Daphne said. She has the same powers as Kalayne.'

'Bullshit,' Shella said. 'I was there at the birth, and saw Karalyn loads over the next few thirds. There was nothing crazy about her.'

'And how old was she when Daphne left Plateau City?' asked Laodoc.

'Nearly seven thirds.'

'She's grown a fair bit since then,' Bridget said.

'I never saw anything out of the ordinary,' Laodoc said, 'but I wasn't the most sociable back then. I didn't pay much attention to the child, I'm afraid.'

'Could it be true?' said Agang. 'This child of Daphne Holdfast and Killop, could she possess the same powers as Kalayne?'

'In Rahain,' Laodoc said, 'scientists believed that the Holdings and the Kellach peninsula were once a single continent, long ago. If that's true, then maybe the powers of Kalayne belong to both their peoples.'

Agang's eyes widened. 'That's it,' he said. 'This is the answer.'

'What?' said Shella.

'Kalayne may be dead,' he said, 'but this girl lives.'

He stared across the table.

'We need to find her.'

CHAPTER 24
REARGUARD

S hield Mountains, Imperial Holdings – 7th Day, First Third Winter 507

'Kara-bear?' Daphne called, her eyes scanning the crowded camp. 'Where is she? Celine?'

The Holdings woman glanced over. 'What is it?'

'Where's Karalyn?'

Celine frowned. 'She was right here, I just saw her...'

'Karalyn!' Daphne cried.

'Look, here's her toy,' Celine said, kneeling by the fire where the girl had been playing moments before. 'She must have run off.'

'Dammit,' Daphne muttered, walking round the fire where the others were eating their breakfast in the dawn light. Kylon caught her eye, and walked over.

'Help me look for Karalyn,' she said, before he could open his mouth. 'She was here a minute ago, now she's gone.'

'I'll check the caves,' he said.

'Alright, go.'

She turned, and pulled on some battle-vision, her enhanced eyesight taking in every detail around her. She examined the area next to the busy campfire, then searched by the haphazard jumble of tents, trees and carts, extending her vision out to the paths at the edge of their new base as far as the sentries.

Nothing.

'I don't understand,' said Celine, worry creasing her brow, 'she can't have just disappeared.'

'She's not in the caves,' Kylon said, his eyes dark. 'I'll start searching the tents. We'll tear this place apart until we find her.'

'Wait,' Daphne said. 'Maybe she's still here. Maybe we just can't see her.'

'What?' said Celine.

'If she can hide from the Emperor, she could be hiding from us.'

'Do you think you can find her?' Kylon said.

'I'll try.'

He nodded. 'I'll get a search party organised while you do what you can here. Signal me if you find her.'

Daphne watched the Kell man stride away, as Baoryn stepped out of the crowd to follow him. She sat on the rough ground, and lit a cigarette.

Celine knelt next to her. 'Should I send a messenger to Killop and Chane?'

'No,' she said. 'Not yet.'

She stubbed out her cigarette, and closed her eyes. She took a few deep breaths, steadying herself. She softened her focus, allowing her mind to break free of her body in the way Kalayne had taught her, rather than use the more forceful Holdings method. Her vision gazed down on the camp. She saw herself, seated, with Celine crouching next to her, biting her nails.

Two yards to her left was a tree, with low hanging branches. Under them, Karalyn was crouching, her knees drawn up, her eyes closed. Daphne glided down.

What's wrong, little bear?

Mummy.

Are you scared? Everything's all right, you don't need to hide.

Mummy hide too.

Mummy's here because I was worried, Daphne said. *Please don't hide from mummy, Kara-bear.*

No, mummy hide now.

Why? What are you hiding from?

Karalyn's eyes opened. *The bad man's coming.*

Daphne's vision shot back to her head and she opened her eyes. She could see Karalyn, crouching under the branches of the tree. Daphne held out her right arm, and the girl ran to her.

Celine gasped. 'Where did you appear from, young lady?'

Daphne held Karalyn close, her mind racing. She needed to calm herself. Karalyn was sniffling in her embrace, but she cleared her mind, and sent a flash of line-vision up to the nearest mountain peak, half a mile to the north. From there, she scanned the approaches to their base. There were only two ways to access the narrow valley where they had camped. Daphne looked first to the west. In a clearing a few miles away lay several Rahain flying carriages, their hatches open. Dozens of soldiers were spilling out of them. Daphne spun round, and sent her vision east. The same, except this time the soldiers were accompanied by a tall figure in black armour.

She pulled her vision back and retched, holding Karalyn clear as she threw her breakfast up onto the ground. Several troopers stared at her from the fireside.

'I need Killop,' she gasped at Celine, who was sitting open-mouthed, 'and Chane, Mirren, Kylon, everyone. Now.'

'Are you alright, ma'am?' a trooper called over.

Daphne spotted an officer, and staggered to her feet. 'Lieutenant,' she cried. 'Get over here.'

He approached. 'Yes, my lady?'

'To arms,' she said, her gaze steady. 'Get everybody up and ready. No fuss. Now.'

The lieutenant's eyes widened. 'At once, my lady.'

He turned, blew a whistle and began crying out orders to the camp. More officers approached.

'Send for Killop and Chane,' she said, rocking Karalyn in her arms.

'We're here,' said Killop.

She turned, and saw him walk into the clearing by the fire, Chane at his side.

'What's wrong?' he said.

Daphne waited until her officers were gathered.

'Let me take her,' Celine whispered.

Daphne shook her head. 'Get me a table.' She glanced up. 'Chane. Map.'

Celine carried a folding table to where Daphne stood holding Kara-lyn, and Chane laid a map on it. Mirren arrived, drawn by the crowd. She pushed her way through the troopers, until she stood by Killop and the other officers.

'Lady Holdfast,' she said, 'are we compromised?'

Daphne nodded. 'The Emperor's forces are only a few miles away, blocking both exits to the valley.'

The crowd stared at her, their faces frozen.

'I thought he was a hundred miles away,' said Chane.

'He's flown in on winged gaien, straight to our location.'

'The Emperor's here in person?' said Mirren.

'He is,' Daphne said. Some in the crowd grew restless, looking over their shoulders.

'Someone has betrayed us,' cried a trooper.

Daphne swallowed. The trooper was right. She glanced at Killop.

'We'll worry about that later,' he said. 'Right now, we need to hold our nerve and find a way out of this trap.'

'What do you suggest, Commander?' said Daphne.

Killop stepped forward and glanced at the map. 'Show me the positions of the enemy forces, my lady.'

Daphne pointed at the two locations.

'And at which end of the valley is the Emperor?'

'The eastern.'

He nodded, staring at the map. The rest of the officers gathered closer in silence.

'All right,' he said, straightening, 'here's what I suggest. I'll take three raiding squads, and make for this position here in the east. We'll hold the Emperor up, while every other available trooper attacks the Rahain at the western end of the valley. Chane, you take command of this force. Break through the enemy as fast as you can. Once you're clear of the valley, head north towards the coast, and I'll catch you up with my three squads later.'

Daphne stared at him.

'My lady?' he said.

'You'll catch us up?'

'Aye,' he said, 'we will.'

She faced the others. 'You heard the commander, those are my orders. The Emperor thinks he's got us trapped like rats in a bag, but he doesn't know we're waiting for him, or what we're capable of. Let's show him.'

She stepped back, and the camp descended into chaos. Troopers ran around, pulling on boots or armour, and grabbing crossbows. Officers were bawling and shouting to be heard over the pandemonium, screaming at their soldiers to get into position. Killop and Chane were locked in a heated discussion, their voices low.

Daphne glanced at Celine.

'We'd best get ready.'

Celine nodded, and they walked into the shallow caves where Daphne was based, pulling back the long curtain that shielded the interior from eyes and the wind. Daphne put Karalyn down into her cot, and picked up her armour.

'Help me,' she said, and Celine began fastening the buckles at her side.

'Who do you think...?' she said, then stopped as the curtain flapped and Kylon walked in.

'I heard,' said the Kell, his face stern. 'This is bad. You know what it means, don't you?'

'Yes,' Daphne said. 'Either the Emperor can see through Karalyn's vision shield, or someone has betrayed our location to him.'

'Exactly,' Kylon said. He turned, as Baoryn walked in.

Karalyn let out a low whimper, her face crinkling in fear, and Daphne's eyes narrowed.

'Celine,' she said, 'take Karalyn to the cave at the back, and stay there until I tell you.'

Celine gave a slight nod, picked up the child, and disappeared behind her. Daphne stepped forward, buckling on her sword belt. She smiled, and entered the Rahain man's head. She ploughed in deep, her power ripping through his thoughts. Baoryn staggered and fell to the ground, twitching. Kylon cried out, and dropped to his knees beside him, but Daphne carried on searching through the Rahain man's mind, looking into all the dark corners. She stopped. There, hidden away, she sensed the mage threads of the Emperor, nesting inside his brain like a parasite. She recoiled in disgust, and let out a fierce blast of power, scouring it clean.

Baoryn screamed, and Daphne pulled her vision back.

Kylon stared up at her, his eyes enraged. 'What have you done?'

She glanced down, her breath calming. Baoryn was lying still with his eyes open. Foam and spittle covered his chin, and the veins in his head were bulging.

'The Emperor got to him,' she said. 'He was watching us through his eyes.'

'And you killed him for it?'

She shook her head. 'He'll live. He might have a sore head for a while. I burnt the Emperor's presence out of him.'

'He didn't know it was there,' Kylon said. 'He couldn't have.'

'I know,' she said. 'That's why he's still alive.'

Kylon nodded.

'I need to ask you something,' Daphne said, 'and I want a straight answer. Did you ever speak to Baoryn about my daughter?'

'I told him it was our job to protect her,' he said, 'but not why. Do you think the Emperor was listening?'

'We'll have to assume he might have been, whenever Baoryn was in earshot,' she said. 'Get him out of here, and get ready to go. We'll be following Chane's force down the valley to the west.'

He picked up Baoryn, nodded, and left the cave as Killop walked in.

'What happened to him?' he said.

'He was our spy,' she said. 'How they knew we were here.'

'Shit. The Emperor was in his head?'

'Yeah.'

'How?' Killop said. 'I mean, how did he know that Baoryn knew us?'

'I don't know,' said Daphne. 'I'm guessing that it was bad luck, and that the Emperor was messing with the heads of the scouts he was sending up into the mountains to hunt for us. I dealt with it, though. He's blind to us again.'

Killop nodded. 'I have to go. Just came to see you before we head off.'

She put her arm around his waist. 'Please don't do anything stupid out there.'

'I won't.' He kissed her. 'Where's Karalyn?'

Daphne turned her head. 'Celine!'

The Holdings woman walked out, carrying the girl.

'I'll get out of your way,' she said, passing Karalyn to Killop and retreating. He held his daughter close.

'See you soon, wee bear.'

'Daddy hide from the bad man,' she said, touching his cheek.

'I will if I see him,' he said. He put her down in her cot.

'Get out of here as fast as you can,' he said to Daphne. 'And don't look back.'

They kissed, and he left the cave.

Daphne sat on the bed and lit a cigarette. Celine emerged from the rear of the cave, dragging two large packs.

'He'll be alright,' she said.

She nodded. 'Ready to go?'

Celine gazed around the cave. 'So we'll be sleeping rough from now on?'

'Looks like it,' Daphne said, 'unless you can get everything packed up in the next two minutes.'

Celine dropped the packs. 'Two minutes?' She raced round the cave, gathering blankets, clothes, and anything lying around, and stuffing them into the already bulging luggage.

An officer parted the curtain. 'Ma'am, Captain Chane's force is preparing to leave.'

'Thank you, Lieutenant,' Daphne said, picking up Karalyn. 'Time's up, Celine.'

Troopers entered the cave. They began to lift the packs, and Daphne walked back outside into the morning light. Only a few tents remained where dozens had stood ten minutes before, and the camp-fires were out. Troopers were lined up, their weapons and kit strapped to their belts and backs.

'This way, ma'am,' said the officer, and they followed him past the first rows of troopers, towards the western entrance to the valley. They reached Mirren, who was surrounded by her personal guard. Kylon stood close by, brooding.

'Here we are, ma'am,' said the officer.

Daphne stopped, and her own guard formed up round her.

'Where's Baoryn?'

Kylon nodded ahead. 'Up with the sick and injured.'

Daphne gazed down the long line of troopers. Twenty yards ahead were a dozen carts, laden with bags, crates and those unable to walk.

'I'm sorry I had to hurt him.'

The Kell man shrugged. 'You did what you thought was right.'

Mirren strode over to her.

'Quite a morning, Lady Holdfast,' she said.

She nodded, glancing up the line ahead, which was just starting to move off.

'I suppose you wish you were up there?' Mirren went on. 'Leading the charge.'

'Yes,' she said. 'It's what I do best. I'm not used to being at the rear.'

'You may be needed here,' Mirren said. 'If the Emperor breaks through your commander's blocking force, then I imagine the rear-guard could get a little busy.'

They began moving, their guards flanking them by the sides of the path. They crossed the campsite, walking between the abandoned tents and equipment, and the extinguished fires, where breakfast dishes lay stacked. The line slowed as they reached the narrow neck of the valley, and began to descend the long gorge. The carts had to be lifted over several large boulders blocking the way, and Daphne opened her cigarette case while they waited.

'It was very brave of your commander,' said Mirren, taking an offered cigarette.

Daphne lit Mirren's, then her own.

'Especially considering the fact that he gave Captain Chane his best squads.'

Daphne frowned.

'You didn't know, my lady?' Mirren said. 'They had quite the row about it. Captain Chane felt that Commander Killop should take them, but he insisted.'

Daphne said nothing, a knot forming in the pit of her stomach.

'It makes sense,' said Kylon. 'He wants us to have the best chance of escape. The quality of his soldiers won't make any difference against the Emperor anyway.'

Mirren stared at the Kell man, a mixture of contempt and distaste in her eyes.

They began to move again.

Daphne held on to Karalyn, and kept her eyes fixed on the path.

They walked for over an hour through the long and narrow gorge, high cliffs on either side. Troopers hauled the carts ahead of them, while behind, the rear guard marched in silence. Water from the early rains of winter was tumbling over the side of the cliff to their left, joining a stream that ran along the foot of the gorge. Caves had formed behind the waterfalls, and Daphne gazed at their beauty, for a second forgetting why she was there.

A shout rang out from far ahead, and she looked up the gorge. The other troopers were also staring, as the sounds of steel and the cries of the wounded and dying reached them. Squads began to move up the line, rushing towards the fighting.

'Chane'll smash them,' said Celine. She glanced at Daphne. 'Your arms must be aching.'

'Thanks,' she said, passing her Karalyn. The girl tried to cling on, but Daphne pulled her fingers from her hair.

'Don't worry, Kara-bear,' she said, stretching her right arm. Her left, ensconced in its Rahain armour, was stiff and painful. She reached into a pocket and took out a stick of keenweed. Kylon lit a match for her, and she smoked, her pain receding, and her senses quickening. She gazed upwards. The sun was behind a bank of clouds, somewhere overhead. Impatience spread through her. She turned, facing the way they had come. Over the heads of the rearguard, the cliffs loomed, casting deep shadows across the floor of the gorge.

'I'm sure he's all right,' said Mirren. 'Your commander is a very capable soldier.'

Daphne's nerves flared. Why had she let him go? She should have told him his place was with her and their daughter. He couldn't stand up to the Emperor, no one could. She felt a desperate desire to range with her vision, to scan the camp and the valley where Killop was positioning himself, but feared that she might give their location away to the Emperor.

The Creator. She had to remember who it was they were fighting.

A messenger arrived.

'My lady,' she said, catching her breath. 'Captain Chane reports contact with the western Rahain force. She wishes you to know that she is engaging them with all strength in a full frontal assault on their positions.'

'Thank you,' Daphne said, stubbing the weedstick out beneath her heel. 'Let her know the rear remains secure, and pass on my best wishes.'

'Ma'am,' the messenger bowed, then sprinted back down the gorge, following the line of the stream towards the sounds of battle.

Sacrifice

Daphne gazed around. 'Where's Kylon?'

'Gone to check on Baoryn,' said Celine.

'I heard that he was the Emperor's eyes and ears,' said Mirren. 'Most unfortunate. I had deemed you a better judge of character, Lady Holdfast.'

'I didn't delve deep enough into his mind when I first looked,' she said, 'but I believe he was unaware he was being used.'

'Well, it's too late now, I suppose. The damage has been done.' Mirren gazed back up the path. 'The thing that killed Guilliam is hunting us, with nothing to protect us except Killop and a few young troopers. I fear our rebellion may soon be at an end.'

'It's not over yet,' Daphne said. 'We get through this gorge, we can flee north. Without Baoryn, the Emperor has no chance of finding us. We're going to get out of this, Mirren.'

'He hasn't come all this way to give up now,' she said. 'He wants us, and the mages.' She leaned in close. 'Maybe if we led him to the mages, he might be satisfied, and leave. Then we'd be safe. You and your daughter would be safe.'

'We can't betray them.'

'I know. It was just a foolish thought.'

Daphne frowned. 'If you have any more, keep them to yourself.'

Mirren gave a gentle bow, and walked to where her troopers stood.

'Do you think she was serious?' whispered Celine.

'She's scared,' Daphne said.

'She's not the only one.'

Twenty long, nervous minutes passed. The rearguard waited by the carts, smoking and casting glances back up the path.

Daphne sat on a boulder. Celine was next to her, rocking Karalyn back and forth in her arms as the child slept.

Kylon was close by, leaning against the side of the cliff, his long

361

black coat trailing on the ground. He caught her eye, and glanced towards the carts.

Daphne turned, and saw movement. She jumped off the boulder.

'We're moving,' she called out. 'Everyone up.'

The troopers got back into their positions as the carts began to roll forwards. The messenger ran up the path towards them.

'My lady,' she said, 'Captain Chane reports that the path is clear, though she warns that there are still pockets of hostile Rahain forces in the valleys on either side. She requests that the rearguard make all haste.'

'Tell her we're on our way,' Daphne said.

The messenger ran off.

Daphne faced the troopers.

'I want half of you up with the carts,' she said. 'Get them moving as quickly as we can. The rest, watch out for attacks from the flanks. Go.'

Squads of troopers peeled off from the others, their sergeants bellowing orders. The carts began to move faster, and Daphne urged the rearguard on. The gorge widened, with caves and sharp crevices on either side, while the sounds of boots, cartwheels, and the rushing stream blotted out every other noise. The first body appeared, a Holdings trooper shot though the stomach by a crossbow bolt, lying by the bank of the stream. Others came into sight, a mixture of Rahain and Holdings, their bodies piled by the side of the track. Large birds circled overhead in the grey light, waiting for them to pass.

'I might have to give her to you soon,' said Celine. 'My arms are getting sore.'

'Just let me know,' Daphne said. 'Is she still sleeping?'

'Out like a light. She's the only one around here not shitting their pants.'

'I've been in worse situations than this,' Kylon said.

'Oh shut up, you miserable bastard,' Celine said. She glanced at Daphne. 'Should I wake her up?'

Daphne looked at the sleeping child. Her eyes were twitching behind her closed lids. She thought of Killop.

'No,' she said. 'She might be vision-dreaming.'

Daphne's ears picked out a low rumble.

She turned, gazing back up the track, and her heart froze. In the far distance, a new force of Rahain were streaming towards them through the gorge, and in their midst strode the figure in black armour.

'Run!' she cried, plucking Karalyn from Celine's arms and racing towards the carts. To her left, she glimpsed Mirren, her face drawn in terror. The rearguard rushed down the gorge. It narrowed ahead, and carts were being squeezed through two abreast. Troopers were scrambling round them, climbing a few feet up the rocky slopes and leaping down to the other side.

Daphne turned, Kylon by her side, his hand on his sword hilt.

The approaching Rahain were only a few hundred yards away, their lead units sprinting towards them. She pulled on her battle-vision.

'Celine, take Karalyn, and get into the caves. Quickly.'

She stretched out her arms, and Daphne passed her the sleeping child.

'Go, go,' Daphne cried, and Celine and Kylon sprinted off, dodging the retreating troopers, and heading for the deep caves under the high cliffs by the track.

She drew her sword, and opened her mouth to scream orders at the troopers, but the earth beneath their feet buckled and rippled, and a force like a wind threw them to the ground. Daphne landed on her side, then scrambled back to her feet. She stared over to the cliffs, but there was no sign of Karalyn or her two protectors.

You thought you could hide from me forever, Daphne Holdfast, said a voice piercing her mind.

Daphne staggered.

Ahead, the figure in black raised his arms. The Rahain around him drew aside, clearing a path as he approached.

There was a crack like thunder, and the rock face behind the Holdings rearguard shook. Stones began to fall, and the cliffs on either side toppled over and collapsed, blocking the gorge, and killing those trying to haul the last carts through the gap. The troopers round Daphne and Mirren stared, their mouths open.

'Get into lines!' Daphne cried. 'Shields up.'

The troopers began to obey, moving into a rough line, their backs to the blocked gorge. As the Emperor grew closer, he lifted his finger at a trooper, and his head disintegrated in a flash of red. Daphne felt Mirren grab her arm, her face a mask of terror.

I see you, Holdfast. And you, faithless queen.

Daphne turned, staring as the troopers of the rearguard began to fall to the flicks of the Emperor's finger. He was only fifty yards away, scanning the crowd, looking for her. He nodded to his soldiers.

The Rahain charged the rearguard, their shields battering into the line of troopers. Daphne darted forwards, her sword arcing through the air, slicing deep into the neck of a soldier. The Rahain pushed the troopers back, overwhelming them with their greater numbers. Daphne and a handful of troopers were forced to their left, as the Emperor strode forwards, striking down any Holdings close to him.

Daphne looked over her shoulder. Between the jutting edges of the cliff was a deep, narrow ravine, and as the Rahain pushed forwards, troopers began to fall down into it, screaming. She glanced over the edge. It was a fifty foot drop, with a dark stream tumbling at the bottom. With her feet braced half a yard from the lip of the ravine, Daphne lunged out with her sword, killing another soldier, her small group of troopers protecting her with their shields.

The Emperor swept his arm to the side, and around where Mirren stood, a dozen troopers fell, blood exploding from their eye sockets. The rest of her guard dropped to their knees and threw down their weapons. The queen stood among them, her head lifted, but her eyes hollow in defeat.

As Daphne swung her sword down again, she felt the Emperor in her head.

It's over, Daphne. I don't want to kill you. Surrender, and you shall be the mightiest mage in my service, and will stand at my right hand.

The words felt sweet in her mind, and she felt her resolve fade, as if resistance was being drawn out of her. She stared ahead at where the Emperor stood. Next to him, Mirren was being shackled in heavy chains by Rahain soldiers.

'Never,' Daphne whispered. She drew on her battle-vision and stepped back off the edge of the cliff.

For a few seconds, she felt nothing but the air rushing past her, the roar it made almost drowning out the cry of rage from the Emperor. She hit the side of the ravine, and spun, falling deeper. She crashed into the shallow waters of the freezing cold stream, powering her battle-vision to its limits. Her armour pulled her to the bottom, but she struggled up, scrambling to the bank. She pulled her head out of the water, choking for air. Her legs felt numb from the cold, and she could see blood seeping from the wounds she had earned in the fall.

As she crawled from the stream, she glanced up at the narrow sliver of daylight at the top of the ravine. A figure was leaning over the edge, staring down into the darkness of the crevice.

It saddens me that you would rather die than surrender, Holdfast, the Emperor said, *but if that is your wish, so be it.*

He lifted his arms, and brought them down in a lunging motion, and Daphne saw the cliffside around her crack and collapse. The rocks split, and boulders fell, splashing into the stream, and sending fragments flying. She saw a low lip of rock, and crawled under it, as the bottom of the ravine filled with rubble, and the light faded into darkness.

———

When Daphne regained consciousness, she couldn't move. Rock and stone hemmed her in on all sides, but it was loose under the shelter of the lip of rock, and she could breathe. All around was the cold, damp darkness, and she heard nothing but the sharp ringing in her ears.

Mummy?

Daphne gasped, and tried to move her head.

I'm here, Kara-bear, mummy's here.

Daddy.

Daphne fought back tears. *I don't know where daddy is, little bear.*

It's all right, mummy, don't cry. Daddy's here.

A shaft of daylight appeared above her head, and she blinked, blinded. A hand reached in and touched her face.

Killop.

Blood covered the left side of his head, and his armour was bent and blackened by fire. By him was a group of Holding troopers, helping to dig her out. Killop put a water skin to her lips, his eyes never leaving her face. She drank as the rocks were lifted from around her. She was pulled from the rubble, clinging onto Killop's neck as he held her close, her legs trailing.

He rested her against a boulder by the bank of the stream, and they kissed. He examined her for injuries, his hands unbuckling her battered armour. He stopped at her right leg and cut the ripped leather away, revealing an ugly wound, bloody and covered in river mud. He dipped a rag in the stream and began to clean the dirt and blood away.

'You came for me,' she said.

He gazed at her. 'Karalyn led us.'

She looked up, and saw Celine hurry towards her, the girl in her arms.

'Mummy!' Karalyn squealed, as Celine handed her to Daphne.

'Little bear,' Daphne said, pulling her close.

'We saw you fall,' said Kylon, walking towards her. Behind him, Daphne saw Baoryn. The Rahain man was sitting slumped against a boulder, his head and chest covered in bandages. He nodded to her, a grim smile on his lips, as Kylon approached. He handed her a lit cigarette.

'Has the Emperor gone?' she said, taking a smoke.

'Aye,' said Killop, as he cleaned the wound on her leg.

'Hours ago,' said Kylon.

'How did you get away from him?' Daphne said.

'He didn't look for us,' Kylon said. 'He was only after you and Mirren.'

Daphne nodded, then glanced at Killop. 'What about you?'

'He blasted the eastern end of the gorge with fire,' he said. 'Karalyn came to me when she was dreaming, and even though I was awake, I could feel her in my head, helping me.'

'How's the leg?' said Celine.

'Bruised,' Killop said. 'Nothing's broken, but there's a deep cut.'

'I hit the cliffside on the way down,' Daphne said.

'Should heal in a few days,' he said, wrapping a bandage around her calf. He turned to the small group of troopers. 'Get a stretcher made up, and we'll carry Lady Holdfast out of here.'

He stood, brushing the dirt from his battered armour, the dust billowing up in the breeze.

'What now?' said Kylon.

Killop glanced at Daphne.

'It's over,' she said, 'the Emperor's won. He captured Mirren, and even if she doesn't tell him where the four mages are, he'll scour it out of her head anyway.'

Kylon frowned. 'Which means he'll have the full set. The last time he had every type of mage, he was able to grant himself godlike powers.'

He stared down at Daphne.

'What will he do this time?'

CHAPTER 25
TWO TO ONE

Outside Plateau City, Imperial Plateau – 21st Day, First Third Winter 507

Keira frowned. 'Sitting by the window isnae going to make her get back here any quicker.'

'I know,' said Kallie. 'I'm just restless. I might go and check the traps.'

'Again?' Keira said. 'Ye were only out there an hour ago.'

'Anything to take my mind off food.'

'Come and have a smoke,' Keira said, holding out a weedstick. 'Keenweed suppresses yer appetite.'

'So ye keep telling me.'

'It does, but.'

Kallie shook her head. 'If only I had my longbow.'

'Aye, well, ye don't, so stop whining about it.'

'Whining? We've had no food for four days, Keira. The plateau's a wasteland. Every farm's deserted, and there's no animals or folk for miles around. Your invasion last year kicked the arse out of the countryside.'

'A hundred thousand Sanang had to eat something,' Keira said, 'and anyway, it wasnae just me. Agang Garo brought an army up through the Plateau the year before I did, he started it.'

Kallie stared out of the window. 'What was it like when ye arrived, at the head of yer great big army?'

Keira shrugged. 'Wheatfields, cattle, vineyards, wee market towns...'

'My point exactly,' Kallie said. 'Now look at it. No trees, just mud and stumps and burnt-out barns.'

'I don't know what yer fucking problem is, hen. It's just land; it'll recover. Shit'll grow back, and before ye know it, everything will be all nice and green again, and it'll happen a damn sight quicker than it will in Kell.'

'It's not the land that bothers me, it's the lack of food.'

'Come and have a smoke,' Keira said.

Kallie sighed, and got up. She walked across the empty kitchen of the small cottage where they were staying, and sat down next to the warm stove, heated by burning what remained of the furniture. She took the offered weedstick.

Keira cackled.

Kallie frowned at her, and took a smoke. She looked confused for a moment, then her eyes widened.

'This feels... different,' she said, as Keira laughed. 'Everything's brighter, and sparkly.'

'It keeps ye awake as well, does the old keenweed,' Keira said. 'The Sanang used to take it before they went into battle.'

Kallie leaned in closer to the stove, wrapping her cloak around her. 'How much longer do ye think Flora's going to be?'

'How the fuck should I know?'

'You've been to Plateau City before. You told me ye used to live there. You should know how long it takes to walk to the gates and back.'

'Aye, but what about the bit in the middle? Ye know, the bit where she's got to get inside the city and get us some food? Could take her days.'

'We should have gone, not her.'

'It had to be her,' Keira said. 'We don't know if Kellach are allowed in.'

'I think we should go now,' Kallie said. 'See if she's in trouble. She could be in trouble. I cannae stand sitting here doing nothing. If we left before...'

Keira plucked the weedstick from Kallie's hand.

'That's enough for now,' she smirked.

Kallie's face reddened. 'I feel funny. Anxious, like my heart's about to burst. And my mouth's all dry. I need something to drink.'

Keira chuckled as Kallie leaned over and picked up the large jug of water they had scooped from the nearby stream. She raised it to her lips, and glugged down half of it.

'Steady,' Keira said.

Kallie got up and paced about the small room, puffing her cheeks in and out, cradling the jug in her arms.

'Maybe the keenweed's not for you,' Keira said. 'Come and sit down. Talk to me.'

Kallie sat. 'About what?'

'Any old bullshit. I don't know. What about Daphne? Tell me about when ye met her.'

'No,' Kallie said. 'I'm not going to talk about her.'

'Aye, but we're heading up there, eventually,' Keira said. 'Once the Emperor's gone. Daphne's the mother of my niece, and I've still never met her.'

'I'll not be meeting her,' Kallie said, 'or Killop.'

'It's too late for that, Kallie. We've come all this fucking way. Ye're not bailing out now.'

'I cannae handle this conversation, it's doing my head in. Maybe you should talk. I want to know what happened with you and Kylon.'

Keira shrugged. 'He became a right over-bearing wee prick. Zero sense of humour, and he kept trying to tell me what to do all the time. I couldnae stand him by the end.'

'I don't believe you,' Kallie said, shivering by the stove. 'If he turned up here right now, ye'd wet yerself.'

'Would I fuck, ya radge wee cow.' Keira frowned at her. 'Are ye cold?'

'I don't know.'

'Right, that's it,' said Keira, standing. 'No more keenweed for you, ever.' She grabbed a blanket, and threw it over Kallie's shoulders, but she continued to shake.

'I've got an idea,' Keira said, reaching into a bag by her chair as she sat. 'Dreamweed.'

'Not more weed, please.'

'Aye, but this should counteract the other stuff, bring ye down again.'

She lit the new weedstick.

'Are ye sure?' said Kallie.

'Aye, trust me.' Keira took a long draw, and settled into her chair. She wished she had some whisky left, but they had run out of that days before. Maybe Flora would return with a few bottles of rum, or brandy, or any old shit, wine even. That'd be nice. She picked up her mug of water and noticed Kallie staring at her, her eyes bloodshot.

Keira laughed. 'I forgot all about ye for a minute, hen.'

She passed her the dreamweed. Kallie frowned at it for a moment, then took a draw.

Keira's thoughts went back to Flora.

'Annoying wee cow,' she muttered.

'What was that?' Kallie said. 'Who's a cow?'

'Eh?' Keira said. 'Oh, I was just thinking about Flora.'

Kallie nodded, and took another draw.

'Feeling any better?' Keira said.

'Aye,' Kallie said. Her shivering had stopped, and she was swaying gently in her seat. 'Floaty.' She started to smile. 'Thinking about Flora? What kind of thoughts?'

'Not those kind, ya cheeky cow.'

Kallie started to giggle. 'She loves you.'

Keira frowned, watching as Kallie rocked in silent laughter.

'It's not even funny.'

'Aye, it is,' gasped Kallie, her laughter subsiding. 'It's a shame for

Flora, but. I like her. She's good company, and she doesnae take any shit from ye either. I hope she's alright.'

'Me too.'

Kallie started laughing again. 'What was that? Keira actually admitting she has feelings? That's a first.'

'Fuck off.'

'Admit it, ye like her.'

'She's alright, I suppose.'

Kallie leaned over, her eyes heavy, and pointed. 'You love her.'

Keira shook her head. 'I'm beginning to think the dreamweed was a mistake.'

'No,' Kallie said. 'I feel fine, sitting here with you, just the two of us, talking. Ye know, ye can be a right selfish cow at times, stuck up and cocky; but right now I'm glad I'm with ye. Ye've given my life some purpose, after years of not knowing what to do with myself.' A tear made its way down her cheek, and Keira groaned.

'I'm serious,' cried Kallie. 'Don't ruin it.'

'Fucksake, don't get all weepy on me.'

'After we left Killop and Bridget in Rahain, all I wanted was to go home, as if that was even possible. I mean, I knew that Kell had been turned into a desert, but somehow I thought that if I could just get back there, then everything would be alright.' She paused, sobbing, and took another draw. 'But then we ran into a group of bandits in the borderlands with the Plateau. Bunch of nasty wee bastards. At first we were just happy to get fed, and speak to folk after so long on our own, but pretty soon we wanted to leave. Only they wouldn't let us.'

She paused again, her features darkening. She wiped her cheek.

Keira watched her as she smoked from her own weedstick. The thought of Kallie in the hands of some arseholes made her angry, but she didn't want to show it.

'We got away in the end,' Kallie said. 'Ran as fast as we could, and made it back to Kell.'

Keira said nothing.

'Look,' Kallie said; 'I know you had it worse. My story must seem like nothing compared to being forced to kill all those frog-folk, but it was a rough time for me. I... It was bad.'

'I didn't say anything.'

'I know, but I can see it in yer eyes, that smug look of superiority. You've done so much crazy shit that the lives of everybody else must look trivial. You actually think yer a goddess, don't ye?'

'Aye.'

Kallie stared at her, shaking her head.

'There's no point in being modest about it,' Keira said. 'I've got folk in Sanang worshipping me in their wee temples and forest shrines, praying to me on their knees. I've got freaks in Domm who think I'm on this earth to save them all, and who follow me about like sheep. I'm the most powerful mage in the world. I've obliterated cities and brought down kingdoms, and I've come back from the dead.'

She shrugged. 'I'm a fucking goddess.'

'Yeah, right,' said a voice from across the room.

'Flora!' cried Kallie. 'Yer back!'

Keira turned. 'Did ye bring any booze?'

The young Holdings woman raised an eyebrow, and slung her pack off her shoulder. She sat by the stove, dressed in an over-sized coat, and with a woollen hat pulled down over her ears.

'I was worried about ye,' said Kallie. 'So was Keira.'

The fire mage snorted.

Flora looked from one to the other, her nose sniffing. 'Let me guess,' she said, 'you've been smoking in here non-stop since the moment I left?'

'Quite possibly, hen,' said Keira. 'How long's it been?'

Flora shook her head. 'I've been gone for three days.'

'Aye?' Keira laughed.

'I've not,' said Kallie.

Flora turned to her.

'I've not been smoking since ye left.'

Flora spotted the weedstick in her hand. 'You?' she said, her voice high. 'Kallie?'

'Keira said it would stop me feeling hungry.'

'And has it?'

'No,' Kallie said. 'I'm absolutely starving.'

Flora leaned over and opened her pack. She pulled out a paper parcel, and set it on the low table in front of them.

Keira stared, her stomach growling like an angry bear. Kallie leaned so far forward, she nearly fell off her chair. Flora laughed, and unwrapped the parcel. Inside were dried old apples, a pound of hard-looking bread, some over-ripe cheese, and a curling slab of cured beef.

'I think I love you, Flora,' said Kallie.

'Dig in,' she said. 'I've already eaten this morning.'

The Kell women were reaching for the table before Flora had finished speaking. They tore the food to pieces, stuffing their mouths.

Flora shook her head. 'It's like watching wolves.' She picked up Kallie's discarded weedstick, and re-lit it off the stove. She pulled off her hat, and her long black hair fell down her shoulders.

She smiled. 'I'm glad to see that you haven't killed each other while I was away.'

'It was close once or twice,' Kallie said, her mouth full of food.

Keira took the last apple and devoured it in two bites. She sat back, rubbing her belly.

'That was braw. Got any more?'

'Fraid not,' she said. 'That's all I could steal.'

'Ye stole it?' Kallie said.

'We've got no money,' Flora said. 'What did you expect? Food's hard to come by in the city. Scarce and expensive. There are a lot of people starving in the streets.'

'Any Kellach about?' said Keira.

'A few. Nothing like before, though.' She shook her head. 'Plateau City's in a right mess. Well, half of it is. All the rich bastards are doing fine in the New Town, but the rest of the city is lawless, run by gangs. The Kellach quarter, the Old Town, the peasant district, it's all just one giant slum now. The gates to the New Town are locked up and guarded, but I heard rumours about tunnels under the walls.'

'Did ye get in?'

'Not into the New Town. I had no money to pay to use the tunnels, and the guards wouldn't let me through the gates. No papers. I ended up staying in the Old Town. The great fortress there, that joins on to the New Town, is being used as the palace now, after you destroyed the old one.'

Keira smirked.

'The Emperor's not there though, is he?' said Kallie.

Flora shook her head. 'He's still in the Holdings. Some rumours say he's up in the mountains, searching for mages, while others claim he's on his way back, having crushed the rebellion and burnt half the country to ashes.'

'I'm sorry,' Kallie said. 'I hope your family's alright.'

'Thanks.'

'So, what's the plan?' Keira said. 'I reckon we should wait here until His Imperial Arsehole gets back to town, and then we leg it north to the Holdings, and check out the damage. We'll look for Flora's folks first, then see if we can find my wee brother.'

'We don't even know if he's in the Holdings,' said Kallie.

'It's the most likely place, but. And we have a lead. The Holdfasts are meant to be a big, important family, right? We find them, we'll find Killop, if he's up there.'

Kallie frowned.

'Ye don't have to come,' Keira spat. 'Ye can stay with Flora when we find her family. I'll look for Killop on my own.'

'I'll help you,' said Flora. 'If my family are dead, I'll have nowhere else to go; and if they're alive, then they'll still be alive if I take some time out to help you. They might even know where the Holdfasts are; my Hold followed them in their stupid rebellion, after all.'

Kallie said nothing.

'Aye,' Keira said. 'Alright, hen. We'll look for my wee brother together, and moany-face here will just have to make her mind up about whether she wants to come with us.'

'I'm feeling a wee bit sick,' Kallie said. 'I might have to lie down.'

'Ach, ye'll be alright,' Keira said. 'Fight it, it'll pass in a minute.' She raised an eyebrow at Flora. 'First-time smokers, eh?'

'Drink some water,' Flora said. She leant over, picked up a mug and filled it. Kallie took it from her, and sipped.

'Pity there's only water,' Keira muttered.

Flora smiled. 'I'm a professional.' She reached into her pack, and produced a stoppered jug.

'Ya beauty,' Keira crowed, as Flora yanked the cork free. She poured a clear liquid into three mugs on the low table.

Keira picked one up and sniffed. 'White rum?'

Flora shrugged. 'I didn't stop to check the label when I snatched it.'

The fire mage took a drink. 'Ye done good, my wee Flora. Ye done fucking good.'

She put her feet up, and lit a fresh weedstick. 'This is like a wee holiday.'

Flora picked up her mug. 'I'm guessing we won't be moving for the rest of the day, then?'

'Moving?' Keira said. 'Why would we be moving?'

'To the city.'

Keira snorted. 'Why the fuck would we go there?'

Flora frowned. 'Because there's nothing to eat up here. The Emperor could take days to get back, a third maybe, who knows? If we intend to eat in that time, then the only place where there's food is the city.'

'I ain't going back there.'

'So you're going to sit here and starve to death?'

'I'll eat Kallie,' she smirked, glancing at the Kell woman. She was sitting huddled by the stove, the blanket wrapped round her, a green tinge on her face. 'You alright?'

Kallie nodded, puffing her cheeks.

'Let us know if yer going to spew,' Keira said, 'so I can get out of the way.' She glanced at Flora. 'If ye think this is bad, ye should have seen her on the keenweed.'

'No wonder she's messed up,' the Holdings woman said. 'Anyway, don't change the subject. We need to talk about going down to Plateau City.'

'It's not happening,' Keira said, 'and I'm not going to fucking repeat myself again. Take a telling, hen.'

'Fine.'

'Fine?' Keira laughed. 'What happened to the real Flora? Who is this impostor sitting before me? Yer not telling me that yer giving up on the argument already?'

Flora shrugged, and sipped her rum. 'All I have to do is wait.'

'Aye? For what?'

'For hunger to change your mind.'

'I'm from Kell. You'll break long before I do.'

'Then I'll see you down there when you arrive.'

Keira shook her head. 'Ye don't get it. I cannae go back there.' She shuddered, as her head filled with memories of standing before the walls as the Emperor annihilated her army, and then struck her down. Even with the bastard out of town, the thought of seeing those walls again set off an alarm in her brain. It was where she had died, and Agang wasn't around this time to bring her back.

She looked over at Flora, but the Holdings woman was gazing with concern at Kallie, and Keira felt a tightness in her stomach.

'Maybe she should go to bed,' Flora said.

'No,' said Kallie. 'I'm fine. Feeling a bit better.'

'You don't look it,' said Flora.

'Have a drink,' Keira said. 'That'll perk ye up.'

'Or tip her over the edge.'

'She'll be alright,' Keira said, lifting Kallie's mug of rum and passing it to her. Kallie took a sip, grimaced, then took another.

Keira belched.

'Charming,' said Flora. She crossed her legs, balancing her mug on her right knee as she smoked. 'When we eventually get to the Holdings, and go looking for the Holdfasts, it might take a while. That's if any survived the Emperor's invasion. Their names would have been at the top of his wanted list. I heard a lot in the city about the last rebels fighting it out in the Shield Mountains. If the Holdfasts are alive, that's where they'll be.'

'I thought the Holdings was all flat,' said Keira. 'You keep going on about the endless fucking plains.'

'The Holdings is mostly flat, but there's a long range of mountains in the north, which protect us from the ocean storms. No one lives up there.'

'You been?'

'No. I'm a plains girl. Never saw a hill until I first went to the Plateau with the cavalry. When I was little, I thought the whole world was filled with sugar cane, just rows and rows going on forever.'

'Sugar cane?' Keira said. 'Is that some sort of vegetable?'

Flora cackled with laughter. 'I can't wait to see your face when you taste it.'

Keira frowned. 'Unless it's all been burnt to the ground.'

Flora quietened, her smile fading.

'Don't be a cow,' said Kallie.

'It speaks,' Keira muttered.

Kallie straightened, and let out a long breath. 'I think I'm starting to feel normal again.'

'I've got some dullweed to complete the trio,' said Keira.

'Don't even think about it,' snapped Flora.

'Ach, come on; it'll be a laugh.'

'No, it won't,' said Flora. 'A laugh is the opposite of what it'll be.'

'What does dullweed do to ye?' Kallie said.

'It numbs you,' Flora said, 'kills all feeling, which, you know, is great if you're wounded and your leg's hanging off or something. That's what it's meant for; it takes away all pain.'

'All pain?' said Kallie, taking another drink. 'I might give it a go. I could do with feeling nothing for a while.'

'I'm up for it,' said Keira.

'No,' said Flora; 'you might like it.'

'Is that not the fucking point?' laughed Keira.

'But then you'll want to do it again and again. Keira, you must have seen the dullweed addicts in Rainsby, the first time we were there.'

'That was my second time,' she said. 'The first time was much worse. Half the Kellach I saw there were wasted out of their fucking minds, lying about like the dead. But I've had it a few times, and I'm fine.'

Flora sighed. 'Do what you like, then.' She watched as Keira dug about in the weed sack, pulled out a handful of crushed dull-leaf and began to prepare a weedstick.

'I'll make some tea,' Flora said. 'Anybody want any?'

The Kell women shook their heads. Flora stood, and took an old kettle from the large sink by the window. She filled it with water, and placed it on top of the stove. She dropped some tea leaves into the bottom of a mug, and sat. Kallie glanced over.

'Were you two talking about going to Plateau City before?'

'Yeah,' Flora said. 'We'll need to move down there if we want to eat.'

'Not this again,' said Keira.

'I'd quite like to see it,' Kallie said. 'It's meant to be the most beautiful city in the world.'

'Maybe it used to be,' Keira said, 'but it's not any more.'

Flora smirked. 'I wonder why that is.'

'I'd still like to go.'

'Fine,' Keira said. 'You two go. I'm sure ye'll have a lovely time together.'

The kettle whistled, and Flora poured boiling water into her mug.

'We need to stick together, the three of us,' she said, 'and that means Keira should come to the city, and Kallie should help us look for Killop.'

She smiled as the two Kell women scowled at her. She turned to Kallie. 'Come on. This whole thing with Killop was years ago, wasn't it? You turn up in the Holdings, and he'll see that you're doing fine without him. Maybe it'll help you get past it.'

'I am past it,' Kallie said. 'I hadn't thought about him in ages before you lot turned up. No, he and his new woman will just think I'm there because I still love him or something, which is bullshit, cause I don't. It'll be too awkward.'

'But what's the alternative?' Flora said. 'We just leave you somewhere on your own? We can't do that, not after we've come so far. We should agree, right here and now, that we each have one vote when we decide stuff, and if any of us are out-voted two to one, we just have to accept it.'

Keira raised an eyebrow, as she finished making up the stick of dullweed.

'You've out-voted me on smoking that,' Flora said, pointing. 'I don't like it, in fact the thought of you two taking it makes me feel a bit sick, but you know, two against one. I just have to put up with it.'

'I guess I could agree to that,' Kallie said.

Flora grinned. 'So you'll help us look for Killop?'

'Fine,' she said, 'but only if we all agree to this voting thing, and Keira comes to Plateau City with us.'

They gazed at the fire mage as she lit the weedstick and took a long, slow drag. She smiled, as all the little aches and pains she had been carrying disappeared into a fug of hazy well-being. Flora was shaking her head at her, but she didn't care. She didn't care about anything.

'I'll come to the city if it makes ye happy, my wee Flora,' she said.

The Holdings woman narrowed her eyes. 'Is this a trick?'

Keira's brows furrowed. 'A stick?'

'A trick, you dozy bitch,' Flora said. 'Are you trying to trick me?'

The mage thought for a minute. Why was Flora accusing her? Paranoia seeped up into her mind. She shook it away, then realised she had forgotten what they had been talking about.

'Are ye going to pass that or what?' said Kallie.

'Eh?'

'The weedstick.'

Flora sighed. 'You still want it after you see what it's doing to her?

Kallie plucked it out of Keira's fingers, and took a sniff.

'It reeks,' she said.

Keira settled into her chair, vaguely aware that Flora and Kallie were speaking, but not paying them any attention. Her eyesight focussed on a large knot in the wooden beam over their heads, and she stared at it, the pattern swirling before her. So much complexity in such a tiny piece of wood, and she felt a moment of oneness, with the wood, the world, the universe.

She smiled, her eyelids growing heavier with each passing moment.

When she awoke, the kitchen was cold and dark. Kallie sat sleeping in the chair opposite her, her chest rising and falling under the blanket. Next to her, Flora's seat was empty. Keira rubbed her head, her tongue as dry as a badger's arse. She picked up the water jug, and swallowed a large mouthful.

She staggered to her feet, nearly knocking over the chair, then stumbled through the darkness to the small room at the back of the kitchen, which had the cottage's only bed. She pulled off her coat and leathers, climbed over Flora, and got in. She pulled the blankets round her, stealing the warmth that Flora's body had generated, and was asleep within seconds.

'You two have completely stitched me up,' Keira said, as they stood in the grey light of morning, the rain starting to soak through their clothes.

'You agreed,' Flora said, swinging her pack over her shoulders. 'The two-to-one rule.'

'Aye,' Keira said, clutching the weed-sack. 'So ye say. I cannae mind agreeing to anything, but.'

Flora shrugged. 'It's not my fault you were out of your face.'

'Come on,' Kallie said, her face lined and weary.

'How you feeling after yesterday?' Flora said.

'Like shit,' she replied. 'How long will it take to get there?'

'About four hours,' Flora said, leading off, the two Kell women trudging along the track behind her, the cottage fading into the distance. 'We should catch sight of the city in three hours or so,' the Holdings woman went on, 'but we'll need to walk round to the other side, to the gate next to the old Kellach quarter. It's the only one that'll let us in.'

'Shit,' Keira said. 'You mean, we'll have to walk right past...?'

Flora nodded.

'Walk past what?' Kallie said.

Keira spat onto the muddy track.

'Where the Emperor killed me.'

'And me,' said Flora.

Keira glanced at the young Holdings woman.

'Aye, Flora,' she said, 'and you.'

CHAPTER 26
LOYALTY

S hield Mountains, Imperial Holdings – 22ⁿᵈ Day, First Third Winter 507

Killop gazed past the waterfall, his eyes tracking down the rapids to where the wagon had landed. Shattered beams of wood and the spokes from a broken cartwheel were poking up from the white water. He clambered down the slope, keeping to the rocks by the river's edge, his clothes wet from the spray. A small group of troopers were by the smashed wagon, pulling whatever they could salvage from the water. Large sacks of flour had split open, their contents spilling into the river, while others lay submerged, ruined.

The troopers saluted him as he approached. He leaned over and began to help, lifting a crate from the rushing waters, and carrying it to a dry patch of earth where a sergeant was checking over the pile of salvaged goods.

'Put it down there, sir,' she nodded to him, as she inspected the crate he was holding.

'What happened?' he said, placing it by some others.

'Just an accident, sir,' the sergeant said, looking away. 'A wheel slipped, and the wagon went off the track.'

'One slip, and half our flour supply's gone.'

The sergeant nodded, her eyes examining the crates and sacks.

'Is there something you're not telling me?' Killop said.

She pursed her lips, pretending not to have heard.

'Sergeant?'

'I'd rather not say, sir.'

'Major Chane was over-seeing the supply train,' he said, 'wasn't she?'

'Yes, sir.'

'Anything you'd like to add?'

'No, sir.'

Killop frowned. 'Major Chane's lucky to have you as her sergeant.'

'Thank you, sir.'

'An accident, then,' he said. 'Get everything you can save back up onto the track by noon. There's a wagon up there waiting for you.'

'Yes, sir,' the sergeant said, and Killop turned and walked away. He leapt up the steep path, bounding from rock to rock until he reached the track at the top. An empty wagon was parked there, with a handful of troopers sitting next to it.

'Where's Major Chane?' he asked them.

'She left while you were down there, sir,' said one. 'She's gone back to the camp.'

He frowned, and the troopers glanced at each other.

'Wait here for the others,' he said. 'They should be finished by noon.'

He turned without waiting for a response, and strode down the track, anger fuelling his steps, as hunger filled his thoughts. He felt sickened by the waste he had just seen. That wagon had been transporting the first supplies they had seen in days, and now half of it was lost. He glanced at the desolate mountains; their bare, jagged flanks a dull grey in the morning light. Little grew up there besides lichen and wiry thorn bushes. The great plains of the Holdings were closer than they had been since they had left Royston at the Red Hills, the lack of food pushing them back towards the lowlands. Though he couldn't see them, he knew that the plains lay just over the high ridge to his left, less than a day's walk away.

He veered off the track, keeping to a line of cliffs to his right, and descended a narrow path to a shallow dell, where they had camped. The survivors of the rebellion, less than forty folk altogether, sat around a fire, their heads bowed in hunger and defeat. Next to Daphne crouched Celine and Kylon, while Karalyn sat between them. Baoryn, he noticed, was skulking at the edge of the group, his eyes on the horizon.

Daphne glanced up at him. She stood and walked over, a long winter coat over her shoulders.

'How bad is it?' she asked in a low voice.

'Lost about half.'

'Damn. Still, half's better than nothing.'

'It's only enough to last us a few days.'

Her face fell.

He frowned. 'And we need to speak to Chane.'

'I know,' she said. 'Was this one her fault too?'

'Sergeant wouldn't say.'

'Let's deal with it now.'

'Where is she?'

Daphne gestured, and they walked along a small track by a stream until they were out of sight of the camp. Sitting under the branches of a pine tree was Chane, her head low.

Killop and Daphne approached.

'We need to talk,' he said.

Chane narrowed her eyes. 'What is it this time?'

'Don't take that tone with us,' Killop said, but Daphne put her hand on his arm.

'Is something wrong?' she said.

Chane looked up, her eyes bloodshot. 'The world's completely screwed, and you ask if something's wrong?'

'You're drunk,' said Killop.

She laughed. 'Is a Kellach about to lecture me on drinking too much?'

'You're on duty,' he said. 'We've just lost half of our food supply...'

'The wagon slipped, right,' she said. 'Don't know what the fuck you think I'm supposed to do about that.'

'You've been drinking heavily for days,' Daphne said.

'As I said, the world's screwed.'

Daphne shook her head. 'There's something else going on. You were fine until about four days ago, but since then you've been walking about in a drunken rage, and you're making mistakes.'

'We can't all be perfect like you.'

Killop watched as Daphne bit her tongue.

'We want to help you,' he said.

'I don't want help.'

'Then I'm removing you from your command.'

Chane laughed. 'Why not, eh? It's not the first time it's happened to me. You should never have made me an officer in the first place. I'm a mess.'

'I could read your mind if I wanted to,' Daphne said, 'and find out the truth that way.'

Chane's expression darkened. 'Don't you fucking dare, Holdfast.'

'I'm not going to,' she said. 'You're my friend, even though you seem to have forgotten it.'

'I'm not your friend,' Chane said, her eyes empty. 'I've been lying to you. Friends don't lie to each other.'

'Then tell the truth now.'

'You got a cigarette?'

Daphne produced her silver case, and offered her one. She took another for herself, and lit them both.

Chane took a draw. 'You know how I said that there's no weed left? I haven't exactly been honest with you.'

'So you've been keeping a stash of weed, so what?' Daphne said. 'It's not a big deal, Chane.'

'It was dullweed.'

Daphne paused, her brows crinkling.

'There were wounded troopers, and you had dullweed?' she said, after a while. 'I don't understand; I've never seen you smoke it.'

'I don't smoke it,' she said. 'I have it in a tincture. Just a couple of drops each morning into my water bottle, would do me the whole day.'

'Every morning?'

'Yeah.'

'How long?'

'Since the River Holdings, though it got worse after the battle at Red Hills.'

Daphne's eyes lit in fury. 'Damn it, Chane. You've been addicted to dullweed since before you came to Hold Fast and you never bothered to tell me? And you held out on it when we had troopers with broken limbs and crossbow wounds?'

'Sorry.'

'And I assume that four days ago, you ran out?'

She shook her head. 'I had enough for thirds. I lost it.'

'You lost it?'

'Yeah. When we arrived at this camp, I looked for it in my pack, but it wasn't there. I must have left it behind somewhere. I ran all the way back to the old camp, and searched everywhere, but couldn't find it.'

'Is that where you were?' Killop said. 'You lied about that as well.'

Daphne gave him a quick look.

'Look, I don't know how long it'll take you to come off dullweed,' she said, 'but we'll give you that time. As Killop said, you're off command, but only temporarily. You can go back to work once you're well again.'

'Just stay out of folks' way until then,' Killop said.

'Is that it?' Chane said. 'I thought you'd be more angry.'

Daphne stood. 'We'll give you a shout when the food arrives.'

Killop got to his feet, and they headed back up the path, leaving Chane under the branches of the tree.

'I thought you'd be more angry too,' he said.

'I'm absolutely furious,' she said, her face as calm as it always was, 'but I didn't want to show it. We need her working again as soon as possible. She's the best officer we have, as well as my friend.'

'She withheld medicine from the wounded.'

'That's what boils my blood,' she said. 'She had enough for thirds, and she couldn't spare a few drops? The dullweed has rotted her mind.' She shook her head. 'I know I've had my own problems in the past. In Rahain, when I was an assassin, I took dullweed to numb myself. I remember how bad it was coming off it, once I found out I was pregnant. So, even though I'm cross with Chane, I know I need to help her. She'll be back to normal soon, I hope.'

They reached the camp.

'Listen, everyone,' Daphne said. 'Captain Chane is unwell, and is being taken off duty for a while until she recovers. I would appreciate it if you would all give her some space. The good news is that food is on its way, enough for the next few days. When we eat tonight, we shall discuss our next steps.'

She nodded and stepped back, as the troopers round the fire went back to talking. Daphne and Killop sat on the cold ground next to Karalyn, with Celine and Kylon close by.

'Unwell?' said Celine. 'That's one word for it.'

'Don't, Celine, please,' Daphne said. 'Chane's earned our respect.'

'So we're not going to talk about it?' said Kylon.

'It's the Holdings way,' Celine said, 'at least, among the upper classes. There's never a problem large enough that it can't be politely ignored.'

'And that's what we're going to do,' said Daphne. 'Politely ignore it. Starting now.'

Celine shrugged. 'So. Food. Mmm.'

'For a few days?' Kylon said. 'I thought there was going to be more.'

'At least we'll eat tonight,' Killop said, 'and there was tobacco too. The Holdings troopers were quick to save that crate from the river.'

Daphne smiled. 'We trained them well.'

The wagon arrived in the middle of the afternoon, and the crates and sacks were unloaded. The fire was stacked up, and dinner was prepared as the troopers stood in line to receive their allowance of cigarettes and rum. Daphne left to go on a walk up the ridge facing the great plains, and Killop played with Karalyn for an hour, as the sun set over the mountains to the west. It grew colder, despite the roaring fire, and the troopers wrapped their winter cloaks around themselves. Daphne reappeared as food was being served: plates of warm flat-bread and cooked meat in gravy.

Silence descended upon the camp as they ate. Killop heard low groans of relief from folk who hadn't eaten in days. He noticed Chane near the back of the group. She took a filled plate, and stole away to be on her own.

When they had nearly finished, Daphne banged her mug against a rock.

'Everyone,' she said, 'now that hunger's not the only thought in our heads, we need to discuss what to do next. First though, I have some news.'

Every pair of eyes gazed at her.

'The Emperor has left the Holdings,' she said. 'He's taken the four mages and Queen Mirren, and they've crossed the border back into the Plateau. I saw him with my own eyes. He's gone.'

She lit a cigarette, while they waited for her to go on.

'I think the time has come,' she said, 'to go back down to the plains. If we don't, we may well starve up here in the mountains over winter. There's no guarantee of when we'll be able to bring in any more supplies and, as we know, there's very little to hunt up here this time of year. Down on the plains, we'll be able to see the damage the Emperor has caused, but the Holdings is vast. It's impossible for him to have destroyed it all. There will be survivors, and food, though I imagine conditions will be grim everywhere this winter.

'If you take my advice, and advice is all it will be, since none of you owe me any fealty after our defeat, then we should travel east, to Hold Fast. I know of scattered settlements on the edge of the desert, far from the main roads, where my own people will shelter us. It's a tough life out there, but one where we should be safe. The Emperor thinks I'm dead, and if we keep our heads down, there's no reason he'll ever go that way.'

The thirty troopers sat round the fire in silence.

'Should we vote?' asked Killop.

'Not yet,' Daphne said. 'I'd like to hear from anyone who disagrees first.'

A trooper raised his arm.

'Speak,' said Daphne.

'Are we really giving up, ma'am?'

'We lost,' she said. 'The Emperor got what he came for, and now we need to begin the long, slow job of rebuilding our country.'

'But the Emperor's still in charge.'

'I know,' Daphne said, 'but there's not an armed force anywhere in the world left to oppose him. All five peoples have lost countless numbers in the wars. Right now, our aim is survival.'

'He could come back.'

'Yes,' she said, 'he might, and we'll fight him again if he does.'

An older trooper raised her arm. 'Ma'am?'

'Yes, sergeant?'

'I just wanted to pick you up on something you said. You mentioned earlier that our fealty to you was at an end. Excuse me ma'am, but that's bullshit. You're Holder Fast, and the oath I swore was to you and your family. That oath doesn't break because we got beaten, ma'am. If anything, it makes it stronger.'

The other troopers nodded and murmured their agreement.

Daphne sat in silence, her face calm, but Killop knew her heart was racing.

'Thank you,' she said. 'It means more to me than I can say.'

Killop glanced around. 'Anyone else wish to speak?'

No one replied. 'Alright, time to vote. Those in favour of Lady Hold-fast's plan, say aye.'

'Aye,' roared the thirty voices.

Sacrifice

'Carried,' Killop yelled over the noise. 'We leave tomorrow, and head down to the plains.'

The troopers cheered, and settled back to their meals and rum.

'I think I need some fresh air,' Daphne said, standing.

'I'll keep Karalyn here,' Celine said, as Killop got to his feet as well.

'Thanks,' Daphne said. She waited for Killop, and they began walking up the trail to the ridge. When they were out of sight of the camp, Daphne stopped. She put her right arm round Killop, and started to cry. He held her close, saying nothing as her tears fell.

He gazed out over the rough, jagged mountains as the last light of day faded in the western sky, and thought about Daphne's plan. Somewhere safe with his family, that's all he wanted, and if it had to be on the edge of a desert, then so be it.

He heard a cough, and turned.

'Sorry for interrupting,' said Kylon, standing in the darkness of the trail. 'May we speak?'

Daphne wiped the tears from her face, and faced the Kell man.

'What is it?'

'I didn't want to say anything in front of your troopers,' he said, 'but I disagree.'

'I thought you might.'

'Then you know what I'm going to say.'

'I think I can guess,' Daphne said. 'You want to stay in the mountains. You think it's too dangerous down on the plains. Too much of a risk for Karalyn.'

Kylon said nothing.

'Am I close?' she said.

'The plains are too risky,' he said. 'If anyone recognises you, then the Emperor will be back as fast as a flying gaien can carry him. And return to Hold Fast? I saw what he did to it the last time he visited.'

She shook her head. 'You only saw a tiny fraction of the estate. Hold Fast is huge, one of the largest in the country. There are areas up by the desert where we'll be able to disappear.'

'Maybe, but you'll have to get there first. It's a long walk.'

'But down there is where the food is,' she said. 'We have nearly forty mouths to feed.'

'Then maybe we should cut those numbers down. Send the troopers on their way, we don't need them.'

'I'll not abandon those who've proved their loyalty to me. And with the devastation the Emperor brought to the land, there might be groups of bandits roaming the Holds. We'll need the troopers then.'

'As I said, the plains are too risky.'

Daphne frowned. 'But you'll be there to protect her, won't you?'

He glared at her. 'I will always protect her.'

'When we head down to the plains tomorrow, you'll be by her side, protecting her with your big, brooding presence. And if anything happens to me and Killop, I know you'll be there to look after her.'

'Of course,' he said.

'Then this conversation is over. Thank you for raising your concerns.'

Kylon chewed his lip, his eyes smouldering. He nodded, then strode off down the path in the darkness.

'We should get back,' Killop said. 'Get some sleep before tomorrow.'

Daphne nodded. She took his hand, and they walked down the slope to the camp. Most of the troopers were still up, though they had put down their rum, and were cleaning their equipment, wiping the old blood and rust from their swords.

Killop and Daphne sat by Celine, who was cradling Karalyn next to the fire.

'She been sleeping long?' Daphne said.

'Ten minutes or so,' Celine said.

'We should get her to bed.'

They got up and headed for their tent. Killop crouched as he went in, and followed Daphne to a curtained-off section at the back, where Celine put Karalyn into her makeshift cot. They kissed her goodnight.

Kylon appeared.

'You all going to bed?'

'Aye,' Killop said.

Kylon nodded. 'I might have a drink first. I managed to get my hands on one of the few bottles that Chane hasn't drunk yet.'

'I might stay up for one,' Killop said.

'Alright,' said Kylon. 'I have one of Chane's maps, we can look over the route to Hold Fast.'

'Let's all have one before bed, then,' Daphne said.

They ducked back through to where Kylon's sleeping pallet lay by the tent's entrance, and sat. Daphne lit a cigarette as Kylon laid the map on the floor. They gazed down at it. Daphne pointed. 'We're here, and Hold Fast is over here.'

Kylon filled four mugs with rum, and passed them round.

'Where on the map is Hold Clement?' he asked. 'Chane's Hold?'

'Oh,' Daphne said, her finger moving south. 'That's way down here, we won't be going anywhere close. I intend to take us this route, and stay up north, in case we have to get back into the mountains in a hurry.'

'And the desert?' Killop said.

'Hold Fast goes all the way out to here,' Daphne said, her fingers gliding across the paper to the far east, right up to where the great ocean lay. 'This whole coastal strip is desert. Sand dunes and barren, dry wastes. The estate takes in hundreds of miles of it.'

'Why?' said Killop, sipping his rum. 'What's the point of owning desert?'

'The hunting,' she said. 'All sorts of fabulous wild beasts roam the wastes. My father used to love going out there in spring with the Hold Fast Company. When he returned, there was always another head to be mounted in his study. The bit I like best though, is the strip between the grasslands and the desert, where it's not quite either, and where people can live, if they're careful. That's where we're headed.'

'Show me where you're from, Celine,' Kylon said.

'Me?' she laughed. 'I'm from over here.' She pointed to the region south of the capital, by the great river. 'Hold Castor, very minor aristocracy, as I'm sure Daphne would agree.'

'You're an aristocrat too?'

'I'd have to be,' she said, 'to be allowed to marry the heir to Hold Fast. Daphne's mother had me interviewed several times. I had to write an essay stating my reasons why I felt I deserved to wed her son.'

'Vince was her golden boy,' Daphne said. 'She was never going to approve of his wife, no matter who he married.'

'I can't believe we're all that's left of the Holdfasts,' Celine said. 'I miss Ariel so much.'

'Me too,' said Daphne, 'and Father, though I'm glad he's not around to see what the Holdings has become.'

'Hopefully the worst is behind us,' said Kylon. 'The Emperor's gone, and tomorrow marks a new start.'

Daphne nodded.

'I'm knackered,' said Celine. 'I'm going to crash out.'

She crossed to her own sleeping pallet, and got under the blankets.

Killop finished his rum.

'Another?' said Kylon.

'No,' he said. 'I'm pretty tired myself.'

'See you in the morning, then,' he said. 'I might stay up for one more on my own.'

Daphne and Killop got to their feet, and went back to the curtained-off area. Daphne collapsed onto the bed. Killop sat, and pulled off his boots. Across from him, Karalyn lay sleeping, a warm blanket covering her.

He smiled. Even though the world was falling apart around them, he still had Karalyn and Daphne. The only two people in the world he cared about. He still loved his sister, and always would, but it had been so long, and he had no idea what she was doing. Kylon remained his friend, but he was more distant than he had been back in Kell during the Rahain invasion, and sometimes Killop wondered if he really knew him at all.

Who else was there? His mind floated over the faces of those he knew. Bridget, Larissa, Kallie. He fell back onto the bed. He shook himself and rubbed his eyes.

'Daphne?' he said, but she was lying fast asleep on top of the blankets.

His head fell back against his pillow. He knew he should get undressed, get under the blanket, and get Daphne under it too, but he couldn't move, he was so tired. A strange feeling that something was wrong crept over him, but he was so comfortable that his eyes closed, and within seconds he was asleep.

———

'Killop!' cried a voice. 'Wake up!'

A palm struck his cheek, and his head stung. He groaned. A mug of water landed on his face, and he spluttered and sat up. Daphne was on the bed in front of him, her eyes raw with tears.

'She's gone.'

Killop focussed, the words taking time to make sense. He stared at the empty cot. 'Celine? Kylon?'

'She's there,' Daphne said. 'He's not.'

Killop jumped out of bed, still wearing his clothes from the previous day. He charged through past the curtain. Celine was sitting on her bed, rubbing her head. Kylon, and his pack, were missing. Killop ran out of the tent, his feet bare against the rough ground. The sun was rising above the hills to the east, and the camp was busy with troopers preparing their breakfasts. There was no sign of Kylon, or Baoryn.

'Sergeant,' he said, trying to keep his voice calm.

'Yes, sir?' said the sergeant, getting up from the fire, and brushing crumbs from her uniform.

'Get some troopers and search the camp. Find Kylon, and bring him here. And the Rahain, Baoryn, if you see him. Do it as quickly as you can.'

'Yes, sir,' she nodded, and pointed at a few troopers. 'On your feet.'

Killop turned, and went back into the tent. Celine was still sitting on her bed.

Killop knelt by her. 'Did you see or hear anything?'

She shook her head. 'I didn't wake up. I feel like I'm still sleeping now.'

'Kylon drugged us,' said Daphne, walking past the curtain while she buckled on her armour.

'What?' said Killop.

'Chane didn't lose her dullweed,' she said, her face dark with fury. 'He stole it. Get your boots on, we're going after him.'

He ran to the back of the tent, and pulled his boots from under the camp bed. As he pushed his feet into them, his eyes caught sight of the empty cot, and a mixture of anguish and rage built up inside him. If Kylon had taken his daughter, he would rip his head from his shoulders. He grabbed his sword and leather cuirass, and went back through to the other side of the tent.

Daphne glanced at him, her right hand forming a fist.

'Let's go.'

They walked out of the tent, leaving Celine sitting in a daze. The sergeant saw them, and hurried over.

'No sign of them, sir,' she said. 'Kylon and Baoryn are not in the camp.'

Daphne frowned. 'They could be miles from here by now,' she said. 'They could have left hours ago.'

'Have you questioned the night sentries?' asked Killop.

'I'll do it now, sir,' said the sergeant, and ran off.

Killop heard Daphne's breath quicken. Her eyes were screwed shut, and her right fist was trembling. He pulled the silver case out of her belt and lit her a cigarette.

'We need to think,' he said. 'Where would he go?'

'We need to get somewhere high,' she said, her eyes snapping open. 'Somewhere I can range for miles. We'll find him.'

She sprinted for a mountain track, and he ran after her. They climbed up the steep trail, leaping over rocks, and leaving the camp far behind. They came to a rocky ridge, where a cold wind cut through their clothes. Daphne sat, and gazed around, smoking.

'Alright,' she said, as he knelt beside her. 'I'm going to look for Karalyn. If she's out there, I'll find her.'

They kissed, and her eyes glazed over.

Killop watched her for a moment, then got to his feet. He stared down into the mountain wilderness. Lifeless grey peaks were crisscrossed with deep gorges, where they had been hiding for so long. By now, Kylon knew the ways across the Shield Mountains as well as any. He could hide and never be found. Killop smiled, faint hope keeping his heart from despair. Karalyn would tell them where she was.

He turned as Daphne let out a cry.

'I can't find her, Killop,' she wept, as he crouched by her. She reached up and pulled him close. 'I can't find her anywhere.'

Killop's heart sank.

'I've always been able to find her before,' Daphne cried. 'I searched for miles, nothing. She's not anywhere.'

'But Kylon wouldn't hurt her,' Killop said. 'She's not dead, she can't be.'

'How else could I not see her?' she said, her eyes breaking his heart.

Killop's mind raced. 'Maybe he's drugging her too?'

Daphne breathed, and her tears slowed. She frowned.

'Maybe he's putting it in her water,' he said. 'Daphne, she's still alive.'

She wiped her face.

'Kylon knows she would try to contact us,' she said. 'That bastard's keeping her drugged.'

'We're going to find Karalyn,' he said, their eyes locking in shared fury, 'and Kylon.'

'When we do, we're going to kill him.'

He nodded. 'Together.'

CHAPTER 27
SANCTUARY

Snow blanketed the mountainside in a thick layer of white, and sheets of ice flowed down the river that wound through the small town of Silverstream. Smoke came from a hundred chimneys as the inhabitants kept themselves warm through the winter's day. Agang, Laodoc and Bridget sat out on their veranda, drinking heated rice spirits, their breakfast bowls lying empty on the decking by their wicker chairs. The two men were wrapped up in coats and scarves, while the Brig woman sat bare-armed in her leathers, her feet up on the wooden railing. After several days of snow, the sky above was blue, and the sun was shining.

The mountains in front of them shone bright as the sun rose into the sky behind them.

'A fine morning,' Laodoc said. 'The town looks beautiful, now that the blizzard has stopped.'

'It looks good,' said Agang, 'but it'll be cold and wet to travel through. Still, we should be thinking of making our move, snow or not.'

'Is there any point?' Bridget said. 'Shella's not coming. And there are worse places to spend the winter than Silverstream.'

'We've already stayed too long,' Agang said. 'I'm impatient to be off.'

'Off where, though?'

'You know where. To the Holdings, to find Daphne's child.'

Bridget sighed.

'Back through Rahain,' she said, 'then all the way up the Plateau? It'll take us half the year to get there.'

'We could try the tunnel through the Grey Mountains.'

She shook her head. 'Ye saw how heavily guarded it is now. There's no way we're getting through there without imperial papers. We'll have to go the long way round, halfway back to Kellach Brigdomin.'

Laodoc glanced at her. 'Do you want to go home, Bridget?'

'I don't know,' she said. 'I mean, the whole point of us being here is so that we can get Shella and Keira together, only neither of the stubborn cows wants to budge. So now Agang's got this new plan to go to the Holdings to search for Karalyn Holdfast, but... to be honest, it seems like we're clutching at straws.'

'We can't give up, Bridget,' said Agang. 'We must stop the Emperor, or he will destroy the world.'

'Aye,' she said, 'that's what we keep telling ourselves. But is it true? Let's face it, all of our evidence comes from a dead guy who said he could see the future, who only one of us here has met.'

'I saw what the Emperor did to the Sanang army,' Agang said. 'Do you doubt the evidence of my own eyes?'

'No,' Bridget said. 'From what you and Shella have said, I believe he has new powers, and he exercised them to defend his city.'

'But, Bridget,' Laodoc said, 'Shella also believes that Kalayne could see the future. If you believe her about the Emperor, then why would you doubt her about Kalayne?'

Bridget scowled. 'Oh shut up, lizardman.'

Laodoc smiled.

'Alright,' she said, 'say it's all true, then what? We find Daphne, and just ask her if we can borrow her daughter? I'm sure she and Killop will be delighted about that.'

The smile on his face faded.

'See?' she smirked. 'Ye've not thought this through. Ye just can't accept that we've failed, and are grasping at the first idea ye come across. Laodoc, you and me used to live with Karalyn. Be honest, did ye sense anything in Slateford that made ye think she was going to save the world?'

He shook his head.

'But it was you that told us she had powers,' Agang said.

'She does. But she's a bairn, Agang. She can't help us.'

'I won't accept that,' the Sanang man said, leaning back and folding his arms.

Bridget shrugged, and sipped her warm drink.

'You don't need to make any decision now,' Laodoc said to her. 'If we do travel to the Holdings, then when we reach the Plateau, you can decide where you want to go next. It goes without saying of course, but I would very much like you to journey with us. I think Killop would be glad to see you.'

'More than he would you, that's for sure.'

Laodoc bowed his head. 'I greatly regret what I did. I should never have opened my mouth to Daphne about Douanna, but my longing for revenge blinded me to everything else. I am to blame for them leaving us, and I know you still harbour some resentment towards me because of it. I'm sorry, Bridget.'

She frowned, and looked away.

'It's done now,' said Agang, 'and they're probably in the Holdings. The people we need to bind together are scattered to the far corners of the world, while the Emperor sits in the middle, laughing at us.'

'You're taking it very personally,' said Bridget.

'How could I not? He killed me.'

'And ye want to give him the chance to do it again?'

'No, next time I want to be prepared.'

'By using a bairn as a shield?'

'She might be the only person in the world who can hide from the Emperor.'

'So, what, we send her in with a knife?'

The Sanang man's temper rose, his face reddening.

'Come now, Agang,' said Laodoc. 'She has a point.'

'What?' he said. 'Are you losing heart as well?'

'Not at all, my friend, but we do need to think through our plan very carefully.'

'You need to work out how to persuade Daphne, you mean,' said Bridget. 'I'd give up now if I were you. After all, your charms haven't worked on Keira or Shella. The only dumbass to fall for your bullshit is me.'

'I'm sorry you feel that way, Bridget,' said Laodoc.

'Aye,' she said, sipping her drink, 'me too.'

Agang nodded at Laodoc, and he turned to follow his gaze. Two Rakanese in long winter coats were striding along a wooden walkway towards them.

'The scouts I asked for,' he said.

Laodoc smiled as they approached.

They nodded, and said a greeting in their own language.

'I'll translate,' Bridget said.

Laodoc watched as she spoke to the two scouts, her Rakanese lessons having continued apace. He breathed in the cool mountain air, listening to the sounds of the river beneath them.

The scouts nodded again, and left.

'Well?' said Agang.

'Bad news, I'm afraid,' she said. 'They say that every route out of Silverstream is blocked with snow. I guess we're stuck here a little longer.'

Agang stood, and glared at the white mountains. He turned, and began to walk away.

'Wait,' said Laodoc. 'Where are you going?'

'To speak to Shella.'

'Why?'

Agang stopped, and faced him. 'Because they're lying to us.'

'What?' said Bridget. 'Why the fuck would they do that?'

'They don't want us to leave.'

Bridget snorted. 'You're being paranoid.'

'No,' he said, 'I'm not. Are you coming?'

'Yes,' said Laodoc. 'Please wait a moment while I get to my feet.'

Bridget stood, and helped him up. He took his walking stick, and they joined Agang.

'This should be amusing,' said Bridget, as they left the veranda, and headed along a slatted walkway. A foot below, the waters of the river glistened with ice floes as they passed, and their breath misted in the crisp air. They nodded to a few Rakanese on the way. Bridget got more greetings than the other two, and she replied in their own tongue. They reached Shella's house, a large wooden apartment standing alone, with lines of high trees on either side.

Agang knocked on the door.

Bridget took Laodoc's hand, and he leant on her as they went up the steps.

Agang knocked again, and the door opened.

'Master Thymo,' said Laodoc, 'how are you this morning?'

The boy stared up at them.

Agang frowned.

'Is Shella at home?' he said. 'Come on, boy, you know who we are.'

Thymo said nothing.

Bridget crouched down by him. 'Is your auntie home? Can we see her, please?'

'Who's there?' said a voice from within.

Shella appeared at the door, wearing a dressing gown, her hair a tangled mess. 'Oh, it's you.'

'Mage Shella, we need to talk at once,' Agang said.

'Really? Must we?'

'We would be most obliged, madam,' Laodoc said.

Shella frowned. 'Well, drag your asses inside, out of the cold.'

She stood to the side to let them pass, then closed the door.

'Thymo,' she said, 'go to your room. I don't want you to hear all the bad language.'

'Yes, auntie,' the boy said, and ran off.

'I hope there won't be any need for bad language,' Laodoc said.

'Depends what you're here to say,' Shella said. 'Want a drink?'

'Aye,' said Bridget.

Shella led them through to a comfortable living room, with long, low couches covered in throws and cushions, and a fire burning in the corner. She gestured for them to sit, brought over a tray from the sideboard, and put it down on the table in front of them.

'Help yourself,' she said.

Bridget picked up the jug from the table and poured out four cups of clear spirit. Shella sat opposite them.

'Sorry if we got you out of bed,' said Laodoc.

'What do you want?'

'You know what we want,' said Agang. 'The question is, why are you trying to stop us?'

'What?' Shella said. 'Is this a Sanang riddle?'

Bridget laughed. 'The boys have this paranoid theory that Silverstream is conspiring to keep us all here.'

Shella puffed out her cheeks, and half-smiled.

'It's not true, is it?' Bridget said.

'I'm not supposed to say anything,' she said.

'I knew it,' said Agang, slapping his thigh.

'But why?' said Bridget. 'I thought you wanted us to go? When we first got here, you were constantly nagging us about it, asking us why were we still here, or when we were leaving, and now you want us to stay?'

'I don't want you to stay.'

'Has the town council made a decision?' said Laodoc.

'They might have.'

Bridget put down her cup, glaring at the Rakanese woman.

'See?' Agang said. 'What did I tell you?'

Laodoc glanced at Bridget.

'I thought you liked it here,' he said to her.

'That's not the fucking point,' Bridget said. 'This is bullshit. They can't stop us from leaving.'

'They might try,' said Shella. 'I honestly don't know how far the council would go.'

'I assume you disagreed with their decision?' Laodoc said.

'You assume right.'

'Then why didn't you stop them?' said Bridget.

Shella raised an eyebrow. 'What power do you think I have in this town? I'm not on the council, and as there's no election due for a couple of years, I'm unlikely to be on it any time soon. As the founder of the town, I guess they treat me as an honoured guest or something, but I'm not in charge. I can't force them to do anything.'

'I don't understand,' said Bridget. 'Why do they want us to stay?'

'Isn't it obvious?' said Agang. 'The entire town has been free of disease and injuries since we got here. I've treated half the population, from sick children, to pregnant women and old people with dislocated hips. Do you think they want to go back to the way it was before?'

Shella shook her head. 'You conceited bastard, Agang.'

He smiled. 'Am I wrong?'

'You're partly right.'

He folded his arms. 'You can tell your council that we intend to leave, with or without their permission. I am not their captive, and my skills are not theirs to abuse.'

'Tell them yourself,' Shella muttered.

Agang paused, frowning.

'Are you serious?' asked Laodoc.

'Yeah, I am. The council are in session today, why don't you march your asses up there and tell them what you think?' She shrugged. 'This has got nothing to do with me.'

'And would they let us speak?' Laodoc said.

'Probably,' she said. 'You might have to make an appointment.'

'How dare they,' Agang cried. 'They're trying to hold us hostage here, and they want us to make an appointment?' He stood. 'No. I shall go, and tell them that their treatment of us is unacceptable.'

'But, my friend,' Laodoc said, 'we need Shella to accompany us. To translate.'

'She can do it,' Shella smirked, pointing at Bridget.

'What?' said Bridget. 'I can't speak to the town council.'

'Why not? You did it before.'

'That was a speech it took me days to learn off by heart,' Bridget said.

'She's right,' said Laodoc. 'Bridget's Rakanese is certainly better than mine or Agang's, but arguing in front of the town council is perhaps asking too much.'

Shella glanced away. 'Not my problem.'

'I could make it your problem,' Agang said.

'Oh yeah, ape-man? And how do you think you'd do that?'

Agang smiled. 'I will withdraw my labour from the clinic, and when people ask why, I will tell them it is because you refuse to help us. Pretty soon, half the town will be knocking on your door.'

'You'd refuse to treat the sick?'

'I would.'

'You petty-minded, arrogant asshole,' Shella said. She took a sip of rice spirits.

'Okay,' she said, 'here's the deal. If I help you today, by speaking to the council on your behalf, and translating everything for you, then no matter what happens next, you keep me out of it. Whether you stay or go, I don't care. Just leave me alone.'

'Deal,' said Agang, his eyes dark.

'Hold on a minute,' said Bridget. 'This is a rubbish deal. How about you speak for us today, and then you help us get out of here if the council try to stop us. Then we'll leave you alone.'

'Too late,' she said, standing, 'Agang has agreed to my terms. Let's go.'

She strode to the door, grabbing a long, black overcoat on the way, and Agang followed. Laodoc and Bridget glanced at each other.

'How was he ever a king?'

Laodoc shrugged, and gripped his walking stick. She helped him up, and they walked out of the living room after the others. Shella didn't wait for them, and went out onto the street, Agang keeping up with her.

'This is a right mess,' Bridget said, as they trailed behind.

'Indeed, Bridget,' Laodoc said. 'Our Sanang friend can be a little impetuous at times.'

Bridget snorted.

'He doesn't like being powerless,' Laodoc went on. 'I suspect he feels the need to try to exert some sort of control over his life.'

'We're all powerless now,' she said. 'He was a king; you were the chancellor of Rahain. Even I was a clan chief, if just for a short while. We've all had to adjust.'

He glanced at her. 'What should we do, Bridget?'

'We carry on,' she said. 'What else?'

They reached the tall council building, and climbed the steps to the hall's entrance. Agang was sitting in the lobby, his right boot tapping on the wooden floor.

'She told me to wait,' he said as they approached.

'And you did,' said Laodoc, smiling.

'She said that she'd get us in there, to see the council.'

Laodoc sat on the bench, next to him.

'Let us hope that she is successful.'

'I don't trust her,' said Agang.

'I'll be listening,' said Bridget. 'I can understand more in Rakanese than I can say, if that makes sense. I'll know if she's telling us a load of crap.'

'Good,' nodded Agang. 'Thank you.'

'You seem less... angry,' Laodoc said.

'I'm sorry,' Agang said. 'Shella can be so frustrating at times. Sometimes I think she's doing it deliberately.'

'Of course she's doing it deliberately,' said Bridget. 'Look, I think she really does want us to go, and if so, then she'll be in there now, trying to argue our case. We have to accept that she doesn't want to leave. You have to accept it. And let's face it, why would she? She's got a comfortable, safe life here among her own folk. Why would she want to risk it all, and go back out there?'

'I agree,' said Agang. 'We should give up on her, for now at least. But eventually, the prophecy will have to be fulfilled.'

Laodoc said nothing. There must be some way to reach the flow mage, but he didn't know what.

Shella appeared through a doorway, and beckoned to them.

'Come on,' she said, 'you've got five minutes.'

They stood, and Shella ushered them into a dark hallway.

'Listen,' she said, 'I've already told them why you're here, and argued that you should be allowed to leave.' She glanced at them. 'They now want to know if you wish to speak to the council in person before they make their decision.'

'Of course we do,' Agang said.

Shella nodded. 'That's what I thought.' She gestured to a door. 'Through here.'

Agang opened the door and strode through. The others went after him and entered the council hall, a large oval chamber. In its centre was a semi-circular row of tables, around which two dozen Rakanese sat. Tiers of long benches rose on either side of the hall, and there were several officials and spectators present.

They all turned to stare as Agang, Laodoc and Bridget made their way to stand before the semi-circle. Shella followed, then stepped in front of them, and began speaking in Rakanese.

Laodoc glanced over the half-circle of tables. The council members were young, with none looking over forty. They were listening to Shella speak, though many were staring at the three foreigners.

Shella turned to them. 'Okay,' she said. 'Agang, you go first, and I'll translate.'

The Sanang man nodded.

'I would like to thank them for their hospitality,' he said, Shella relaying his words to the council as he went along, 'but tell them that it is time for us to leave.'

A woman at the head of the council spoke.

Shella turned. 'The council regret to inform you that you are forbidden to leave Silverstream.'

Agang gasped. 'I thought they hadn't made their decision?'

Shella shrugged.

'I thought you wanted us to go?' Agang glared at her.

'I do,' she said, 'but I'm only one person. That's democracy for you.'

Agang's temper flared.

'Inform them that I shall refuse to carry out any more healings.'

'Okay,' she said, then turned and spoke to the council.

The woman spoke again, this time for longer, and Shella waited until she had finished.

'Alright,' she said. 'The council say that it's your power, and no one can force you to use it to help the sick if you refuse. But it makes no difference, you are still forbidden to leave.'

'Why?' cried Agang.

'Hold on,' Shella smirked, 'I'm getting to that. The council say that they cannot endanger Silverstream, and you leaving would put the town at risk. Right now, they say, everyone who knows where Silverstream is located, is here. The outside world may be falling apart around us, but while no one knows we're here, we're safe.'

Agang glanced at Bridget. 'Is she telling the truth?'

'Aye,' said Bridget, 'though she made up the bit about the outside world.'

Shella frowned. 'I was merely elaborating.'

Bridget glanced at her. 'I want to know what they'll do if we ignore them and leave anyway.'

Shella nodded, then spoke to the council. Again, she waited while they replied. She turned back to the three strangers.

'They say that you're still free to move about the town, but all sentries have been instructed to stop you from leaving by any of the mountain paths. Also, you're forbidden from stockpiling food, weapons or any other supplies, and your house might be searched now and again. Apart from that, though, they'll leave you alone.'

Laodoc could see Agang about to explode.

'May I speak?' he said.

'Yeah, go for it, professor fork-tongue,' Shella said.

'Then please inform the council that we respect their decision, but need some time to consider its consequences.'

Agang glared at him.

'Whatever it is you want to say, my friend,' Laodoc said, 'losing your temper in front of the council will not help us. We need to discuss this alone.'

Agang's nostril's flared, but he nodded. Shella turned, and passed on Laodoc's words to the council members.

The council replied.

'What did they say?' asked Laodoc.

'This meeting's over,' said Bridget. 'Come on, let's get out of here.'

They filed out of the council chamber.

'I know you must be disappointed,' Shella said, once they had reached the lobby. 'I'm disappointed, too; but if you like, you can come back to my house, and we can have a drink and talk it over.'

Agang scowled. 'I thought you wanted nothing more to do with us?'

Shella chuckled as they left the building. 'No, I said that I wanted nothing to do with your crazy plans, but if you have to stay here, then we can't just ignore each other.'

'Thank you,' said Laodoc, 'a drink would be gratefully accepted.'

They walked back along the wooden walkways, following the long tree-lined avenues, until they arrived at Shella's house. She let herself in, and they entered after her, and returned to the warm living room. They sat, and Shella poured from the bottle that they had left lying on the table.

'I'll have to break it to the others,' Bridget said. 'They're not going to be happy. Especially Dyam, she's been wanting to leave for ages.'

'They won't be able to stop us once the snows have cleared,' said Agang. 'There must be other ways out of here apart from the passes they're guarding.'

'But without supplies?' said Laodoc.

'We'll work it out, somehow.'

Laodoc turned from the brooding Sanang man, and glanced at Shella.

'I'm sorry for your loss,' he said.

'What?'

'Your brother, Sami,' he said, 'and your friend. Jayki, was it?'

Her eyes narrowed.

'They were both in Silverstream, weren't they?' he went on. 'If no one outside knows about it, then I'm assuming they must have died.'

'Oh,' she said. 'Yeah.'

'What happened?'

She took a sip from her cup. 'Jayki was murdered by the One True Path.'

'He was a good man. And your brother?'

Shella blinked, her face reddening a little.

'He died too.'

Laodoc frowned. 'I'm sorry to hear it. How?'

She paused.

'I want to speak to you alone.'

'All right,' he said. He got to his feet. 'Lead on, madam.'

Shella went to a side door, and Laodoc walked after her, passing Bridget and Agang on the way. They went into a small study, with scrolls and maps lying on a desk.

'If it's too painful to talk about,' he said, 'I understand.'

Shella said nothing, biting her lip.

'Did you see him die?'

'Not exactly.'

'But you know he's dead?'

'Yeah. Probably.'

Laodoc's tongue flickered. 'Probably?'

'You have to keep this to yourself,' she said. 'The truth is, I don't know what happened to Sami after I fled the city. I'm sure he's dead; I mean, he has to be, right?'

Laodoc's heart pounded. 'When was the last time you saw him?'

'When we were arrested,' she said. 'He was dragged off somewhere.'

'And that's the last you heard of him?'

She shook her head. 'Just before the ritual that transformed the Emperor, he spoke to me, Guilliam I mean. He said that he was making Sami a prince.'

Laodoc stared.

'But that was when he was still Guilliam,' Shella said, 'before he became the Creator.'

Laodoc sat down in the room's only chair, his mind whirling.

She frowned at him. 'What are you thinking?'

'When you escaped,' he said, gazing up at her, 'were the other mages, the ones who'd taken part in the ritual with you, were they all dead?'

She nodded.

'Oh Shella,' he said, 'don't you think someone might have noticed that your body was missing?'

Her face darkened. 'Of course I've thought about it.'

'The Emperor might be looking for you.'

'I'm not stupid, I know that.'

'But if he's looking for you, then what would stop him from reading Sami's mind, and discovering the whereabouts of Silverstream?'

She began to pace the floor. 'Because,' she said, 'if the Emperor had made him a prince, and wanted to keep him under tight control, then he would have put him in the palace. And Keira destroyed the palace; she razed it to the ground if I remember correctly.'

She turned to him. 'He's dead.'

'Maybe he is,' Laodoc said, 'maybe he's not. The truth is, we have no idea. You've strung together a series of assumptions to salve your conscience, but in reality, you have placed Silverstream into a position of great peril.'

She said nothing, her face turning a shade of grey.

'I will have to inform the town council about this,' he said, 'for we are all in danger. I will have to tell them that your brother may well be alive, and if he is, then there is a high probability that the Emperor knows the location of Silverstream, and the fact that you might be hiding here.'

'You treacherous bastard,' Shella cried. 'You can't do that.'

'I don't see that I have any choice.'

She glared at him, and raised her hand. 'You're old, and weak. It wouldn't take much to push your heart too far.'

'Oh, my dear Shella,' Laodoc sighed, 'tell me it hasn't come to this. Threatening old men? But if you must, then I suppose you had better get on with it.'

She lowered her hand. 'What do you want?'

He smiled. 'You know what I want.'

'Either way,' she said, shaking her head, 'my life's over.'

'Then make your choice, Madam Flow Mage.'

'But if I go,' she said, 'Silverstream will still be in danger.'

'Not if we stop the Emperor.'

She turned to face the desk, her head bowed.

'Take Agang and Bridget,' she said, 'and go back to your house.'

'And?'

'I'll be there at midnight to collect you.'

Agang hadn't stopped grinning in hours. Every time he passed Laodoc, he slapped him on the back, much to the old man's discomfort. From the outside, their house was quiet, with every window shuttered against the wind and snow; but inside it was bustling, as the strangers packed up their belongings and gathered all the food they could find.

'It's not enough,' said Dyam, gazing at the meagre pile. 'Not nearly enough. We'll be travelling the rest of winter through Rahain, and probably won't reach the Plateau-Kellach border until New Year. What are we going to eat in all that time?'

'Lola has her bow,' Agang said. 'Don't worry, we'll manage.'

'Do we have a plan for getting past the sentries?' said Bridget. 'If we leave the way we came in, then they'll probably be posted by the woods where Laodoc broke his leg.'

'I'm afraid that Shella left out the details,' said Laodoc. 'We're in her hands now. We have to trust that she's thought it all through.'

'I still don't know how you did it,' Agang said, raising his hand.

'Please,' said Laodoc, flinching, 'my back can't take any more.'

Agang laughed. 'Sorry, my friend.'

There was a tap at the back door. Agang bounded forward and opened it an inch. Laodoc watched as he spoke through the doorway for a moment. He turned.

'It's time.'

Bridget and Lola pulled their packs over their shoulders, and Laodoc stood.

'Dean!' Dyam cried. 'Get yer lazy arse out here.'

The young mage emerged from his room, and joined them as they left the house. Shella was waiting outside, sitting up on a small cart, holding on to the reins.

'There's only room for one more on this,' she said, 'but you can load up your packs.'

Agang gestured to Laodoc, who stepped forward. Bridget gave him a hand as he climbed up next to Shella. The others put their packs on the back of the cart, alongside the supplies that Shella had brought.

'Stay close,' she said to them, 'and stay quiet.'

She pulled the reins, and the two gaien began to lumber down the wide walkway, lit by lanterns hanging above them. After a short distance, she veered the cart to the right, and took a dark and narrow path north towards the mountains. The gaien heaved, and pulled the cart through the foot-deep snow.

'Where are we going?' said Laodoc. 'This isn't the way.'

She smirked at him.

Agang ran to the front of the cart.

'Are you trying to trick us?' he said. 'We're going the wrong way.'

'Settle down,' she said. 'We're going to the pass through to the Plateau.'

Agang's mouth fell open.

'There's a pass?' Laodoc said.

'How do you think I got here?' she said. 'Do you imagine I walked all the way through Rahain?'

'It's the first we've heard of a pass.'

'The town council were hardly likely to tell you about it,' she said. 'I was lucky to find it myself. The truth is, I was lost in the mountains, and scouts from Silverstream found me and Thymo, and led us to the town.'

'And where is Thymo?' Laodoc said.

Shella's face fell. 'I left him a note.'

'Did I hear right?' said Bridget, approaching. 'Are we going directly to the Plateau?'

'Yes,' said Agang. 'If she's right, it should take thirds off our journey.'

The Brig woman frowned in the darkness, as a light fall of snow began.

Laodoc smiled at her. 'It means we won't be passing Kellach Brigdomin any more. You'll have to make your decision now, I'm afraid.'

Dyam, Dean and Lola joined the others at the front of the cart.

'What do you guys think?' Bridget asked them.

'Now that Shella's coming with us,' said Lola. 'I say we go.'

Dean nodded.

Dyam stared up into the dark mountains as the snowflakes fluttered down.

'Aye,' she said. 'Let's go.'

'Right then,' said Bridget, gazing at Shella. 'We'll go to the Plateau, and we'll find Daphne.'

'Great,' said Shella. 'Now, if you'd all get out of my fucking way before these dumb gaien are snowed in, I'd be much obliged.'

They moved to the side of the track, and Shella lashed the reins.

CHAPTER 28
FOOTSORE

S hield Mountains, Imperial Holdings – 27th Day, First Third Winter 507

Daphne's eyes scanned the horizon, her attention focussed on the sharp ravines that led down from the mountains ahead. She put a cigarette to her lips and inhaled. Her body was exhausted, and she had lost count of the number of times she had used her vision skills in the previous few days, but she ignored her pain and discomfort.

Five days they had been searching for Karalyn, a time in which Daphne had eaten almost nothing, and had traversed mile after mile of steep tracks through the Shield Mountains.

She pulled on her mage powers, and felt for her daughter, pushing her vision deep into the ravines below.

Nothing.

She didn't react. It was just one more disappointment to add to the growing pile festering in her mind. She knew she was on the edge of breaking down, but while she could still walk, and range, she would keep going.

She turned to Killop, who was crouching by her side. She shook her head and they got to their feet, beginning the long descent to the valley beneath them. She pointed up at a high range to the east.

'There next.'

He said nothing. She kept her gaze away from him, unable to look at his face. The guilt they bore was driving a wedge between them. She knew it was her fault, but it was his, too. They should have realised that Kylon would betray them, but they drank the drugged alcohol, and allowed him to steal their child.

Kylon. She would enjoy scouring his mind when they caught him.

Behind them walked Celine and Chane, and a handful of troopers. The sergeant was still with them, along with a few other Holdfast loyalists, but the rest had gone. Sent to collect food and supplies from the plains to the south, they had never returned. The sergeant had said that they were probably lost in the mountains, but Daphne knew the truth.

A bitter wind blew down the mountainside, blowing dust from the track up into their faces. She shielded her eyes, bloodshot from lack of sleep, and continued down the slope. The track led on for miles, and she kept going, her thoughts forced from her head as she concentrated on putting one foot in front of another.

She felt a hand on her shoulder.

'They need to rest,' Killop said.

She gazed back down the track. The others had lagged behind, spaced out along the way they had come. She glanced up at the high ridge.

'We need to climb up there before it gets dark.'

Killop followed her gaze. 'There's not enough time left in the day.'

She frowned, and looked for the position of the sun, but thick clouds were covering the sky.

'Is it past noon?'

Killop paused, his eyes narrowing. 'It's nearly evening, Daphne. We've been walking all day.'

She lit a cigarette, and sat on a boulder, realising that her legs were aching.

'I'll scout for a campsite,' he said, and walked off.

She waited for the others to reach her. Chane arrived first, leading a pair of young troopers, who collapsed by the side of the track. Chane was sweating, her breath coming hard. She pulled a hip flask from her belt and took a drink, then held it out to Daphne.

She shook her head. Chane shrugged and sat down.

The sergeant came next, with another trooper. She passed round the water skin she carried over her shoulder, and they all took a turn.

Three more troopers were the last to reach where Daphne sat. They were helping Celine, who was limping. The troopers lowered Celine to the ground, and the sergeant knelt by her.

'What's the trouble, miss?'

'My knees,' Celine groaned, 'my ankles, they're all sore.'

'Not surprised, miss,' the sergeant said. 'We must have walked more than twenty miles today.'

Daphne glanced back at the high ridge. It was at least another ten miles from where they sat, and Killop had been right, the daylight was beginning to fade. She swore to herself. A wasted day. She should have picked a nearer peak, but her exhaustion had caused her to miscalculate, and now she had no time or light in which to range out for Karalyn.

'Dammit,' she muttered.

Chane sat by her. 'You alright?'

Daphne said nothing.

Killop re-appeared. He took a long drink from the water skin.

'There's a dell a couple of hundred yards up the track,' he said. 'It's flat enough for the tents, and there's wood and water close by.'

The sergeant stood. 'Lead on, sir.'

The rest of the troopers got to their feet, and they trudged up the track, two supporting Celine as they went. Daphne and Chane waited until they had gone, then slid off the boulder and followed them.

'I'm here if you want to talk,' Chane said.

Daphne ignored her. Part of her blamed Chane. If her mind hadn't been addled with drink and drugs, then she might have been of some use, she might have somehow prevented Karalyn from being taken.

They reached the small clearing that Killop had found, and the troopers began to pitch the three remaining tents. The sergeant built a fire, and Killop sparked it up for them, his fingers generating fire out of nothing as the others watched.

The sergeant grunted. 'I'll never get used to seeing that.'

Celine was laid on the ground, with a cloak for a pillow. She clenched her eyes in pain as the troopers gazed at her. One got her a blanket, while another began to rub her calves, but Celine swore, and pushed them away.

Daphne sat next to Killop on the other side of the fire from Celine, her thoughts elsewhere. The sergeant made up some weak tea from a few dry leaves she had in a pouch, and they got a mug each.

'Keep your chins up,' the sergeant said to her troopers. 'We'll find the girl soon.'

Daphne drained her mug, and stood.

'I'm going for a walk.'

'I'll come with you,' said Killop.

'I want to be by myself.'

She turned and walked back down the path, the light fading as she grew further from the fire. She reached a bend in the track that she remembered passing on the way up, and sat on the edge of the cliff, gazing down into the dark valleys below her.

She dropped her mask, and began to cry.

Killop sat down beside her.

'Not now,' she said.

He said nothing, just looked out over the valleys.

'Please go.'

'No,' he said. 'I can't.'

She wiped her cheek with her right hand. 'Have you come to tell me that it's not my fault?'

'No.'

'It is my fault. It's our fault.'

'Aye.'

She paused, feeling the pressure of their combined guilt like a weight upon her shoulders. She wanted to get up and walk away, but her heart was joined to his, and walking away now would feel like walking away forever.

'We let Kylon into our lives,' she said. 'We trusted him.'

He bowed his head. 'Aye, we did. We willingly gave him responsibility for our daughter.'

'At least you got to spend time with her,' she said. 'I was never there, never had time to play with her, or watch her grow and learn. I was so busy with the rebellion, and Celine and Kylon were available, and it was easy just to leave her with them, and you. And then my family were killed, and Karalyn nearly was too, and again I wasn't there for her. After that, I was afraid to get too close to her, in case I lost her too.'

She started to cry again, and Killop took her hand.

'And I lost her anyway,' she said, weeping, 'and all that time I could have been with her, I wasted.'

He put his arms round her.

'If I could only have her back,' she said, her face in his shoulder, 'I promise I would do better.'

She cried in his arms as he held her close, and for that moment, the distance between them faded to nothing.

Daphne's dream-vision rose above the valleys, as it had every night since Karalyn had gone. She looked down at the glow of the low fire, a couple of troopers still up and awake, then scanned the mountains around her. The jagged peaks were only visible as a faint contrast against the blackness of the night sky, clouds obscuring the seven stars.

She frowned. Aside from the campfire, all around was an endless ocean of silent darkness. She listened for Karalyn, but heard nothing.

Kara-bear, she said, *it's mummy. If you can hear me, but can't answer, just know that daddy and I are looking for you every day, and we'll find you soon. We love you, little bear.*

She released her vision, and floated back down to the tent where her sleeping body lay, tears falling down her cheeks.

She awoke, sobbing, and felt Killop's arm around her.

Mummy?

Daphne shot up.

Mummy?

The voice was faint, as if from a long distance away. Daphne concentrated, feeling out with her vision.

Karalyn? she cried. *I'm here, baby. I'm here.*

Silence.

She bowed her head.

'What happened?' Killop said.

She opened her eyes to see him lying next to her, his eyes wide. She lay back down again.

'She's alive,' she whispered. 'I don't know where, but she's alive.'

The dawn was grey and cold as they crawled out of their tents. The sergeant and Killop got the fire going, and the troopers washed and sat, warming themselves against the flames. Daphne glanced at them, and saw how thin they were, and how close to despair.

'Karalyn's alive,' she said.

Everyone turned to look at her.

'I got a message from her last night. It was faint, but it was her.'

'Where is she?' Chane said.

'I don't know,' said Daphne, to the sound of sighs and groans. 'I couldn't tell.'

'So what do we do now, ma'am?' said the sergeant.

'We keep to the plan,' she said. 'We climb the ridge we were aiming for yesterday, and take a look into the next valley. Chane, you got a map handy?'

Chane nodded, and reached for a satchel. 'Kylon stole most of them, as you know,' she said, 'but I have one of the region we're in just now.'

She unrolled a chart and laid it on the ground, using stones to keep the corners down.

She pointed. 'We're here.'

'Alright,' said Daphne, 'then the ridge is here.'

'Is that the start of the plains at the bottom of the map?' asked a trooper.

'Yeah,' said Chane. 'We've circled right round this area, and are almost back at where we started.'

'Then,' the trooper went on, 'we're less than a day's walk from those farms.' He pointed to a settlement marked on the plains. 'We could be there by nightfall.'

'Who asked for your opinion?' said the sergeant. 'If Lady Holdfast says we're going to the ridge, then that's where we're going.'

The trooper's face twisted into a snarl.

'We can't go on,' said another. 'I'm sorry, ma'am, and sergeant, but we've not eaten in days. We want to help find the child, but we can't if we starve.'

'Shut your mouth,' the sergeant cried. 'All of you.'

The troopers backed off, but their eyes remained defiant.

'We have another problem,' said Chane.

Daphne glanced at her.

Chane gestured at Celine, who was sitting by the fire on her own. Her eyes were red, and she was staring at the ground.

'Can you walk today?' Chane said to her.

Celine looked up and shook her head.

Chane crouched down by her side. 'Let me see your feet.'

Celine pulled off her loose boots, revealing bloody blisters, and swollen bruises round her ankles. Her face fell at the sight.

'Shit,' said Chane.

'We'll have to carry her,' said the sergeant.

'All the way up the ridge, sergeant?' said a trooper.

'You'll carry her all the way to Kellach Brigdomin if I say so, trooper.'

'No,' Celine said. 'Just leave me here. You can come back for me.'

Chane turned to Daphne.

'We might not be coming back this way,' she said.

Chane shrugged. 'Sorry, Celine.'

The sergeant bit her lip. 'May I have a quiet word, ma'am?'

Daphne nodded.

They walked away together, Chane and Killop following.

'What is it, sergeant?' Daphne said, once they were out of sight of the troopers.

'Maybe we need a day or two to rest and get some food, ma'am,' she said. 'We could be on the plains by this evening, and get settled into a barn or somewhere suitable. Once we've rested, and purchased supplies, then we can come back and resume the search for your daughter.'

'No,' said Daphne.

The sergeant glanced at Chane.

'They have a point,' she said to Daphne. 'They'll soon be too hungry to think straight.'

Daphne shook her head. 'We'll lose three days, at least. We can't.'

'Maybe you could all go,' said Killop, 'and I'll stay up here looking until you've recovered.'

Chane frowned. 'Surely even the Kellach have to eat?'

He nodded. 'And I have been.'

'What?'

'There are roots, berries, and fungus up here that I can eat,' he said. 'Stuff that would poison any of you lot, but they don't affect me. I could live in these mountains indefinitely.'

Chane shook her head. 'You've been eating all this time? I've not seen you eat once.'

'I didn't want to rub your faces in it,' he said. 'I know how hungry you all are. But the point is that I can keep searching, while you re-supply. I can move faster on my own, and will be able to cover a few more valleys. We can arrange a place to meet in three or four days.'

Daphne glanced at him. 'If you're staying, then so am I.'

He looked at her for a long moment.

'No,' he said. 'You need food and rest. You'll be no good to Karalyn if you starve.'

'Forget it,' she said, her voice rising. 'There's no way I'm going back to the plains while you're up here. What if you find them? You'll be out-numbered. No.'

Killop frowned. 'I can take Kylon.'

'You're good,' said Chane, before Daphne could speak, 'but Kylon's the best sword-fighter I've ever seen, apart from Daphne on battle-vision, obviously. And what if Baoryn puts a bolt in your back while you're busy with Kylon?'

The Kell man said nothing.

'If I can speak my mind,' said the sergeant, 'I'd say we should all go down to the plains.'

'I agree,' said Chane.

Daphne's temper flared. 'Am I the only one that gives a damn about finding Karalyn?'

'No,' said Killop, while Chane and the sergeant lowered their eyes, 'you're not.'

'It seems like it,' she said.

'That's why you need to rest,' he said. 'You're so tired and hungry, you're not thinking straight.'

'Don't speak to me like I'm a child.'

Killop's eyes narrowed, but he closed his mouth.

Daphne felt like she was about to explode, as anger, fear and guilt tore through her.

'None of you understand,' she cried. 'If we waste another three days, then Kylon will be even further away, and we'll never find her. Is that what you want?'

'No, ma'am,' the sergeant said.

'Then tell your troopers to get ready to go.'

'Yes, ma'am.'

The sergeant saluted, and walked back up the track, her shoulders bowed.

Chane shook her head. 'They'll desert, first opportunity they get.'

'I don't care,' Daphne said. 'If they don't want to help, then I don't want them around.'

'They're your most loyal troopers,' Killop said, his eyes tight. 'They're the ones who've stayed, but they need to eat, Daphne; we've pushed them too far.'

'It's alright for you,' she said, turning her anger on him. 'You don't need to worry about food, you can stay up here, mocking the rest of us weak Holdings. But you're not staying up here without me, no matter what you say.'

He gazed at her.

'I'm going down to the plains,' he said, 'because if you stay up here with me you'll die.'

Daphne screamed, and lashed out with her armoured left arm, striking the side of the cliff-face. The wrist-guard tore away a chunk of rock, sending an excruciating pain up her arm, her elbow on fire. She grasped her wrist in her right hand and sank to her knees, weeping. She closed her eyes, feeling Killop's arm over her shoulder.

Deep inside, she knew they were right, but frustration scourged her.

'Kara-bear,' she sobbed. 'I'm sorry.'

———

It rained during the afternoon; a short downpour that drenched them as they trudged along the track towards the plain. Daphne hardly noticed, her mind a torment of conflicting emotions. Ahead of her, Celine was being carried on a stretcher by two troopers. She seemed in better spirits, now that she knew they were going to the plains to buy supplies. They all seemed in a better mood, except for Killop, who had been silent the entire way.

She glanced at him.

She knew he was hurting, she knew he would rather be searching, instead of retreating down the mountain with the rest of them, but her anger with him remained. She felt betrayed, as if she were the only one prepared to sacrifice everything to find her daughter.

The grey clouds scudded overhead, mirroring her mood.

Chane offered her a cigarette, and lit it for her.

'Thanks.'

'I'm feeling a bit better today,' Chane said. 'Sounds stupid, I know, but this morning when I woke up, my first thought wasn't about dull-weed. I guess my hunger's overpowered my craving, for now at any rate. Anyway, I wanted to say thank you, for helping me get through the worst of it. I don't deserve you as a friend.'

Daphne said nothing.

'I know you blame yourself,' Chane went on. 'You shouldn't, it was my fault. It was me who introduced you to Kylon. I knew he was dangerous, but I didn't think he'd turn out to be a treacherous bastard. No one did, Daphne.'

'You talk like she's dead,' Daphne said. 'She's not.'

'I know, you heard her voice last night, and it's given me renewed hope. Maybe that's part of why I'm feeling better today. We're going to find her, I know it; but maybe we need to think about changing our strategy.'

Daphne glanced at her. 'Go on.'

'We need money,' Chane said, 'enough for more people, and more supplies. We need to widen the net, and cover more ground. We will find her, but it might take more time than we'd thought.'

'We'd need to go to Hold Fast for that,' Daphne said. 'Kylon stole most of my money, and the only place where I could gather all the people we'd need is back home.'

Chane nodded. 'That's what I was thinking too.'

'More time wasted,' she said. 'I don't think I could cope with all the waiting, and the work organising a large search party. All I want to do is look for her.'

'We could send Celine? That sort of work would suit her better anyway. She's the only one here who's never been in the army, and all the trekking through the mountains has nearly made her lame. And, of course, she's a Holdfast.'

Daphne thought for a moment, then nodded.

'I'll speak to her later, if you want,' Chane said, 'when we get closer to the plains.'

'Alright,' Daphne said. She glanced at her friend. 'Thanks.'

Chane nodded. 'How's the arm?'

'Sore.'

'One thing's for sure,' Chane said; 'that cliff won't be hassling us again.'

Daphne almost smiled. They caught each other's eye for a second, then glanced back at the track, trudging on.

The daylight was beginning to fade as they descended a low foothill, the great plains spread out like the ocean before them. Patches of sunlight illuminated fields and grasslands as the clouds broke up to the west, and despite her longing to be looking for Karalyn, Daphne's heart rose at the sight.

They reached a paved road at the bottom of the slope, and turned right, their stride adjusting to the unyielding surface beneath their boots. After a further hour's walking, they saw the buildings of a settlement in the distance, and reached it as evening fell.

There were around two dozen houses, some lining the main road, others scattered by barns and other farm buildings. Most of the houses were spilling light from gaps in their thick shutters.

'Where are we again?' said Killop. 'Which Hold?'

'We're in Hold Terras,' said Chane. 'Well, a small part of it. The Emperor never came this far north-west, which is why these houses are still standing. It's wheat land,' she went on. 'This whole area, in fact. Wheat fields in every direction.'

Killop glanced around at the empty fields, and Daphne wondered whether there were enough people left in the Holdings to sow them when spring came.

As they got to within twenty yards of the first house, a bell rang out, and they halted. A crossbow bolt flew through the air, skidding off the road in front of them. The troopers bunched together, Daphne at their centre.

'Go back the way you came,' cried a voice. 'We don't want your kind here.'

'Our kind?' muttered Chane. 'What's that supposed to mean?'

'We just want to buy some food,' Daphne called out, 'if you have any to sell.'

'Not if you're with one of them.'

'What are you talking about?' Chane yelled. 'One of who?'

'One of those Kellach bastards.'

They all glanced at Killop.

He raised his arms. 'I'm not a threat.'

'That's what the last one said,' cried the voice.

Daphne strode forward.

'And when was the last one here?'

'A few days ago.'

Daphne swallowed. 'Did he have a young girl with him? A Holdings girl?'

There was silence for a moment, as Daphne's heart raced.

'Yes.'

She shook her head, unable to speak.

'That Kellach is the bastard we're looking for,' cried Killop, 'and his Rahain friend. If you've seen them, then please help us.'

There was another pause.

'Why should we help you? That Kellach and his friend killed three of our townsfolk, after we welcomed them, and fed them.'

Daphne stared at the row of houses.

'Because that girl is my daughter.'

There was a rustle, and a small group of armed Holdings emerged from behind the first house in the row. They looked Daphne up and down, and scanned the rest of her group.

Killop drew his sword, and the group aimed their crossbows at him. He stepped forward and laid the weapon onto the ground.

'I understand your anger,' he said, 'and I'm prepared to walk into your town unarmed to show I'm not a threat.'

One of the townsfolk picked it up.

'I'll need it back when we leave,' Killop said. 'I intend to use it to cut that bastard's throat.'

The leader of the townsfolk nodded. 'Come with us.'

They followed the group up the street, and entered a large house on the right, where they were shown to a dining hall. Celine was carried in, and placed by the head of a long table.

'We can feed you,' their leader said, 'but we're not rich round here.'

Daphne nodded, as the troopers found seats round the long table next to Celine. She pulled a pouch from her belt, and withdrew twenty coins. The man smiled, and took the money.

'We'll get the kitchens fired up,' he said, 'but we'll have bread and ale for you in a few minutes.'

'Tell me about the Kellach man,' she said.

'In a moment,' he said, walking off.

Daphne sat down at the table next to Killop.

He caught her eye, and she could see the hope he was carrying.

Townsfolk entered with trays, and unloaded plates of bread, and jugs of ale, along with a bowl of apples and some strong-smelling cheese. The troopers launched themselves at the food.

'Steady with the ale,' said the sergeant. 'Wait until you've eaten something first.'

Daphne ignored the food, her eyes on the doorway where the man had left.

'Have we been searching in the wrong place?' she said to Killop, who was also staring at the door.

'I don't know,' he said. 'What was Kylon doing here? Stocking up?'

'Then why would he kill those people?' she said. 'It doesn't make sense.'

Her heart quickened as the man came back into the dining hall. He was with two women, dressed as stable workers.

They sat down next to Daphne and Killop.

The man looked at Daphne. 'You said the girl was your daughter?'

'Yes. Did you see her?'

'Yes,' he nodded, 'though she was always sleeping.'

'Why was Kylon here?' said Killop.

'Kylon?'

'The Kellach man.'

'He said he was here just to buy food, but he was a liar. In the middle of the night, he broke into the stables, and murdered three of these women's friends, who were sleeping there. He then stole two horses, and killed the only other two we had left.'

'I saw them leave,' said one of the women. 'They all rode off on the one horse, leading the other one behind them. The Kellach man, the Rahain man, and the girl, who was being carried in a bundle between them.'

Daphne let out a sob, bowing her head. Killop took her hand.

'Did they take supplies?' he said.

'Yes,' said the man, 'the ones they'd already paid for.'

'Enough for how long?'

He shrugged. 'Ten days, if they're frugal.'

Daphne sensed Killop's anger burn. She lifted her head.

'Which way did they go?'

The man took a drink of ale. 'South.'

'South?' Daphne said.

'Yes,' he said, 'towards the road to the Plateau.'

Daphne nodded. The Plateau. She turned to Killop, and their eyes met.

The doors to the hall swung open, and more trays were carried in, this time loaded with large bowls of cooked meat and vegetables. The smell reached Daphne's nose as the troopers let out a cheer, but her mind was blank to all else but where her daughter might be going.

'Where's he taking her?' she said, her voice a whisper.

'I don't know, miss,' said the man, 'but I hope you find him, and your girl.'

'And when you do,' said one of the stable women, 'make sure he suffers.'

CHAPTER 29
NO WAY BACK

Plateau City, Imperial Plateau – 7th Day, Second Third Winter 507

Keira sat with her feet up on the window ledge, a mug of ale in one hand, and a weedstick in the other. She was up before noon, early for her. Rising as the sun was setting had become more usual since they had arrived in Plateau City to begin their wait. She gazed out through the open shutters at the quiet streets of the old Kellach quarter. Only a few thousand of her folk still lived within the city walls, a fraction of the previous number. Many tenements were burnt-out shells, and others lay abandoned, or had been taken over by Holdings squatters from the peasant districts.

The signs of the Emperor's brutal suppression of the quarter were still visible everywhere she looked, but the authorities seemed to have lost all interest in controlling what remained of the population. To her right lay the old Emergency Wall, built to protect the completed half of the city when Agang had invaded. It now functioned to separate the rich New Town beyond from the slums of the poor. The gates between were sealed shut, and Keira had never seen them open in the fifteen days they had been living in their tenement apartment.

No soldiers or church wardens ever ventured into the poorer half of the city, and the folk there had taken the law into their own hands; and the slum districts were now controlled by a series of gangs, who fought over the few trades still making any money.

Her gaze went to the towers of the Great Fortress, at the corner of the Old Town, where it dominated the southern half of the city. The imperial flag had been raised at dawn, a banner of white with a golden star.

'You ever going to pass that?' said Kallie.

'Smoke yer own.'

'I cannae be arsed making one.'

'Tough shit.'

Kallie turned to Flora. 'Will you make me one, please?'

The Holdings woman tutted and put down her book.

'You're much better at it than I am,' Kallie said.

Flora sighed. 'Pass me your stuff.'

Keira chuckled as Kallie handed a leather pouch over to Flora.

'We shouldn't get too wasted,' Flora said, as she began to prepare a weedstick. 'We've got a lot to do today.'

'No, we don't,' said Keira, her eyes turning back to her view over the city's narrow streets. 'We have exactly one fucking thing to do today. Leave.'

Kallie shrugged as they gazed out of the window. 'You wouldn't even know the Emperor was back,' she said. 'I thought there would be parades, or something.'

'And where's his army?' Keira said.

'Hopefully lying dead on the plains of the Holdings,' Flora said.

'What'll he do now, do you think?' Kallie said.

'Fuck knows,' said Keira. 'So far, he's flattened Rainsby, Frogland, and now the Holdings, but it looks like he's run out of soldiers.'

'I'm sure Ghorley could squeeze some more out from Rahain,' said Flora. She smiled. 'They should be freezing their arses off about now.'

She passed Kallie the completed weedstick.

'Thanks,' she said, lighting it. 'He's bound to have heard about what we did in Kell. The next army he raises will be heading down there, to get the mines running again.'

'Maybe,' said Flora. 'Depends if he's got any Kellach mages.'

Kallie frowned.

'We know he's been hunting mages again,' the Holdings woman went on, 'just like he did before. If he's got a hold of the full set, then I'm not sure he'll give a shit about whether a few lizards are feeling the cold this winter. I mean, look around. Does it seem like the Emperor cares about actually ruling? The empire's falling apart. Trade's collapsed, there's no money or food, or work. All those folk killed, just so he could get his hands on more mages.'

'Is he going to use them to become even more powerful?' Kallie asked.

'Maybe he's just getting rid of the competition,' Keira said.

'Kylon said he was trying to destroy the world,' Flora said.

Keira scowled. 'Who cares what that wee prick said?'

'Either way,' Flora said, 'the Emperor's up in that fortress right now, with all the mages he captured from Rakana, Rainsby and the Holdings, and any others he had left over from the last time.'

They gazed out of the window at the high towers of the fortress, gleaming in the morning sunshine.

'If anything happens,' Kallie said, 'how will we know?'

'There was an earthquake,' Flora said, 'and Keira lost her powers.'

'You did?' Kallie said, turning to her.

'Aye. For a couple of hours.'

'Must have felt terrible.'

Keira thought back, and remembered the feeling of looking for her well of power, and finding it not empty, but gone. Relief had been her first emotion at the time, as if a great weight had been lifted from her, but now she was glad to have it back. She was going to need it.

She shrugged.

'Well, if it happens again,' Kallie said, 'we'll hopefully be long gone from here.'

Keira glanced at their bags, lying packed by the front door of their rented apartment.

'The last stretch,' she said.

'Holdings for the spring,' Flora said, 'then we'll see what the bastard's done to it.'

'And then maybe Frogland,' Keira said.

The two other women frowned at her.

Keira shrugged. 'Why not? I'll have been everywhere else. I always wanted to see the world.'

Flora shook her head.

'Rakana? Really? I thought you wanted to avoid them?'

'It's not like I'd go around telling them who I was, ya daft cow,' Keira said. 'Just fancy seeing it.'

'You might bump into Shella,' Flora smirked, 'the mage that Kalayne said you were going to meet.'

'I wouldnae know her if I passed her on the street.'

'I wonder if Agang's found her yet,' Flora said. 'It'd be funny if he has, and then takes her back to Domm to look for you...'

Keira laughed. 'Aye, I can imagine the look on that uptight Sanang prick's face when Kelpie tells him we've gone. And that old lizard bastard.'

There was a rap at their front door.

'About time,' said Keira, as Flora got to her feet. The young Holdings woman crossed the room, and opened the door an inch, then unlatched the chain.

'Good morning,' said a large Kellach woman, entering. She was followed into the apartment by two enormous Kellach men, both armed.

The woman glanced at the bags piled by the door. 'All ready to go, I see?'

'Aye,' said Keira. 'Have a seat. Want a drink?'

'Aye,' the woman said, 'why not?'

She sat by the window, and Kallie passed her a mug of ale. Her two minders stood by her shoulders, keeping their eyes on them.

'Cheers,' the woman said, raising her mug.

'Aye, cheers,' Keira said.

They drank.

'Everything's arranged,' the woman said. 'Wagon, horses, supplies. Everything that was on your list.'

'Everything?' Kallie said, her eyes lighting up.

'Aye,' the woman said. She glanced at one of her guards and snapped her fingers. The man reached inside his overcoat and pulled out a longbow, wrapped in oilskins, and a quiver full of arrows. He passed them to Kallie, who grinned.

'Thanks.'

The woman shrugged. 'That's what five pounds of weed gets ye.' She reached into her coat, and produced a large pouch. 'And this.'

Keira took the pouch, and looked inside. Gold.

'That's what's left over,' the woman said, 'after taking off your accommodation, food, booze, the wagon and horses, and everything else. It comes to just over three hundred.'

Keira nodded.

'They grow weed in the River Holdings now,' the woman said, 'or at least, they did before the Emperor went up there and kicked their arses. You sure about heading up there? It's meant to be a wasteland.'

'Aye,' said Keira. 'Looking for relatives. We were just waiting until the Emperor had cleared out.'

'Aye,' she said. 'Now that he's back in town, you're not the only ones leaving the city. Folk remember what he did the last time he was here. Was thinking about relocating to Rainsby myself, if things get too rough.'

'There's always the tunnels.'

'Aye, that's what saved us last time, when the Emperor was going mental through the Kellach quarter. We sat tight down there until he'd left, and when we got back to the surface, the streets were filled with bodies.' She glanced out of the window at the towers of the fortress rising above the tenement roofs. 'With that bastard back,' she went on, 'it's no surprise folk are wanting to leave.'

She sipped her ale. 'Mind ye were asking if I'd keep my eye out for any odd-looking folk?' she went on. 'This morning, I got paid a fortune by someone arriving in the city, and wanting to hide. While everyone else is leaving, this crazy bastard is paying me to stay.'

Keira nodded, drinking her ale.

'And that wasn't the only weird thing about him,' the woman went on. 'He had two folk with him, a shabby looking Rahain guy, and a Holdings girl.'

'That's not that weird,' Flora said. 'People are mixing more with each other all the time.'

'Aye,' the woman said. 'This Holdings girl was only a bairn, but, and ye don't see that often.'

Keira frowned.

'A Kellach guy with a wee Holdings girl?'

'Aye.'

'What did the guy look like?'

The woman shrugged. 'Twenties, miserable bastard. Was wearing a long black coat.'

Keira spat out her drink. The woman raised an eyebrow, wiping ale from her leg.

'What was his name?' said Flora.

'I didn't ask,' said the woman. 'Just like I've not been asking you lot any questions. One thing the guy did ask me though was if I'd seen a Rakanese woman that he's looking for.'

'Do you remember what she was called?'

The woman rubbed her chin. 'Cilla?'

'Shella?'

'Aye, something like that. I told him to go down to the docks. There's not many frog folk left in the city, but that's where she'll be if she's here, I told him.'

Keira tried to think, but she couldn't imagine how the news could be anything but bad.

'Where are they now?' she said.

'In the tunnels under the Old Town,' the woman said. 'I offered him a big apartment, after all, he had plenty of gold on him, but he said he wanted to stay hidden.'

Kallie smirked. 'And yet you're telling us about him.'

'You're leaving,' she shrugged. 'What's the difference?'

'We're not leaving just yet,' said Keira. 'We're going to visit the Old Town first.'

'Hold on,' the woman said. 'He's paying me for protection. I can't be having ye going round and beating him up or anything.'

'It'll be fine,' Keira said, 'we just want to talk to him. Will ye show us where he is?'

The woman frowned. 'Aye, alright.' She gazed at her. 'No trouble, mind.'

'It cannae be Kylon, surely?' Kallie said, as they walked along the quiet streets towards the Old Town.

'It had better be,' said Flora; 'otherwise we're wasting two hours for nothing. We should be on our way.'

'We will be soon, my wee Flora,' Keira said. 'Patience.'

'And this bag's heavy,' Flora said. 'I packed it thinking it was going straight onto a wagon. I wasn't expecting to be lugging it around town.'

The large woman raised an eyebrow at Keira. 'Does she always complain?'

'No,' Keira smirked. 'They take it in turns.'

The woman grinned. They took a right, crossing over an open sewer running down the middle of the street. Keira crinkled her nose.

'I'll not miss the fucking smell,' she said.

They passed an alley with a long row of burnt-out tenements. Their roofs had collapsed, and the blackened walls looked like they could follow at any moment. At the end of the street was the Old Town wall, cutting across the Kellach quarter, and running up to where the Emergency Wall sealed off the New Town. The gates to the Old Town were open, with no one guarding or watching who passed back and forth.

They went through, and the character of the city changed. The streets were narrower, and the buildings lower and older. The fire damage was also less severe, the Emperor having restricted his rampage to the Kellach quarter, but the poverty and squalor were as bad as anywhere she had seen, even Rainsby. The population were mostly Holdings, with a few scattered Kellach and Rakanese. Many were crippled, and sat on street corners, begging.

Compared to the quiet streets of the Kellach quarter, the Old Town was bustling. A few market stalls had stock for sale, and several taverns and shops were open for business. More were boarded up and closed, however, and the food being sold was poor quality at exorbitant prices. They pressed on down a busy thoroughfare, then came to a square. Ahead loomed the gates and walls of the massive fortress. It stood at the corner of the Old Town, its other side facing the New.

Its gates were closed, and though no soldiers were on duty outside, the local populace were giving the building a wide berth. Every window on the Old Town side had been bricked up, and the building seemed lifeless.

'He's in there, is he?' said Keira.

'Aye,' said the woman. 'The queen's back too. He captured her up north and brought her home.'

'I bet she's fucking ecstatic about that.'

The woman chuckled. 'There's rumours that she'll be hanged at a big public execution, but that's all it is, a rumour. No one knows what's going on inside, and anyone who tells you different is a liar.'

They went down a side lane, losing sight of the fortress. They reached an old tavern and the woman knocked. The door opened, and a man looked them over.

'Ma'am,' he bowed to the woman, and let them in. They went to the kitchen, and the man pulled away a rug, revealing a trapdoor beneath.

Flora shook her head. 'Right under their noses.'

'That's right, little lady,' the woman smiled.

The man opened the trapdoor, and they climbed down. The woman left one of her minders by the entrance to the trapdoor, and the other followed along. At the bottom of the ladder, she led them through a series of winding tunnels, well lit by wall lamps. They passed chambers and caverns where supplies and weapons had been stockpiled, and rooms where folk huddled and hid. They went down another ladder to a lower level, where damp from the Inner Sea stained the walls, and left puddles on the rocky ground.

'Here we are,' the woman said, pointing to a cavern with a curtain pulled across the entrance. 'Remember,' she said, 'you're here to talk. If you feel the need for violence, come back out here and we'll negotiate, but for now, the occupants of this chamber are under my protection. Don't forget it.'

Keira nodded.

The woman snapped her fingers, and her minder pulled the curtain back. Keira walked through, followed by Kallie and Flora.

The chamber was lit by a single lamp. There was a row of low pallet beds, with bags sitting on two. There was also a table, with four chairs. On one sat a Rahain man, who looked up as they entered.

'Baoryn, ya auld bastard!' Keira cried, throwing her backpack to the ground. 'I've not seen you in years.'

The Rahain man stared at her.

'This is Baoryn,' Keira said to Flora and Kallie. 'Met him in the Brig Pass. He was a prisoner, but joined our side. Was always a useful wee bastard, back when we were fighting the Rahain, as they'd never be expecting one of them to be working with us.'

Keira laughed, then noticed that Baoryn hadn't moved an inch since she walked in, his features frozen. She walked over to the table and sat. Flora and Kallie pulled off their packs, and slung them to the ground.

'Hi,' said Flora to the Rahain man, who didn't respond. She raised an eyebrow. 'Talkative fellow, isn't he?'

She and Kallie sat at the table. Baoryn started to edge backwards.

'So,' Keira said, 'where the fuck is that arsehole?'

'Who?' Baoryn muttered, his tongue flickering.

Keira smirked. 'Don't give me your shite, ya wee lizard bawbag; ye know fine who I'm talking about.'

His eyes darted to the curtain at the cavern's entrance.

'Thinking of running?' Keira said. 'Try it. I'll be more than happy to beat the information out of ye, if ye don't feel like talking.'

A bead of sweat rolled down his forehead.

'Keep yer hands on the table where I can see them,' Keira snarled. She drew a knife from her boot, and poked him in the ribs. 'Now, I'll keep this simple. Yes or no answers. First, you came into the city with Kylon, right?'

He nodded.

'And a wee Holdings girl?'

He paused, and she jabbed the knife a fraction deeper. He flinched. Kallie moved her seat round so she was behind him, and held her own knife to his back.

He nodded.

'My niece?' Keira said.

'Yes.'

'Are Daphne and Killop alive?'

'Yes,' Baoryn said. 'I think so.'

'Thank fuck,' she said. 'I thought you being here meant they'd been killed or something.' She shook her head. 'Still, them being alive means that either they asked you to take their child into danger, or you stole her. Which is it?'

Baoryn said nothing.

'Ye stole her, ya pair of shitstains?' Keira said, her eyes tightening. She moved the knife up to his throat. 'Now answer this, ya bastard. Where are they? What's that arsehole doing with my niece?'

Baoryn shook his head, and his eyes flickered towards the back of the cavern. Keira frowned, and stood.

'Keep that knife on him,' she said to Kallie, and walked by the row of pallets, to where baggage had been heaped. Her eyes looked over the packs and trunks, and a thick pile of blankets.

Her mouth opened.

In among the blankets, a young girl was lying asleep, her dark-skinned face almost hidden under the covers. Keira lifted the blankets.

The girl was dressed in a simple tunic, her arms and legs stick-thin, her face gaunt.

'What the fuck?' she muttered, gazing at the girl. She looked more unconscious than sleeping. 'Flora, get over here.'

The Holdings woman approached. 'What is it? Oh. Oh shit.'

'Is she alright, do you think?' Keira said.

'I'm not a physician,' Flora said, 'but no, she looks far from all right.'

Keira felt anger grip her. She clenched her teeth and stood, turning to face the Rahain man. She strode across to him and grabbed him by the throat, lifting him clear of the chair.

'What have ye done to her, ya piece of shit? I'll fucking rip yer head off.'

The Rahain man choked, his hands trying to pull her grip away. She squeezed tighter.

'Yer going to kill him,' said Kallie. 'Not that I mind, but he probably knows where Kylon is.'

Keira threw the Rahain man against the wall, his body cracking off the side of the cavern and collapsing onto a bed pallet. He rolled off and hit the floor.

Kallie stared. 'Ya radge cow. Ye've killed him.'

Keira said nothing, her eyes on the twisted shape Baoryn's body was making on the ground.

The curtain parted and the woman walked in, her minder lurking nearby.

'What the fuck did I say?' she said, glancing at the Rahain man. 'This is my town; ye cannae just come in here and tread all over my rules. These bastards paid me...'

'Look what they've done to my niece,' Keira said. 'Sorry for breaking the rules, but this one's personal.'

The woman went to where Flora was crouched, and gazed down at the girl.

'Pyre's arse,' she muttered.

'They abducted her,' Keira said. 'The bastards stole her from my brother.'

The woman straightened, and turned to Keira. 'This girl is from the Holdings.'

'Aye.'

'Then how can she be yer niece?'

'Her mother's Holdings,' Keira said. 'Look; I don't give a shit what ye think, I'm taking that girl out of here with me. There's no way I'm leaving her with the bastard that stole her.'

'Well, ye've already killed that one,' the woman said, pointing at where Baoryn lay.

'Aye, and I admit it, I'm probably going to kill the Kellach guy as well.'

The woman folded her arms. 'It'll cost ye.'

Keira bared her teeth. 'Ye want me to pay to take my own fucking niece?'

'I've only your word for that,' the woman said.

'Flora,' Keira said, 'pick up the girl.'

The Holdings woman gathered the sleeping child in her arms. 'I won't be able to carry her and my pack out of here,' she said, grunting.

'I'll take it,' said Kallie, edging across the room.

The woman stared at them.

The child squirmed in Flora's arms, then threw up down her leathers. She began to shiver, her body convulsing.

'This isn't good,' Flora said. 'We can't put her on a wagon in this condition.'

Keira frowned.

'If I blow this whistle,' the woman said, pulling a chain from round her neck, 'these caverns will be full of guards within a minute. Put the child down, and step away.'

'Don't fucking try to stop us,' Keira said.

The woman's minder put his hand on the hilt of his sword.

The curtain parted, and Kylon walked in.

Keira stared at him. His black hair fell about his shoulders, framing his permanently down-turned expression. His long coat trailed along the ground behind him, and he had a sack over one shoulder. His eyes widened as he saw her.

'You know these folk?' the woman said.

'Aye,' he replied, his eyes never leaving Keira's face.

'This woman claims that the girl is her niece,' the woman went on.

'She is,' Kylon said.

The woman raised an eyebrow. 'It seems I owe you an apology.'

Keira shrugged. 'Ask him if he stole her.'

The woman glanced at Kylon. 'No,' she said. 'This is family business, and I'm not getting involved in that. Your wagon though, will ye still be needing it?'

'Aye,' said Keira, 'but not today.'

'It's three gold a day to keep it stored and ready to go at short notice. And it'll be more if yer thinking of staying on in yer apartment until the girl's better.'

Keira reached into her pouch of gold. 'Here's fifty for now. Come and see me if we're still in the city when it runs out.'

The woman nodded. 'Been a pleasure doing business with you.' She gestured to her minder. 'Let's go.'

'So I can kick this guy's arse?' Keira said.

'If he kidnapped yer niece,' she said as she was leaving, 'feel free to do worse than that.'

The minder pulled the curtain for her, and they left.

Keira leapt forward before anyone else could move, and swung her fist at Kylon's face, striking his nose. Blood gushed, and he staggered. Kallie drove her heel into the back of his knee, and he toppled over. He reached down to pull his sword from its scabbard, but Keira stood over him and punched him again, unleashing all her strength and rage. Her fist dislocated his jaw and he went down, his head striking the side of a bed pallet on the way to the ground.

'Tie him,' she said, rubbing her bleeding hand. 'I've got a few questions for the fucker.'

Keira paced the wooden floor of their apartment, cursing her strength. Kylon was still unconscious, and hadn't stirred once while they had transported him, Karalyn and all of their belongings back to their rented place in the Kellach quarter. More coins had been spent on arranging the disposal of Baoryn's body, and the entire operation had taken over three hours.

Flora was through in their bedroom, watching over Karalyn. Keira could hear the girl's groans and soft cries, and wondered why she hadn't just killed Kylon. Kallie handed her an ale and a lit weedstick.

She nodded, gazing into Kylon's broken face. She may have scarred his nose for life. It looked swollen and bent to the right, the blood trailing down over the deep bruises under his eyes.

'He's not so pretty now,' Kallie said.

Keira said nothing.

Kallie walked round the chair where they had propped up Kylon, and checked that the ropes were tight. She glanced up at Keira.

'Are ye ever going to wake him?' she said. 'Ye cannae just stand there staring at him all afternoon.'

'What?'

'I said, are ye ever actually going to wake him up?'

'Aye,' she said, frowning. 'Alright.'

She threw her mug of ale over him.

Kylon spluttered, the ale mixing with the blood on his face. His eyes opened a crack and he gazed around the room.

'Where's the child?'

'Safe,' said Keira.

'Baoryn?'

'Dead.'

He closed his eyes, and sobbed.

'This is happening all wrong,' he said.

'Ye've got that right.'

'You being here,' he said, his words slurring, 'is better than I could ever have imagined. It's fate. Kalayne told me to trust that you'd be here, all I had to do was get the child to Plateau City, and you and Shella

443

would find us. You're here, and Shella is surely on her way, just as he foretold.'

He gazed up at her.

'It's all coming true, just like he said.' More tears spilled down his face. 'That's why I left you, during the battle before the walls of this city. Kalayne told me I had to protect the child, and bring her here when the time was right.'

'What's wrong with her?' Keira said.

Kylon paused, and swallowed.

Keira leaned over him, her face inches away. 'What have you done to her?'

Kylon closed his eyes. 'Dullweed.'

Keira and Kallie stared at him.

'You fucking...'

'...prick.'

'Flora!' Keira cried. 'Get yer arse through here.'

The Holdings woman came through to the living room, and Keira glanced over at her.

'We're dealing with dullweed withdrawals,' she said.

'Shit.'

'How long?' Keira asked Kylon.

'Fifteen days,' he whispered.

Flora's face fell. 'She might not make it, Keira. She's dehydrated, and malnourished, and the withdrawal symptoms will only make things worse. Right now, a fever's burning her up, and I don't know what to do.'

'Get a doctor,' Keira said. 'Use whatever gold we have.' She threw the coin pouch to the Holdings woman.

'On it,' she said, clutching the pouch and rushing to the door.

Keira pulled a chair close to Kylon, and sat.

'Why?'

Kylon opened his eyes and gazed at her.

'I'm sorry.'

'Fuck yer apology, ya lowlife piece of crap,' Keira spat. 'Why would ye drug a wee girl?'

'So her mother couldn't find her.'

'Ya sick bastard.'

'I did what had to be done,' he said. 'It pained me, but I had to do it.'

'Fuck you. It's always the same. Ye only do bad shit because it's for the greater good, or so ye believe. Ye've gone too far this time, but. You fucked with my family. There's no coming back from that.'

'Are you going to kill me?'

Keira sat back. 'I don't know.'

Kallie glanced at her. 'Not feeling sorry for this arsehole, are ye?'

'No,' she said, 'but maybe we should keep him for Daphne and Killop. I'm sure they'd want a quick word with him.'

'Aye,' Kallie smiled. 'I'm sure they would.'

CHAPTER 30
CHASE

Hold Stringer, Imperial Holdings – 7th Day, Second Third Winter 507

Killop had never been on a boat upon the Inner Sea, but being in the middle of the Holdings plains, with nothing but an ocean of flatlands surrounding them, made him feel like he could imagine it. He sat at the entrance of the little tent, watching the sun rise in the east. At that moment in Kell, snow would be covering every glen and hillside, but in the Holdings, another warm and cloudless dawn beckoned.

The rays of the sun warmed everything they touched, removing the chill from the air in just a few minutes as the night slipped away, and the new day arrived.

He picked up a leather pouch. It was almost empty, but he took a pinch of tealeaves, and sprinkled them into the bottom of two mugs. He placed them by the fire, where a pot of water was starting to boil.

He lifted his own mug of cold water.

'Happy birthday, wee bear.'

He closed his eyes for a moment and listened to the silence, sending his love to wherever his daughter was.

The tent rustled behind him, and he moved out of the way to let

Chane pass. The Holdings woman crawled outside and slumped down next to him.

'Morning,' he said.

She grunted, and lit a cigarette.

Killop took the pot of water from the low fire and filled the two mugs.

'Tea?'

Chane took a mug, and rubbed her head, her long hair tangled and falling over her face.

He turned and opened the tent.

'Daphne, tea?'

'Coming,' groaned a voice.

She emerged from the tent, her face tired, but her green eyes burning. She kissed him, and sat next to the fire, picking up her mug. Chane offered her a cigarette.

'Thanks.'

'Well,' said Chane, stretching, 'we made it through another day.'

'Not just any day,' Daphne said.

'You're right,' said Chane. 'I almost forgot. It's Karalyn's birthday.'

'I can't believe she's two already,' Daphne said, shaking her head. 'This time last year, we were preparing to leave Slateford.'

'Aye,' Killop said, 'and we had that wee party for her.'

Daphne smiled.

'You can hold the biggest party ever when we find her,' Chane said.

Killop threw some roots into the pot, and put it back onto the fire.

Daphne glanced away, her stomach rumbling. Chane pulled a notepad and pencil from a bag and began scribbling.

'Seventeen miles yesterday,' she said. 'That makes two hundred and eleven altogether, since we left Celine and the others.'

'We're slipping,' Daphne said. 'We need to do over twenty today to catch up.'

'I don't have any maps of this region,' Chane said, 'but I think we're close to the border between Holds Nestor and Stringer. Shit, I've been down this road before, but it was ages ago. I remember passing a large settlement in Hold Stringer, where there were dozens of big tobacco warehouses, and cigarette factories.'

'Wonder if any of it's still standing,' Killop said.

Chane shrugged. 'Hold Stringer wasn't part of the rebellion, so it might have been spared.'

'I don't think the Emperor cares,' Daphne said. 'Every Hold he passed through has been devastated, whether they were with the rebels or not.' She sighed. 'And we should stop calling him the Emperor. It's the Creator, not Guilliam.'

'I know,' said Chane, 'but it's hard to get my head around. I mean, why would god come down to earth?'

Daphne shrugged. 'Maybe he didn't mean to.'

'It would explain why he's so pissed off.'

The women stubbed out their cigarettes.

'Ready?' Killop said, and they nodded.

They packed the tent and belongings up, and Killop slung the large pack over his shoulder. He stamped out the fire, and tucked the boiled roots into his belt. They walked to the road and faced south.

'Will we run for an hour?' Daphne said.

They nodded, and set off.

Killop let his mind wander as they travelled, keeping his eyes on the straight road as it cut across the vast plains. The sun rose higher in the sky, and the day warmed up. They passed empty fields of low stubble for most of the morning, while they alternated between running and walking. At noon, they went under a monumental stone archway across the road.

'Hold Stringer,' said Daphne, as Killop gazed at the enormous blocks of marble.

The crops by the side of the road changed from barley to tobacco, but the fields were as empty as before, the cut stalks of the tobacco plants marking row after row into the distance.

'At least they got the harvest in,' Chane said as they strode down the road.

They slowed as they saw a cluster of cottages and outbuildings ahead. As they approached, they could see the fire damage. The roofs of the houses had gone, and the walls were blackened and scorched. The decomposing bodies of several dogs lay out by the front of the cottages, flies buzzing around them.

They walked on, and rounded the far side of a large burnt-out barn. They stopped. Against the wall of the barn lay over a dozen corpses lined up in a row, their heads missing.

Chane shook her head. 'Why did the Creator make us, if he hates us?'

'He wants to terrorise us,' Daphne said, 'make us too afraid to disobey him again.'

A wind caught up, blowing ash from the barn into their faces. They turned, and continued down the road.

They passed more small settlements, each treated in the same way, with no survivors. As the afternoon wore on, and the sun descended the western sky, they saw a town in the distance. To its left ran a long line of large, low warehouses that took up an area far larger than the town itself.

'Stringerton,' Chane said. 'That's where half the tobacco in the Holdings is stored. Somewhere on the other side of town are the factories.'

Killop squinted. 'Nothing looks damaged from here.'

They walked on, approaching the town. They passed the first buildings, a pair of abandoned cottages, their windows smashed, and front doors wide open. Trails of clothes and household items were scattered across the ground.

The sun dipped to the horizon, and it grew darker.

Around them the town loomed, the empty, silent streets branching from the main road, with dark houses and stone tenement blocks. The seven stars appeared over the eastern horizon, and Killop used their faint light to keep to the road.

'I can't see a thing,' said Chane. 'There's no one here.'

'Wait,' said Killop. 'What was that?'

'I don't know,' Daphne said. 'It sounded like a door closing. Come on.'

They went down a side street bordered by high houses, and a low glow of illumination appeared. They turned a corner, and saw a tavern by the side of the road, light escaping from under its front door.

'Stay where you are,' said a man's voice.

A lamp was un-hooded, and they blinked in its bright light.

'What are you doing here?' the man said.

'We're travelling south,' Daphne said. 'Looking for my daughter.'

'You got any food?' said Chane. 'We've got money.'

There was a long pause.

'You'll have to leave your weapons at the door.'

'Alright.'

The lamp was hooded again, and the tavern door opened. A woman and a man, both with crossbows, came out on to the street. The man glanced around, peering down the dark roads.

'Were you followed?'

'No,' said Daphne.

The man nodded. 'Inside.'

They went through the entrance, the woman ushering them in. The man came in last, and closed the door, sliding a long bolt home. He stared through a slit opening.

'Stack your weapons by the wall,' the woman said.

Daphne nodded, and unbuckled her sword belt. They arranged their swords and knives by the door, and the woman gestured for them to follow. She led them into a large room, lit by dozens of oil lamps, and crowded with Holdings folk. They were sitting round tables eating and drinking, a mixture of the young and the old, many of whom had cross-bows resting against the benches.

'They're armed, I see,' Chane muttered.

'You're the strangers here,' the woman said. 'Sit.'

Killop looked around for seats as many of the folk stared at him.

They moved to the end of a long table, where locals shifted down to give them room on a bench. They sat, and three bowls of broth were placed before them, along with a chunk of bread each.

'Thanks,' Daphne said. 'How much do we owe you?'

'We don't want your money,' the woman said, sitting opposite them among a group of children, who were all eating the same broth. 'What in the Creator's name would we do with it?'

She watched as they ate.

Killop finished his bowl first, and pushed it back. 'Thanks,' he said. 'Is this all that remains of the townsfolk?'

The woman nodded.

'Used to be over a thousand people living here,' an old man said, 'until the damned rebellion.'

'It wasn't the rebels who did this to us,' the woman said. 'Put the blame where it's due.'

'What happened?' said Daphne.

'The Emperor,' the woman said. 'He killed them all.'

'A thousand folk?' said Killop.

The woman nodded, her eyes grim. 'He marched everybody out of the town, to a field by the warehouses. Got them to dig a big hole in the ground, then lined them up and slaughtered them like cattle, while his Rahain soldiers kept anyone from escaping.'

'How did you get away?' said Daphne.

'I wasn't there,' she said. 'I'm a teacher, and I hid in the school cellar with my class.' She glanced at the children sitting by her.

'I saw it,' said a young woman. 'I was lined up with the others at the edge of the pit. The Emperor was standing, raising his hand at the lines of people. There was blood everywhere, coming from people's mouths, and eyes...' She paused. 'I fell into the pit, and a body fell on top of me. They must have thought I was dead too.'

'We found her,' said the man sitting next to her, 'when we went out at night to see what had happened. She was the only one who survived the pit.'

'And the Emperor?' Daphne said.

'He'd gone by nightfall,' the older woman said, 'after his army had ransacked the town for supplies.'

'If he's gone,' said Killop, 'why are you still hiding?'

The woman frowned. 'Two days after they left, some of his army came back. They've occupied the factories on the southern edge of town.'

'Why?'

'There's a full year's crop sitting in the warehouses,' she said. 'They've begun transporting it away south. Must be worth a fortune.'

'The bastards come into town sometimes,' the old man said. 'Root about, looking for food, or anything they didn't steal when they first came through. They know we're here, but leave us alone, so long as we don't interfere with them.'

'How many are there?' Killop said.

'A few hundred, we think,' the woman said.

'Why?' the old man smirked. 'You thinking of taking them on, son?'

'Aye.'

'You'll do no such thing,' the woman said. 'You'll have to promise us, that when you leave tomorrow, you'll go nowhere near the factories. There's a path to the west that we can show you in the morning.'

Daphne nodded. 'I need to ask you something else,' she said. 'Have you seen any other Kellach pass through here since the Emperor left?'

The woman nodded at Killop. 'Is that what he is, a Kellach?'

'Yes.'

She shook her head. 'He's the first one of that kind I've ever seen.'

'The man we're looking for may have been cloaked,' said Daphne. 'Have any other groups of strangers been here?'

'Just a few Holdings,' the woman said. 'Nobody like him.'

'They could have gone around the town,' Chane said, 'especially if they wanted to avoid meeting anyone.'

Daphne nodded.

'You two sound awfully posh,' said the old man. 'Are you cavalry officers or something?'

Daphne glanced at him. 'Used to be.'

'Rebels?' he said, narrowing his eyes.

'Does it matter any more?' Daphne said. 'The Emperor made no distinction when he slaughtered the people of this town. He doesn't care about any of us, and he would have invaded anyway, with or without the rebellion.'

The old man snorted. 'What utter nonsense. The rebels brought this disaster upon us, and each one of them deserves to be hanged.'

Some in the crowded room growled their support at his words, while others looked at the floor.

Daphne stood, her face set firm, and looked around the room.

'I am Holder Fast, leader of the failed rebellion against the insane rule of the Emperor.'

The room fell into silence.

'I'm on my way to the Plateau to rescue my daughter,' she went on, her green eyes shining, 'and then I'm going to kill the Emperor, to avenge the fallen of the Holdings, and to stop him from ever returning.'

She stared at the old man.

'If you want to hang me, come and get me.'

Killop and Chane rose, and stood by her side.

No one moved in the silence, as the townsfolk stared at them.

A child began to cry.

The woman stood.

'Lady Holdfast,' she said, 'we'd be honoured if you and your party would stay with us tonight, but we'll also be happy to see you gone in the morning. By being here, you endanger us all.'

'I'm grateful for the offer,' she said, 'but we'll not be staying. After this is over, we Holdings will have to come back together, and rebuild our country from the ashes up.'

'You'll never stop the Emperor,' cried the old man, 'but if you want to walk right into his arms, I'll not be standing in your way. He'll kill you, Holdfast, and I won't be shedding any tears for the end of your line.'

Daphne smiled. 'We'll see ourselves out.'

They turned and walked for the door, folk parting to get out of their way. They went through to the entrance hall, and picked up their weapons.

'Wasn't expecting you back so soon,' said the man by the front door, rising from his seat.

'Thought it better to avoid any trouble,' Daphne said.

The man frowned.

'Wait,' cried a voice.

They turned, to see a young man rush towards them along the hallway. Killop stepped in front of him.

'Aye?'

'That old man in there doesn't speak for all of us,' he said. 'I'm Mannie, Lady Holdfast.' He bowed. 'And if you like, I can help guide you through the town.'

Killop noticed a slight haze pass over Daphne's eyes.

'Alright,' she said. 'Thanks.'

'I want you back by sunset tomorrow, at the latest,' said the older woman, striding down the hall. She stopped in front of the young man, and patted down his unruly hair.

'Yes, mum,' he said.

'Here,' the woman said, passing a bag to Killop. 'Some food for your journey. Good luck.'

He nodded.

The front door opened, and the man peered outside.

'All clear,' he said.

Daphne shook the woman's hand, then walked out, Chane a step behind her.

'Take care, Mannie,' the woman said, kissing her son.

Killop followed Mannie outside, and the door was closed. Mannie took a small lamp out of his cloak, and opened a side shutter, sending a beam of light shining down the road.

'I'll take you to a house on the edge of town,' he said, 'where you can sleep. It's next to the path that goes round the factories. Follow me.'

They set off. Killop stayed at the rear, keeping his night vision away from the light spilling from the lantern. The streets of the town were silent as they passed down a long, wide road. They took a turn to the right, and after a further ten minutes' walk, Mannie stopped.

He shone his lamp around.

'These are the last houses before the fields start,' he said. 'The road goes west for about three miles, then sweeps south. By the time it reaches the highway, you'll have passed the factories, and the lizards shouldn't see you. Watch out on the road though, they go up and down it with wagons, taking the tobacco harvest away.'

He turned to a row of cottages. 'This is where we'll stay for the night.'

He walked to a low stone-built house and opened the front door. He gestured for them to follow, and they went inside, where Mannie closed the shutters and turned the lamp up full.

Killop gazed around the small living-room.

'You can light a fire,' Mannie said. 'No one will see the smoke out here.'

There was coal sitting in the fireplace, and Killop dropped the two bags to the floor, went over, and knelt by it. The two women sat close to the fire as he lit it, Chane unpacking their blankets while Daphne opened the bag of food.

'Thank your mother for me,' she said to Mannie. 'This should keep us going for a few days.'

Mannie sat by them.

'Are you really going to kill the Emperor?'

'I wondered about that myself,' said Chane, lighting a cigarette.

Daphne laid out her blanket on the floor. 'I think we have to.'

Killop glanced at her in the firelight.

'Otherwise,' she went on, 'he'll destroy us all.'

Killop stepped away from the fire and sat down next to her on the floor.

'I'm going to sleep,' she said, lying down, and pulling a blanket over her.

He watched as she closed her eyes. Was she serious? He lay down next to her.

'Nineteen miles today,' he heard Chane mutter from her chair, as he closed his eyes.

The endless line of wagons stretched into the distance, each one full of slaves. There were nearly a hundred crammed into the wagon where Killop, Bridget and Kallie were chained. Many had died, but there was no way to get the bodies out of the wagon, the steel and wire mesh keeping everything in. The smell was overpowering, and inescapable. Killop closed his eyes, his fingers stroking Kallie's hair as she lay with her head in his lap.

'The ocean,' said Bridget, her voice a whisper.

'We're going to die on this journey,' said Kallie. 'Death is all that's left for us.'

Killop said nothing, despair threatening to crush him.

'Yer wrong,' said Bridget. She attempted to smile from where she sat, squashed up next to Killop and Kallie, her blood-streaked skin inches from them. 'We're going to live, ye fucking hear me?' She rattled her chains. 'These won't last. The three of us sitting here together in this shithole on wheels, we'll make it. I believe it. We've just got to stick together, and help each other...'

A long, low plaintive wail entered Killop's dream, and his surroundings dissolved as it grew louder, shrieking in pain.

Karalyn.

In a second, Daphne's sleeping consciousness was by him.

She's found us, she cried. *Our baby's found us.*

Where is she?

This way.

She soared away, pulling Killop after her, and they flew south, tearing over the plains of the Holdings, the land a blur beneath them. His heart pounded as he heard the voice of his daughter again, crying out to them.

We're coming, wee bear, he growled.

He saw mountains ahead, and they rose up and rushed over the snow-covered peaks. Daphne increased her speed, and after a few moments they cleared the mountains and saw the Plateau spread out in front of them. They heard Karalyn cry out again, and Daphne raced down, towards a city on the shore of the Inner Sea.

The Imperial Capital.

Before Killop had time to think what that could mean, they were inside Karalyn's head, somewhere within the great walls of the city.

Mama.

We're here, Kara-bear, Daphne sobbed.

Help me.

We will, said Killop, aching at the pain his daughter was in.

Her thoughts were fading in and out, as if her mind was on the edge of falling into a deeper unconsciousness, like the one she had been trapped in for days.

We're coming to get you, wee bear.

Daddy, she said, *come soon.*

Can you open your eyes for us, little bear? Daphne said.

Killop watched as Karalyn's eyes opened a crack. Her vision was blurred. A cloth came down, and wiped her face. Her sight focussed on the face of a young Holdings woman as it loomed close.

The woman gasped.

'Get in here,' she shouted. 'She's opened her eyes.'

Two figures appeared at the door, and approached.

Keira and Kallie.

His heart froze. His sister was alive, and she was with Karalyn. He felt Daphne's shock next to his own thoughts.

'She's a wee fighter,' Keira said, her hand stroking away strands of Karalyn's hair from her face.

An older Holdings man, dressed as a physician, approached from the other side of the bed. Karalyn's eyes flickered over as he held out a cup for her.

'Drink this,' he said.

Karalyn's lips touched the cup, and at the same time, the connection to her parents was severed, and their minds hurtled back to their bodies in Stringerton.

Both of them shot upright on the floor by the low fire. They embraced, sobbing, Killop holding her tight. For a long time they sat there, their bodies close, as they wept in silence.

Killop opened his eyes. Chane and the Holdings boy were both sleeping on the big armchairs to either side of the fire. He took Daphne's hand, and they stood. They crept out of the cottage, and Killop gazed up at the seven stars in the night sky, wiping the tears from his face.

'We know where she is,' he said.

'And who she's with,' said Daphne, lighting a cigarette.

'My sister,' he said, shaking his head, 'and Kallie.'

Daphne frowned. 'What are they doing with our daughter?'

'Trying to help her, from what I saw.'

'Kalayne, Kylon, Keira and Kallie?' Daphne spat. 'Tell me this is not some twisted Kell plot.'

'But she's off the dullweed,' Killop said, 'or whatever it was keeping her quiet. And they've got her a healer, that must have been Keira's doing. And we didn't see Kylon anywhere.'

'Of course she's off the dullweed,' Daphne cried. 'They're in Plateau City, ready to do whatever insane plan Kalayne cooked up.'

She clenched her fist, her face dark with rage.

'We need to get there as soon as possible.'

'That's what we've been doing.'

'No,' she said, 'we can go faster. Did that boy in there not say there were wagons going up and down the road? If there are wagons, there will be horses.'

'At the factories?'

'Yes.'

He thought about the promise they had made to stay clear of the Rahain, in case they sought revenge on the townsfolk.

'We should do it now,' he said, 'while there's a few hours of darkness left.'

She nodded.

'What about Chane?' he said.

'I've left her once before,' Daphne said. 'I won't do it again.'

They went back into the cottage. Daphne went to where the boy lay on a chair, and raised her hand.

'That should keep him asleep for a while,' she said.

Killop knelt by the fire and rolled up their blankets, while Daphne crossed the room to Chane. She kicked the chair, and Chane opened her eyes and groaned.

'Up,' she said. 'We've got work to do.'

The first glow of dawn was spreading in the east, lighting up the road as the six horses thundered down it. Far behind them, appearing as tiny wisps on the horizon, tendrils of smoke were rising from the cigarette factory they had raided. By that time, Killop thought, the entire garrison would be out searching for them. At least twenty Rahain soldiers lay dead, and over a dozen wagons had been destroyed, along with crates of food supplies and weapons.

As the sun rose, Daphne slowed her mount to a walk. Chane and Killop did the same, and they trotted three abreast, each trailing a spare horse connected to their saddles with ropes.

'We'll let these three cool down,' Daphne said, 'then we'll swap over.'

Chane nodded.

'Are ye alright to take a quick look back,' said Killop, 'just in case they're following us?'

'I've already checked,' Daphne said. 'No one's on the road.'

'The town?' said Chane.

Daphne nodded. 'Soldiers have gone in.'

'Shit. I hope those people are alright.'

Killop caught Daphne's glance, but they said nothing.

After a few minutes, Daphne halted, and they dismounted. They began to switch their packs over from the spare horses.

'We need to talk about Keira,' said Killop.

Daphne nodded, her eyes narrow.

'I know you're worried,' he said, 'but my sister would never do anything to hurt Karalyn, or allow anyone else to hurt her.'

'She's a sadistic maniac,' Daphne said, fitting the saddle to her spare horse. 'She's slaughtered thousands without remorse. Forgive me if I don't share your optimism.'

They walked their spare horses to the front, and remounted.

'You're wrong,' he said, gathering the reins, and securing the rope of the horse trailing behind.

'Yeah?'

'Aye. This is different.'

'How?'

They began to trot down the road, the sun's rays shining onto the plains and warming the land.

'Keira gets it,' he said. 'It's family.'

She glanced at him, kicked her heels, and they took off down the road.

CHAPTER 31
FOUR MAGES

Southern Plateau – 13th Day, Second Third Winter 507

'This is a lovely part of the world,' Laodoc said from the wagon's bench, as they travelled down the narrow path. On their left a steep cliff rose, but to their right they had a grand view over the rolling foothills of the Plateau. They had followed a river from close to its source, where it had emerged as a patch of boggy ground, before widening as the miles went by. According to their map, it meandered all the way across the Plateau, before emptying into the Inner Sea.

'At least the snow's gone,' Shella said. 'Hate the stuff. It's still freezing, though.'

'It's warmer here than it was in Silverstream,' Bridget said, sitting in the empty space at the back of the cart. 'Fuck knows what it'll be like further north when summer comes.'

Shella smirked. 'I can't wait to see you Kellach savages sweating your asses off. Even Plateau City's roasting in summer. The Holdings will be like a furnace.'

'I'm looking forward to it,' said Agang, walking alongside the wagon. 'All this cold down south, it's not for me.'

'Will our skin turn dark like the Holdings folk?' asked Dean, from the other side of the wagon.

Shella frowned at him.

'No,' said Laodoc, 'though you might tan a little.'

Shella laughed. 'Yeah, Dean. You'll go bright pink.'

Laodoc shook his head. 'That's where you're wrong, Shella. The Kellach Brigdomin don't sunburn. It might be something to do with their healing powers, but I never saw a single one with burns when we were last in the city.'

'Fucksake,' Shella said. 'Those big bastards get all the breaks.'

'The poor wee Rakanese,' Dyam smirked, as she walked along beside them. 'Shit eyesight, shit hearing, keep catching stupid wee diseases like colds, whatever the fuck they are, being short, not able to eat loads of stuff in case ye get poisoned...?'

'Come on,' said Shella, 'there must be some poison that'll kill you.'

'I don't believe there is,' said Laodoc. 'Back when Bridget was my captive in the Rahain Capital, a professor belonging to my research institute once tried to prove it.' He glanced at the Brig woman. 'Do you remember?'

'Aye,' she said, rolling her eyes.

'I was unaware at the time that the experiment was going ahead, but I read the results afterwards,' he went on. 'The professor administered a dose of cyanide to Bridget and Killop that should have killed them in seconds. She had a hypothesis that the Kellach constitution would be able to expel it before death occurred, and she was proved right.'

Shella stared at him.

'You experimented on them? Like animals?'

'We did. We believed at the time that the Kellach were inferior beings. Some argued that they were barely sentient, and unfit for anything other than manual labour.'

Bridget laughed. 'Charming, eh?'

'You seem surprisingly okay about it,' Shella said.

'There's no point dwelling on it now,' Bridget shrugged. 'Past is past, and anyway, Laodoc was quick to realise the error of his ways.'

'Indeed,' he said. 'In fact, my sympathy for them led to my downfall at the time. We did some good work, once they'd been moved to better accommodation and the physical experiments ceased. We wrote volumes of research on Kellach culture and history.'

'I have a small confession to make about that,' Bridget said, stifling a laugh.

He frowned.

'We might have made a lot of that up,' she said.

Shella sniggered.

Laodoc said nothing.

'It was me and Kallie, mostly,' Bridget said. 'We had a right laugh inventing stuff for your book.'

Laodoc's tongue flickered as the two women chuckled.

'But why?'

'There were things we didn't want you to know about,' she said, 'in case the Rahain used it against us. We were your captives, and you were going on about getting your book published. We didn't want all your folk knowing our secrets.'

'What secrets?' said Shella.

'Oh, about fire mages and the existence of sparkers. And stuff about being twins, and what that meant to us.'

'Twins?' said Agang.

'Aye,' she said, her smile fading. 'It seemed so important to us back then, but it means nothing any more. It's all gone.'

'What does it mean, though?'

Bridget turned to him. 'All Kellach Brigdomin are twins, well, most of us. There are the odd few singles about, like Dyam.'

'So you have a twin?' Agang said.

'No,' Bridget said, 'I'm different again. I was part of triplets. I had two sisters, who were identical. We were all born on the same day, but.'

'Had?'

Bridget nodded. 'Both died in the war.'

'Sorry,' said Shella.

Bridget shrugged. 'Seems a long time ago now. And most of the other Kellach survivors, the same thing happened to them. I doubt that many twins are still together, except maybe in the deepest glens of the Domm Highlands.'

'It'll return,' Laodoc said, 'once new generations are born.'

'Aye,' she said, 'as long as the Emperor never goes down to Domm, and the folk there are safe.'

Agang frowned. 'Would I be right in saying that Killop and Keira are twins?'

'Aye,' Bridget said, 'and ye could see it, whenever they worked together, like two halves of the same person, even though they're completely different.'

'That doesn't make any sense,' laughed Shella.

'I know,' Bridget said, 'but the fact that they're both mages only adds to it. A thrower and a sparker together, the two sides of Pyre's gift. That's what we believed, anyway.'

'A sparker?' said Agang.

'Aye,' Bridget said, 'someone who can generate fire from nothing. Keira can throw fire that's already there, but she can't make it. Only a sparker can do that.'

'Did you know this?' said Agang to Laodoc. 'This is all new to me.'

'Killop never told me anything himself,' he said, 'but I had a fair inkling, from listening to people talk in Slateford.'

'I knew,' said Shella. 'Daphne told me about Killop, and Bedig told me about twins.'

Laodoc glanced at Bridget, but the Brig woman didn't react.

'So the Kellach mage powers are split between twins?' Agang said. 'Do you think the Emperor possesses both?'

'You were the one who was there,' said Bridget, 'you saw him.' She turned to Shella. 'You did, too.'

'I saw him throw fire,' said Agang. 'He destroyed the Sanang regiments that had breached the city walls by hurling balls of fire at them.'

'The Kellach mage he killed in the ritual,' said Shella, 'she was a thrower. That's what she told me anyway, while we were all in a cell together.' She shook her head. 'She was crazy. She actually volunteered, can you believe that? She gave herself up to the Emperor, even though the Kellach in the city were trying to hide her from the One True Path.'

Bridget gazed out at the vast land to their right, the foothills undulating in the morning sunshine.

'Do you remember her name?'

'Lilyann,' said Shella. 'Young. In her teens, I would guess.'

Dean let out a cry, and wept, putting his head in his hands. Dyam strode over, reaching her arm over his shoulder.

'Lilyann?' said Bridget.

'You knew her?' said Shella.

'Aye.'

Dyam looked up. 'She was the fire mage that fought under Killop at the battle for the gates of the Rahain Capital. She practically won the war for the alliance.'

Bridget's eyes hardened. 'Then the religious fanatics from the Holdings poisoned her mind.' She glanced at Dean. 'They tried to get to him, too.'

Shella pulled on the reins, bringing the wagon to a halt, as Dean remained standing, tears flooding down his cheeks.

She glanced at Bridget. 'Were they...?'

Bridget shook her head. 'Just friends. We found them in a camp for slave children in the Rahain highlands, where the authorities had forgotten all about them. That prison was all they'd known for years.'

Laodoc clenched his fist. 'How I wish I could undo the evil that my nation brought to yours, my Kellach Brigdomin friends. How I wish I could erase the past few years and start again.' He paused, tears coming to his eyes. 'I'm so sorry.'

Bridget leaned forward and embraced him as he began to weep.

'It's alright, ya auld lizard,' she said, patting him on the back.

'It's not though, is it?' said Dyam, her pale blonde hair blowing in the breeze. 'Our folk might survive, if we defeat the Emperor, but we'll never be the same.'

'None of us will,' said Shella. 'Let's face it, even if the Emperor hadn't gained all his new powers, we were probably going to kill each other anyway.'

'I wonder what he's been doing?' said Agang. 'It's been nearly a year since I fled the imperial capital with Keira. We know he attacked Rainsby, but what else has he done in our absence?'

'Gathering more mages, I'd guess,' Shella said. 'That's what Kalayne said he'd be doing. So he could try again.'

'Then he could be anywhere,' Bridget said. 'Pyre's arsecrack, we're unprepared.'

Laodoc frowned. 'Maybe we should go to the imperial city first,' he said, 'and learn what's been going on in the empire, before we do anything else.'

'We have to find Daphne Holdfast's daughter,' Agang said. 'The most obvious place to start looking is in the Holdings. Besides, we're bound to hear word on the road about what's been going on, once we get down to the Plateau, at any rate.'

'Traveller's gossip?' Laodoc said. 'Damn it, how I wish we had a vision mage with us.' He glanced around, his frown turning into a crooked smile. 'It's the only one we're missing. We're one mage short of a ritual.'

Shella shook her head at him. 'I keep forgetting that you're one too.'

'A poorer specimen you'd be hard put to find,' he said. 'I can make sand quiver, well I could, it's been forty years since I tried that particular party trick.'

Dyam ruffled Dean's hair, and glanced up to Shella. She pulled on the reins, and the wagon moved off again. They continued along the path as it descended the side of the hills. After a mile, the view of the Plateau was lost as they entered a narrow gorge.

It grew dark in the shadows of the steep cliffs, and the path became wet and slippery from water running down the rocks. Ahead, Laodoc noticed the opening of a cave.

'Are we going through there?'

'Yeah,' said Shella. 'This is the reason I couldn't find the pass when I came south from the Plateau. The cave goes through a spur of the mountain, and emerges under a waterfall. You could walk right up to it from the other side, and never know there was a tunnel there.'

She took a lamp from under the driver's bench, and lit it as they entered the cave. The walls were smooth, as if the tunnel had been formed by flowing water many years before. The way was narrow, and the others on foot had to go ahead of the wagon. Shella attached the lamp to a short post by her side, and they travelled on, the only sound coming from the clipping of the stones under the gaiens' clawed feet. The tunnel descended at a gradual pace, and after twenty minutes, they began to hear the roar of water. Shella extinguished the lamp as a circle of shimmering grey appeared.

'The waterfall,' she said. 'Through there's the Plateau.'

Agang looked up at them. 'We should scout the way first.'

'I'll go,' said Lola.

'Alright,' said Bridget. 'We'll wait for ye.'

The Lach woman took her longbow from the wagon, and pulled it free from its covering. She picked up a quiver of arrows, nodded to Bridget, and set off for the waterfall without a word. She squeezed to the left of the tunnel, where the falling torrent was lighter, and disappeared through the curtain of water.

'Four mages sat here,' said Shella, 'and we send someone without powers.'

'Lola's a good scout,' Bridget said. 'It's her job, it's why we brought her.'

'I hope you're paying her well.'

Bridget laughed. She stopped, as she noticed the look on Dean's face.

'Sorry about Lilyann,' she said. She climbed down from the wagon. 'Here. It's your turn, anyway.'

Dean clambered up, and huddled down among the crates and sacks of supplies, as Bridget stretched her limbs.

'So are there farms and shit in this part of the Plateau?' she said.

'I passed a couple,' said Shella, 'though I gave them a wide berth.'

'Our half of the Plateau has been sparsely populated since the old

wars with the Holdings ended,' Laodoc said. 'The opening of the Great
Tunnel through the Grey Mountains was meant to herald a new wave
of settlement. Instead, it merely allowed the alliance army to reach
Rahain quicker.'

'It's the same in the Holdings half,' Agang said. 'My information
said that there would be farms and towns, but it was mostly deserted.'

'Such a waste,' Shella said. 'It's all good land. If we'd been allowed
to settle there, then the Migration would have succeeded. The Holdings
and the Rahain were just too greedy, though. Neither side wanted us
anywhere near them.'

Bridget nodded, then glanced up at Laodoc. 'I'm starting to feel a bit
bad about inventing all that stuff for yer book.'

'I understand why you did it,' he sighed. 'I can see why you wouldn't
want your secrets read out in every school and academy in Rahain, but
I admit it does hurt a little. Simiona spent many days working on it, and
I know how much it meant to her.'

'When this is all over,' she said. 'We'll get a few bottles of whisky, sit
down together, and do it properly. For Simiona. We'll dedicate it to her
memory.'

'I would like that.'

Dyam snorted. 'If ye want it done properly, then don't listen to
anything she tells ye. I taught Kellach history and culture in Slateford's
schoolhouse. I'll help.'

'Thank you.'

'She'll just tell ye about how great she thinks the Domm are,'
Bridget said. 'Those conceited arseholes are always forgetting about the
rest of us.'

'Aye?' smirked Dyam. 'And what is there to know about Brig, except
that they reek of sheep shit, and their ale's crap?'

Laodoc smiled. 'I'll need to ask Lola about the Lach, then. And later,
someone with the Kell point of view.'

'Ye'll have Killop for that,' Bridget said, 'when we finally meet up
with him. Though watch out; the Kell are up their own arses almost as

much as the Domm.' She shook her head. 'They think they're special. Keira's a prime example, and Kylon wasn't far behind.'

Shella raised an eyebrow. 'You're all just barbarian giants who live in caves and eat dung as far as I'm concerned. Kylon was alright, though. I even fancied him a tiny bit.'

'That moody bastard?' laughed Bridget.

'I did say a tiny bit, I wasn't infatuated or anything. But unlike the rest of you, at least he had some dress sense. And washed occasionally. And, you know, brushed his hair more than once a third.'

Bridget and Dyam frowned at her.

'Yer a right cheeky wee cow,' Dyam said, 'for a shortarse.'

'She's just jealous,' Bridget said. 'She wishes she was Kellach.'

'Yeah, right,' said Shella. 'Great lumbering oafs that stink of alcohol, whose every second word is fuck?'

'Better than maggot-eating swamp frogs,' Bridget said. 'Can yer tongue catch flies?'

'Got a problem with flies, have you? Maybe you should take a bath.'

'Bloody women,' muttered Agang. 'Always bickering.'

'Shut it, ya monkey-arsed reject,' said Bridget.

'Yeah,' smirked Shella, 'when we want your opinion we'll ask for it, ape-boy.'

'I wouldn't interfere,' said Laodoc, glancing at Agang as he seethed. 'I seem to recall that the Kellach Brigdomin use insults as a form of endearment. The worse the epithet, the more they like you, or so I believe.'

'Yer arse,' said Dyam.

'As for Shella,' Laodoc went on, 'she derives a curious pleasure from seeing how far she can push people. If you rise to her bait, then she'll come back again and again for more.'

'You're a wise old lizard sometimes.' Shella said, 'though mostly, like now, you're just a pain in the ass.'

A wry smile settled on his lips as Shella, Bridget and Dyam laughed.

'I hope Lola's back soon,' muttered Agang.

Two hours later, the bottom-left corner of the waterfall shimmered and Lola walked through, her clothes and hair drenched.

'How'd it go?' asked Bridget.

'Not great.'

She reached into a sack on the back of the wagon, and took out a wrapped chunk of ryebread. She tore off a piece and shoved it in her mouth.

'Well?' said Agang.

She turned to him.

'They're waiting for us.'

'Who?' said Laodoc.

'Imperials. About a company or so of Holdings troopers. They've been up here, scouting round the waterfall, but they didn't see the tunnel. I saw tracks outside and followed them down the hill. They're camped about three miles from here.'

'Can we go round them?' said Bridget.

'Not if we want to keep the wagon,' Lola said, chewing the bread. 'We could climb, and take a detour to the west, but there's no way the gaien will be going up those slopes.'

'So we lose the wagon and walk to the Holdings,' said Agang, 'or we fight.'

'We can't fight a whole company of troopers,' said Laodoc.

'You know,' said Shella, 'I suppose I could go down there and kill them all.'

The others quietened.

'If you want,' she said.

'Alone?' said Bridget.

'Well, I'd want a couple of you with me, to give me cover,' Shella said, 'but you can leave the killing to me.'

'I'll go,' said Agang. 'I'll need to borrow one of the Kellach's shields.'

'Take Dean's,' said Dyam. 'It's not like he knows how to use it.'

Laodoc glanced at the boy, but he said nothing, his gaze on the floor of the wagon.

'I'll come as well,' said Lola. 'I know the way.'

'Alright then,' said Shella, sighing. 'Holdings, eh? I hope they have some cigarettes on them. I'll be needing one later.'

'Wait,' said Laodoc. 'Is this the right thing to do? These soldiers have probably been conscripted, and sent out far from their homes and families. It's not their fault the Emperor is evil.' He bowed his head. 'If it weren't for me, we wouldn't even need a wagon. I'm the one who'll slow us down if we have to walk, and so I cannot help but feel responsible if you slaughter these Holdings youths.'

'Don't worry, old man,' said Shella, touching his arm, 'there's no way I'm walking to the Holdings.'

She jumped down to the ground and strode forwards. Agang took a shield from the back of the wagon, and he and Lola followed the Rakanese mage.

Shella turned.

'We'll be back in a couple of hours,' she shouted over the roar of the waterfall.

Laodoc nodded, and Shella went through the curtain of water, followed by Agang and Lola.

Bridget and Dyam glanced at each other, while Dean remained silent in the back of the wagon.

'That's fucked up,' said Bridget.

'No shit,' said Dyam.

Two hours passed, and Shella had not returned.

Dyam had kicked Dean out of the wagon, and was sleeping in the back, while Bridget sat up on the driver's bench, next to Laodoc. Dean had disappeared, though Laodoc suspected the boy was sulking in some dark corner of the cavern.

'I hope he's all right,' Laodoc said. 'The boy.'

'What, Dean?' Bridget said. 'He shouldn't have come. It's my fault, I should've been firmer at the start, and said no.'

'Don't blame yourself, Bridget,' he said. 'I was there too, and I didn't

471

object to him coming along either. You and Dyam, you've tried your best for him, but the boy's not suited to magehood.'

'He's too sensitive,' Bridget said. 'Needs to find a nice lassie and settle down.'

They heard a noise from the waterfall, and turned to see Lola emerge into the cavern.

'It's done,' she said.

Bridget and Laodoc glanced at each other.

'Shella...?'

'She killed them all, just like she said she would,' Lola said, shaking her head. 'It was quite a sight.'

Bridget nudged Dyam awake.

'We're going,' she said, then gazed around the cavern. 'Dean?'

Dyam rubbed her head and sat up. 'Where is that boy?'

'He's down at the Holdings camp,' said Lola. 'I thought you'd sent him.'

'No,' said Bridget, frowning, 'we didn't.'

Dyam clambered down from the wagon, and pulled a tarpaulin over the crates and sacks.

'That should keep it dry,' she said.

Bridget yanked on the reins, and the two gaien began to lumber towards the waterfall. Lola and Dyam slipped through first on foot, then Laodoc and Bridget closed their eyes and went through. The roar of the water was deafening, and the torrent soaked them as they passed out of the cavern. The wheels of the wagon climbed up a bank, and Laodoc looked around.

The waterfall fed a sparkling stream that flowed to their right, while around was a forest of tall conifers mixed with spruce. The ground was sloping away in front of them, and a track wound its way down the mountainside. Above them, the sky was blue, with patches of white clouds. Bridget shook her head, spraying water over Laodoc as she laughed.

'Welcome to the Plateau,' smirked Lola, from where she leant against a tree. 'This way.'

Lola set off down the track, as Dyam climbed back up onto the wagon, pouring the pools of water from the tarpaulin onto the ground. Bridget pulled on the reins, and they took off, following Lola down the hillside.

Laodoc scanned the ground ahead, but the trees were too thickly spread for him to see much. The ground was piled in brown pine needles, and the wagon was gouging deep ruts in the mud. They carried on down the track for an hour, the gaien slow and awkward on the slope. As they reached an area of flatter ground, Lola turned to them.

'I should warn ye,' she said, 'the camp's just up ahead. It's not too pretty in there. And there's something else.'

'What?' said Bridget.

'Shella and Agang, they took a prisoner,' Lola said. 'Some Holdings mage-priest that was with the troopers. They were... questioning him in his tent when I left.'

'And Dean?' said Dyam.

'The lad was in there with them.'

Bridget flicked the reins, and they carried on. At the base of a tree, Laodoc caught sight of the first bodies, a pair of Holdings sentries, streams of blood running from their eye sockets. They went another hundred yards, and passed a low embankment marking the edge of the square-shaped camp. On the other side of the bank, the scale of the carnage became clear. Dozens of bodies littered the ground, men and women in imperial uniforms. Some were in full armour, while others were half-naked, lying dead at the entrances of their tents.

Laodoc's tongue flickered as the wagon stopped, the path ahead blocked by corpses. They climbed down, and made their way on foot towards the large command tent where Lola was leading them. They stepped over and around the bodies. Laodoc tried not to look at their faces, but his sight was drawn. Each had been killed in the same way as the sentries; their eyes gone, the hollow sockets raw, red holes in their faces. Blood streaked their uniforms and the sides of the tents pitched in rows, and had formed into pools on the ground.

'Fucksake,' he heard Bridget mutter, as they passed a low campfire. It was still burning, and around it lay the bodies of a dozen troopers, some still clutching bowls of food in their dead hands.

They walked past two dead guards and into the command tent. Inside were tables and chairs, and a row of low camp beds. Bodies lay scattered where they had fallen. At the end of the tent, Laodoc saw Shella and Agang. They were standing in front of a man who had been tied to a chair. His head was lolling forwards, a blindfold covering his eyes, his face a red pulp.

'Shall I heal him again?' said Agang.

'Nah,' said Shella. 'He's given us everything he's got.' She clicked her fingers, and the man in the chair made a choking noise, and his head fell forwards.

Bridget walked up to the figure in the chair, as Shella and Agang turned.

Dyam snarled as she spotted Dean, sitting in the corner, his eyes transfixed on the body.

'Get out of here,' she said. 'This is no place for a bairn.'

'What?' he said, looking up. 'And out there's better?'

Bridget frowned at Shella and Agang.

'Yer a pair of sick wee bastards.'

'Didn't know you were so sensitive,' said Shella.

'We got a lot of information out of him,' said Agang, 'some good, some not so.'

Laodoc said nothing.

'I'm going to clear the road,' said Bridget, 'so we can get out of here as fast as possible.'

She left the tent.

'We'll help,' said Dyam, grabbing Dean by the collar, and hauling him out after her.

Shella lit a cigarette, her fingers red.

'Don't look at me like that,' she said.

'I wasn't aware I was looking at you in any particular fashion, madam mage,' Laodoc said.

'Yeah, right,' she said. 'You think I'm a cold-blooded bitch.'

'Why would he think that?' said Agang. 'We were only doing what was required. I don't see the problem.'

She glanced at him. 'Maybe in Sanang the torturing of prisoners is routine, but Laodoc lives to a higher standard. It's fine. Let him have his moment of moral superiority. He'll still benefit from what we learned.'

Agang frowned. 'Say something, my friend.'

Laodoc let out a long breath. 'I don't know what to say. My heart is burning with a fierce mixture of anger and disappointment, and guilt, at my part in this.'

'Grow up,' said Shella, heading for the entrance to the tent.

Agang stood for a moment in silence, then followed her out. Laodoc gazed at the body of the dead Holdings mage-priest. He should be feeling glad at the death of an enemy, a member of the church that had brought ruin to his country, but he felt nothing but emptiness.

He felt a hand on his shoulder.

'Bridget?' he said.

'Come on,' she said, 'I've got something to show you.'

She took his hand and they left the tent. She led him through the rear of the camp, until they came to a clearing where the others were standing.

Laodoc's mouth opened. Ahead of them was a paddock, where a dozen winged gaien were chained to posts. Beyond them stood a row of flying carriages.

Shella nudged Agang. 'Told you he'd be happy.'

'See, my friend,' Agang said, 'with one of these, we could be in Plateau City in days.'

'Plateau City?' said Laodoc.

'Yeah,' said Shella. 'It's time to kill the Emperor.'

He glanced at her. 'But what about Daphne's child? Don't we need her protection?'

'Not any more,' Agang said. 'Not from what the priest told us.'

'Let's go back a bit first,' Shella said. 'You were right, Laodoc, about Sami. The Emperor read his mind, and found out about Silverstream.

He sent these guys out to try to find it, and the mage-priest had to report back to the Emperor regularly. Now, do you want to know what the Emperor's been doing since he got his powers?'

'Indeed,' said Laodoc.

She lit another cigarette. 'He took a Holdings army into Arakhanah City, and annihilated half of my people.'

'Oh Shella, I'm sorry,' Laodoc said.

She shook her head, suppressing her tears. 'He took every mage he could find, but they committed suicide, so in a rage, he burned the city to the ground, then broke the sea walls and flooded it.'

'It gets worse,' said Agang.

'How?'

'After Rakana, he took a Rahain army into the Holdings, after the Holdfasts organised a rebellion against his rule.'

'The Holdfasts?' said Bridget. 'Daphne's family?'

'Yes,' said Agang, 'acting with others. The Emperor has only recently returned to Plateau City, leaving the Holdings in smoking ruins.'

'And Daphne?' said Laodoc. 'Do we know anything of her?'

'The Emperor destroyed her family,' he said, 'then chased her through the mountains. She fell off a cliff and is presumed to be dead.'

The others stood in silence.

'I don't believe it,' Shella said. 'Not Daphne. She's alive.'

'Maybe,' said Agang, 'maybe not.'

'And Karalyn?'

'The priest didn't know,' said Agang.

'This is grim news indeed,' Laodoc said, 'but it doesn't explain why you want to go to Plateau City. Shouldn't we be looking for Daphne?'

'Because now's our only chance,' said Shella. 'The Emperor's weak after using so much power in such a short time. He over-reached, and exhausted himself. He's locked up in his fortress in Plateau City, trying to recover.'

'If we hit him now,' said Agang, 'we have a chance. But if we wait, he'll grow strong enough to undertake another ritual. He has all the mages he needs, but he's too weak to do anything about it. We must strike now.'

Bridget frowned. 'And how would the priest know all that?'

'Like Shella said before,' Agang said, 'he was in regular contact with the Emperor. There aren't many mages of his calibre left, he must have been high up in the imperial government. He was entrusted with finding Shella.'

'And how long will the Emperor take to recover?' said Laodoc.

'He'll be back on his feet within a third,' Shella said. 'If we fly, we could be there in under ten days.'

'We get as close as possible to the fortress,' said Agang, 'then get inside, and destroy him.'

'Alright,' said Bridget. 'We've come this far, let's finish it.'

'One question,' said Dyam. 'Does anyone know how to fly one of those things?'

They all turned to Laodoc.

'Me?' he said.

'Come on,' said Shella, 'surely you know?'

'Well,' he said, 'I did some basic training, but it was a long time ago, when I was in the army.'

'You were in the army?'

'Yes,' he smiled. 'Fifty years ago.'

Shella laughed.

'Let's hope you've got a good memory.'

CHAPTER 32
THE NIGHT BEFORE

Outside Plateau City, Imperial Plateau – 18th Day, Second Third Winter 507

Three horses had died on the way to the imperial capital. Killop had lamed two, and the third had slipped and broken a leg while being ridden by Chane. Daphne had put all three out of their misery, before cutting long strips off their flesh. They had dried out in the sunlight, and Daphne, Killop and Chane had eaten little else in days.

Daphne slowed her mount to a walk as they approached an abandoned farmstead, four miles from the city. She slung her leg over the saddle and dismounted by a long water trough, tying the reins to a post as the horse drank from the muddy rainwater.

Chane and Killop followed her lead. Killop groaned as he landed, rubbing his back.

Daphne smiled at him. 'We made it,' she said. 'There should be no more riding for a bit.'

'My arse will be grateful,' he said. He gazed up at the sky. 'It'll be dark soon. Will we head straight to the city?'

'Not yet,' said Daphne. 'We've no idea what we're walking into. I'll need to scout the city to find out where Karalyn is, and to do that, I'll need to rest.'

Killop nodded. He pulled down the pack from where it was secured by his saddle, and they walked into the empty farmhouse. Half of the roof had collapsed, and there were birds nesting in the beams. Chane kicked off her boots and fell into a creaky old chair.

'I've never felt so knackered,' she said.

Killop unpacked food onto a table.

Chane flinched at the sight. 'I can't face having horse again. Seven days.'

She glanced at Killop as he began raking through the kitchen cupboards.

'Don't know why you're bothering. This place has been ransacked by every army that's passed through in the last few years. To be honest, I'm shocked there's any furniture left.'

Killop shrugged. 'You never know.'

Daphne listened to them from where she stood by a broken window, her gaze on the grassy hillside in front of the farmstead. Somewhere on the other side was Karalyn, and the Emperor. She bit her lip. This was happening. She was going to walk into the heart of the empire... and do what? Rescue her daughter, but then what? Her mind told her to flee. Snatch Karalyn, run north back to the Holdings, and hide. Hide forever.

'Ha!' cried Killop. He glanced at Chane. 'Tea. No good to me, but I'll put some water on to boil for you.'

'Nice one,' said Chane.

'The armies that passed through were Sanang,' said Daphne. 'I guess they had no use for tea.'

'I'm surprised they didn't try to smoke it.'

'They probably did.' She glanced at Chane. 'How you feeling about the dullweed? It's been a while.'

Chane shrugged. 'I'm still functioning, I suppose. What about you? I bet you wish you had some keenweed.'

'I've told you,' she said, 'it helps with the vision powers.'

'If you say so.'

'There's no point in arguing,' Daphne said. 'We haven't got any, and that's that.'

Chane picked up the sack and took out a pack of cigarettes.

'We do have plenty of these though,' she said.

Daphne walked over, and took one. Chane lit hers and Daphne's as Killop got a stove burning, a small pot of water sitting on the flame.

'What about you, big man?' Chane said. 'You must be missing the booze. I know I am.'

Killop shrugged.

'Maybe we can find a drink in the city,' Chane said.

'Forget it,' Daphne said. 'We can't afford to screw this up.'

'I meant pick up a few bottles for later,' she said, 'for when it's safe again.'

'Safe again?' Daphne said. 'It'll only be safe again if we kill the Emperor.'

Chane puffed out her cheeks. 'You need to think this through. You know the only way to get close to the Emperor is by using Karalyn to shield you.'

'No,' she said. 'There must be another way.'

'You let me know when you think of one,' Chane said. 'Until then, it's a crazy idea.'

Killop brought over two mugs of hot tea.

'Thanks,' Daphne said, taking a sip.

The tea was stale, and bitter without any sugar, but it was still the best thing Daphne had tasted in many days. She leaned against the table, smoking and drinking. She surged a small thread of battle-vision, and felt her energy return. She gazed over at the window. It was getting dark outside, and the interior of the farmhouse was bathed in shadow.

She stubbed out her cigarette and took a long breath.

'I'm ready,' she said.

Chane tossed her the pack of cigarettes.

'Thanks. I'll be back soon.'

She kissed Killop, and left through the front door. She passed the horses and continued up the long grassy slope to the top of the bank. In the far distance was the city, discernible with her vision-enhanced eyesight as a faint blur on the horizon. She sat down on the bank, and focussed. She longed to see Karalyn, but knew that the search could take a while. She remembered the look of the building from when she had dream-visioned there before, but it was in a street she hadn't recognised, and she didn't know the exact location.

Over the ten days since discovering Karalyn's whereabouts, Daphne had joined her mind to her daughter's on only three more occasions. The other times, Karalyn had either been too sick to reach out with her powers, or too feverish and confused to make any sense. In all that time, Daphne had caught only glimpses of life within the apartment where she was recovering,

Her vision soared up from her body, and crossed the miles of grassy plains to the walls of the great city. The gates by the New Town were sealed shut, with soldiers up on the gatehouse towers. She moved south, past the gate leading to the cathedral and merchants' quarter, which was also closed and guarded. She came to the breach in the walls that Keira had created, and Daphne marvelled at the power Killop's sister possessed to have caused such destruction. Barricades had been constructed across the hole in the wall, and at least two companies of Rahain soldiers in imperial uniforms were stationed just behind.

She went further south, and came to a stretch of wall she had never seen before, jutting out past where the old Kellach camp had been. A large gate stood there, but it too was closed and guarded. New towers flanked the river, and a large area had been walled in on the other side. A heavy steel gate lay across the flowing water, and soldiers patrolled the walled banks.

Daphne paused, stunned. There was no way in. She hadn't realised how much the city had changed in her absence. They would have to wait for dawn, and try to walk in.

She pulled her vision up, and over the wall into the Kellach quarter, where she guessed Keira's building was most likely to be. It lay quiet and still beneath her, full of empty tenements and abandoned or burnt-out shops. A few pockets of life lit up the dark district of the city, where the remnants of the Kellach population lived alongside Holdings squatters.

In the distance, she recognised the large tenement block where Karalyn was being held.

It was time to confront Keira.

Daphne pushed her vision through a gap in the shutters of Karalyn's bedroom. She smiled. Her daughter was up, playing with the young Holdings woman who had been caring for her. Daphne sent her vision through to the living room, where Keira was sitting alone, smoking and looking out of a window. Daphne entered her head. She looked out through the Kell woman's eyes, and projected an image of herself onto the glass.

'Hello, Keira,' she said.

Keira's eyes widened. She looked over her shoulder, and Daphne moved her image round, so that she appeared to be standing in front of the Kell woman.

'Who are you? And how the fuck did you get in?'

'I'm Daphne Holdfast, and I'm not really here. I'm in your head.'

Keira reached out her hand, and her fingers passed through the image.

Her jaw hung open.

'How did ye find me?'

'Through Karalyn,' Daphne said.

'The bairn?'

'Did you not know she has mage powers?' frowned Daphne.

'No, why the fuck would I?'

'That's why Kylon took her,' Daphne said. 'She's like Kalayne.'

'Really?'

'So,' Daphne said, 'what exactly are you doing with my daughter, Keira?'

Keira picked up a bottle from the floor by her feet and took a long swig.

'This is mental,' she said. 'You can make yerself appear wherever ye want?

'Karalyn,' Daphne said. 'What do you and Kylon want with her?'

Keira frowned. 'What are you on about? What do I want with her? I fucking saved her life. Aye, me. That wee prick Kylon had her strung out on dullweed, and was slowly killing her. For ten days now, me, Kallie and wee Flora have been looking after her. Fucksake, more than once I thought she was going to die on us, but she pulled through. She's a wee fighter. And now you come and accuse me of... what the fuck are ye accusing me of?'

Daphne paused. She knew Keira was telling the truth.

'Thank you for looking after her.'

Keira smirked. 'That's better, hen. So I'm guessing ye thought me and Kylon were working together or something. Well, come and see this.'

She got to her feet and walked to a door of the living room. She unlocked it, and eased it open. Daphne peered inside. In the darkness lay a figure on a bed. He was tied down with ropes across his chest, and binding his wrists and ankles to the bed-frame. A hood was covering his head.

'Hey, Kylon, ya fud,' Keira yelled. 'Ye'll never guess who's come to visit.' She turned to Daphne. 'Shall I take his hood off, so ye can see him?'

'No thanks,' Daphne said. 'You kept him alive, then?'

'Wee Flora's been feeding the dipshit,' Keira said, 'and keeping him docile with the same stuff he used to drug the wee one. We thought you might want him.'

'Thanks, sister.'

Keira grinned. She closed the door, and sat down again.

'Now we know where we stand,' she said, 'let me take a look at ye.'

She stared at Daphne. 'Killop's woman, eh? Mother of his child. Hope yer good to him. I take exception if anyone messes with my wee brother.'

Daphne smiled. 'I love him more than anything,' she said, 'except for Karalyn.'

Keira nodded. 'I'm family now as well. That wee lassie's my niece, and even though I usually find bairns to be a right pain in the arse, I have to admit she's alright. She's a bonnie wee thing.'

'So how did you and Kallie end up in Plateau City at the same time as Kylon and Karalyn?'

'It does look weird, I know, but we were here well before Kylon turned up. There's not that many Kellach folk left in the city, and I heard about him arriving and paid him a visit. The reason we were in the city at all, though, was because we were coming to visit you.'

'Kallie was coming to visit me?'

Keira laughed. 'She just came along to help wee Flora get back home to the Holdings. That's the other reason we're here. I don't suppose ye know what happened to Hold Cane?'

'Is that where Flora's from?'

'Aye.'

Daphne shook her head. 'The Emperor passed through Hold Cane. Not much of it's left.'

Keira nodded. 'I should tell ye, if ye ever meet Flora, she's not too impressed with the Holdfasts. I think she blames your family for getting her folks involved in yer rebellion.'

'She's not the only one,' Daphne said, 'but my father's dead now. The Emperor killed every one of my family, except for Karalyn. Apart from my sister-in-law, we're the only Holdfasts left.'

'The Emperor kicked yer arses, eh?'

'Yeah. He did.'

'So where are ye now?'

'A few miles outside the city.'

Keira snorted. 'Ye made it down here fast.'

'We went through a few horses on the way.'

'Wait a minute. Is my wee brother with ye?'

'Yeah.'

'Killop rode a horse?'

'All the way from the Holdings.'

Keira laughed. 'I pity the poor beast carrying his fat arse.'

Daphne raised an eyebrow.

'Hey,' Keira said. 'I'm allowed to slag him off; I'm his big sister. So, what's the plan?'

'We'll enter the city tomorrow, and come here.'

Keira nodded. 'Or, we could come to you. The wee lassie's well enough to travel now, and I've got a wagon and supplies locked up and waiting for me. The city's crawling with soldiers, maybe best if ye don't come in.'

Daphne hesitated.

'Aye,' Keira said, 'that's what we'll do. We'll pick ye up on the road, and get on our way to the Holdings.'

Daphne bowed her head.

'We can't.'

'Why the fuck not?'

'The Emperor. If we don't stop him, he'll destroy us all.'

Keira groaned. 'Not this again; ye sound like Kylon. Look, I get that the Emperor's a fucking nutter. He's wrecked his way through Frogland, and your Holdings, but I've gone up against him before.' She shook her head. 'Let's get out of here, Daphne. The Emperor's not our problem.'

'He killed my family.'

'Most of them. Do ye want to lose the ones ye have left?'

Daphne felt her will begin to crumble.

'Let the bastard sit on his throne and fester,' Keira said. 'Ten days he's been back, and not a fucking peep from him. There might be plenty of soldiers in the city, but it's an illusion; he lost his Holdings army in Frogland, and most of his lizard soldiers in the Holdings. He's spent.'

'It sounds like a reason to strike now.'

'No, Daphne,' Keira said. 'Like a bear with his paw in a trap, he'll be most dangerous cornered. Let's leave him be. There are plenty of places in the world where we can hide, and live in peace. With me and you side by side, nobody'll fuck with us. I hear yer quite a fighter, and yer not bad with yer vision tricks. I keep forgetting yer not really here.'

Daphne chewed her lip. 'How early in the morning could you be ready?'

'Dawn? That's when the gates open. Where are you?'

'At a farmhouse a mile off the road to the Holdings, about four miles altogether.'

'We'll be there an hour after dawn. Wait in sight of the road, you'll see us.'

Daphne nodded. 'I have to go soon,' she said, 'I'm running low. Walk with me through to Karalyn's room.'

Keira got to her feet and they went to the bedroom, where Flora was on her knees playing with the girl.

'Mama!' Karalyn cried when she saw her.

Daphne crouched down as her daughter drew near. She paused in front of the apparition, smiling.

'I'm here, Kara-bear,' Daphne said.

Flora stood, and gazed about.

'See mama soon?' Karalyn said.

'Very soon,' she said.

'What's going on?' Flora said. 'Who's she speaking to?'

'Her ma,' Keira said.

'Daphne's here?'

'Aye, but she's in my head, so ye cannae see her.'

'Karalyn can.'

Keira shrugged. 'She's a fucking mage.'

Daphne glanced up at her. 'Do you always swear in front of my daughter?'

'Keiwa say silly things,' Karalyn said.

'You've got that right, kid,' said Flora.

'I have to go, little bear,' Daphne said, turning back to her daughter. 'Daddy and I will see you tomorrow. We love you.'

She blew her a kiss and disappeared, as Daphne pulled her vision back the long miles to where her body sat motionless on the grassy bank. She blinked open her eyes, a headache pounding behind her temples. With nothing to take the edge off, her mind felt flayed and raw. She lit a cigarette, and sat for a few more minutes, stretching out her limbs as her headache grew.

She got to her feet, and stumbled down the grassy bank in the darkness, towards the farmhouse. Inside, Killop and Chane were sitting round the stove, where a hatch was emitting a low light from the fire within.

'Shit, you look rough,' Chane said.

Killop stood, and gave Daphne his seat.

'Did you see her?'

'Yeah,' Daphne said, sitting as Chane thrust a mug of lukewarm tea into her hand. 'She's doing well. Up and about, playing with the Holdings girl we saw her with.' She smiled. 'I spoke to her, told her we were going to see her tomorrow.'

'So we're not going in tonight?' said Chane.

'The city's changed,' Daphne said. 'It's much more secure now. And I had a chat with Keira.'

'You did?' said Killop. 'How is she?'

Daphne glanced at him. 'You were right, Killop. I'm sorry for doubting. Your sister's not part of any conspiracy with Kylon, in fact she's got him tied up in a room in their apartment. She's also got a wagon, and supplies, and I arranged to meet them tomorrow morning by the northern road.'

'So we won't have to go into the city?' Chane said, puffing her cheeks out.

'What else did she say?' Killop said. 'Keira, I mean.'

'You look nervous, big man,' said Chane.

'I've not seen my sister in years.'

'She was in good spirits,' Daphne said. 'She got annoyed that I had my suspicions, but we worked it out.'

'Did she seem like a crazed mass murderer?' Chane said.

'You don't know anything about her,' Killop scowled.

'I was in Sanang,' Chane said, 'when the firewitch was rampaging through the forest, slaughtering thousands. I heard the stories of the things she did, and saw with my own eyes the atrocities carried out by her worshippers.'

'She was worshipped?'

'Yeah,' Chane said, 'half of Sanang believed she was a goddess.'

'I bet she believes it too. Her head will be the size of a fucking mountain,' Killop said, starting to laugh. 'Tomorrow's going to be something else. Getting Karalyn back, and seeing Keira again.'

Daphne smiled at him despite her pounding headache, and ignored his swearing. She had a feeling she would be hearing a lot more of it, once Keira joined them. It was good to hear him laugh; it had been a long time.

'Does this mean that we've given up on trying to take the Emperor down?' Chane said, lighting a cigarette.

Daphne's expression fell. 'I don't know. Let's get Karalyn clear of the Plateau, and we can have another think about it. Having Keira with us will change things.'

'No kidding,' Chane said. 'The two most powerful mages in the world together?'

'You're forgetting Shella,' Daphne said.

Chane shrugged. 'You and Keira will have to do. Shit, we'll be on the road again tomorrow.' She turned to Killop. 'Your arse will be back up on the saddle.'

He shook his head. 'If Keira has a wagon, then we'll be going slow. I'll walk.'

'Let's get some sleep,' Daphne said. 'We need to be up at dawn.'

Chane nodded. 'I'll take the back room.' She stood, and picked up her blanket roll from the pack. 'See you in the morning.'

'Night,' Daphne said.

Killop laid out their own blankets by the warmth of the stove.

'Just one more night,' she said, as they lay down. 'One more night till we get our baby back.'

He put his arm round her and kissed her.

'One more night.'

For much of the night, Daphne's sleep was dreamless, her exhausted mind and body resting in Killop's warm embrace. A few hours before dawn, she felt her senses stir, as her consciousness was nudged.

Mama.

Kara-bear? she said, her mind groggy and thick as it moved into a state of dreaming.

Mama come.

Daphne felt her vision dragged from her body, and pulled towards the city at lightning speed. Her sight hurtled over the walls and through the New Town, right up to the high towers of the Great Fortress. She blinked, and found herself in the mind of the Emperor, her daughter's consciousness hiding alongside hers.

He was gazing at a fire roaring in a hearth. No lamps were lit in the hall where he sat, and the only light was coming from the flames. His breathing was steady, but his heart was racing with anticipation.

'Not long now, my darling queen,' he said, his eyes never leaving the fire. 'The time draws near when I will be bidding you farewell.' He frowned. 'If it works this time.' Anxiety rippled through him, and he shuddered. Then anger, and hatred took over. How he loathed his creation. Miserable and weak; stupid creatures. He could kill them all as one stood on an insect. Only Keira had ever shown any real spirit, and she was dead. As for the rest of the mages, the Holdfast woman had revealed early promise, but had thrown it away to play at being a mother instead, before falling off a cliff. Shella, though... He smirked.

There was a knock at the door. It creaked open.

'Your Imperial Majesty,' bowed Arnault.

Daphne gazed at the Holdings man through the Creator's eyes. He was stooping, and his face seemed to have aged by decades since she had last seen him.

'What is it?' said the Creator, his contempt for the man seeping through his thoughts.

'Everything is prepared, your Majesty,' Arnault said, his eyes lowered. 'The mages are ready.'

'Good,' he said, rising.

'I've checked everything three times, your Majesty,' Arnault said. 'I know that this might well be our last chance.'

The Emperor smiled, and began walking to the door, passing a long table on his left. Halfway along it, he paused, and turned to face the row of thrones.

'Wish me luck, my darling queen,' he said.

The lifeless eyes of Mirren stared back at him, and Daphne grimaced. Her throat had been cut, and she looked like she had been dead for several days, as she sat slumped on the throne.

Karalyn pulled their minds away, and Daphne felt herself hurtled upwards as the girl fled from the fortress, weeping.

It's alright, little bear, she said as her daughter slowed, far above the city.

Aunty Mirrie, she sobbed.

Daphne felt terror surge from the girl, and tried to radiate love and reassurance, but her own fear was rising. She gazed down at the Great Fortress. Somewhere in there, the Creator was about to re-enact the ritual that had granted him more power than any other being in the world. What would it do this time?

Go back to your bed, she said, *and wake up Keira.*

No. Stay with mama.

Daphne's heart tore as Karalyn wrapped her thoughts close to hers, and all her instincts cried out to hold on to her and protect her.

I'm sorry, little bear, she said, *but you have to wake up Keira, and tell her to get you all out of the city as quickly as you can.*

Karalyn said nothing, but clung on tighter.

Daphne sighed. *Alright, we'll go down together.*

Daphne pulled her daughter down over the city, gliding past the Great Fortress and over the Kellach quarter. The city was quiet and dark, with only a handful of windows leaking light onto the streets. She found Keira's apartment block, and went through a shutter and into a dark room. The Kell fire mage was lying asleep on a large bed, her chest rising, and a pool of saliva seeping from her open mouth.

Daphne hesitated for a second, then went into her mind.

Fire. The skies burned, and falling wreckage was striking the blackened land where Keira stood, her arms raised. All around, trees were burning, and scorched corpses littered the ground.

Keira, said Daphne.

The fire mage turned, tears and ash streaked down her face. She frowned at Daphne and Karalyn as the background faded out to nothing.

We've just seen the Creator, Daphne said. *He's re-enacting the ritual.*

Now?

You need to get out of the city.

Shit.

And I need to get back to the farmhouse and wake up. We'll head for the gate into the Kellach quarter. I'll contact you again once we're there.

Keira nodded.

Daphne turned to Karalyn.

Keira will look after you, she said. *Do what she says, and be a good girl. I'll see you soon, I promise.*

No! Don't go!

I have to, little bear. I'll see you soon.

Daphne pulled herself free of Karalyn and soared away, blocking her daughter's cries from her ears. She surged over the city. As she was reaching the walls, a booming wave of power burst out over the streets, from the direction of the Great Fortress. Tenements crumpled and fell in the surge of energy, and Daphne's consciousness tumbled through the air. She gazed out in panic as the ground under the city rippled and buckled, sending houses, towers and walls crashing to the ground. Above the half-ruined streets rose the Great Fortress, the largest building left standing in the city. She stared at it and in an instant her vision power ceased, and she was back in her own head, a flashing pain surging behind her eyes.

She got to her knees, her right hand covering her face, her head feeling like it was about to explode.

The ground rocked under her as the shock waves reached the farmhouse. The roof fell in on top of them, and a swinging beam struck the stove, driving it into the wall in an explosion of fire and sparks. Killop grabbed hold of her, and they ran from the building, falling onto the grassy bank.

Daphne lay on the grass, clutching her head in agony, Killop's hand on her shoulder. He stood, and she watched him race back into the farmhouse, before her eyes closed.

CHAPTER 33
LAST ONE DOWN

P lateau City, Imperial Plateau – 18th Day, Second Third Winter 507

'I have to go, little bear,' Daphne said, turning to her daughter. 'Daddy and I will see you tomorrow. We love you.'

The Holdings mage blew her a kiss, and disappeared.

Keira shook her head. 'Fucking show-off.'

'Has she gone?' Flora said.

'Aye.'

'What did she say?'

Keira rubbed her chin. 'We'd better get Kallie.'

Flora wandered out of the room, and Keira knelt down by Karalyn.

'Ye'll see yer ma soon,' she said. 'Play here for a bit, while the rest of us talk, aye?'

Karalyn picked up her toy horse as Keira walked from the bedroom, and entered the living room. She poured herself a large rum and lit a stick of keenweed. It felt good to be going; and it felt even better that she was going to see her wee brother soon.

Flora and Kallie came into the room.

'Flora tells me ye've been hearing voices in yer head,' Kallie said. 'I knew it was only a matter of time.'

'Ye better sit down,' Keira said. 'Cause ye won't be laughing when I tell ye who it is you'll be seeing tomorrow.'

Kallie frowned. 'Daphne's close?'

'Aye,' Keira grinned, 'and my wee brother, too. We're meeting them in the morning.'

Flora poured Kallie a drink and handed it to her.

'Where?' the Holdings woman said.

'Out of the city,' Keira said. 'A few miles up the road towards the Holdings. We're getting out of here at last.'

Flora sat.

'Let's put some distance between us and that mad bastard in the fortress,' Keira went on. 'This has worked out perfectly. Instead of wasting time searching for them, Daphne and Killop have come to us. All we need to do now is get you back to Hold Cane.'

Keira hesitated, as she remembered.

'What is it?' said Flora. 'What's wrong?'

Keira gazed at the Holdings woman. 'Daphne said that the Emperor had been in Hold Cane when he was rampaging through your country. He didn't leave much behind.'

Flora clenched her fists. She got up from her seat and walked to the window facing the Great Fortress, and gazed out into the evening sky.

Keira turned to Kallie. 'Ye look like someone's taken a shit in yer breakfast.'

'I don't think I'm ready for this, Keira,' she said. 'Seeing them together, I don't know how I'll react.'

'Ach, come on,' Keira said, taking a swig of rum. 'It'll be awkward for the first five minutes, then it'll be fine.'

'I thought we still had a third or so before I had to decide,' Kallie said. 'Tomorrow's too soon. I might stay here.'

'What? No way, Kallie, not a fucking chance.'

'I couldnae take seeing Killop with his new family. Sorry.'

Flora walked over. 'If she's staying, then so am I.'

Keira gawked at her. 'Yer giving up looking for yer family?' she cried. 'Just like that? They might still be alive; it's worth a shot.'

'I am going to look for them,' Flora said, 'but I'm not travelling to the Holdings with Daphne Holdfast. I'll wait a couple of days, then go by a different route.'

'I'll go with you,' said Kallie, 'if you want.'

Flora smiled. 'Yeah, that'd be great.'

Keira narrowed her eyes. 'Ya back-stabbing wee cows. After all we've been through, yer abandoning me because ye might feel a wee bit awkward? Look, come with us, even for a few days; try it at least before ye fucking quit on me.'

They said nothing.

Keira felt her temper close to exploding.

'Sorry, Keira,' said Flora.

'Fine,' Keira snarled. 'Fuck the both of ye. Ya pair of useless tossers. I don't care about yer personal bullshit, Daphne's ma sister now, so if ye fuck with her, ye fuck with me.' She stood. 'Flora, do something useful for once and get yer lazy arse down to the tunnels. Let them know I'll be needing the wagon at dawn. And make sure ye pick up the keys.'

Flora stood. 'Alright, but you'll have to put Karalyn to bed.'

Keira frowned. 'How hard could it fucking be?'

Flora smirked, and walked to the front door of the apartment. She pulled a long cloak from a hook, and left, slamming the door.

'Ye can't blame her,' Kallie said. 'The Holdfasts are responsible for destroying her home.'

Keira turned to her. 'Yer an eejit. The Emperor destroyed her home. The Holdfasts were only doing the same as what I did last year, and fighting the bastard. He kicked their arses, just like he kicked mine, but at least they had the guts to try.'

She downed her rum.

'Ye turned her against me,' Keira went on. 'Ye knew she liked me and ye couldnae handle it. Ye wanted her for yerself; well, now ye've fucking got her.'

'What are you talking about?' Kallie muttered, as Keira stormed from the room.

495

She walked into the bedroom and saw Karalyn playing on the rug with her wooden horses.

'Bed,' she said.

The girl ignored her.

'Bed.'

Nothing.

Keira frowned. She didn't have time for this. She was needing to be packing, so she could squeeze in a few rums and a smoke before bed. Shit, why had she promised to leave at dawn? She wondered if Daphne would object to the still considerable amount of weed she was carrying. She snorted. Killop would be more likely to find some pious reason to complain about it. Daphne seemed alright. A better sister than Kallie, anyway. She'd better leave her some, she thought. Enough to see her by for a while.

She leant down and picked Karalyn up.

'Right, ya wee toerag,' she said, as the girl wriggled in her arms. 'Time for bed.'

'You're a stinky poo.'

'And you're a cheeky wee cow.'

'Cows go moo. You're a stinky poo.'

'Aye?' Keira said, putting the girl down, and raising her hands like claws. 'If you're a cow, then I'm a big fierce bear, who's going to fucking eat you, em... who's going to eat you.'

The girl shrieked, and ran round the bed. Keira got down on all fours and chased her, roaring and growling as Karalyn half-laughed, half-screamed. Keira cornered her against the wall. She picked her up and threw her onto the bed. She sat down next to her and grabbed her foot.

'I'm going to eat this first,' she growled, and the girl wept in laughter as Keira tickled her toes.

Keira smiled down at her. This auntie shit was alright.

Keira rolled over and fell out of bed, crashing down onto the floor.

She groaned, opening her eyes as her dream came back to her. Had Daphne been in her head again? Taking fucking liberties, just coming in like that. What if she'd been thinking about guys or something? She would have to speak to her about it.

Her eyes widened as she remembered Daphne's message. At the same time, she heard a wail coming from Karalyn's room.

'The Emperor,' she muttered, scrambling to her feet. She pulled on her clothes, and made it to the crying child's room in a few strides.

'It's alright,' she said, picking the girl up and rocking her. 'We need to get dressed and go.'

She put the girl down and lit a lamp. She was in the middle of pulling out some clothes for Karalyn as Flora walked in, scratching her head.

'What are you doing?' she said. 'You leaving now? Without saying goodbye?'

'Shut up and get dressed,' Keira said, as she pulled a woollen dress over Karalyn's head.

'Eh?'

'We need to get out of here. Now. That mad fucking bastard's about to perform the same shit that he did last year, and he's doing it right now. You remember? Earthquakes, crazy mage shit? A hundred thousand heads exploding?'

Keira finished tying Karalyn's boots, and had picked her up as the tremor hit the tenement. She was knocked from her feet, landing on her back on the floor, Karalyn held tight to her chest. The lamp smashed against the rug, setting it alight, as the floor buckled. The walls curved and swayed, and the roof fell in on them. Keira rolled over, shielding Karalyn, and crawled under the bed. The floor gave way, and they soared down, crashing into the floor below, landing on a table. It collapsed, and Keira lay still, every part of her aching, Karalyn whimpering in her arms. A cloud of dust descended on them as the tremors stilled.

'My fucking back,' she groaned. She gazed up at the dark hole in the ceiling above, where flames were licking the sides of the bed. She tried to move her legs, and they responded. She wriggled her toes, then gazed at the girl lying on her chest. 'How ye doing, ma wee toerag? Ye alright?'

Karalyn looked up at Keira, her eyes wide. She didn't seem to be injured, so Keira edged off the table as debris fell through the hole from the floor above. Keeping Karalyn held tight in her arms, she staggered to her feet. She was in an abandoned apartment, stripped of anything valuable, and covered in a thick layer of dust. She stumbled to a broken window and gazed out.

'Shit,' she said, her eyes taking in the scene of devastation. A dozen fires were burning in the Kellach quarter, and half of the buildings had collapsed. The Great Fortress loomed tall and undamaged amid the rubble and ruined streets. She tried to reach out to the nearest flames, but her powers had gone. She remembered back to when the Emperor had annihilated her army. It had taken a few hours for her powers to return that time, but whereas before she had felt relief at the loss of her skills, now a feeling close to panic was creeping through her.

'Don't get carried away,' she muttered to herself.

'I want to see mama,' said Karalyn.

'Aye, I'm sure ye do, hen,' Keira said. 'That might not be the easiest thing right now, but.'

'I want mama!'

'Alright, alright,' she said. 'We cannae leave Kallie and wee Flora, but. We have to go upstairs and help them.'

She carried the child across the room, hearing the floorboards creak and move under her boots, and made it to the front door. It was locked, so she stood back and kicked it open, sending splinters of the door frame flying out. They went into the stairwell. It was in darkness, but Keira knew where the steps were, and edged towards them.

Halfway up the stairs, she put her foot down on a step that gave way, and they nearly toppled over the edge. Keira dived back, staying close to the wall.

'That was close, eh?' she laughed. She peered up into the darkness.

'This is fucked up; I cannae see a thing.' She took a breath. 'Flora!' she yelled.

Nothing.

'Where the fuck are they?'

'Karalyn find them,' the girl said.

'What? Are your powers fine?'

The girl didn't respond.

Keira remained still in the darkness of the stairwell, her back against the wall, wishing she had stayed in Domm.

After a minute, Karalyn wriggled in her arms.

'Flora coming,' she said. 'Karalyn woke her up.'

'Good lass,' Keira said, kissing her on the head.

A door above opened, and Flora staggered out onto the landing, holding a lamp in her outstretched arm. She was still dressed in her nightgown, smeared with patches of blood and dust. She squinted down at Keira and Karalyn, swaying in the lamplight.

'Where's Kallie?' Keira cried.

'Here,' the Kell woman said, coming out behind Flora. She was fully dressed, and had a large pack over her shoulder, next to her longbow. 'I managed to grab the stuff ye'd packed.'

Keira noticed smoke coming out of the doorway behind the two women at the top of the stairs. Flora staggered, and Kallie caught her by the arm. She took the lamp, and clasped her other arm round the Holdings woman's shoulder.

'Watch the steps,' Keira said, as they began their descent. She began to move down herself, avoiding the gaping hole she had made on the way up. She made it to the next floor's landing, and put Karalyn down.

'Yer wee, but yer heavy,' she said, as the girl clung on to her leg.

She leaned back against the wall and watched as Kallie helped Flora down the stairs. When they reached the landing, the Kell woman lowered Flora to the floor, where she slumped.

'Hey, don't stop,' Keira said. 'There's another four fucking floors to go.'

Kallie grimaced, and pulled Flora back to her feet. Keira sighed, and picked up Karalyn.

Keira glanced at Kallie as they made their way to the next set of steps.

'Looks like it's the Kell doing all the work again.'

It took an hour of slow and tiring effort to negotiate the four flights of stairs to the ground floor. Many of the wooden steps were loose and cracked, and parts of the roof continued to fall around them. Halfway down, Keira realised, in the light of Kallie's lamp, that Karalyn was asleep in her arms. Flora struggled the whole way, with only Kallie's strong arm keeping her upright.

When they reached the last step, Keira staggered forward into the hallway and put Karalyn down. She took the pack from Kallie's shoulder and found a cloak, which she rolled up and placed under the child's head. She dug into the pack, and found a small pouch. She took out a stick of keenweed and lit it as Kallie lowered Flora down.

'What now?' said Kallie.

'We see if our wagon's in one piece,' Keira said. 'The building where it's being kept is on the way to the gates, so if it's fucked we should still be able to get out of the city.'

Kallie nodded down at Flora.

Keira frowned. She took a long drag, and crouched down next to the Holdings woman.

'You alright?'

Flora looked up at her, but her eyes were bloodshot and half-closed.

'She might have whacked her head when she fell,' Kallie said.

Keira touched Flora's head, feeling through her hair. She withdrew her hand and squinted in the lamplight at the blood on the tips of her fingers.

'Yer going to be alright, wee Flora,' she said, but even to her own ears she sounded like she was lying.

Kallie joined her by Flora's side, and they crouched in silence for a moment.

'We'll have to carry her and Karalyn,' Keira said. 'That's if yer coming?'

Kallie nodded.

'Good. I'll take the pack and Karalyn, you take her.'

'Aye.'

Kallie took a long woollen tunic out of the pack, and pulled it over Flora's shoulders, trying to avoid the wound at the back of her head. She picked her up in both arms. Keira stubbed out the weedstick, feeling the false energy flow through her. She tied up the pack and slung it over her back, then lifted Karalyn in her left arm, holding her close.

The two women caught each other's eye, and nodded.

With her free hand, Keira pushed open the door to the street and stepped outside. Though it was still night, the sky was lit up by the fires burning through the Kellach quarter. In the light of the flames, Keira gazed at the half-ruined street. Some of the tenements had collapsed completely, while others like her own were still standing. Debris littered the road, with roof tiles, masonry and splintered wooden beams strewn around. A few Kellach were wandering around, or were standing gazing at the devastation.

Keira looked up at the Great Fortress. Its walls seemed more solid than before, and light was spilling out of the windows on the top floor. What was that bastard doing up there?

'Come on,' said Kallie. 'We haven't got all night.'

'Aye,' Keira said, turning. They began to walk down the road towards the gates, and Keira stopped again.

'Shit!' she cried. 'Pyre's arsecrack.'

Kallie frowned at her.

'That wee prick, Kylon,' Keira said. 'We fucking left him up there.'

Kallie glanced at the tall tenement. Its outer walls were fractured, and smoke was belching from the broken windows of the upper storeys.

'I'm not going back in there,' she said. 'The fire'll get him, anyway.'

'Aye, probably,' Keira said. She spat on the ground. 'Shit way to go, but.'

'He deserves it.'

Keira glanced down at Karalyn nestling into her left side. 'Aye, I guess he does.'

They turned and set off down the road again. After ten minutes they came to Welcome Square, the central point of the Kellach quarter, where a crowd had gathered. Most were armed, and several were brandishing burning torches, while families huddled together near the derelict fountain in the middle of the open space.

Nods greeted them as they passed a collapsed tenement and entered the square. Down one side, bodies were being laid onto the ground in rows, and relatives and friends of the dead mourned over them. Lamentations filled the air, along with angrier voices. Keira and Kallie kept moving through the crowd of Kellach and Holdings until they reached the other side.

'We're nearly there,' Keira grunted, shifting Karalyn to her right hip.

They turned a corner and followed a narrow street for a hundred yards, avoiding the fragments of debris covering the road. In the distance, Keira saw the walls of the city. Some stretches were intact and standing tall, while others had collapsed. They arrived at a low stone building, and stopped at a closed gate. Keira took a key from her pouch and unlocked the large wooden door, and they stepped inside.

'It's pitch black in here,' she said. 'Get the lamp lit.'

Kallie entered the building and put Flora down onto the floor. She unhooked the lamp from her belt, and found her box of matches.

'That's better,' Keira said, as Kallie lit the wick, sending light outward from where they stood. 'Shit.'

The central section of the long roof had collapsed, and large shards of glass and twisted wooden beams lay blocking the passageways between the rows of storage sheds.

'What shed's the wagon in?' said Kallie.

Keira glanced at her keys. 'Fourteen.'

'Right,' she said. 'You stay here. I'll find it.'

The fire mage nodded, and Kallie took the lamp and the keys and walked towards the sheds. Keira sat down by the door next to where Flora lay, the light from the fires in the city providing a low level of illumination. Karalyn was still asleep in her arms, so she put her down next to the Holdings woman. She slung her pack off and found a blanket, then covered the girl with it. She glanced at Flora. Her eyes were closed. Keira placed a finger under her chin, and felt around, but there was no pulse.

'Don't you fucking die on me,' she cried. 'It's not allowed.'

Keira put her ear to Flora's mouth, listening for breath.

Nothing.

She touched her skin.

Cold.

Keira fell back against the wall and clenched her fists, tears spilling from her eyes. Silent sobs wracked her chest, and her heart ached. She had first seen Flora in the Kellach camp outside Plateau City, then led her halfway round the world, only to get her killed in the same place they had met. Her wee white-faced witch. Why had she never told her how she felt?

What did she feel?

She gazed down at Flora, then took another blanket from the pack and lay it over her still body, kissing her on the forehead.

'Goodbye, wee Flora.'

She leaned against the wall, and wondered what everyone in the World's End was doing. Sleeping probably, she realised, remembering the hour. She thought back to her comfortable bed at the rear of Kelpie's tavern, and shook her head. What was she doing in the imperial capital? The one place she had never wanted to see again, and somehow she had been lulled into complacency, even after the Emperor had returned from the Holdings. No. That wasn't right. She glanced at Karalyn. The lassie was why she had stayed, and it was her job to make sure the girl was kept safe, at least until she could be handed over to her parents.

She heard distant cries from outside, and a scream. She peered through the crack in the door, but saw no one out on the street. She leaned her head back against the wall, and closed her eyes.

Someone kicked her.

'Get up,' yelled Kallie.

Keira opened her eyes. 'Flora.'

'I know,' Kallie said. 'It's a shame, but there's nothing we can do for her now.'

'Did you find the wagon?'

'Aye. It's fine,' said Kallie, 'but the horses are dead.'

'Shit.'

'We have to move, Keira.'

'Aye,' she said, stretching her limbs, her gaze on the covered body of Flora. 'I know.'

'No, we have to move now. Something's happening outside.'

Keira squinted through the gap to the street. There was no one there, but the cries and shouts were much louder, and closer. Mixed in was the sound of steel striking steel, and the thud of boots on the cobbles. She caught a glimpse of uniforms at the end of the street as they dashed by.

'Soldiers?' she said.

'The Emperor must have sent the army out.'

Keira got up. She pushed the door open another foot, and glanced down the street. To her left, the sky was lightening, a faint glow appearing above the remaining battlements. She ducked back inside as another group of soldiers rushed by, heading in the direction of the gates.

'What the fuck are they doing?' she muttered. She turned back to Kallie. 'We'll have to get out on foot. We'll walk up to where Killop's staying.'

'If we can get through the walls,' Kallie said.

Keira felt for her power.

Nothing.

Maybe this time it was gone for good.

She pulled the pack over her shoulder and picked up Karalyn, who stirred.

Keira took a breath, and stole a last look down at Flora.

'Let's go.'

They ran down the street, keeping to the thick shadows of the buildings on their left. They paused at a crossroads, then sped down the road towards the gates. A hundred yards ahead of them stood the gatehouse. It remained upright, though long, jagged cracks marked the stonework, and the wooden gates were hanging off their hinges. In front of the gates, a handful of Kellach and Holdings folk were fighting a group of Rahain infantry in imperial uniforms. The soldiers were kneeling in lines, firing crossbow bolts into the civilians, who were charging them with swords and axes.

Keira and Kallie raced up the street. The Rahain were facing away from them, and Keira dived into a doorway when they were only twenty yards away.

'Look after the lassie,' she said to Kallie, putting Karalyn and the pack down and drawing her sword.

Kallie stared at her. 'Use yer powers.'

'I cannae,' Keira said.

She ran back into the street before Kallie could say anything else, and charged the backs of the Rahain soldiers, her sword raised. When she was a yard away, an arrow flew past her shoulder, and struck a soldier in the back of his neck, almost taking his head off. Keira screamed, and lashed out with her sword, cleaving the nearest soldier from the neck down. The others turned to her in shock. She felt the old memories of countless fights take over, and ploughed through the group of Rahain, while arrows continued to strike those out of her range.

She was joined by the group of armed Kellach and Holdings civilians, and together they slew the last of the soldiers.

'Thanks,' panted a Holdings man, leaning on his long axe. 'You saved our arses there.'

'Nae bother,' said Keira, taking an offered bottle of something from a tall Kellach fighter. She took a swig. 'Cheers.'

'We'd better get out of here,' said another. 'More soldiers are coming.'

'What the fuck are they trying to do?' Keira said.

'Seal the quarter,' said the Holdings man. 'They're rounding up everyone, and taking them to the Great Fortress.'

'You getting out of the city?'

'Aye,' said the Kellach. 'I'm not hanging around for the Emperor to turn up. I was here last time he paid us a visit.'

'We'll come with ye,' Keira said.

'We?'

'Aye, wait a minute.' She ran back to the doorway. Karalyn was standing next to Kallie, peering out.

'Come on; let's go,' she said, picking up the girl.

'No, want to walk,' cried the girl.

'No fucking time for that,' yelled Keira, as she and Kallie ran out onto the street. They joined the group, and together, they ran for the gates.

When they were halfway there, a Holdings fighter shouted, 'Get down!' Keira glanced up and saw a great mass of dark red fire fly over their heads. It struck the gatehouse with a blinding flash, and the structure went up in thick, oily flames. The heat was intense, and the group juddered to a halt, and started to retreat.

Keira.

The fire mage froze. She recognised the voice.

I'm intrigued to see you alive. Intrigued, and also glad. You will make a fine specimen for my next attempt.

'Keira, move,' cried Kallie. 'The fire's spreading, but we can run to the collapsed part of the wall. Don't stand there gawking, come on.'

Keira's legs refused to obey.

I'm coming for you, fire mage.

Karalyn screamed, and Keira blinked. She glanced at Kallie, who was staring at her. The fire from the gatehouse was starting to engulf the nearby buildings, and the other fighters had scattered. They were alone.

'The bad man's here,' whimpered Karalyn.

'What?' said Kallie, looking around.

'It's me he's after,' Keira said.

'How does he know yer here?' Kallie cried.

I see all, said the voice of the Emperor inside Keira's head. *I see every mage in the world. All of them. You can run, but I'll find you. I'll find all of them.*

'Sounds like a fucking challenge,' Keira muttered. She glanced at Kallie, then ran, the Kell woman sprinting after her. They raced down a street away from the burning gatehouse, then turned and headed towards a section of the wall where it had collapsed. A few civilians were already there, climbing over the rubble in the direction of the rising sun.

Keira heard the stamps of boots, and swerved to her right as ranks of Rahain soldiers charged down the street past a burning tenement block. In their midst strode a figure, standing taller and broader than any Kellach Brigdomin, clad in a full set of black armour that glinted in the firelight.

Kallie skidded to a halt, her eyes wide, and started to back away. Keira joined her, and they retreated into the doorway of an abandoned and closed-up shop. They huddled in the corner as the Rahain sped by. The Emperor raised his hand, and the civilians trying to flee over the rubble dropped like scythed wheat.

Keira swallowed, and put Karalyn down.

'Stay with yer Auntie Kallie,' she said, kissing her. She gazed at the Kell woman. 'Look after her.'

She stood, and strode out into the street.

'Couldnae get enough of me the first time, eh?' she sneered at the Emperor.

Keira flexed her fingers and felt for her powers as the Emperor

turned to face her, silhouetted by the flames from the burning tenement. The company of Rahain continued on towards the collapsed wall
until the two stood alone in the street, the Emperor towering over her.

'Ye think yer smart, wee man,' she cried, 'just cause ye've grown a
foot or two? I've seen bairn's shites that were harder than you.'

'The things I'm going to do to you,' the Emperor said from behind
his iron mask. 'I'm going to enjoy breaking you.'

Keira squinted. 'Is that supposed to make me feart? Oh, I'm fucking
quaking here.'

Just a little bit longer, keep him talking a little bit longer.

He raised his hand.

'Don't ye want to know how I escaped last time?' she said.

'I'll find out everything I want when I have you in chains.'

'Nah,' she said, her hand poised behind her back, 'I have a better
idea.' She whipped her hand round and spread her fingers. With a
deafening roar, the fire raging in the tenement toppled down from
above and fell upon the Emperor, drowning him in an inferno of
flames. Keira was thrown off her feet by the force of the explosion, and
she landed in a heap by the wall of the building opposite.

She raised her head, groaning. Her vision spun, and the stink of her
singed hair filled her nostrils. All she could see were the flames roaring
on the street only a few yards in front of her. She began to crawl away
from the heat when she noticed something move. She stared as a figure
rose from the flames, tall and dark.

Keira groaned. 'Now that's just bullshit.'

The Emperor strode towards her, his armour glowing hot, its black
enamel blistering off.

'You want me to kill you?' the Emperor said, his voice raging and
booming in her head. She flinched. 'I will,' he went on, 'but not before I
have shredded and flayed your mind and your body.'

'Dream on,' she gasped, as he leant over her.

His head whipped back as an arrow pierced his right eye socket. He
staggered, and Keira felt hands grab her shoulders.

'Run, ya stupid cow,' screamed Kallie, hauling her to her feet. As

Keira got up, Kallie notched, aimed and loosed another arrow, striking the small gap between his helmet and armoured shoulder where the flesh of his neck lay undefended. The arrowhead drove deep behind his ear, and the Emperor fell to his knees. Kallie turned and ran, pulling Keira along with her. She shoved open the door of an empty shop where Karalyn was sitting. She was on the floor, rocking back and forth, her knees up at her chin.

'It's alright, wee one,' cried Kallie. 'I found her.'

Karalyn reached out with her arms and Keira embraced her.

'Come on,' said Kallie. 'Two arrows won't stop him for long. We need to run.'

'It doesn't make any difference,' she said. 'He'll find me wherever I go.'

Kallie slapped her.

'Don't talk shite, and don't give up. Take Karalyn and follow me.'

Kallie slung the pack over her shoulder and pulled an arrow from her belt quiver, her longbow resting in her left hand. She ran to the back of the shop and kicked the door down.

Keira picked up Karalyn, and stumbled after the Kell woman, her body aching.

'Hold on tight, wee one,' she said, as she kept up with Kallie. They ran down alleyways, but soldiers were now occupying every weak point in the wall around the Kellach quarter. They kept running, Kallie turning back towards the centre of the city, and the Great Fortress. She stopped at a small squat building, and pushed the door open. Keira followed her in, her knees buckling.

'Down here,' Kallie said, shoving furniture out of the way to reveal a trapdoor.

'The tunnels?' Keira gasped. 'Aye. You go first.'

Kallie lifted the trapdoor, and climbed down the steps dug out of the ground. Keira put Karalyn down, and looked out of the open door onto the street.

'Go after yer Auntie Kallie,' she said. 'He won't find you if I stay up here.'

'No, Keiwa come,' Karalyn said, starting to cry as she stood by the trapdoor.

Keira knelt by her and stroked the hair out of her eyes.

'If ye go down there, Auntie Kallie will keep ye safe, but if I go too, then the bad man will find us all.'

'Don't be silly,' the girl said, sobbing. 'Karalyn hide with you.'

Keira gazed at the girl. Had the Emperor been telling the truth about being able to see every mage? The more she thought about it, the more like bullshit it sounded. And even if it was true, then she'd make sure Karalyn got away, even if the Emperor did find her. Now that her powers were back, she wouldn't be easy to capture.

She smirked.

'Alright then, ya wee toerag,' she said. 'Let's hide in the tunnels.'

Karalyn reached out and took her hand.

Last one down's a stinky poo.

CHAPTER 34
MADE TO ENDURE

Outside Plateau City, Imperial Plateau – 19th Day, Second Third Winter 507

O utside Plateau City, Imperial Plateau – 19th Day, Second Third Winter 507

Killop gazed at Daphne. Her eyes were closed, and her chest was rising and falling in time with her breath. Her dark skin glowed in the reflected lamplight within the small stables where he had laid her body down. He had checked her for injuries, but had found nothing, ruling out a blow to her head, and he was starting to believe something or someone had harmed her mind instead.

The Creator. It had to be. Daphne had been unconscious for nearly an hour, since the moment the earthquake had ceased. The two events were connected somehow, and both had something to do with the Creator, he felt certain of it.

He heard the door to the stables open behind him.

'How is she?' said Chane.

'The same.'

The Holdings woman walked over and crouched by him. She looked exhausted, and was covered in smeared ash. She lit a cigarette as she frowned at Daphne.

'I've taken care of the horses,' she said. 'Moved them a quarter of a mile up the track and put them in a barn. Took a while to calm them down. The earthquake and fire freaked them out.'

He nodded, his mind elsewhere.

'I saw the city from the top of the slope,' she went on. 'The sky's all red and flickering, as if the city's in flames. The earthquake must have hit it hard.'

Killop said nothing.

'We need to re-think the plan,' she said. 'I doubt that Keira will be meeting us at the time and place we arranged.'

'She'll be there.'

'But, Killop, the city will be in chaos...'

'Then maybe I should go in.'

Chane eyed him. 'On your own? You've no idea where your sister or daughter are.'

'Then what do you suggest?'

She shrugged. 'I'm all out of suggestions, big man. Look, it's only an hour or so till dawn. We could wait and see if Keira comes along in her wagon, and then decide. But, I'm worried.'

'Of course yer worried,' said Killop. 'Daphne's unconscious and Karalyn might be in danger.'

'Not just about that,' she said. 'The earthquake, that's what I'm talking about. Kylon told me there had been an earthquake when the Emperor got his powers. We know the bastard's in the city, and he's got his captured mages with him.'

'Shit,' Killop said. He remembered something Daphne had mentioned a long time before, about how she had lost her powers when she had been captured by Douanna. He glanced down at his fingers, and willed a spark to arc between them.

Nothing happened.

His mouth dropped open. For the first time in his life since he was in his teens, his powers had gone.

'You're right,' he said, looking up at Chane. 'I can't spark. Daphne said the same thing happened to her the night the Emperor got his powers, even though she was hundreds of miles away.'

'He's performed another ritual? I wonder if all the mages he captured are dead. There will hardly be any left at this rate.' She shook her head. 'Do we assume that the bastard's even more powerful now?'

'I think we have to.'

Chane stubbed out her cigarette and lit another one.

'Thanks,' she said. 'You know, for pulling me out of the farmhouse.'

He nodded.

'I know I've not been the easiest to get along with,' she went on. 'I know that I screw up most things I try, but Daphne's the only friend I have in the world, and I'd do anything to help her. What I'm trying to say is that if you need me to go into the city to look for Karalyn, then I'll do it. That way, you can stay with Daphne.'

'No thanks.'

'Are you not even going to consider it?'

He stood. 'I need some air.'

Without waiting for Chane to speak, he pushed open the door of the stables and stepped out into the chill night. To his left, a hint of dawn was appearing as a light smudge on the eastern horizon. Though he had slept only a few hours, his head was buzzing with pent-up frustration. He bowed his head and turned to his right, and strode up the grassy slope to the top of the low hill.

In the distance, he glimpsed the city. Karalyn's birthplace, and the centre of the world. The clouds above it were reflecting the red glow of the fires burning beneath, and his eyes picked out flames. If he ran, he could be at the walls in under an hour. If he was quick, he could be in, and back again before Daphne awoke. That would be a good way to surprise her. He smiled. To have her open her eyes to the sight of Karalyn would signal the end of their nightmare.

Chane was right, though. He had no idea where to begin looking, and the city looked immense in size. And if the Creator was even more powerful than before, then he would be no match for him if he was discovered.

He swore under his breath as helplessness rubbed his nerves raw. His only respite was the knowledge that his sister was looking after

Karalyn, and if anyone could keep his daughter safe, it was Keira. Even without her powers, she was a resourceful cow.

He turned to walk back to the stables, but halted, his mind conflicted. He needed to do something, he would explode if he had to sit for hours by Daphne's side, while the city burned and his daughter and sister were still inside. It was stupid, it was selfish, but he had to go. He had to look for them.

A scream tore through the air, coming from the stables. He ran down the slope and burst through the door.

Daphne was sitting up, her eyes wide.

Killop rushed to her side.

'Karalyn,' she gasped. 'The Creator. Earthquake.'

'The earthquake was an hour ago,' Killop said. 'Are you alright?'

She caught his gaze. 'I saw the Emperor. He was ready to perform another ritual. Then I spoke to Keira, told her to get Karalyn out of the city, and then... then the earthquake, and I can't remember anything else. Except Karalyn, just now, she woke me, somehow...'

'How are you feeling?' said Chane, offering her a water skin.

Daphne frowned. 'Fine. My head feels... fine.'

'Karalyn fixed you,' Killop said, 'just like she fixed me before.'

'Yeah,' Daphne said, 'maybe.' She gazed at him. 'My vision powers have gone.'

'Mine too.'

'It feels like I'm blind.'

'How long did they take to come back last time?' Chane said.

'A few hours,' she said, lighting a cigarette. 'I can't really remember. They came back gradually though, not all at once.' She took a draw. 'What time is it?'

'Less than an hour before sunrise,' Killop said.

Daphne stretched her neck and rolled her shoulders.

'Thanks for waiting for me,' she said. 'Are we ready to go?'

Killop nodded. 'Can you run?'

She got to her feet.

'Let's find out.'

514

For almost an hour, Killop, Daphne and Chane raced across the grassy slopes and fields towards the city. Behind them, the glow of the coming dawn was growing, lighting their way. Ahead, the city loomed closer with every step. Countless pillars of smoke were funnelling up from behind the half-ruined walls. Battlements and towers had toppled, and the gatehouse leading to the Kellach quarter was awash with thick dark flames.

They slowed as they approached, reaching a steep embankment a hundred yards from the walls. They halted, and lay down along its ridge, gazing at the city.

'I can feel my vision returning,' said Daphne. 'It's not all there yet, but it's coming.'

'Excellent timing,' said Chane. 'Something's going on in there. Do you see the soldiers guarding where the earthquake ripped holes in the wall? Why would they do that? They're stopping people from getting out. And there's more up on the battlements.'

'But not by the merchants' quarter,' Daphne said, pointing to the right of the Kellach district. Killop looked over. There were several breaches in the walls, but no soldiers could be seen.

'So the Emperor's sealed the Kellach quarter?' he said. 'Can we get in from anywhere else?'

'There's a wall separating it from the New Town,' Daphne said. 'The gate there will probably be guarded as well, but it's our best option.'

'But what if Keira breaks out while we're in the New Town?' he said. 'She might be fighting her way to the walls right now.'

'We can't just wait here,' said Daphne.

Killop turned to Chane.

She frowned. 'No way.'

'A while ago, you said you would do anything.'

'I'm not staying out here while you two go in,' Chane said. 'No chance.'

'You don't need to,' said Daphne. 'My vision powers are returning. I should be able to contact Karalyn or Keira soon, and then we'll know where they are.'

Chane winked at Killop. 'You're not getting rid of me that easily.'

He said nothing as they slipped down the slope and ran north, following the line of the ridge away from the Kellach quarter.

'The Merchant Gate,' said Daphne, pointing ahead as they raced through the grass. Killop glanced up. The gates were lying open, and a group of civilians were gathered outside. They turned to gaze at the three arrivals, and Killop noticed that most were dressed in dust-stained night clothes.

Daphne ignored them, and headed straight for the entrance.

The group quietened as they passed, but no one tried to stop them. Killop and Chane followed Daphne through the large gates, and into the city. Inside, a scene of destruction awaited them. Fires were raging out of control in several places, and more than half of the grand stately mansions and buildings had collapsed. Civilians stumbled around in small groups, gazing with wide eyes, or mourning over the bodies of the fallen.

They reached a large crossroads, and Killop saw the vast shells of the imperial palace and the cathedral, both derelict ruins that covered acres of space within the walls. Immense heaps of rubble lay piled by their gutted and flame-scorched carcasses.

'That's what your sister did,' Daphne said, seeing where he was looking, 'the last time she was here.'

'This doesn't feel right,' Chane said. 'No soldiers, no church wardens. I thought there'd be someone in authority to check us coming in.'

'They must all be in the Kellach quarter,' Daphne said.

'That's what worries me,' Chane said. 'Why would every soldier be sent there, unless they knew Keira was in the city? I can't think of any other reason why the Emperor would abandon the rest of it.'

They took the left-hand street at the crossroads, and headed through a large open marketplace, its stalls empty and deserted. Behind it loomed a high wall, its stonework rough and irregular, compared to the smooth ashlar blocks of masonry that comprised the other great walls of the city.

'That's the old Emergency Wall,' Daphne said as they strode towards it, 'built when Agang brought his army to the city two years ago. It separates the Kellach quarter from the New Town.'

They paused as a gatehouse came into view. Dozens of soldiers were clustered at the great double doors that led through to the Kellach quarter. A barricade had been constructed, and Killop could hear the sounds of violence coming from the other side. His hand went to the hilt of his sword, and he had to force himself not to charge the gates.

There were no civilians within a hundred yards of the wall, and several of the soldiers were staring in their direction. Daphne turned, and began to walk towards the other side of the market.

'We're not getting through that way,' she said, as Killop raised an eyebrow, 'but there are other ways in.'

Killop gazed up. The sun was breaking over the eastern horizon, and daylight was revealing more of the damage. Smoke filled the sky above, and with no wind, the great towers of soot and ash were combining into a dark cloud over the city. In the streets, the fires were growing, burning unchecked and spreading from house to house.

Daphne coughed, and tied a strip of cloth over her face as the smoke thickened.

'This way,' she said, and set off down the road, Killop and Chane a step behind her. Daphne raced away from the Emergency Wall and towards an enormous fortress ahead, which seemed to Killop to be the only undamaged building left in the city. Its high walls stood firm and solid amid the destruction, and a great banner was flying from its tallest tower, displaying the imperial star. As they got closer, he realised that every opening on the walls of the fortress had been blocked up, except for the upper storey, where light was coming out of a series of narrow windows.

'Where are we going?' he said.

'On the other side of the Great Fortress, there's a gate leading to the

Old Town,' Daphne said. 'We can try to access the Kellach quarter from there.'

'Is that where he lives?' Killop said, glancing up at the fortress. 'In there?' She nodded.

They passed the fortress and reached a wide street, filled with civilians making their way towards the gates to get out of the city. All of them were Holdings, and many looked dazed and frightened, clutching on to bundles of possessions as they trudged along the road.

Daphne ploughed into them, pushing her way against the flow of people. They turned a corner, and Killop saw the gates ahead, leading into the city's Old Town. It was blocked with civilians trying to flee. A great mass of Holdings were pushing and cramming through the opening in the wall, all attempting to get into the New Town.

'Shit,' said Chane, pausing to catch her breath. 'How are we getting through there?'

Daphne, Killop and Chane shoved their way to the side of the road to get out of the press of folk heading in the opposite direction, and reached the eaves of a line of shops, all boarded up.

'What'll we do?' said Chane.

'I'm thinking,' Daphne said.

Killop gazed around, wishing he knew the layout of the city. He had once seen a map of it on the Holdfast estate, but had paid it no attention at the time. He swore. So close to his daughter, yet it felt like she was a hundred miles away.

'Are your powers back?' he said to Daphne.

'I'll check,' she said. Her eyes went hazy, then she nodded. 'Kick in the door for me.'

Chane and Daphne stood clear, and Killop battered it down. They entered, and Daphne found a chair, and wiped the dust from it.

'Cover me while I take a look,' she said, sitting.

Chane took up position by the door, and Killop crouched next to Daphne, her eyes clouding over again. Killop took a long, slow breath, his heart pounding. He glanced down at his fingers, feeling his own power come back. Keira's must have returned by now as well, he thought, if she was still alive.

Daphne let out a cry of pain and terror and flew back off the chair, landing on her back on the stone floor. Killop raced to her side.

She opened her eyes, groaning.

'What happened?' he said. 'Are you alright?'

'The Creator,' she gasped. 'He sees us. He knows where we are.' She sat up. 'He's coming.'

'Karalyn?' Killop said. 'Did you see her?'

Daphne shook her head, and scrambled to her feet. 'No. Or Keira. I was searching the Kellach quarter when the Creator entered my mind.' She stared at him. 'He's more powerful than I believed possible. He could have killed me in an instant.' She shuddered. 'I've never felt so weak, so vulnerable.'

'We need to get out of here,' cried Chane. 'We have to hide.'

'It's no use,' Daphne said. 'I can still feel traces of his power in my head. He'll see me wherever I go.'

Killop took her hand.

'Then we fight,' he said. 'We go down fighting the bastard if we have to.'

'He wants me alive,' she said, her eyes more full of despair than he had ever seen before. 'He told me what he wants to do, what his plan for me is...'

'Fuck his plan,' Killop said.

'I don't want him to take me alive, Killop,' she whispered.

He gazed into her green eyes. 'It won't come to that.'

'Come on, guys,' Chane cried. 'We can talk about this shit later. We need to go.'

Killop pulled Daphne along by her hand to the door. She seemed to be in a daze, as if the Creator had dulled her mind, or filled it with hopelessness. Outside, the street was as packed as before, with hundreds of Holdings civilians moving out from the gates to the Old Town on their left.

'Let's mix in with them,' Chane said. 'He'll never see us among this lot.'

'You don't understand...' said Daphne, as Killop led her along. They moved into the crowd, allowing it to shepherd them away from the gates. On either side of the road, the collapsed streets loomed in the morning sunshine, and smoke lay in thick pockets. A fire was raging unchecked a street away to their left, tearing through the stone tenement blocks.

He heard a scream in the distance behind him, and turned. He squinted through the smoke at the Old Town wall, and saw an enormous figure standing upon the battlements. His right hand was raised, and the screams intensified. The crowd panicked as the cries grew louder and nearer, and groups tried to shove their way forwards. Killop pulled Daphne close as the masses of civilians tried to run. Chane was separated from them in the crush of folk, and Killop lost sight of her in the panic. The screaming grew closer, and he saw the reason. Like a ripple on a pool of water, a wave of power was spreading over the crowd, and wherever it reached, people were falling, clutching their chests in agony, and lying still on the road in heaps.

Killop put his arms round Daphne and braced himself as the wave reached where they stood, but it passed them, felling every civilian on either side, and continuing up the street. Killop stared at the hundreds of bodies carpeting the road, his legs frozen to the spot. He and Daphne were the only two standing. His eyes scanned for any sign of Chane, but there was nothing but piles and heaps of corpses.

The Creator approached, striding through the carnage, a good head taller than any Kellach Brigdomin.

Killop drew his sword. Next to him, Daphne did the same, her eyes defiant.

The Creator laughed.

'Daphne Holdfast. I should have known that a cliff's edge wouldn't stop you. And Killop of Kell, partner of Daphne and brother of Keira, you are also a mage? A mere sparker, but still, I'll take what I can get.'

He halted ten yards from them, his black armour burnt and smoking. Patches of blood covered his shoulder guard, and there was a hole punctured through the right eye socket of his mask.

'What are you waiting for?' said Daphne, her sword held high. 'Come and get us.'

'You won't be dying today, Daphne,' the Creator said. 'Tomorrow perhaps, but not today.'

Daphne glanced at Killop

'I meant what I said before,' she whispered. 'Don't let him take me.'

Killop stared at her, unable to put what he was feeling into words. He nodded, then turned to face the Creator, his knuckles white on the hilt of his sword.

The Creator raised his arms. His fingers splayed out, and he grunted in effort.

Around them, the heaps of bodies began to move. An arm juddered, a leg, then gasps of breath as the dead took in their first air for several minutes. Killop and Daphne stared as scores of corpses heaved themselves to their feet. Their eyes were empty, their mouths open, their arms hanging loose by their sides.

The Creator waved his hand, and the dead turned to face him.

'Take them,' he said. 'Alive.'

Without a sound, the raised dead lunged at Killop and Daphne, reaching with their arms to grab them.

Killop slashed out with his sword, severing hands and cleaving a man in two, as behind him, Daphne did the same. The dead were slow, but had no fear, and advanced from every direction. Killop's sword arm swung again and again, spraying blood across the ground and slicing the undead into pieces, but still they came. Unarmed, they clutched at his clothes and hair, some crawled and took hold of his legs. He kicked out, and struggled, picking one up by the throat and hurling him through the air.

At his back, he could hear Daphne start to toil, and he remembered her words.

He turned, pushing away more arms as they reached for him, and saw Daphne two yards to his right, surrounded by raised Holdings peasants, drowning in their midst. At the edge of the mob, he saw Chane. Her eyes were dead, and she was advancing like the others, scrambling over the bodies of those that Daphne had sent to their deaths for a second time. Daphne saw her too, and turned to face Killop. He caught her eye, and they stared for a moment at each other. Killop tried to lift his sword arm, but a dozen hands were pulling it down. He raged and writhed as more piled on top of him. His head hit the ground as he toppled over under the weight, and his eyes closed.

Killop felt a spark blast through his mind and he cried out in pain, awakening. He opened his eyes. He was hanging by his arms from chains attached to a hook in the ceiling, his feet inches off the ground. The room was small, and there were old stains of dried blood on the walls and floor. A window was lying open to his left, and he glanced out. He was somewhere high up, overlooking the burning and ruined city. The upper floor of the fortress, it had to be. From the light outside it was still daytime, but there was too much smoke hovering above the city to be more exact.

He had failed Daphne, and allowed her to be captured alive, but at that moment he was glad. If she was alive, then there was still hope. He remembered the way the Creator had been able to raise the dead, and hold them to his will, and any hope he had faded. The Emperor, or Creator, whoever the being was, it now had more power than every mage in the world combined. If he wasn't a god before, he was one now.

He cursed Kylon's name, and hoped his sister had killed him.

His chains rattled as he tried to relieve the pressure on his arms. His shoulders were in agony, and his wrists were on fire where the iron bands dug into his skin. He tried to raise himself, straining with the muscles in his arms, pulling his body up, and he lifted his head as far as his bending elbows, but it was too much, and he fell back, jolting his shoulders and back.

He heard a low laugh.

'You are most amusing to watch,' the Creator said from the shadows of the room. 'Other races would weep or despair, but my mighty mountain warriors keep going, no matter how awful the odds. I made you well.'

Killop said nothing.

'I can see the spark power burning within you,' the Creator went on, 'just as I can now see every mage in the world, wherever they may be. All except one.'

He emerged from the shadows, clad in a fresh set of shining black armour, the jet enamel tracery gleaming in the light from the window. He still wore the same mask as before, and Killop could see his blood-shot right eye through the ragged hole.

'As you are her brother,' he said. 'I thought it prudent to read your mind, to see if you knew her whereabouts, but that only raised more questions than it answered. Questions that I need you to be awake for. Answer me, and your death will be quick. Obstruct me, and you will suffer.'

He came closer, to within a few feet.

'Do you understand?'

Killop lifted his head, and spat at him.

The Creator laughed.

'Someone has tampered with your mind,' he said, 'and made certain memories impossible for me to read. I see them in there, but when I try to grasp them, they slip from my reach like fish in a river, glinting just beyond my touch.'

Killop tried to blank his thoughts, but they flashed to his daughter, and how she had repaired his mind long before.

The Creator gazed at Killop and smiled. 'You know of what I speak. Good. Yet even now, while your foolish mind is remembering it, I cannot read you. So, you must tell me. Who did this? And don't say Daphne. I have already read her mind, and know she is incapable of such a subtle use of power.'

Killop laughed.

The Creator narrowed his eyes and lifted his fingers.

Excruciating pains ripped through Killop's body and he convulsed, shaking like a rag doll from the chains, his head lolling as every nerve within him burned.

The Creator lowered his fingers, and the pain ceased.

'Now answer me, or I will do that again. And again.'

Killop opened his mouth, blood and saliva rolling down his chin.

'You lost Keira,' he gasped. 'That's funny.'

He screamed as the pains shredded him again, and he longed to lose consciousness.

There's no escape, the Creator said in his mind. *I can keep you awake through the worst pain imaginable. Tell me who meddled with your brain, and it will end.*

The agony eased, and Killop swung from the chains, his head bowed.

'Well?' said the Creator.

Killop said nothing.

'I see that you think I need to keep you alive,' the Creator said. 'That is the hope sustaining you. You think I need you for the ritual.' He smiled. 'You're wrong. I don't need you or your sister. A young fire mage happens to be approaching the city at this very moment, along with the other mages I require. After scouring the earth for them, now I find I need only sit here, and they all come to me.'

The Creator stared at Killop. 'Now, that's funny.'

He laughed. 'And now you despair. I feel it. Good. Know that there is no hope. One more ritual, that's all it will take. My mind encompasses all things, and so now I see how close I am to my goal, and there's nothing anyone can do to stop me. All you can do is lessen your suffering.'

He raised his hand.

'So,' he said, 'are you ready to answer my question?'

Killop spat out a mouthful of blood. 'I can take whatever you throw at me. You can burn me, flay me, shred my mind, but I'll never help you. Deep down, you know it's true. After all, you made me, didn't you?'

The Creator narrowed his eyes, and the pain began again.

CHAPTER 35
DOWN TO EARTH

O utside Plateau City, Imperial Plateau – 19th Day, Second Third Winter 507

'Dolphins,' said Laodoc, gazing out of one of the carriage's round windows at the waters of the Inner Sea as they sped past. 'How wonderful.'

'Why?' said Shella, squinting through the glass. 'Are they tasty?'

'They are beautiful creatures,' he said. 'I can't imagine eating one.'

'I can,' she said. 'They're huge. Could feed a family for a week. Maybe we could stop and try one.'

'No,' said Agang, from the other side of the carriage. 'We'll be in Plateau City by this evening. We don't have time to stop.'

'I thought you were sleeping,' she said, 'or maybe I just hoped you were.'

Laodoc frowned. The bickering between the pair had increased since they had begun travelling within the close confines of the carriage. Although they stopped and camped each day at sunset, they spent most of their waking hours within the narrow wooden tube, hurtling over land and water. For the first couple of days, Laodoc had nearly exhausted himself by taking the controls, but the Kellach women were quick learners, and soon Bridget, Dyam and Lola were taking turns to pilot the vessel. They had also navigated, using the sun, and the position of the seven stars, to plot their way north-west, towards the imperial capital.

Laodoc smiled. It was strange, but he felt free, as if no matter what awaited them in the city, everything would be alright. They would either defeat the Emperor or die in the attempt, and he was at peace with whatever fate ordained.

'Maybe we should stop,' Shella said, 'then we'd be fresh in the morning when we arrive.'

Agang sighed. 'What? You mean we've raced all this way, just to ease up at the last stretch? Every day matters, Shella. You know that.'

'Oh shut up, you sanctimonious asshole,' Shella said.

Laodoc heard Bridget chuckle from where she stood by the pilot's controls at the rear of the carriage.

'The sooner we get there,' Agang went on, 'the sooner we can put an end to the misrule of the Emperor, and bring peace to the world.'

'Are you out of your ape mind?' Shella said. 'In the far from certain event that we do manage to stop that mad bastard, do you really believe that wars will suddenly end? We were fighting each other before the Emperor went nuts, and we'll do the same after.'

'You're wrong,' Agang said. 'You're missing the point. The empire was a success, if only for a short while. It points the way, it shows us what we need to do. Unite the peoples of the world under a single banner, with one law for all, and one government to rule fairly.'

Shella laughed. She opened her flask and took a sip.

'And I don't suppose,' she said, 'that you have any suggestions about who should rule? Or were you thinking about constituting a democracy?'

'I feel no shame in stating the simple truth,' he said. 'We should rule. After we have killed the Emperor, we will be in the heart of government, ready to take the reins.'

Shella started laughing again.

'We each have experience of governing,' he went on, ignoring her. 'I was king of Sanang, while you, my friend, were chancellor of Rahain.

Even Shella here,' he smirked, 'was a princess. We would make a formidable team.'

'And Bridget too,' said Laodoc.

'Indeed,' said Agang. 'I include her in this also.'

'What a fucking honour,' Bridget said, rolling her eyes. 'I get to be in Agang's club.'

'Think it through, Bridget,' Agang said. 'The four of us, we could rule the world.'

'Being in charge sucks,' said Shella. 'I'd have thought being king would've taught you that.'

'And how long were you king for?' said Bridget.

'Eight thirds,' he said, glowering. 'Longer than you were chief.'

'This conversation's pointless,' Shella said. 'Let's focus on beating the Emperor, not waste our time with this bullshit.'

'Spoken like a true leader,' Agang said.

Laodoc gazed out of the window. He could see land approaching.

'We're only a couple of hours from the city,' he said. 'Shella, you know it best. Where should we land?'

The Rakanese mage frowned. 'That depends. We should fly over the city first, to see what's happening. The city might be armed to the teeth, ready to fight us off. I don't know how many ballista it would take to knock out our flying snakes, in which case our fly over should be high.' She shook her head. 'Either way, we'll be letting the world know we're arriving or, well, they'll know somebody's arriving.'

'We do have the option of landing further from the city,' Laodoc said, 'and travelling the final miles on foot. That way, we could enter the city unannounced.'

'Speed and surprise,' said Agang. 'These are the most formidable weapons at our disposal. We land as close as possible to the Emperor, and unleash Shella upon them.'

'Excuse me?' she said. 'Is that how you see me? As some sort of killing machine?'

'I've witnessed your power with my own eyes,' he said, 'but you won't be alone. When we land, I will be at your side, shielding you as I did at the camp, and ready to heal you if you are wounded.'

Shella frowned, and lit a cigarette. 'And we'll be doing this in a couple of hours? Shit.'

Lola switched places with Bridget, and the Brig woman came and sat next to Laodoc, who was gazing out at the green fields racing by beneath them. Bridget picked up a bottle of wine, liberated from a farmhouse they had passed a few days before, and took a swig.

'I'll watch your back,' she said, 'while they're off doing their heroics.'

'Thanks,' he said. 'It's at times like this that I feel my age, while my younger companions are getting ready to fight. Are we being rash, Bridget?'

She laughed, then took another swig. 'Laodoc,' she said, 'we're about to fly right into the heart of the imperial capital, where the mad Emperor is either waiting for us or not, is weak... or not. Rash doesn't even begin to cover it.'

'Yet I feel,' he said, 'somehow confident.'

'Aye,' she said, 'me too. Been feeling it all day. Like it's what we're meant to do.'

Laodoc smiled. 'Maybe it is.' He reached for his blanket. 'I'm going to try to get some sleep now, or at least rest. I imagine we have a busy time ahead.'

'No problem,' Bridget said. 'I'll be sure to wake you when it all kicks off.'

Laodoc stretched out on the wooden bench and lay down. He closed his eyes, feeling the rocking of the carriage, and hearing the low chatter of the passengers. He tried to sleep, but his head was full of thoughts. Although Agang's enthusiasm hadn't spread to Shella, Laodoc felt it seep through him, and he daydreamed about the benevolent rule they would bestow upon the empire. Power held no interest for him, and he agreed with Shella's remarks regarding being in charge, though he might have expressed it in a less vulgar manner. He had no desire to be the sole ruler, but Agang's idea of the four of them acting as a team was worth considering. He allowed himself to picture them basking in the roars and cheers of a liberated and free populace, waving at them from the steps of the palace, then remembered that Keira had destroyed it.

He frowned.

He had failed as chancellor of Rahain. He had tried to please everyone, and had ended up despised by all. The Old Free, the New Free, the Holdings church, they had all been happy to see him go in the end. And now, Governor Ghorley ruled in the Emperor's name, with an iron fist, crushing all dissent and heterodoxical thought, transforming Rahain into an obedient and subservient colony of the empire.

Things would be different once they had secured power in Plateau City, he was certain of it.

Laodoc felt a hand shake his arm.

'We're nearly there,' said Bridget.

He opened his eyes and sat up, feeling groggy. Bridget was dressed in her patched-up and worn fighting leathers, a sword at her belt, and a crossbow over her shoulder. She was eating from a dish with her fingers, and his stomach rumbled.

She handed him a bowl.

'Eat up,' she said, 'then get yer boots on.'

'Yes, ma'am,' he smiled. He glanced around the carriage. Agang was pacing back and forth, mouthing words to himself, lost in his thoughts. Shella was frowning at him while she smoked another cigarette and sipped from her flask. She seemed confident, but there was a slight twist under her left eye. Lola was sitting next to Dean, checking her longbow, as the boy stared at the book lying open in his hands. Dyam was at the rear of the carriage, handling the controls, and maintaining a long glide.

Laodoc took some food and gazed out of the window while he ate. In the distance, he could see the imperial capital, bathed in the red glow of the sun as it lowered in the western sky.

'This is the first time I've seen it,' said Bridget, as she sat on the bench beside him. 'Not as big as I thought.'

'The seven cities of Rahain are all much larger,' he said, 'but the Holdings are a young civilisation, new to building cities. It's not bad for a first attempt.'

'If the Holdings are barely civilised in the eyes of the Rahain,' Bridget said, 'no wonder you thought the Kellach were tree-climbing savages.'

Shella glanced over. 'I knew you'd see sense in the end.'

Bridget laughed.

Laodoc's smile fell as he stared out of the window.

'The city,' he said, 'I think it's burning.'

The others gathered round the windows and peered out. What Laodoc had thought was the reflected glow of the sunset was more than that. Flames were raging throughout the city, and what lay above was not a cloud, but smoke.

'Shit,' said Shella.

'Maybe Keira arrived before us,' said Agang, his eyes wide. 'Maybe she attacked first.'

'The walls look damaged, too,' Bridget said. 'Something's fucked the place up.'

They gazed in silence as the flying carriage approached. Dyam pulled on the controls, and Laodoc lost sight of the city as they gained altitude, climbing upwards. He felt his stomach lurch, and he put down his bowl of half-eaten food.

'I hate this bit,' Bridget groaned, gripping the sides of her seat.

They levelled out, and the city came back into view. He could see the outline of the great walls, and began to understand the extent of the devastation wrought below. Entire streets appeared to be nothing more than piles of rubble, and half a dozen huge fires were consuming about a quarter of the area within the city boundaries. As he expected, the palace and cathedral were hollowed-out ruins occupying the northern section of the city, but south of that, only the Great Fortress seemed to be standing. Its high towers and walls were gleaming orange and red in the flickering light of the fires raging around it.

'Pyre's bawsack,' muttered Bridget. 'What a mess.'

Agang nodded over to Dyam.

'Take us down.'

'Alright,' she cried out. 'Strap yerselves in!'

The passengers settled into their seats, and pulled the leather belts over their shoulders. Laodoc sat back and took a long breath as the carriage began its descent, lowering through the air in wide, lazy circles. Laodoc could see the city every time they banked and turned, getting closer with every second.

Shella yelled as she stared out of a window. 'Stop!'

She unstrapped herself, and ran towards Dyam.

'Turn back,' she screamed. 'Now!'

Dyam stared at her, then yanked on the controls, heaving them forward, and the carriage jolted and began to spin.

'What are you doing?' Agang yelled, ripping off his straps and racing up the carriage. He swayed as they banked and twisted, Dyam fighting with the controls.

'Keira didn't wreck the city, you fucking idiot,' Shella cried, as she hung on to the side of the carriage. 'There's been an earthquake. Do you remember the last time there was a earthquake?'

Agang paused, his eyes widening.

'We're too late!' she screamed at him. She turned to Dyam. 'Get us out of here.'

'I'm trying,' she grunted. 'Just give me a second to get the beasts under control.'

Laodoc's hands began to shake as the carriage juddered and rolled through the sky. Dyam heaved on the controls, and they straightened, levelled, and began to rise.

Laodoc turned and stared back out of the window. The city was only a hundred feet below, and pillars of smoke rose above them on either side. Dyam steered the carriage between them, gaining altitude.

They banked, and he saw the Great Fortress. There was movement on the roof, and he gasped as a burst of flame shot towards them.

'Look out!' he cried.

He felt the heat of the firebolt as it raced past the window. There was a great cry from above, and the carriage slowed and banked.

'Someone's bringing down the gaien,' cried Bridget.

Laodoc stared out of the window as another bolt of fire roared past them. On the roof of the Great Fortress, a figure was standing, raising his arms into the air. The carriage shook as a second gaien was hit. They started to descend.

'We're going down,' yelled Dyam.

Laodoc closed his eyes as they dropped through the air. The remaining two gaien above were straining against the weight, but were achieving nothing more than slowing their fall. They passed the height of the roof of the fortress, a few hundred yards away, and crash-landed in a long skid, bumping and jolting at speed until they came to a grinding halt.

Bridget was the first to rise. She unbuckled her belt and turned to stare out of the nearest window.

Laodoc rubbed his head. Every bone in his body felt wrenched and sore. He tried to unfasten the belt buckle, but his hands were trembling.

'Everyone alright?' said Bridget.

'Fine,' yelled Dyam, unstrapping herself from the controls.

She rushed to where Shella was clinging on to a railing, and helped the Rakanese mage down. Agang staggered to his feet.

Bridget helped Laodoc out of his seat as Lola began to open a side hatch.

'Wait,' said Bridget. 'We'll do this properly, just as we planned. Shella, Agang and Lola will lead, the rest of us will follow with crossbows.' She clapped her hands. 'Come on, move.'

Agang picked up his shield, and made his way to stand next to Lola, as the others reached for their crossbows. Shella lit a cigarette and walked to the hatch. She peered out of the window as Lola grabbed the handle.

'Do you know where we are?' Laodoc said.

'We're in the Old Town,' she said, 'not too far from the docks.'

'You mean we nearly landed in the water?' said Bridget.

Shella frowned. 'Right now, I'd rather be taking my chances with the Inner Sea.'

She nodded at Lola, and the Lach woman threw open the hatch. She stepped forward, her shield raised, and Agang followed. Shella winked at Laodoc, and went out after them.

'I'll take the rear,' said Dyam, a crossbow cradled in her arms. 'Dean, you stay by me.'

Bridget nodded, then she and Laodoc left through the hatch and stepped down onto the cobbles of the street. The light in the west was starting to fade as he gazed around. The area was deserted, and in ruins. He could see at least two fires burning within the Old Town, and the earthquake had toppled many of the buildings. Their carriage had left a long gouge down the middle of the road, ploughing up cobbles and ripping aside paving slabs.

'Nice landing,' said Bridget.

'Cheers,' said Dyam, ushering Dean out of the carriage. She clambered round the side of the wooden structure and released the two remaining winged gaien.

'Go on home, boys,' she yelled, as they flew away.

Laodoc glanced at Shella and Agang, who were arguing a few yards up the road, while Lola scouted forward. He gazed around. Down a narrow street to his right, he could see the arches leading to the port of the city, where the trading ships had once berthed, loading and unloading goods from every corner of the world. Laodoc knew that the Old Town was one of the poorer districts of the imperial capital, but the squalor that surrounded them was worse than anything he had seen on his previous visit. Heaps of refuse were piled high in the streets, and the tenement blocks that hadn't collapsed or been burnt to the ground were dilapidated slums. The place stank, of smoke and human waste.

Lola returned.

'There's no one here,' she said. 'If we're heading to that fortress, the way is clear.'

She pointed up at the high towers that rose above the roofs of the Old Town, and they turned and stared. As Laodoc gazed up, he felt any confidence within him dissolve. What a stupid old man he was, to think he could stand up to the Emperor. He shuddered.

Shella frowned, and rubbed her head. She glanced round at the others.

'Did anyone else feel that?' she said.

'Feel what?' said Bridget.

'I don't know exactly,' she said. 'Like my mood just crashed, and all of a sudden I felt nothing but black despair.'

'I felt it,' said Laodoc.

Shella scowled. 'Don't you understand? That mad bastard up there's messing with our heads. No wonder we were so cocky about coming here. He's been playing us, filling our heads with crap, then pulling away the rug.'

Agang's face fell. 'He knew we were coming.'

'He led us right here,' Shella spat, 'and like idiots, we fell for it.'

'What are we going to do now?' said Dyam. 'We can't exactly fly out of here.'

Bridget smirked. 'Does anyone know how to sail a boat?'

'Whatever we do,' Laodoc said, 'we can't stand here arguing. The Emperor is no doubt aware of us now, even if he wasn't before.'

Shella nodded. 'Snake-eyes is right. Come on.'

She set off, skirting the damage caused by the carriage's landing, and the others followed. They kept to the same order as before, with Agang and Lola flanking the flow mage, and the rest behind. Laodoc began to feel the heat from an immense fire devouring whole streets to their left, the tenements and shop fronts belching flames. Smoke was billowing out from the roads leading to the inferno, sending thick grey and black clouds in their direction.

Laodoc coughed, as the smoke began to envelop them.

'Keep moving,' yelled Agang. 'It's clearer up ahead.'

Bridget grabbed Laodoc's sleeve as the visibility fell. His eyes were watering, and the stench of burning filled his mouth and nostrils.

'This isn't natural,' he heard Shella cry, though he couldn't see her through the dense grey smoke. 'This is the Emperor's work.'

'Don't stop,' Bridget said, pulling him along the street. His feet slipped on the greasy cobbles, and he staggered, choking.

'I can't breathe,' he gasped, then he realised that Bridget had gone. He gazed around, but could see nothing but smoke. He heard voices, but they seemed to be coming from far away, whispering. He fell to his knees, crying out in pain as he struck the hard cobbles, but the smoke was thinner nearer the ground, and he was able to breathe again. He sensed a dim glow in the distance, and began to crawl towards it, over the piles of steaming refuse. He gagged, every inch of him repelled by the smell and the smoke, but kept going, his hands deep in the rotting waste in the gutters of the road.

He continued crawling, but there seemed to be no end to the smoke, and so he followed the road on and on towards the light. Above him he could see a patch of sky, dark now that the sun had set below the horizon. He gazed around, but it was like being lost in a thick fog, and every direction looked the same.

Exhausted, he collapsed into the gutter, a trickle of oily water running under his legs and past his head. Ahead, the light seemed closer, and it gave him hope, although he knew he had failed and the Emperor had won.

He didn't mind. He would lie there until the last breath left his body, and then he would be at peace.

Don't give up, he heard a voice call to him. *You're so close, Laodoc. Just a little further.*

Laodoc lifted his head, straining to see where the voice was coming from. There was a wisp of movement ahead of him, a flash of a white robe, and he stared.

'Simiona?'

He pulled himself up and stood, his knees shaky. The clouds of smoke were thinning, and the light in front of him brightened. He saw a door in a wall. It was lying open, and he caught a glimpse of the white robes disappearing inside.

Laodoc staggered forward, his heart bursting with longing and grief. He nearly fell, but kept on, his feet shuffling over the cobbles. He reached the door and peered into the darkness within.

'Hello?' he called out.

Nothing.

He stepped inside, and the door closed behind him. A row of wall lights burst into flame, lighting up a long corridor. At the end of it stood a young woman in white, her back to him. She turned her head, smiled, and began to ascend a flight of stairs. He stared at her as she moved out of view, tears rolling down his cheeks.

He shook his head, but there was no room in his mind for anything other than following his lost Simiona, and he placed one foot in front of the other and walked onwards.

Keep going, Laodoc, my dear. I'm waiting for you.

He wept, and quickened his step. His knees were aching and his breath ragged, but he ignored the complaints coming from his body, his will stronger than his frail shell, his love more powerful than his weakness.

He reached the stairs, and collapsed.

———

Pain rippled through his body and he awoke screaming.

'Come on, wake up,' said a voice. 'You lazy old reptile.'

Laodoc opened his eyes. He was lying on his side on a low wooden pallet, in a small windowless room. Chains were attached to his wrists and ankles. He raised his head. In front of him was standing an enormous figure in black armour.

'Did you enjoy your little illusion?' he said. 'I'd hoped that your will to see that slave girl again would have been enough to bear you to the top of the fortress on your own, but no; I had to come down and get you myself.' He laughed, an ugly guttural sound. 'The others practically ran up the stairs, so keen were they to join the party.'

Laodoc said nothing, his eyes on the Emperor.

'I'm learning, you see,' he went on. 'I went out first to collect Keira the fire mage, but I got a burning house dropped on me and two arrows in my head for my trouble. For Daphne Holdfast, I killed and then raised a few peasants to capture her, which was tiring; so for your group I decided to simply sit here and wait for you to come to me.'

Keira? he thought. Daphne? His heart broke in despair. The Emperor had them all.

'Pathetic,' the Emperor said. 'How easy it is to manipulate you creatures. Fill you full of hope, then snatch it away again, like playing with puppets.'

'Who are you?' Laodoc gasped.

'You know who I am,' he said. 'I am the Creator of this universe. I made everything in it, the mountains, the ocean. You.'

'I don't believe you.'

'Of course you'd say that. Laodoc, the ever-sceptical atheist, seeker of scientific knowledge and truth. To be honest, I don't care if you believe in me or not. In a few hours, it won't make any difference.'

'But if you created us,' Laodoc said, 'why did you put suffering into the world? And don't say free will. Free will doesn't cause disease, or famine, or drought. You could have made a world where children didn't die because of sickness, or even placed a tiny sliver of more compassion into people, to blunt their crueller instincts. You could have done all of that and still allowed us free will.'

The Emperor shook his head. 'Your questions are meaningless. They assume I care whether or not you suffer. Do you think my heart bleeds when one of you is hurt? My world and yours are so far removed from each other that I feel no more empathy for you than I would an insect. As a mage, you are worth a little more to me than the average, but only as a tool to fulfil my purposes. Nothing more.'

'You are evil.'

'Evil?' the Emperor laughed. 'Are you evil if you swat a fly? If it weren't for me, you wouldn't be here; none of this world would exist. I gave you life. All the emotions you feel: love, pity, friendship. Hate. They're only there because I made you capable of feeling them. But what is in my power to give, I can also take away.'

'Do you have children?'

The Emperor paused. 'What?'

'I had two sons,' Laodoc said. 'My wife and I gave them life, and when they grew up, we let them go out into the world, to become men. Though in my heart I always loved them, they were no longer mine to control. I had no right to take their lives from them. If I had done so, I would be evil. It is the same with you. Once you made us, we no longer belonged to you. We are free.'

The Emperor stood in silence for a moment, then he turned and left the cell. Laodoc watched the door shut, then lay his head down on the low pallet, the chains digging into his skin.

His eyes closed, a tear escaping and rolling down his cheek. He was going to die in a few hours, knowing that although he had been wrong his whole life, he had left god with nothing to say.

CHAPTER 36
DEFIANCE

Plateau City, Imperial Plateau – 19th Day, Second Third Winter 507

'Why is mummy angry?' asked Daphne, from high up on her horse.

'Shh,' said Ariel, glancing at their mother, who was riding her own stallion in front of them on the path.

Daphne frowned, her hands clutching on to the reins of her mount. She gazed around at the endless grassy pastureland and fenced-off fields, where dozens of horses grazed and cantered in the bright after-noon sunshine. She usually loved her daily trip out with her elder sister and mother. The two girls would ride their horses, dressed in their smartest clothes, their hair groomed and faces clean. Often their mother would chat to them, and tell them stories, or teach them how to be ladies, and Daphne would listen with keen ears and wide eyes.

'Head up, Daphne,' she heard her mother say. 'Shoulders back.'

'Yes, mummy.'

'Ariel, stop chewing,' her mother went on. 'You look like a hired hand.'

'Sorry, mummy.'

The two girls glanced at each other, their expressions a mixture of mischievousness and fear. Mother had a temper, which was mostly directed at their father, but occasionally the children would be on the receiving end of an angry tirade. In recent days these seemed to have become more common, and Daphne had been on edge, trying her best never to say or do anything which might make her angry.

That day however, they were all supposed to be happy. Daphne had never seen her father so delighted. A man she rarely saw, let alone talked to, her father's moods had long been a source of anxiety to her, but after the priests had departed the estate house that morning, he had been whooping and grinning, and hugging Vince as if they hadn't seen each other in a long time.

'What does it mean?' she whispered to her sister who, being three years older, was considered by Daphne to be very wise. 'What's a vision mage?'

Ariel's eyes widened. Before she could say anything, their mother pulled on the reins of her mount and brought it to a halt. She turned to face the girls.

'It means your brother is special,' she said. 'He has been given a wonderful gift by the Creator.'

Daphne smiled. 'That's nice, mummy.'

Her mother frowned, her features darkening in a growing fury. Daphne edged back in her saddle, and she sensed Ariel do the same.

'It also means that Vince will be leaving us,' she went on. 'He will go and join the cavalry when he is old enough, and he will be lost to me.'

Daphne's heart sank. 'He can't go!'

'He's not leaving yet, you silly girl,' her mother said, 'but it's inevitable.'

'Father seems happy about it,' said Ariel.

'Well, yes,' she said, 'of course he is. He gets to brag to his friends about his son having battle vision, just like him.' She looked away, her eyes gazing into the distance. 'No doubt he also hopes it will increase his standing with the queen.'

Ariel's nine-year-old face frowned. 'Father said that Vince is lucky to be a mage, and that anyone who says bad things about them is just jealous.'

'He would say that, wouldn't he?' their mother said. 'But he's wrong. Maybe the very highest mages are envied for their power, those closest to the prophet, but I feel sorry for them all. Being a mage is a burden and a curse. A life of thankless duty awaits Vince. They will take my gentle boy away and train him to be a killer.' She looked at her two daughters. 'And I have three other children still to be tested by the priests, when your time comes.'

'I hope Jonah has the vision,' said Daphne. 'I want him to leave. I hate him.'

Their mother narrowed her eyes at her, then flicked the reins.

'Your father may have won the first round,' she said, turning her mount, 'but there are three more battles ahead.'

She kicked her heels, and her horse trotted off. Daphne and Ariel glanced at each other, and followed.

Her body beaten, Daphne lay curled up in the straw and dirt on the floor of the dark cell. Her leathers had been stripped from her, and she shivered in her long undershirt. The beautifully crafted armour that had protected her crippled left arm had been ripped off in the frenzied assault by those the Creator had raised from the dead. She had killed dozens of them when they had attacked, sending them to second deaths, only minutes after their first. It had been the sight of Chane among her attackers that had undone her. She had frozen for a moment, and her eyes had caught sight of Killop, swinging his long sword amid a swarm of risen peasants. A moment had been enough. Dozens of hands had taken hold of her, and she had fallen, kicked, scratched, punched and bitten, until she had almost been crushed to death under the mob.

Some small part of her mind remembered every long minute that followed, of being dragged over the cobbles by her arms, then carried into the Great Fortress. Rahain soldiers had taken custody of her, stripped and chained her, then thrown her into the cell where she now lay.

Blood trickled from her mouth, and she clasped her left arm in her right, holding it close to her body. Her crippled elbow felt broken, the fierce agony tempered by battle-vision, but she was weak, and it took all of her concentration to block out the pain. If she let go, she would slip into an unconsciousness from which she might not awaken. She remembered asking Killop to make sure she wasn't captured, but despite everything, she was glad to be alive. Being alive gave her another chance to fight.

No matter what happened, she would go down fighting. She was a Holdfast, and she had been captured and tortured before, and she would not shame the family; she would not give in. Let her defiance stand for everything and everyone she loved. Killop, Karalyn. She would never betray them.

She lessened her battle-vision a fraction, allowing more pain through in order to conserve her energy. She could take it. It was no worse than when B'Dang had shattered her arm in the Sanang forest over four years before. She had endured that, she could endure this. As her pain levels rose, so did her anger. She hoped Kylon was dead. She hoped Keira had made it slow and painful. If it weren't for him, they could all be living safely in the desert borderlands of Hold Fast.

She knew she would probably never see her daughter again, but the future wasn't fixed, and even the tiniest hope would keep her strong and sustain her through the worst nightmare. She took a long breath, taking the cold air in through her nose, and out through her mouth, clearing her mind. The cell she was in was sealed and in utter darkness, with no windows or cracks in the door to allow her vision through. There were two air vents built into the wall, but both were fitted with a series of meshes too fine for her vision to penetrate. A cell designed for a vision mage. She had no idea of the time, but it felt as if she had been lying in the cell for hours.

A blinding light split the room, and Daphne clenched her eyes shut as she heard the door of her cell open. She squinted, and saw a Rahain guard hook a lamp to the wall and walk out. Her eyes adjusted to the light as an immense figure appeared in the doorway. He stepped inside, and the door closed behind him.

He towered over her.

'Holdfast,' he said, the voice coming from behind a steel mask.

She wiped the blood from her mouth. 'Creator.'

'We meet again.'

Daphne turned and pushed herself up so that she was sitting with her back to the wall. She rested her crippled arm on her lap, and gazed up at the figure in black armour.

'You got a cigarette?'

The Creator stared down at her, and she heard a low mocking laugh from behind the mask.

'The Holdings were always my favourite people,' he said. 'Made in my image, did you know that? Of course not, how could you comprehend anything about me? For long millennia, I was alone. I witnessed everything, but could do nothing. And then, finally, the first prophet appeared, five hundred years ago, and then at last I could speak with another being. I guided your nation for five centuries, preaching my message of unity, dreaming that one day the peoples I created would live together in peace.'

'Peace?' Daphne said.

'Yes, for only through peace would the conditions arise to allow all five types of mages to be gathered together.'

'I thought for a moment you were saying you cared for us.'

'Don't be ridiculous, Holdfast. When I created this universe, and designed the beings that would live in it, I admit I held some foolish views regarding your worth. However, millennia of watching you slaughter each other, and then, when the five continents were melded into one, and the land settled down, what did you do? You continued to slaughter, only this time you fought the other races. Forgive me, but I lost any sympathy for the inhabitants of this world a long time ago.'

Daphne shook her head. 'I don't believe you had any to begin with.'

'Maybe you're right. What does it matter now? It'll all be over soon.'

'You're going to kill us all?'

'Yes. Not personally, of course, but you will all cease to exist. The universe will collapse, and everything in it will be as if it never was.'

'And you?'

'I will be home,' he said; 'free of this grotesque charade. It was a mistake, all of it. I should have listened.'

'Why are you telling me this?'

'I thought someone should know,' he said, 'even if your life will be over soon, along with everything else. I thought about telling Laodoc, but all he wanted was to debate theology.'

'Laodoc?'

'Yes,' he said, mirth behind his voice. 'He obliged me greatly by flying in on a carriage earlier this evening. And he wasn't alone. In one glorious day, I've had handed to me on a plate all the mages I require for a final ritual. There's you, of course, and Laodoc. He is indeed a poor mage, but the excellent standard of the others will cancel out his weakness.'

She stared at him. 'Who else?'

'You'll see soon enough.'

Daphne shook her head. 'This will be what, your third attempt? Fourth?'

'There have been many more than that, Holdfast,' he said, 'especially before I came down and took Guilliam's form. Arnault failed me often.'

'You'll fail again.'

He snorted. 'Your ignorance is matched only by your stubbornness, Holdfast. A trait you share with your Kell lover. It took a great deal of torture to get from him what I wanted.'

Daphne kept her face still. 'I don't believe you.'

The Creator took a step closer, and loomed over her. She felt his power surge through her mind, ripping through her memories, and raiding her darkest thoughts. She relaxed, leading him to all of the places that Kalayne had taught her how to make, places where she could reveal to the Creator nothing but what she wanted him to see.

He shook his head. 'Where is Keira?'

Daphne said nothing.

'By what means can she hide from me?'

'Was that a yes or no about the cigarette?'

'I can inflict great pain upon you.'

'You already have.'

He stepped back. 'What does it matter?' he said. 'The knowledge and power I received at the last ritual gave me the understanding of what I need to do to ensure success this time. It will be midnight shortly, and the preparations are well under way.' He put his hand on the door. 'We will meet again, Holdfast. Soon, and for the final time.'

He turned to the cell's entrance and stepped back outside into the corridor. The door closed behind him, and Daphne stared at it, the lamp on the wall continuing to light the cell.

Laodoc was captured, she thought, along with her and Killop. And others.

But Keira was still free, and that meant that Karalyn was safe.

She closed her eyes, clinging on to that hope.

No sound entered the cell to distract Daphne, and she concentrated on her breathing. Despite her vision being unable to leave the room, she ordered her mind. She could not prevent the Creator from penetrating her thoughts, but she knew that he was as blind to her dream-vision abilities as he was to Karalyn or Kalayne whenever they had hidden from him.

Her thoughts went to her daughter. She pictured her face, framed by unruly brown curls of hair, her expression wearing that look of concentration she had when she was playing with her toys. Daphne wished she had played with her more, wished she could have a second chance to be a better parent, wished she could see her, and hold her one last time. She caught herself as she was about to spiral into self-pity and regret. She wasn't going to give up, not yet. She went through the words of the Creator, trying to find a weakness.

He wanted to go home, and she felt a twinge of sympathy for him. She would still kill him if the opportunity arose, but at least now she could partly understand his motives. After spending thousands of years trapped and alone, was it any wonder that he was desperate enough to destroy everything if it meant he could be free?

The cell door opened, and two Rahain guards stood in the entrance.

'Get up,' said one, his crossbow pointed at her stomach.

She stood, her chains clanking against the floor. She kept her expression calm and serene.

'Move,' the guard said, and she walked forwards. They let her walk between them, then they prodded her back with their crossbows.

She walked down the stone corridor, lit by wall lamps every few yards, until they came to a steep set of stairs leading upwards. She went up, the guards close behind, her chains thunking on each step as she climbed. Up and up they went, past landings leading to other levels of the fortress, but the guards kept her to the stairs. She was tired, and her left arm was in agony. The steel band round her withered wrist was weighing it down, pulling on her fractured elbow. She kept her battle-vision working at a low level, all of it focussed on keeping the fiery pain from becoming too much to bear.

She reached the top of the stairs and emerged out onto the flat roof of a high tower. It was circular, with a four-foot high parapet enclosing its perimeter. In the centre was a low platform, and positioned around it were five metal posts, which had been driven into the flagstone roof. Surrounding them, the city was swathed in the glow of the fires raging through the streets. She gazed around. Apart from her and the guards, no one else was there.

Without hesitation, she shot her range-vision off the side of the tower, reaching a section of the Old Town wall close by. She pivoted her sight round, taking in the devastated streets. Ahead of her was the Kellach quarter, and her heart pounded at the thought that Karalyn was somewhere in the desolate and deserted district of the city. The fires in the quarter had been extinguished, and she could see soldiers patrolling the streets in numbers.

Despite her longing to see her daughter, she paused.

I know you're watching, she said in her mind. *I know you want me to lead you to Keira. The truth is, I don't know where she is, or if she's still alive, and I wouldn't tell you if I did.*

Her vision snapped back to her body as she felt her chains being pulled by a powerful force. She fell to the ground, her eyes opening. Standing over her was the Creator, his black armour blotting out the light from the fires. He dragged her by her chains across the roof, and she screamed in agony as her left arm was wrenched and twisted. He threw her down next to one of the five posts, and leant over. With one hand, he ripped the post from the flagstone where it was embedded. He looped her chains around it, then drove it back into the solid slab. The stone seemed to grow soft and viscous as the post was rammed deeper, pulling the chains with it. He touched the stone, and it hardened again.

He stood by Daphne, who lay with her arms out-stretched, the chains swallowed up into the rock by the post. Without a word, he turned and walked away to the stairwell. Daphne lay still, her face clenched, as the pain from her arm overwhelmed her. For a second, she longed for death.

She heard movement around her, but the pain was all-consuming. Her name was called, or it might have been, she wasn't sure. She withdrew into herself, her mind slipping between consciousness and oblivion. She heard her mother telling her to sit up straight, act like a lady, smile and, above all, always be polite.

A cruel laugh mocked her. She felt a surge of power ripple through her, and the pain vanished in an instant. She gasped.

As much as I enjoy watching you suffer, Holdfast, the Creator said in her head, *I need you lucid, in order to extract the maximum life from you.*

She opened her eyes. Around the roof in a circle, attached to the other posts, were faces from her past. Was she dreaming?

'Hey, Daphne,' said Shella, sitting on the flagstones a few feet to her left. Her hands and wrists were enclosed in large metal gauntlets, and her chains were sunk into the rock by the base of the post.

Daphne stared, her mind foggy and distant, despite the absence of pain. She could feel that her arm was still broken, and realised that the Creator had numbed her. She gazed round the circle. To Shella's left was Agang, squatting by his post, his fists clenched. After him was Dean, the young fire mage from Slateford, and lastly, between Dean and Daphne, was Laodoc. He was sitting cross-legged by his post, gazing at her.

'Are you all right, miss?'

Daphne sat up, and pulled her nightgown down over her knees. She cradled her left arm across her legs.

'This is a right laugh, eh?' said Shella, holding up her metal-encased hands. 'What a bunch of dumb asses we are. The Emperor must be pissing himself laughing at us. I came all this way ready to fight him, and I walked right into a fucking cell.'

'What did he make you see?' said Agang.

'My brother Sami,' she said. 'You?'

He bowed his head. 'An old friend.'

'Dean?' said Shella. 'What about you?'

The boy raised his head to look at her. His face was ashen, and covered in bruises. His fists were also bloodied.

'Lilyann,' he said.

'Looks like you put up a fight, at least,' she said.

He shrugged.

'What about you, professor fork-tongue?'

'Simiona.'

Daphne gazed at them. 'He trapped you all with visions?'

'Like distracting kids with candy,' said Shella. She looked Daphne up and down. 'Judging by your appearance, you went down fighting.'

'He raised hundreds of dead peasants. They overwhelmed us.'

Agang stared at her. 'He raised them?'

'Yes,' she said, 'just after he'd killed them.'

'Then he's a true soulwitch now,' Agang said. A tear ran down his cheek. 'What else can he possibly want? He is the most powerful being in the entire world, and he rules it. What more does he need?'

'He wants to go home,' she said. 'He told me.'

The others stared at her.

'He wants to leave?' said Laodoc.

She nodded.

'And he needs us to do it?' said Shella.

'Perhaps the level of power required is of an order of magnitude greater than any one mage could achieve,' said Laodoc.

'It's greater than many mages could achieve,' said the voice of the Creator, booming across the roof. They turned to see him emerging from the stairwell. Rahain soldiers followed him, and took up position around the length of the parapet, surrounding the five posts.

'Why do you think it has taken so many attempts?' the Creator said, striding up onto the platform in the centre of the roof, Arnault shuffling after him. The Creator gazed at each of the mages. 'This, however, will be the final attempt. You each have enough in you that, combined with my own power, will be sufficient to trigger the collapse of this universe.' He laughed. 'And just in time. There are so few mages left in the world that it's unlikely I would be able to assemble another group. Yours will be the last faces I see before I am free of this wretched world, and all of its miserable inhabitants.'

'Hurry up then,' said Shella. 'So you can fuck off.'

'Patience, my little amphibian witch,' he said. 'You should have stayed in Silverstream. Instead, you shall have the honour of being the only mage to participate in two rituals. I hope you told the others how painful it is to have your life force slowly drained from your body?'

'Where's Killop?' said Daphne.

The Creator turned to face her, and she felt his vast power bore into her mind.

'Where's Keira?'

You're going to fail, she said, pushing her words into his head.

He ripped his mask off and stormed towards her, his eyes red, his face blistered, and she flinched back against his raw power. She felt her mind raided, and fell to the ground writhing as he scoured her thoughts, sending every nerve aflame. She screamed, her head feeling like it was about to explode.

'You're hiding something,' the Creator cried, his rage seething above her.

'Leave her alone,' said Laodoc.

The Creator turned to face the old Rahain man, and Daphne felt his presence leave her mind. He stared at Laodoc. For a moment, Daphne thought he was going to strike him, but he turned away.

'In a short while,' he said, striding back to the platform, 'I will be laughing about this.'

Daphne pushed herself back into a sitting position, leaning against the post. Her pain had been numbed again, but she was exhausted.

'I can see why you wore that mask,' said Shella.

'It is only Guilliam's worthless flesh,' the Creator said. 'My powers may have disfigured his features, but my own body lies pristine, waiting for me to return to it.' He turned to Arnault, who was standing in silence by the platform, his head bowed. 'Shall we begin?'

The Lord Vicar looked up, his eyes glazed over and vacant. He clapped his hands together, and more soldiers filed up the steps, leading a row of chained prisoners. They were Kellach Brigdomin, and each had been beaten. They shuffled onto the roof, crossbows aimed at their backs, their shackles binding them closely together.

The Creator strode from the platform and approached them. He waved his hand and, grunting, the Kellach fell to their knees before him, as if a weight had fallen on their shoulders. He walked to the end of the line, and placed his hand on the forehead of a Kellach woman. Her face seemed to shrink into itself, and she choked, but her body remained frozen to the spot where she knelt. Her eyes melted, and blood flowed down from the sockets. The Creator lifted his hand, and she toppled to the ground. The other Kellach stared in horror, straining against the invisible force keeping them on their knees.

Daphne stared, unable to pull her eyes away as the Creator flung the body of the woman over the edge of the parapet and moved on to the next prisoner. One by one, he drained them of their lives, and each time he seemed to grow a little taller, his shoulders and arms thicker and stronger, while sparks seemed to fly across the surface of his armour as he threw each body from the top of the Great Fortress. When he had drained the last of the prisoners, the Creator turned to Arnault.

'You have been a most incompetent servant,' he said.

The Lord Vicar raised his eyes.

'Still,' the Creator went on, 'it would be a shame to waste your remaining vision power.'

He placed his hand round Arnault's throat, and watched as the life was drained from him. The Lord Vicar's body hung limp, his eyes hollow and empty. With a flick of his wrist, the Creator sent Arnault's body flying over the rooftop parapet, where it disappeared into the darkness.

The Creator stood in silence, staring up at the night sky with a look of ecstasy on his face, his eyes shining.

Daphne glanced at Shella. The Rakanese woman was looking with disgust at the Creator, contempt dripping from her.

'You're a coward,' Daphne yelled at him.

'Damn right,' said Shella. 'Everyone hates you. Why don't you kill yourself, and leave this world to those who love it?'

'You, love it?' said the Creator. 'You're a cynical, bitter woman with a heart full of murderous deeds that you feel no shame or regret for.' He gazed at the mages, 'Each of you has been responsible for evil acts. Murder, torture, the death of children and the slaughter of innocents.' His eyes stopped at Dean. 'Except the boy here, but that is more due to his youth than to anything good within him. If he were a better fire mage, then no doubt he would have killed many by now.'

He shook his head at them.

'This world was my mistake,' he said; 'and tonight, one year from when I came down to inhabit this material form, I will end it.'

He stood up onto the platform, and raised his hands.

The black clouds of smoke above the city began to swirl around, and everyone on the roof stared upwards as a tight whirling vortex was created.

Daphne felt a firm grip envelop her mind, as the Emperor entered. At once, she sensed the links reaching out from him to the other mages, and could see inside all of their minds at the same time. Fear, panic and awe rolled in waves through her from the others, and she could pick out the individual terrors that held them in his grasp.

He lowered his arms, and Daphne's head fell forwards, released. She took a breath, and gazed around. The other mages were doing the same, and she caught Laodoc's eye.

They looked up at the Emperor. He was frowning.

'It's still not enough,' he said. 'The three strong should balance out the two weak, but something else is missing.'

'Might as well give up then,' gasped Shella. 'Break out the gin and call it a night.'

The Creator ignored her, instead turning to stare at Agang.

'That thought you just had,' he said. 'Interesting.'

Agang widened his eyes.

'A sparker and a thrower?' the Creator said. 'Very perceptive, Agang. Thank you.'

He turned to a soldier. 'Have someone fetch Killop.'

'He's alive?' Daphne said, her heart soaring.

'Of course he is,' said the Creator, as the soldier ran off to the stairs. 'A little bruised, perhaps.'

'You bastard,' she said. 'You're going to fail.'

The Creator smiled. 'My crippled little Holdfast, defiant to the end? I expected no less.'

He turned and walked to the edge of the parapet, gazing down at the city. Daphne watched him, then heard sounds coming from below. Steel striking steel, and cries of agony filtered up to the roof. She drew on her reserves, and flew a line of vision to the top of the parapet. The streets below in the Kellach quarter were filled with movement. Imperial soldiers were battling a mixture of Holdings peasants and Kellach Brigdomin around barricades, and through the main square. She zipped her vision back to her head, and glanced at Shella.

'There's fighting in the Kellach quarter.'

'Good,' she said. 'Who's winning?'

'Couldn't tell.'

The Creator turned. 'There are hundreds of soldiers inside this fortress, and no one has ever broken into it by force in all the years it has stood here. I have also wrapped the building in false visions, enough to blind anyone who gets too close, and also to alert me if a mage approaches. No one will be interrupting us, so calm yourselves.'

Shella smirked. 'It's not us who's panicking.'

There was movement by the stairwell. Daphne's eyes narrowed as she watched a squad of Rahain carry Killop up the steps. His arms were trailing on the ground, and his head hung down.

'Here he is,' said the Creator. 'The sparker. At times, I almost forgot I made them, but now they prove their worth.' He gestured to the soldiers. 'Set him down, then leave the rooftop. All of you. Your presence is required below, to ensure I am not disturbed.'

The soldiers carried Killop onto the roof and put him down by the platform. They bowed low, then filed back down the steps, leaving the Creator alone with the mages.

Daphne stared at Killop's unconscious body. His face had been beaten, and his leathers were torn and bloody. She felt for him with her dream-vision, and found his mind wounded but intact. She sensed where their daughter's protections were already starting to rebuild scoured areas of his mind. A tear escaped her eye.

She refocused as the Creator raised his arms.

'Goodbye,' he said.

The clouds of dark smoke began to rotate again, gaining speed as they whirled and spun. Flames from the burning city were sucked up into the vortex, which began to glow, the clouds on fire.

Daphne felt him in her mind again, clamping it down and holding her tight. She retreated to a safe space, from where she watched as his presence filled her body from head to toe. Around her, she could feel the other mages bound to him as she was, and she sensed Killop too, his body possessed by the Creator's spirit.

The Creator drew on them, and she felt her life being drained out of her. At the same time, the vortex above them grew brighter, and spun faster, blurring in a circle of fire. Her eyes began to close. She tried to dream-vision out to Karalyn, heedless of the risk; her desire to see her daughter one final time over-powering her caution, but her energy was disappearing.

She was weakening, as were Killop and the others, and the Creator exalted in his power.

Daphne struggled, resisting with all her strength, fighting to the end.

CHAPTER 37
HACKED OFF

Plateau City, Imperial Plateau – 19th Day, Second Third Winter 507

Keira kicked the chair where Kallie was sleeping.

'Wake up, ya lazy cow.'

The Kell woman grunted, her red hair falling over her face. Next to her, Karalyn was sleeping on a low mattress, her form lit by the glow of a flickering oil lamp, hung against the damp walls of the deep cavern where they were hiding.

'Get up,' Keira said, kicking the chair again.

Kallie opened her eyes, grimacing. 'What's happening?'

'Nothing,' Keira said. 'Just been sitting on my own for fucking hours, watching you two get yer beauty sleep. I'm bored.'

'Why don't ye get some rest?' Kallie said, rubbing her face.

'I cannae sleep,' Keira said. 'My head's buzzing.'

Kallie shrugged. 'There's plenty of booze that'll knock ye out.'

'I cannae get wasted. Not when I'm looking after her.'

She flicked her eyes over to the sleeping child.

Kallie reached down and picked up a bottle. 'Well, I'm having another one. My head's splitting.'

'No wonder,' Keira said. 'Ye put a barrel-load away earlier.'

'So?' Kallie said, filling a mug with spirits. 'Flora's dead, Keira. And the Emperor... well, maybe you can stay sober after going through that, but I couldnae handle it.'

'Ye did alright at the time.'

'Aye,' Kallie said, 'but my nerves were shredded. I thought he was going to kill us, I really did.'

Keira rummaged in her pouch, and lit a stick of keenweed.

'Is that how ye've managed to stay awake?' said Kallie. 'Have ye been smoking all day?' She looked around. 'What time is it anyway?'

'How the fuck should I know?' Keira said, taking a draw. 'Evening? Night? And anyway, there was another reason I had to stay awake.'

'Daphne?'

'Aye.'

'Has she been in contact?'

'No.'

'Shit. Ye got any dreamweed?'

'Aye. Ye're not getting any, but.'

Kallie frowned. 'Why not?'

'I need ye ready, ya daft cow,' Keira said.

'Ready for what? I thought we were going to hide down here until it was safe to leave the city?'

'Something's wrong, Kallie. Daphne should have sent a message hours ago. If something happens tonight, I need ye able to shoot yer longbow. Ye'll be useless if yer wasted.'

Kallie sipped from her mug, and coughed. 'Shit, this stuff's rough. Alright, give me some keenweed, then.'

Keira narrowed her eyes.

'Ye'll get some when ye need it.'

'Yer treating me like I'm a bairn,' Kallie said. 'Nothing's going to happen tonight, anyway. Hopefully, Daphne's just waiting to see how things settle down, and then we'll be on our way.'

'You still drunk?' Keira said. 'Yer fucking delusional. You saw what the Emperor did, right? How exactly do ye think things are going to settle down?'

Kallie gazed around at the damp walls of the small cavern.

'Alright,' she said, 'things are bad; I admit it. The Emperor's no doubt still searching for you, but I think we're safe down here for now. Hang on,' she said, frowning, 'if the Emperor can't see us down here, then maybe Daphne can't either. Maybe she's been trying to find us.'

Keira felt annoyed that Kallie had thought of this before her.

'She's the best fucking vision mage going,' she said. 'She'd find us.'

Kallie said nothing, sitting back in her chair and nursing her mug. Keira shifted in her seat, the leathers digging into her skin. She longed to be able to wash and clean herself, but there were no toilets or baths that deep in the caverns. Already, the smell coming from the bucket in the small cave behind her was starting to reach her nostrils. They had no food, and little water, and she was keeping what they had for Karalyn.

She watched as Kallie's eyes began to close. She stubbed out her weedstick and got to her feet, stretching her limbs, and gazing down at the sleeping child. Her dark skin shone in the lamplight, and Keira smiled. She reached down and spread the twisted blanket back over the girl's legs, covering her, then went to the entrance of the cavern. It opened on to a long, low tunnel, which stretched into darkness on either side. There were other caverns close by. Some were empty, while others were sealed with iron grilles, and locked up.

She needed a plan.

Flora would have known what to do. Or, rather, Flora would have told her the right thing to do. For a long time, Keira had allowed the young Holdings woman to act as her conscience, her moral filter. It had given her free rein to behave any way she wanted, always knowing that Flora would still be there, no matter what crazy shit she had just done.

But she had lost Flora, and gained Karalyn. And the child, her blood, needed protecting. Keira would fight like a bear to stop anyone from hurting her, and that simple truth had shifted her priorities. She tried to imagine a time in the future, long after this was all over, when Karalyn was back with Killop and Daphne, and she was free to... do what, exactly? Go back to being the town drunk at the World's End in

Domm? Or, if she wanted to, she could rule the world. She smirked. She knew there was a joke in there somewhere.

What did she want? To see her brother again. To be free from the fear that the Emperor was trying to kill her would be nice as well. She realised that she would never be free while the Emperor lived. Even if she hid alone in the most remote corner of Domm, every morning when she awoke, she would wonder if she was witnessing her last sunrise, if that would be the day the Emperor would find her.

But how could she kill him? She had already tried, and had been lucky to escape with her life. The first time she had faced him, she hadn't even managed that. And now he was more powerful than ever. She gazed up at the tunnel ceiling, glistening with moisture. Somewhere above her head, through hundreds of feet of earth, was the Emperor. What was he doing? She remembered him saying that he would be able to see her wherever she went, but they had been in the cavern all day, and through the evening, and there had been no sign that she had been discovered.

Maybe Kallie was right. Maybe nothing was going to happen that night. She should have a drink, and switch to dreamweed, and get a good night's sleep, so she was fresh for the morning. The idea tugged at her, but her mind was already made up. She was Karalyn's aunt and guardian, and that was that. Losing her would be..., it wasn't something she could bring herself to imagine. She thought about how Killop and Daphne must have been feeling all this time without their daughter, the worry must have tormented their every moment. How could they bear it? All the Kell knew loss. She and Killop had seen friends torn apart by crossbow bolts and swords, yet if Karalyn were to die, Keira knew that everything she had ever felt would be dust and ashes.

What should she do? What would Flora say?

The white witch would tell her that she had to get Karalyn out of the city, no matter what it took.

Keira felt her eyes begin to well up, and she shook her head. No time for that. She turned, and walked back into the cavern. She knelt by her chair and packed her bag, stuffing it with their things. She took two sticks of keenweed from her pouch, then slipped it on to her belt.

She nudged Kallie.

'Not again,' she groaned. 'What is it this time?'

'We're going,' she said. 'Time to leave.'

Kallie rubbed her eyes. 'What? Now? Is it morning?'

'I've no idea. I think it's probably the middle of the night, but fuck knows.'

'What about her? You going to wake her?'

'Not if I can help it. We'll carry her up to the caverns closer to the surface, see if we can pick up some food for her, and find out what's been going on.'

'And then?' she yawned.

'And then we get out of the city. Maybe you were right about Daphne not being able to see us down here. Either way, if we get a good pace going, we can put some distance between us and the Emperor before dawn.'

Kallie sat in silence, her eyelids heavy.

'What if the exits to the city are guarded?'

'We fight our way out.'

'Huh.'

'Here,' Keira said, holding out a weedstick. 'Smoke this.'

Kallie took it from Keira's fingers, and lit a match.

'Light mine as well,' Keira said, holding up her own.

Kallie lit both, and took a long draw.

'It's a terrible plan,' she said. 'The Emperor could be searching the Kellach quarter for you right now, and we're just going to oblige him by emerging from our hiding place? How do you know he's not waiting for us to make this very mistake, eh?'

'That's why we find out what the fuck's been going on first,' Keira said. 'When we get to the upper caverns, there'll be folk there we can ask. If the Emperor's searching for me, they'll know.'

'And then we call it off?'

'Fucksake. Let's wait to see what they have to say first.'

'And how are you going to fight, if you're carrying Karalyn? I mean, I can't shoot everybody.'

Keira frowned. 'Let's worry about that shit when we step in it.'

'Alright,' Kallie said, standing. She stretched her arms. 'Pyre's arse, we're manky. We're still stinking of smoke from the fires, and covered in dirt, blood, and who knows what else. And yer hair, it stinks from when it got singed.'

'It's like being back in the war.'

Kallie smirked. 'Which one?'

'Take yer pick,' Keira laughed. 'I've fought in three so far.'

'Come on, then,' said Kallie, picking up the pack and slinging it over her shoulder. 'Let's get on with it.'

Keira shook her head and stood. She strapped her sword to her belt, and crouched down by Karalyn, watching her sleep for a moment. She gathered up the girl, wrapped in the blanket, and stood holding her in both arms.

Kallie smirked.

'Don't start,' Keira frowned.

She shifted Karalyn onto her left hip, her head nestled onto her shoulder. The girl groaned and wriggled, but her eyes stayed closed. Keira smirked back at Kallie, and strode to the cavern entrance. Kallie unhooked the lamp, and followed.

They walked up the tunnel, lowering their heads to avoid hitting the ceiling. Pools of water had collected along the path, and Karalyn stirred against Keira's side as she stooped through the tunnel. Kallie's lamp lit the way, and after a few minutes the passage widened, and began to slope upwards. They clambered up the steep path until it levelled out onto a short landing. At its end was a rope ladder, disappearing up into the darkness.

'You go first,' said Keira.

'No way,' said Kallie. 'If you drop the girl, I want to be here to catch her.'

'I'm not going to drop her,' she said. 'Alright, I'll go first, but only because you have the lamp. Make sure you hold it up for me; I don't want to be climbing that fucking thing in the dark.'

She walked to the ladder, her left arm keeping Karalyn close. She reached out with her right hand and grabbed hold of the rope, pulling herself up to the first rung. Kallie came close, and her lamp shone up. Keira swore, gazing at the height she was going to have to climb one-handed. Karalyn had been awake when they had descended the rope earlier that day, and had clambered down it easily.

'Get a move on,' said Kallie. 'My arm's getting sore holding the lamp.'

'You are fucking hilarious,' Keira said, climbing the ladder. Each time she got her feet up onto the next rung, she had to grab the rope higher up, while keeping Karalyn steady. She kept going, losing her temper and patience as she went, until they reached the top. She emerged into another earth-walled cavern, and sat, her left arm aching, and waited for Kallie.

'You look knackered,' she said, lifting the lamp clear of the tunnel, and climbing up next to Keira. 'Are ye still sure it's a good idea to go outside carrying the bairn?'

'We'll be fine,' Keira said, getting back to her feet. She switched Karalyn to her right hip, and stretched her left arm.

They set off again, following the tunnel that led from the cavern. She saw the flickering light of lamps ahead, and began to hear voices. The passageway opened on to a much wider tunnel, with booths dug out on either side. Men and women, both Kellach and Holdings, were gathered. Many were busy, pulling on armour or buckling swords to their waists.

'What's going on?' Keira asked a small group, who were unloading a crate of crossbows.

The group glanced at them.

'It's all kicking off in the streets above us,' said one.

'The Emperor?'

'No sign of him,' the man said. 'Apparently he's locked himself up in the Great Fortress.'

'This is our best chance,' said another. 'If we can keep the garrison busy, we can break out of the city and run for it.'

'What's he doing?' said Kallie. 'The Emperor, I mean.'

'Pyre alone knows,' said a Kellach woman. 'His soldiers took over a hundred folk captive, and led them off into the fortress a few hours ago. The Emperor's not been seen since.'

'You both look fit,' said the Holdings man. 'You coming to help?'

'Aye,' said the Kellach woman. 'Ye can leave the bairn here with the old folk, she'll be safe enough.'

'I cannae,' Keira said. 'I promised the girl's mother that I'd stay with her.'

'I can fight,' said Kallie, tapping her longbow.

'Do ye know how to use that, hen?' said the Kellach woman.

'Ya cheeky cow,' said Keira. 'She's the best shot around. I can still fight, though.'

'Aye?' said the Kellach woman. 'With a bairn on yer hip?'

'Aye.'

'How ye going to draw yer sword?'

Keira frowned. She looked down. Karalyn's legs were around her waist, covering the hilt on her belt.

'Here,' said the Holdings man, handing her a long knife. 'Stick that in yer boot.'

'Cheers.'

The group moved to the side of the tunnel to allow a dozen armed civilians to pass.

'Come on,' said the Kellach woman. 'Let's go.'

The group moved off. Keira and Kallie tagged along at the end, and followed them through the tunnels, passing groups of elderly and injured civilians, and stores of food and water.

'Hang on,' said Keira. She ducked into one of the storeroom booths.

'I need water and food,' she said to an old woman sitting on a stool by the supplies, 'for the girl.'

'Staying or going?'

'What does it matter?'

The old woman shrugged. 'If you're staying down here, I can give you some rations, but if you're leaving, then you'll need to trade something for them.'

'Why?'

'Those are the rules, take it or leave it.'

Keira glanced at Kallie. 'Got any money left?'

'Nope.'

'Shit.' Keira lowered her voice. 'Do you take weed?'

The old woman frowned. 'If you have any dull for the injured, then I'll take it.'

Kallie turned round, and Keira opened the pack strapped to her back. She rummaged around and pulled out a small pouch.

'Here ye go,' she said, handing it to the old woman.

The woman inspected the contents of the pouch, then reached down and picked up a packed bag.

'Pleasure doing business with you.'

Keira took the bag, and stuffed it into Kallie's pack.

They walked back out into the main tunnel.

'Pyre's cock,' Keira muttered. 'We've just been fucking robbed. That was about forty gold's worth I just gave her, for a wee bag of food and a flask of water.'

Kallie shrugged. 'Just as well we still had it.'

'Aye, she said, as they walked down the tunnel. 'Let's hope we don't need it.' She patted her belt. 'Still got plenty of keenweed left, but. We'll not be sleeping tonight.'

The civilians they had been following were out of sight, so they got in behind another group, and continued through the tunnels for several minutes. It seemed like every surviving civilian from the Kellach quarter was sheltering in the caverns. Small fires were burning in alcoves, and the place was bustling.

'Go get the bastards!' an old Holdings peasant called out as they passed, and the others around them cheered. Keira felt her back slapped as the peasants crowded the tunnel, offering words of encouragement to the fighters. They squeezed through, and came into another, narrower tunnel, which sloped up at a gentle gradient. At the top was a rope ladder, leading to the surface.

One by one, the members of the armed group ascended. When the last had gone up, Keira approached the ladder. At its base stood an armed Holdings woman.

'Hey,' she said. 'You can't take that kid up there. It's too dangerous, there's fighting in the streets.'

Keira smiled and walked up to her, a good head taller.

'Aye?' she said. 'You going to stop me?'

The Holdings woman hesitated, then reached out and grabbed hold of Karalyn's blanket.

The girl stirred, and Keira snarled.

Kallie stepped up, and removed the woman's hand from Karalyn.

'I wouldn't do that, hen,' she said. 'Best if ye just let us go.'

The Holdings woman cowered back as the two Kell towered over her.

'I have orders,' she said, her eyes darting around. 'Only fighters are allowed up.'

Karalyn opened her eyes, blinked, and looked around.

'Where's mummy?' she said.

'That's where we're going, wee one,' Keira said. 'Just you hush now.' She glared at the Holdings woman. 'Ye can go and report us or whatever, it doesnae matter. I'm taking the bairn up there, so get out of my way.'

The Holdings woman looked terrified, but stood her ground, blocking the rope ladder. 'You can't take a little girl up there.'

Karalyn gazed at the guard. For a second the woman looked back, then her eyes clouded over and she fell to the ground.

'Woah,' Kallie said, her eyes wide. 'Either she just fainted, or... or...'

Keira stared at Karalyn. 'Was that you?'

'Aye,' the girl said. 'Lady sleepy.'

'Good trick,' Keira smirked. 'Mind ye never use it on me.'

She reached up, and grabbed the rope. 'Here we go again.'

Ten minutes later, Keira and Kallie stepped out of the small cottage where the hidden entrance to the tunnel was located. Karalyn was still awake, though she kept yawning and rubbing her eyes. In the distance on their left stood the Great Fortress, and a cacophony of noise was coming from that direction. To their right was the road leading to the gates in the walls of the Kellach quarter. The night sky above was lit by the reflected glow of the huge fires that were burning in other parts of the city.

Keira scanned down the streets, but no one was in sight. She nodded to Kallie, and headed off to their right.

'No!' Karalyn cried. 'Go the other way.'

'Shush,' Keira said. 'We're getting out of here, wee one.'

'Wrong way,' the girl said, struggling and wriggling in Keira's arms.

'Stay still,' Keira said. 'We cannae go that way, that's where the crazy Emperor is.'

She put her foot forwards, and nearly fell over as a pain tore through her head.

Keira go to fortress, she heard the child's voice say in her head. *Not leave city.*

Keira staggered, while Kallie stared at them.

'Be fucking reasonable, wee one,' Keira cried, her head splitting. 'We need to find yer ma and da.'

Mummy and daddy are in the fortress. Bad man hurting them.

Keira stopped, and turned to face the towers of the Great Fortress. The pain in her head ceased.

'Are you sure?' she said.

'Sure about what?' said Kallie.

Keira frowned at her. 'I'm talking to the bairn.'

Karalyn pointed. 'Mummy and daddy there.'

'Shit,' said Kallie, standing next to Keira as they gazed at the fortress.

Keira glanced at her. 'Ye don't have to come,' she said. 'I cannae ask ye to do that. But if Killop's in there, I'm going in to get him.'

Kallie said nothing.

'Well?' said Keira.

'I'm not leaving ye now,' Kallie said, as she unslung her pack. 'But I'm not lugging this with me.'

She pushed aside the broken door of the nearest building, and placed the pack inside.

'We'll come back for it later,' she said.

Keira frowned. 'Alright.' She gazed down at Karalyn. 'Let's go rescue yer mummy and daddy.'

They set off, racing down the street, keeping to the shadows. Ahead, the noise grew. They darted down a side street and cut across a series of alleys, trying to work their way around where the fighting was taking place. They came out on to a wider road, and almost ran into a crowd of Rahain soldiers. Keira skidded, and sprinted in the other direction, Karalyn clinging on, her fingers digging into Keira's neck. Some of the soldiers turned and saw them, but most were occupied with fighting a large group of civilians that were attacking from the other side. One reached for his crossbow, and Kallie put an arrow through his neck, sending him flying.

Keira barged down another alleyway. Noise was coming from every direction, and she gazed up to get her bearings. Ahead, the tall towers of the fortress loomed. She shifted Karalyn to her left hip, and ran on, rushing across a street where groups of soldiers were engaged in a running battle with armed civilians. Rocks and crossbow bolts sped past them as they charged into a narrow alley on the other side, and kept running.

The sounds of fighting began to die down as they raced through the tight streets near the walls of the Old Town, and soon it was quiet. They slowed to a walk. Keira's heart was pounding, and she caught her breath. They walked into a small square, the air heavy with mist. Not a sound of the violence behind them reached their ears.

'This is weird,' whispered Kallie, glancing around.

Keira looked up. Above the mist, the high walls of the Great Fortress rose into the night sky. All around was a dull red glow, as the clouds of smoke reflected the huge fires devastating other areas of the city. On the other side of the square was a short street leading to the gates of the fortress. It was close, just thirty yards away, but Keira's legs felt heavy, and she stopped, and sat down by a low wall. She put Karalyn down next to her, while Kallie crouched close by, her gaze on the square and the fortress gates.

'I want mummy,' wailed Karalyn.

'I know,' said Keira. 'Soon. Just need a rest first.'

She reached into her pouch and pulled out two sticks of keenweed. She lit them both and handed one to Kallie, who took it. They sat by the wall for a moment, smoking, the mist drifting by.

'Here's what we're going to do,' Keira said. 'You're going to stay here with Karalyn, and I'll go in.'

Kallie said nothing, chewing her lip.

'No,' said Karalyn. 'Me go too.'

Keira laughed, though it edged into tears. 'No, wee one, I'm not taking you into that place.'

'Karalyn hide from bad man.'

Keira frowned. 'Aye. You hide out here with Auntie Kallie.'

'No, hide with Keira.'

Keira glanced at Kallie. 'Look after her.'

She stood, and was preparing to leap the low wall when a blinding pain ripped through her skull. She fell to her knees, holding her head in her hands.

'No,' said Karalyn, glaring at her.

'Fucking stop that,' Keira gasped, and the pain vanished. She fell back against the wall, panting. 'Pyre's arsecrack, my fucking head.'

Kallie stared from her to Karalyn. 'Did she do that?'

Keira nodded. She picked up the dropped weedstick and relit it. She turned to Kallie.

'What are we going to do? She's not going to let me go in there alone.'

Kallie shrugged. 'I don't know. Wait until she falls asleep?'

Keira frowned at her. 'That's the most stupid idea I've ever heard. That could take hours.'

Kallie looked away. 'I was only trying to...' Her eyes widened.

Keira turned, and spat out the weedstick. Ten yards away, Karalyn was running through the little square, towards the gates of the fortress. She stopped, turned and gazed at them.

'What she doing?' Kallie cried, as Keira jumped to her feet. They vaulted the low wall, and sprinted through the mist towards the girl, who laughed and ran away. Keira lowered her head and raced towards her, heedless of the risks. She caught up with her a few yards in front of the gates, and scooped her up in her arms. Her eyes darted around, but no one was about. One door of the gates was lying open, and Karalyn pointed.

Keira glanced at Kallie, and walked forwards. She peered through the gap into the fortress. Inside, lamps were lighting the walls, and a large group of soldiers were in the hallway. Half were wearing battered armour, and looked exhausted, while the others were fresh, and getting ready to leave. Before Keira could move, a Rahain officer glanced in her direction. She froze, but his gaze passed over her as if she wasn't there.

'Karalyn hide Keira,' the girl whispered in her ear.

Keira stayed still, gazing at the soldiers. Several more looked over at the door, but no one seemed to notice them standing there.

'Why can't they see us?' murmured Kallie, from over her shoulder.

Keira said nothing, and put a foot up onto the threshold of the gate. She squeezed through the gap in the doorway, and entered the fortress, Kallie at her back. They stood there a moment, as the soldiers went about their business. The fresher infantrymen were beginning to line up, an officer at their head. Keira stepped to the side, and they watched the soldiers march out past them.

Keira smirked, her confidence returning.

They strode up the passageway, ignored by the exhausted soldiers resting by the walls. Karalyn pointed again, and they followed her lead, coming to a tight set of spiral stairs leading upwards.

'At least it's not a fucking rope ladder,' Keira said, as Karalyn raised her finger.

They entered the stairwell, and climbed the steps, up past other floors, unseen by any of the soldiers stationed there. Twice Keira paused, certain that she could hear someone following them, but each time, she decided she was hearing the echo their boots were making on the iron steps.

Their pace slowed as they passed a fifth level. Keira's calves were aching, but her pain was overshadowed by the pressure of mage energy coming from above. It felt like a barrier of sheer power, and moving was like trying to trudge through knee-deep mud.

'What is that?' Kallie gasped.

Keira said nothing, her strength focussed on climbing the last steps. She reached the top of the stairwell, and peered over the edge, Kallie joining her. Karalyn scrambled down, and the three of them stared out on to the roof.

In the centre was the Emperor, his hands raised, while above, the sky was burning. The clouds swirled round in a blur, the wind howling, almost deafening her. On the roof, surrounding the Emperor, were five figures, chained to posts. Daphne was there, her head bowed, along with Agang, Dean and Laodoc, who sat slumped against their posts, and a Rakanese woman she didn't recognise.

'Mummy,' cried Karalyn. 'Daddy.'

Keira's eyes went to the ground by the Emperor's feet. On the stone slabs lay another figure.

'Wee brother,' whispered Keira.

She lifted her right hand, and tried to draw upon the closest fire raging in the city, but nothing happened. She looked within herself, her heart racing, but found an absence where her mage power should be.

'Bastards,' she groaned, her will almost breaking.

'He's killing them,' Kallie said.

Keira gazed at Karalyn, but the girl was in near hysterics, weeping and staring on to the roof. Keira loosened her scabbard. She kissed Karalyn on the head, drew her sword, and climbed up onto the roof.

She stood there for a moment, feeling the power of the Emperor gust around her like a warm wind, the eddies swirling against her face.

She stepped forwards.

'Get away from my wee brother,' she yelled.

The Emperor didn't move, his gaze remaining upwards as the energy surging over the roof grew in intensity. She struggled forwards, fighting the waves of power rippling through the air.

'I said,' she screamed, 'get away from ma brother, ya fucked up maniac!'

The Emperor looked down, his eyes confused. He saw her, and smirked. Without interrupting his ritual, he nodded in her direction, and she was blown back by the explosive power as it hit her. The sword was wrenched out of her hand as she flew through the air. She collided with one of the five posts and collapsed to the ground, several ribs broken, and bruised all over.

Keira opened her eyes, and saw double for a moment, the hazy images drifting in and out of focus. The Emperor was continuing, paying her no more attention. She tried to move, but her body felt broken. She raised her head a fraction, blood coming from her forehead and obscuring her vision.

She noticed movement by the stairwell, a struggle. Kallie was wrestling with someone, a man, who lashed out and struck the Kell woman. Kallie fell back down the stairwell, disappearing from sight. The man picked up Karalyn. He turned, and saw Keira.

'Kylon,' she groaned. 'No.'

He hesitated for a second, staring at her, then gripped Karalyn under his left arm and jumped up onto the roof. In his right hand, he held a spear. His long black coat was fire-stained and ragged, and his face a swollen mass of bruises, but his eyes shone like black diamonds.

Karalyn cried out, struggling, and Kylon rushed forwards, running towards the Emperor. He paused by the body of Killop, and drew back his right arm. At the last moment, the Emperor saw him, and lowered his head, frowning.

Kylon's arm flew forwards, releasing the spear. It shot through the air, striking a gap in the Emperor's armour under his left shoulder. The Emperor flinched, and the vortex above began to falter, the impetus lost. The Emperor flicked a finger, and Kylon's head exploded.

Keira stared as his body fell to his knees, Karalyn struggling to be free of his dead grip. Around them, the mages stirred. Agang lifted his head, his eyes bleeding. Next to Keira, a woman groaned.

The Emperor looked down at Karalyn. He frowned as the vortex swirled in slow circles above them. He pulled out the spear from under his shoulder, as the girl freed herself from Kylon's arm. She was weeping, and staring at the body of her unconscious father.

'You?' the Emperor said. 'All this time, I've been blinded by a little girl?'

He raised his finger.

An arrow flew over Keira, striking the Emperor in the throat. He staggered back a step, making a choking noise.

Keira lifted her head. The Emperor was clutching at the arrow in his throat, as Karalyn raised her arm towards him. He let out a long shriek that pierced the night air, and at once his mage powers vanished, and the swirling vortex dissolved, the glowing light within extinguished.

'Now,' said the voice of a woman lying chained to the post beside Keira. She turned. It was one of the frog folk, with big, wide eyes and long black hair. She was holding Keira's knife, which had fallen from her boot. She pushed it into the fire mage's hands. 'Save us.'

Keira stumbled to her feet, and began to run. Her legs screamed in pain, but she ignored it, charging with her fading strength towards the platform where the Emperor stood. She passed the headless body of Kylon, then leapt over where Karalyn knelt hugging her unconscious father, her wee brother.

She landed on the platform, and sprang at the Emperor. She swung her left arm round his neck and plunged the knife in. He dropped to his knees as she twisted the blade in his throat, sawing through his windpipe and severing the arteries. He reached up with his right hand and grabbed her throat, squeezing. Her right arm moved in a frenzy, hacking and sawing as his blood pumped out all over her, spraying the platform as he fell. His grip on her throat increased, and in the seconds before her neck snapped, she felt her knife cleave air.

She toppled to the ground, her closing eyes watching as the Emperor's head bounced off the platform.

Keira smiled as her breath slipped away.

I am a goddess.

CHAPTER 38
THE FIRE GODDESS

Plateau City, Imperial Plateau – 20th Day, Second Third Winter 507

Killop's heart was pounding in anticipation as the chill wind swept the drifting snow across the frozen glen. Ahead of him on the steep path was a priest of Pyre, his guide to the mountain retreat where they had taken his sister. He hadn't seen her since the priests had removed her from the village following the deaths of the Kalliver family, when Keira's powers had been revealed. That had been back in the summer, and nearly half a year had elapsed. Killop had missed his twin. They had done everything together, and barely spent a single day apart in the years since their birth. Now it was the morning of their fourteenth birthday, and although he couldn't wait to see her, he was worried.

Would she have changed?

The priest reached the top of a ridge, and waited for him to catch up. As he neared the summit, he saw the priest point. In the distance, nestled among a stand of fir trees, was a low building, built of stone, with a thatched roof. Smoke was coming from a chimney. On the threshold sat a girl.

Killop blinked, and ran towards her, joy and relief flooding his heart at the sight of his sister.

She glanced up at him as he approached. He could tell she wanted to jump up to greet him, but she kept her smile wry. Despite the weather, she was wearing a loose tunic, and he could see the muscles in her upper arms. She looked fit, and strong.

'Happy birthday,' he said, stopping a yard from her. He longed to hug her, but felt awkward, as if he had remained a boy, while she was becoming a woman.

'Aye,' she said. 'You too, wee brother.'

He lowered his eyes. 'I missed you.'

'Of course ye did,' she smirked. 'Ye must've been bored out of yer mind without me to entertain ye.'

He smiled, but couldn't find the words to describe how empty the house had felt, or the long silences and angry glares from their ma and da, or how often he had wanted to speak to her. He started to cry.

'Fucksake,' she muttered, her face reddening.

The priest ambled towards them. He gazed at the tears rolling down Killop's cheeks, and dug into the pockets of his long robes.

'Big lads like you don't cry,' he said, looking embarrassed as he passed Killop a hanky. 'Come on now.'

Keira stood, and punched Killop's arm.

'Snap out of it, ya eejit,' she said, with a smile on her lips. 'We're not bairns any more. It's time to grow up.'

Killop felt a surge of energy flow through his body, jolting his heart and touching every part of him, his fingers, his toes, his skin. All pain ceased, and he felt the wounds and bruises from the beatings he had endured disappear, healed in an instant.

He opened his eyes. A Sanang man was sitting before him in the grey light of dawn, looking exhausted.

'Killop?' he gasped.

'Aye,' he said, lifting his head from the stone slabs.

'I am Agang,' the Sanang man said. 'Welcome back.'

Killop sat up, remembering. 'Daphne?'

'She's fine,' Agang said, pointing over to his left. Killop's eyes followed, and he saw her, dressed in her nightgown, her crippled left arm held close to her side. She was crouching down, embracing their daughter. Before Agang could say another word, Killop leapt to his feet and ran to them. Daphne gazed up at him, tears falling down her face as she smiled.

'Daddy,' said Karalyn, reaching out with her arms.

He embraced them both, holding them as they held him, crying and laughing together, wishing it would never end.

Killop stopped, as his memories continued to return. He pulled back.

'The Emperor?'

'He's dead,' said Daphne.

'The bad man's gone,' said Karalyn.

Killop frowned. He glanced around. They were high up on a roof overlooking the city. Around them were a few dozen armed fighters, made up of Kellach Brigdomin and Holdings folk. Most were standing clustered together, gazing down at something. Killop recognised Bridget and Dyam among them, their eyes wide.

He picked up Karalyn and stood, Daphne taking his hand. They walked towards the group, and folk got out of their way to allow them through. Bridget saw him, and rushed forwards. She threw her arms around him.

'She did it,' she said, as she started to weep against his shoulder. 'I'm sorry.'

He looked down. The enormous body of the Emperor, clad in black armour, was sprawled headless on a low platform. A yard away was his severed head, once again enclosed in its enormous steel helmet. Lying next to it was another body.

Killop said nothing, his face crumpling as Daphne took Karalyn from him. He fell to his knees and wept over the body of his sister. He took her cold hands in his, staring at her, oblivious to anything else around him, his heart breaking as uncontrollable tears spilled down his face. The others who had gathered around said nothing as he broke down in front of them. Daphne put a hand on his shoulder.

'I couldn't save her again,' he heard Agang say. 'My powers came back too late.'

'No one's blaming you,' said Daphne. 'You healed the rest of us.'

'I know,' said Agang. 'I'm just sorry.'

'She saved us all,' said another voice. 'I saw her do it. I gave her the knife. That asshole Kalayne was right all along. I did meet Keira, in the end.'

'You saw it, Shella?' Daphne said.

'Yeah,' she said. 'Keira ran at him, but the Creator flicked her away like an insect. But then Kylon appeared with Karalyn. He threw a spear, and distracted the Creator for a second.'

'Kylon?'

'His body's over here,' said Dyam.

At these words, Killop turned his face, and saw the headless corpse lying a few yards away. Someone had covered him with a blanket, but a long black coat was trailing out from under its edges.

'And then,' Shella went on, 'as the Emperor was about to kill Karalyn, someone shot him in the throat with an arrow.'

'What?' said Bridget. 'Who?'

'I never saw,' said Shella.

'Who else was up here?' said Daphne.

There was silence for a moment, then the crowd parted, and a woman approached.

'It was me,' said Kallie. She looked like she had been up fighting for hours, her face streaked with dirt and tears, her red hair blowing in the chill breeze. 'I shot the arrow.'

Daphne reached out and embraced the Kell woman, who remained stiff, but didn't back away.

'Thank you,' said Daphne.

'And then,' Shella said, and they all turned back to her, 'then Keira hacked the bastard's head off with a knife.'

'He broke her neck,' Killop said, his voice a low mumble.

'Yeah,' said Shella. 'She died for us.'

'The firewitch will never be forgotten,' said Agang. 'The forests of Sanang will mourn when they learn of her death.'

'They'll be weeping in Domm, too,' said Bridget, 'and composing songs to remember her. We'll get a stretcher, and carry her off the roof. We can bury her with her kin in the Kellach quarter of the city.'

'She'd want to go back home,' said Kallie, 'to Kell.'

'The Sanang have as good a claim to her as any,' said Agang. 'She is worshipped throughout the forest.'

'She hated Sanang,' said Kallie. 'You're not taking her there.'

'Enough,' said Laodoc, walking into the centre of the crowd, leaning on his stick. He gazed at them. 'Do any of you understand what has taken place here? The creator of this universe is no more, and yet here we are, living amid his creation. Godless and alone, with no one watching us from above. All we have is each other, living together on this world. Do not overshadow our first moments of freedom with ill-tempered arguments.' He gazed at Keira's body. 'As her twin, Killop is the only one here who has any say in what happens to the fire mage. No one else.'

Bridget nodded. 'Aye, that sounds right.'

Killop kept his eyes on his sister, as the others waited for him to speak. Whatever he did, he knew that Keira's name and life would be fought over, her legacy claimed by different folk, who would forget she had been a real person, with failings just like anyone else. He did not want them fighting over her body as well.

'No one's getting her,' he said, standing. 'We'll cremate her here, where she fell.'

'Alright,' said Bridget. 'You heard him, everyone, back off.' She turned to him as the crowd dispersed. 'I'll get it arranged. There's food and water by the parapet.'

She leant over, and picked up the head of the Creator, gripping on to the enormous helmet with both arms.

'We'll burn the Emperor's body first,' she said, 'but I'm keeping hold of this. Proof.'

A Holdings civilian with a crossbow strapped to his back came running from the stairwell. He halted before Bridget, staring at the huge severed head in her arms.

'Aye?' she said.

'Ma'am,' he said. 'The last imperial soldiers in the city have surrendered. The commanders are wanting to know what to do with the prisoners.'

Bridget chewed her lip. 'We need to save as much of the city as we can,' she said. 'Get them working in the streets, putting out the fires and protecting anything that's not been burnt to ashes.'

'Yes, ma'am,' the man saluted, and returned down the stairs.

Bridget hauled the Creator's head over to the parapet, set it down by the wall, and sat on it.

Dyam rolled her eyes. 'Bridget thinks she's the empress now. That's her new throne.'

The Brig woman shrugged.

'How exactly did you find yourself in charge, Bridget?' asked Laodoc.

'After we lost you guys in the smoke,' she said, 'Dyam, Lola and I realised you'd gone into the fortress, but we couldn't get in, so we broke through the wall into the Kellach quarter. There were riots happening all over the place, but they were disorganised. All I needed to do was rally them, and point them at the fortress. If I hadn't, we would never have got in.'

'You fought your way up here?' said Daphne.

'Aye,' she said, 'floor by fucking floor.'

'Empress Bridget, eh?' Laodoc smiled, his tongue flickering.

She laughed.

'I'm serious,' he said. 'Right now, you are in command of the only armed force in the imperial capital, and hence you control the seat of government, the centre of the world. I could think of worse rulers.'

Agang frowned. 'We agreed that we would rule as a team of four.'

'Who agreed that?' said Daphne.

'Me,' he said, 'along with Laodoc, Bridget and Shella, on our way here.'

'I agreed nothing,' said Shella. 'I'm not doing it.'

'And I'm too tired, my friend,' said Laodoc. 'I've had my fill of trying to control the events of this world, and am more than happy to swear allegiance to Bridget.'

'Count me in,' said Shella.

'Aye, me too,' said Dyam.

'And me,' said Killop. They turned to look at him.

'No way,' said Bridget. 'Absolutely no chance.'

'Then I'll do it,' said Agang.

'Forget it, Agang,' said Shella. 'As of this moment, I'm acting as the new empress's personal bodyguard. If you want to be emperor, ape-boy, you'll have to go through me first.'

'Alright,' said Daphne. 'If it's a choice between Agang and Bridget, I choose Bridget.'

'It seems the world's most powerful mages are in agreement, my friend.' said Laodoc.

Agang fumed. 'Then what am I supposed to do?'

'Go home,' said Bridget. 'Do all the things to improve Sanang that you said you were going to do, only this time, actually do them.'

He stared at her. 'Are you placing me in charge of Sanang?'

She frowned for a moment.

'Aye, alright.'

Agang got down on one knee.

'Then I swear allegiance to you, Bridget of Brig, your Imperial Majesty.'

The others around her did the same. Killop glanced at Daphne as they lowered themselves to the stone slabs of the rooftop. Karalyn squirmed free, and ran over to hug Bridget's leg as she sat on the giant helmet. All across the wide rooftop, the groups of armed Holdings and Kellach Brigdomin saw what was happening, and within a few seconds, they were all on their knees.

Dyam raised her arms.

'Hail her Imperial Majesty,' she cried, 'Empress Bridget of Kellach Brigdomin.'

Bridget looked awkward as she took in the cheers and applause from the crowd on the roof.

'Of Brig, ya cheeky Domm cow,' she muttered under her breath.

The others retreated to the parapet, as two large pyres were constructed in the centre of the roof; one for the Emperor, and one for Keira. Wood was collected from the lower floors of the fortress – door frames, tables and chairs, and heaped into great piles. The new Empress sat on the steel helmet of the Creator, while next to her stood Laodoc and Shella. They were giving their advice on setting up a new constitution, while Dyam took charge of getting the pyres built.

The young fire mage Dean wandered over, and sat down alone, a few yards from the others.

Killop sat with Daphne and Karalyn, his tears mixing with laughter as the sun rose higher in the morning sky. The fires in the city were dying down, in part because entire areas were burnt out, but also because the remaining citizens had been roused, and were on the streets, carrying buckets of water, or clearing firewalls. The gates of the capital had been opened, and folk were coming and going, as the devastated city struggled back to life.

'What will we do now?' Killop said, as Karalyn climbed onto his back.

Daphne shrugged. 'Hold Fast?'

He nodded.

She smiled. 'I hope Celine's been looking after the place.'

'And who will rule the Holdings?'

'Shh,' said Daphne. 'If Bridget hears you, she might well appoint me on the spot.'

'You're Holder Fast,' he said. 'You must be in the running.'

She frowned. 'Do you want me to?'

'No,' he said, 'but maybe you should. You'd be a great leader. It's probably the right thing to do.'

'I'm sick of doing the right thing,' she said. 'I just want to be with you and Karalyn, and leave the world to its troubles. I long for a normal life.'

'Sure you wouldn't get bored?'

'After all this?' she said, lighting a cigarette. 'I crave boredom.'

He gazed at her.

'There is something Bridget can do,' he said. 'Come on.'

They got up, and walked to where the new Empress sat.

'Your Majesty,' Killop said, bowing his head.

Bridget winced, 'Please don't do that.'

'I need a favour.'

'Aye?'

'I need you to overturn a law.'

'Which one?'

'The one that says folk from different races can't get married.'

Bridget laughed. 'Aye, sure. Consider it revoked.'

'Thanks.'

'Fuck it,' said Bridget. 'If I'm Empress, then I proclaim you both married, as of this moment. Congratulations.'

Daphne blinked.

'I knew I'd get ye married some day,' Bridget smirked. 'Sorry it took so long.'

Shella laughed. 'I'm not sure that was the wedding they were hoping for.'

Daphne turned to Killop. 'Lord Holdfast.'

He smiled. 'Holder Fast.'

They kissed. Bridget and Shella pretended to vomit, while Laodoc smiled.

A Kellach woman approached.

Killop drew back, and saw it was Kallie. Daphne glanced up at the tall red-haired woman.

'Sorry for interrupting,' said Kallie. 'I've got something I want to give to Karalyn.'

'Aye?' said Killop.

'Aye,' she said. 'It used to be yours, so I hope you don't mind, it's just that I think Keira would want her to have it.'

She dug into her pack and took out a small wooden toy, then crouched down to Karalyn's eye-level as Killop and Daphne watched in silence.

'Yer Auntie Keira made this long ago,' she said, holding out the wooden bear. 'It's travelled halfway round the world, and now it's yours.'

Karalyn took it from her hands.

Killop frowned. 'Keira made it?'

'Aye, after she broke the one yer da made for ye.'

Killop gazed down at his daughter as she held on to the old toy, running her fingers over the teeth and claws.

She smiled. 'Wee bear.'

'Thanks, Kallie,' said Daphne. 'What do you think you'll do now?'

The Kell woman stood. 'Go back to Kell, I suppose.'

'Whatever you do,' she said, 'good luck.'

Kallie nodded. 'You too.'

An armed civilian approached, stopping before Bridget.

'The pyres are ready, your Majesty.'

Bridget rose, and the others quietened. Killop glanced over at the two huge mounds of wood. On one lay his sister, while on the other was the headless body of the Creator.

The Empress strode forwards, flanked by her mages and friends. A tall Kellach man in armour handed her a lit torch, and she approached the first pyre. She gazed up at the black armour of the Creator and without a word, she touched the end of the torch to the pyre, keeping it there as flames took hold of the wood. She stepped back, and the crowd watched as the fire spread. The breeze helped fan it, and the flames rose, licking the black armour. No one spoke as the fire began to lash the Creator's body, the flames and thick, dark smoke rising into the sky.

Bridget glanced at Killop, holding out the torch.

He shook his head, and turned to Dean.

'Come with me, mage.'

The boy looked up at him.

'I can't,' he said.

Killop held out his hand. Dean swallowed, his eyes red. He stepped forwards, and they walked to the foot of the pyre where his sister lay.

Killop knelt before the boy.

'I'll spark,' he said. 'You throw.'

'What if I fail?'

'You won't.'

The boy raised his hand, and stared at it for a moment. Killop lifted his hands, and focussed. An arc of white fire leapt across the gap between his fingers, and Dean pushed out with his hand. Killop felt the boy's strength pull the energy from him, and a burst of flames flew out from the sparks, setting the pyre alight.

Killop stared at the flames.

Bridget approached, putting her hand on Dean's shoulder. Killop got to his feet, Daphne taking his hand, while Karalyn hugged his leg.

The crowd on the roof watched as the flames rose higher and higher, the fire spiralling up through the heaps of wood, sending smoke rising into the bright sky, and consuming the body of Keira.

Killop went over all the things he wished he could say to her, how proud he was of her, and how much he loved her. Tears fell down his face.

Karalyn gazed up at him and smiled.

'Don't be sad, daddy. Wee bear will look after you.'

AUTHOR'S NOTES

JUNE 2019

Thank you for reaching the end of *The Magelands*.

The last ten chapters were the toughest to write of the whole series. In some ways I didn't want it to finish but after two and a half years of writing I was determined to give it the best ending I could. I hope you enjoyed it.

... and if you're not finished with The Magelands and want more, look out for the two book–length Origin Stories. One (*The Trials of Daphne Holdfast*) relates to Captain Daphne Holdfast's adventures in the Sanang forest where she meets Agang and B-Dang for the first time. The second (*Retreat of the Kell*) follows the Rahain invasion of Kellach Brigdomin from the point of view of Killop, and includes a lot more Keira.

There is also a novella-length book, *From the Ashes*, featuring the exploits of the fire mage just before the opening of *The Queen's Executioner*.

ABOUT THE AUTHOR

Christopher Mitchell is the author of the Magelands epic fantasy series.

For more information:
www.christophermitchellbooks.com
info@christophermitchellbooks.com

Printed in Great Britain
by Amazon

42479925R00341